ALSO BY JENNIFER HRITZ

I, too, Have Suffered in the Garden
Smoke and Glass

THE CROSSING

A Novel

Jennifer Hritz

Cover art: Stephanie Estrin
Cover design: Susan Michalski

For M,

who started everything

&

for Gus,

who keeps me going

Author's Note

I'm happy to introduce you to the rerelease of *The Crossing*. You won't find much that's different in the interior of this version; I simply fell in love with the painting I had commissioned from Austin artist Stephanie Estrin for the cover of *Smoke and Glass,* my third novel. In the interest of keeping my collection uniform, I decided to ask Stephanie to paint something for each of the novels. I've also done a simple copyedit, cleaning up a few errors that had been overlooked in the initial publication.

I'd like to thank Stephanie for her gorgeous painting, which perfectly encapsulates what I imagine Joel feels throughout so much of this novel.

I'd also like to thank Susan Michalski for her work in getting this novel to publication the second time around, and especially for how beautifully she has (yet again) taken one of Stephanie's paintings and crafted the perfect cover.

A quick note that the font and typesetting have changed from the original version.

PART ONE

Jennifer Hritz

1

October 1991

No one's at the spring this late in the season, and I stretch out on the bank, my legs crossed at the ankles as James makes his way across the rocks, his arms held out from his sides like airplane wings. We're barefoot, our shoes cast aside as easily as our afternoon class. Sun soaks our skin, and I yawn with shuttered lids, steeped in calm. At the park above us an occasional whistle from the train punctuates the muted sound of preschoolers at play.

Fuck *me*, that's cold, I hear James say as he drags his toes through the water. I lean back on my elbows, watching as he braces himself, the muscles in his calves tensing. Then he's submerged, and when he breaks farther out ten seconds later, he's whooping at the chill. C'mon! he calls. Too cold, I call back, and he slams his hand through the water like he's trying to soak me with the spray. Pussy! he shouts. At least I'm a warm pussy! I yell. He laughs and says something I don't catch before he flips over and starts a lazy backstroke.

I stare up at the sky as the wind sifts through my hair, reminding me of every dive I've ever taken, the shock of sun on my wet skin when I rise from the depths, the breeze that contradicts those very rays. I haven't been diving in almost a year, not since last Christmas when my father forced us to take a trip to Belize we would've been better off canceling. The diving rivaled any I've experienced, but our accommodations reflected the country's rustic infrastructure to a degree that my father had failed to anticipate. At first I spent a fair amount of time under the water, but my mother looked so miserable every time I left her at what I jokingly started to refer to as "our compound" that I started staying behind with her. That infuriated my father more than her refusal to accompany us on our dives, and we ended up flying home several days ahead of schedule. You're going to regret this next semester, he told me as we packed our equipment, When you're ass-deep in coursework. Diving's the one commonality we possess, the only activity we share without antagonism. That day, my father made it clear that I'd ruined everything.

I glance around for James, who's never been scuba diving himself, an infraction I'm determined to correct. This past summer I tried to persuade him to head to Mexico with me, but he never has cash, and he seemed reluctant to let me pay for the ticket myself. Instead, we spent our time at the pool, where he'd landed a job as a lifeguard as well as a girlfriend, and I worked on my tan. At some point, though, I'm going to convince him to take off with me.

Once I locate his casual freestyle, I close my eyes and give myself up to the sun. The colors I worked with all morning hold me close, and I linger over the palette in my mind, along with the canvas that's waiting for me at home. There's a part of me that can't wait to get back.

James and I live off of 29th Street, just west of Guadalupe. There's a little too much traffic, and the houses all show signs of wear, but trees arch over the sidewalks and will likely drop bushels of pecans this fall. Our house, white frame with a pine green trim, boasts a ramshackle roof and a rickety swing we frequent every evening regardless of the weather. I love every inch of the place, couldn't care less about the sagging front porch and alarmingly low ceilings my father pointed out at the beginning of last summer when he drove up to inspect what he'd leased at my insistence. I'm too taken with the weathered hardwood floors, the sixty-year-old windows that will leave us shaking with cold when the temperature drops. I'm too enamored of the room I call my own.

Windows line three of the walls, offering me better light than I've entertained in all the years I've been painting, and the same ancient hardwoods that greet my feet the moment I step from my bed each morning catch the kaleidoscope of colors that drips from my brush in the back room. I don't even bother to clean up. Instead, I'm reminded of what I've done, what I might be capable of doing, and when late afternoon sun casts shadows beneath my feet, I almost don't care what I've had to give up in order to get to this point.

My father finds artists frivolous and self-indulgent, and I know he's never been able to reconcile himself to the fact that he traded one in for another. My mother abandoned her work early in their relationship, but I've been holding a paintbrush since I could walk. My earliest memory, in fact, shows me plunging a thick tuft of brush into a well of scarlet, then sucking the paint off the end. My mother was appalled, but I dimly recall thinking the color tasted exactly as I expected.

The more painting enraptured me, the greater my father's resentment grew. Even now, the memory of him throwing my paints in the trash when I was six remains one of the most vivid of my childhood and the first time I can remember him losing his temper so viciously. I honestly don't recall the offense that precipitated the event. But I do remember my father sweeping my paintings from the kitchen table and tossing them along with my watercolors into the trash compactor. When he flipped the switch and everything was chomped into bits, I burst into tears, then threw myself on the floor in a full-fledged tantrum. He was hauling me up by my arms when my mother rushed in and plucked me away from him. Edward, she said as I sobbed into her shoulder, How could you, how could you?

My father has an impatience for anything he can't quantify, anything he can't control. That's why when I found the house last May I didn't play up the sun porch that could serve as my studio. Instead, I made the slightest of references to what he did to me over Spring Break.

He capitulated, like I knew he would. My Ford Explorer served the same fucking purpose.

But look what I got in return: an amazing house, big enough for James and me to each have our own bedroom, and a place for me to work as well. I've never before had so much space. This past summer, for the first time, I bought the materials I need to stretch and gesso my own canvas. There's something satisfying about shaping the frame myself, something sacred about applying the gesso with quick, even strokes. When it's finished, when the gesso's dry, I don't bother with pencil. There's a term for that, I think, some Italian word I can never remember. What if you make a mistake? James asks, and I laugh. Not because I don't make them, but because half the time they lead me somewhere I never intended, somewhere far better than I envisioned.

Sometimes James asks how I classify myself, and I almost always shrug. Abstract expressionist, he'll say, throwing out a word he knows only because he took Art Appreciation last semester, and I'll roll my eyes. I'm not looking to be categorized. Instead, I'll tell him who inspires me, who moves me, who leaves me breathless. Gorky, I'll say, Rothko, Pollock. All abstract expressionists, he'll inform me, and I'll tell him I'm not an idiot. Aren't you interested in anyone alive? he'll ask. Aren't you a History major? I'll snap back.

What surprises him, I think, doesn't seem to be the expense of what I'm doing or the tedium of preparing my own canvas. I think more than anything he's stunned by how easily the back room holds my attention. He catches me in there at all hours of the day and night, finds me barely able to hold a conversation because I'm so lost in the paint. I gesso canvas after canvas, undeterred by each new stretch of white.

I'm still drifting when James hits the ground beside me, shaking his head like a dog and scattering drops of spring water that hit my arms like tiny icicles. Sorry, he says, seeing me wince. He scrubs at his hair, letting his towel fall around his shoulders when he's finished and closing his eyes. Autumn light burnishes every shadow gold. I've had moments lately when I've felt such an intense rush of belonging I've had trouble breathing.

+ + +

James turns twenty at the end of the month. Twenty: the number feels huge, portentous, in a way that sixteen didn't, in a way eighteen never could. There's something about twenty that shimmers, even though James will still have to buy his beer tonight with a fake ID. I have four more months at nineteen myself, but I can't help thinking that somehow, turning twenty will change everything.

The morning of James's birthday, his father drives down from Fort Worth to take him to lunch. I'm quietly impressed by the interest Dr. Fielding takes in his son's life, by the way he's scheduled a day off of work to spend time with him. For my last birthday my father sent me a monogrammed leather planner. I've known you for six months, James told me, And even *I* know that's not your taste. After the fact I think he felt bad for saying anything, but it's not like his comment was some big revelation. If anything, I was more struck that this guy I roomed with, one I barely saw for the first three months of school and spent a month away from over the holidays, knew me better than my own father.

James insists that I accompany them to lunch, so I tag along, pleased to be included but feeling at the same time completely awkward in his father's presence. Dr. Fielding is an American Studies professor, and given the current state of my grades, I'm reluctant to open my mouth. But I figure out soon enough that there's no reason for me to worry. He and James converse with little input on my behalf, and I sit there watching them, knowing that I've never experienced with my own father what I'm witnessing right in front of me. Their conversation seems so fluid, and when James pauses long enough to shove a forkful of barbeque in his mouth, his father turns to me. James tells me you're an artist, he says. Sort of, I mumble, casting a scathing glance at James, but he's already talking me up, telling his father that when we get back to the house, he should take a look at some of my work. I don't know whether to be flattered or alarmed. What're you doing? I ask in a low voice as we're walking out to the car, and he gazes back with an innocence he couldn't possibly contrive. I don't want your father combing through my shit, I tell him. Okay, he says, shrugging, acquiescing so easily that for the rest of the afternoon, long after his father has left, I'm still second-guessing myself.

We go out that night, hitting one bar after another, meeting up with friends and a few of James's fraternity brothers. There's a girl James likes, too, but I keep mostly to myself, mulling over our lunch today and my missed opportunity, thinking of what James had to say about my paintings. I wonder what would've happened if I'd invited James's father into the back room, whether his reaction would have mirrored what I imagine my own father's might be if I were to extend the same suggestion to him. My father and I would've gotten stuck on my grades, on my homework, on the classes I've been skipping. I would've been compared to James, a model student and a fraternity member to boot, characteristics my father admires and which would normally make me puke, if it hadn't been for the casual slide of James's hands in his pockets that first day we met at the beginning of freshman year, if it hadn't been for the way he hooked his gaze on mine when I confessed my aspirations mere hours after I saw him for the first time. My father's not to be trusted with the secrets I hold, with the paintings I breathe into being. I don't know if I can trust James's father either. My mother's a given, but then, she's my mother. She gave me my first brush the way she would've given over her own blood.

James is something else, something I can't wrap my head around under the best of circumstances and which tequila renders downright impossible. He's mystifying, a puzzle exquisite in its intricacy, the one thing I want to figure out. At the same time, he's the simplest thing I know right now, my one constant other than the painting, as sure as the feel of that brush in my hand.

Or maybe I'm just drunk. I take a long, lingering drag of my cigarette; across from me James has lost the girl, and he sucks on a cigarette of his own, an affectation for both of us that sooner than we expect will become the first thing we reach for in the morning. One by one our friends say their goodbyes, and by last call we're alone, licking from our lips the foam off our beers. Thanks, he says after a minute. For what? I ask, embarrassed, and he gives me a look. I shrug.

+ + +

The day before Thanksgiving, my parents' house sprawls around me, five thousand square feet of luxury. As I step into the living room, the smell knocks me back a dozen years. An outsider wouldn't think twice about the scent of vanilla wafting from the lit candles or the lingering aroma of my father's Cuban, but I feel as if whatever progress I've made distancing myself in the interest of self-preservation has already disappeared, the months I've been away feeling at the same time like the gravest sort of mistake. I embrace my mother, the thin blades of her shoulders beneath my palms like the wings of the most fragile bird. She's forty-two and still pretty, though *pretty* probably isn't the right word. Striking, maybe, in a haunted sort of way. Like something John Williams Waterhouse might have painted. I've seen her only twice since Spring Break, once in May when my semester ended and once over the summer, both trips cut short because I just can't handle the tension anymore. Now I'm worried that the strain in her voice may have everything to do with my absence. You got your hair cut, I say, and she blushes in a way that tells me I'm the only one who noticed.

We don't have much time before she expects my father home from work, and she gestures me into the kitchen, where she's preparing a meal far too elaborate for the night before a holiday. I take a doubtful look around me, at the salmon I know she's going to roast with citrus, at the almonds she'll have to toast for the rice: she's making one of my favorite meals, and I have a feeling that if I open the refrigerator, I'll find a pumpkin cheesecake she'll insist on cutting tonight. Mom, I say, We could've ordered a pizza.

She seems hurt by the suggestion and waves away my offer to help. I'd much rather talk, she says, so I give up and pull out a chair. Now, she says, offering me a smile, Tell me everything.

I provide her with an edited version of the past couple of months, skirting her hesitant question about my grades but obviously not well enough to prevent a crease of concern from appearing on her forehead. I've been sketching some, I say to divert her attention, and she raises her eyebrows. Have you brought anything to show me? she asks. I shrug, quelling the mixture of shyness and excitement I always feel when she asks. But she shakes her head; she knows me too well. Come on, she says, Let's see.

I run upstairs. Buried under the clothes in my suitcase, I find the sketchpads I've brought, then carry them downstairs and watch from the corner of my eye as she settles herself at the table to look over what I've done. She pauses at the drawing I like best, James hunched over his Chemistry text, tugging on a handful of hair. I used to sketch him on the sly, afraid he'd be pissed if he knew what I was doing, but the first time he caught me, early our freshman year, he just stepped closer. He stared at the sketch for a while before giving me a curious glance. You're good, he said, sounding surprised, and without waiting for an invitation he took the book from my hand and leaned back against his desk so he could start from the beginning. Now I don't even bother to hide what I'm doing. You know what you're looking at, don't you? he asked last week when he saw the sketch my mother's now examining, A four-point-oh.

I roll my eyes at the memory as my mother touches the wave in James's hair, the line of stubble along his jaw. This one has interesting texture, she says. Yeah? I say, and she nods, tapping her finger on James's collar. I like the contrast here, she says. I know exactly what she means, the rumpled softness of a tee shirt James likely pulled right from his dirty clothes next to that near-beard. I hadn't had to labor with my pencil either. The sketch just bled from my fingers, a feeling that's pretty much the best one I've found so far in this world.

My mother nods her approval, and a starburst of satisfaction starts in my chest and spreads outward from there. I value her opinion more than anyone's—and not simply because no one other than James has really seen my work. My mother was an artist herself once, and though the only reason she picks up a brush these days might be to baste a turkey, she knows what she's talking about when it comes to art. If she can find something promising in what I've sketched, then maybe I'm as good as I hope.

The back room makes all the difference, I tell her, and she says, The back room? My studio, I say, still finding myself uncomfortable with the term. Having the space to work, she agrees, and I nod. I wish you could see it, I add. Soon, she promises, though I have my doubts. My father has been to Austin only twice since I started college, and the likelihood that he'll make the trip anytime soon seems about as possible as me ending the semester with a perfect grade point, the chance that my mother would come without him even more improbable.

Mom? I say, hesitating, because though I've asked her about her own work many times, she never divulges. I don't understand how she could give it up, not if she felt the same way about her work as I feel about mine. I'd rather give up my breath than my brush. But before I can tell her what I'm thinking she's murmuring over another sketch, one from last summer. We'd just come back from the pool, and James had collapsed in the shitty, threadbare chair I'd confiscated from a neighbor's trash pile, then peeled his damp shirt over his head. He'd still had his lifeguard whistle around his neck, and the chrome against his tan was what had gotten me. I'd sat down right across from him with a pad of paper and a pencil. Don't I get any privacy? he'd asked, taking his mouth away from the phone just long enough to ask the question, and I'd ignored him because he let me. My pencil had moved, full sweeps down the line of his torso, scrawls of loose spirals in his hair, still slick from the pool. I'd half-heard his voice, teasing his girlfriend as I teased out the contrast of that whistle against his skin. And his eyes: every so often he'd glance over at me, and I worked that in, kept working that in until his conversation ended. D'you get what you needed? he asked, Or are you going to follow me into the shower?

The front door slams shut, and I yank the books away from my mother, then slip them onto the chair next to mine. She's already on her feet, opening the oven door. Joel, she says, Would you mind setting the table?

The request comes just as my father rounds the corner, timed impeccably for his benefit. I stand and shake his hand, and he loosens the tie around his neck, looking me up and down until I straighten. Taller, he claims, though I haven't grown at all since summer. Even if I had, I wouldn't be able to look him in the eye; he'll probably always have a few inches on me. But we have the same hair, thick and dark, the same full mouth. Eyes the color of gunmetal.

Didn't your mother ask you to set the table? he asks, as if his arrival isn't responsible for delaying my response to my mother's request, and I duck into the dining room, where I find the table already set. The pool beckons just beyond the windows, glimmering in the light of a full moon. I can hear my parents in the next room; I feel a constant, low-level wariness, listening to them. But there's not even a hint of tension in the soft lilt of my mother's voice, and I lean my forehead against the glass, my eyes on the moon. Maybe I'll slip outside in the middle of the night and swim despite the cold.

Finished already? my father asks, and I turn, then glance at the dining table, where my mother has shaped the napkins into fans. But he doesn't seem to notice. Your mother, he confides, gesturing outside at the pool, Has been angling for a heater. She doesn't even swim, I say, and he says, That was *my* point.

We exchange a rare, guarded smile. I have to admit, he muses, Swimming in November has a certain appeal. Not without a heater, I tell him, and he nods. You were contemplating a night swim though, he says, Weren't you? I frown, disliking the way he's read my mind, but he just shrugs. You've done it often enough, he adds, Over the years.

Even though he's obviously talking about something too far in the past to warrant repercussions, I tense. How do you know? I ask. I've seen you, he tells me, Once or twice. You've seen me? I say. The first time, he confides, You were fifteen.

He'd come outside for a brisk, middle-of-the-night swim, he says, only to find that I'd beaten him to the pool. He was on the verge of interrupting me—he didn't think it was safe for me to be swimming by myself at night—but then he saw me dive. Your form was flawless, he says, and I flush at the belated compliment. He'd watched me surface, then glide through a dozen laps and a dozen more without effort. Back and forth, washed in the light of a moon as full as the one we can see tonight. You finally pulled yourself out of the water and sat on the lip of the pool, he says, And for a second I thought you saw me, but then you tilted your head back to the sky.

He's staring at the water now as if he can see me out there. Hell, I can almost see me myself, and I take a veiled glance in his direction. He looks downright nostalgic, and when he speaks again, he sounds wistful enough to startle me. A part of me wanted to join you, he admits, But the moment was too private.

Sometimes I think I have him pegged so wrong.

Dinner's ready, my mother says, appearing in the doorway, and my father gives me a quick smile. Too cold tonight anyway, he says.

+ + +

By the time I head downstairs the next morning I've managed to convince myself that we might actually be capable of enjoying an amicable holiday celebration. Not once has my father mentioned my grades, and though midnight didn't find us swimming, we did accept second helpings of that pumpkin cheesecake my mother had baked. I'm not deluding myself; we're not going to end up sitting around the fireplace this afternoon, reminiscing about Thanksgivings past. But there's at least a chance that we'll be able to get through the day with something resembling civility.

My father's already at the table with a mug of coffee and *The Wall Street Journal*. You're up early, he says, raising his eyebrows. I thought I'd help, I say, glancing at my mother, who's already prepping for dinner. I like your initiative, my father tells me, though he clearly has no intention of joining us, and my mother smiles. Chopped fine, she says, handing me an onion.

We're good. We're more than good, and I can feel myself relaxing and agreeing to the cup of coffee my mother offers me. Breakfast in a bit, she adds, like I can't get myself a bowl of cereal. My father complains about the economy as he peruses the paper, but in a mild way, then asks my opinion.

His interest appears genuine rather than a test to see whether or not I've been paying attention in class, and in a hesitant voice I tell him what I think. He nods, musing as if I've given him something substantial to ponder, and I can't help remembering James's birthday lunch and the easy banter between him and his father. This morning might be the closest I'll ever get, and I sip my coffee, appreciating the ease of this moment, my mother quiet but attentive as she shells and peels chestnuts for the stuffing.

We've never shared this holiday with anyone else. My mother's parents died just after she graduated from high school, and for reasons that have still never been explained to me, my father has distanced himself from his own family. Occasionally, my parents open our house to my father's colleagues, and I can recall more than one dinner party my mother has thrown at his request. But holidays we spend alone, and this Thanksgiving is no exception. For just a second I wonder about James's Thanksgiving, a holiday he's spending with his parents and little sister, and an aunt and uncle and cousins in town from West Texas. For the first time I consider myself lucky that today belongs to just the three of us.

I've chopped my way through several onions and have started on the celery before my father finally stretches his arms over his head and announces that he's thinking of making a few calls in spite of the holiday. I sneak a quick look at my mother, who keeps her eyes on the butter melting in the pan in front of her. But I know what she's thinking. However pleasant the morning has been so far, now we'll have the chance to continue our conversation from yesterday. I can tell her about the oil paints I've been using, maybe try to ask her again about the work she did when she was younger, before she met my father, before I was born. She can finish her thoughts about the sketches she saw yesterday, tell me which ones she likes best. I need her input, need someone other than James looking at what I've done.

My father gets to his feet as I'm planning our conversation, and when he lingers, I glance up, impatient. Good to have you home, he says to me, and the same satisfaction that filled my chest when my mother was looking over my sketchbooks yesterday flows through me now, followed by the worst kind of confusion. I need him to be more than the caricature I've created, but I just don't know how to reconcile two decades' worth of evidence to the contrary. He smiles, my own macabre benefactor or a father ready to bestow a new beginning. An image of him standing in front of the dining room windows last night talking about my fifteen-year-old self decides my reaction.

I return his smile, and he squeezes my shoulder, too hard. Beneath my skin, my muscles brace themselves, adrenaline flooding my system so suddenly my breath turns audible, and though I want to jerk away from him, I stand rooted to the spot, my hand still gripping my knife. At the change in my expression he frowns, confirming what I already know: that in this moment he has no desire to hurt me. But I swear I smell smoke, and as the realization of my rejection narrows his eyes, I turn to my mother, who wears her fear like a shroud.

Then he's gone. I'll be in my office, he says over his shoulder in a voice so casual I wonder why I'm shaking. I place both hands—one still holding the knife—palms down on the counter. Joel? my mother says, and the words leave my mouth before I can stop them, before I have time to predict their potential for damage. Sometimes I hate him, I say.

I know my mother has no idea what happened over Spring Break; for years I've kept this shit to myself. But at the very least she's aware that my father and I don't get along, that he refuses to see me for who I am, that he's bent on creating me in his own image. She's witnessed firsthand the emotional abuse, and I suspect she's been dealing with some of that herself since I've been gone. She might even be suffering more, and my hand clutches the knife I'm holding, thinking about what she might have been made to endure.

If I'm looking for commiseration, I'm not going to get it. How can you say such a thing? she asks. I lower my eyes at the tremor in her voice, the tears I fear will follow. I know you have your differences..., she says.

She doesn't finish her thought, and when I take a step in her direction, she blocks me with a look. Go, she says, I have my hands full.

I call James that night after a dinner so fraught with tension that our very silence vibrated. My father, apparently deciding that he's done wasting time on displays of affection, grills me about my grades. My mother does nothing to intervene, and while I'm glad of that—I work my ass off to ensure that she's never in the middle—I know that at least part of her silence stems from my behavior this morning. I try to make up for what I said, but she's done with me, too, and my offer to help with the dishes she soundly refuses. What's up? James asks when I reach him, and I close my eyes.

We talked only a handful of times on the phone before school started our freshman year, resigned to rooming together even though we'd never met. But our first night in Austin I realized just how much I'd covet the ease with which he yawned, without bothering to cover his mouth, the casual thrust of his hands in his pockets when he leaned against the desk in our room. Every gesture I wanted for my own, and half the time, I found myself scrawling through my sketchbook, trying to loosen the feeling.

For the most part I rarely saw him those first few months, involved as he was with his fraternity and the part-time job he'd taken on in order to pay for it. Then one night, in the middle of November, he called and confessed in a rush of desperate, uncharacteristic breath that he'd gotten pulled over on his way home from a party, refused a breathalyzer, failed a round of sobriety tests. By the time I arranged for a gritty bail bondsman to release him the day was dawning, and I barely had enough time to take in the smudge of shadow under his eyes before he was grabbing me in a brisk, unanticipated hug, reeking of cigarette smoke and beer. Thank you, he said.

No problem, I shrugged, embarrassed by the fervor of his arms but touched by his sincerity.

I knew there was no way he could pay me back without getting his parents involved, without jeopardizing his standing with the fraternity he was on the verge of pledging. I knew that was why he'd called me, and when we climbed in my Explorer and he drummed his fingers on the leg of his jeans, my heart hammered an unexpected accompaniment. Just buy me a beer or something, I said, and that night we ended up in my Explorer, armed with a six-pack, enough to whet our desire but not so much that James would end up back behind bars. Heading north, we chased stars across darkened farm roads, bullshitting about classes and parties, then turning more serious, our eyes on the sky. That was the night I realized he has an idyllic sense of family I can't even envision, and after a while I shut down, pulling silently on my beer. Later, on the way back to the dorm, he let loose a scream, laughing as the bottle between my legs sloshed into my lap. Try it, he insisted, so self-assured that I was left wretched with jealousy. When I opened my mouth, the sound floored us both. We took turns screaming in between swallows of beer the entire way back to Austin. The release of energy liberated me, and I felt a sudden burst of strength. We can do anything, I thought. Anything.

Talking to James, I can forget for seconds at a time that I'm in my father's house. I can forget the clamp of his hand on my shoulder, the look in my mother's eyes the moment I disappointed her. I can forget everything but the sound of James's voice, and I keep my eyes shut and will it to take me home.

+ + +

Finals kick me in the gut, starting with my Ethics exam. I've stayed up late all weekend, cramming, but at this stage of the game the effort's moot. If you just read the material when it's assigned, James says, loitering in the doorway of my bedroom on Sunday night as I'm realizing the sheer folly of highlighting something I'll never reread, Then you'd barely need a review. You sound like my father, I mutter. Isn't that defamation of character? he asks.

The next day, I flip through the pages of my exam with mounting anxiety. I see names, writers, I don't even recognize. In just fifteen minutes I've answered every question I can, and when I run my eyes down the Scantron, I realize I'm totally screwed. I bubble in the circles until I have a shape resembling a sickle, the kind I'll obviously be using to slit my own throat in order to avoid another confrontation with my father. When I'm finished, I trudge up to the front of the room, two hundred pairs of eyes boring a hole in my wayward back.

This isn't a good sign, James tells me when I get home hours ahead of schedule. Falling into the chair across from him, I bury my face in the arm of my sweatshirt. That bad, he muses. Worse, I mumble. So what's next? he asks. Spanish, I say, Tomorrow. What a relief, he says, You're practically fluent.

That night, I listen to him brag about how he's aced his Chemistry exam. He's earned nothing less than an A since he started college; you'd think it would rub off. You have five minutes to open a present? I finally ask, interrupting as he outlines the rest of his week. You got me a present? he says.

She's a tabby, all teeth, one of many from the litter next door. The closest you've come to pussy all semester, I tell him, handing her over. You've been waiting all day to say that, haven't you? he asks. He lifts her by the scruff of her neck, and she mewls, paws flailing. I'll take care of her shots, I tell him, but he's not listening. He's already smitten, and he christens her, then murmurs her name over and over.

+ + +

James leaves with Pandora in tow at the end of the week, but I stay at the house through the weekend, afraid to face my mother, afraid of the punishment my father will mete out the second he sees my grades. Concern for my mother finally forces me out the door, and when I make it to Houston, I see that I was right to worry. The shadows under her eyes rival those she wore at Thanksgiving, and there's a tremor in her hands I've never seen. What's wrong? I ask, What's going on? I'm just tired, honey, she says, The holidays don't plan themselves. Well, can I do anything to help? I ask, and she gives me a smile that doesn't quite reach her eyes. You're sweet, she says, But no. Is it him? I ask in a lower voice, and she sets her mouth in a way that makes me wish I hadn't asked. I watch her, hating that she's unhappy, hating myself for wanting to go back to Austin when I've just barely arrived.

With sincere trepidation I check the mailbox for the next few days. I know I have an A in World Civilizations, thanks to James, and I might get away with a B in Government, but I've got a solid C in Biology, and I'll be lucky to get one in Spanish. Ethics—a D would surprise me.

On Christmas Eve my father comes home from the office in a foul mood. We tiptoe around him, afraid of saying the wrong thing; I don't think he believes me when I tell him I still don't have my grades. Do you think we're hiding them from you, Edward? my mother actually asks, and I take a step between them, assuring my father that I'll deliver the grades into his hands as soon as they're delivered into mine. We make a pretense of exchanging a few obligatory gifts before I head upstairs, where I lie awake for hours, dreading tomorrow and all the tension it promises.

The next morning, I find my parents lounging around the dining room table with an insouciance that leaves me dumbfounded. You slept late, my father grunts, and I cut him a quick, defensive look. But he's teasing me, and I offer him a smile he surprises me by returning. When he puts his arm around my shoulders, I'm embarrassed by the tears that come to my eyes. Dressed in a crisply starched shirt and new tie, he touches my mother's hand, and I wonder, not for the first time in my life, if maybe it's not as bad as I sometimes think.

Jennifer Hritz

2

January 1992

James and I haven't spoken since we left Austin, not since we threw ourselves down the front steps and into the night, not since I tossed him the keys to my Explorer. Next to me, he grips the steering wheel with an urgency he rarely possesses.

There's been an accident, that's all I've been told, and I slide my hand up and down the worn leg of my jeans, reliving the past few weeks, hearing the beginning of every message she left on my answering machine. I erased them all the second I heard her voice.

I haven't spoken to her—to either of my parents—in almost a month, since the day after Christmas. I'd knocked on the door of my father's study, a semester's worth of shitty grades in my hand and a tremor in the pit of my stomach, and when I saw the smoke coiling from his cigar, I pulled out a last-ditch effort as a means of survival: I threatened him. Enraged, he told me something monstrous. I fled, bawling, then got the fuck out of there. My mother begged me not to go, but I was adamant, knew that I needed to absolutely, irrevocably, cut the cord. By the time I reached Austin city limits I'd cried as much as I'd allow myself.

Remembering that miserable drive, I curl my hands into fists, my nails slicing half-moons in my palms. I've defended her, to James, to myself, when in reality it wouldn't take much to indict either one of my parents.

But then there's the painting. She gave that to me, indulged my obsession in direct defiance of my father. Edward, she said over my shoulder as she rocked me back and forth, How could you, how could you?

I pick at a hole in the knee of my jeans, worry it until I can fit two fingers through the threads. James glances at me in the thin light from the dashboard, his baseball cap crammed low over his eyes. I have to stop for gas, Joel, he says. He sounds almost apologetic, and I'm struck by how readily he's accompanied me the night before classes start, by the reluctance with which he accepts the cash I offer him when we pull into a service station. Every so often, when I want to fuck with him, I remind him that he still owes me coin from bailing him out of jail. Dude, I've more than paid that shit back, he'll say, I have to *live* with your ass.

Night this far out in the middle of nowhere glitters with stars, and I stare out the open passenger window into a cold, silent wind that stings my cheeks and burns my eyes. Even the sideview mirror can't begin to decipher the rash of emotions fighting for dominance in my expression, the fear of what I might have set in motion, the regret already building at the back of my mouth.

A rage so fine and pure I shimmy along with the sky.

You okay? James asks as he climbs back in the Explorer. That West Texas accent causes his words to linger, and I shake my head, taking note of the set of his jaw, the purse of his lips. He's not usually so quiet, and I realize that his silence means he's preparing himself for the worst.

I've managed to fit my fist through my jeans by the time we reach Houston, and I wrestle my hand from the hole when I see the police car in my parents' driveway. I should have imagined my father's complicity, and I sprint across the lawn, then throw open the front door with such force that the officers inside automatically cradle the butts of their guns. But I have eyes only for my father.

I've never seen him so disheveled, and I falter taking in his crumpled clothing, the tie that hangs unknotted from his neck. After a horrified moment I realize he's crying. Any thought that he could be responsible vanishes. Dad? I say, but his expression's suddenly so venomous I take a step back. I want him to come toward me, need him to tell me there's been a mistake, but it's an officer who approaches instead. I catch a brief glimpse of James, his hand to his mouth.

They try to stop me as I tear through the living room, as I burst through the bedroom into the master bath. She's gone, but there's still so much blood. Falling to my knees, I clasp my hands behind my head, execution style. I don't recognize the language that spills from my mouth. And then James kneels in front of me, folds me into his arms. Okay, he says, Okay. The word's a disconnection from what's in front of me, a promise of what's to come, and without question the one thing I can hold onto. I latch on and don't let go.

+ + +

At the hotel—where my father has insisted we go despite the arrival of the cleaning service—I escape to the bathroom, where I crouch on the floor beside the tub with my head in my hands. I can hear James talking on the phone in a hushed tone to his parents; I'm lost in Thanksgiving, the scent of vanilla, the thick stench of my father's Cuban. Sometimes I hate him, I said, and I was both shamed and wounded by her tears.

Joel, James says through the door. I close my eyes without answering, bite the inside of my lip until I feel the sweet release of blood fill my mouth. Joel? James says again. He tries the knob, but the door, which I've neglected to lock, sticks. Open the fucking door, Joel, he says, and before he can throw the full force of his weight behind it I stand and reach for the knob, nodding and shaking my head at the same time like a mental patient. I need sleep, I say. He trails me as I yank back the covers on one of the beds, but I shut him up and crawl inside.

An hour later I listen to him breathe. Eyes closed, I try to picture the layout of our dorm room last year: the window, grainy with dust; the water stain on the ceiling in the corner by the closet; the glare of the fluorescent light. Carried away by the images, I let myself float, James's breathing background music. Despite everything, I sleep.

+ + +

The night of my mother's visitation, I dress in a charcoal suit I've bought for the occasion, knot a tie around my neck. I've gotten my hair cut, and I run my fingers through what's left. Thick, dark, short, my hair accentuates the hollows my eyes can't quite fill, the stark bones in my face. I've lost weight the past few days, and though my parents' housekeeper made James and me lunch today—tomato soup, grilled cheese sandwiches, chocolate milk, all of which made me feel five years old—I couldn't eat a thing.

At the funeral home I stand with my father. The casket's in the background, closed at his insistence, though the decision's immaterial. Suicide renders the atmosphere downright bitter, and I'm acutely aware of my father's humiliation. Groping for breath, I try to ignore James, who watches my every move from across the room. You should take off for a while, I told him earlier today, self-conscious about everything he's done for me. Don't be ridiculous, he said flatly, I'm not leaving you here by yourself.

My father's colleagues murmur their condolences, but I barely hear their voices. I keep combing through the holiday, the tension on Christmas Eve, my father's repeated requests for my grades, which still hadn't arrived. Do you think we're hiding them from you, Edward? my mother asked. But the next morning she laughed when my father teased me about how late I'd slept, twisting the bracelet I'd given her the night before around and around her wrist. Maybe, I thought, watching my father touch her hand, maybe it's not as bad as I sometimes think.

Now I'm drowning in a sea of mourners, and when my vision starts to gray, I mumble my apologies, then skirt the edge of the room until I find an exit. Outside the sky swims above me, a haze of cloud and reflected light, and I lope the length of the funeral home, gulping dizzying mouthfuls of air. Even with my eyes squeezed shut I can see her, framed in white Christmas lights the moment I drove away. I sway on my feet, then bend over, my hands on my knees. Joel? James says, and I whirl around.

Back off, I growl. Okay, he says, Sorry. Stop! I cry, Stop being so fucking *nice* to me! He hesitates, and I ball my hands into fists. Give me one goddamn minute to myself, I say, Would you please. He turns, and I back up against the wall, then slide down until I'm squatting on my haunches. Trembling, I release my breath, guess that I've got maybe five minutes before my father comes looking for me. I cry for two, then press my hand to my forehead. The pain doesn't go away.

+ + +

I poured the first drink with my father's knowledge, the second while he was mingling with the handful of guests who've escorted us back to the house. As I tipped the decanter the third time, he caught my eye and gave his head a slight shake, a gesture I pretended I didn't see. Now he murmurs alongside his guests, holding a scotch of his own, his shirt perfectly pressed, the meticulous attention to detail. I've needed him to reach out, needed to know he's not blaming me for what happened. Instead, he's kept his distance, and over the past few hours I've come to the conclusion that he's punishing me.

Eschewing conversation, I slouch against the sofa cushions, James beside me wearing one of my ties. I haven't apologized for my outburst at the funeral home, but he doesn't seem to care. He's more concerned with whether or not I'm holding it together, with what I've told him so far. And there's still so much he doesn't know.

At this point I'm just drunk enough to imagine that I see her through the dining room windows, out by the pool in the musky dark. She's beautiful but haunted, with long hair as thick as mine and hollow cheeks that complicate her eyes. I couldn't paint her if I tried.

When ice clinks against my teeth, I gaze into my glass, then get to my feet. Don't, James says in a low voice, and despite my inebriation, I have to admire his insight.

I think you've had enough, my father says, appearing beside me as I'm unplugging the decanter. I happen to agree, but I pour a generous shot anyway. My father glances behind us at the assembled crowd. Joel, he warns as I raise the glass to my lips.

Under normal circumstances he'd have to say nothing else; under normal circumstances I'd never so blatantly disobey him. But I've had one too many drinks, and there's no one left to protect, and I honestly don't think my father will retaliate, not in front of his guests.

I swallow a mouthful of liquor. My father's face petrifies. *You*, he hisses, so low only I can hear, *You*. His voice smolders with rage, with the truth, and I close my eyes as if that could shelter me from what's coming. *You* pulled the fucking trigger, he says.

I sink to the floor under the eyes of a dozen guests, under the weight of an accusation I've been expecting since the initial phone call. His words penetrate my skin, burrow into the furthest recesses of my anatomy and take up root. Hands covering my eyes, I writhe, my softest tissue threaded with barbs, guilt a slow, insidious crawl through my veins.

Then James has me by the arms. Upstairs, he says under his breath, and something about the way he says the word, some odd combination of tenderness and authority I never knew existed, moves me in the direction he's pointing.

20

+ + +

Despite the morning's morbidity, the sun shines with a vengeance, and I follow my father to the front of the church and slide into a pew next to him. I have a sinister headache, and I dig my fingers into my temples, glancing behind me to find James. Last night, he paced back and forth at the foot of my bed as the room spun around me. I'm ashamed of my behavior, of what he's been made to witness the past few days.

My mother's casket rests in front of us, illuminated in an incongruous shaft of sunlight, and I shift my focus to my hands. Over the past few days I've bitten the nails to the quick, and they bleed at the slightest provocation. I pick at them, paying scant attention to the service. My father, past the point of shedding tears, sits stoically beside me. I'd thought he might have words for me this morning, thought he might apologize or blame what happened on too many drinks of his own. But he took one look at me and turned away.

I could scream, right here, for hours.

My father has insisted on driving the Mercedes to the cemetery, and I watch from the sideview mirror as the line of cars snakes behind us. I'm living now for the moment I can leave, the moment that will take me back to Austin, the moment that will take me home. In the meantime I've started to tremble, and I squeeze myself together, trying not to fall apart.

Do you think you can do without the money? my father asks, pulling up behind the hearse, and I turn to him, confused. What? I say, and he kills the engine. One look at his expression has me fumbling for the door. Do you? he asks, holding me back.

I try to recall that moment last night when I stood in front of him and summoned the courage to meet his eyes with my own. But this morning I have nothing, and my father adjusts the collar of my shirt. An impartial observer would interpret the action as paternal, but I know better. Your choice, he tells me, But I don't think you'd last long.

I don't breathe as he leaves the car, as he steps toward my mother's remains. My lungs simply shut down, and when they finally open again, I can't control the shaking any longer. My teeth chatter so hard I have to cover my mouth; still I can barely hold back my scream. Instead, I bite, sinking my teeth into the soft flesh of my hand.

I will never be free.

+ + +

My professors have already been notified of my situation, and most of them tell me to ease into the semester and let them know if I need a little extra time with assignments. After faking through each of my classes at least once I hole up in the back room under the pretense of working. But despite what I feel brewing, I can't bring myself to pick up a brush. I have a feeling I won't be able to bear seeing what comes out the other end. Instead, I sleep. Solid, black sleep that I fall into easily, dreamlessly.

James worries over every class I skip, every dinner invitation I decline. We stop just shy of argument every time he suggests I leave the house. He's been more friend than I expected, more friend than I've deserved. So when he coaxes me outside one afternoon under the guise of a shared cigarette, I follow him without complaint, and we settle ourselves on the back steps beneath a threatening sky.

So, he says, sliding a Marlboro from the pack between us and reaching in his pocket for a lighter. Behind us Pandora scratches the screen. She's been more work than we anticipated—we came back from Houston to find claw marks gouging the furniture—and I'll find James bitching at her in one breath, then cradling her in his arms the next. Now he casts an idle glance in her direction, then squints up at the clouds when we hear the low rumble of thunder. You're a Business major, he says.

For the past year and a half I've managed to keep my major a mystery, explain away my failure to register for art classes by telling him that I want to get as many core classes out of the way as I can. I heard you on the phone with your father, he admits, and I feel the blood rush to my face. What, were you fucking eavesdropping? I ask, and he gives me a look suggesting I should know better. Weren't you going to take Drawing Foundation this semester? he asks.

The class I'd quietly dropped after the holiday, even though that meant a twelve hour course load instead of fifteen.

It's *your* life, you know, James reminds me. Yeah, well, I mutter, reaching for a cigarette, It's *his* money.

We sit with that unhappy proclamation, inhaling and exhaling into the swollen sky. I spent several months during that first year James and I roomed together worrying about whether or not he thought me pretentious given the difference in our finances. But I was the one he called the night he was arrested for that DWI, even though at the time we barely knew each other. Since then, we've had only one blowout regarding money, and that was because I lied about the cost of our rent. I couldn't help myself. I knew when I pulled up to this house at the end of our freshman year that I wanted to live here, and I knew James had financial limitations. So I softened the numbers. Fuck your intentions, he said when he found out, You can't take it upon yourself to pay for everything and not expect me to feel indebted. He ticked off a list: beer; dinner every other night; a hotel room I booked when we flew on a whim down the interstate to San Antonio. I half-expected him to bring up the DWI, and when instead he let me off with a warning, I breathed a sigh of relief. He could've told me he was moving out.

The sky opens, and as raindrops spatter around us, we duck under the safety of the porch. What's the worst that could happen if you told him to go fuck himself? James asks, and I think back to that moment in my father's Mercedes when he threatened me with the only thing he has left. He'd cut me off, I say. James shakes his head, smoke streaming from his nose. You could make a go of it on your own, he says, but he offers the suggestion tentatively, as if he can already imagine my response. I don't disappoint, shoot him a withering look. You're more interested in what you've got going on in there anyway, Joel, he says, nodding in the direction of the back room. So? I say. Maybe you should consider dropping out of school, he says. How am I supposed to *live*? I ask. Wait tables? he suggests, as if that's a legitimate possibility. Wait tables, I repeat. Or whatever, he mumbles. I'll never have time to paint, I tell him. You wouldn't have to answer to your father, he points out.

I grit my teeth, but I can't expect him to understand, can't expect him to know the ways my father owes me. I deserve this money. I deserve the house and the car and more fucking clothes than I can wear in a year. I deserve more than my father can ever repay.

James takes a deep breath, grinding out his cigarette, and for the briefest moment I think he's going to belabor the point. Instead, he gets to his feet. What're you doing? I ask as he pads down the steps, but he just throws his arms wide and lets out a *whoop*, the sound both invitation and encouragement. I'm right back at the spring, and I close my eyes, trying to feel my way to that moment in the sun. October, barely four months ago, when she was still alive.

C'mon! James calls, cold rain soaking his skin. You're certifiable, I mutter, but when I reach him, I tilt my head back and open my mouth to the sky.

+ + +

I can't risk losing my life here, can't risk losing my father's financial support. I'll never survive without him, so I erase the past month and shove everything so deep inside I won't be able to find it again. Then I reinitiate relationships with my professors and struggle to make up enough work to avoid failing notices mid-semester. James follows me to the library since I'm too easily distracted staying home. He's always got work anyway, busts his ass trying to ace every paper, every exam.

I turn twenty at the end of February, but I don't feel much like celebrating. At least let me take you to lunch, James says in between classes, and so I do, picking my way through a hamburger as he complains about his fraternity. He's done nothing but since he pledged over a year ago. Most of the time I keep my mouth shut. I've never understood his interest in the Greek system, other than that he's obsessed with the source itself: Greece's history, its mythology. Otherwise, I just don't get it. He's subject to late-night meetings and volunteer work and party planning that goes way beyond filling the bathtub with a few bags of ice and a couple cases of beer. But I don't say a word. I'm just thankful for the time I get with him. He could've decided to move into the fraternity house this year instead of with me, and if he had, I might have never seen him again.

Today he tells me that some of his older brothers have started accusing him of taking his responsibilities too lightly. There's a dinner tonight, he says, one he forgot about entirely until Shelton reminded him this morning. Shelton's a dickwad with an obnoxious nasal twang and a vested interest in Ralph Lauren, judging from the limited range of his wardrobe. My father would love him. I don't want to go, James whines. So don't, I say. But he tells me that at the rate he's accumulating black marks they'll kick him out of the fraternity before he can make the decision to quit himself. So go, I sigh. It's your birthday, he reminds me, and I say, Big fucking deal.

But after he leaves I'm sorry I encouraged him. I've had a sad little day, kicking around memories of my mother and the birthdays she planned for me during my childhood, quiet affairs that usually involved an excursion to an art museum and lunch. I never denigrated those times; I never wanted the kind of birthday party I knew my classmates shared with their friends. I relished the relative solitude of the museum, the velvety coolness of a chocolate milkshake afterward, my mother sitting across from me, lit from within from what she'd just seen. This year she's no longer here to call me, and my father phoned so late in the day and so briefly that I couldn't help but feel like an afterthought.

I'm staring at my reflection in my bedroom window when James appears in my doorway midway through the evening, too early to have seen his dinner through to the end. What're you doing here? I ask, and he shrugs, his hands in the pockets of his jeans. He has longish, wavy hair I've seen girls swoon over, and I watch as he shakes it from his eyes. Let's go out, he suggests. Nah, I say, but he's already kicking my boots in my direction. C'mon, he says, We'll go to Mount Bonnell. At this time of year? I ask, and he tells me we'll have the place to ourselves because of the weather. I bought a bottle of Bacardi, he adds.

James doesn't often spring for liquor; he can't afford the expense. That fraternity eats up every available penny he earns. But he's made a special exception because of my birthday, and I don't know whether to accept this gift he's offering so freely or give in to the resentment in my chest. I don't want to be pitied. C'mon, he says, taking my silence for agreement, I didn't come home so you can sit on your ass.

Wind rocks the trees at the top of the cliff, and we stare down at the lake and then at the black sky above us. Stars skitter back and forth beneath the clouds. We're drinking the rum straight, small nips that warm our chest and flow toward our fingertips. Even so, my toes feel numb, and I curl them in my boots, heavy Redwings I've worn so often over the past year and a half that the leather has softened like a kiss. James wears them, too, his own pair he probably squandered all of his Christmas money to afford. He kicks them idly against the rock wall circling the edge of the cliff.

I quit the fraternity, he says.

I turn to look at him, but his hair, wild in the wind, obscures his expression. Everything feels frivolous, he adds, You know? I nod without speaking; the few times I've seen him head out the door with a basketball under his arm over the past couple of weeks have practically undone me.

How'd they react? I ask, and he reaches for the Bacardi. Not well, he admits, taking a sip. He hands me the rum, and I watch as he hoists himself onto the wall, then gets to his feet. I light a nervous cigarette.

The day we met, we had an informal meeting with the R.A. on our hall. I'd spent the afternoon driving up and down the Drag, that eclectic mix of restaurants and shops on the edge of campus, listening to Jane's Addiction and contemplating whether or not I should just cut town, keep driving and never return. By the time I made it back to the dorm I barely had enough time to take a quick shower, my first in the community bathroom. I remember the tepid temperature of the water. I remember noticing how ropy my arms had become from swimming all summer, and my tan.

After my shower I made my way to the TV room, where the meeting was being held. Guys already sprawled across the sofa. I sat with my back against one of the chairs, and when James appeared, he nodded in my direction but sat well away from me, near the door. I felt the slight the way I would a paper cut, sharp and keen.

For the next ten minutes I paid half-hearted attention as the R.A. introduced himself and went over some bullshit rules, but I balked when he suggested we say a few words about ourselves. I cast a quick glance at James, then, who was sitting with one knee to his chest, picking at his toenail. The depth of his tan shocked me, as did the thin, embroidered bracelet he wore around one ankle. He caught me watching and raised his eyebrows.

Knowing that he was going through Rush, I expected him to introduce himself with a nod in the direction of whatever fraternity he espoused, expected him to tell us that he was majoring in Business. Instead, he confessed that he was aching for his summer gig as a lifeguard. I miss my little sister, too, he said. How old? some idiot yelled out, leering. She's six, James said. His bare feet, crossed at the ankles, rocked slowly back and forth. What's your major? the R.A. asked, and James shrugged.

We moved on, but I kept stealing glances at him. I couldn't help myself. I felt so strange in my own skin, and I sensed, looking around the room, that I wasn't the only one. Some guy would hasten a joke, and everyone would cut their eyes at James to see how he'd respond. Meanwhile, I waited in agony for my turn. I just wasn't sure what I wanted to reveal.

I'm Joel Grayson, I finally admitted when the guy to my right finished up, I'm an artist.

I'd never said those words before, and the declaration sounded good coming from my mouth. I actually had to stop the smile I could feel sprouting at the edge of my lips. So you're an Art major? the R.A. asked, and I hesitated, ultimately refusing to spoil the moment by announcing that I'd end up with a Business degree. Instead, I tried a shrug. Miraculously, the affectation worked, and before I knew it the next guy was introducing himself. Then I did smile, so quickly I thought no one saw. When I felt eyes on me, I looked up. James's expression didn't change.

Even then I knew he had something. Even then he pulled me in, and I watch him now as he balances on a ledge no wider than his boot. C'mon up, he says, offering the invitation as if it's mine to receive. No fucking way, I say. Where's your sense of adventure? he asks. I had it beaten out of me at a young age, I mutter, and he frowns, as if he can't decide whether or not I'm serious. Then he spreads his arms like he's thinking of taking flight. The view's beautiful up here, Joel, he says. But I shake my head, and he finally jumps away from the edge and back toward solid ground. Happy birthday, he says when he lands. Thanks, I say, and he grins.

+ + +

For the first time since I've known him, James has some legitimate freedom, and we spend the next few days indulging in the kind of camaraderie we should have from the beginning. I'm so fucking glad I *quit*, he admits, his drawl thick and slow from the pot we've been smoking. I laugh and he smiles, a lazy, luxurious smile that looks so good on him I can't keep the thought to myself. That fraternity was sucking you dry, I say, and he tilts his head to the side, looking thoughtful. I think I just outgrew them, he says. They were never a good match, I tell him flatly. He fixes his eyes on me, and I shake my head, fortified in part by the pot we've shared but more because of the decision he made the other night, the trip he made to Houston with me last month. You don't need them, James, I say, You never did.

For just a second I think I might have overstepped my bounds, and I'm about to mumble an apology when one corner of his mouth slides to the right in a gesture of unabashed admiration. You should be candid more often, he says.

That night, I wake from a nightmare that pales in comparison to the ones that plagued me as a child. I'm thrown into a sitting position, biting back screams, soaked in a sweat so cold I doubt I'll ever get warm again. Moaning, I duck back under the covers, willing my heart to ease, my ragged breathing to taper. Slowly, the specifics of my dream start to fade, and when I've finally settled enough to sink back into sleep, the nightmare takes me again.

I attribute the dreams to the pot we smoked, but the next night, I'm in the exact same position, bolt upright in bed, sweat-slicked and shivering, just as terrified that I've awakened James as I am of drifting back to sleep. Instead, I make my way to the back porch, where I smoke in the dark. Then I creep into the living room and turn on the television. Buried in an afghan on the sofa, I dream again.

By the end of the week I'm sick with exhaustion and afraid to close my eyes. Haven't you slept? James asks when he gets up for his eight o'clock and finds me on the porch, where I've smoked the better part of a pack of cigarettes. In a hoarse voice I tell him I'm not really all that tired; I'm just having a string of weird dreams. And no, I definitely don't need to see anyone.

Later that afternoon, I stretch out on the sofa in front of the television. You look like shit, James tells me. He's on his way to the library to do some research for a paper he has to write for his Greek & Roman Mythology class. I've already berated him for spending his Friday afternoon doing homework, but he was too excited to take me seriously, and I finally had to admit that maybe this whole obsession he has with Greece, right down to the map he hung on the wall next to the dartboard I picked up over the holiday, might be the real thing. Now I comb my fingers through my hair with half an eye on the television and half an eye on James, who's slinging his backpack over his shoulder. You want me to stay? he offers, and I make a face. Why? I say, When you can hear the Sirens calling?

After he leaves I rub my temples. Whoever came up with the idea of keeping people awake as a means of torture had a good idea. I feel like I'm in a prison camp and I'm being beaten slowly and methodically into submission. Another night of this and I'll confess anything. I've never needed sleep so desperately, and I plead to whoever's listening to just give me an hour. One hour of uninterrupted sleep, one hour of peace. *One hour*, I think as Pandora curls beside me, and with my hand in her fur I close my eyes.

I'm perched on my childhood bed, sunlight spilling through the open blinds. I'm painting: a tree, a sun, a house, nothing I've ever painted, and when the knock comes, I laugh a child's high, piercing laugh, ignoring whoever's at my door. The knock grows louder, insistent, but still I don't move. I just laugh, and paint, and paint, the brush strong in my hand, my happiness fierce in its intensity. Then the door swings open. I hear my heartbeat, feel it in my throat, stare at the blackness beyond the doorway. When I look back down, my painting's gone. But there are my hands, my adult hands, covered in so much blood I almost don't see the torn skin under my nails.

I come to with a muffled cry and find James standing across from me. When I sit up, stars dance along my line of vision. Dude, you have *got* to see someone, he says. I hold my head in my hands, too exhausted to disagree.

Monday morning, I pick a doctor out of the phone book, and when I tell the woman who takes my call that I'm happy to pay in cash, she squeezes me right in. The doctor's young, brisk, asks if I've been dealing with any stress. Yeah, I mumble, My mother killed herself six weeks ago. He glances up at me. You should probably talk to a counselor, he admits, and before I can tell him that's never going to happen he hands me a prescription for a tranquilizer.

I take it that night and sleep so shallowly I might as well have never gone to bed at all. Well? James asks the next morning as I collapse at the kitchen table. I didn't dream, I tell him. Good, he says, and I can't explain why he shouldn't be relieved, why the drug was every bit as exhausting as the nightmares themselves.

I forego the pills. The nightmares come back. Swallowing tears of frustration, I end up alternating between the drugs and the dreams until eventually, over the course of the next few days, the dreams stop altogether. A good thing, because I'm almost out of pills and I don't know if I'd be able to con a refill out of that doctor since I've ignored his advice about counseling. I awaken one morning drug-free, then stop mid-stretch when I realize I've slept for more than eight hours without a nightmare. Cool, I whisper in the quiet of morning light. I'm cautiously optimistic.

At my father's request I go to Houston for Spring Break, and when I pull into the driveway, I linger in the Explorer for a while before I shut off the engine. There's no sign at all of what transpired here two months ago, and that makes me more nervous than if I'd found a body bag on the front lawn. Gnawing on my cuticle, I gaze at the azaleas flouncing their showy selves on either side of the arched doorway. They coax me back in time to a Spring Break I'd just as soon forget. I take a quick look in the rearview mirror. A neighbor across the street offers his hand in a tentative wave. I lower my eyes without responding.

I know my father's still at work; I'd planned my trip this way so I'd have a few moments alone in my mother's house before he had a chance to sully the memories I wanted to recollect. But now I'm wondering if I made the right decision. I feel the way I do in those first petrifying moments after I've awakened from a nightmare, and I find my way to the front door with a dread I can't describe.

Nothing's out of place, and as I loiter in the foyer, I honestly anticipate my mother rounding the corner, smiling her quiet smile. *Show me*, she'll say, *Tell me what you've been working on.*

But she's not here. She's not here, and I take a hesitant step into the living room, where everything's the same: the crystal lamps on the end tables, the spill of the drapes, a mélange of curiosities on the shelves in the corner. No one would guess that for the past two months my father has been living here alone; the house even smells the same.

How can she be dead if the house smells the same?

And the quiet. The quiet's like nothing I've ever heard, nothing like the silence the times I've been left alone here because my parents went out for the evening or my mother had errands to run. Instead, the house holds its breath, and I stand on the fringe of the living room, my heart quickening, chill bumps scuttling along my spine.

Then I bolt, through the back door and toward the pool, kicking off my sandals and yanking my shirt over my head. Into the water I fly, where I crank out lap after lap until I've outrun the feel of that house. When exhaustion begs me to stop, I float, the sky above such a perfect blue that tears come to my eyes. I let them fall for half a minute before I swallow what remains and drag a raft into the water. Hauling myself up, I close my eyes.

My skin's burning by the time my father gets home from work. I climb from the pool, figuring that he's probably pissed to have found me out here in the sun instead of huddled over one of my Economics texts at the dining room table, but when I take a closer look at him, I see that his own skin holds the beginning of an early summer tan. So he's been taking advantage of the pool, too.

I'm not sure I love the idea. Shouldn't he still be in mourning?

But that evening, I realize that he's not as together as he seems at first glance. Tension lingers beneath his expression, and he makes reference, twice, to bouts of insomnia. He fails to invoke my mother's name, but despite his generalizations, I gather that the past couple of months have been difficult for him. I'm glad you could come, he admits, and I wonder if he might need me as much as I need him.

Just because I'm on vacation doesn't mean my father isn't working, and I spend the next several days by myself, mostly outside by the pool. But I awaken Friday to rain, and when I finally drag my ass out of bed and trudge downstairs, the sound of the water plinking against the windows unnerves me, and the tan I've acquired looks strange in the bright light of the kitchen. I hike into the living room, where I consider turning on the television, thinking that mindless daytime talk shows might settle the nervous-as-hell feeling in my stomach.

Then I catch the shimmer of light in the hallway leading to the master suite.

I might as well have never left. It takes no imagination at all for me to be right back at that moment, and I have to sit on the edge of the tub with my head between my knees. When I think I can stand up, I do and open the door to the closet. I don't understand why my father hasn't gone through her things. As I pull the plastic from one of her dresses, the scent of her perfume finds me, and I have to press my lips together to keep from crying.

I should've known I couldn't make it through the week without a lecture, and that night, when my father and I go to dinner, he wastes no time. He seems frustrated that I don't have a job lined up for the summer, and when I point out that it's barely the middle of March, he informs me that Permian has already hired everyone they need. What are your plans? he asks. I guess I thought I could take a break this summer, I admit. He narrows his eyes at me, frowning. Because of everything that happened, I add lamely. That doesn't sound very productive, he tells me. I look down at my plate, at the pink flesh of my salmon. The problem with you, Joel, he says, Is that you don't want to work for anything.

I'm not sure that's fair given that I'm still trying to reconcile the image of my mother with a .38 in her mouth, but before I can protest he asks about James. He's taking summer school, I mumble. Well, that's something, my father muses. I force another bite of fish, my appetite dulled by the fear that he'll insist I come back here for the summer, but by the time he makes it through another glass of wine we've worked out a compromise. I take two classes in summer school, business classes, and I can stay in Austin.

I'm relieved enough to order dessert.

+ + +

I have a few weeks of free time after my semester ends, before the summer session starts, and I suggest to James that we get out of town for a while, even if we just road trip to South Padre. My treat, I add, knowing he doesn't have cash. Don't start that shit again, Joel, he says, so I sulk, then spend my time watching shitty television and dodging his questions about why I'm not painting. I'd finally pulled the door to the back room shut midway through the spring semester, and I haven't opened it since.

I'm so restless as a result that I'm almost ready to walk into a business class the first week of June. But one week of lectures about economic theory and I'm ready to fling myself off the 360 bridge. Meanwhile, the heat becomes more untenable with every passing day. Even the spring does little to allay my restlessness, and by the end of the month I'm trying again to convince James to take off with me, just for a few days, someplace where we can swim and maybe do a little diving. I don't have the *cash*, he says, and I urge him to consider the trip an early birthday present. Fine, shit, he finally says, Where do you want to go?

We land in Cancun a couple of weeks later and take a shuttle to our resort, where we park ourselves in front of the pool and start ordering cocktails. James cranks out laps while I yawn, and by the end of the day he's lost the look of tension that's followed him around the past six months, and the sun has tanned his shoulders a deep, nutty brown. You were right, he admits as we're walking back to our room before dinner, This was a good idea.

While he showers, I lean over the balcony, watching the sun slip beneath the horizon. I ease a careful breath from between my lips, the rocking I've felt in my heart since January slowing to a manageable beat. I honestly think I could paint, for the first time since she died.

That night, we hole up in a bar that caters to college students and end up flirting with a couple of girls who tell us they're leaving the next day. They're desperate, James says when they head into the restroom, Close out your tab. I do, shaking my head. I know without asking which girl he wants; I've known him for two years, know he wants something just to the left of conventional, just short of predictable. That's why I ended up with Melissa last summer, who by traditional standards had everything I should've wanted: perfect body; great tits; long, silky hair that just skimmed the top of her ass. Her best friend, Cathleen, was the complete opposite, quiet and wicked shy, with shorn hair and a boyish figure that had nothing on Melissa's curves. But James totally dug her and moped around for weeks when she dumped him just before school started.

So I'm not surprised when the girls return and he slides his arm around Patricia, who wears her hair cropped close, a thin, silver barrette over her ear. Her breasts hover small and high beneath a gauzy, white blouse. I turn to her friend, whose expression borders on disbelief; I get the impression she expected to be able to choose, and I try to soften the blow. I don't want to deal with a princess complex all fucking night. Your sandals kick ass, I lie. They're bronze and high-heeled and twine around her ankles like a pair of snakes, and the second I bestow the compliment, she smiles. Thanks, she says, leaning into me, and when James looks over his shoulder, I roll my eyes.

We go for a walk on the beach, then follow the girls back to their hotel, where we drink copiously from the mini bar. I watch as James and Patricia slide from where they're sitting on the bed into something more prone, his voice low, persuasive. Then I glance at Patricia's friend, whose name I've chased with several drinks. C'mon, she says, taking my hand and pulling me onto the balcony.

Sliding the door shut behind us, she invites me into the shadows, and I find it ironic that James has once again chosen a girl who most likely won't give up a damn thing when her friend's already grinding against me, whispering suggestions she has every intention of making me follow. Here, she whispers, guiding my hand up her skirt, Right here.

Oh my god, you *suck*, James says to me on the way back to our resort, You nailed her on the fucking *balcony*?

I never know what kind of expression I should wear under these circumstances, whether I should feign modesty or elaborate on what transpired. Mostly, I just feel guilty keeping this secret from him. God knows the work it takes to deflect suspicion exhausts me. But I'm still getting used to admitting what I want, even to myself.

The first time, I was fifteen. I knew he was gay; everyone at school knew, and when he approached me one day and asked without apology if I wanted to drive to the beach with him, I didn't know whether to feel flattered or terrified. Mostly, I wanted to know how he knew I'd be interested when I'd barely figured things out for myself. But I was too afraid of the answer, and I flicked my eyes around to see who might be watching us together. I don't think so, I said, and he smiled like he'd known I might be a challenge. Why not? he asked, leaning closer. I gulped in the scent of him, then reared back in confusion. I'll tell you what, he said, and he gave me instructions on where to meet him the next day if privacy was my concern.

I didn't sleep that night. I couldn't, and the next day, I jittered through my classes, pretending to weigh the pros and cons when I knew full well what I planned to do. When I came up beside his car, parked strategically a few blocks from the school, he didn't look surprised. An hour later, he kissed me, a hot ocean wind rushing around us, and I opened my mouth and kissed him back. Afterward, I couldn't believe how I'd let myself go, and the next day, even though I couldn't help replaying that entire hand job in my mind, I couldn't bring myself to look at him. I felt his eyes on me anyway. He knew what I was, and he had the power to tell anyone he chose.

I've carried that fear for the past five years, run interference for James over and over again because I can't imagine telling him the truth. The sex I'll chase once I'm back in Austin serves as my only solace, sex that's impersonal and furtive, sex I'm always sure will lead me back to myself and never does.

You're the fucking *man*, James says now, and the vehemence of his admiration further crushes me. I'm a fraud. But when he bumps my shoulder and tells me I look awfully fucking morose for someone who just got laid, I conjure a grin. Your time will come, I tell him in my most condescending tone, and he gives me the finger.

At least my laugh feels real.

+ + +

I awaken the next morning with a shiver in my spine. Today I get to dive, and that's no small feat. I haven't been under the water since that botched trip to Belize, and I'm ready to get my breath back, to feel even for a moment like everything's right with my world. In the absence of painting there's not much left for me to claim. But I can dive, and oddly enough, I can tell my father about my trip after the fact and know he'll consider this money well-spent.

This is completely safe, right? James asks at the dive shop I've found, as he's signing several pages worth of waivers. The dive master chuckles, winking at me; he's thin, a little older than I'd thought when he first introduced himself, his arms tan, toned, smooth. I make it a point not to return his gaze.

Because James isn't certified, he's required to complete a trial dive in the pool, and we head out there with our tanks in tow, then sink into the water, into the quiet blue. My breath already feels easier after ten seconds than it has in months. I could stay down here forever, and I close my eyes, the muscles I've held in a death grip since the holidays finally beginning to unwind. In that moment of relaxation I think about my mother. She never understood why I wanted to go beneath the surface, declined to accompany my father and me on any excursions. And I've had plenty, starting when I was seven, in Cabo, Aruba, Fiji. My mother waited on shore, anxious and alone, and when we'd return, she'd throw her arms around me and spare an accusing glare in my father's direction as if he'd tried to steal me away from her. Really, Mom, I'd say, The water's so beautiful. But she didn't believe me, not enough to experiment herself.

I miss her.

The thought swims toward me, and I brace myself for sudden impact. But the water and the slow intake of my breath envelope me, and I'm able to acknowledge the emotions those three words raise and then let them go. I take another breath and open my eyes.

I'm alone.

I find James sitting on the steps at the shallow end of the pool, his head buried between his knees. The dive master croons to him in a voice so tender James would probably elbow him in the gut if he wasn't struggling to catch his breath. He's okay, the guy assures me as I approach. But I can see James shivering, and I instinctively touch his arm. What happened? I ask. James shakes his head. Tears well in the corners of his eyes; I watch, stupefied, as he pinches them with his thumb and forefinger. I've never seen him so inhibited, and for a second I feel the way I might if what tethers me to the planet suddenly disappeared. I think he just panicked, the dive master murmurs, and I have to refrain from reminding James that he's a lifeguard, for Christ's sake. There's no reason for him to be scared.

I think we're done here, the dive master adds, and I agree. As disappointed as I might be, I have no interest in coercing James into doing something he doesn't want to do. But he stops us both. How deep? he asks, squinting in the direction of the ocean though he already knows the answer. Thirty feet, the dive master says. And we don't have to *go*, I add. No, he says, Just give me a minute.

A half hour later, he's managed sixty seconds in the pool, but I can tell he still isn't sold by the way his gaze dwells on the strip of hotels as we motor away from the coastline. I show him the backup again. I promise, I say, You'll forget you're breathing with a tank. He nods; I get the impression he wants me to shut up so he can obsess in peace. Go fast, the dive master says under his breath when we finally reach the drop, Before he changes his mind.

The water catches me in a warm embrace, the kind I've been longing for since I watched the sun disappear from our balcony last night. I let the waves cradle me, then move to the side to make room for James; he stares down as if I'm leading him to his execution. Relax, I say when he hits the water beside me, flailing for his mouthpiece, You're going to be fine.

We inch down the rope, then glide along the reef. The colors stun me as they always do, and my fingers tingle thinking about what I could do right now given the right paints, the right brush. I eye James; he's clenching his teeth so hard my own jaw starts to ache. So I give up on convincing him to enjoy himself and concentrate instead on the beauty of my breathing.

After thirty minutes we surface, slow and easy. I haven't felt this calm in months, and after the dive master helps us into the boat I turn to James. I guess you're not joining me tomorrow, I say. No fucking way, he blurts out, and the dive master and I share a conspiratorial smile. He's dark, his hair thick with golden highlights, and for one powerful second I let myself wonder what might happen if I reached over, right now, and ran my fingers through its damp heft. The thought compromises my breath, and I don't trust myself to answer when he asks if we're college students. Juniors, James says, and the dive master glances in my direction. You must need a vacation, he says, With all that homework. I don't spend a lot of time studying, I admit, and he takes his time looking me up and down. I bet you don't, he says.

That guy was totally hitting on you, James says on the way back to our resort. Maybe, I concede, ransacking his tone for clues that he disapproves, that he's disgusted, that he's ready to book the next flight home. Maybe, my ass, he says, He was practically on his fucking knees.

A ridiculous blush crawls up my neck, and James guffaws. That turn you on or something? he says, and there's a part of me that wants to seize this moment and break my silence once and for all. Mere seconds pass as I consider my options, but I've hesitated just long enough. James watches me with a wariness I can't combat; I have an uncomfortable recollection of this guy I met a few times last summer for quick hookups when I was sleeping with Melissa. Don't you have a *girlfriend?* he asked when I showed up at his apartment unannounced, and I'd wondered if I'd ever come to a point in my life when desire wouldn't be coupled with shame. Fuck you, I say now in a voice so weak I can't imagine I'll convince him. But James grins. For a second there, he says, You really had me going.

I never do get around to painting. There's no opportunity, really, during our time in Cancun, and after we're back in Austin I'm too preoccupied with my failed attempt at coming out and the approaching semester to sort through how I feel about the back room. Why don't you concentrate on your real work? James asks once school starts up again and I complain about the business classes I'm taking. I shrug and tell him I'm busy, but the bottom line is that after eight months without working I'm more scared of a paintbrush in my hand than the remote for the television. So I keep the door to the back room shut, repress what I'm feeling, and find that I've got quite a knack for keeping everything in my life just beneath the surface.

3

I go for a run the first time the weather falls below eighty degrees, and I can't seem to make myself stop. I feel fantastic, hesitate to light up on the back porch the few nights dreams drive me awake because I'm afraid that inhaling so much smoke might affect my lung capacity the next day. You're obsessive, James tells me as I'm tying the laces of my very new, very expensive running shoes for the third time in a twenty-four period. Come with me, I offer, but he tells me he'd rather sit on his fat ass and watch television.

The running becomes a huge stress release for me. I eat better, think twice before I get trashed, knowing a hangover will affect my run. James remains in a state of denial until after his birthday, and then he starts running with me. He catches up quickly, and we run together every other day. The off days I run alone, unwilling to give up the endorphin rush. It's raining, he whines one night, and I say, Grow some balls, man. I'll go regardless of the weather, regardless of how tired I feel. It's the one thing, since I've given up the painting, that I can count on to relax me.

James invites me to go with him to Fort Worth for Thanksgiving, and I jump at the chance, unable to envision the occasion in Houston without my mother. Though a barely suppressed tension permeated every one of our holidays, I wasn't immune to the pains my mother took to make them special, as if all the preceding years might be erased if only she had the right decorations or the perfect chestnut stuffing. She tried, the only way she could. I can't imagine going back without her.

I hope you're not imposing, my father tells me when I break the news, and I assure him that I talked to James's mother myself, already feeling guilty about ditching him. I hate thinking that in order for me to breathe over this holiday he's going to be sitting in Houston alone. But he tells me he's going to Mexico City that week. Wait, I say, confused, What if I wasn't going to Fort Worth? Well, that hardly matters now, he says, Does it?

I hang up, stunned. What was he thinking? That he'd let me get a little closer to the date and then tell me he'd be out of the country? What would I have done if James hadn't invited me to Fort Worth? Cook my own goddamn turkey?

So we're good? James asks, pausing in the doorway of my bedroom, and all I can do is nod. I can't tell him my father wasn't planning on seeing me anyway. That rejection would just be too humiliating to voice.

I don't feel like running that night. I skip, telling myself one day won't hurt, that I'll pick it back up again tomorrow. But the next day I skip again. One day piles on the next, and before I know it two weeks have gone by. I'm tense, my temper short, and the fact that each day brings us closer to the holiday season makes me that much edgier. The exercise is nothing but a salve anyway; I have larger issues at stake, not the least of which is that without the painting I've got absolutely no sense of direction whatsoever. Go for a run, man, James finally says at the beginning of Thanksgiving week, and I tell him to go fuck himself in a tone of voice that makes me uncomfortable recalling it later that evening.

When we get to Fort Worth, we find a welcome home note from James's mother, and from that moment on I'm second-guessing my decision to spend the holiday with them. I might have been better off kicking around the house alone in Houston or planting myself in front of the television in Austin. I feel my mother's absence keenly, and I've retreated into silence even before James's parents get home from work. I stand to the side when they finally arrive; everyone seems so happy to see each other, and I have to grit my teeth to keep from bursting into tears.

At dinner the next afternoon I barely say a word. There's not much of an opportunity, to be honest; I can't compete with James's analysis of every lecture he's heard in his Classical Literature class or his sister's chatter. Ashley's a cute little thing with blondish hair and an upturned nose that pairs perfectly with her wide open eyes. She hangs on her brother's every word, and twice her parents have to tell her to sit down, though James seems just as reluctant to loosen his hold on her as she seems to let go. I know how much he hates being away from her, how torn he felt the summer after our freshman year when he was faced with the decision of living in Austin or going home to his family. I couldn't blame him then, can't blame him now. They're everything I never had myself, and I concentrate on my plate, looking up occasionally as if I'm interested in the conversation and not the past.

You know, James says later that evening as I stand outside inhaling one cigarette after another, The point in bringing you here wasn't to make you feel worse. I'm fine, I tell him. He glances over his shoulder into the living room, where his parents and sister have started a game of Monopoly. Do you realize you've never once talked about what happened? he asks.

He should know better, and I mentally calculate the glasses of wine he drank at dinner. But he stands steady in front of me, his eyes holding mine. You're not my therapist, James, I say, That's not what I need from you. What *do* you need? he asks. How about leaving me the fuck alone? I ask, and he turns on his heel and slams the door behind him. I crouch down in the corner of the porch, inhaling my cigarette like I'm drowning and I've just been offered a regulator. I hate the way my fingers shake every time I think about her. And yet I can't help myself, can't stop the memories that a day like this conjures for me.

Once, when I was nine, I dropped to the floor with my paints right in the foyer. My mother was on the phone; I could hear her murmuring in the background, the perfect soundtrack for what I held in my mind, and I curled over a fresh sheet of paper, so ready to begin that I couldn't wait for her to finish, to help set me up at the kitchen table where we didn't have to worry about a mess. A thin sheet of paper, too thin for the fury of my fingers, and I was too mesmerized to notice. When she caught her breath beside me, I looked up, then glanced back down at my painting. Even before I lifted the paper, I knew what I'd find: crimson and wine and sea green, seeping into the hardwood floor. I stared up at her in dismay, then watched her gift me a smile. Show me, she said, Show me what you've done.

The paint didn't come up, though she scrubbed the floor herself, and that afternoon she brought the rug from the dining room into the foyer. Just some redecorating, she said when my father came home from work that evening and eyed the rug with suspicion, and he grunted, accepting the scotch she offered him. I half-expected him to guess her motivation, and I trembled imagining his reaction. But she distracted him with a question, and the next time he was out of town on business, she arranged for the hardwoods to be redone.

There's no hiding anything from James though. He knows me too well, and nothing I do this weekend can disguise the fact that I'm hurting. Irritated, I get to my feet. Behind me the Monopoly game is in full force; I just can't bear going back inside. Instead, I turn my face to the wind and make my way down the front steps. The bare branches of the trees scrabble at the night sky.

I walk for hours, ducking down side streets, retracing my steps when I think I might be lost. I'm cold, but every moment brings me that much closer to the clarity I've needed.

Without him I'd have no one.

When I get back to the house, his parents and sister have gone to bed, and I make a mental note to apologize in the morning for leaving without explanation, without a thank you for asking me to spend the day with them. James I find in the kitchen in the half-dark, constructing an elaborate sandwich from leftover turkey and stuffing, a bottle of beer open on the cabinet beside him. Hungry? he asks, indicating the loaf of bread. Maybe, I say, reaching for a beer of my own. Tossing the bottle cap on the counter, I lean back against the refrigerator. Just be my friend, all right? I say, and he looks up, surprised that I've spoken or that for once I've admitted what I need. I shrug, like my confession isn't a huge fucking deal. Yeah, he says, Okay.

That night forces me to acknowledge that I need something in my life besides the running. I can't imagine therapy; I can barely talk to my best friend. Instead, I opt for the back room, hesitate just outside the door the day we get back to Austin. Go on, James encourages at the end of the hallway, and I take a deep breath and plunge through my fear.

There's a place for me in this space. I feel it as I step through the doorway, and my bare feet tread over worn floorboards to my easel, to a canvas raw and wide. A waft of linseed oil, colors I'd never find in my dreams, not the kind I've had the past nine months. Then the brush, easing into the paint. I slide the excess along my palette until there's nothing left but the merest hint of gold.

Still she turns toward the door, glancing back at me over a devious shoulder. I can't explain her eyes. Gritting my teeth, I force her forward, move her mouth until she smiles. Her hair coils like snakes, and I pin handfuls back, away from her neck. Beneath my brush her eyes soften, calm. In her hands a bird, an egg, a brush dripping paint. In her hands, mine. I'm five years old.

By the time I'm finished my forearm is stiff, my muscles rigid. Well? James asks from the doorway, and I look over at him. A year off hasn't done me any favors, I admit, and he comes over to see what I've done, then shrugs. I get the feeling he's more impressed by the brush I'm holding than the canvas in front of us. Maybe I should find a different subject, I mutter. Maybe, he says, You should stop thinking so much.

I take his advice. I start with Pandora, and when my brush finally loosens, I move on to the light, scattered through the branches of the pecan trees. The swing on the front porch, James's hand around a bottle of beer: this is what gets me through Christmas, the first in Houston without my mother. I spend half the time in my old room upstairs with a ream of paper and ink, the easiest materials to hide if I hear my father's footsteps on the stairs; I have no desire to further arm him. On Christmas Day he gives me cash, telling me he had no idea what to buy and I should just get whatever I want. I could be hurt, but I've given him a gift certificate, so I don't have much room for complaint. There's no tree, no decoration to speak of other than the poinsettias his colleagues have sent en masse, and we sit in the living room, the two envelopes on the coffee table the only evidence of gift exchange. He doesn't mention my grades, though they've improved, and neither one of us mentions my mother. The day after Christmas, I lock the house behind me before I head back to Austin; he's been at the office since early morning, in one way or another has been at the office my entire life.

+ + +

In the weeks after the holiday I linger over the palette, drawing out that moment before my brush touches the canvas. I use a palette knife to mix oil paint with a thin wash of linseed oil, well aware that whatever I create will likely take forever to dry. I'm okay with that. The canvas necessitates this sort of deliberation, and I get sucked in, so lost in my head I can't shake myself loose even when James raps on the doorframe and wonders if I want to spring for a pizza.

D'you ever worry you'll tap out? he asks one afternoon. What do you mean? I say. We're in the back room, where I'm flicking a paintbrush idly back and forth across my jeans. Paint stains the denim, so thick and vibrant I almost can't bring myself to wash it. I have a half a dozen tee shirts in the same condition, and I wear them more often than anything else I own. They let me know I've found my way back, remind me of the year I've just lost. I never want to be in that position again.

James sprawls by the window, one leg hooked over the arm of the chair, and he stretches his arms above his head. What if you didn't have anything to say? he asks, What if you lifted the brush and nothing happened?

I find the idea laughable and a little insulting. There's always something, I assure him. Wouldn't it suck though, he says, If one day there wasn't?

I could drive myself insane if I thought about the possibility long enough. But the material's everywhere around me, expectant, luminous, and I cast an eye back through the wreck of my childhood, the past year, and tell him there's more than enough subject matter to last me a good, long while.

I spend the anniversary of my mother's death in front of the canvas, the way I think she would've wanted, and though I don't mention my motivation to James, he's figured out on his own, and he settles down across from me with an open book midway through the afternoon. Time passes without a word, the stroke of my paintbrush against the canvas and the turn of an occasional page the only sounds we hear. There's a good feel in here, he admits when twilight falls, and I glance over at him.

I know exactly what he means.

+ + +

Since James and Cathleen broke up over a year and a half ago, he's dated only sporadically, girls that rarely last longer than dinner and a movie. But one night he hooks up with some girl in one of his classes, and from that point forward he's whipped. Elisa's actually pretty cool: smart, savvy, a bit on the edge with her butcher-block, blond hair and long, dangly earrings. She's different, I admit. God, isn't she? he says before he catches himself. He shrugs, but he's blushing, a slow creep of crimson I can't help pointing out. He's too crushed to care.

I'm a little jealous. For one thing, I'm not used to having to share James with anyone. He and Elisa spend most of their free time together, and I'm lucky to get a weeknight with him, let alone a Saturday. But at least Elisa and I get along, and they're both quick to include me, even if they're just hanging out at home.

Watching from the sidelines as they fall for each other, I realize for the first time that I want the same thing. I envy them their eagerness, their excitement. Why don't you set me up with one of your friends? I ask Elisa, caught up in their enthusiasm, and she cocks her head. I get the feeling she suspects, and I back off, then throw a few carefully staged comments her way, thinking that might ease her suspicions. But Elisa's not buying it.

We're in the living room one night, James asleep with his head in Elisa's lap. We've been smoking a little pot, listening to The Black Crows, and I watch, yawning, as Elisa slides her fingers through James's curls. She has nails every bit as ragged as mine. Sometimes I catch James pulling her hand away from her mouth, chastising her in a voice so sugary I'd roll my eyes if I didn't want the same damn thing for myself. You shouldn't bite, he murmurs, kissing her, and the next thing I know they're excusing themselves and shutting his bedroom door behind them. Now she touches the back of her neck with her free hand. She just got a haircut; if I saw her from behind, I'd take her for a guy. Or maybe I wouldn't; those earrings glitter with their own kind of fire, nearly touch her slender shoulders. Can I ask you something? she asks. Sure, I say, feeling expansive and magnanimous from that joint. Why haven't you told James? she asks.

My eyes widen, and I hasten a shrug to mask my panic. There's no point in pretending I don't know what she means. Casting a glance at James to be sure he's really asleep, I come up with a thousand retorts and settle on the most benign. The timing hasn't been right, I mumble, implying that given the right circumstances, I'll be happy to tell him everything. She gives me a look that begs to differ. This is none of your business anyway, I mutter. He'd be more understanding than you think, she says, and I moan. Elisa, I say, Please tell me you haven't said anything to him. Of course not! she says, giving her head such a vigorous shake her earrings fly, It's not my place.

I'm not sure I believe her, but what choice do I have? He hasn't confronted me, that much I know. So she could be telling the truth.

Keeping this a secret can't possibly be working for you, she adds. Didn't I just say this is none of your business? I ask, and she gives me a wry smile. Sometimes I just can't help myself, she says.

Though I'm annoyed by Elisa's forthrightness, she has a point. I'm tired of sleeping with girls, tired of accepting accolades from James that make me feel hollow and duplicitous. I'm tired of pretending like I know what I'm doing. The last girl I went out with—which I did solely to appease James because he wanted to double-date—expected me to go down on her, practically pushed my head between her legs the second she got me in her bedroom. I couldn't stay down there long; thirty seconds and I'd totally lost my hard-on. At least fucking her I could pretend I was somewhere else. At least with a blowjob I can close my eyes and go wherever I need to go.

I want to see a movie with someone and not feel condemned. I want to bring them home afterward and collapse on the couch, the windows shut tight against a bitter February night, and know I don't have to walk into my bedroom alone. I want to wake up with someone beside me, our day wide open, ready to be filled however we choose.

So a few days later, in the middle of my Rhetorical Theory class, I meet this guy's eye. He's been watching me for the past month, trying to figure me out, and I've avoided every glance. For one thing, we have a class together; I'm used to encounters that end swiftly and cleanly, and the thought that something could happen between us that we'd have to revisit every Monday, Wednesday, and Friday doesn't appeal to me in the least. But he also has a reputation, one that scares the shit out of me. I don't know that I'm ready to be frank. I don't know that I'm ready to be honest. I don't know that I want to be seen with him, and though I realize just how hypocritical that makes me, I'm still not sure if I'm willing to take the risk.

But as I'm slouched in my chair, listening to a lecture that would probably leave my father frothing at the mouth with excitement, I have a quick image of Elisa's expression the moment I tried to blame my reticence on timing. I'm so tired of pretending.

I lift my gaze, and he rewards me with a tantalizing smile I can't believe I was ever willing to reject. I smile back, then realize I'm sitting in a full lecture hall, surrounded by my peers. Shifting my eyes to the professor, I jot down a few notes I'll see later and won't be able to decipher. Then I glance at him again through lowered lids. He's writing something on a sheet of paper, which he folds a moment later and sails through the air in my direction. The note lands beside my boot with a *thunk*, drawing the attention of everyone around me. I hesitate only a second before curiosity bends me over. *You, me,* he's written. *Movie. More.*

My stomach swims, heat already making its way into my crotch. Contemplating, I slide my pen in my mouth, then withdraw it and touch the paper. I've drawn a little sketch before I realize what I'm doing: the two of us walking under a crescent moon, stars swirling in the night sky. I immediately crumple the paper in my fist, then glance in his direction. He's not looking at me, but he's been watching; I can tell by the clench of his jaw and the way he's sitting upright in his chair. *Shit.* That's not what I meant.

Smoothing the paper with my open palm, I take the pen again, then realize there's nothing to write. I fold the note with careful fingers and send it back the way it came. He opens the paper with a tentative hand; he's afraid of what I've written, and I feel so guilty I almost don't care about the half a dozen students who've taken an interest in our exchange. For a minute he just looks at what I've drawn. Then he smiles, a different smile from the last one he bestowed, and traces a heart in the air with the tip of his finger. I bite my lip as the girl next to me raises her eyebrows. The guy behind her doesn't look as friendly, and I duck my head, snatching the note from beside my boot this time without looking up. *The Dobie,* he's written. *Tonight. 7:30.* I give him the barest of nods.

I meet him that night outside the theater, terrified that I'm going to see dozens of people I know and dizzy at the thought of sitting beside him in the dark. Do you even know my name? he asks as we're standing in line at the concession stand. Paul, I say, and he laughs, a dimple appearing in his left cheek. He has hair the color of the sun, eyes like a river. I'm not sure I'm going to be able to sit through the movie. Did you know my name before this afternoon? he asks, Or did you have to do some research? Are you kidding? I say, and he shrugs. You haven't looked at me once all semester, he points out.

I'm not about to tell him why, though he can probably guess, especially when he slips his arm around me as we're heading into the theater and I shrug away from him, whispering quick apologies. Do you know who *I* am? I ask once we're seated and the lights have dimmed. Yeah, he says, You're the guy who's going to break my heart.

I don't know what to say. I feel like I'm in a position of power and submission at the exact same moment, and I realize that eliminating any real intimacy from my prior sexual experience has laid me bare in a way I haven't expected and don't know that I particularly like. I'm half-tempted to flee, right now, before this can go any further.

The soundtrack from the previews reverberates through the floor beneath us, and Paul beckons me closer, then lowers his mouth to my ear. You're a junior, he says, And a Business major, though I'm not sure why. I close my eyes. I can feel myself unfolding, abandoning all sense of caution. I've been fantasizing about your mouth all afternoon, he whispers, Joel Grayson.

But he makes no move to kiss me. Instead, he tilts the box of popcorn in my direction; I reach in and take a handful. For a minute we examine the screen in front of us without speaking. How do you know I'm going to break your heart? I finally ask, and he gives me a smile, patient and wounded, like he's been here a thousand times and knows exactly what to expect. I dip my hand in the box of popcorn again, and he catches my fingers. I'm never going to make it through this movie, and I hold my breath as he twines his hand through mine. Yeah, he whispers, as if he's reconfirming what he suspected all along, You'll break my heart.

+ + +

Paul's a senior, a Radio/Television/Film major with no discernible goals other than graduating in May and getting a job so he can upgrade his ride. I find his lack of motivation refreshing, precisely because I know what my father would think—and that's without him suspecting what we're doing every second we're alone.

For the first time I don't feel the need, as soon as I come, to make my getaway. But my answers to personal questions I keep short, and Paul tells me more than once that I'm not the easiest guy to get to know. I shrug, self-conscious and close-mouthed, and he gives up and kisses me instead, long and hard before I extricate myself and hole up in his bathroom to shower. I like you, he says when I reappear. I like you, too, I choke out, and he smiles.

Though I'm careful about where I go with Paul and who sees us together, I worry that James might find out. I have a feeling he'd be substantially more pissed if the news reached him secondhand, and more than once, I debate telling him, back out every time because I'm too afraid of what might happen if Elisa's wrong. Without James I have no one other than a questionable father and a pseudo-boyfriend who in all likelihood will be taking a job somewhere else in less than three months.

But that doesn't stop me from concocting whatever lies I have to in order to get out of the house. Luckily, James seems lost enough in Elisa that he pays little attention. I skip classes, waste entire afternoons lounging in Paul's bed with a bottle of Rolling Rock, Stone Temple Pilots on his mediocre stereo. Sketch me, he says, and so I do, making sure to leave the evidence behind when I leave. He follows me out to the Explorer, then gets inside and sucks me off, in full view of whoever might be watching from the various balconies of his apartment building. I know no one can see; it's late, and I've tinted the Explorer's windows too dark. But the possibility: that's an aphrodisiac I never expected, and I drive home still shaking.

Elisa turns twenty-one the first week in March, and though James has a private celebration in mind for her birthday, he suggests we go out the following night, the three of us, to take advantage of the buttery nipples at one of the bars on Sixth. I've already abandoned my own fake ID less than ten days prior; my birthday, though a mere two weeks into my relationship with Paul, marked our first argument. Let me get this straight, he said when I got to his apartment that afternoon to find a lopsided cake and a sink full of dishes, You came here to get laid and then you're going out to dinner with friends? He had a streak of chocolate on his chin, and I wanted to lick it clean, but he yanked away when I stepped close to him. I'll come back after dinner, I promised. Oh, could you? he said, Could you go out and celebrate your birthday and then slink back here when you're finished?

I didn't say anything. He had every right to be angry, and for a long moment we just stared at each other without speaking. Then he ran his hand through his hair. This is what I was talking about, he said, This is what I meant. Paul, I said, I can't— I know you can't! he snapped. I watched his eyes, and when I thought they wouldn't narrow, I took a step in his direction. Look, I said, trying to soothe him, We're good here, okay? He didn't move, and I kissed him: his mouth, his chin, tasting chocolate and what was quickly becoming the familiar flavor of his skin. I liked that, this familiarity, the way I'd figured out what turned him on, the way he was beginning to know me the same way. Everything seemed easier; I didn't have to work as hard, except to cover my tracks. We're good, I murmured, unzipping his jeans, and he gave in.

But I had my work cut out for me when I bailed on James and Elisa after dinner that night. I'm meeting someone, I mumbled as they protested, Just a friend, for a drink. Ask him to come with us, James insisted before Elisa finally figured out what was going on and told him she was kind of tired anyway. I gave her a grateful look, though I obsessed later about what she might have said to James in private. No matter what she promised, I'm not entirely sure I can trust her, and when we go out for her birthday, I realize that once she's drunk, all bets are off.

I don't think she means to corner me the way she does. We're actually having fun, we're actually happy to be out together, and the fact that Paul's cramming for a Latin exam means I don't have to think about what I'm missing. I can just go along with James and Elisa, I can knock back a few shots, I can spend time with my friends knowing that tomorrow night I can see Paul. In reality I'm suspended between two worlds, committed wholly to neither one, and after she's had a few shots Elisa eyes me, her lips pursed around a cigarette. You should be *with* someone, she says, exhaling. What do you mean? I ask, and she waves her hand as if we're all friends here, as if we don't have any secrets. I give her a tight, eat-shit-and-die smile. She watches me through a stream of smoke, her chin resting on her palm, and I flick a glance at James, who gazes back with a directness I don't like. For just a second I wonder if I'm being set up.

Then he shifts his eyes to the ashtray in front of us, where he taps his cigarette. I half-expect him to change the subject or at least tell his girlfriend to shut up; even if he doesn't know why, he can tell I'm not happy. But he doesn't say a word, and Elisa, swaying slightly to the music in the background or maybe from the shots, closes her eyes. We could double, she says through a drag, We could go camping over Spring Break. I'm going to Houston for Spring Break, I tell her. We could come with you, she says. Elisa, James warns. Hey, I'm just looking out for him, she protests, like I'm not even here, I just want him to loosen up. Fuck off, Elisa, I say. Okay, James says, This is getting out of hand. Looping his arm around Elisa's waist, he helps her to her feet. Time to go, birthday girl, he tells her.

The next morning, Elisa finds me on the back porch where I'm smoking a cigarette, still a little too shaken to go for a run. Hi, she says, touching the earring that drips toward her shoulder. I'm really not in the mood, I tell her, and she hesitates, then sits down beside me anyway. I owe you an apology, she says, keeping her voice low. She's been biting her nails again; her fingertips look tender and sore. I shouldn't have had that last shot, she admits. This is my life, Elisa, I tell her, and she looks up at me. I know, she says, but I shake my head. No, I say, You really don't.

From that point on my rapport with Elisa cools considerably. I have my escape, and I take it every chance I get. James doesn't ask where I'm spending my time, and though I make the assumption that he's too wrapped up in Elisa to care, he also might be giving me the chance to do what I need. At this point I'm not sure what he knows.

I go to Houston for Spring Break, a small concession in my father's mind, given the figure he deposits in my checking account every month, but one that rankles me nonetheless. I'd rather be with Paul, who's spending the week in Corpus Christi, bunking at his aunt's and soaking up the sun. I have a feeling he's getting some ass, too, though he denies that when I ask. Are you saying you miss me? he wants to know. Maybe, I admit.

I'm going to bury you with that goddamn phone, my father growls once I've finally hung up, Who the hell have you been talking to? J-just this girl, I stammer, and he raises his eyebrows. Well, he says, I guess there's hope for you yet.

+ + +

My father's comment might be the impetus, or maybe I'm just sick of having to yank Elisa's bras from the shower rod before I take a bath, but I start to realize over the next few weeks how much I want Paul in my own bed. I want his mark in my space, his toothbrush beside mine. I want, in a driving rain, to be huddled with him at my own house instead of behind the wheel of my Explorer, driving to the only place we can be together without fear of discovery.

One night, I leave his apartment around midnight, afraid that if I stay any later I won't go home at all. I don't want to have to answer any questions, especially since James has already asked me about my plans for the evening. Test coming up, I said, Econ notes. On a Friday night? James asked, and I'd been forced to shrug and mutter something about my father and my grades. Don't go, Paul moans when I get to my feet and reach for my clothes, but after that first objection I get dressed in silence. I'll call you, I say, and instead of walking me to the door or trying to convince me to stay, he just nods.

When I get home, I expect to find James and Elisa crashed out in front of the television, but they're already shut in James's bedroom, oblivious to my arrival, the headboard of his bed whacking against the wall. I take a shower, a long one, the water as hot as I can stand it. Turning off the faucet, I can still hear James and Elisa going at it.

Come over, I say to Paul on the phone the following afternoon, and he pauses like he's trying to figure out if I'm fucking with him. We haven't spoken all day; he's been punishing me or maybe just protecting himself. Really? he finally asks, and I mentally calculate a worst-case scenario of when James and Elisa might be back. Really, I say.

Ten minutes later, he's pulling into the driveway. You're not going to show me around? he says when I reach for his jeans, and I don't want to admit that we've got an hour at best. I'd rather get right to the point, I tell him, leading him into my bedroom. Muscled and thick-veined, he leaves me riddled with hunger. We pull our tee shirts over our heads at the same moment, and I lick the trickle of sweat on his neck, inside the crease of his shoulder, his skin flushed. In this moment I'm not thinking about the fact that if I want to be honest, we have little in common other than a Rhetorical Theory class and a mutual admiration for Nirvana. I just want to fuck him, in my own house, and my tongue travels the length of his body with a practiced certainty that feels like years in the making.

I linger too long. Half of me understands what I'm doing, knows the risk I'm taking and simply doesn't care. The other half freezes when I hear the slam of the front door. Get dressed, I hiss, shoving him away from me. We stumble into our clothes like a fucking comedy act, knocking shit over, ramming toes into the bed frame. The second he yanks his tee shirt over his head I throw open the door. James and Elisa pause at the end of the hallway. I thought you were gone, I blurt out, nixing with one sentence any chance of avoiding suspicion. We were, James says as Paul steps behind me.

James's eyebrows raise, and I immediately blather something about Paul being in one of my classes. Right, Paul says so flatly I flinch, We're study partners. He's on his way out, I add, and silence descends like a shroud. James gives me a long, searching look it takes all of my strength to return, and then without a word he and Elisa head into his bedroom.

Look, I get it, Paul's already murmuring, I know. He's keeping his voice low, his hands to himself, but I can't help darting a glance over my shoulder. When I look back, he's drawn in tight, and I have a brief, conflicting image of him sprawled across my bed just five minutes ago. I can't do this anymore, he whispers.

He wants me to stop him from leaving. He wants me to pull him into my arms, to kiss him, to invite James and Elisa back into the living room and behave in front of them like lovers. He wants something I'm in no position to give, and the fold of my arms across my chest saves me the humiliation of opening my mouth.

From the back porch I can hear his truck jump to life. Everything okay? James asks through the screen door. I bring a cigarette to my lips, watching as smoke drifts into the afternoon sky. Want a beer? he adds, and I clear my throat. Sure, I say, Why not?

+   +   +

James finds a job waiting tables over the summer while I resign myself to the drudgery of business classes. When I complain about the tedium of homework on the few occasions I crack a book, he shuts me up with a look. Since I broke up with Paul, there's been nothing to distract me, and I've been sketching James lately and Elisa too, though my drawings of her I can never get right. You need to stop, James says one night, You need to stop following her around with a fucking sketchpad. What about you? I ask, and he says, No fucking way.

But he always relents, always, and I come home from class one day in the middle of July, intent on convincing him to sit for me. I had him up until four o'clock in the morning a couple of nights ago; he's a good subject, complicated in a way I find gratifying. It's a challenge trying to pin him down, and I like watching his reaction when I show him what I've done.

Today I find him on the back porch, a cigarette in his hand and a full ashtray beside him. I can smell him from the doorway, the stink of that restaurant, refried beans and mesquite-smoked meat. What's up? I ask, letting the door swing shut, and he shrugs. I drop down beside him and reach for a cigarette. Where's Elisa? I ask, and the muscle at the back of his jaw spasms. I'm trying to decide if I should just give him some space when he buries his face in his hands.

Whoa, I say. He moans like he's being gutted from the inside out, then starts bawling, wracking sobs that almost paralyze me. For just a moment I picture him sitting on the steps of that pool in Cancun. Once again, the world's axis tilts as the boundaries of everything I know to be true disintegrate. I can't stand seeing him so stricken, and I slide a cautious arm around his shoulder. He collapses into me, and I hold him as he cries, until he finally pulls away. His cigarette has burned almost to the filter, and he crushes it out in the ashtray with the others. She's pregnant, he says.

What? I say, but he doesn't repeat himself. I stammer the only question I can, a ludicrous one under the circumstances. How? I ask. I don't know, he says, She's on the Pill. Are you sure? I say, I mean, did she— She took a test, Joel, he tells me. He digs the heels of his hands into his temples, trying to kill whatever headache plagues him. She took a lot of tests, he says wearily.

No wonder he's been begging me not to sketch her. No wonder he's been acquiescing in her place, and I think back to the chalk drawing I made of him the other night, the one that caught him off-guard, the one that made him eye me with something bordering on suspicion, as if I might be a fortune teller, as if I could reach for his palm and tell him everything he needs to know. I don't know, I'd mumbled, not sure how to explain myself, You look kind of full. And he did, even then, even at four o'clock in the morning as he stood across from me and stared at what I'd done. He looked like he was holding everything inside, like he had an entire world just beneath his surface.

Now I'm half-awed, half-horrified by the insight in the stroke of my fingers, even more so when I realize with a sharp stab of fear that I could be looking at the beginning of the end. If Elisa has this baby, he'll never stay here. What're you going to do? I ask, and the tears that still glaze his eyes spill onto his cheeks. I know before he says a word what Elisa wants, and as much as I long to bask in a moment of self-involved relief, I can't get past the anguish in his expression. I don't think I have a choice, he says.

Five days later, Elisa has an abortion. I haven't seen her once; she's been holed up at her own apartment, and James spends the night with her, then leaves for the restaurant in the morning without bothering to come home first. When I see him between shifts, he keeps to himself, avoiding my eye, as if I might be casting a judgment on him he couldn't possibly handle. I finally stop him the day before Elisa's appointment as he's on his way out the door. Are you okay? I ask, realizing even as I speak the futility of my question, Do you need anything? He looks at me with a hollow expression and answers without a trace of emotion. What could you do, Joel? he says, What could you possibly do?

I know enough not to offer him money.

The next morning, I skip my classes, too preoccupied thinking about what he's going through to listen to a lecture about comparative economic systems. *Frivolous*, he said last year at the crest of Mount Bonnell, and I understand all over again what he meant. I want to be here in case he calls, in case he comes home, though I can't imagine he will. He'll stay with Elisa, and I doubt if I'll see him again before tomorrow.

But I hear the front door slam late that afternoon, and I drop the book I'm pretending to read and head into the living room. He's standing just inside the door, and when he sees me, he bursts into tears. She doesn't want to see me anymore! he wails.

I pour him shot after shot of tequila because I know why he's really crying. I've seen the way he looks at his sister. I know the way he's taken ownership of our friendship the past couple of years. He can't bear to think about what Elisa's done, and when he finally passes out, face down on his bed, I pry his shoes off of him myself. I know he'll never be the same.

He doesn't talk to Elisa again. Instead, he works while I trudge through the second summer session. When we have free time, we play darts, make small bets because James always has petty cash. By the end of the summer he starts to look more like himself, until one night, just when I think he's moved on, we catch sight of Elisa across a crowded bar. I wait for him to approach her, but he just watches her for a minute, then stares into the palms of his hands. Why don't we take off, I say, and he follows me without a word.

I drive to Mount Bonnell; beside me James doesn't protest, and when we reach the bottom of the cliff, I park the Explorer, and we hike the steps to the top. Eighteen months have passed since the last time we stood in front of this view, though now a summer breeze winds through our hair and sweat stains our shirts. James leans against the ledge, and I think about the last time we were here, the precarious way he see-sawed on top as if he'd take any risk he was offered. I think about what he's lost.

I saw Melissa the other day, he says. Yeah? I say, D'you talk to her? Briefly, he admits. He lights a cigarette, exhaling through the side of his mouth. She says she doesn't talk to Cathleen anymore, he adds.

In the dark I can't make out his expression, and I flick the ash from my own cigarette in the direction of the lake, so far below us that its surface seems like nothing more than a thin sheet of black. That could've been us, he says. What do you mean? I ask, and he's quiet for a minute. What if we'd never met? he finally says, What if we'd… drifted apart or something? You mean if I hadn't bailed you out of jail, I say, going for levity, and he gives me a ferocious look that catches me off-guard. I'm fucking serious here, Joel, he says, Don't you ever think about this shit? I shrug, though I do. Of course I do. I don't know, he says, I guess I'm just… trying to figure out what's random and what's preordained.

I have a sudden lump in my throat that I can't seem to swallow. I'm haunted by the same questions myself.

I'm not sure I want to know the answers.

4

James buries himself in preparations for the GRE, convinced he wants to stay on at UT and get a PhD in Archaeology. I refuse to entertain plans of my own, stymied by the castigation that's sure to ensue the moment I break the news to my father that I'm not interested in an entry-level business position after I graduate next May. I just want to paint. On the other hand, I've managed to keep my work so much to myself that at this point I'm not sure I have the courage to show anyone what I've done. So now I'm in this weird place where I'll have a degree I have no interest in utilizing and a roomful of paintings no one other than James has ever seen. I need time to figure out what the hell I'm going to do next. There's got to be something I can say to convince my father for a little extra time.

One tawdry encounter follows another. Since Paul, there's been no one consistent, and to be perfectly honest, I'm getting a little tired of the bullshit. I'm sick of not being able to bring anyone to the house, haven't been willing to run the risk since James almost caught me with Paul. I hate the way I feel having sex on the sly, coming home afterward with the taste of guilt in my mouth. I hate feeling like I'm regressing.

I'm also being unfair. James keeps nothing from me, nothing, fell into my arms the day of Elisa's abortion and sobbed as if someone had wrenched that baby from his own body. It's time for me to be honest.

The night I decide to tell him over a quiet beer at a bar down the street, he gets a phone call from one of the professors in the Classics department. There's some problem with a conference paper she's supposed to present the next day, and she can't get in touch with her teaching assistant. We're literally on the way out the door, but James jumps at the opportunity to help, knowing that every gesture, every overture, raises his chances of getting into the graduate program. I watch him leave, feeling like I've been taken to the brink of orgasm and then pulled abruptly back. I had my speech all ready, anticipated ahead of time the range of possible reactions I could expect. Now I have no idea whether I should concede defeat and try again another time or if I should just wait up for him.

By the time he gets back I've made the mistake of dressing for bed, and I'm already regretting my pajama bottoms, which seem to give me a distinct disadvantage. You still want to grab a beer? I mumble, crossing my arms over my tee shirt, and he peels a couple from the carton in the fridge and kicks the door closed without breaking stride. There's a bounce to his step, an excitement borne from the evening and the impression he made on his professor, and as much as I hate to break his high, I know that if I don't say something soon, I'll lose my nerve. Steadying myself, I speak, in the space between my heartbeats. James, I say, I'm gay.

He blinks. I get the impression he's less surprised by my revelation than that I've finally spoken the words aloud. You knew, I say, and he slides his hands in his pockets like maybe he's embarrassed or I've accused him of something far worse than holding my secret close. I live with you, he says. But you never said anything, I protest, and he gives me an impatient look. What did you want me to say, Joel? he asks, It's not as if I didn't give you plenty of opportunities to tell me.

For just a second he sounds almost hostile, and I wonder what he's thinking about, who he's bringing to mind: Paul; the dive master in Cancun; any one of a number of guys I slept with surreptitiously but who might have gossiped after the fact. I'm not sure I want to hear how he finally guessed, and I'm overcome by a wave of shame despite the fact that if he suspected all along but didn't confront me, he's more friend than I've ever known.

I lift my eyes and find him studying me with a concentrated expression, the way he might pour over a map if he was lost and trying to find his way home. I'm sorry, I say, but he shakes his head. You don't have to apologize for who you are, he tells me.

Tears fill my eyes; I don't know what I've done in my meager life to afford such friendship. Relax, he says, kicking my bare foot with his boot, All right? I take a deep breath, not quite believing my luck. So we're okay here, I say, We're good. James flicks his eyes around the living room. Are you kidding? he says, I could never afford this place by myself.

+ + +

There's a part of me that worries James will change his mind, that despite his reassurances, he'll admit he can't deal with what I've told him. Though he says nothing, does nothing, to indicate that his acceptance of what I've confided is anything other than sincere, I'm just paranoid enough that I hold back from behaving in a way that might be misinterpreted, misconstrued. I don't want him thinking that he's going to wake up every morning to a different guy walking out the front door. So I start out by mentioning, casually, that I'm headed to a certain bar, a certain club; in the past I would've lied about where I was going or I would have not gone out at all. Not once does he react in a way I'd consider judgmental. In fact, he shocks the shit out of me by suggesting that he come along. Why would you want to do *that*? I ask, and he looks so defensive I check myself. Here I am, making him feel like he's done something wrong when he's just trying to offer his support. Maybe, I say, backpedaling, I'm not really into that scene.

I'm lying, sort of. Bars afford me the oddest combination of anonymity and acceptance, and sometimes I bask in that elixir, tucked into a corner that I make my own as I watch who comes and goes. Eventually, I'm approached; I'm too new, too young, too vulnerable to overlook, and I let whoever had the balls to come up to me coax me into the back, where I lean against the wall and wonder how I could ever bring James here.

I head to Fort Worth for Thanksgiving for the second year in a row. I'm just glad you have an invitation, my father informs me when I tell him of my plans, and I spend a few minutes feeling hurt that once again he's chosen to travel during the holiday before I compartmentalize that emotion and start to worry instead about how James's family will receive me now that they know I'm gay. James told them himself without consulting me first, and even though he insists that they couldn't care less, I'm not sure I believe him. I can only imagine my father's response if he heard the news, and the idea that James's parents have accepted the information without reservation I want to call out as the bullshit I believe it to be. Just because Mrs. Fielding called me herself to invite me doesn't mean that James didn't have to strong-arm her into picking up the phone.

I'm actually less concerned about James's mother than I am about his father. I think about how kind he was to me when he came into town for James's birthday the year before last, the attention he paid me in regard to my work; he offered me more respect in one afternoon, with one kindly placed question, than my own father ever has. And yet I can't help thinking that he'd rather I wasn't coming for the holiday, wasn't an influence in his son's life. Maybe he'll even try to persuade James to move out. After all, if I'm gay and his son is living with me, then what does that make his son?

By the time we arrive on Wednesday afternoon I've managed to convince myself that I'm walking into a situation where I'm absolutely not welcome, where best-case scenario, I'll be ostracized, and worst-case scenario, I'll be asked to leave. I hesitate behind the wheel, but James has his hand on the door, and before I can open my own Ashley's flying down the front walk into her brother's arms. We're making pumpkin pie! she crows, and that fast she's pulling us both toward the house, where James's mother smiles from the doorway. Welcome home, she says, and that sentiment, the one I've been missing the past two years, brings tears to my eyes. They're not lost on her, and she doesn't hesitate before she offers me a hug. We're so glad you could come, she says. She smells like her kitchen, like brown sugar and cinnamon, and I linger longer than etiquette probably allows, grateful for her arms, straightening only when James's father appears behind her. Self-conscious all over again, I watch him greet his son, the way their handshake moves smoothly into an embrace. Then he looks at me; his gaze doesn't waver. Joel, he says, extending his hand, Good to see you.

A few nights later, satiated from yet another home-cooked meal and an acceptance so dense and unexpected I almost can't believe it's real, I agree when James suggests that we go out for a drink. I know he'll want to drive;

he likes showing me where he used to hang out, likes to reminisce, and I flip him my keys. I'm happy to sit back and listen as he points out, not for the first time, where he went to high school, where his first girlfriend lived, where he took piano lessons when he was eight.

Where to now? he asks after we've crawled through downtown. I crack the window and light a cigarette. At this point I'm so relaxed I'd agree to anything, and when he tells me he knows where we should go, I just let him drive. A cold wind steals the smoke from my mouth, my cigarette pressed between my lips, ash flicked into the night. Up 7th Street, then University, but before we can get to I-30, James pulls hard to the right, into the Botanic Gardens. I cut him a look as he grinds to a halt at the back of the parking lot. What're you doing? I ask. Let's go for a walk, he says. I examine the iron gates with dubious eyes. How're we going to get in? I ask. He just opens his door and grins.

Instead of approaching the gates, we skirt around the side of the parking lot, then duck beneath an overhang of brush. I follow him as he crashes through the bracken, thwacking aside tree limbs. You would've made a shitty Indian, I mutter as we come up against another fence, not as formidable as the one at the entrance but still guaranteed to impale us if we attempt to shimmy across. James curls his hands around the bars and stares into the garden on the other side. Now what? I say. I think we have to climb, he admits, and I groan. But he's already using the soles of his boots as traction, and he hoists himself up, hand over hand until he reaches the top. Don't try this at home, he says, and then he's jumping to the ground on the far side. I follow him, shoulders straining. Watch your ass, he says as I'm swinging over the top, and I laugh, slipping just enough that I have to catch myself with my hands when I hit the ground.

There's no trail that I can see, and the moon's barely a sliver above the trees. You know where you're going? I ask as we start walking. Not really, he says. At least I'm wearing a coat; he's in nothing but a sweater, and I blow on my hands, still cold from gripping the fence. Through the underbrush we go, leaves crunching under our feet, and we fall into a silence we don't break until we stumble upon a path five minutes later. Now the way's easier, and I slide my hands in my pockets as we wind among the trees. My breath comes in wild plumes, and I glance at James and wonder how he's not feeling the cold. He looks over at me, intuiting my question. Feels good, he says, shrugging.

We stop at a bench under a gazebo that gives us temporary shelter from the wind. Without a cigarette my hands have nothing to do, and I shove them in the pockets of my coat and stretch my legs out in front of me, crossing them at the ankles. Beside me James rakes his fingers through his curls. You bring your dates here when you were in high school? I ask, and he laughs. Only in the dead of winter, he tells me. We're not quite there yet, I say, and he shrugs. Coming soon though, he says. He glances at me, sidelong. You could come here for Christmas, you know, he says.

I let myself think for a minute about how that might work, about the space that would afford me, the time I could spend at the museums here, the same ones I hit today because they have a few acquisitions—a Picasso, a Munch—I wanted to see for myself. I think about what it might be like to wake up on Christmas morning in James's old room, because that's where I stay when I'm here, in one of two single beds split by a lamp so dim I wonder how James made it through childhood without needing glasses. I think about Ashley and the rush of excitement she must feel waiting to see if Santa came. For her the morning's still magical, and I wonder what it might be like to share that time with her, share that time with James. He's inviting me himself, and given the way his parents have treated me the past few days, they'd likely welcome me back.

And yet, I'm not a part of his family. I'm not, no matter what James says, no matter how many weekend trips we make north. I'm a friend, a roommate, someone his family likely feels sorry for because how could they not? Less than two years ago, my mother killed herself, and now I've just come out and they probably think that's one more reason to pity me. Even if I'm wrong, even if they'd create a place for me, my father won't allow it. He doesn't travel over Christmas, and as long as he's in town, as long as he's paying for my education—and my house and my car and every fucking cigarette I smoke—he'll expect me to come to Houston.

I need to talk to him anyway. I need to tell him that in six months when I walk across that stage I'm not planning on walking off and into an office. I have no interest in some shitty job at Permian or anywhere else my father, with his contacts and influence, thinks he can place me. I got the Business degree he wanted me to get; now it's my turn to make a decision.

Where *are* you? James asks, and I turn to look at him. He combs my expression in the dark. I'm not sure what he's seeing, what the night reveals. I have to go to Houston for the holiday, I say, But thanks. He looks away, out onto what might be a rose garden in the spring. You've had a good weekend, Joel, he reminds me. So? I say. Then, thinking I've sounded ungracious, I say, I appreciate you including me. You make it sound like I invited you because I felt sorry for you, he says. Did you? I ask. Jesus, he mutters, getting to his feet. All right, I say, following him, I know you didn't. What the fuck happened? he says, I just thought you might want to come here for Christmas. I do! I tell him, and he says, So what's the problem?

I don't want to remind him that my father and I have a transactional relationship. And if I tell him there's a part of me that, despite everything, hates thinking of my father spending the holiday alone, he probably won't believe me. I'm not sure I trust the thought myself.

I just have to go to Houston, I say, and he sighs, his breath a whirl of white. Are you at least going to tell him? he asks, and I nod. A few more weeks, I say, And he's going to be hounding me about applications anyway. What? he says, I'm talking about you coming out to him. Why would I do that? I ask, and he says, Because it's time? I don't think so, I say. My parents were fine with it, Joel, he points out. They probably wouldn't feel the same if *you* came out to them, I tell him. That's bullshit, he says. Maybe, I say, But *my* father isn't *your* father. He might surprise you, he tells me. No, I say, He won't.

At first I think he's going to argue with me. I can see the words on the tip of his tongue, can hear them even before they're spoken. Then he shrugs, and I know he's giving up, at least for now. Holding his head back, he examines the sky. I join him, my breath a fog. I'm freezing my balls off, I inform him when he shivers. Coffee? he says, and I say, Thank god.

+ + +

Another holiday without my mother, and I realize on Christmas night that my father and I aren't even trying to go through the motions. There's still no tree, and while I have a feeling that seeing one might reduce me to tears, I'm also aware that at the basest level I feel a loss so profound I have to sequester the emotion to the same corner of my mind that holds the rest of my past. I can't think about what I've given up either, the time I could be spending with James and his family; I have business to take care of, and after my father hands me an envelope containing my Christmas check I clear my throat. My father eyes me over the rim of his scotch. Here's where we share a sort of fellowship, with liquor complicated on the tongue.

After I graduate, I say, I want to take some time off to paint.

My words sound strong, my intention formidable, but I have less than a second to bask in their validation. I'm not sure I've ever seen my father with an expression of such disbelief, and any thought that James might have been right and that I might be able to segue into an admission of my sexuality dissipates immediately. With a look my father has managed to accuse me of wasting my degree, his money, my life, and what comes out of my mouth next astonishes me all the more as a result. Unless you want to cut me off, I add.

I can't believe I've said the words. I don't know where they came from, and I'm afraid he'll call my bluff and I'll be forced into the unfortunate position of having to grovel, to plead for forgiveness, to tell him I didn't mean a word. God, and if that's the case, I'll be working on top of everything else, cranking out numbers in some windowless office the moment I get my diploma. I actually feel faint, and I take another stout swallow of scotch as fortification.

But I should've known that he's too self-conscious of what his friends and colleagues would think if he were to take me up on my threat. I catch the finest glimpse of wariness in his eyes, so quick I can't be sure I've interpreted what I've seen correctly, and then he's grumbling his concessions. One year, he says, I'll give you one year, and then we'll reevaluate. I nod, quelling my nerves with my drink. I had a similar opportunity after college, he confides.

He might be lying, though if that's the case, he's a master of embellishment; he has the anecdotes to prove his claim. But as I listen to him brag about his own youthful jaunt through Europe, I find myself having to hide my glee behind my glass. I have a year, a year with no responsibility other than my work.

For the time being I can pretend my life's my own.

+ + +

I use the cash my father gave me for Christmas to upgrade our furniture, a leather sofa and a recliner that James insists we'll argue over until I finally tell him he can prop his ass there any time he wants. When the furniture's delivered, we hold our breath, wondering if Pandora will take to the leather with her claws. But she stretches herself across the bar as James takes a couple of beers from the fridge and settles himself in the chair. I hit the sofa, swinging my boots onto the ancient coffee table, which I hadn't thought until now about replacing. I think I prefer the room this way anyway, this blend of old and new, this nod to where we've been and what might come next. Well, James says, winking at me, All we need now are some girls.

Instead, I bring home a guy, though he couldn't be any straighter if he tried. I'm taking a Microeconomic Theory class, and one afternoon after our professor cordons us off in fours for group work, I stare at two girls I've never met and this guy named Peter Gilcrest that I've had the misfortune of sharing classes with since freshman year. Though he's not in a fraternity, he probably should be. He'd fit right in with that razor-short hair of his, not to mention the pole someone rammed up his ass. A likely misogynist, Elisa said when we saw him out one night, and we'd both laughed. Now I sigh, tuning him out as he starts siphoning off work for each of us to do in a brittle, authoritarian tone that leaves little room for negotiation. With a half-chewed pencil I sketch a little instead.

After class I step outside, and the air's so light and dry, the sky such an intense blue, that I think I might be able to touch it if only I tried. I close my eyes, lingering at the top of the steps. The sun warms my face, and for just a minute I picture myself under the sea, rippled in light, the sand a ribbon beneath me.

Hey, someone says practically in my ear, and I jump. Peter's standing beside me in a raunchy, long-sleeved tee shirt advertising some sorority party. His hair's so short I can see his skull. What do you want? I ask. You're an artist, right? he says, overlooking my tone and cramming a stick of gum in his mouth. I give him a suspicious look. I have a feeling I'm about to get reamed for refusing to participate. Yeah, I admit, but he just nods. Thought so, he says. He offers me the pack of gum, and I take a piece, sparing a glance at my watch. So, he says, You want to get something to eat?

I almost choke, and he smacks his palm between my shoulder blades as one of the girls in our group—Megan, I think—sidles up to us. Am I interrupting? she asks, and the seconds I take finding my breath give Peter the time to announce that we were just about to grab lunch. Want to come? he asks her. Sure, she says, and because I have no idea how to retreat without seeming like a total prick, I trudge along after them.

Ten minutes later, Peter's telling us that he's been interviewing for shitty jobs he has no interest in taking but has to at least consider because come May, he needs employment. I just want to stay in Austin after graduation, he confesses, but Megan tells us she's willing to move wherever she can find work. I have nightmares, she says, Of not being able to pay my rent. What about you? Peter asks. I'm taking a year off, I admit, and their expressions furrow with envy. I have half a mind to tell them what I've had to put up with the past twenty-two years to earn three hundred sixty-five days to myself. Are you going to travel or something? Megan asks. Joel's an artist, Peter says, like we've known each other since kindergarten, Didn't you see what he was drawing in class? I narrow my eyes, but Peter takes another bite of his sandwich as if he's just making conversation. So are you going to use the next year to work on your art? Megan asks, turning to me. That's the plan, I tell her, and she sighs. She has barely-there cleavage, berry-tinted lips, and when she threads her way through the restaurant to refill her iced tea, Peter gazes after her. God, she's hot, he mutters, and to get him back for roping me into this lunch, for calling me out because I was drawing in class, I say, Yeah, I'm gay, man.

I expect his mouth to drop, for him to shift in his seat and avoid my eye. But he just crunches on a handful of chips. Yeah, he says absently, I think I heard that somewhere.

His reaction's so bland that I tell James about him as soon as I get home from campus. I'm confused, he says, Are you interested in him or something? I don't want to convert the guy, I tell him, I just think I underestimated him. Whatever, he says, but when we hook up with Peter the next afternoon to shoot some hoop, they immediately hit it off. That ramrod frame of Peter's helps us on the court, too, and later we invite him to hang on the front porch with us, drinking beer and swapping stories about stupid shit we've done the past four years. He's cool, James admits after Peter leaves, and I smile.

Peter nails a job just before Spring Break as an investment advisor for a fledgling brokerage firm. I'd be hunting around for the nearest shotgun, but he's so happy to be staying in Austin that he doesn't seem to care. I can't blame him; I wouldn't want to be anywhere else, and neither does James.

Though I haven't admitted as much, I'm terrified thinking about what might happen if James doesn't get into UT's graduate program. He's applied to a half a dozen other schools, so in that regard he's covered. But I have a hard time picturing myself tagging along after him to Chicago or Virginia or somewhere without seeming like an obnoxious ex-lover. Faced with his departure, I start to wonder what the hell I'm doing, what I'll ever accomplish. If he leaves and I stay behind in this house, what will my life look like? In his absence who do I really have? A well of loneliness carves itself a place in the pit of my stomach, and I find myself pulling away from him, preparing for what I'm starting to think might be the inevitable. He's going to move on without me.

And why shouldn't he? He has goals, a plan, a vision. What do I have? A vague commitment to making my way as an artist, evidenced by the fact that I've done nothing in four years, nothing, to find out how I go about doing that. A semi-closeted sex life. A dead fucking mother and a father with a penchant for expensive cigars.

I start grinding out my frustration in whatever sex I can find instead of in the paint, where I belong. James just raises his eyebrows when I skulk through the front door long after midnight, my lips bruised red, the lingering brush of facial hair along my jaw. Nowhere, I mutter though he hasn't asked a question, and he stares at me through the glasses he finally admitted he needs for reading. I don't give him a chance to comment. I'm already moving down the hallway.

But he corners me one afternoon on the back porch where I'm sitting with my customary pack of Marlboros and a third beer. We spent Spring Break in Padre, a last hurrah before we graduate, and we brought that balmy weather back with us. Every day we swelter a little bit more. What's up with you? he says, plunking down beside me as I wipe sweat from my brow. What do you mean? I say. My eyes find the sky, where storm clouds pile up, thick and premonitory. I have a quick recollection of the conversation we had on this porch our sophomore year after my mother's funeral. He'd plunged down these steps into a driving rain, and I knew at that moment I'd do anything to be near him.

Tipping the beer to my mouth, I realize he hasn't answered, and I risk a quick glance in his direction. He actually seems concerned, and instead of being touched, I'm catapulted into an ire so vast and wide I'm honestly frightened. I turn my attention to my cigarette, taking note of my shaking fingers. C'mon, he says in a voice that presumes I'll confide in him, and I bristle with a ferocity that should widen his eyes. C'mon *what?* I growl.

I expect him to get to his feet and slam the door, but instead he shrugs me off, drawing a cigarette from my pack. I smolder watching him light up. Kind of pissed, aren't you? he muses. Did I invite you to join me out here? I ask, and he tilts his head to the side, considering. Smoke swirls around us, trailing upward into the heavy sky. I take another drag, the cords in my neck tight enough to snap. You want to tell me what's eating you? he says. Nothing's eating me, I mutter, and he smiles, a loose curl of his bottom lip that calls bullshit on my claim. I shake my head, watching as he shifts his position, stretching his legs out in front of him and crossing his feet at the ankles. He's settling in for the long haul, and I glower at him, my cigarette spitting ash. Been going out a lot lately, he says. So fucking what? I say. So nothing, he says, shrugging, I'm just making an observation. Now *that's* bullshit, I tell him, and he grins. He must have worn a baseball cap to campus earlier; his hair's crushed down around his ears, and he combs his fingers through his curls, looking thoughtful. You haven't been working much either, he says. Who the fuck are you? I snap, My father? Mephistopheles, you mean? he asks.

I laugh without forethought, and he nods, satisfied. Anyway, he says, Your father would have no complaints if you gave up the painting for good. Kind of a backhanded way to get me moving, I mumble, and he says, Did it work? I mash the butt of my cigarette in the ashtray between us. It's not that simple, I tell him. He gives me a quick smile. At the risk of sounding like I know what I'm talking about— he starts. Do you ever shut up? I say, but he's already lifting his hand, ready to signpost. You're graduating, he says, And you have no idea what you're going to do. I'm going to *work*, I tell him, and he says, As hard as you're working now?

Fuck *you*, I say, getting to my feet, I don't have to take this shit. Wait a second, he says, Let me finish. Why, so you can berate me? I say, I do a good enough job of that on my own. Do you think I don't know that? he asks, and I say, Then what are you doing here? Sit back down and I'll tell you, he says, flipping me the pack of cigarettes.

I watch him lean his head back as he inhales, then slowly lower myself to the top step. You're graduating, he says as I light another cigarette, And you have no idea what you're going to do. I shake my head, sucking in smoke; he holds up finger number two. You want to paint, he says, But you haven't bothered to figure out how to get your work into anyone else's hands. Is this supposed to be making me feel better? I ask, but he ignores me, holding up finger number three. In classic masochistic fashion, he says, You're avoiding the back room. He thinks for a minute, then holds up another finger. And you're probably fucking everything that moves, he says, Because in your warped world view, that's somehow going to make you feel better. Go to hell, I say, and he laughs. I shake my head, trying to kill the emptiness I already feel knowing that someone who understands me so well has every intention of leaving me in a few short months.

So, he says with a self-satisfied air, Did I hit the nail on the fucking head or what? You forgot one thing, I say as he stubs his cigarette in the ashtray. Oh? he says, What's that? I show him my hand, five fingers spread. You're leaving, I say.

He looks startled. Who says I'm leaving? he asks. All right, I concede, There's a chance you could get into UT— A good chance, he interrupts. Bullshit, James, I say, You've already told me that most programs don't take their own undergraduates. You should have more faith in me, he says, and I roll my eyes. You're more likely to end up across the country, I remind him. You're not coming with me? he asks, and I cut him a look that says not to fuck with me. He gazes back with an innocence that would shame Christ himself. You seriously want me to come with you? I say. Well, what else are you going to do? he says, It's not like you have something holding you here. That doesn't mean you want me following you, I point out. You're not a dog, Joel, he says, And anyway, what's the point of staying here when you can come with me and help pay for my apartment?

I give in to his smile, the massive burden of my fury beginning to unravel. Now, he says, clapping his hands together as if his work here is done, I'm starving.

I paint. I paint with a frenzy I've never felt in my life. I barely sleep, and when James appears in the doorway one afternoon a few weeks later, I tell him he can come in or get out, but I can't talk right now, I can't. I don't ever want to stop. Can I at least tell you I told you so? he asks.

I look up, and he flashes what must be his letter of acceptance. Are you shitting me? I say. You should've had more faith, he says, but I'm already pulling him into a congratulatory hug. When we part, the paint stains on his tee shirt mirror my own. Another year, I tell him, and he smiles. Four, he says.

+ + +

There's an air about the campus, the spring weather combined with the scent of freedom, and as those last few weeks before graduation wind down, I can't help thinking: this is the last exam I'll take before finals, the last trip I'll make to the library, the last time I'll sit in a classroom on a Friday afternoon. Life after graduation beckons, sweet and carefree, from just around the corner. Even my father's imminent arrival for commencement itself can't squash the happiness I feel deep in my chest, a happiness more exquisite than any I've known.

On graduation day I sit through my ceremony, get fifteen seconds of fame and endure a couple hours' worth of everyone else's. Afterward, my father says he'd like to take me to dinner, and we head to a restaurant of his choosing, somewhere he's managed to get a reservation on short notice. He couldn't be more gracious, ordering champagne, congratulating me, and when he puts a brief arm around my shoulder, I can't help feeling a foolish rush of pride.

I wonder what my mother would think. Would she be happy with what I've accomplished, or would she know that deep down I don't give a shit about the degree, that I've never needed anything other than the paint? Would she slip me a graduation present surreptitiously? A tube of oil paint in a provocative color, a bouquet of my favorite brushes? Or would she sit quietly while I accepted my father's present, an envelope containing another hefty check?

I'd do just about anything to know.

My father's sending me to Europe for the summer, says he hopes I'll use the time wisely. You have a year, he reminds me, But you need to start thinking about what comes after that year. I keep my mouth shut. I've already come to the conclusion that I'll do whatever it takes to stay away from the business world, at all costs.

+ + +

James and I spend the week after graduation lounging around outside in dilapidated lawn chairs, working on our tans. At night we wander through bars we've frequented for so long now they're as familiar as our own back porch. What the fuck would I do if I hadn't gotten into UT? James asks one night as we stumble up our front steps. I hook my arm around his neck and pull him close. He smells like summer sweat and beer, and he gives me a loose grin before he smacks his shin against the screen door. I let him go as he curses, kicking the door for emphasis. I'm rolling my eyes, but I swear I'd contemplate giving up my trip to Europe if we could just stay here, our life strung with moments like this one. I'm not so sure I need much else.

But the week comes to a close, and James starts working full-time in an attempt to save money before he starts graduate school in the fall. My summer jobs suck more with every passing year, he tells me, I've gone from lifeguarding to waiting tables to answering phones at a security company. You can handle three months, I say, trying to rally his spirits, and he stares at me like maybe he's regretting his decision to stay in Austin after all. You're leaving the country, he reminds me. Do you want to come? I ask, a free ride implicit in my invitation. Don't tempt me, he says flatly.

The morning before my flight, I wake feeling mildly celebratory. There's a storm coming; I can smell the rain when I open the front door and step onto the porch. I'd been thinking about a trip to the lake, but instead, I'm looking at a sky full of thunderclouds. And if I don't leave right this second, I'm going to be heading out for breakfast tacos in the rain.

The sky starts to fall as I pull into the line at the drive-thru, the storm gaining momentum as I inch forward and reach through the rain for my breakfast. I toss the sack beside me, then lift from the seat to replace my wallet. I'm edging the Explorer forward at the same time to make space for the car behind me, and even though I see the guy standing under the awning, I completely miscalculate his timing. He makes a break for his car at the exact moment my foot hits the accelerator; the Explorer skids on the wet pavement in excruciating slow motion.

I miss him by half an inch. He gapes at me through the windshield, and I throw the Explorer in park and scramble out from behind the wheel. When I round the hood, he backs away like he thinks I'm going to beat his ass for darting in front of me. I'm halfway tempted. He scared the shit out of me. Instead, I shout at him through the rain. Are you okay? I ask. He nods. You sure? I say, stepping forward and touching his arm. He's younger than I thought, probably still in college. You almost killed me, he says, and for some reason we both laugh. Lightning crackles around us. I should..., he says, gesturing to his car. Let me buy you breakfast, I say, glancing at the soggy bag he's clutching, and he hesitates, looking over my shoulder at my Explorer, now clearly holding up the line at the drive-thru. I like the look of his eyes, the way he tilts his head to the sky for a moment like maybe he's standing in the shower at home instead of in a downpour. Or you can come to my place, I say, letting my eyes slide down his torso, I live right around the corner.

This isn't the sort of chance I usually take. I have a very strict protocol as to where I'll pick someone up, and the taco shack down the street isn't on the list. If I'm in a bar, if I have time to scope someone out on campus, then I have an idea of what I'm getting into. But I don't know this guy, and an unwelcome proposition could turn this situation ugly in a hurry.

I've never brought anyone back to the house either, not since I came out to James. A handful of times I've let someone swing by to pick me up on the way somewhere else, but I haven't let anyone in my bed, not since Paul, mostly because I think that just because James threw out an invitation to accompany me to a gay bar as a show of solidarity doesn't mean he wants to find some stranger lounging in my bed.

But James works until five.

You have a name? I ask. Aaron, he says. I'm Joel, I say, thunder underscoring my words. You have a dryer, Joel? he asks.

He follows me back to the house, where I lead him into my bedroom on the pretense of getting a towel. He scrubs one across his hair, rainwater smacking against the windows, running in rivulets down his chest as he pulls his shirt over his head. His nipples stand hard and erect; I want to cover them with my mouth. Where should I...? he says, and I take his sopping shirt into the bathroom and wring it out in the sink, my own shirt a second skin. From the corner of my eye I can see him unzipping his jeans, peeling them away from his hips. He doesn't look my way, and for just a second I wonder if I've misread him the same way I misjudged the moment he stepped in front of my Explorer.

But not this time. I can tell by the way his eyes drift to my crotch, then linger. I take the opportunity to look him over, the way he's standing in my room in the middle of a Friday morning, the storm outside casting a gloomy light over the length of his body. Half of me wants to idle right here, in this wash of appreciation for what I've done, the risk I've taken, the knowledge that even if James comes home early, I'm not doing anything I haven't already confessed. The other half of me wants to push Aaron toward my bed and tumble down with him into whatever madness we can create.

I've waited too long to make a move, and Aaron draws himself in, confused; I understand his expression because I've worn it so many times myself. I was probably wearing it sixty seconds ago. *Did I read something wrong? Am I about to get my ass kicked?* I place a reassuring hand on his chest. His skin's cool to the touch, like he just pulled himself from a swimming pool. His mouth warms under mine.

He ends up spending the day, appropriating my bed like maybe he's thinking of making it his own on a permanent basis. I might balk a little more if he hadn't admitted that he has a boyfriend. Your boyfriend know how you're spending your time? I ask. He's propped on the heels of his hands, his lips a whisper away from mine. Dry, his hair's the color of champagne. Oh, I'll tell him the whole story, he assures me. Seriously? I say, pulling back to look at him. Oh yeah, he murmurs, bringing his mouth back in line with mine, The whole story.

I like him, maybe enough that I'm a little disappointed he has someone waiting for him at home. But in the meantime I like seeing him walk across the hardwoods in my bedroom to adjust the volume on the stereo. I like wandering into the kitchen for a couple of beers to drink with our cold tacos, and then coming back to find him waiting for me. I like the way he winds his legs around mine when I climb in bed. You're the best near-death experience I've had, he informs me as the day starts to dwindle.

The rain has tapered over the past hour, a breeze unlikely for this date in May leaching the last of the humidity from the air. Aaron opened my bedroom windows himself, and we'd let that cool wind wash over us, then ducked, laughing, under the covers. Now he's in the shower, and when I hear James's footsteps on the front porch, I feel a familiar, momentary panic. But I'm also kind of proud of myself for not chasing Aaron away, for not kicking him out before I was ready, and I square my shoulders and head into the living room as James tosses his keys on the bar. Hey, I say, I kind of have someone here. Really? he says, surprised.

As if on cue, Aaron appears in the doorway, naked and glistening, drying himself off with one of our towels. I scuttle forward but not before I catch an expression of pure astonishment on James's face, like despite what I've told him in the past, he's failed to understand until now how that might translate into reality. Come with me, I say to Aaron, taking his arm and steering him toward my bedroom. What's up? he murmurs. James isn't gay, I say, and he gives me a quick look of concern. I shake my head. He knows, I say, He knows, but you need to get dressed.

Depositing Aaron in my bedroom, I make a grim turn and head back down the hallway. James has a bottle of beer in his hand, and he's rubbing the lip back and forth with his thumb, gazing at nothing. When he sees me, his eyebrows raise. Sorry about that, I mutter, and he shrugs. I yank open the dryer and grab Aaron's jeans and shirt, his boxers. Let me just…, I say, gesturing toward my bedroom, and James nods.

Everything okay? Aaron asks as I hand over his clothes. Yeah, I say, We're good. I watch him get dressed, then find his sandals for him under the bed. So, he says when he's ready, running his hand through his hair.

A year ago, I sent Paul packing. I refuse to do that again.

C'mon, I say, reaching for Aaron's hand, Let me introduce you.

He follows me into the living room as James comes out from behind the bar. I scrutinize their handshake, but when I search James's expression, I fail to find the slightest hint of disapproval. You want a beer? he asks Aaron, who flips me a smile. Thanks, he says, But I can't stay. I'll walk you out, I offer.

On the front porch he slides his arms around my waist, and despite what the neighbors might think, I sink into his kiss. Sorry I almost killed you this morning, I murmur. So worth it, he tells me. Yeah? I say, smiling. Bet your ass, he says, and then I look over his shoulder, through the screen door. I must imagine the narrowing of James's eyes, because the second our gaze locks, his mouth slides to the right in a gesture both benign and congratulatory, the antithesis to my nightmare. Later, Aaron says, and I watch him walk down the front steps and cross the yard. Look both ways, I call as he reaches the street, and he laughs.

So how'd that happen? James asks once I'm back inside. I almost ran him down this morning, I admit. You almost ran him *down*? he says, Where? Taco place down the street, I say. And that led to you getting laid how? he asks. I don't know, I mumble, but he's clearly not going to let this one slide. I don't know, I repeat, shrugging, I just... asked if he wanted to come home with me. And that was it? he says in disbelief. Well, that's not verbatim, I mutter.

He stares at me as if he's trying to figure out exactly how I spent my afternoon. You want another beer? I ask, trying to distract him, and he looks at his half-empty bottle and shakes his head. I get one for myself, stalling on the far side of the bar. How does that even work? he asks. How does what work? I say, but I have a feeling I know what he's asking. That whole... dynamic, he says. I don't think it's that different, I tell him, and he looks impatient, like I'm intentionally withholding information. I suppose I am, and I finally sigh. There's a certain amount of negotiation involved, I admit. He nods, the movement slow and contemplative. I can imagine, he says.

+ + +

That night, James and I sit in the swing on the front porch, peeling the labels from our bottles of beer. He's sulking; we were supposed to go to dinner tonight since I'm leaving tomorrow, but Aaron has thrown me off-track, and the errands I should've knocked out at some point this afternoon I ended up running after he left. You're welcome to come with me, I said to James, and he gave me a shitty look. I've been working all day, he said, The last thing I feel like doing is running your errands.

By the time I finished he was starving and pissed. I'll order a pizza, I told him, but four slices have failed to soften his mood, and I'm starting to worry that the issue has nothing to do with dinner and everything to do with what he walked into earlier. Look, I finally say, I didn't mean to catch you off-guard. Like I give a shit who you fuck, he says.

I'm trying to dissect the hostility in his tone when he says, I hate my fucking job. I know, I say, and he rolls his eyes like there's no way I can possibly commiserate; he's probably right. Other than that week I spent at Permian, I don't know what it's like to be shut up in an office all day. And you're going to be hiking around Europe for the next few months, he says, like he's accusing me of something far worse than international travel. My father has a pretty tight schedule laid out for me, I mumble, It's not like I can just do whatever I want. He shakes his head. You should hear yourself, Joel, he says, You sound like such a prick.

I'm stung by the insult, but I don't say a word, and for a long minute he keeps his complaints to himself. Then he starts swinging slowly back and forth. I know you have issues with your father, he says, But c'mon. C'mon what? I ask. You have no idea how lucky you are, he says, his gesture encompassing the house, the Explorer, and everything in between.

A well of ice hits the pit of my stomach. You have no idea what you're talking about, I tell him, ready to end this conversation before we cross impossible lines. I have some idea, Joel, he says, And this poor little rich kid act is getting really fucking old.

His words suck at my equilibrium. I struggle to my feet, then grapple with the front door and slam it shut behind me. Even if he doesn't know the details of my relationship with my father, he knows enough. He knows enough.

I finish packing, then hunt around for my passport, waiting for his apology. I don't get one. Thinking the first move shouldn't be mine, I hold my ground, then finally give up before he can get to sleep. I don't want to leave the country with this argument hanging over my head.

My flight's early, I remind him, standing in the doorway of his bedroom. So? he says.

I want to tell him that I'm going to miss hanging out with him this summer, the longest amount of time we've been apart since we met. I want to tell him that however ridiculous it sounds, I'd rather be in Austin with him. But I'm thwarted by the expression on his face. I'll send you a postcard, I promise instead. Whatever, he mutters, I'm not holding my breath.

5

I spend most of my time alone over the next couple of months. I follow my father's schedule for me, visit a few obligatory tourist traps, dedicate some of my time to the museums in each city. But I leave feeling not so much inspired as intimidated. How can I not, coming face-to-face with the work of the masters? Even the paintings in the smaller galleries I visit possess a presence that demands respect. My own work, remembered from half a world away, seems puerile in comparison, and I realize for the first time what a mistake I've made not letting anyone other than James see my work. I have no idea if I'm any good at all.

I force myself to sketch a little anyway, sitting in cafés in London, Paris, Rome. Then I pick apart what I've done. Every pencil line, every smudge, becomes cause for scrutiny. I criticize until the trash can at my hotel overflows, until my sketchbook's empty and my motivation's shot. With an empty bottle of wine beside me, I fall into sleep, where I dream in languages not my own.

What I need right now is a compliment. What I need is reassurance. But I haven't talked to James since the night before I left Austin, the postcard I promised him never sent. I can't erase the image of his face the night before my flight, his insistence on withholding an apology knowing he wouldn't see me for months. Just because his own summer looked like shit didn't mean the bastard had to dump all over mine.

Or maybe I'm the one who fucked up, bringing Aaron back to our house. How did I expect James to react when Aaron showed up naked in our living room? I should've apologized more profusely, should've promised him that he'd never have to deal with anything so blatant again. Instead, I led Aaron onto our front porch and kissed him in plain sight of everyone.

Still, James could have been honest with me. *Like I give a shit who you fuck,* he said. But maybe he does. Maybe that's the point. Maybe he's fine with what I'm doing behind closed doors, but he doesn't want to have it thrown in his face.

And yet I didn't do anything in front of him that he hasn't done himself with any number of girls. Can he really be upset about a kiss viewed through a screen door? I'm sorry that Aaron made an impromptu appearance, but I lived with Elisa's tampons in my medicine cabinet for six months.

The longer I go without speaking to him, the more stubborn my grudge becomes, and the deeper my insecurity. The one thing I have going for me right now, the only thing, seems to be my dick. I'm enough of a novelty and have just enough of an American swagger to find myself presented with more opportunities than I expected. I cultivate an attitude of indifference I didn't know I had the balls to pull off, take risks I shouldn't, and think every time I coax someone back to my ridiculous suite at the top of the Spanish steps that I couldn't come up with a better way to say *fuck you* to my father if I tried.

One night at the end of July, I find a guy squatting outside the Pantheon, stroking a cat that looks so feral I hesitate to approach. *Scusami*, I say when I get too near and the cat bolts. The guy looks up at me, annoyed. *Parli l'italiano?* he says, getting to his feet and brushing grit from his hands. No, I admit, and he purses his mouth in a grimace I find attractive despite its downturn. American, he says, the word declarative and loaded with assumptions. I shrug, lighting a cigarette and offering him the pack. He rolls eyes heavily lashed, then gazes at me with a look so languid I drop my next line. My hotel's nearby, I say, taking a chance that his English is better than my Italian. He squints, concentrating on extracting a cigarette from my box, hiding his surprise. Then he nods.

I wake the next morning to the quiet click of the door. I'm hungover; I can tell the second I turn my head. There's an oppressive feel to the air, and when I manage to get to my feet long enough to pull back the drapery and pry open the window, I'm assaulted by a wave of heat. I might as well be in Houston, and I crank the window back in place and throw myself on the bed. Lucio or Lucino or whatever the fuck his name was didn't have to slink out without waking me. I wasn't going to try to convince him to stay. But he could have at least thanked me for inviting him here last night. I spent a goddamn fortune on room service.

You should hear yourself, I can almost hear James say, *You sound like such a prick*. Fuck you, I mumble, but as I sprawl there in my king-sized bed, naked and flushed, staring out the window into the Roman sun, I'm caught off-guard by a wave of discomfort. Two months I've been gone, and for two months James has been working. Peter, too, and Megan, who moved to San Antonio the week after we graduated to take a job as a customer service representative somewhere. Meanwhile, I'm wandering the catacombs to escape the heat, staring at paintings hundreds of years old and calling it research. *That's the plan*, I said last spring when they asked if I'd be spending my time painting, but I have no more than a dozen sketches, each one less sophisticated than the last.

When Lucio told me he wasn't into condoms, I let him fuck me without one.

Hesitating, I pick up the phone. Where are you? James asks sleepily, and the homesickness I feel hearing his voice nearly abducts my breath. Italy, I say, reaching for my cigarettes, I'm in Rome. He yawns as I light up, then reaches for a cigarette of his own; I can hear the lighter and his sharp inhale, the creak of the wood under his feet as he walks through our house. Almost six thousand miles away the screen door slams. How's work? I ask. Predictable, he says, settling into the swing. You swimming at all? I ask. Some, he says, It's hot as shit here.

I take another drag from my cigarette and listen as he does the same. How's Europe? he asks. Amazing museums, I admit. I bet, he says, and we fall silent. Together we smoke, all the way through to the end of our cigarettes without speaking another word. Finally, as I'm dropping my butt into the near-empty bottle of wine beside my bed, he clears his throat. So I'm an asshole, he says, Did you really have to make me wait eight weeks before you called? Why didn't *you* call *me*? I ask, and he says, Because I didn't know where you were, you idiot.

He's shaking his head. I can't see him, but I know he's shaking his head. Have I been punished long enough? he asks, Are you ever coming home?

I laugh despite the furious rush of tears behind my eyes. Yeah, I say, so relieved that he wants me back I couldn't care less if he hears the quaver in my voice, I'm coming home.

+ + +

I land in Houston a few weeks later, stumble off the plane jet lagged and exhausted, and spot my father just outside of customs. Why are *you* here? I ask, and he conjures up a wounded expression. Can't I pick up my son at the airport? he asks. *Not without arousing a good deal of suspicion*, I think. Instead, I offer him a half-hearted smile, letting him take my luggage. You must be tired, he says, and now I'm sure he has an ulterior motive. I'd imagined him walking in the door from the office this evening and getting right to the cross-examination no matter how weary I felt. He's definitely up to something, and I trail behind him as we head toward the car, trying to summon the energy for whatever's coming.

At some point over the summer he bought a new Mercedes, and he opens the door and invites me inside with a proprietary air. I sink into the softly cushioned leather; I can hardly argue with him about such a beautiful automobile. When you're rested, he says, You can take it for a drive. Sure, I say, not quite believing him. I've never been behind the wheel of any of his cars, not since I was sixteen and he returned from a business trip overseas. Anxious to show him how much my driving had improved, I offered to take him to the office. Pulling into his reserved space, my foot accidentally found the accelerator instead of the brake, and I'd plowed forward, right into the concrete wall. I'm still convinced that the only reason he didn't beat the shit out of me right there was because we were in full view of one of his colleagues.

So tell me, he says now as I peel myself from the memory, Was Europe everything you imagined?

I tilt my head as if I'm considering, though I've instantly thought of Lucio. I have a hard time not smirking. Europe was good, I say, Europe wore me out.

But he's not even listening to me. Permian plans to open an office in Dallas, he tells me as if we're in the middle of a conversation about his job. Are you moving? I ask, startled, and with impatience he brushes my question aside. I'm talking about a real opportunity here, Joel, he says, Now I know you don't have much work experience, but that Business degree coupled with my recommendation—

I'm already groaning. You don't seriously mean that I should get a job at Permian, I say. I can ensure you a strategic position, he informs me, like maybe the real reason I don't want to work for him has to do with starting at the bottom rather than knowing that six weeks in his employ will likely find me following in my mother's footsteps. Doing what? I ask. Marketing, he says, Or even sales. He glances at me; I have a feeling I look every bit as much like a recalcitrant teenager as I feel. I know we've talked about you taking a year off before you start work, he says, But I'm hoping you've had time this summer to reconsider your priorities.

He didn't waste any time, did he? I can't even see the skyline yet, and he's practically finished his sales pitch. Frankly, I'm surprised he didn't wait a couple of days so he could ease me into the idea. But maybe his intention was to catch me off-guard, so fresh from vacation I'd agree to whatever he wanted. Well, that's not going to happen.

You promised me a year, I remind him.

His expression changes, and he sits back, exasperated. Well, you did, I tell him sullenly. You're going to lose ground if you wait a year, he tells me. I don't care, I say, and he assures me that I'm going to care when next year at this time I'm scrounging to pay rent. What do you think you can accomplish in a year's time anyway? he asks, as if I don't have the self-discipline to paint the fucking walls. How am I supposed to know until I try? I say, and my father gives his head a grim shake. I'll be the first to admit that I know little about art, he says, But I'm not naïve enough to believe that just anyone can earn a living painting. He eyes me over the top of his sunglasses. Do you really think you have the talent? he asks.

My father has no clue whether or not I'm any good. The last work of mine he saw I handed him my freshman year in high school. We'd gone skiing that year for the first time, and the mountain was frigid, my mother timid. After the first couple of days I started hanging out with her in our condo, drinking hot chocolate and painting. My mother smiled when I showed her what I'd done, but my father just stared at the paintings and then me in disbelief. I spend thousands of dollars so you can ski over Spring Break, he said, And you sit inside and *paint* instead. Hearing that word turned blasphemous, I'd vowed never to show him anything again.

My point, he continues now, Is that you have to start asking yourself whether you're foolish to pursue a dream that will never materialize. Don't question my talent when you've never taken the slightest interest in anything I've done! I say. I don't know how you've deluded yourself into believing you're an artist, he mutters, Even your mother didn't think you have what it takes.

My mouth drops, and for a moment he looks as if he wants to snatch what he's said from the air between us. We haven't mentioned her directly since her death, and he averts his eyes, knowing he's used her name to hurt me. I strangle the sob that's fighting to break away from the back of my throat, mentally combing through years' worth of conversations with my mother. I don't think she'd have ever said anything derogatory about my potential, but there's an unfortunate piece of me, especially after what I've experienced in Europe, that believes him.

Joel— he starts, and I say: You promised me a year. He's quiet for a moment, and then he nods.

The next morning, when I come down to breakfast, he tells me he's been thinking about my transportation situation. You've had that Explorer for four years, he reminds me, stirring his coffee. I pour myself a cup, watching him from the corner of my eye; he waits, silent, a regular fucking salesman. Yeah, all right, I finally say, and he rubs his hands together. We'll go out today, he tells me, mollified.

I drive back to Austin behind the wheel of a brand new, black BMW 325i convertible, having promised to sell the Explorer. James steps onto the front porch as I pull into the driveway, and there's a small second when the memory of our last conversation here constricts my breathing. But he's smiling, and I let the window slide down. Want a ride? I say.

That night, as the blinds bleed the last of the day's light, I stretch out across my bed. You still jet lagged? James asks from the doorway. We've played catch-up for the past few hours, tripping over each other's words as we cruised through Austin with the top down, and now I'm whipped. So, he says, leaning against the doorframe and adopting a casual tone, D'you suck any dick this summer? I wince, fearing a flare-up of whatever angered him before I left for Europe, but he shrugs. Just checking, he says. What about you? I ask. Did *I* suck any dick this summer? he says. I roll my eyes. Actually, he confides, assuming a self-pitying posture, I had a depressingly lonely summer. You had the whole house to yourself and everything, I remind him, and he says, A lot of good that did me. Rapping his knuckles against the door, he straightens. 'Night, Joel, he says, turning and heading back down the hallway.

I watch the light shift, twilight merging into nightfall so effortlessly I might have blinked and missed the show. Five minutes more and I'll be fast asleep in my own bed for the first time in months. Just the thought relaxes me, and I let myself sink into the sheets, the ceiling fan a whir above me. Glad you're back, James hollers from the living room just before my eyes slide closed, and I ride his words into sleep.

+ + +

James settles naturally into graduate school, but my own work doesn't come as easily. There's a threatening element to the painting that didn't exist before I left for Europe, before that demoralizing conversation with my father, and after a couple of weeks I give up and start sleeping. You're still in bed? James asks when he finds me asleep at noon. I bury my head under my pillow, and for the moment he leaves me alone but asks when I drag my ass into the kitchen what the hell is wrong with me. I'm bored, I lie. The look he gives me isn't sympathetic.

That night he forces me to sit through a lecture about the time I'm squandering, the opportunity I'm wasting. Don't you realize how lucky you are? he asks, the question sounding far too similar for my liking to the one he posed on our front porch the night before I left for Europe. I swing the bottle of beer I've pulled from the fridge back and forth across the bar without saying anything. He purses his lips, watching me. What do you want from me? I finally ask. I want you to answer the question, Joel, he says. Forgive me, I say, If I decline to classify my life as *lucky*. That's not what I meant, he says, And you know it. You sound an awful lot like my father, I mutter. Don't be a dick, he says, Just answer the question. *What* question? I say. Why aren't you painting? he asks, enunciating each word. I don't know, I say just as carefully, but he shakes his head. Yeah, you do, he tells me. You know, I really don't need the psychoanalysis, I say. That's debatable, he mumbles. Oh my god, get off my ass, James! I say. Someone's got to ride you, Joel, he says, Because you're letting yourself get sucked into a vortex of inertia, and it's going to take an act of god to pull you out. Maybe it should fucking occur to you that you don't always know what you're talking about, I say, My father— This is your own goddamn choice, he interrupts, Don't delude yourself into thinking otherwise.

He's right. That's the bitch of this whole situation; I know he's right. But I can't just ignore what happened this past summer, can't forget what my father claims my mother thought of my talent. How am I supposed to go into the back room with those words as an accompaniment?

Instead, I surrender to the television, let malaise swallow me whole. I wallow in self-involvement, neglect to ask James about his first semester of graduate school, his first semester teaching. I barely notice the oversight. Every phone call from my father delivers a fresh dose of pessimism, and with what little energy I have I head downtown to see what I can find. There are times I don't even make it out of the bar, times I leave with someone I shouldn't. And then I start bringing guys back to the house, where I skirt past James and lock my bedroom door, the unarticulated rule I made about parading a series of men through our house conveniently forgotten.

Can you turn off the television for two fucking minutes? James finally asks one afternoon, finding me crashed out on the sofa. I've been awake for maybe three hours, a quick trip to Taco Cabana and back-to-back episodes of *The Facts of Life* all I've managed so far. I dig around for the remote as he sweeps the remnants of my breakfast off the coffee table and eyes the handful of beers I've already allotted myself. He's probably still pissed about last night, when he walked through the front door to find the guy I'd picked up earlier that evening fumbling with the button of his jeans like a toddler newly mastering the skill. I'd followed James's gaze as he took in my trick, who was half-dressed and high and older than me by a good fifteen years, with pockets of flesh under his eyes that suggested either an alcohol addiction or some serious sleep deprivation. He looked every bit as sketchy as he probably was, and I suddenly couldn't imagine what had made me nod when he approached me a couple of hours earlier.

The energy in this house is malignant, man, James says. Hey, just because you don't like who I'm bringing home— I say, and he groans. *You* don't like who you're bringing home, Joel, he tells me. I force myself into a sitting position but fail to find a defense. Seriously, he says, I don't know how much more of this self-sabotage I can handle. What is that, a threat? I say, You going to move out? He folds his arms across his chest. Well, be my guest, I tell him, And good luck paying that rent. Fuck you, he says, turning on his heel. But when he reaches the door of his bedroom, he turns back. I haven't put up with your shit for the past four years because of the money, he says, *Asshole*.

After he slams his door I go into the bathroom and stare at my reflection. I'm afraid I favor my father. I've seen pictures, know I'm right. Before she died my mother showed me a photograph taken his senior year in college. I found the resemblance so disturbing I had to make light of the similarities in our features before I handed the picture back to her. She didn't know, after all, the extent of the damage.

Spreading my arms, I examine the scars high on the insides of my biceps. I remember exactly the violation responsible for each instance of discipline. One for lying about a score on a math test in sixth grade. Another for skipping school when I was fifteen and being stupid enough to forge my father's signature on the note I turned in. A third for blowing off curfew the summer before my senior year and wandering in the back door, drunk, in the bleak, pre-dawn hours. And the one that got me where I am today, the one that brought me to this house.

Standing in front of the mirror, I can conjure the smell of my skin smoldering, the taste of blood in my mouth.

I don't like the inertia any more than James does. I don't like walking in the back room and feeling a wave of fear so sharp I'm almost knocked off my feet. But the fact remains that right now, in this moment, I can't stand in front of the canvas any more than I can wave my paintbrush as if it's a magic wand and erase my history.

Still, as shitty as I might feel, I can't risk losing James. He's been upfront with me; he's told me he doesn't know how much more he can take. So at the very least I have to show him I'm willing to make an effort.

The next morning, I go for a run, a lousy run that simply serves to remind me that I haven't laced up my shoes in months. But James's expression upon my return placates me just enough to go again the next day, and then the day after that. For four weeks I run, sometimes twice a day, once in a downpour so thick I can't see more than two feet in front of me. The exercise barely lifts the veil of depression that has surrounded me since the summer, but I'm able to function at least enough to pull myself out of bed by the time James wakes up in the morning. I make him toast, like a dutiful housewife, then stand in the middle of the living room after he leaves for class, willing myself not to fall prey to the TV. Instead, I run. I read, though nothing so heavy or dry I might end up asleep. I reorganize the CDs. I do anything I can to prove to James that he has no reason to worry, and when he asks if I'm coming with him to Fort Worth for Thanksgiving as usual, I just nod.

+ + +

The weekend before the holiday I come down with a cold, or what I think might be a cold, until the fear I've been ignoring for the past few months worms its way forward. I dig my fingers into my neck, checking my lymph nodes, which might be swollen because I have a sore throat or because I'm staring headlong into an abyss. Panic causes me to push myself to run without a day off, disregarding the ache in my lungs and a sinus headache worse than any I can remember. You're going to get pneumonia, James tells me, watching me lace my shoes again on Sunday night, Why don't you give it a rest? I'm fine, I tell him, stifling a cough, but by the time I get back to the house I'm shivering, and my fever, which was borderline when I left and which I'd been deluded enough to believe I could sweat out of my system, has skyrocketed. I drop to the sofa as James shakes his head. You're going to the doctor tomorrow, he says, Because you can't take this shit to Fort Worth.

The next morning, he insists on driving me. I don't have it in me to argue, and I lean my flushed forehead against the passenger window, my hands tucked between my knees. Here, he says, cranking up the heat and cracking the driver's side window just enough so he can breathe. As we pull up to the same office complex I visited just before Spring Break my sophomore year, I don't even try to convince him that he should wait for me in the car.

While he reads through a stack of undergraduate papers outside the examining room, I tremble as the doctor—a different one than I saw two years ago—places a cold stethoscope against my chest. How long have you had the fever? he asks. A couple days, I say, and he nods, sliding a tongue depressor from his pocket.

If he doesn't suggest the test, I'm going to have to bring it up myself.

How many other men are sitting in doctors' offices around the world right now, allowing their glands to be prodded, worrying about their diagnosis? I stare straight ahead, fighting against tears, thinking about all those lives, all that fear. Why not me? Why should I be any different?

Well, there's not much I can do for you, the doctor's saying, jotting something down in his chart. Can't I get an antibiotic or something? I ask, and he shakes his head without looking up. If you're not better in a few days, he says, handing me a form to take to the front desk as he's getting to his feet, Give me a call. What about HIV? I ask.

He stops. I can't look him in the eye.

Do you have reason to believe you've been exposed? he asks. I'm silent, wondering what else he's going to say, if he's going to dredge up my most private moments, shame me into admitting what I've done. But he just shakes his head, scrawling something across another form and passing it to me. You'll have to go to the second floor for the blood work, he mutters. His hand's already on the door; I picture him ducking into the next room and scrubbing up like he's about to perform surgery. When will I have the results? I ask. They'll tell you at the front desk, he says over his shoulder.

The receptionist, all smiles when I first hand her my form, drops her voice to a near-whisper as she schedules me an appointment for next week. There's a chance the lab will be running behind because of the holiday, she says, We'll call you if that's the case. I can't stand the pity in her expression, and I lurch back to the waiting room, where James looks up. Virus, I croak, digging in my pocket for a tissue. Shit, he says, No antibiotic? I shake my head as he shoves his papers in his bag. I have to get some blood drawn, I mumble. Okay, he says, getting to his feet. But outside the office he turns to me. Wait, he says, Why do you have to get blood drawn?

An awful moment, this one, as he stares at me with parted lips. It's just a test, I say. But why? he asks, Do you... does the doctor think...? I groan, holding my congested head in my hands. Don't interrogate me, I moan, and before he can say anything else the elevator doors slide open. I'm *fine*, I say, sloughing him off as he follows me, Just wait for me in the car.

But he holds his ground, shadowing me so closely that the lab technician upstairs probably pegs him for my boyfriend. Mr. Grayson, she says, gesturing me forward, and here's where I draw the line. *Wait*, I tell him, and he backs away, shoving his hands in the pockets of his jeans. I go with the tech to a room in the back, where I lean my head against the wall as she preps my arm, protected by a pair of latex gloves. Though I want to turn away, I watch the needle leach my blood, ruby-colored and potentially lethal.

Back in the waiting area James jumps to his feet, his skin so ashen that for just a moment his expression reminds me of something I think I'd rather shake. Next week, I tell him, and he lets out a breath, scrabbling in the pocket of his coat for a pack of cigarettes so that by the time we make our way out to the parking lot he's primed for the lighter. Back in my car the steering wheel spins under his hands as he leaves the parking lot, bumping us up over the curb. If you know you're fine, he says, Then why'd you have your blood drawn? I close my eyes. Do you *need* to be tested? he asks, and I curl toward the window, huddled inside my coat. Please, I say, Just drive.

+ + +

My fever breaks on Wednesday morning. James isn't here; he's at campus, his classes wrapping at noon for the holiday. For the past two days he's brought me cold washcloths and aspirin, hot tea with lemon and honey that he must have made a special trip to the grocery store to buy. Not once has he tried to reinitiate our conversation from Monday.

I stretch, then get to my feet and go into the bathroom, where I shower for the first time in days. As long as there's hot water, I stand under the stream with closed eyes. My hands, my chest, my legs. For now, at least, I'm fine.

You feel up to the trip north? James asks when he gets home and finds me dressed in jeans and a sweatshirt, a mug of coffee in my hands. You still want me to go? I ask, and he gives me a look that tells me there's little I could've said that would've pissed him off more.

We leave that afternoon, James behind the wheel and Pandora pacing the backseat. She doesn't like the car, but the neighbor who usually looks in on her when we're out of town told us she was heading to Florida, and we don't want to take a chance with the furniture. Florida. Even there I could do some diving. Maybe that would relax me. Maybe a handful of inhales through a regulator would soothe me in a way the cigarette between my fingers can't.

As if my lungs want to remind me of what I'm putting them through, I start to cough. James raises his eyebrows, alarmed in a way he wouldn't be if we didn't have these test results hanging over our heads, and I crack the window and toss my butt into the wind. I'm fine, I say, and he just nods as if he's putting as little stock in my claim as I am.

For the next forty-eight hours we don't talk about what happened at the doctor's office or what I have waiting for me next week. Instead, we hang out with James's parents and Ashley, who for the third year in a row treat me like one of their own. I hold tight to that feeling, to Ashley's hand in mine as she skips along beside me at the grocery store on Wednesday night, where we've been sent for extra whipped cream. I try to place myself in the moment when James's mother gestures me into the kitchen the following afternoon and hands me the potato masher and butter. Sitting around their dining room table, I finger the glass of wine they've poured me, wine I brought them myself and probably shouldn't be drinking but which I still hold on my tongue, trying to decipher its nuances despite my lingering cold. At the Kimbell on Friday afternoon I brood over *Girls on the Pier*, losing myself in the pucker of that full moon, and when I turn, forgetting and thinking myself alone, I find James, standing close enough that I could touch him with the merest extension of my fingers. For the past three years he's been the only real family I've known.

+ + +

Something wakes me our last night in Fort Worth, a scrambling on the roof, a clatter of claws across the shingles which causes Pandora's ears to prick up. Then nothing, and I throw back the covers and slip out of the bedroom and across the hall to the bathroom. James's parents have a small house, built forty years ago and barely remodeled, the bedrooms so close together that I find myself holding my breath for fear of waking anyone. There's a nightlight in the bathroom, and I piss in its dim glow, my dick in my hand and my reflection in the mirror moments later a shadowy reassurance.

I'll be fine. I'm sure I'll be fine, and I creep back down the hall and burrow under the covers. Though the bed's small—even when I was a kid, I didn't sleep in a single—I'm comfortable here. I can hear James breathing, and the sound soothes me the way it did the night my mother died, the way it did most of my freshman year when we were living in the dorm. I remember wondering that first night how I was supposed to jerk off with James only an arms-length away, the way my dick hardened just slightly at the thought that he might be jerking off too. I don't know if he ever did, and I tried to relegate my own moments to the times when he wasn't in the room.

I've stiffened at the memory, and without thinking I slide my hand beneath the waistband of the pajama bottoms I'm wearing. I tug once, twice, then stop, partly because I'm not alone but more because I'm not sure I want to touch my own poisonous cum. Self-loathing rises like bile at the back of my throat, and it's all I can do not to go into the bathroom and wash my hands with water so hot my skin burns clean away.

I've never been tested until now. I've never been tested because I feel fine, because most of the time I use condoms. Every so often I'll get a look of impatience, a roll of the eyes that—especially when I was first experimenting—made me feel ridiculous for bringing up the suggestion at all. And Lucio. I squeeze my eyes shut and think back to that hotel room, the bottle of wine that was almost empty, the condom I reached for and Lucio's expression when he saw what I held between my fingers. *No, no, no,* he said, *No preservativi.* I looked at him, at the taper of his waist and thick swirls of hair above his cock, which was long and firm and uncut, and knew I should protest. *Non mi piaciano i preservativi,* he said, and I groaned. C'mon, man, I said, reaching for him, but he pulled away when I tore the wrapper. *Niente preservativi,* he insisted, so I tossed the condom in the trashcan along with the drawings I'd torn from my sketchpad earlier that evening and let him fuck me without one. Twice.

Now I'm waiting to find out if a half a dozen stupid mistakes will cost me the heart that's still beating. I run my hands through my hair, then lightly, lightly, slide my fingertips across my eyelids, my cheekbones, my lips. Beside me James breathes. I don't want to disappear.

+ + +

The lab calls Monday and tells me my results won't be in until the end of the week. The delay almost brings me to tears. The holidays are enough of a stretch, the knowledge that I've put James in a position where he's unable to concentrate on the end of his first semester of graduate school leaving me so guilt-stricken that I can barely look him in the eye. Normally, I'd lock myself in the back room and paint myself out of this nightmare, but I can't even open the door. The last thing I need is to confirm my own suspicions, that my father wasn't lying, that my mother knew I don't have what it takes. Instead, I sit in the chair beside the fireplace and hold my head in my hands, looking up mid-week to find James staring at me with a horrified expression. I don't know anything, I tell him, I won't know anything until Friday.

Thursday's nasty, hot and humid in a way that reminds me of Houston and the trip I'll be making in a few weeks to see my father. As long as he's covering my expenses, I'm required to join him for the holiday, and I shudder thinking about what that trip might look like under the cloak of a positive diagnosis. I can't even imagine life beyond my appointment tomorrow, and I pace back and forth in front of the windows that night, waiting for James to get home from campus. Pandora, curled on the windowsill, watches me with unblinking eyes.

When James still isn't back by nine o'clock, I go into my bedroom and put on my running shoes. I can't take another minute alone here, and I slam the front door, breaking into a run before I reach the street. My breath comes hard, then easier, my lungs gradually loosening until I'm running at a full sprint. I run until I can't take another step, until there's a stitch in my side I can't ignore. Sweat drips from my hair and stings my eyes.

Back at the house I prop my foot on the railing of the porch and stretch my hamstring, looking over my shoulder when James's car pulls to the curb. You go for a run? he asks, climbing the steps, and I nod, switching legs. He leans against the railing, watching me. Cold front's coming tomorrow, he says after a minute, and I straighten, wiping my forehead with the back of my arm. Light from a passing car momentarily illuminates the stubble along his jaw. You working tonight? I ask, and he shrugs. He can't concentrate any more than I can, and I follow him into the house, where I head into the kitchen and hunt around for a glass I can pass off as clean.

Joel, James says, dropping into a barstool, Are we ever going to talk about this? There's nothing to talk about, I say. But why now? he asks, and I sigh. Because I've never been tested, I say. Never? he says. Have you? I say. I don't sleep with other guys, he tells me, and something in his tone makes what he just said sound like an indictment, though I can hardly give him some bullshit lecture about his risk factor when I'm the one who picked up a stranger in Rome and then shrugged when he told me he didn't like condoms. Well, I say, I *do* sleep with guys. Without protection? he asks.

It's unfair that I have to answer these questions, that I have to explain myself. I didn't say a word when he brought Elisa home, when he convinced me to follow those girls in Mexico back to their hotel. I've never once asked if he uses condoms. And yet he's sitting across from me with an incredulous expression, judging the half a dozen moments I rejected common sense in favor of sensation. I feel an intense rush of anger, and I lean across the counter, my voice even but my teeth gritted. You want me to explain myself? I say, You want me to ask you for absolution? All right, Joel, he says, getting to his feet. You want me to tell you about the guy in Italy who didn't like condoms? I ask. And you slept with him *anyway*? he says.

I hurl my glass against the wall. Shards fly through the air and skitter across the floor, and I hold my hands to my head, then turn to look at James, who gapes back at me. For a long moment we stare at each other, until he finally releases his breath. Okay, he says, but I brush past him, snarling when he reaches for my arm. Don't *touch* me! I say, and he lets me go.

+ + +

The next morning, I'm hunched over a bowl of Raisin Bran when he comes into the kitchen, dressed in jeans and an old tee shirt and looking suspiciously like he's not planning on teaching his class. You're not coming with me, I inform him through a mouthful of cereal, but he just sits down across from me and reaches for the box. I withhold comment as he digs around and comes up with a handful of bran flakes, then starts picking out the raisins. Elisa was a lesbian, he says. *What*? I say, and he nods. I drop my spoon in my bowl. Elisa was a *lesbian*? I ask, What the hell was she doing with you? He shrugs as if we're talking about something that's all in the past, something he doesn't think about every day: that if he was just Elisa's diversion, then that baby never stood a chance.

Why are you telling me this? I ask. He gazes down at his hands, then starts cracking his knuckles. I want you to understand why I haven't been tested, he says. Lesbians get AIDS too, I say uncharitably. He squirms, like he'd rather not have to divulge his secrets; his discomfort gratifies me more than I'd ever admit. Let *him* confess the particulars of his sex life. Let *his* experience be picked apart. Well? I say when he doesn't answer. Except with Elisa, I've always used condoms, he says. Every single time? I ask, and he looks away. Yes, he says, Both times.

I scour his expression for a glimpse of the truth, then realize as his cheeks flush that he's not lying. I think about the girls he tends to go for, girls quiet and shy and defiantly dogmatic about what they're willing to give up. I think about how much time he spends on campus, how much time he spends studying. I think about how little time we spend apart.

Whatever, Joel, he says, as if he knows what I'm thinking, I can't just walk in a bar and end up with a blowjob. Well, you *could*, I point out, and he shoots me a furious look, then lets a smile slip through his anger. I'm grateful; this conversation must be pissing all over his pride. C'mon, he says, getting to his feet, You're going to be late. You're not coming with me,

I tell him again, and he says, Joel, what're you going to do if you get a shitty result? I've got a .38 in the glove box, I tell him. That's not funny, he says, and I sigh. The doctor's going to think you're my boyfriend, I say. So? he says. Don't you care? I ask, and he actually laughs. By the time you got around to coming out, he says, Every one of my old fraternity brothers thought I was fucking you.

My jaw drops, and I realize suddenly what he must have had to deal with before I came out, what he must still have to maneuver when he tells someone his roommate's gay. The assumptions about his own sexuality must make him crazy.

Look, if I cared that much about what everyone else thought, he says, I would've moved out a long time ago.

Well, he's probably right about that.

I'm going with you to get those results, he says, and this time I nod.

+ + +

An hour later I'm sitting across from the doctor, suspended in time. Rough-worn jeans, rough-worn boots, a sweater unraveling at the wrists. Fingers free of paint, hands cleaner than they've been in months. A tightness in my muscles borne of tension and fatigue, of regret and fear. Beside me James has his eye on the doctor, trying to glean something from his body language, from the open folder on his desk. There's a strong smell of coffee and an undercurrent of nicotine, cigarettes stolen between every painful diagnosis, caution abandoned in the stress of the moment. Photographs of another life, one lived outside the confines of this office; they have nothing to do with me.

Mr. Grayson, the doctor says.

Every misstep, not just of mine but of everyone who came before me, everyone who's sitting in an office right now with a different diagnosis: I feel them all. For just a minute my body's not my own. I'm shackled, paralyzed, bereft of breath. And then James brings me back. James always brings me back, and this time, it's his hand on my shoulder, his mouth near my ear. I follow the sound, and in that moment everything else falls away: the doctor, this office, a million voices crowding my head.

You're okay, James says, You're okay.

6

Even though he downplays his fanaticism because of me, I don't know anyone who likes Christmas more than James does. I suppose I can't blame him; if I had a Dick and Jane family, I'd probably want to preserve the whole bullshit holiday, too. He totally gets off on shopping for his little sister, spends money he really doesn't have on earrings and pajamas and books he thinks she should read. I tag along, having nothing better to do these days, give him my opinion on which CDs Ashley might like best. Pink or purple? he asks, deliberating over tiny, spangled purses. I give him a helpless shrug. Isn't this supposed to be your area of expertise? he asks. I'm not the one lingering over the lip gloss, I tell him.

I think if James had his way, he'd insist that we stop on the way home from shopping to pick up a Christmas tree. There's a part of me that feels like indulging him. Blessed with a negative HIV result, I feel a spark of magnanimity. At the same time, I don't know that I want to be reminded every time I walk in the door of not only my past but what the current holiday has in store. So I keep my mouth shut, then lean in the doorway at home as he twines a strand of colored lights around the railing of the front porch in a gesture of compromise. There's a moment just before he plugs them in that I find myself holding my breath. But the muted colors lend an atmosphere to our porch that reminds me more of our favorite bar than my childhood, and I settle myself in the swing with a beer and a satisfied friend beside me.

We're sitting there the week before the holiday, a couple of days after James has finished his semester. He's leaving for Fort Worth in the morning, and he's trying to convince me to come along. You can go to Houston for Christmas, he says, Just come to Fort Worth for a few days first. Nah, I say, and he puckers his mouth around his bottle. Why not? he asks, irritated. I just want to hang out here, I say. Why, he says, So you can paint?

Since October, I've been trying to make my way without my work, and I've logged more miles running in the past couple of months than I ever could've imagined. But I'm living in a fog, and the only relief I've felt since my father met me at the airport last summer was that moment in the doctor's office a couple of weeks ago, a moment that should've spurred me into action. I know I need to work. I know I need to paint. I know that without a brush in my hand I'm nothing. But I can't set foot in the back room. I can't bear to find out she was right.

Beside me James is already back-tracking, throwing out something that's supposed to pass for an apology, telling me he just doesn't get why I'm wasting the one year my father's giving me. I mean, seriously, Joel, he says, What're you doing here? The best I can, I mumble, and he gives me a long, hard look. That, he finally says, Is the biggest load of crap I've ever heard.

+ + +

I arrive in Houston on Christmas Eve, late because of heavy traffic and a profound reluctance to get this party started. In my absence my father has made his way into the scotch; he holds his liquor well, but as I watch him pour what's probably a third and then a fourth drink, I start to get annoyed. I can't explain my frustration because I quickly catch up. Instead, I mentally remove myself from our celebration, the two of us with a bottle of scotch and a catered meal, forcing small talk. I hate that we need to anesthetize ourselves in order to carry on a conversation.

The next morning, my father tells me he can't make it to brunch as planned. Why not? I ask, already dressed in a coat and tie. Work, he says, Something came up at work. On Christmas? I ask, and he gives me the sort of look that lets me know I'm an ungrateful son-of-a-bitch. Go by yourself if it's that important to you, he says. Go to brunch by myself on Christmas, I say, and he takes a frustrated step in my direction. I lurch backward, stumbling over my feet, and we stare at each other until he presses his fingers to his forehead. We'll have dinner, he says, circumventing apology. Fine, I mutter.

After he leaves for the office I go to the cemetery. I have no idea why. I haven't visited my mother's grave since the day we buried her, but something steers the BMW in that direction, and once I pull to a stop, I roam among the tombstones for a while before I stumble on the exact location purely by chance.

Standing with my hands in my pockets, I read her name again and again. Do you have any idea...? I ask, then start as I realize I've spoken aloud. I clear my throat and take a quick look around for interlopers, but I'm the only one here, the only one alone on Christmas Day. My own father declined to spend the day with me despite that I've driven all the way down from Austin to see him, despite that what I gave up in order to make this trip would have fulfilled a need so prodigious it almost terrifies me.

Reaching out, I trace the first letter of my mother's name. The stone's cold, the ground hard under my feet; I have to squeeze my eyes shut at the thought of what rests beneath them. When I open my eyes again, I see what I should've noticed all along. Someone's been here before me. Maybe not today, but recently enough that the flowers tilted toward the sun look plenty fresh. Recently enough that the winter weeds cropping up around the base of some of the surrounding headstones have been plucked away from my mother's. I hunch my shoulders and pretend to contemplate, but I have a feeling I know who came this way.

That night, I want to make a connection. When my father gets back from the office, I pour him a drink myself, watching as he rubs his hand back and forth across his jaw. He looks tired and melancholy, and feeling soft-hearted, I offer up my afternoon excursion as a sort of gift. We can talk about her, I think, talk about how difficult the holidays are without her, talk about how much we still miss her. But my confession doesn't induce my father to open up. Hey, I know, I say, noting the flicker of guilt in his expression and comparing it with my own, I know how you feel. With an awkward hand I touch his shoulder; he doesn't move. Dad? I say, and the word seems to shake him. I have work, he says. What about dinner? I ask. He stares into his glass, then tells me I can order out, that he's not up for going anywhere. But Dad, I protest, and he meets my gaze with a conviction that astounds me. Joel, he says, I have work.

James calls my car phone as I'm backing out of the driveway, like he has some sort of pulse on my emotions. You okay down there? he asks. I'm leaving, I say. What do you mean? he says, You're going back to Austin? I'm already gone, I tell him.

Four hours later, I pull up to our house, frowning at the subdued bits of color from the strand of lights around the porch railing. I've had a long drive, longer than I should have; I'd stopped outside of Sealy to take down the BMW's top, wanting the cold wind in my hair, then drove so hard and fast into the night that I flew right past the exit for Highway 71. I was halfway to San Antonio before I realized my mistake, and freezing my ass off to boot. Now I climb from the convertible and squint at the swing. James raises his hand in a solitary greeting. What're you doing here? I ask, climbing the steps, and he shrugs. He must have packed as soon as I hung up with him. It's Christmas, man, I say, regretting the interruption to his family's celebration, but he just holds out a tin of homemade cookies, his expression illuminated by a hundred colored lights. That's supposed to be my line, he says.

The nightmares return that night. I'd half-expected them, but the prediction does nothing to lessen their severity. You should go back to bed, I mutter as James follows me onto the porch, but he shakes his head and lowers himself to the swing beside me. I light a cigarette and pull the acrid smoke into my lungs. James sets fire to a cigarette of his own, then leans back, bracing his heel against the porch and pushing away so the swing starts to sway. He's had the foresight to throw a sweatshirt over his head, but I won't last long out here wearing nothing but a short-sleeved tee and pajama bottoms. Even without the smoke I'm exhaling I can see my own breath.

Can I ask you something? James asks, as if he knows I'm rationing my time, and I feel the same shock of panic I felt when Elisa asked me why I hadn't told James my secret. I guess, I say, steadying myself with another drag. Do the nightmares have anything to do with your father? he asks.

The smoke I was set to exhale winds up in my lungs. James whacks me on the back, and when my breath finally returns, I twist my arm so he can see. My father, I say, Had an affinity for Cubans.

I don't know why I answered the phone that day my freshman year a week before Spring Break; James and I were well into an ample joint, and I scrambled for sobriety when I heard my father's voice on the other end of the line. Am I interrupting? he asked as James snickered beside me. I lingered too long over the question, half-tempted in the midst of my high to admit the truth before reason coaxed me back. No, no, I said, and I could tell that he'd misinterpreted my hesitation. He thought I was with some girl, and I glanced at James, hanging halfway off his bed, his eyes on the ceiling of our dorm room, the joint pinched between his lips. He was staring at the water stain in the corner by the closet, a blemish the color of dog shit that would've driven even Rorschach mad if he'd been forced to worry over it night after night. Now's fine, I said, and my father cleared his throat. Even under the influence I found myself on guard. I've managed, he said, To secure you an internship at Permian Energy.

I groaned out loud. I was already dreading the summer, that stretch of time between my freshman and sophomore years, knowing that my father wanted me back in Houston. I wanted to stay in Austin even though a part of me couldn't help feeling like I was abandoning my mother. It's time, she'd insisted the previous fall when I was packing for college, but since then, I'd been careful to check in with her on an almost daily basis. She never gave me anything but inane news: what they had for dinner, where the neighbors were going on vacation, until one night I came right out and asked if she was okay. Of course! she exclaimed, Why wouldn't I be?

You realize, my father said, That these are prestigious positions. I understand, I said, glancing at James, who rolled his bloodshot eyes. You realize, my father continued, The kind of groundwork I had to lay in order to get you this position.

He meant my grades, which weren't fantastic in high school and hadn't improved much since. A clean slate, he'd suggested when I left for college, but he wouldn't let me take the art classes I craved, saddling me instead with classes fit for a preliminary business major. My grades that first semester reflected my resentment.

These are competitive internships, Joel, my father said, and I cradled my forehead in the palm of my hand. I was starting to feel swimmy, and when James leaned over and offered me another toke, I shook my head. I'd rather get a job waiting tables, I confessed, and my father actually laughed. Really, Joel, he said, Waiting tables? I shut my eyes, listening to the same old bullshit about how much I had to learn, the responsibility I had to my future. Whatever opinions I had weren't worthy of discussion, and without thinking I reached for a pad of paper and a pencil. James watched as I scrawled across the page, and by the time my father finished one fucker of a lecture I'd drawn a pretty decent sketch of me with a noose around my neck. James sucked away the last of our joint as my father delivered the final, satisfying blow: I'd get a taste of what the summer would be like the very next week because I'd be working over Spring Break.

What are you going to do for us, Joel? McGarrity, the President and CEO, asked on my first day after he shook my hand, and I looked to my father for help. I'm thinking about letting him organize the research on those strategic limited partnership arrangements we've been discussing, he said. McGarrity lifted an eyebrow. My father laughed at his expression, then placed his hand on my shoulder. I expect great things from Joel, he confided, and though I couldn't help feeling gratified, I was also rendered speechless by his claim. He'd pretty much managed to convince me that he expected nothing of the sort.

How was your day? my mother asked that evening, and I looked at my father, half-expecting him to tell her that he wasn't sure I had the aptitude for this after all. But he gazed at me with such unaccustomed affection I squirmed. Not bad, he said. My mother glanced at me for confirmation, already looking pleased, and for just a second, knowing there was still time before dinner to hit the pool, I wondered if maybe my mother had been right the previous night when she told me in private that my father was simply looking for a way for us to spend more time together. Four days, I thought. I can handle four days.

For the next three I kept my head down and did whatever I was asked no matter how menial the task. My father didn't give me any real responsibility, but twice he used me as a sounding board regarding the strategic limited partnerships he'd mentioned my first day. He included me in his lunch plans with his colleagues, and though I spent most of the hour listening to, rather than joining in, the conversation, I couldn't help but bask in his good graces.

But after a week of menial labor I was done. Friday morning, kneading the back of my neck as I stared out at another flawless sky, I realized that I hadn't spent even one day in the pool. For all practical purposes Spring Break was over. I'd be leaving for Austin in the morning, and I'd have my work cut out for me trying to bring my grades back up to the level my father expected.

When I got to the office, I tried to have a good attitude. I really did try, but if I caught a glimpse of blue through the windows, if I thought about James sitting on his ass in the sun, I felt sick at what I was missing. The thought that I had an entire summer of the same shit made me want to scream.

Late that afternoon, I followed my father to a meeting with McGarrity and a few others, where I sat off to the side of a sleek mahogany conference table, idly sketching the men around me as they talked numbers. I honestly couldn't see how they worked like this every day. I'd put a bullet in my temple, and I threw together a hasty self-portrait, showing just that. Then I yawned without covering my mouth. The movement seemed vaguely familiar, and I'd just remembered James yawning in exactly the same way the day we met when I felt my father looking at me. I bolted upright, and as I did, my drawing slid from my lap. McGarrity reached for it.

Horrified, I watched as he scrutinized what I'd done, my father straining from across the table to see why I'd captured his boss's interest. McGarrity eyed me over his shoulder, looked me up and down. A good likeness, he finally grunted, and my father, understanding at the very least how I'd been spending my time, seemed like he might launch into an apoplectic fit right there. McGarrity handed back the portrait, clearing his throat. Where were we? he asked, and my father gave me a final, black stare before he turned his attention again to the meeting.

I expected a reprimand as soon as we were finished, but my father didn't say a word. He simply held out his hand, and I relinquished my drawing, which he slipped into his briefcase without bothering to peruse. I was too afraid to puncture his silence with an apology, and we drove back to the house without speaking, the tension between us so toxic I could barely breathe.

My mother could tell the second we walked in the door that something was wrong, and she trailed my father as he fixed himself a scotch. Get out of that suit, he barked at me. I moved, ducking upstairs, where I changed into shorts and a tee shirt and rinsed my face with shaking hands. I was tempted to stay up there, to hole myself up in my room in the hope that he'd forget about me, but I didn't want to leave my mother alone.

Downstairs, though, she was nowhere to be found. Only my father waited for me in the doorway of his study, and when he gestured me inside, I closed the door and lowered myself into the chair across from his desk. He had my drawing in front of him, a cigar poised between his fingers, his silence a sure sign of his fury. But I was nineteen, and the mere fact of my age gave me a sense of confidence I usually didn't feel. I was older, and even my father had his limits.

I'm sorry, I mumbled, figuring I should start off with an apology, but he didn't seem appeased. Spending your time sketching instead of paying attention, he said, Would've been seditious enough. He leaned forward, taking up my drawing between his thumb and forefinger like it was a piece of offal. This, he said, Is inexcusable.

He let the sketch fall back to the desk, and I glanced down at McGarrity's heavy jowls and beady eyes, at my own self-portrait, a gun to my head. Under the circumstances I hadn't done a bad job, and I took an extra second hunting for flaws before I realized what I was doing and looked back up at my father. He tapped the ash from his cigar, then picked up the phone. You owe that man an apology, he said.

I knew better than to argue, and I watched as he dialed McGarrity's number, then hit speaker so I could listen in on the conversation. My son, he said when McGarrity answered, Has something to say to you. He gestured me forward, and I leaned over the desk like the automaton I knew I was. I'm sorry about what happened in the meeting, I muttered.

McGarrity made a gruff noise I wasn't sure how to interpret, and I glanced at my father, who narrowed his eyes. My behavior was inexcusable, I added in a lower voice. All right, then, McGarrity said, and my father nodded his approval, then turned back to the phone. Johnson— he started, but McGarrity, obviously not realizing that he was on speaker, emitted a belly laugh that caught us both off-guard. Oh, don't be so hard on him, Ed, he said, Spring Break's an institution for these kids, and you've had him at the office all week.

My father's mouth dropped. Hell, McGarrity chuckled, Half the time even I don't want to be there. Yes, my father managed, Thank you.

I was already on my feet, babbling apologies, when he gripped my shoulder and shoved me back down. Don't you stand up! he said, Who the hell do you think you are?

Somewhere out there my mother was waiting for me. She couldn't know, and after a minute I stopped struggling against him.

The cigar, crushed against the inside of my arm, brought tears to my eyes. I blinked them away before they could run down my face, bit my tongue until I tasted blood. I didn't make a sound. I knew his fingers would leave bruises where they gripped my arm, but I didn't try to wrench away; I'd made that mistake in the past. Instead, I counted—

one, two, three—until he finally pushed me away from him. Get out, he said, Get the
fuck out of here.

That night, my mother and I had dinner alone. My father had fabricated an
emergency at the office, and when my mother asked if we'd had an argument, I took note
of the worried lines around her mouth and shook my head. She'd run to the store, she'd
told me, not realizing she needed a lemon for the sauce she was making. I'd scoured their
medicine cabinet, and I sat across from her with my eyes at half-mast thanks to what I'd
found. Honey? my mother said, Are you sure you're okay? Of course, I said, Why
wouldn't I be?

James stares at me, the cigarette between his fingers heavy with ash. I
indicate the ashtray, and he starts, then taps the butt against the edge of the
swing instead. The first time, I offer though he hasn't asked, I was eight.
When did it stop? he asks. I take a final drag on my own cigarette,
ruminating, then grind it in the ashtray. Not soon enough, I say.

The next morning, I wake at dawn with a shimmy in my spine that
reminds me of my trip to Cancun with James the summer after my mother
died. Something's there, something I can no longer ignore, and I take a
breath, the sort I need to ground myself. Then I make my way to the naked
wall that separates the living room from the kitchen table. Trailing my hand
along its texture, I feel the paint, rough and uneven. I don't have a brush in
my hand yet, but the painting's already in front of me, perfect and
complete.

By the time James stumbles into the kitchen a little before noon I'm
spent. Jesus, he says, gazing from one end of the wall to the other. It's an
arm, I tell him. Yeah, he says, I can see that.

The arm, unblemished, runs from the shoulder down through the hand.
Thick streaks of sapphire leak from the nails, the fingers long and thin. I
run my own through my sweaty hair. The wall was too white, I confess, and
he nods. Okay, he says.

+ + +

My motivation comes back with a rush, my focus so intense that I
come to in the morning from blissful nights of sleep with my fingers
shaking. The second they touch the brush they steady, and I paint until I
feel a release so sweet it's better than any orgasm I can remember. I could
work forever like this, ignoring everything but the canvas in front of me
and the paint staining my hands.

One night, I come down long enough to take a break, and I head to a
bar, where I light a cigarette and shiver on the sidewalk in a tee shirt
splattered with crimson-colored paint. I could've taken more time to make
myself presentable, but my negligent grooming habits never seem to matter;
if anything, they have a tendency to work in my favor, and I'm eyeing a guy
lingering outside with a couple of his friends, the sole of his shoe pressed
against the side of the building and his hair in his eyes, when someone sidles
up to me. Big honking breakfast burritos, he says, blinking seductively. My
eyes widen, and I look around for a means of escape, but he holds me back,

manicured fingers clutching my sleeve. I slip from his grasp, trying to be judicious. I don't think so, I say, but he manages to look offended. You've been out what now, honey, he says, A year?

I don't like how easily he's been able to read me, and I mumble something about having been around as he raises his eyebrows. I've never seen *you* here, I add. I don't see how that's possible, he tells me, I'm an icon in this city.

Now I'm nervous, and I take a short, quick drag on my cigarette. Maybe he's someone I should know and I'm completely fucking up by blowing him off. I look him up and down, trying to figure out what I'm missing: short, balding, a soft little paunch he should probably kill with a gym membership. Long eyelashes and the sort of limp gesticulations that do nothing for me. As he poses, I realize that only a lifetime of money can buy the kind of glittering confidence oozing from his pores.

The guy I was watching a few minutes earlier chooses that moment to stroll past, turning his eyes to mine at the last possible second. I stare right back until the one vying for my attention clears his throat. Inhaling one last time, I crush my cigarette beneath my boot. Look, I sigh, and he says, Do you have any idea who I am? Should I? I say, taking a step in the direction of my evening. Didn't your daddy teach you better manners? he shrieks.

I grind to a halt, though I'm not pissed by his presumption. Instead, I feel chastened. The second he sees my expression, he softens. Let's start over, he says in a kinder voice, extending his hand, I'm Kyle. Joel, I mumble. Joel, honey, he says, stepping closer, Where've you been hiding yourself? I flush, and he rubs my paint-stained shirt between his fingers. Have you buried the body yet? he asks. When I laugh, he smiles, pleased with himself, then links his arm through mine. Now, he says, How about that breakfast?

Over the burritos he promised I find out I was right about the money. Kyle has a house overlooking Lake Austin, a sweet boat docked out back. Daddy's little boy, he says, winking, and I grimace. What about you? he asks. What about me? I say. Is there a special someone? he asks. I don't want a special someone, I tell him. So instead you're breaking hearts, he muses. I don't hear anyone complaining, I say, and he cocks an eyebrow as if I've just announced that I give a serviceable blowjob. I wipe my mouth with my napkin. Are you seeing anyone? I ask, and he waggles his fingers. Sweetheart, he says, I've been through more sad little stories than I care to recall.

I take a closer look at him, at the silk shirt he's wearing, the careful way he's parted his hair to hide recession, his wide, full lips. He's not *that* bad. He's just out, more out than I've ever been and way more effeminate than makes me comfortable. More coffee, he coos at our waiter, and it's exactly that sort of unrestrained display that makes me cringe and—I have to admit—fascinates me at the same time. I can't imagine being so unselfconscious. I hold my breath, waiting to see how the waiter responds, but he just refills our mugs without a word.

So you're alone, I say to Kyle, getting back to our conversation, and he tilts his head. How can I be alone, honey, he says, When I'm sitting here with you?

+ + +

I invite James with what I hope passes for enthusiasm to come with me to Kyle's for a party. Despite his offer last year to accompany me to a gay bar, I've been careful to keep my sex life and my life with James neatly bifurcated. But now that I've met Kyle—now that I've hooked up with him a half a dozen times for dinner and let him drag me along to a Valentine's Day gala—I think it's time. Where've you been? James asked last night when I stumbled in the front door giddy with champagne and a sky full of stars viewed from Kyle's boat. Just out, I said. He sulked for a while before he finally broke down and asked if I was full of shit when I said Kyle and I were just friends. Once you meet him, I said, You'll see what I mean. Yeah? he mumbled, When's *that* going to happen?

I chew on my thumbnail as I look him over, paying close attention to the wave in his hair, the glasses that, should he choose to wear them on Saturday night, will inevitably inspire some kind of teacher-student fantasy in the post-frat boy crowd, the way his jeans cling to his hips. He's open enough to intrigue, straight enough to be a challenge. You checking me out? he asks, smirking, and I say, I'm trying to prevent you from getting mauled.

Three times on Saturday James comes in my room to ask what he should wear, and I finally think about telling him that once someone makes their way into the pool Kyle keeps heated year-round, he might not need to worry about clothing at all. Instead, I sigh and walk over to my closet. How much attention do you want? I ask. He looks startled. Don't give me that virgin shit, I say, stripping a plain white tee from a hanger, You knew what you were getting into when you said you'd come tonight. He offers up a muffled protest as I dig up a thin cashmere sweater I bought just before Christmas, thinking I'd need something tasteful if my father invited me to get a drink with him one night over the holiday. This still has the tags, he says, like that's going to stop him from borrowing it. I watch as he pulls it over his head. It's too clingy, he says, squirming, and I grab his hips. Be still, I tell him, adjusting the material. I step back and fold my arms across my chest. It's too small, he says mournfully, but I shake my head. Trust me, I say.

Thanks to that Valentine's Day gala, I already know a good number of Kyle's guests, but Kyle himself accosts me before I can approach any of them. And who's this? he asks, air-kissing me but keeping his eye on James. Kyle, I say, James Fielding. Kyle lets a shriek bleed through the fingers he holds to his lips. The roomie? he gasps, and James glances at me, then nods. Kyle steps back, clutching my arm as he looks James up and down. I thought you said he was straight, he says to me in a mock-whisper, and

James flushes. Joel dressed me tonight, he says, unwittingly digging himself deeper. Your very own Barbie doll, Kyle says to me, and as the color in James's cheeks deepens, I groan. This is exactly the sort of shit I wanted to avoid. Let's get a drink, I say, yanking James in the direction of the bar. *That* was Kyle? he asks along the way. I told you so, I say.

The party's mixed, but James stays close for precisely the reason I anticipated. Without me glued to his side he's fair game; to be honest, he's fair game either way. A half a dozen guys scope me out for an introduction, and I watch James fall into conversations that probably aren't as benign as he thinks. Within an hour I'm tweaking from anxiety. I just can't handle the responsibility, and even though there's a part of me that wants to protest when he heads back to the bar with some guy spouting existentialism— leave it to James to find the only academic at the party—I take the opportunity to duck onto the deck with this guy I've hooked up with a couple of times. He's about my age, works at the Texas School for the Blind. He's not much of a conversationalist; to be honest, he's not really my type. He has darkish hair that would look much better in a Caesar cut, and tonight I tell him so. You think? he asks, and I tilt his head to the side with the tip of my finger. Definitely, I say.

When I finally head back to the party, James pulls me aside. Who's the guy? he asks in a low voice, and I make a quick assessment of the living room. Which one? I ask. The one who's had his tongue down your throat for the past thirty minutes, he says. Oh, I say, embarrassed, That's Luke. Uh-huh, he says, You leaving with him? I don't know, I say, Maybe. We both glance in Luke's direction; he gives me a look that's impossible to misinterpret, then edges his way through the room and comes up behind me. So who're you? he asks James, sliding his arms around my waist. I'm a friend, James tells him. Yeah? Luke says, You joining us tonight, friend? Jesus, Luke, I say, but James just laughs.

The next morning, he confesses that he's jealous. Of *what?* I groan, hoping he's not going to make some generalization about gay men and promiscuity. Hey, I'm not saying you have it easy, he tells me, But just for the sake of argument, I'd like to know how many guys you've slept with in the past year. I don't know, I say, Five? He tells me I'm intentionally underestimating. But whatever, he says, Do I need to remind you how many girls I've been with this year?

I venture a generous guess despite what he's told me. One, he says, One girl and I'm telling you, it was a fucking battle. I try not to smile. Honestly, he says, leaning over the bar to snag an apple, I'm thinking of a little experimentation myself just so I can get laid. Well, you can always give Luke a call, I say. Not my type, he tells me, polishing his apple on his shirt and taking a bite. I roll my eyes; he shakes his head, then wipes the juice running down his chin. Not yours either, he says.

+ + +

I take advantage of the last of the cooler weather and run outside as much as I can, knowing that soon the combination of heat and pollution will make even a morning run intolerable. Sometimes I can persuade James to join me, but he's usually more inclined to park his ass on the sofa than to tie up his running shoes. You're going to look like shit this summer, I tell him, and he says he doesn't care. I allow him the delusion until I talk to Peter, who belongs to a gym and manages to sell me on the idea of joining. I try to convince James, but he isn't enthused. I can think of better ways to spend the thirty bucks every month, he says, And anyway, I have to save some money for Greece.

He's spending almost three months there this summer on a dig with a couple of his professors and a few graduate students, a remarkable feat given his short tenure in the program. Underneath all his bravado he's nervous about being the only first-year graduate student invited and self-conscious about the fact that some of the older students were slighted in favor of him. Fuck 'em, he says when I offer my analysis, but I know him well enough to understand that he's uncomfortable with his position. You need this trip, I tell him, You deserve this trip, and you know I'm right.

Saying these words isn't easy for me. I want him to go; I know he needs the experience. But last year's excursion to Europe after my graduation constitutes the longest amount of time we've been apart, and I'm daunted by the thought of stretching that record. That I'll be the one left behind doesn't help. I have no idea what I'm going to do with myself.

Determined not to get sucked into a summer of slack, I work on plans of my own. I'm finally ready to get something resembling a portfolio together, and I drop by one of the galleries on 6th where the owner takes pity on me and strikes up a conversation. I still feel too self-conscious to produce anything more than talk. I guess I'm a little nervous about my one-year deadline; I've blown off most of the past twelve months, first in Europe and then because I was caught up in my own inertia after my return. Now I feel like I'm at a crossroads, and I really want to see what I can do here given the chance. My father hasn't reminded me even once about our agreement, and I'm not sure what to think. All I know is that I want a little time to get on my feet. In the interim he has plenty to share.

Now I need to reorganize, clean shit up, restock. I start the morning James leaves, flip through drawings I've scribbled over the past six months, make a list of what I need. I could spend hours in an art supply store, alternately my sanctuary and my own private hell depending on how much I've been working. Right now I'm feeling good, though, and Pandora watches from the windowsill as I jot down what I want. After a while I take a break and rub the soft fur behind her ears, trying to concentrate on the work I have ahead of me and not how empty the house feels with James gone. She stretches her neck like a slinky, and I draw my fingers across her throat. You and me, girl, I whisper, We've got nothing but time.

I miss James, but I keep busy running, painting, getting together for drinks with Kyle. He throws party after party, and the weather's too pretty not to take him up on his invitations. I spend half my time on his boat, and he graciously sets me up with an array of friends. I point out which guys pique my interest, work my way through a half a dozen in the first few weeks alone. What do you think? he asks one afternoon as the sun beats down on us. I'm examining my tan line, and I'm not the only one. Sure, I say, meeting Simon's eyes across a crowded deck, Why not?

I dump Simon after a week. He's crushed. This is what Kyle tells me: You've crushed him, he says. Tough shit, I say, He knew this wasn't anything serious. Some day, Kyle says, You're going to get royally screwed, and I'm not going to feel the least bit sorry for you. Whatever, I tell him, I'm just having a good time.

By the beginning of August I've gotten a couple of postcards from James. He talks about his work in the first one, but in the second he sounds homesick. He'll be back the tenth, he writes. He's sick of eating cheap Greek cuisine, and he wants nothing more than a plate of enchiladas and a cold Shiner. I can read between the lines: he's homesick, and I suck more satisfaction from that than I would have imagined. I'll admit that it's been cool, having the place to myself for a while. But honestly, I'm just ready for him to come home.

+ + +

My god, it's good to see you, I confess, pulling him into my arms the second he opens the front door. You too, he says, laughing, You too. Breaking away, I examine him: his tan, his overgrown hair, the stubble thick along his jaw. What, I say, They don't cut hair in Greece? You don't like it? he says, running his hand through his waves. You look fantastic, I say, and he grins. You do too, he says, You do too.

I've bought a bottle of tequila, and I pour us each a shot. I want to know everything, I say, Tell me everything. He knocks back his drink, smacks his glass back down on the bar. Amazing, he proclaims. Yeah? I say. Trans-fucking-formative, he says.

Maybe it's his enthusiasm. Maybe it's the way he talks about his summer, the dig, the thrill of excavation. Maybe it's simply that the house feels alive again, in a way it hasn't for months and I don't think I even noticed until he appeared again in our doorway. But I'm already wary when he jumps to his feet and unbuttons his shorts. Check this out, he says.

I've never seen a tattoo so intricate. His hip blazes with the sun, dozens of rays spiraling outward from a hot center. Meanwhile, the surface boils, a complexity of vermillion and saffron and a color so pale it might as well be bone. This is the work of an artist, and without thinking I reach out to touch him. He doesn't miss a beat, blathering on about the pain and how he couldn't get the tattoo wet for two weeks; I'm on fire. My finger burns as tears come to my eyes. I don't realize that I've melted to my knees.

You miss me or something, Joel? James says, and the shift in his voice lifts my eyes. He's staring down at me, half-puzzled, half-amused. I scramble to my feet, prattling excuses he shrugs away. I knew you'd be into it, he confides, buttoning his shorts. I pull my gaze away from his fingers, and he winks. I just didn't expect you to drop to your knees, he adds.

That night, he gives me a souvenir from his trip, thick black rope strung with a single pendant. I touch the spiral shell of something long dead. You don't like it, he says flatly. Not true, I say. I unscrew the clasp and try to fasten his gift around my neck. Here, he says, stepping behind me. His fingers spit fire. When I glance in the bathroom mirror, he smiles. I stare at our reflections, his arm hugging my chest. Then he unwinds himself and gives my back a fraternal smack. Don't say I never gave you anything, he tells me.

The next morning, he heads to Fort Worth to see his family for the first time since May. Normally, I'd feel cheated seeing him for such a short time after a long summer of drought, but instead, I'm relieved to see him go. I need the time to obsess about the hours we spent talking last night, the way he threw his arm around my shoulder and told me he was so glad to be home. I close my eyes; the memory of his sun radiates heat throughout my body, stockpiles in my groin.

I'm confusing missing James with something else. I'm misinterpreting a work of art, infusing emotion where none should exist. James is nothing more than he's ever been, and I call Simon and coerce him into coming over. I miss you, I say, which is only partially a lie because I do miss the sex. Well, he says, Maybe just for a little while.

Late afternoon sun paints the walls of my bedroom gold. I stretch out across my bed, my hands in Simon's hair, my eyes closed to the light.

I can't get James out of my mind.

Jennifer Hritz

PART TWO

Jennifer Hritz

1

September 1995

I start running early in the morning. I'm usually outside as the sun's rising, and I breathe in the gray dawn to the rhythm of whatever I've got in my Walkman, my feet solid on the asphalt. Sometimes I miss James's company, but I don't invite him on my morning excursions. A few weeks into the semester he's already up every night working, sleeps as late as he can in the morning before he has to head to campus.

I date a little, I fuck around. It's not so hard, really. The trick is to concentrate on the moment, on whoever I'm with, which more often than not these days is Simon. He's likable, eager to please, and while I realize deep down that I'm stringing him along, I can't seem to help myself. I need the diversion.

You're toying with him, Kyle says, You shouldn't be cavalier about sleeping with someone who's so taken with you. Simon knows this is nothing serious, I say. He also thinks he can change your mind, Kyle tells me. Not my problem, I say, and he raises his eyebrows. I skirt his gaze. Hmm, he says, leaning in close, What aren't you telling me? Nothing, I mumble, and he shakes his head. Honey, he says, I don't believe that for one second.

Simon becomes my unwitting subject. I sketch him, quickly, in the lamplight of my bedroom long after he falls asleep. He never stirs. My own bouts with nightmares come and go, and I usually find myself awake in the middle of the night, curled at the foot of the bed, gingerly moving aside covers so I won't wake him. The soft scrawl of my pencil melds with the murmur of his breathing.

I don't tell Simon what I'm doing and keep my drawings hidden. There's something so melancholic about each pencil line that looking at the entire collection in tandem makes me want to weep. One in particular always stops my breath. I'd caught him after an especially vigorous hour in bed, and his skin's damp, his hair mussed. He looks used, or maybe used up, and for days afterward I can't bring myself to look at it.

Then one morning, I watch from the bed as he gathers his clothes, pulling his jeans to his waist. His abs disappear into the V of his zipper; I know how hard they are, what they feel like against my own, and when he reaches for his shirt, I'm suddenly reluctant to see him go. Wait, I say. Moving toward the edge of the bed, I slide two deft fingers between the button of his jeans and his navel. I'm not through with you yet, I tell him, and he catches my hand and holds it fast. Joel, he says, sounding hungover and heartsick. I sit back on my heels. Why don't you stay, I say.

+ + +

We have a few short, contented weeks, during which I spend virtually no time with James. I'm avoiding him, and I suffer spasms of guilt when he asks why I'm always so busy. I miss him, from a purely platonic standpoint, and when he finally suggests going with some friends to see the Longhorns play, I agree. I guess you can bring Simon, he mutters.

I get the impression James doesn't like Simon, or at the very least doesn't like the time I'm spending with him. I don't deliberate over why that might be the case and invite Simon anyway. I'd love to come! he says. It's just a football game, I say, already annoyed by his enthusiasm. I don't care, he coos, I just want to be with you.

Game day dawns wet and humid, and Simon eyes the clouds warily from the front door. I watch him, ill-humored. I'm ready to cut him loose. The novelty's worn off, and I'm starting to realize that convenient, easily accessible sex isn't worth feeling imprisoned. It's barely drizzling, I tell him before he can say a word. Looks like it's going to pour, he says. So don't come with us, I say, hoping he'll comply. He gives me a hurt look, glancing at James to see whether or not he's paying attention. Don't look at him, I say, He won't run in this shit, but he'll sit through a fucking football game.

Simon goes. We all go: me, Simon, James, a couple of James's friends from school. In the stands we tuck ourselves under a plastic tarp, watching the soggy mess on the field, and when the rain turns a little colder, I just hunch my shoulders into my shirt. Simon looks miserable, and I suddenly feel sorry for dragging him out here when I know he doesn't even like the game. I'm just about to apologize when he sees me watching him. This is so hetero, he confides, and by the way James shifts beside me I know he's heard.

Sympathy disappearing, I stand. Where're you going? Simon protests. To take a shit, I say, and he flushes, moving his knees to the side to let me pass. A few seconds later, I hear James clattering behind me. Why are you following me? I ask over my shoulder. Why do you think? he says, a barely perceptible smirk beneath his expression, I have to take a shit too.

We stand in the rain without speaking. Water runs down James's cheeks and into the collar of his shirt. Would it be wrong for me to just leave him up there? I finally ask. You know what your problem is? he says without answering me. Enlighten me, I say. He just shakes his head, flinging water droplets. I should go back up there, I mumble, and he says, Dump him,

Joel. He nods as if the matter's decided. You're gonna do it anyway, he says, Why waste a good game?

I wait though, until the game's over, until I can get a moment alone with Simon at home. This is all because of a stupid football game? he asks in disbelief. No, I say, I'm just not interested anymore. His face crumples; I'd have preferred a swift kick to the groin. By the time I manage to peel myself from his embrace I feel as if I need a shower.

Have you been eavesdropping? I ask James once I've kicked Simon out. Yeah, he says without taking his eyes from his book, I've got nothing better to do. Dropping onto the sofa, I cross my legs on top of the coffee table and jiggle my feet. What's my problem? I ask, and he frowns. At the game, I remind him impatiently, You were going to tell me what my problem is. Ah, he says, remembering. He leans back in his chair, then takes off his glasses and holds one stem to his mouth. Sitting in that armchair in front of our fireplace, he might as well be somebody's grandfather. I brace myself for his advice. You want something more than a fuck, he tells me. What? I say. You want something more than a fuck, he repeats, Because *just a fuck* is all you've ever really had. I don't understand, I say. C'mon, Joel, he says, Don't you get a little bored? Bored? I ask, and he shakes his head. Look at your body language right now, he says.

He has a point. I'm all choked up, legs crossed, arms folded on my chest. I'm the picture in the dictionary alongside the word "defensive." Look, I'm not saying there's anything wrong with what you're doing, he continues, I'm just saying that you seem a little bored. Bored, I repeat, and he says, Enter Simon. Simon wasn't boring, I protest. That's debatable, he says, But what's really important is that Simon bored *you*. You don't know what you're talking about, I mumble, and he shakes his head. You fuck these guys with little discrimination, Joel, he says, Maybe you should try to find someone who actually *does* something for you.

I think I already have. I'm afraid I already have, and I stare at him until he tilts his head. What? he says, Did I actually get through to you? You're a fucking sage, I say, standing. In my case, he adds, as if he's not ready to end our conversation, I've done the relationship thing, and now all I'm really interested in is someone to fuck. He holds up his right hand as a case in point. I'm getting a callous, he confides, and I roll my eyes. Examining his hand, he sucks on the skin between his thumb and forefinger. Ink, he explains, and I say, Right.

+ + +

The weekend before Halloween, we're crawling along 6th Street, hitting bars, talking about catching some band James wants to hear. Half the people we pass wear costumes, and we duck among witches, black cats, skeletons, passing a cigarette back and forth. My footsteps keep time with his.

We've had a good few weeks. I've caught some shit from Kyle, both because of the way I've screwed Simon over and because I've made excuses just about every time he's tried to convince me to meet him out somewhere. If you think I'm such a menace, I finally asked him, Why are you so interested in setting me up? He told me I had a point, and I basked in the sudden absence of obligation. I'd rather hang with James anyway, and I tell myself that I'm just making up for the time we lost while I was otherwise engaged.

At the next bar we snag a couple of beers before we manage to score a table near the band. James turns his mouth to my ear; I only catch half of what he says, but I nod anyway and offer him my lighter when he bums a cigarette. You made it, he says when Peter approaches. Exhaling from the corner of his mouth, he leans across me. Music thrums in the pit of my stomach.

Later, when the band takes a break, Peter tells us about some girl named Amy he's just started seeing. I order another beer, watching the orange glow of James's cigarette in the half-light. He's leaning back in his chair, one arm draped over the back, and though he's only wearing a tee shirt and jeans, I have a quick image of his Dracula cape and fangs from Halloween, freshman year. He taps his cigarette lazily against the ashtray, glancing with mild interest at the girls next to us, who started to grind at the first strains of The Knack. Nice, he murmurs, jutting his chin in their direction, and taking note of their black dresses, black heels, straight blond hair, I say, I can't even tell them apart. He laughs, flicking his cigarette, but when one girl raises her arms above her head, revealing a smooth, white belly with a scrawl of tattoo and a navel ring, James leans forward. Huh, he muses.

Any doubt about what I've been feeling since he came home from Greece dissolves. He might as well have punched me in the gut for all the breath I can draw into my lungs. I watch as he leaves the table and makes his way toward her, touching the filmy material of her dress, the bare skin of her shoulder. She smiles and says something I can only imagine. When he slides his hand down her arm, I shudder. Joel? Peter says, and I jerk my eyes in his direction.

I'm saved from trying to explain myself when James appears in front of us, introducing Kristen, making space for her at our table. I hate the gleam of triumph in his smile. What's with you? he asks as the band starts up again and I hit ten minutes with barely a word. I shrug, avoiding Peter's eye, dragging methodically on my cigarette until it disintegrates in my hand.

Listen, don't tell her you're gay, James says when Kristen ducks into the bathroom. What? I say, and even Peter looks dismayed. I'm trying to get laid here, James reminds us, adding that I should be happy for him, that I've given him shit for the past year because he hasn't hooked up with anyone. You're going to totally kill the mood, he tells me. What do you want me to do? I ask, and he shrugs. I don't know, Joel, he says, Just… act straight. How about if I hit on her? I say, That way there won't be any confusion.

I shut down, answer every question I'm asked with short, I-could-give-a-shit answers, and when we finally leave the bar, James holds me back. You could try a little harder, you know, he says, Maybe give her a fucking chance. You don't need *me* to like her in order for *you* to fuck her, I tell him. Maybe if you got to know her— he starts. I know, I know, I interrupt, I'd want to fuck her myself. Why are you being such an asshole? he says. *I'm* the asshole? I say, When she's the one who infiltrated our evening? Infiltrated? he repeats in disbelief, Infiltrated? He shakes his head. She's not the enemy, Joel, he tells me, And I'm not your fucking boyfriend.

I leave for the airport four hours later, bound for a six a.m. flight for Cancun. James went home with Kristen, and when I got back to our house alone, I stood in the middle of my bedroom trying to figure out exactly where I'd gone wrong. I half-expected James to come walking through the door, and when he didn't, I decided that getting out of the country was my answer.

So I head to Mexico, where I sit on my ass for hour after hour without doing a damn thing. Every morning, I stare into the water, rediscover that there's nothing better than being barefoot twenty-four hours a day. I nurse myself with margaritas, sleep away the afternoons under a turquoise umbrella near the water's edge. The sun burns itself into my skin, and I soothe myself with lotion. I eat on the patio outside my room, indulging in crab legs and lobster, cold bottles of beer. While the rest of the resort sleeps, I walk the beach, keeping company with the ocean as starlight pricks the sky above me.

In my less sane moments I think about calling him, decide against it only because I'm not sure what hearing his voice will do to me. I'm okay here, and I convince myself that by the end of the week I'll be okay there, too.

The day before I leave, I talk to the girl who sets up diving tours. Carla has long, dark hair, a smile remarkably like my mother's, and she's led the three excursions I've taken this week, each one more tame than the last. I want something solo, I tell her, Something different. Three hundred U.S., she says without blinking. I don't care about the cost, I say, Just don't treat me like a novice. For a long moment she looks at me, as if she's sizing me up. Then she nods. Tonight, she says, her English careful and precise, We will go tonight.

I meet her at midnight in the parking lot of the hotel. Already there's a subversive feel to the evening, and as we pull onto the highway, the wind whips her hair around her face. We drive for at least twenty minutes with little conversation. She's taken my privacy request seriously, and I feel indebted. A good dive tonight and I can handle anything, even my return trip home. A few days ago, I'd think of James's hand on Kristen's arm, and my stomach would cave in on itself. But I've worked with that image until I can hold it for moments at a time with relative calm. A little underwater breathing and I'll be able to look him in the eye.

Carla finally pulls off the highway onto a dirt road heading inland, and after another half-mile, she stops the truck and beckons for me to follow her. The vegetation's dense, the mosquitoes monstrous, and I blink away the sweat dripping into my eyes. My sandals squelch through the muck, and after ten minutes I start to question my judgment. I'm in the middle of the fucking jungle, in the middle of the fucking night, with some girl I don't know. How likely is it that I've made this decision rashly? My foot finds a root tangled in the earth, and I trip, barely catching myself before I hit the ground. My guide doesn't even turn to check on me. I stumble after her; my gear's getting awfully heavy. How much longer? I finally ask, but she doesn't answer, and I take a look behind me, wondering if I could find my way back to the road by the light of the meager moon. Maybe I should make a break for it while I'm still alive.

There! she suddenly exclaims, and I peer past her into the gleam of her flashlight. A black pool waits in front of us beneath an outcropping of rocks, the epitome of anti-climax. You've got to be kidding, I say, but she ignores me, slipping her tank over her shoulders and crouching at the edge of the water. I whack at the mosquitoes clamoring for my blood. They will not bother you in here, she reminds me, slipping backward, and I sigh, then climb into my gear.

But I've failed to test the water, and my heart stutters as I enter the pool. If I had told you how cold it was, Carla laughs, hearing me gasp, You would not have come! Why didn't you tell me I needed a wetsuit? I ask, but she's already gesturing for me to turn on my light. When I do, nothing happens. Shit, I say, flipping the switch back and forth to demonstrate. She shrugs, unconcerned. Stay close, she tells me, as if it wasn't her responsibility to make sure I had a backup, and then she ducks under the water before I can protest.

We're down maybe fifteen minutes, only ten feet or so from the surface. Only once does she glance back to make sure I'm okay. I'm giving her a half-hearted thumbs up, wondering how long I have before hypothermia sets in, when I realize we're heading into a cave. The rock's narrowing, what was once the ceiling dipping into the water just above my head, and I automatically pull back. In all my years of diving I've never been in a cave. A night dive presents enough of a challenge; I like the way the sun shines through the water, the patterns it creates on the sand, the idea that I can see exactly what I'm doing if something happens, if I lose my regulator, if I start to panic.

I don't think I can do a cave.

I watch Carla's light fade, then grit my way to the surface, where I spit out my regulator. Even when I wave my hand in front of my face, I can't see a thing. If I wanted to backtrack, I'm not sure I could find my way, not without a light.

It's really fucking cold. And so quiet. I could die here and not make a sound.

When Carla finally clears the water beside me, I'm so angry I'm shaking. A cave? I say, Without a goddamn light? One light is enough, she says. I like the option of coming up if I need to, I tell her. This is fine, she insists, You will be fine. I'm cold, I complain, and she gives me a look. I am not a novice, she says in a mocking tone. I stare at her in disbelief, then watch as she repositions her mask. She's going back down, and I have no choice but to follow her.

Ahead of me she ducks beneath the rock, and I realize as I slip beneath the surface and enter the cave that if my tank goes now, I'm screwed. I overcompensate, take in too much oxygen. Please, I think, feeling slightly faint, please let this be over soon. Please let me get out of this alive. Up ahead Carla turns a corner, her light dimming, and I flounder in the dark, my tank scraping rock. Every muscle I own seizes up at the sound. Sheer will propels me forward, and I round the corner.

Colors blend soft-hued beneath Carla's light, like the best kind of palette. We hover just inside the mouth of the cave, luxuriating in the temperature shift, watching as fish stream by. Everything's alive, teeming. I don't know where to look, there's so much to see. Plants wave gently back and forth in the sand; tiny sea creatures dart between my legs. I hover above the ocean floor, and the fish that pause at my outstretched hands nibble my fingers. A school of fish trails through the water just ahead of me, cherry-colored, and after a while I stop trying to chase them. Green-backed, a turtle brushes by me, and I look into his eye, transfixed. He's beautiful, and I want to cry.

We stay ten minutes before Carla touches my arm and taps her wrist. The mouth of the cave recedes into darkness, but I know what's there, and I swim, calm, behind her light. I can't hear a sound except my own breath.

+ + +

The time I've spent away from James disappears completely the second I walk through our door. I stand in front of him, trying to retrieve the feel of my last dive, finding it hard to believe that only fifteen hours ago I was breathing underwater. Well, well, well, he's saying. I can barely look at him, but from the corner of my eye I can see him shaking his head. How was your *vacation*? he asks, though it's pretty clear from his antagonistic tone that he has no interest in hearing the details. Fine, I mumble. You should've *called*, Joel, he says. I left you a note, I tell him, and he reaches for the slip of paper he's obviously been harboring in animosity. *Went to Mexico*, he reads as if he doesn't know the damn thing by heart, *Don't know when I'll be back*. Smacking the note on the bar, he throws up his hands. What the fuck, Joel? he says, What was I supposed to do with that? I wasn't sure how long I'd be gone, I protest. Then you should've *called*, he says.

Pandora inches toward me and pounces on one brown, sandaled foot. I scoop her up, concentrating on her whiskered face as James glowers at me. Even in his ire I want him, and the thought turns me inside out, makes me feel vulnerable and exposed and consequently, pissed. What was I supposed to do? Staying here would have only made everything worse. Who knows what I might have said, what I might have done that morning after he slept with her? I'm already dreading what he's going to tell me next. What if in my absence he's fallen for her? Look— I start, but he's shaking his head. You left the country because I hooked up with someone, Joel, he says, Could you be any more passive-aggressive? Next time I'll just beat the shit out of you, I mutter, and he says, You're missing my point. No, you're missing mine, I say, hearing the words at the same time I try to usher them back into my mouth, I left because…

I catch myself before I fly right over that goddamn cliff.

Because…? he says, and even though I don't say a word, my expression must be the picture of angst. Well, if I haven't told him outright, he's sure to guess now. But he suddenly hunches his shoulders, averting his eyes. You're right, he says, And I'm sorry.

What?

I never should've asked that of you, he adds, and I realize that he thinks I left for Mexico not because I've made the mistake of falling for him but because he asked me to act straight. I throw a prayer to the gods that he was such a prick that night, then fold my arms across my chest like maybe I haven't decided whether or not to forgive him. If your sexual landscape didn't resemble a wasteland, I say, You wouldn't have to be such an asshole. He grimaces, leaning against the bar; I have a sudden, fleeting image of him the day we met.

Later, he sits with his hand curled around his beer as I tell him about my dive. His hair winds just below his ears, the exact same color as the hardwood floors beneath us. I've been unaware of the thickness of his lips for five years. Joel? he says when I trail off. Yeah, I say, I'm just glad to be home.

+ + +

I move through the next few weeks in a stupor, vacillate between saturating James with attention and flat-out avoiding him, afraid he'll guess what I'm thinking. He's been my best friend for five years, and I've never envisioned him as anything else. He's not my type; he never has been. It's not that he's not good looking. I'd be the first to admit that he has great hair, an infectious smile. I can see that right now sitting across from him.

But for whatever reason, everything I would've overlooked in the past appeals to me in a way I never would've imagined: that he's lost a little weight, leaving his jeans loose around his hips; the furrow of his brow when he's grading papers; the way his hair, newly cropped, hugs the back of his neck as if it doesn't want to let go. I reassess his physical attributes and come to the conclusion that he's still not my type. I'm simply seeing him now in a way I never have before. He's just James, suddenly beautiful to me for no apparent reason, and I almost groan. I'm every straight guy's nightmare.

The self-castigation doesn't make a difference. I'm unable to quell what I'm feeling. We sit across from each other, a random bar on a random Friday night, and I don't know how to make my voice any less transparent. He smiles at me over his beer, oblivious, regaling one anecdote after another from his semester, and I notice with a start the small lines around his eyes, the soft curve of a crescent on one side of his mouth. I want to trace it with my finger, and I have to grasp my beer mug to keep my hand still.

Hanging on to the time I spent underwater, I dive into the paint, try to coax forth those same colors, the sensation of that temperature shift. I carve a moon into the night, full, weighted like the prelude to a kiss. I give up on the details and count on the stroke of my brush. I end up with a canvas so rich and wet it's all I can do to keep my hands to myself. Hibiscus, teal, key lime: I carry these colors every morning when I run, carry them into my dreams.

Every day he moves me more.

Thanksgiving approaches, and for the first time since my sophomore year I debate going to Houston for the holiday. The thought of sleeping in the same room with James, of lying so close to him and listening to him breathe, seems like the worst kind of torture. On the other hand, I have no desire to see my father, especially since my one-year deadline has lingered longer than I think either of us anticipated. I feel like I'm living each day like there's a gun to my temple.

And I hate this game we're playing. I hate that my father has the power to make me feel infantile, that every inkling of confidence or self-possession I have I question after five minutes in his presence. I wish there was a way I could get what I want—what I deserve—without having to put myself in an undesirable position. Instead, I'm twenty-three years old and tied to my father in ways I can't even fathom.

I end up tagging along with James to Fort Worth, where I'm welcomed like a second son. I can't help but imagine how his parents would respond if they knew how I really felt, if they knew that what I really want involves a locked bedroom door and James's mouth covering mine. At the same time, I can't get over how they continue to accept me, how readily they include me in their holiday year after year. So I smile in the appropriate places, banter back and forth with Ashley, chat with James's father about the class he's teaching this semester regarding popular culture and social mores. When Mrs. Fielding pulls me aside to ask if I have any ideas for Christmas gifts for James, I have a list ready: boots, a Discman, a wallet to replace the one that's fraying at the seams.

But as I'm whispering with her in the corner of the kitchen, I'm watching him from lowered eyes. I'm sucking in an inaudible breath when he stands and stretches. I'm asking the thoughtless gods what the hell they were doing, burdening me with feelings that will never be reciprocated, that leave me racked with confusion and shame.

What're you two plotting? James asks, opening the refrigerator and letting out a tremendous belch. James! his mother says. Incorrigible, he agrees, giving her a wink, and she laughs in spite of herself. You better watch out, I tell him, Or you're going to be looking at an empty stocking. He snorts. This woman, he says, indicating his mother, Can't resist me. She's the only woman who can't, I mutter. Coal in your stocking, buddy, he says, opening a beer and nudging my shoulder, but his mother shakes her head. Joel's a good boy, she tells him, and James rolls his eyes. You have no idea, he says, How *naughty* we're talking here. C'mon, man, I say, shrugging him off, and his mother adds, I think you're embarrassing him, sweetheart. Am I embarrassing you? James asks me, feigning innocence, Should I not tell her what's on your Christmas list? I narrow my eyes as he takes a generous swallow of beer. What's on my Christmas list? I ask. A man, he says solemnly.

His mother and I groan at the same time, and he squeezes my shoulder. My mission for 1996, he promises. Give him a break, honey, his mother begs, but he grins. Mark my words, he says, Next year at this time, you're going to be thanking me.

+ + +

My father insists that we get together with some of his friends for Christmas, a suggestion I foolishly second when I think about the debacle of our last holiday. As soon as we arrive at the home of one of his colleagues, my father points me in the direction of his daughter, who tells me she just graduated from Rice University with an Engineering degree. Within five minutes I'm positive that I'd never encourage a friendship with this girl, let alone anything as intimate as I think my father's hoping given the looks he's sending me over his glass of champagne. You went to Rice, right? I finally ask her after listening to an earful of propaganda about Permian, where she plans on starting work in January. Well, she admits, Rice was a little laidback for my taste. She asks what I do for a living, and hesitant to tell her in my father's company, I say, What do you think I do? Well, she says, eyeing me, Something with computers? My smile disappears as my father tries to quell one of his own, and I make the decision at that moment to let my hair grow. I want it long.

Are you trying to set me up? I hiss as we're ushered into the dining room, and my father gazes at me with such deprecation that for just a second I think he knows. Feeling queasy, I make my way to my seat and mobilize my defenses. I launch myself into a full-scale discussion with our host's daughter, laugh at her inane jokes, agree whole-heartedly with her politics, pretend to be someone I'm not. It's not really all that difficult, to be honest. I've had years of practice.

By the time our host suggests coffee and dessert my father has cast a couple of approving glances my way, and I'm thoroughly disgusted with myself. I pick my way through the chocolate on my plate, drink enough coffee to counter the alcohol. I end up jittery and anxious, jiggling my leg and pining for an escape.

That wasn't so bad, my father says on the way home. I run my fingers through my hair, still shaky from all that caffeine. No, I lie, I had a really great time. My father cuts me a look that suggests I'm overdoing it, and I start to worry all over again. We lapse into silence, and as we turn down my father's street, every house laced with lights, I'm struck by the strangest sense of déjà vu. Saliva floods my mouth, and I almost don't hear my father suggest that he's ready to hear what my plans are for the new year. I've been more than patient, Joel, he says, pulling into the garage and cutting the engine, But I've spent the past eighteen months waiting for you to come to your senses.

I shut my eyes. I can't believe I have to deal with all of this in one day. Smoothing the material of my coat, which I've folded over my lap, I listen as the engine clicks, cooling down. I don't want to work in the business world, I finally tell him. You don't want *any* job, he says, You just want everything handed to you. That's bullshit! I tell him, and he says, *What?* You heard me, I mumble, and he nods, pissed. Fine, he says, yanking open the door, You can take that to the bank next month.

I jump from the car. Hey! I say, and he turns back. I deserve more time, I tell him. Oh? he says, Why is that? You know why, I say.

He stares at me, and I watch the play of emotion on his face: anger, impatience. Regret. I brace myself, frightened by which is going to win, and then he nods briskly. Six months, he says as if we're bartering, and I shake my head. A year, I say. He glances away from me, then allows that maybe another year's in order. But no more, he tells me, I'm tired of having to explain away your lack of motivation.

A few days later, back in Austin, I'm rifling through one of the drawers in the kitchen, looking for a pack of cigarettes and telling James about the obstacle course I had to maneuver over the holiday. What the hell do you expect, man? he asks once we're outside on the back porch, where I smoke furiously. He picks a leaf off the steps, crumbling it in his hand as I exhale, the smoke in my lungs mingling with my cold breath. Would *your* father try to set you up? I ask. My father's not trying to figure out whether I'm gay, he points out. I scowl, tapping my foot, and ask if he thinks, then, that my father knows. Who gives a shit? he says. I do! I tell him. You're almost twenty-four years old, Joel, he says, Aren't you tired of keeping this from him? You know I can't tell him! I say, He'll cut me off if he knows! So *that's* what this is about, James says. He stands up, brushing pieces of leaf from his jeans. You know what? he says, There are worse things than working for a living. I stare at him, incensed, then crush out my cigarette on the top step. That's interesting coming from a professional student, I tell him, and he walks past me and slams the door.

I'm in the back room later that evening, though I'm not working. Instead, I'm standing in front of the easel, staring at the canvas I started earlier this afternoon. My palette waits beside me, a container of brushes on the table. My hands smell like linseed oil no matter how many times I wash them. This is where I belong, and I take a deep breath, then glance over when James appears in the doorway. Don't bring your shit in here, I warn. I wouldn't, he says, falling into the chair against the windows. He's wearing jeans and one of my shirts, and he runs his hands through an unruly mop of hair. What're you working on? he asks. I shrug. You ever take anything by that gallery on 6th? he asks. Next week, I say, though I know I won't. I'm not sure why that's the case, why every time I get close, I feel myself retreating. Fear of rejection, probably, stemming from abandonment issues caused by a suicidal mother and a father whose love I still question. But now, in light of our argument on the back porch, I feel foolish using that as an excuse. At some point don't I have to take responsibility for whether or not I succeed?

I wander over to the window. Night blankets everything, and more than the bare branches of the pecans, I see James's reflection. He's watching me, probably working hard to keep his mouth shut as promised. I feel like I should give him something, but I certainly can't face him, certainly can't tell him what I've been thinking the past five months. I press my forehead against the glass. What if he walked up behind me, right now? What if he stood close enough for me to feel his breath on my neck? What if I turned to face him?

I need to get out of this room before I taint everything that matters, and without a word I turn and walk past him. He finds me in the kitchen, where I'm standing at the sink, scrubbing paint from under my nails. I don't want to be polite and vague with each other, he informs me. Okay, I say. I don't want to censor what I say to you, he tells me. No one said you should, I say, and he shakes his head. I get the impression you'd rather I keep my thoughts to myself, he says. I rinse my hands and shut off the water. You don't make things easy, I admit. Why should I? he says, Why shouldn't I tell you what I think? Because you don't know what you're talking about, James, I tell him, Because you weren't there when I was eight years old and getting the shit burned out of me.

I can feel myself shaking, that familiar tremor in my hands, at the back of my mouth. I'm saying too much, and I swallow whatever words might follow. They leave a sour taste, rankle the pit of my stomach. I realize that what I want, what I need, is to be able to take two steps forward and bury myself in his arms. Instead, I take a long breath that gets me nowhere. His money shackles you, Joel, he says, Every bit as much as those cigars.

I slam my fist on the counter because if I don't, I'll hit him. I'll smash his beautiful jaw into a million glittering pieces and grind them beneath my boot. The money gives me time to work! I say, The money pays for this fucking house! I take those two steps forward until my breath meets his. To his credit, he doesn't move, and I stare into eyes that seconds ago I looked to for release. Shut the fuck up, I whisper, Do you understand? He looks away from me, then nods. Shut up, I say, Or I will never speak to you again.

+ + +

For three weeks we barely acknowledge each other. Instead, we're polite and vague, exactly what James said he wanted to avoid. The nightmares that rip me from sleep on an almost nightly basis I suffer through myself. He has no idea what he started, and I slip onto the front porch in the middle of the night and watch the moon, my pathology my only companion. I've never felt so alone.

My father calls. He's in Austin on business and wants to get together for drinks. I feel like weeping at the thought. But I have no room to decline his invitation, and when I meet him downtown, I order a scotch and manage to suck at least half before he comments on my hair. I smooth the ends self-consciously; I'm way overdue for a cut. You're looking well, I say, trying to change the subject. He's in a coat and tie, his hair both conservative and rakish enough to make him appear younger than his age, which must be fifty or maybe fifty-one. He brushes off the compliment and asks what I've been up to. That's how he phrases it: *What have you been up to,* and the question sounds accusatory rather than casual. I shrug. He doesn't say a word when the bartender replaces my empty glass with a fresh scotch. What about you? I ask. I'm getting married, he says.

I wait for the punchline.

We'll have a private ceremony at the beginning of December, he continues, A reception on Christmas Day. You're getting *married?* I say, and he purses his lips. I realize this comes as a surprise, he says.

I don't believe this. I was just there last month, and he didn't say a word. Who is she? I ask. Her name is Catherine, he tells me. I pleat my cocktail napkin, obsessive folds that do nothing to stall the trembling in my fingers. How old is she? I ask, and my father's face tightens just slightly at the question. Thirty-four, he admits. I feel like throwing up. Trust me, he says as if that's a valid option, You're going to like her.

I stop on the way home and buy a bottle of twenty-five-year-old Macallun scotch. Sitting in the driver's seat of my BMW, I wrench the cork from the bottle and take a long swallow, then ease through the three blocks toward home. No one's there except for Pandora, and I snag her under the belly and plant myself in the chair next to the fireplace with the scotch and my cigarettes.

My mother doesn't know I smoke. She never saw this house. She has no idea I have a convertible, that I've decided to grow my hair long. The back room she never saw. If I showed her my most recent work, would she even recognize it as my own? I've graduated from college, spent time in Europe, fallen for my best friend. Four years she's been gone, and so much has happened that if I could sit down beside her now, I wouldn't know where to begin.

I've managed to get along without her. I never would've thought that possible, and I feel a pang of guilt for moving on. At the same time, I have an ache so deep inside when I think of her I feel like a football player who's taken a helmet to the gut. Her absence still takes my breath away, and that my father's capable of filling the void with a woman closer to my age than his own seems to me such a blatant disavowal of the commitment he made to my mother and our family that I want to cry.

By the time James gets back from campus I'm fairly fucked up, and I watch him shrug out of his coat as he takes in the bottle of scotch and the ashtray beside me. What's going on? he asks. My father's getting married, I say. What? he says, and I indicate the scotch with a wave of my hand. You want a drink? I offer. He examines the bottle. Went straight for the good shit, huh? he asks. Why not, I say, My father's paying for it, remember?

He leans over to crack the window next to my chair without comment. We watch the smoke from my cigarette drift into the night sky. She's thirty-four, I tell him as he extracts a cigarette of his own from my pack. He shakes his head, flicking the lighter on and off with an idle hand. In the glow of that orange flame his features soften, and I feel a wall of tears behind my eyes.

I can't live like this. I can't live the way we've been living the past few weeks, as if we're nothing more than roommates, as if at semester's end we'll go our separate ways and never see each other again. I take another gulp of scotch, the one that will nail me to the bed tomorrow until well past noon. I don't want to fight with you, I say.

He takes the scotch I pass him, but he doesn't drink. I don't want to fight with you either, he says.

Even that concession fills me with relief, and I rest my head against the back of the chair. That last shot pulls me under, and I close my eyes, drifting as he murmurs that he's sorry, he crossed a line, we're fine, we're good. Okay, I whisper, and he knocks my knee with his own. Okay, he says.

+ + +

I force my father and his remarriage out of my mind, the way I do everything else. I have no plans to go to Houston, and I don't intend to make the trip for a good, long while. My father gives me space, doesn't push the issue, mentions Catherine just enough to remind me that she's a presence in his life and she's not going to go away. There's no talk of the wedding, no suggestion that I get to know her—though that's inevitable—and I concentrate on the immediacy of my own life, my own problems.

So, James says one night. We've been kicking around the idea of going out, but the weather sucks, and every time there's another clap of thunder we edge closer to the fireplace, which we lit on a whim. How's that vow of celibacy working for you? he asks. I give him a sharp look. I'm not taking advice from someone who never gets laid, I inform him, and he snorts, smart enough not to mention that one night with Kristen. I spend all of my time working, he says instead. As if you've never considered your students fodder for dating, I mutter.

I look at him, crashed out in the chair beside the fireplace, his arms draped over the side. I don't want to hear about his students or anyone else. I don't even want to go out. I just want to sit here, steeped in conversation and the wine we're sharing, that fireplace a backdrop right out of a Victorian novel. I'm happy to spend the rest of the day here, the rest of the night. I just don't want to talk about who he wants.

But he's not interested in his potential conquests. He wants to talk about mine, or rather, the fact that I've been missing in action for months from whatever scene I embraced last summer. I don't know what to tell him. I can't be honest with him. But my behavior must seem as ludicrous to him as it does to Kyle, who can't begin to understand the apathy I've exhibited since the fall. Sitting across from James and listening to him dissect the reason I might be holing up in the house—I've been too busy painting; I'm preoccupied with my father's remarriage; I'm self-conscious about my hair (I answer that one with my middle finger)—I start to wonder if I'm running the risk of discovery. If I thought for even a second that he might return what I'm feeling, I'd go to him now, kneel down in front of him and let the light from our fireplace color whatever happens next. But one hint of what I'm thinking might have him packing his bags. With a sinking heart I realize that I need to take action, if for no other reason than to deflect suspicion.

That weekend, we both have dates. I go out first, on Friday, with this guy I met a few months ago and haven't considered much since. Will's nice, nice enough that I feel a little shitty when we head back to his apartment. I'm using him. But I haven't had sex in four months, and I'm so reluctant to find out where I'll go once I close my eyes that I haven't been jerking off much either. I need someone's hands on me, and the second Will closes his front door, I pin him against the wall. I don't think he was looking to get laid tonight; that he made reservations at a restaurant I mentioned the first time we met tells me he's hoping for something more. But he lets me get his jeans down around his ankles, his protests meager enough that I ignore them altogether. I don't have a condom, Joel, he murmurs, and I yank one from my pocket and hand it over.

When I get home, James emerges from his bedroom, his finger marking the page in the book he's reading. You have any fun? he asks, and I shrug, tossing my keys on the bar. I actually feel worse than I did when I left the house. I have the distinct sense that whatever I'm feeling for James isn't something I can fuck my way through, at least not with someone like Will, who paused long enough to ask me what I like. I'd almost groaned. Where the hell is Lucio when I need him? That night in Rome, he fucked me raw, until I begged him to stop. He didn't give a shit what I wanted; at the very least he was willing to find out by trial and error. The last thing I needed tonight was something tender. The last thing I needed was the sweetest kiss in Will's repertoire or to be asked to stay.

James leans against the wall as I collapse on the couch; if I didn't know better, I'd swear he was looking for details. He's a good-looking guy, he finally offers. *You* want to go out with him? I ask. Not my type, he says, like he's actually considering the possibility. No? I say, Who's your type, James?

I know what he's doing. He's pulling us back to that conversation we had after Kyle's party when he tried to convince me I have it easier in regard to sex. But I'm not laughing, not the way I did last year when he told me Luke wasn't his type or mine either.

My type, he muses, tapping the edge of his book against his thigh. He's wearing pajama bottoms that might be mine. Who can tell anymore? I watch him give my question some thought, as if there's some legitimacy here, as if anything's riding on the outcome. When he finally gets a look at my expression, he straightens. I'm just fucking with you, Joel, he says. Yeah? I say, reaching for the remote, Well, I don't feel like being fucked with right now.

Saturday evening, I sit on the front porch as James gets ready for a date of his own. He's left me alone for most of the day, giving me plenty of time to conjure up a good dose of self-pity. Everyone I know has plans tonight, and I rock back and forth in the swing, feeling sorry for myself. You've got to figure this out, man, Peter mumbled earlier this afternoon, dropping by for a beer before he left to meet his girlfriend, and I'd been doubly humiliated: that he knows the truth and that it's clear I'm still drowning.

Now I wait in the swing for James to leave, scraping paint from the wood with my thumbnail. I don't know the details of his evening, and I don't want to know. I just want it to end.

What do you think? he asks. I look over at him; he's standing in the doorway, his arms spread wide. He's wearing jeans and one of my sweaters, a v-neck tinted such a light shade of gray the color's almost silver. No, I tell him. I can't borrow it? he asks, surprised, Or it looks like shit? Looks like shit, I say, turning my attention back to the swing. I feel the tiniest bit smug, then instantly guilty. From the corner of my eye I see him glance at his watch, hesitating. Then I look down at what I'm wearing, a cranberry sweater barely two weeks old. Take it, I sigh, stripping, and he grins. I watch as he pulls my sweater over his head, his tee shirt hiking up just enough that I see his navel. When he tosses the other sweater to me, I forget to breathe; I know the material will still be warm from his skin. Yeah? he says, holding out his arms again. I give him a cautious look; the color's perfect for him, and I hold back from touching the fold of material at his waist. Yeah, I say. He turns, checking out his reflection in the window, then settles on the swing beside me. Don't you need to leave? I mumble. You trying to get rid of me? he asks. I force a laugh, staring at the paint embedded in my nail. If I'm careful not to breathe too deeply, I can ignore the scent of shampoo that accompanies him every time he changes position.

After he leaves I sit in front of the television with a beer and the remote, trying not to envision a play-by-play of his evening. I have half a mind to pick up the phone and return the call that Will made earlier today, but he's not the one I want, and calling Will or anyone else I've hooked up with over the past year isn't going to accomplish a thing. I settle back on the couch with Pandora and contemplate a cigarette. I have a feeling I've got a long night ahead of me.

But he's home early, and my heart flips in my chest at the sight of him. That was fast, I say. Lousy date, he tells me, falling into the chair and swinging one leg over the other. He looks fucking amazing in that sweater. I'm bored, he adds, and I'm suddenly wary. What do you mean? I ask. He puckers his lips. They're the moon I painted after my trip to Mexico, and I swallow the saliva filling my mouth. I don't know, he admits, I'm just bored. I comb my fingers through my shaggy hair, trying to think of something to say that won't incriminate me. You want to get high? I finally ask.

We smoke, taking our time, passing the pipe back and forth. I feel really good right now, he says, sliding from the chair to the floor. He scratches his head, then starts raking his fingers back and forth across his skull. Yeah, I say without taking my eyes from him, and he reaches again for the pipe, holding a lungful of smoke, then easing it out between his lips. I have an immense urge to reach out and touch him. The energy it takes to hold back sobers me considerably, and I focus my attention on my bottle of beer as he scoots the pipe across the coffee table in my direction. I'm done, I say, and he raises his eyebrows but doesn't press.

By midnight we're both lying facedown on the floor in front of the fireplace. Well, at least the night ended on a high note, he mumbles. No pun intended, I add. He laughs softly; I crumble a stray marshmallow from the Lucky Charms we've been eating. Why'd your date suck? I ask, and he shrugs without sitting up. Dunno, he says, Why aren't you going out with anyone? I went out with someone last night, I remind him. Right, he says, dipping his index finger into the marshmallow I've crushed, You going to see him again? I don't know, I say though I'm pretty sure I'm not, Why? He shrugs, sucking on his finger; I'm suddenly impatient. Why are you so interested anyway? I ask. Why are *you* so agitated? he says. Because you're fucking with me again, I tell him. I just asked if you were going to see him! he says, When did we get to a point where I couldn't ask you about the guys you're dating?

He sounds genuinely wounded. The whole reason I went out last night was to make sure he didn't figure me out, and here I am, so tangled up that I'm fighting with him instead. I shake my head, and he nudges my calf with his boot. Seriously, he says, What's going on?

I look at him. I don't speak; I just look at him, and he stares right back. We're close enough that I can see the gold in his eyes. I want to mine it for meaning, steal it from its depths and try to set it on fire. I want right now to pull him toward me, the palm of my hand cupping the back of his neck. I want the moment that everything begins.

His mouth slides to the right, and then he's laughing, still a little stoned. I let loose a smile of my own, and he toys with it, leaning closer, apart, closer, apart, the potential unnerving. Stoned and magnetized, I could change everything.

In the end I do nothing at all. In the end I watch as he gets to his feet, yawning, stretching his arms above his head. 'Night, he says, heading toward his room.

I break down as soon as I close my bedroom door. It's been too long, the pot too potent, the evening too provocative. Sliding between the sheets, I'm already closing my eyes, his necklace heavy on my throat. I try jerking off slowly, but it only takes about sixty seconds for me to come, his image plastered all over the inside of my eyelids. Afterward, I press the heels of my hands into my eyes, wondering if he'd be appalled or amused by what I'm visualizing, and which is worse.

The next morning, in a fit of desperation, I invite him to go somewhere over Spring Break. How about Padre? he asks, surprising me, and I agree, quickly, to whatever he wants.

Padre's in six days. Padre's the key.

+ + +

We're flying down the interstate, top down, the sky clotted with clouds. We've been fighting over the wheel, so happy to be heading out of town, away from responsibility. Only once last night did James voice a nervous confession about escaping from the avalanche of work that usually consumes him; I just turned up the volume on a Bob Marley CD and cracked open a beer. He watched me, his arms crossed over his chest. Pujan's using this week to catch up on his grading, he finally informed me. Pujan needs to get laid, I told him. Pujan nailed every one of the answers on our mid-term, he said grimly, and I told him that was probably the only thing Pujan has nailed lately. Didn't Aristotle say there's no genius without madness? I asked. I don't remember, he said, But my professor told me that I need an A on my final paper if I want to maintain my grade point. I offered him my beer, the quintessential pusher, then nodded when he took a swallow. Tell you what, I said soothingly, If we get to Padre and you're still feeling tense, we'll just turn around and come back. You know as well as I do, he said, That's never going to happen.

But today he couldn't be in a better mood, and we head south without regret. With every mile I lose a little more of my inhibition. I could reach over, right now, take his hand and thread it through mine. I could pull to the side of the road, put the BMW in park and tell him what I've been aching to admit for months. I could wait until tonight, until we've had a couple of drinks, until we're standing on the balcony of our condo. And then, as the waves usher in an ancient rhythm, I could step toward him. Mouths open, we meet in the middle. His sun sheds a fiery light.

I couldn't be any more wrong. Padre's insane, the beaches packed, college students everywhere, and there's no escape because our condo's right on the water. A loose word, *condo*, to describe our accommodations. What a shithole, I say when we open the door, but James shrugs, unwilling to comment since I'm footing the bill. I silently accept the beer he hands me, the first of many dozens I drink over the course of the next week. Even with the sliding glass door closed I can hear snatches of conversation and drunken laughter. Bikini-clad girls cross my line of vision not ten feet away, and the second James grins, I come close to dropping my head in my hands. What was I thinking? I should've booked us something out of the way, somewhere so isolated we would've had nothing to distract us but possibility. Let's get out there, James says without taking his eyes from the party on the beach, and struck dumb by my naïveté, I tell him I think I'm going to smoke first.

The week passes in an alcohol- and pot-induced haze. We stay out late crashing parties, crawl back to the condo in the rough hours before dawn, then get up after a few hours of sleep and crawl back to the beach. In my more lucid moments I watch James flirt with different girls, then flee to the condo for quick, mind-numbing hits from a hastily wrapped joint when I can't take anymore. At the end of the week I shut myself in the bathroom and look in the mirror. James is outside within shouting distance, engaged in a sexually charged conversation with some girl from Oklahoma, and the experience has driven me back to the condo under the guise of getting more beer. He's disappeared in the middle of the afternoon twice so far this week, leaving me in a lugubrious stupor of self-pity, returned both times with an expression of such satisfaction that I'd wanted to stab my eyes out with the key to our condo just so I wouldn't have to look at him. Now he's on target for a third encounter, and I just want to go home, back to Austin, where he sees no action whatsoever.

I turn on the faucets, fill my hands with tepid water, and lift them, dripping, to my face. My hair's sweaty, overgrown, and I gather a chunk in my hand and sit on the rim of the tub with my elbows on my knees. The combination of marijuana and sun-warmed beer muddles my sense of time, and I'm moaning softly when James bangs on the door. What're you doing in there? he calls, Whacking off? I don't answer, and he opens the door a crack. Are you sick? he asks, Or just loaded? Loaded, I decide, and he comes in, giving off a profound scent of tanning lotion. Good for you, he says.

Turning to the mirror, he smooths a curl above his ear with the heel of his right hand. You going back out? he asks, meeting my eyes, and I shrug. The knobs of his vertebrae disappear into his swimming trunks, and without thinking I reach out and brush a thin blur of sand from the back of his shorts. Copping a feel? he asks. I let out a nervous laugh. So are you coming or not? he says, turning to go. I stare at the floor beneath my feet. Well, I'm going, he announces, Wish me luck.

I call Kyle the day we get back to Austin. I thought you were out of circulation, he says, I thought you were waiting for Prince Charming. Never fucking mind, I snap, and he says, Oh honey, you need to get *laid*.

I meet him and a few friends that night for drinks. You're going out? James asked, surprised when he saw me standing in front of the mirror trying to figure out what to do with my hair now that it's grown out of anything resembling a style. Yeah, I said, What's so strange about that?

Darryl's tow-headed, with broad shoulders highlighted by a button-down in an unfortunate shade of shit. I slide my hand up his wrinkle-free khakis, figuring he'll look a hell of a lot better once I get him undressed. He doesn't miss a beat, his fingers curling around mine. Damn, I think. This isn't so difficult after all.

2

Darryl's way more into me than I am into him, but he brushes my concern aside. I know, he confides, Kyle said you've been caught up in someone. Kyle said that? I ask, startled, and he shrugs. I'm not worried, he says, putting his arms around me. There's a good connection between us, though I suspect that has more to do with sexual drought on my part than with chemistry, and I refuse to think too much about the fact that under normal circumstances we'd probably have never made it past the first night. Darryl's fine. He's nice enough, good-looking enough. He's fine.

Darryl's a driver for UPS, gets up most mornings well before dawn. The nights he stays with me I barely hear his alarm, pull the covers up over my head to muffle the light when he goes into the bathroom. He's usually through with work by the middle of the afternoon, but that's when I'm holed up in the back room, painting. By the time I'm finished and ready to go out Darryl's winding down. I can't function on five hours of sleep, he informs me as if I'm still in college, still partying every night. I get that, I say, But I'm not interested in heading to bed at nine o'clock. After a few minor disagreements and one full-blown fight we finally settle down, agreeing to disagree, deciding that he's better off going to bed himself and getting the rest he needs than wasting time arguing about when I'm going to join him.

Spending the night at Darryl's place isn't an option because it's such a hole. No furniture? I said the first time I walked into his bedroom and saw a mattress on the floor. He pretended to be insulted, but I don't think he gives a shit. He makes decent enough money, if I can take what he tells me at face value, not that I expect him to pay for much of anything. There's no reason; I have plenty of cash, and while I don't want anyone taking advantage of me, it's obvious Darryl needs his paycheck for basic necessities. What the hell does he spend his money on? James asks when I tell him what passes for a bed in Darryl's apartment. His wardrobe? I suggest, and we share a laugh, at Darryl's expense.

+ + +

In May, as James finishes up his semester, he tells me that in less than a year he's going to be taking his qualifying exams. Once he passes those, he'll be at the dissertation stage. He looks every bit the part. Does this come with the territory? I ask when he leaves for campus on his last day of classes wearing a sport coat with jeans, Are you going to come home with a pipe? Come with me to Fort Worth this weekend, he says, ignoring me, We'll get my mom to cook for us. Nah, I say, I've kind of got something going with Darryl. He looks briefly pissed and takes off by himself for ten days. I relish the opportunity to be in the house without him; I have an idea of the damage I could've caused if he'd stayed in town with nothing more pressing to occupy his time than the preliminaries for his exams.

While he's gone, I make myself available to my boyfriend. He cooks me dinner one night; the food sucks, but the gesture's kind, and we drink enough wine between the two of us to color our perception of the entire meal. I like having the house to ourselves, he says, threading his fingers under my shorts, and I close my eyes.

I don't take this for granted. I'm barely two and a half years removed from a time when I wouldn't invite a date into my home, wouldn't open myself up to a blowjob in the middle of the living room regardless of whether or not James was in town. Now I don't have to make apologies, and I give Darryl my full attention, subscribe to the pithy notion of loving the one I'm with.

I don't talk much to James while he's gone. When he calls, our conversations feel brief, perfunctory. He's sleeping a lot, he says, and he's feeling guilty about that since he has so much work to do for next year. I tell him he needs the rest. You're probably glad to have me gone, he says, and I'm struck by the hint of jealousy in his tone. I have to remind myself not to be fooled. Don't worry, I assure him, We haven't gotten around to changing the locks yet.

+ + +

Darryl takes advantage of some vacation time mid-June, and we talk about going away somewhere, but the trip never materializes. Ultimately, Darryl's too lazy to take matters into his own hands, and I'm too leery about spending that much time alone with him with no means of escape. We end up whiling away the few extra days watching movies and sleeping late instead. There's something to be said for having someone at my disposal, someone willing to go down on me in the middle of a random Sunday afternoon without having to go through the hassle of picking him up first. But I have a feeling we're making James crazy, turning the house into a den of sloth. More than once I've caught him rolling his eyes at something Darryl said or staring at him with an expression so flat I can only guess what emotions he must be masking. I'm starting to get the impression he doesn't care much for Darryl; he's just humoring me because I've gone so long without dating anyone.

Saturday night, Darryl and I go out to dinner and invite James to come along. It's the least we can do, subjecting him the way we have to Darryl's vacation. I don't expect him to accept, but to my surprise he agrees, and once we get to the restaurant and I'm sitting across from him, I realize just how much I've missed him the past couple of months. I've barely had a chance to ask what he's working on this summer, and I start lobbing questions his way, then sit back and listen as he tells me about the research he's conducting for one of his professors, a follow-up to the dig he took part in last summer. Even though I've read little of what he's describing, he's so passionate, so lost in this ancient world, that he sucks me right in.

The thing about Crete's architecture, he says, leaning forward as if he's letting me in on some great secret, Is that just about everything was made from stone. He talks about the pieces his group found last year, chunks of a temple, shards of pottery that held water and wine. You can't imagine, he says, You can't understand what it's like to see something that no one has seen for centuries. I'm right there with him though, and a quarter of an hour passes before I finally realize that Darryl hasn't spoken. His presence suddenly reveals itself to me as an intrusion. I don't want him here at all. I'd rather be with James alone, and either because he senses my impatience or because he genuinely has to take a piss, Darryl excuses himself to find the restroom.

What'd I say? James asks the second he's gone, and I reach for the bottle of wine with a sigh. I think you intimidate him, I admit. He shakes his head, looking less embarrassed than irate. Look, I'm sorry for the historical diatribe, he says, But am I really supposed to keep my mouth shut for fear of threatening him? Of course not, I say, and he blurts out that he misses spending time with me alone without having to watch what he has to say, for fuck's sake. What do you want me to do, James? I say, Break up with him?

He doesn't answer, and I gaze at him over the rim of my wine glass. He's thrown himself back in his chair in a fit of annoyance, and I hold my breath at the sight of him, at the tan he's managed to acquire with his early evening treks to the spring to swim laps, at his golden throat framed against the white collar of his shirt. With that bronze skin and thick head of hair he might as well have stepped out of ancient Greece itself, and it's all I can do not to wrestle him to the floor right here in front of everybody.

Can I help it if I want you all to myself? he asks. He's half-smiling, admitting how ridiculous his question sounds, but god, if only he weren't joking. I don't know, I say, But you're going to have to try.

+ + +

My father's ready to introduce me to Catherine. Twice he leaves messages, and when I finally call him back early one morning at the beginning of July, he suggests that I come down for the Fourth. That's tomorrow, I remind him, and he says, If you returned my calls in a timely fashion, Joel, we'd be able to plan. I muffle a groan, my hand cupped around a mug of coffee. I already have a commitment, I say, which is halfway true since Darryl and I have kicked around the idea of spending the day at Kyle's. Catherine's starting to get the impression that you're not interested in meeting her, my father informs me. So she's pretty intuitive then, huh? I ask.

Silence fills the line as Darryl bumbles his way into the kitchen in his UPS uniform, smacking open cabinet doors for the cereal and rummaging for a clean spoon. I watch him, vaguely annoyed. Didn't I find his uniform a turn-on at one point?

I understand your reluctance, Joel, my father's saying, But I will not tolerate this disrespect. Sorry, I mumble, glancing up as James appears and mutters a greeting to Darryl as he reaches for the coffee pot. Darryl plunks down beside me and starts slurping. I edge away from him. Look, I'll meet her next month, all right? I say into the phone. Labor Day weekend, my father says, Plan on it, Joel.

I hang up, running my hand through my hair. I'll go with you if you want, Darryl says in between bites. I stare at him as he dribbles milk onto the table. To meet your stepmother, he adds, and from the corner of my eye I see James wince. She's not my stepmother, I say flatly. Well, she will be, Darryl reminds me as James shakes his head. How would I even explain your presence? I ask. *He* goes with you to Houston, he says, pointing at James. No, he doesn't, I say before James can open his mouth, And even if he did, that's different. Why? Darryl asks, and I say, Because I've known him since freshman year, Darryl. But I'm the one you're fucking, he points out. Don't remind me, I mutter, pushing back from the table.

That night, sleep refuses me. I've apologized to Darryl, told him that where my father's concerned, he'd be smart not to push me. I appreciate you wanting to help, I added, but that last insult I'd thrown his way this morning obviously still stung because he fell asleep pouting. Now I'm wide awake, and I finally throw back the covers and pull on a pair of shorts, then make my way into the living room, where I find James crashed out on the sofa, a beer within reach.

Can't sleep? he asks as I fall beside him. Why are you awake? I ask, turning the question around, and he shrugs, a serpentine slide of his shoulders that slices right through me. Without thinking I lean a little closer. He lights a cigarette, then offers me the pack. He needs a haircut and probably a shave. I got laid tonight, he says, keeping his tone casual. Seriously? I say. You don't have to sound so surprised, he says grimly, and I flick the lighter without saying anything. His hand on her arm: the thought can still make my stomach hurt. Who was she? I ask. Friend of a friend, he says, No one you know. I reach for the ashtray; when I lean forward, the necklace he gave me swings forward too, by half an inch. So? I say when he's quiet.

He shrugs again, and his silence tells me everything I need to know. I can feel my insides fall limp with relief. He tilts his head without lifting it from the back of the sofa; for the first time I realize he's drunk. She went down on me, he says, lowering his voice like maybe he's afraid Darryl's going to hear. Lucky you, I say, trying to ignore the way he's spread out across the sofa, trying not to picture anyone kneeling between his legs. He grunts; I lift his beer to see if there's enough to warrant me taking a swallow. She had no idea what she was doing, he adds. That's not usually an issue for me, I admit, and he glowers, as if I'm intentionally trying to antagonize him.

I turn to the television, but I can feel his eyes crawling all over me. I'm not sure what I'm supposed to say, but he's already sitting up and downing what's left of his beer. Let's go for a drive, he says. Now? I say. No, dipshit, he says, getting to his feet, Next week.

Thirty minutes later, he has me north of the city, driving farm roads like it's freshman year. I've stopped at a service station to fill the tank and charge a six-pack, and now James holds a cold bottle in his hands, seventy-mile-an-hour wind tangling his hair. The night swallows his words as he leans forward to crank up the stereo. This is the way I want him. This is the way I've always wanted him, ever since I bailed him out of jail and we took to the road, rationing our beer and biding our time, feeling each other out in a way we never would have if James hadn't knocked back one too many drinks and climbed into his fraternity brother's car. Now I'm here beside him, my own bottle between my legs.

Darryl's going to be pissed if he wakes up and finds me gone. I barely give a shit. This moment already eclipses his anger, and James's smile gets me in the gut. I focus on the road, the stereo's bass, the pounding of my fucking heart. He's there in my periphery, at the same time has always been front and center.

I make a quick turn, accelerating down a rutted road that might be private property. James leans back in the passenger seat with his feet on the dashboard, expostulating about something I can't hear well enough to decipher. I grip the steering wheel in my hands, nodding as if I can hear him, as if I agree. When the bird hits the windshield, I jerk to the left, and for just a second I swear the BMW tilts on its side; as I correct, it's not the road in front of me that I'm seeing but James, sitting on the couch and tilting his head in my direction. Feathers rain down on us like something apocalyptic. I slam on the brakes, and the BMW squeals, pulling up short mere inches from a barbed wire fence on the side of the road.

What the fuck? James says, and together we stumble from the car. I think you killed an owl, man, he says, brushing feathers from his clothes. But there's no sign behind us of what I hit, and I have to shake the feathers from my hair to prove to myself that I didn't imagine that smack against the windshield. Tentatively, I approach the front of the BMW, but the car's unscathed and ready to drive, engine humming, radio blaring some late night KLBJ. I think I spilled my beer, James complains, and I reach into the car and pluck another bottle from the six-pack. Might as well keep you good and drunk, I say, and he winks in a way that makes my dick twitch. I lean over and take the keys from the ignition; silence rushes in to fill the void, and James automatically cocks his head. Man, listen to that, he says, dropping his voice. I murmur an assent, and we trail backward until we're flush against the car, eyes adjusting to the darkness. After a minute he shakes a cigarette from a pack of Marlboros. Got a light? he asks.

We're quiet as he smokes, as I breathe in his exhale. I could sleep out here, he finally admits. Peaceful, I agree, and he drops his cigarette to the ground and crushes it out underneath his sandal, then thinks better of what he's done and picks up the butt, handing me his beer. I watch as he folds himself over the driver's side and stashes the cigarette in the ashtray. How environmental, I say. Only you can prevent forest fires, he informs me. I pass him the beer, but he doesn't take a sip. Instead, he turns the bottle thoughtfully in his hands without comment. I shove my own hands in the pockets of my shorts, one foot crossed over the other. In a matter of hours this sky will brighten; we'll be home again, in separate beds.

You know I'd go with you, James says, and I frown, confused by what I've missed. He shrugs, his arm inadvertently bumping mine. To Houston, he says, To meet Catherine. I'd never ask you to do that, I tell him. But the option's there, he says, If you want me.

I glance over at him, and he gazes back, sweet and earnest and kind. You shouldn't have to go through this shit alone, he says. I'm not alone, I say.

He stiffens, misinterpreting my words, and I want to place a reassuring hand on his arm despite the cost to my sanity. But I'm safer letting him believe I meant Darryl, and he squints in the direction of the horizon. He's been asking questions, you know, he says, Your boyfriend.

He's managed to tinge the word *boyfriend* with just a hint of acrimony.

About your mother, he adds, About how she…

I make a small, unconscious sound that I manage to cut short. Even so, James looks alarmed. What'd you tell him? I ask, clearing my throat, and he shakes his head. Nothing, he says, stashing his empty bottle in the carton, That he was asking the wrong person.

I nod, but I'm shaking the way I always do when I think of her. Hey, he says, and then his hand's cupping the back of my neck, pulling me toward him. You're okay, he whispers, and though I probably shouldn't, I close my eyes.

Less than five seconds we're entwined, but that's enough to send me spiraling. This right here reminds me why I shouldn't be spending time with him, why I shouldn't accept invitations to drive out to the middle of nowhere in the dead of night. I'm already losing myself in his arms, in the beery scent of his breath, the slight stickiness of his skin. I push myself away from him before anything else can happen. C'mon, I say, It's late.

As the sun's rising, I slide into bed next to my boyfriend. I can hear James on the other side of the bathroom, fumbling in his nightstand for the Advil I made him promise he'd take. My lips find Darryl's throat, his nipple, the line of wiry hair below his navel. I can coax him into a hand job, a blowjob, the hardest fuck I can possibly handle. I can wear myself out, then close my eyes and fall so far into sleep that I'll forget the way James's arms felt around me. I can convince myself I don't need him, at all.

+ + +

Darryl and I don't invite James to hang with us at Kyle's for the Fourth. I get the impression that James is hurt, especially since he offered to accompany me to Houston, since he let me burrow myself in his arms in the hour before dawn when he told me that Darryl has been interrogating him. But I'm the one who had to hold back from opening my mouth on his skin, and I have to remind myself that even if James doesn't want me to be with Darryl, that doesn't mean he wants to be with me.

With that thought in mind I turn an eye to my work the day after the holiday and gradually let my gaze soften. A few deep breaths and a paintbrush in my hand and everything else falls to the periphery. With an empty house I can work without distraction, without listening for James, without negotiating Darryl, who stared at the painting on the living room wall for all of five seconds last April before he launched into a solicitous review that did nothing but highlight a sincere lack of sophistication which embarrassed the shit out of me, mainly because I knew James was listening and judging everything he said.

But today James comes home from work early, early enough that I frown when I see him standing in the doorway. He shrugs without explanation. Can I see? he asks, indicating the canvas. He doesn't wait before approaching. I look at what I've done, which isn't much; I couldn't have been standing here more than a couple of hours. Still, I have trees arching over a midnight road, barbed wire choking the moon. He smirks, satisfied, like he's figured me out. I don't know what I'm doing yet, I mumble, crossing uncomfortable arms over my chest and smudging my shirt with paint. You can always ask Darryl for advice, he tells me.

I give him a sharp look. Sometimes I feel like he has a direct line to what I'm thinking.

If that's the case, then he knows what he's doing to me when he steps closer and nudges my shoulder with his own. I really like your painting! he says in an over-eager voice that's supposed to mimic Darryl. I shake my head, caught between laughing at James's impersonation and feeling like I should defend my boyfriend. I mean, look at that moon! he continues, pointing to the canvas, It's like a, what-do-you-call-it, a metaphor or something! All right, I say, and James throws out his chest in a gesture that's so quintessential Darryl I snicker. Special delivery, he says, lowering his voice and grabbing his crotch, and I shove him off-balance. You're a snob, I tell him. Hey, at least you're getting some ass, he says. That's more than you can say, I agree.

He looks pissed. I got laid a couple of nights ago, he reminds me. Does it count if it sucked? I ask. Anyway, he says, I have nothing against UPS drivers. No? I say, and he shakes his head. It's that mediocre IQ that gives me pause, he says. Well, I say, I'm not fucking his brain.

That shuts him up long enough for me to take a breath and try to ground myself. Standing so close to him wears me out, and when he can't come up with a retort, I take my brush between my fingers. I'm working, I say, and without another word he turns and leaves the room, slamming the door behind him.

+ + +

James has reason to be frustrated with the way I've been keeping my distance save for that one late-night drive. We're rarely spontaneous; instead, the time we spend together is carefully planned, negotiated, something we have to build into our schedules. That would be irritating enough if the reason behind the issue was his work or mine, but the fact that there's someone standing in our way, someone James obviously doesn't like and would rather see me dump, he must find intolerable. Last week, we were midway through a lunch he practically had to beg me to share when he turned suddenly morose. What? I said, and he admitted that being with me is like getting laid. Halfway through he's depressed because he knows he's going to have to wait forever until the opportunity comes around again.

But the reason I'm doling out a drink here and a dinner there is because I'm terrified of what I might do if I spend the kind of time with him that I've always spent. How can I be expected to sit here night after night? To accompany him to the spring every day? To talk to him about his work and my work and then just close the door behind me when it's time for bed? I want him to be more than that. I want him to be a part of everything.

Fuck that. I want him to *be* everything.

In the early morning hours of a Saturday at the end of July we make our way to the front porch. He booked this time with me a week ago; I'd told him we could hang out once Darryl went to bed. I half-expected him to tell me to forget it, that he wasn't going to beg me to spend time with him. But he just nodded, and I felt another rush of guilt for holding him so far apart. If I didn't want him so badly, I'd never behave this way.

Have you ever noticed, he says, muttering his usual complaints as I shut the front door behind us, That the middle of the night is the only time I can get you alone? Have you ever noticed, I say, That you're jealous of my boyfriend? He grimaces, dropping down on the swing beside me. I tap a box of cigarettes against my palm, then slit the lid, and we fall into an uncharacteristic but companionable silence. A mellow breeze undercuts the humidity; nights carry me through the brutal daytime temperatures of Austin summers, along with the occasional beer I hold cold against my forehead. Beside me James sprawls, head tilted back, blowing smoke upward from his bottom lip. I'm careful not to misconstrue the way he's sitting, the proximity of his leg to mine, the occasional brush of his sweaty arm against my own as he taps the edge of his cigarette on the ashtray between us. We're close; the swing's tight. We can't help but be compressed between its arms.

You want a beer? he asks, getting to his feet, and I nod. I feel his pull when he leaves me, as I close my eyes and follow the sound of his bare feet walking through the living room and into the kitchen, the thump of the refrigerator door closing. He's the sun to my planet, and I wonder why I'm even bothering to pretend. He holds me in his orbit whether I want to be there or not.

The screen door opens, and he pads back toward me. I clink the butt of a fresh bottle against his as he settles down beside me and reaches for the Marlboros. So you and Darryl, he says, extracting a cigarette.

I have a feeling he wants to ask how long he's going to have to put up with this guy before I come to my senses. But he just turns his head to the side to exhale, and I take a sip of my beer, following the smoke's trajectory until it disappears. Across the street the neighbor's dog barks at shadows. The leaves of the pecan trees rustle together, then quiet down underneath the baleful eye of the moon. In the silence I can feel something building, a restlessness, a shiver of impatience, and when James leans forward, I brace myself. What do you... do with him? he asks.

I don't know whether to be stunned more by the outrageousness of his question or that he expects me to answer him. For just a second I remember the query he lobbed at me when I got back from Europe after graduation, about whether or not I'd sucked any dick while I was away. I'd been taken aback not because his question bothered me; in fact, at the time I would've never considered his curiosity inappropriate. Instead, I was struck by how easily he'd asked. I still wasn't used to being accepted without judgment, and knowing full well the tension between us when I'd boarded that plane to Europe, I was relieved to hear him speak so casually. But there's something intimate in the question he's just posed, something brazen and assumptive about the way he expects me to tell him what he wants to know. I'm shocked, but at the same time I'm so profoundly aroused that even though I should probably tell him that what Darryl and I do together is none of his fucking business, I can't.

What do you want to know? I ask, but now that I've indicated that I'm ready to give him exactly what he wants, he pulls away, withdrawing into his beer. The smoke from his cigarette obscures his expression. My own cigarette's shaking, held between trembling fingers I lift repeatedly, obsessively, to my mouth. From the corner of my eye I watch him, the slide of his beer down his throat, the ropy muscles in his shoulders. My gaze falls lower, to the fold of material in his shorts. For five seconds, ten, I let myself wonder what might happen if I reached over, right now, and made him come alive. He lets out a deep, agitated sigh, and at the sound I yank my eyes back to my cigarette, which I've already sucked into oblivion.

And then he's talking about a lecture he attended a couple of days ago where some scholar brought up the Sacred Band of 300, Theban warriors chosen specifically because they were homosexual couples, the thinking being that against men bound by such intimacy, such loyalty, no army would stand a chance. He's read about them before, of course, he says, but for some reason the lecture struck him in a way he hadn't expected and hasn't been able to shake since. He can't stop thinking about their successes, their eventual defeat at the Battle of Chaeronea, the way they all fell together, the praise lavished upon them by the leader of the very army responsible for their demise. The longer he speaks, the more animated he becomes, and soon he's citing theories, paraphrasing writers unfamiliar to me, pointing to ancient Greece and the practice of pederasty, the depiction of the relationship between Achilles and Patroclus throughout history, before he's circling back to the Puritanical roots of our own culture. Where the hell are you going with this shit? I finally ask.

He reaches for the cigarette I've lit, taking it right from my hand. His eyes flame, and they hold mine, the tension between us so keen that I think I could bridge this distance between us and get away with it. He no longer seems like such an impossibility.

But the front door bangs open. We swivel at the sound. In the doorway Darryl yawns, then rakes his fingers through the hair on his chest, watching us like a territorial mountain lion. When're you coming to bed? he asks me. In a minute, I say, and he nods, glancing at James and then back at me as if he's thinking of joining us. I'm suddenly turned off: by the thick curve of Darryl's naked arms, by the fact that he's pulled on those wrinkle-free khakis without bothering to button or zip them, by his very presence. Give me a goddamn minute, Darryl, I say, my voice harsher than I intended, but he takes his time, his gaze sliding from me to James and then back again before he slams the door shut behind him.

Once he's gone, we don't look at each other. Instead, James starts rocking, slowly, back and forth, the swing creaking beneath our weight. Another minute and I'm caught in his rhythm.

+ + +

Over the next couple of weeks Darryl doesn't say a word about what he may or may not have seen on the front porch. I'm still not sure what *I* saw, if the light in James's eyes was honestly an ember of desire or simply the reflection of a shared cigarette. We'd lingered on the porch for no more than five minutes before I finally mumbled something about getting to sleep. A test, I'd thought, but James nodded without a word. Since then, there's been nothing remarkable about our interaction and nothing unusual between Darryl and me either. Instead, it's Darryl and James who seem to be at odds.

I can hear them arguing now, and I round the corner into the kitchen, where James meets my eyes, then immediately drops them, his cheeks tainted with such a furious flush I have to wonder if Darryl propositioned him. I glance at my boyfriend. He's leaning back in one of the kitchen chairs, his legs spread, wearing an expression of sly self-satisfaction. I half-expect him to cup his balls; he's the picture of a proprietary man. What's going on? I say, and Darryl smiles like maybe he has something on James and intends to use it against him. James has a lot on his mind, he says. Shut the fuck up, James hisses, screwing his hands into fists, and Darryl gets to his feet. James takes a step in Darryl's direction, and incredulous, I block him with a palm to his chest. What's *wrong* with you? I say, and he mutters something unintelligible I'm supposed to take for an answer. Over my shoulder Darryl stands his ground. He looks exactly the way he did on the front porch the other night, like he has something to claim, and he folds his arms across his chest, punctuating his point. I don't know what the hell happened here, I say, But I have no interest in refereeing your shit.

Darryl smirks. You hear that, James? he says, and James snorts, though there's a flicker of fear in his eyes. Before I can figure out why, he's snagging his keys from the bar. You don't have to *leave*, I say, but he slams his way through the front door. I turn to Darryl, who contrives an air of innocence. What was that about? I ask, but he just pulls me into his arms. I'm going to fuck you now, he says in the same conversational tone he might announce that he's going to pick up some beer. You have work, I remind him, And I'm going for a run. But he's yanking down my shorts, sinking his teeth into my neck, and I close my eyes in spite of myself. I think about the blowjob I gave him last night, the same kind I want to give James: slow and methodical and without intent of reciprocity. I could knock on his bedroom door one night after Darryl's asleep and drop to my knees before he can say a word. Once I touch him, he won't want me to stop. I know he won't want me to stop, and I tilt my head back, imagining the slide of his fingers through my hair, the way they'd grip my head as I take him deeper and deeper.

I'm moaning, and Darryl gives one of my nipples a cursory tweak. Not here, I murmur, because I don't want James coming home to find me bent over the kitchen table, and I can tell where this is headed. Here's fine, he whispers, shrugging out of his uniform, Here's good.

Later that afternoon, I'm in the back room, mired in what's in front of me. I've skipped my run in favor of a nap and a quiet lunch of odds and ends since James mistook my keys for his own, and I'm stuck here without the BMW. I haven't heard from him, and while there's a part of me that wants to worry over what happened this morning, I really just want this moment to myself, this moment to paint.

I haven't reached out to local galleries yet, but I swear I'm getting closer. I've gone through my paintings, know exactly what I'll pull should anyone be interested. I need to get some slides, need to buy a light table and a loop. Then I need to suck it up and put myself out there. I'm up against a timeline whether I like it or not. I have until December, but at that point I'll either be looking at another negotiation with my father or worse, some full-time gig guaranteed to push me right over the edge.

Part of me knows that won't ever happen, that I won't ever take a full-time job at Permian or anywhere else. My father can threaten all he wants, but I'll never cave. I'll never give up the one thing that matters most to me.

But I'd rather not have to chase inspiration in the handful of hours I'm not busting my ass waiting tables or tending bar. I want space and time, and after everything I've been through I know I deserve both. I cost him what? Three thousand dollars a month? Four if I've gone out of town or made a run on oil paint? Please. He can afford more than I'm spending.

And it's not as if I'm not working. I've dealt with a few brief periods of inactivity like any other artist. But most days, I treat the back room like my father treats his job; I'm in there at daylight, I work through the weekends. *Summer* doesn't automatically translate into *vacation*. Painting isn't my hobby; it's my lifeline.

So when the phone rings, I'm tempted not to answer it. I'd rather stay right here in this moment, my brush one with my mind. But one glance at the Caller ID has my brow furrowing, and when I answer, there's a tremor in my voice.

James had an accident. The doctors are working with him, I should come as soon as I can. I'm already wiping my hands on my jeans, leaving thick streaks of scarlet paint. I'm already searching for the keys to his shitty car.

I have no concept of my own fear until I get to the hospital and they refuse to let me see him. Can't you at least tell me if he's okay? I ask, and the receptionist just repeats what she's already told me, that she'll let the doctor know I'm here. Why don't you take a seat, she says, eliminating the upswing at the end of her sentence to let me know that she's issuing a command and not making a suggestion.

I sit, combing my fingers up and down my jeans, realizing too late that the paint staining them looks an awful lot like blood. My mind immediately jumps to the accident, and though I don't know a thing about what happened, I create a cataclysmic scene before I can stop myself. Leaning forward, I hang my head between my knees. *This will not end the same way*, I think, and suddenly I'm in the middle of that bathroom, my knees hitting the ceramic tile. His arms around me, that word, *okay*, the only one I needed to hear.

When someone calls my name, I look up with what must be an expression of such pure terror that the doctor immediately sits down beside me. He's going to be fine, she says, and those words cause the ones that follow to blur. She gives me just a moment to catch up before she continues. Even though the airbag deployed, he has a couple of black eyes, a broken wrist, a cracked collarbone. A few of his ribs suffered substantial bruising. He has a concussion, a mild one, and they want to keep him overnight for observation. Please, I say, Just let me see him.

An hour later, I'm sinking into the chair beside his bed. He looks like he's been sucker punched, first in one eye and then the next. His left wrist's wrapped in a cast, his chest bare except for the tape around his ribs. I wrecked your car, he confesses the second he sees me. I don't give a shit about the car, I say. He turns his head in my direction, wincing at the movement. For a long moment he looks at me, his eyes little more than slits, and I know instantly what he's thinking. On an instinctive level he knows what I've just been through, knows what the past couple of hours have dredged up from the muck of my past, and even though he's the injured party, he's worried about the impact of his accident on my state of mind. I'm fine, I say, but he holds my gaze, and I'm struck once again not just by how thoroughly he understands me but by a loyalty so immutable I'm not sure anything could cause its dissolution. I'm awed and utterly ashamed of what I was fantasizing about this morning, and when he starts to apologize, I shake my head. Just rest, I tell him, and finally, he nods.

+   +   +

I stay with him until his parents arrive. I've made the call myself, given them a thorough recounting of what happened, and they insist on coming down with Ashley in tow. She's eleven now, almost twelve, with long, wavy hair that's darkened over the years to the exact same color as her brother's. She has a hopeless crush on me, one I indulge by buying whimsical trinkets for James to deliver to her when he makes the trip north. Maybe by the time I'm old enough to get married, she said the last time I saw her, You won't be gay anymore. You never know, I said, wanting to let her down gently.

Now his family rushes into James's hospital room with an urgency I can't imagine my father exhibiting if the circumstances were reversed. I step toward the door, reluctant to leave but recognizing my place, noticing at the same time the way Ashley hangs back. She looks every bit as scared as I felt five hours ago. Hey, beautiful, I say, slipping my arm around her, and she gives me a smile that misses the mark. I understand why; her mom's crying, and even though James has awakened enough to reassure them, he looks like he's been given a good, hard pummeling from which he might never recover. Honestly, Ashley, I say, tucking a strand of hair behind her ear, He looks way worse than he feels. She doesn't seem convinced, but I nod. I promise, I say, They're going to let him out tomorrow, and he'll probably race you to the car. She relaxes a little at the image, then confides, They'll probably take him down in a wheelchair. Then you're so going to win, I say, and now she giggles. I give her a wink, then nudge her toward the bed. If you don't at least say hello, I tell her, You'll never hear the end of it.

She moves forward, and I watch them for a minute, the four of them, marveling at their intimacy. Then I go home, where Darryl's waiting for me. He's an imposter, no one I want, and though he says all the right words, I have no desire to follow him into my bedroom. Darryl, I say, I think I need a night to myself. He tilts his head, assessing my confession to determine whether or not he should find it suspect. Please, I say, opening the front door, I'll talk to you tomorrow.

+   +   +

James fills me in on the accident the next night, staring at his side in the bathroom mirror, his skin tinged purple. His parents brought him home this afternoon and lingered into the evening, stocked the refrigerator with groceries and picked up prescriptions. I hung out with Ashley while they fussed over him, walked her up the street for ice cream when she reached a patience threshold for which I could hardly blame her. Do you know how much I like you? she said, winding her tongue around the cone I bought for her. She had a button of vanilla on the tip of her nose, and I wiped it off with my finger. How much? I asked, and she said, More than ice cream. That's a lot, I admitted. More than Christmas, she said, giving me a sly smile. Now you're getting crazy, I told her, and she grinned. Walking home, she took my hand in hers, and I let her, gazing down at her every so often. I wouldn't have wanted a sister of my own; I couldn't have handled the responsibility. But something about Ashley tugs me so sweetly, and when we reach the house and her parents tell me they're getting ready to head out, I'm almost sorry to see her leave.

Later that night, I'm suffused with gratitude. He's okay, he's home, and when Darryl calls, I tell him James just got back from the hospital and he's not up for visitors. I'm not calling for James, he informs me, and instead of fighting back, I hang up. Leaning in the doorway of the bathroom, I watch James stroke his ribs. He'd been driving north on the upper deck, he tells me, messing with the radio. I wasn't paying attention, he admits, grimacing as his fingers reach his collarbone. He'd looked up just in time to realize he was crossing over into the next lane. I jerked the steering wheel, he says, And slammed into the concrete barrier so hard I spun around just in time to get swiped by that Suburban. You remember all of this? I ask. With startling precision, he says. What the hell were you doing on the upper deck? I ask, and he catches my eye and then drops it. Just driving, he says.

The next day, I go to check out the BMW, James insistent on accompanying me. Approaching its mangled shell, I'm almost ill. Jesus, I say, You're lucky to be alive. He nods, a little dazed; I don't think he realized quite how close he came. I watch as he buckles his seatbelt one-handed, favoring his wrist, as he tongues the stitches at the edge of his lip. I can feel myself slowly sinking.

+ + +

By the time Darryl comes by that evening I've already made my decision. There's too much work involved here, too much to hide, and I allow him entry just long enough to see James. Damn, Darryl says, gaping at him, You really do look like shit. James gives him a rueful smile, like an unhappy prizefighter. I glance from one of them to the other, bracing myself for animosity given what happened the morning of James's accident. As if he knows what I'm thinking, Darryl steps behind me and slides his arms around my waist. The ploy's deliberate; I know that now. He curls his fingers possessively through mine, and I catch James's reaction, an abrupt aversion of the eyes. Before I can even extricate myself he's on his way back to his room, muttering something over his shoulder that I'm supposed to take for *good night*.

Worming out from under Darryl's arms, I shove him toward the front porch because there's no way I'm doing this with James on the other side of the living room wall. What's your problem? Darryl's saying, but I get him outside and shut the door behind us. Listen, I say, and he gives me an incredulous look, like he already knows where this is going.

He's a decent guy; he deserves better. But I just can't keep this up any longer, and I lower my voice, as if James might be holding his ear to the door. This isn't working, I say. *What's* not working? he says, I haven't even seen you the past couple of days! Darryl, I say, and he sneers so suddenly that I recoil. Don't fucking kid yourself, he says, I know what's really going on!

For just a second I feel the same panic I used to feel before I came out to James, when I thought he might have guessed. What're you talking about? I say. You think I don't *know*? he says, You think I don't see you *watching* each other? I shake my head, both in a gesture of denial and because I can't believe what I'm hearing, I can't believe he's figured out the truth, and what does he mean, what does he mean he sees us watching each other?

James is watching me?

Darryl takes a step closer; I don't think he's capable of hitting me, but adrenaline floods through me, my hands automatically forming fists. Fury twists his face into something almost unrecognizable. The thought that we could have ever touched each other with anything even masquerading as tenderness seems inconceivable. You can *have* each other, he snarls.

He stomps down the front steps, then peels away from the curb in a burst of exhaust that hangs heavy over the street and suffocates the pecans. I'm shaking, and I sink into the swing as if its gentle rocking might calibrate the pounding of my heart. Above everything, the anger that still thickens the air and the rush of hormones still spinning in my system from being *this close* to getting cuffed, I can't stop thinking about what Darryl claims to know, that there's something here and that it's not one-sided. I let my memory rest on James's expression in the living room a few minutes ago, in this very swing the week before last, then suck in my breath. Something's here, and with Darryl gone I've cleared the way. There's nothing to stop either one of us.

He's lying on his bed, propped on one elbow, protecting his good side, and I hold that picture of him when I throw open the door to his room: James, in this space I've seen so often over the past five years, this space where he sleeps and studies and jerks off. This space that has worked its way into my dreams since he came back from Greece last summer, this space with its makeshift bookshelves and battered desk and a low lamp we both swear will probably burn the house down someday because there's no way it's wired correctly, we've scalded ourselves too many times turning it off. He's here in this space, and I want to be here too, I want to brush away the thick locks of hair that fall into his eyes, slide his glasses from behind his ears and decide once and for all if what I think I saw reflected in his gaze on our porch was nothing more than an overactive imagination or wishful thinking. I want to lie down beside him, the radio set to KLBJ, and tell him what I've done. I want to be drunk and foolish and still see the morning with no regret.

I broke up with him, I blurt out, and something, the hint of invitation in my tone or the way I've burst into his room without consideration, widens his eyes. He pulls himself into a sitting position, his finger keeping his place in the book he was reading. Just now? he says. On the front porch, I say, and his expression slides slowly into a mask I'm suddenly terrified I won't be able to penetrate. *You can have him*, Darryl said, but now, standing here, I'm not so sure. Confusion deals me a good, hard blow, and I lower myself to the edge of the bed, noticing as I do the way James pulls his knees to his chest in a gesture of such true defensiveness I blink. At the very least he should be ecstatic that I've gotten rid of Darryl. At the very least he should be thrilled to have me at his disposal. Even if I've misinterpreted his motivation, he should be glad he's not in competition for my time.

You've been after me to dump him for months, I say.

He doesn't deny the accusation; he couldn't. But he's also not looking at me. Instead, he's staring at the book in his hand, and when he flicks his eyes in my direction, it's for the merest second, as if lingering any longer might burn them clean away. The slow dawn of comprehension comes over me, and with a foundering heart I realize that I didn't mistake what happened between us on the front porch. But maybe Darryl, instead of being the impediment to possibility the way I've assumed, allowed James to hold my gaze in a way he never would've risked if he thought for a second I'd take a chance. Now that Darryl's gone, I'm a threat and not a provocation.

If that's the case, I'm more of a fool than I thought.

I have to get back to work, he mumbles, but I wait until he raises his eyes, until he's looking right at me. Next time I have a boyfriend, James, I say, Keep your fucking mouth shut.

+ + +

For the next few weeks James dates one girl after another, a rapid succession of dinners and movies that depletes his checking account and leaves him looking more dissatisfied than I've ever seen him. You trying to prove something to me? I come right out and ask when I return from an early morning run and find a pony-tailed little thing slinking out the front door. What's that supposed to mean? he asks. Hey, I'm happy to see you finally getting some ass, I say, chugging from a bottle of Gatorade and wiping my mouth with the back of my hand, Scrawny though it may be. I happen to like her, James tells me, folding his arms across his chest. Yeah? I say, You going to call her again? I might, he mutters. Was it her quick wit that charmed you? I ask, Or does she just give really fantastic head? He grimaces in a way that tells me one of two things: she gives a shitty blowjob, or she can't be bothered at all. I'm instantly gratified. Knowing he had someone in his bedroom last night just about gutters me; at least I can take comfort in knowing that whatever action he's getting doesn't fulfill him.

I take a step closer; I know what I look like right now, the way I smell, the sheen of sweat on my arms because even at eight o'clock in the morning, a late summer run takes my breath away. Poor you, I say, locking my eyes on him and dropping my tone. He's a good inch shorter than I am, a negligible amount, but I can't help but relish that at this moment I'm looking down at him. I can play this game better than he can; I've had too much practice, and he's too agitated from the night he just endured or because of the way I'm toying with him. He holds still when I lean toward his ear, but he won't look me in the eye. I have to admit, I almost lose my nerve. Did she suck you off? I ask, lowering my voice even more, Or did she not even try? None of your fucking business, he mumbles, and I smile. What do you do with him, Joel? I whisper, D'you suck any dick while you were in Europe?

That gets him. He looks at me from the corner of his eye; I swear I can sense a change in his breathing. I have half a mind to hold my palm in front of his lips just so I can feel his breath on my skin. Why do you want to know so much? I ask. You're the one who's grilling me about Twila, he says. *Twila*? I say, Her name's *Twila*? Shut up, he mutters, but I'm already snorting with laughter. Are you sure you didn't have to pay her? I ask. She wasn't *that* bad, he tries to tell me, and I say, Not exactly an endorsement. You've fucked plenty of questionable guys, he reminds me. And we're right back where we started, I say, With you wanting the details.

I choose this moment to walk away from him. He'll call me back, I think as I head into the shower. He'll call me back because he'll never accept the way I've called him out. But he doesn't say a word, and when I get out of the bathroom, he's nowhere to be found, his car absent from the curb, his wallet forgotten on the counter. He shouldn't be driving yet, not with that cast on his arm; if anything happens to him, I'll never forgive myself.

But after five minutes of guilt and self-doubt I give up. I can't spend the entire morning worrying about him, and anyway, he started this shit. I could've continued to quietly admire him from afar, but he had to start feeding me queer theory. He had to stare into my eyes on the front porch like the only thing he was waiting for was an indication. And now I'm being punished? Now I have to sit back and watch while he screws every girl he can scrounge up just to make a point? Well, fuck that.

I call Kyle. What're we doing today? I ask, and he groans, whining when I tell him to shut up and get his ass out of bed. We have plans.

+ + +

I'm sky high. I should know better; Ecstasy winds me up and then dumps me a few hours later. But right now I'm still thick in its thrall, and I creep up the back steps, giggling through the finger I hold to my lips. Shh, I say to the guy holding my hand, what's his name? Terrance? Thomas, maybe. Thomas, I say, testing it out, and he grins, backing me up against the screen door. He's a friend of a friend of a friend, or something like that. I saw him on the dock before we left Kyle's, and now he's here. How did we get here? I still haven't replaced the BMW. Thomas must have driven us. That's right; Thomas drove us, because I went down on him in his car, the gum I'd been chewing tucked under my tongue. Easy, he groaned, Easy.

I have a swimmy recollection of the evening: the sun setting on the water, a shot or two of tequila I probably shouldn't have drunk. Kyle roped me in. This is the wrong crowd, honey, he said, pulling me away from that guy in the black trunks, the one with the scar running from his knee into the leg of his shorts. How'd you get this? I asked. Water skiing, he said, and I knelt down in front of him and slid my fingers to the scar's tip. I was ready to take him in my mouth right there, his hand was already on the back of my neck, but Kyle yanked me away from him and coaxed me up the stairs to his condo. Wrong crowd, he said, the half a dozen guys who'd shown up an hour after I slipped that blue pill between my lips, the guy in the black trunks and his friends, and when I looked over my shoulder as I followed Kyle, they were watching me, silent, a mass of sexual tension.

We were supposed to go dancing, Kyle gave me the E, he'd given me the E on his boat and we were supposed to go dancing and then we never made it out the door. Or off the dock. Or whatever. He didn't want me to leave. He wouldn't let me leave and then I don't know how it happened, we were in Thomas's car and I was sucking Thomas's cock. Now I twist the doorknob and Thomas turns me around, planting his feet on either side of mine. Are you ready? he says, and I grin.

We make it halfway through the living room before James appears in front of us. James and I haven't spoken since this morning when I walked away from him, and I'm suddenly overcome by a wave of compassion. He doesn't know what he's doing, he just doesn't know what he's doing, and I can make this better. Hey, I say, Hey. I take a couple of steps toward him and I'm touching his jaw, his stubble rough beneath my fingertips, my mouth so close and then he's jerking away from me. What're you *doing*? he asks. Hey, hey, I say, We're okay here, we're okay. I reach for his hand. We're okay, I say, and he yanks away from me. *Jesus*, Joel, he says.

Thomas and I are lying on my bed and his mouth feels good. His tongue slides along my neck, around my nipple, and I like that but he's doing nothing for me. I'm not even hard, I can tell I'm not hard, but I reach between my legs and wrap my fingers around my dick. Let me do that, Thomas says, and so I watch his hand on me as I lift my arms above my head and grab onto the back of the mattress. Something's playing on the radio, some music I don't recognize, something beautiful, and I watch Thomas and I could fall in love with him. He wears a halo of gold, and his eyes look into mine, and I know this is just the Ecstasy talking but he's good, he's so good, he's trying to make me feel so good.

And then he's giving up because there's no way I'm getting hard, but he's a rock and a couple of books crash to the floor, loud enough for James to hear, but he doesn't come in, doesn't knock, and I remember, now I remember seeing him, he's home. He knows I'm in here with someone, someone not him, and I wish, I wish and that's it, then I'm hard and Thomas lifts my legs onto his shoulders and I close my eyes.

+ + +

Morning finds me alone, facedown on my bed, my mouth a desert and my memory a wasteland. I'm twisted in the sheet, and I thrash around until I kick it off, onto the floor with the rest of the bedding. My head throbs, and I squint against the light stealing through the blinds. Leaning over, I reach for the top drawer of the nightstand, then find it open. That means condoms; that's a good sign, and I hang over the edge of the bed, a position which worsens my headache but allows me to grip the edge of the trashcan and tilt it in my direction. Two wrappers, which means either that he fucked me more than once or the first one broke. I have no recollection of either.

I sit on the edge of the bed, getting my bearings. I really should've known better. Ecstasy rocks my world for about four hours, but I suffer the aftereffects more than anyone I know. Every time, I get a bitch of a headache. Every time, I spend the following week in a stupor that borders on downright despair. I run my hands through my hair, my tongue skimming my front teeth. A shower, I think, but when I go into the bathroom, it's all I can do to brush my teeth. I'm tempted to crawl back in bed, but it hardly looks inviting, stripped down to the bottom sheet, the blankets in a heap on the floor.

As I walk down the hallway, the wood creaks, announcing my arrival before James catches sight of me, though when he does, he merely raises his eyebrows, then goes right back to staring at the television. I have a feeling he's not really watching, and I grunt, trudging over to the refrigerator with grim pessimism. I need juice or Gatorade, something to wash the taste from my mouth, but there's not a damn thing in front of me, and I shut the door a little too hard. He doesn't look over; he still hasn't said a word. I decide to take a chance. You want to get something to eat? I ask. I'm not hungry, he says without taking his eyes from the television.

That may be the first time he's turned down free food. Fuck. Without a car I'm either going to need to walk somewhere myself in this goddamn heat or I'm going to have to ingratiate myself enough that he hands over his keys. I look over at him sitting all hunched in front of the television in an old tee shirt and shorts frayed around the edges. He's so fucking hot it hurts. I just want to sit down next to him and tell him how ridiculous this is, this back and forth bullshit. He's all disheveled and rumpled, and he hasn't shaved in days—

Oh *shit*.

I did a little E last night, I blurt out. Yeah, he says, I figured. I rub my hand across my own jaw, then gaze down at my fingers like they hold a secret; I can't believe I've touched him. When I look back up, he's shaking his head. Why'd you take that shit, Joel? he asks, It fucks you over every time. I know, I say, gouging my temples with the heels of my hands, I know, we were supposed to go dancing— And instead you brought that asshole here, he finishes flatly. You're *jealous*, I say. Go fuck yourself, he snaps.

I don't deserve this. The night before last, he nailed some skank, and now he's acting like I cheated on him. What am I supposed to do, hold myself to a vow of chastity in case he gets drunk at some point and decides he wants to experiment? The thought sobers me, not that the E hasn't already dropped me from a high altitude. There might be something here, and he's not willing to examine it. Well, I'm done. He can fuck all the girls he wants. I'm not going to stand in his way.

And he better not stand in mine.

+ + +

The next few days I spend wallowing in a pit of misery, partly because James won't look me in the eye and partly because I'm still suffering the aftereffects of Kyle's party. Why'd you give me that shit? I whine when Kyle calls to find out what the hell happened to me, and he says, Honey, you were out of *control*. Not until you slipped me that pill, I remind him. You practically pried it from my fingers, he protests, and I say, Well, you told me we were going dancing! Honey, he says, You were looking for an escape. I groan. You know what, Kyle? I say, I have a raging headache, and I'm depressed as shit, and if you're going to be cryptic— You want me to speak my mind? he says, Because I can tell you exactly what I think about this obsession of yours. What obsession? I ask. Please, he says, I could see this coming from the first night I met him.

Jesus, how transparent have I been the past year? Peter, Darryl, Kyle… It's a good goddamn thing I don't play poker. What're you doing, Joel? Kyle says, Why are you doing this to yourself? I'm not doing anything! I say, I can't help the way I fucking feel. This will not end well, he tells me. Thanks for the vote of confidence, I mutter, and he says, Well, I'm certainly not going to pretend like you have a chance.

I know I don't have a chance. That's why I don't want to eat, why I don't want to sleep. I don't even want to paint, and as the next weekend approaches, the weekend that I've finally agreed to meet my father's fiancée, I start to realize that this impending marriage might be exacerbating the situation. I haven't let myself think about what my father's remarriage says about his relationship with my mother or the years they spent together. They weren't necessarily happy; this much I know. But my parents shared a span of time together, a time that included my childhood, and I can't help feeling as if my father's remarriage negates everything that came before. He's moving on, and while I can't fault him the timeline—despite my initial reaction, I know that the four years since my mother's death have likely been lonely ones for him—I can't help feeling cast aside.

I also haven't allowed myself to think about what might happen to my financial situation after my father's remarriage. Our agreement ends this December whether I'm ready to strike out on my own or not. But I've suffered for years at my father's hands, and there's no way I'm going to let his new wife push me aside. I have every right to claim what's mine, and I leave Austin with a brusque goodbye to James and fly to Houston determined to make that clear to both of them.

My father and Catherine greet me at the front door before I can even extract my key, and I'm so stunned by Catherine's presence—I'd assumed I'd meet her later in the evening—that I let her draw me inside without protest. I thought I'd have time alone in the house, time to linger over what's left of my mother's presence, time to collect myself. But I realize as I take a quick look around the living room that I'm too late. Catherine's already moved in. What made this house my mother's has disappeared, and I have a feeling that if I ask my father where her possessions have been stored, he'll tell me they're gone for good. I'm terribly hurt that I haven't been told and further discomfited by Catherine's radiance. I'd wondered who my father might choose in my mother's absence, and Catherine stands before me cloaked in an emerald shift and bejeweled heels, honey-colored hair spilling over shoulders obviously carved from daily sessions with a personal trainer. She has none of the understatement my mother possessed, and I accept the scotch she offers with tears in my eyes.

By the time we're ready to leave for dinner a scream hovers behind my lips. Why haven't you gotten around to replacing that BMW? my father asks, taking Catherine's hand. The diamond on her finger catches the late evening sun, piercing the roof of the car with a hot, white light, and I'm too busy clamping down on my tongue to answer him. I hate him for touching her, hate her for even being here.

The next morning, I sit at the kitchen table, my hand wrapped around a thick mug of coffee, trying to nurse a well-deserved hangover. I'd guzzled my way through two stiff drinks the night before, then knocked back a bottle of wine mostly on my own. My father hadn't said a word; I think he managed to delude himself into thinking we were celebrating their upcoming nuptials. They chattered so much between the two of them that I don't think they even noticed my silence, and when we got back to the house and I bid them an early good night, they both smiled as if we'd all shared a companionable evening.

Now he tells us he plans on going into the office for a while. Today? I groan, not wanting to be left alone with his fiancée, and he sets his expression in a way I know too well. I have some work to do, he says, keeping his tone even, And Catherine thought the two of you could get to know each other.

I have no desire to spend quality time with Catherine. But at this point I'm not sure I have a choice, not with my father waiting for my response and Catherine looking so saddened by the vehemence of my reaction. I was just going to hang out by the pool, I mumble, but she brightens. That's fine, Joel, she says, I just want to spend time with you.

She's got to have some kind of agenda. She must be aware of the multitude of ways in which I've disappointed my father over the years, probably knows about the arrangement we have, the money he deposits in my account every month; she can't possibly approve. The best I can expect might be a speech about how she's not here to take my mother's place.

If that's the case, I'm out of here.

I go upstairs to change into my swimming trunks, then trudge back down to the pool, where Catherine beams at me. Have a seat, she offers, gesturing toward the lounge chair next to hers. She's wearing sunglasses, but as soon as I sit down, she pulls them on top of her head as if she wants to be sure I can see her eyes. Her skin's the color of true cream, a direct contrast to her sapphire bathing suit and sarong, and the pink polish adorning her toes. I discovered last night that she has an empire of her own, a clothing boutique near The Village, one that earns a substantial enough income to preclude her from caring about the cash my father gives me. I don't feel the wellspring of relief I expected. Instead, something teases the back of my mind like a word on the tip of my tongue.

I have lemonade, she offers, inclining her head toward a pitcher on the table behind us. Spiked? I ask, and she laughs. I thought you might want something a little less abrasive, she says, After last night.

My eyes narrow. I'm going to get a lecture about how much I drank? Is she fucking kidding? She seems to realize that she's already said something wrong, and for a while we sit in silence, listening to the quiet lapping of the pool. Must be strange, she finally ventures, Meeting me. I don't say anything. I must have come as a surprise, she adds. I shrug, and she looks me in the eye. I want you to know, she says, I was in favor of telling you sooner.

Is that supposed to make me feel better? Am I supposed to thank her? *She's erasing my mother.*

I thought giving you some time to get used to the idea might be less volatile, she continues, But Edward... She trails off. I have no idea how she expects me to respond. Does she want the truth? Does she want to know that my father kept the news to himself because he thrives on a good power trip? That nothing satisfied him more than making his announcement, knowing the blow he was dealing me? He's a fucking control freak, and like a junkie, he'll get it any way he can.

The way she's watching me, I worry I might have spoken aloud. A thin line of sweat worms into my tee shirt, and I wipe the back of my arm across my forehead. I'm starting to regret not taking her up on her offer of lemonade. The humidity's oppressive; my heart rate has ratcheted up a notch in the ten minutes I've been sitting here. I need to submerge myself in that pool, and in preparation I plant my feet on either side of the chair.

He cares about you, Joel, Catherine says, and I turn to her in disbelief. Is she honestly going to try to make the argument my mother made all those years ago? She has no right, knows nothing. I'm the one who endured those years, not her. My father hasn't revealed himself to her, not fully, not truly. She's working with an illusion, and though there's a part of me that feels sorry she's been fooled, I'm not about to let a fledgling sympathy bully its way into making me listen to this shit.

But before I can say a word she's pressing a manicured hand to my arm. I'm sorry, Joel, she says, I so wanted us to get off on the right foot. Then you should probably stop talking about my father, I say, and she grins as if nothing I could've said would have delighted her more. That's the most direct you've been with me since you arrived, she says. Yeah? I mutter, Well, there's more where that came from. She actually claps her hands. Don't tease me, she says, Tell me what you're thinking.

I stare at the azaleas bordering the pool. Though they're not in bloom, they haunt me anyway. Shaking my head, I reach behind me for the lemonade. Catherine watches as I pour myself a glass, then take a long swallow that does nothing to quench my thirst. I'm going for a swim, I mumble.

I can feel her watching me as I strip off my tee shirt and make my way to the diving board. Toes on the edge, I pause, gazing into the tranquil blue. Then I dive, breaking the surface, clean and smooth. The tips of my fingers skirt the bottom, and I propel myself to the far side of the pool, then flip and head back toward the deep end. I'm a strong swimmer, even now, even though I didn't get to the pool much this past summer, and I cut through the water a dozen times before I hear her splash alongside me.

I have to hand it to my father; he has impeccable taste. Catherine's hair, slicked back from her head, highlights the delicate bones in her cheeks, her azure eyes, lips that part in such an arresting smile that for just a second I want to smile back.

I manage to restrain myself.

You're a good swimmer, she tells me. I shrug, and she rolls her eyes with just the right amount of *savoir faire*. I swam in college, she offers. When'd you graduate again? I ask, and she laughs. You're kind of a smart ass, she tells me. My father didn't warn you? I say.

She disappears beneath the surface, and I watch her do a handstand, toes pointed. The gesture's so whimsical, so playful, that I can't for the life of me figure out what my father's doing with her. Or rather, what she's doing with my father given the presumed state of her own financial affairs. How did you meet him? I ask when she reappears. You don't know? she asks, sliding her fingers through her hair, and I shake my head. To be honest, I haven't wanted to know. I haven't wanted to hear anything about them. But now I realize that I need to understand what happened, and I listen as she tells me that my father walked into her shop one afternoon to pick up a token for his assistant. I don't volunteer the information that he was probably sleeping with the woman, but Catherine's smart enough to guess what I'm thinking. She's ready to retire, she confides, a glint of humor in her eye, Not exactly your father's type. She describes their courtship, the weeks my father spent wooing her, the day she gave in because she just couldn't resist him any longer. He was sweet and chivalrous, she says, and I'm horrified by what I know has to be a serious case of delusion or a misinterpretation on my part of all the years I've known him.

I think I've upset you, she says with something that sounds like real regret. I shrug, though I'm not fooling anyone. I've never heard anyone refer to my father as *sweet*, I tell her, and she smiles so gently that I'm suddenly wistful, though for what I can't imagine. You've both had a long four years, she says, and I don't know whether to nod in relieved agreement or let myself feel the incredible rush of anger just beneath the surface of my skin. What right does she have to even allude to my mother?

Instead of confronting either emotion, I duck back under the water. I catch a glimpse of her on my return lap when I come up for air. She's hesitating, trying to decide whether she should wait until I settle down or get out of the pool entirely. I think she surprises us both by joining me.

Her strokes are a startling contrast to the frenzied intensity of my own. My heart's flying, and so am I, chased by a thousand memories I don't want to examine. Every lap gives me greater distance between myself and what I'm trying to avoid: my mother, my father, our tortured past. Catherine and her compassion, which I hadn't expected and frankly, don't want. I'd rather have a wicked stepmother, someone cold and condescending, not this woman who's already killing me with confusion. I want to leave them all behind, and I swim until I can't take anymore, until even Catherine, who clearly spends hours every day at the gym, can't keep up. I swim until my lungs feel like they're going to burst, and then I push myself even further.

By the time I stop, I'm seeing stars, and I hang on to the side, catching my breath as Catherine glides up next to me. That was beautiful! she says, You just plowed through everything! So you're going to be my stepmother *and* my shrink, I gasp. Lucky you, she agrees. She rests her chin on her hands, which she crosses on the lip of the pool. My eye catches her engagement ring, and she sees me watching, then touches my arm. What do you want from me? I say, but my tone holds none of the animosity I should feel. I'm too wiped out, and I run my hand through my hair, which I'm still weeks away from being able to pull into a legitimate ponytail. I guess, she says, I want you to give us a chance.

I don't know what she means. Is she talking about the two of us? Does she mean her and my father? Surely she's not talking about the *three* of us; surely she's not imagining that we could be some kind of family, however dysfunctional. That's not possible. That's just not possible.

But before I can clarify, her pretty brow furrows. Joel, she says, What happened to your arms?

I hid the scars for years: from my mother, from the girls I dated. When I started sleeping with men, I was quick to make a joke before the subject came up. Scattergun, I'd say, Got too close to a rattlesnake and my buddy freaked. A few of them have been gullible enough to believe me, and the ones who didn't, knew better than to press. Only James knows the truth, and even then, I managed to keep my secret for years. We lived together in the same dorm room. We swam together in the summer, dove into the sea in Cancun. He never suspected a thing.

They're hard to see, for one thing, hidden on the underside of my arm. And I took pains to keep them that way, shunning sleeveless shirts, stripping in front of no one without a ready explanation or water to shelter me. But I'm so tired right now that I'm clinging to the edge of the pool without thinking, exposing myself in the process.

Joel, she says, infusing my name with a tone so maternal everything occurs to me at once, in a spectacular explosion of fear and grief. I've been so busy worrying over what I stand to lose financially because of my father's relationship with this woman, so busy lamenting the eradication of my mother, that I never gave a thought to the one possibility that should frighten me the most.

Honey? she says, What's wrong?

I don't wait around to tell her. Without a word I hoist myself over the side of the pool. Joel? she's saying, but I'm already gone.

+ + +

What did you do? my father hisses, covering his phone with the palm of one hand the second I step into his office. I have a feeling Catherine's on the other end; normally, I'd be crushed by the way he's automatically thrown his allegiance in her direction. But I'm too consumed with what I've figured out, and I step forward with a resolve I don't usually possess in his presence. He glowers at me from across his desk, no doubt listening to his fiancée tell him that I took the keys to her Audi right from her handbag. I'd made it to his office in record time, threw a fit when the security guard refused me entry. Just *call* him, I insisted, and as pleased as my father seemed at first to hear that I'd paid him an unexpected visit, the time it took for me to travel twenty-six floors and Catherine to contact him has changed his mind.

I need to talk to you, I say, but he makes no move to end his call. Instead, he's pointing at the chair across from his desk as if I'm six years old and he's on the verge of beating the shit out of me if I don't obey. *Now*, I say, and my tone actually convinces him to hang up. You have my attention, Joel, he says, What's the problem? Is she going to have children? I ask. Who? he says. Catherine, I say, Is she going to have children?

He stares at me, the groove between his eyebrows deepening. *Tell me*, I say, and for a moment longer he looks confused. Then his expression changes, and he stares at me with a repugnance he makes no attempt to disguise. I should've known, he says.

Oh my god, he thinks I'm talking about the money. He thinks I'm here to protect my share. I don't care about the *money*, I say, and he laughs as if he knows me far better than that. For just a second I doubt myself; after all, I came to Houston determined to secure my future. But then I remember that moment in the pool less than thirty minutes ago, the cadence of my name in her mouth. I don't care about the money, I repeat. No? my father says, Then why are you here?

But I don't have to say a word. My father's an astute man, and if I'm not here because of the money, then I must be here because of what he did to me and what I fear he could do to someone else. He doesn't need more than a second or two of silence to understand what I haven't said, and the truth widens his eyes before he succumbs to a fury so well-anticipated I'm already backing toward the door. How *dare* you? he says, How dare you *accuse* me?

I'm not here. I'm suddenly somewhere else, in another office, in another time. Everything's grainy, like an antique photograph, fear a snake coiled in the pit of my stomach. I'm on the verge of a catastrophic memory, and I hover on the edge, ready to prostrate myself, on the cusp of giving in.

Then I throw up. Wrenched from the past, I stagger forward. The floor rises to meet me.

+ + +

I'm lying on the sofa in my father's living room, tonguing the line of stitches on my bottom lip. I'm a little out of it. My head still feels thick, like I've just returned from a faraway land but left my soul behind. The narcotics don't help. My father gave them to me himself from his own ample stash, and I've chased them with wine from the bottle my father has opened despite Catherine's protestations. She's sitting beside me in a flowered armchair that would've made my mother cringe. Can I get you anything? she asks for what must be the hundredth time since my father and I returned from the emergency room. No, I say, Thank you.

I want to go home. But I can't; even I can see that I'm not capable of boarding a plane, regardless of whether or not James picks me up on the other end. I could rent a car if I could find someone stupid enough to hand me the keys. The thought makes me snicker, and both Catherine and my father, who's pacing back and forth in front of a television no one watches, exchange glances. Then Catherine gives me an indulgent smile. She'd make a good mother, I think, which I find ironic. She'll never be one.

My father told me himself after I scrambled into a sitting position in his office, blood dripping from my mouth. I'd busted my lip hard enough to split through my skin. Don't touch me, I managed to choke out, but he tilted my head to the side. You'll need stitches, he said, getting to his feet and handing me a wad of tissues. Vomit clung to the front of my shirt, and without a word my father opened the credenza beside his desk and handed me a fresh one. He had the decency to look away while I changed. I don't want children, he said while his back was still turned, so quietly I might not have heard him, and I closed my eyes. I've suspected that all my life. I can't imagine why I thought Catherine could convince him otherwise.

Joel? Catherine says, Can I get you something to eat? She's wearing a pink tee shirt, her hair scooped back in a loose ponytail. Under different circumstances I might have liked her. But she's sitting where my mother should be, and that's not something I can get past. There's so much in my life I just can't get past.

I'm not hungry, I mumble, touching my lip. My reflection in the bathroom mirror a little while ago told me that my mouth looks like something in progress, something Dr. Frankenstein himself might be assembling. I catch my father's eye across the room. Are you still working? I ask, and he frowns. I start to giggle, amusement bubbling in my chest like a bottle of champagne I should've known better than to shake. I could easily get myself in trouble or incriminate my father; I've seen the glances Catherine keeps darting his way. I don't know what he's confessed so far, but it certainly wasn't the truth. The pitying look she gave me after they snatched a few moments alone when we first got back from the hospital clued me in. For all I know he's told her that I burn myself and that he's done everything he can to stop me.

Maybe you should get some sleep, Joel, Catherine says. Maybe, I agree, but the thought of dragging my ass upstairs to a bedroom that's no longer mine doesn't induce me to stand. Instead, I let myself melt into the sofa.

Something's ringing, and my eyes finally focus on the cell phone Catherine's pressing into my hand. Hello? I say, pulling on the word. Joel? James says, and the sound of his voice fills my eyes with tears. I bury my head in my hands without thinking, then realize too late what I'm doing. But when I look up, my father and Catherine have judiciously left the room, and realizing I'm alone, I fold myself over my lap and cry. He's called, he's called to check in on me despite the past few weeks. What's wrong? he asks, but the pain killers, the tranquilizers and wine, have my tongue so twisted I can't begin to untangle it. I don't know that I want to. I don't know what I might say.

Joel, James says, and I think in my inebriated state that he sounds the way I must have sounded when they wouldn't let me see him at the hospital last month. I don't want him to have to endure what I went through. I don't want to hurt him. I want him here, next to me. I want him to be the one, not the one on the phone, but the one beside me. You're..., I whisper, You're... What? he says, What? I cover my eyes with my hand. Stars spin behind them in a brilliant mosaic of color. I chase them to the croon of his voice. *Take me home*, I think, but he doesn't hear me. I'm there with him; I'm in my bedroom. I can hear the creak of his boots on the hardwoods. There's a paintbrush in my hand. Joel, he says, I'm calling 911.

That pulls me back. Through time and space I fall into a body I can't escape, into scars that define me. My mouth throbs. Don't, I manage. Are you sure? he asks, and I nod, forgetting that he can't see me. Yes, I say. Then talk to me, he says, What the fuck is going on down there?

I take a long inhale, then shudder it back out. Cocking my head, I listen for my father; I don't want to be overheard, and I wonder if I can get to my feet and make my way to a safe place. Swinging my legs over the side of the sofa feels like a blow to the head. I can't, I whisper. You're going to have to tell me *something*, Joel, he says, and I cast around for the water Catherine brought me earlier and take a dribbling sip. I was worried, I confess, I was worried she'd get pregnant. Catherine's pregnant? he asks. No, I say. Are you drunk? he asks. Vicodin and Xanax, I say, And wine I probably shouldn't have touched. But why? he says.

I keep it simple. My father and I had an argument. I tripped. I busted the shit out of my lip when I hit the ground and had to get stitches. When we got back to the house, my father broke open the medicine cabinet as if he might be the neighborhood supplier. I took too many pills because I wanted to kill the moment.

By the time I finish telling him my abridged version of the day's events I've almost managed to convince myself that I might have overdramatized the situation. But I'm trembling, my hands shaking so violently I wouldn't be able to write my name if someone handed me a pen. I want to come home, I tell him, and he says, I'll be there as soon as I can.

+ + +

I leave in the middle of the night. James loads my bag in the back of his piece of shit car; I'm surprised he made it all the way from Austin without incident. My father and Catherine will find out I'm gone in the morning. I've scrawled a barely legible note that I've left on the table beside the front door: *Back to Austin with James.*

Looks like you got cuffed with a hard right, James says, glancing over at me as he puts the car in reverse. Tripped, I say, and he nods. That's what you said, he agrees without challenging me. He pulls out of my father's driveway, leaving the house behind. I lean my head back, into a seat duct-taped into submission. His car smells like a cigarette freshly lit, and I watch as he lights one for me, the press of his lips, the brush of his fingers against mine when he hands it over. I inhale from the good side of my mouth the way I'd take a hit from a bong, letting the smoke travel into my lungs. He lights a cigarette of his own, his wrist still in that cast, and cracks the window. Soft and innocuous, the radio soothes the silence. You want to talk about it? he asks. No, I say. He flicks a trail of ash into the wind. All right, he says.

I might never have him. I might never know what it's like to kiss him, to touch him, to slide my fingers underneath his shirt. My hand might never unzip his jeans. But he knows who I am, and he never asks me to apologize. I've never known such blind acceptance, such unremitting loyalty. I'm not sure I'm worthy, but my god, the way I feel in this moment, breathing the very air he exhales; I will never ask for anything else. I love you, I say, because I mean the words, I mean them honestly, and he flips me the quickest of smiles. I love you, too, man, he says.

Jennifer Hritz

3

I'm determined to be satisfied with what we have: a friendship unlike any I've imagined. If we're never anything more, I'll survive. I've had a taste now of what it's like to not have James in my life; the past three weeks have shown me that pit of emptiness, and at this point I'm willing to settle. I don't know how I'm going to handle the fact that the object of my desire is also my greatest friend. But I make up my mind that I'm going to try.

James thwarts my every intention. Since we've come back from Houston, he hasn't left my side, as if he blames himself for the argument I had with my father, the lip I split as a result. He wants my time, my attention, my Saturday nights. I'll go wherever you want, he tells me so casually that I'm never sure what he means. We end up accepting every invitation we're offered, incapable of saying no. A party one night, a club the next; he follows me around, and I have no idea how to introduce him. The nights we stay home, we fidget through countless hours of television, making a concerted effort not to look at each other, then head toward separate bedrooms before he holds me back. A look, a laugh, a lean of his head against the doorjamb, and then I'm lingering, backed up against the wall opposite his bedroom, denied entry but teased into thinking I have a chance. He has to know what he's doing to me, I think. How can he not see what this does to me? Light low, voices hushed, until the moment he comes to his senses. I should get to bed, he always says.

I. Never *we.*

I buy a new car at the end of September, another Explorer James selects himself. I like the upgraded model, he confides, In red. We go out the night I take delivery, meet up with Peter and his girlfriend, Kyle, a few others. We're an unlikely group, and we slide into a semi-circular booth, order Mexican martinis, and smoke one priceless cigarette after another. I sit between James and Kyle, listening to the two of them argue about whether we should give this place an hour, then try a different bar. Do you let him go *anywhere* without you? Kyle asks. James gives him the finger, his wrist fresh from his cast. Cock block, Kyle snaps back.

Later, I'm crushed between James and Amy, Peter's girlfriend, who keeps trying to read my palm. She holds my hand in hers, tracing lines with the tip of her finger. You don't really believe this shit, do you? James asks her, slinging his arm around my shoulders. I don't hear her response, caught as I am with the weight of his leg against mine, his mouth mere inches from my own. She taps the edge of my wrist, says something about creativity, metamorphosis. No shit, James drawls, a salt crystal clinging to his lips. For a moment, just one, I wonder what would happen if I gave myself leave to brush it away, with my finger, my tongue.

By midnight I'm a little drunk, and James has stayed close at my heels. He's disappeared down the back hallway into the restroom, and I move my martini glass in slow, obsessive circles, waiting for his return. I have Kyle to my right again when he suddenly looks past me. Well, hey there, he says as a friend of his approaches.

B.J. settles in beside me, and by the time James makes his way back to the table the entire lot of us is listening to a story, in a Scottish accent that I'd probably find irresistible under any other circumstances, about some trip across country B.J. made as a roadie for Phish. James lingers, annoyed, at the end of the booth where B.J. is sitting, then gives up and slides in on the opposite side. B.J. gives him a quick look, makes the mistake of failing to introduce himself. James hunches over his glass, a faint flush creeping into his cheeks. From the corner of my eye I see Peter and Amy exchange glances and hear Kyle mutter something I can't quite catch.

Thirty minutes later, B.J. slides his arm along the booth behind my shoulders. I manage to hold his eyes for full seconds before they flick back to James, who's chain-smoking. He's finished off one pack, and he opens another, tearing the little strip of foil from the packet and rolling it between his fingers. He's barely spoken since his return to the table, and when B.J. finally leans over and asks if he can bum a cigarette, James's voice leaves his mouth as scratched as an old vinyl. Be my guest, he says, relinquishing the pack and clearing his throat. He lights a match and holds it to B.J.'s cigarette, then watches, squinting, as the flame licks its way toward his fingers. He doesn't take his eyes from the fire, shakes his hand just before the flame reaches his skin. So B.J., he says, lighting a cigarette of his own and exhaling a great cloud of smoke, Is that a nickname or a blanket invitation?

I'm not the only one to recoil from the hostility in his tone. B.J. sizes him up, decides to be polite. That depends, he says, On who's asking. He glances in my direction, then back at James. Are you asking? he says. James snorts. He's saving himself, Kyle mumbles beside me, and James flushes. I can't look at any of them.

What am I supposed to do with you? Kyle murmurs in my ear a few minutes later as B.J. says his goodbyes. Kyle, I warn when he glances across the table at James. Don't fuck with me, James snaps before Kyle can get started, and Kyle raises eyebrows I swear he has shaped. I place my hands on the table. Can you drive? I ask James, and he nods. I hand him my keys. We leave without looking back.

+ + +

Somehow we manage to be completely anti-social. I don't want to see the same awkward glances from Peter, don't want to defend myself to Kyle, don't want to waste my time trying to hook up with someone when the only one I want sleeps ten feet from my bedroom door. We skip parties, bow out of dinners, manufacture excuses as to why we can't play ball. James insists that he's busy with school; I tell Kyle I'm painting, trying to get my work out there. Uh-huh, he says, letting me lie, and I use the space to concentrate on the one I love.

James's birthday falls on a Saturday a week before Halloween. I take him to dinner, but he's oddly maudlin, and the bottle of wine I've ordered only makes him more morose. You're twenty-five, I remind him, frustrated by his mood, Not fifty. He trails out to the Explorer, where he informs me that he's not sure he wants to go home, but he's really not up for much else. Your call, I tell him, and he shoves his hands in the pockets of his coat, the one I gave him earlier today because he's been wearing the same piece of shit since freshman year. At least, that was my excuse when I saw the coat one afternoon last week when I was shopping for the weather I knew would be heading our way soon. In reality I just wanted to see him in that jacket.

The color got to me first, a color fitting for army fatigues, circa 1972. When I opened the zipper, I did so with reverence, as if I might find his warm body inside. Instead, I saw a fleece lining wholly inappropriate for mild Austin winters. I bought the coat anyway, and he surprised me tonight by reaching for it as we headed out the door. Sixty degrees, man, I said, but he just shrugged.

Let's get a bottle of wine, he says now, And go to Zilker.

We run by the house to pick up the wine, then head to Zilker Park, where we hike past the playground and follow the train tracks to the tunnel under Barton Springs Road. Every time a car passes overhead, the wood shudders. This is a hell of a place to celebrate your birthday, I tell him, passing him the corkscrew and hunkering down against the wall. He eases the cork from the bottle and takes the first swig leaning against the fence overlooking the water. And a hell of a way to drink a Cakebread, I mutter.

Under cover of the tunnel we have some shelter from the wind, but thick strands of hair still blow across my face. I finally broke down last month and had the ends trimmed, but I'm determined to grow my hair long. My bangs I can tuck behind my ears, but only for seconds at a time before they swing forward. Now I sweep them back and take the bottle from James. The wine's cool, but my body warms with the first swallow. So, I say conversationally, handing the bottle back, Why are you in such a goddamn funk? He squints into the dark without answering, and with my eyes I trace his profile, the shape of his mouth as he lifts the bottle to his lips. I'll have to remind him to keep pace; he has work tomorrow—he always has work—and the last thing he needs is a hangover. He takes another sip, then hands me the bottle. Elisa called, he says.

For a brief, hysterical moment I'm afraid he's going to tell me that she lied all those years ago, that she never had the abortion and James has a son. But he just shakes his head, looking grim. She sounds good, he says, picking splinters from the railing and prying them apart, Grounded. And you're pissed, I conclude.

He doesn't say anything, but I know what he's thinking, that she obviously doesn't have a hard time reconciling herself to what happened. I don't point out that he's making assumptions, because I can't imagine what he's still going through. He must look at the calendar every day and wonder where he'd be if he'd been able to convince her to make a different choice. I'd have a three-year-old, he says, and I hesitate, aware that I have to choose my words judiciously. You might not be in Austin, I say, And you likely wouldn't be in graduate school. But he shakes his head. Sometimes, he says, I'm amazed by the regret I carry around every day. He looks at me, the night a perfect shadow for the emotion welling in his eyes. Do you have any idea what that's like? he asks. I manage a nod, and he nods back in commiseration, then squats down beside me. Shit, he sighs. Happy fucking birthday, I agree.

We're quiet for a minute, and then he holds his hand out for the bottle. What about you? he asks, taking another swig, Or do you have to wait until your own birthday to start cataloging your sins? I catalog them every day, I say, and he cocks his head. I peel my eyes from his, examining the water through the bare branches of the trees. The wind has picked up, and I'm starting to regret not grabbing a jacket of my own. Cold? he asks as I get to my feet, and I shrug. But he's already opening his coat, his movement mirroring the moment I imagined last week: James, undressing, for me. Averting my eyes, I reach for the bottle of wine, though we've already killed it. Better? he asks after I've slid my arms through the still-warm sleeves. I nod, and we start walking back through the park, our steps slower than when we first arrived, our silence less frustrated. When he pauses at the top of the steps to the spring, I protest for only a second before I clamber down after him. In the dark we balance on the rocks, arms outspread. How many years since I watched him from the bank? Four, five? That day seems so long ago, but the same rush of belonging infuses me even now, warming me despite the wind, despite the way the temperature's dropping with the night.

Thank you, he says over his shoulder, and I don't know what he means. Dinner? That I've agreed to schlep through Zilker with a bottle of wine as if we're still in high school? Or is he saying something more?

As my mind trolls for the answer, I trip right into him. He stumbles forward, catching himself just before he hits the water. I teeter behind him, the empty bottle slipping from my fingers, and then he's steadying me, his hand on my arm. Shit, he says, laughing, and god, I can't help myself. I smile at him. We stand there, grinning, my heart stuttering as if I've just been dropped from a high-rise. I don't have the breath to scream.

Then he's turning away from me. We make our way back to the Explorer without speaking; I'm too busy mulling over what just happened, worrying it, conjuring up his expression as he stood across from me, the air saturated with possibility. Inside I turn the key in the ignition as he buckles his seatbelt, then wait half a beat before I turn to him. He's windblown, disheveled, and he jiggles his leg up and down, gazing at something beyond the windshield. I could take a chance right now, reach out to touch his thigh, then leave my hand behind. I could move closer, just close enough. I could say his name. I could coax him toward me.

Instead, I put the Explorer in reverse. James slides the window down; that cold wind slices right through me, but James shuts his eyes as if he's standing on a Mexican beach with the sun burning his shoulders.

I go to sleep alone.

+ + +

Thanksgiving approaches, a welcome diversion, an opportunity to focus on something other than what's between us. Despite the way James bailed at Zilker, there's a friction between us that I find impossible to ignore, and I catch him sometimes, staring at me with a penetrating expression. After a minute he shakes his head as though he's been under a powerful anesthesia. I wrestle with the blankets at night, unable to fall asleep. He's just beyond my doorway.

I head to Fort Worth for the holiday even though Catherine called me herself to invite me to Houston. We'd love to have you, she said, and I thought about asking why, if that was the case, my father had left it up to her to extend the invitation. Instead, I thanked her, determined to be polite but equally as determined to avoid shutting myself in the same room as my father and his fiancée and deeming the occasion cause for celebration. I'm already dreading Christmas and their reception, and I do my best to shove that imminent holiday out of my mind and concentrate instead on spending Thanksgiving with James and his family.

We linger in Fort Worth for four days. Each night finds us in beds separated by a heartbeat, but we keep to ourselves, as if even quiet conversation might cross a boundary we shouldn't traverse. Still, I can listen to him breathe, and I take surreptitious sips of the air, claiming as mine what he's already exhaled. When I wake in the mornings, he's gone, and I stumble into the kitchen, where he's drinking coffee and making breakfast for Ashley, who chatters about junior high and band practice and the boy in her Spanish class who doesn't give her the time of day. Hungry? James asks, meeting my eye in the light of the sun in a way he never could in the confines of his old bedroom. I nod, helping myself to the coffee as Ashley informs me that I, specifically, would think this kid was hot. The smile James tosses over his shoulder carries me the rest of the day.

We drive back to Austin late on Sunday in traffic so dense we lament having waited until the last minute to go home. But even the stress of what should be a three-hour drive turning into five doesn't ruin us. James braces his boot on the dashboard when we come to a standstill just past Hillsboro, and we spend the next forty minutes unpacking Ashley's Christmas list, then another twenty dissecting whether or not he should come with me to my father's wedding reception. My contention—that he hasn't been invited—he sweeps aside as inconsequential. I could use the support; I know that. And I'm not going to lie. That he's willing to even consider giving up his holiday touches me in a way I can't describe. But expecting James to skip out on the family Christmas I know he loves simply because my father's getting married and I might crack under the pressure doesn't make me comfortable. You have a life, I remind him, and he gives me a look, like I shouldn't challenge my position within that construct. At least think about it, he tells me, and I nod.

That night, he wanders through the open door of my bedroom like he's looking for something. I watch him pace from where I'm sacked out on my bed, where I've been reading, as he touches a finger to an empty beer bottle, palms a cellophane-wrapped mint. Can I help you with something? I ask, but he shrugs, peeling the mint from its plastic and placing it on his tongue the way he might a communion wafer. He examines the titles in my bookcase with a bent head as if he hasn't seen them a thousand times. Dusty, he proclaims, trailing the tips of his fingers along the wood. I'll get right on that, I tell him as he pulls a book from the shelf and pretends to peruse its jacket.

Then he collapses on the bed next to me and opens the cover.

I stop breathing. His leg beside mine, his head on my pillow; how could I possibly breathe? From the corner of my eye I watch his own scan the page, then lift from the book and rake the room. He's placing himself here, not in this moment but in another, in a time that hasn't happened, but could, could. Our silence feels immense, laden with suspension, and when I can't stand another second, I stand up, the hardwoods creaking under my bare feet as I cross the room. He doesn't ask where I'm going. I escape into the living room, where I pace back and forth, wondering if I was wrong to leave, waiting to see if he'll come out. When I finally peer through the doorway of my bedroom thirty minutes later, he's asleep.

I go to him. I don't touch him; I just stare down at him, at the brush of lash on the swell of his cheek, the part of his lips, the rise and fall of his chest. His slumber gifts me with the time I've needed, and I dream over him, lose myself in the pulse in his neck, the hard curve of his jaw. I take what I want, without giving in, and then I lie down beside him. Buried in sleep, he turns toward me; I shift until we're aligned: arms, legs, shoulders. Mouths. Hips.

I close my eyes.

+ + +

James spends most of the next two weeks on campus finishing up his classes, though he still has papers to write, exams to administer. I welcome the time away from him. I don't know how to behave around him, don't know what risks I'm willing to take. We've never spoken about the night he fell asleep in my bed; by the time I'd awakened the next morning he was gone, and I have no idea at what point he decided to leave.

My father calls to remind me that he's getting married in a matter of days, as if I could've possibly forgotten. We've barely spoken since I fled in the middle of the night in September. I'm not sure what he expects. A heartfelt congratulations? A hesitant offer to stand next to him? I'd rather charge an espresso maker to his credit card and be done with it.

On his wedding day I seek solace in the one thing I know to be true. I'm painting less with oils; acrylics allow me to move at a much faster pace. I don't have the patience right now for all the blending oils require, the worry that if I don't layer everything just right the paint might crack. With acrylics I don't have to prime and gesso the canvas ahead of time either. They're so much more flexible, and if for some reason I end up with something that doesn't work, I don't feel like I've wasted weeks of my life in the process.

Catherine's dressing for the ceremony; I'm standing in front of my easel in my favorite jeans and a tee shirt. My father waits for his fiancée to make her entrance; I'm lost in a hue of blue. A justice of the peace pronounces my father and Catherine husband and wife; I wipe paint from my cheek with the back of my hand. I'm better off where I belong.

In a burst of energy and wanting to have something to tell my father if he brings up our arrangement over the holidays, I summon the balls to hire a photographer so that I can finally get some slides of my work. Then I drop in on one of the galleries I visited forever ago. I open the door, a little awed by my audacity; I still have a hard time imagining that what I do in the back room could compare with what hangs on these walls. I catch a quick glimpse of the painting displayed across from me, the first in what looks like a series of landscapes so lush I falter. *Even your mother didn't think you have what it takes*, and though my father's words were spoken more than two years ago, they're as terrifying to me as the first time I heard them. I stare at the painting in front of me, at the strong strokes of a confident brush. I am not this good.

Can I help you? someone asks, and I turn. He must be the gallery owner, dressed so fastidiously, and I offer my hand. Joel Grayson, I mumble. Cameron Mackey, he says, shaking, What can I do for you? I'm an artist, I admit, and his eyes settle on the portfolio tucked under my arm. Ah, he says with a vague politeness resulting from what's probably years in the business. Yeah, I say, I thought… I trail off, glancing in the direction of the wall across from us. The painting's huge, at least fifteen by twenty. Trees of triangles, the crest of a wave, a smattering of peaks that might be waves or birds or dying leaves. I could never mix colors like these.

Cameron waits with raised eyebrows. I thought you might be interested, I finish, and he strokes a neatly trimmed sideburn. Everything about him is neatly trimmed: his hair, his waist, his fingernails, which I notice when he holds out his hand. Might be a few weeks before I can get back to you, he says, taking my portfolio, and though he's spoken with a sigh, my fortitude returns with a rush. That's fine, I say, Thank you. For the record, he adds, I don't usually accept cold calls.

I feel myself flushing. I should've known to schedule an appointment, and I eye my portfolio, already wondering what, in my lack of sophistication, I've failed to include. I've given him slide sleeves showcasing thirty different paintings, slides I reviewed just this morning with a loop and the light table I picked up over the weekend. That and my contact information are all I have to offer. I'm minus an MFA, minus an exhibition history: should I have included some kind of statement about the direction of my work?

But he's already turning away, and instead of hitting the other galleries I intended to visit today, I decide to mail the rest of my slides instead. I don't want to ruin my chances just because I've broken some unwritten rule. And one of these has to hit, right? Even if one gallery takes just one painting, that would be something. With one painting shown I have a track record. I can go to other galleries, I can tell them my work's out there. One painting's all I need, and I swing into my driveway when I get back from the post office and bound up the front steps. James looks up when I burst through the door. You're not going to believe what I just did, I say.

That night, he comes home from campus with some pot. I'm in the back room, shaking the events of the day from the end of my brush; I've got a studio lamp next to my easel, windows in front of me, flecks of midnight covering the bottom half of my canvas. I have no idea where I'm going, and that's exactly what turns me on.

Looks like a kindergartener got hold of your brush, James says, stepping toward the easel. You really don't have much of an aesthetic, do you? I ask. Let me take a few tokes and I'll get back to you, he says. I bump him, but he holds his ground, then tilts his head, examining the canvas more seriously. Something's gonna break, he says. What do you mean? I ask, and he shrugs. I know you, he says.

Thirty minutes later, we're sitting on barstools, smoking, rocking from side to side. Where'd you get this shit? I ask, coughing through a smile, and he shrugs. The beer we're drinking slides easily down our throats, and we trade empty bottles for fresh ones quickly, recklessly. So you know me, huh? I say, and he doesn't miss a beat, picking up the thread of our conversation from the back room. I've been watching you work for years, he reminds me. Yeah, but *I'm* not sure where I'm going, I say, So what makes you think you have any idea? I told you, he says, offering me the joint, I know you.

Part of me revels in his words. To be known, accepted, cherished; or am I simplifying what might be nothing more than James, stoned? But no. I remember him mere months ago, pointing to the canvas, dropping his voice to mirror Darryl's. He knows me, he's always known me, and I gaze at him for a long moment before I hand him the joint and drift toward the stereo. You going to remember me when you're famous? he asks. Doubtful, I say, You're not right for my entourage. What, he says, I'm not hot enough?

Hot isn't the word I'd use. Sacred: that's what comes to me as I look him over. He's sacred, a god, Eros. Everything I've been the past six years, everything I've done, I owe to him. That I ventured into that gallery today: if he hadn't been there when my mother died, I don't know what I would've done. He's the one, and I gaze at him now, in the sweater I tossed him on the front porch last winter, his hair a scramble, his mouth a pout. Taking your time trying to decide, aren't you? he asks, on the cusp of a smile.

A slip of the letters and *sacred* transforms. I'm scared.

You're fine, I mumble, and he takes a small sip from the joint, the first time I've ever seen him move so delicately. He turns his head to the side to release his smoke, that smile giving the slightest curl to his lips. *Fine*, he muses, Is that what you think of me? What do you want me to say? I ask, and he fixes his eyes on mine. C'mon, Joel, he says like I'm refusing to acknowledge some secret we share. He slides his elbow along the bar, his head propped on his hand. Never has he looked at me so directly, with so little inhibition. He's stoned, and I wade through his high in the midst of my own. C'mon, he says, and I take a step in his direction.

When we kiss, I can't breathe. His lips, his tongue, everything I'd imagined. Is this really happening? I whisper when we break apart. I don't know, he says. But his mouth unwinds under mine.

+ + +

The soft click of the bathroom door the following morning opens my eyes. Hey, he mutters. He's yanking a sweater over his tee shirt, cramming a baseball cap on his head, and after that initial syllable of greeting his eyes dart away from mine. I slide into a sitting position, his sheet to my waist. I have to get to campus, he says, as if I've challenged his industry. Okay, I say. He combs through the loose papers in his bookshelf, dropping some in his haste. An image from junior year comes back to me: Paul's expression as I threw on my jeans when James and Elisa slammed the front door. I pull my knees to my chest. I'll be late, he says.

He shuts the door behind him. I'm capsized by the wave of his absence, and I hold my hands to my head, taking in the remains of last night. The stub of a joint, an empty bottle of beer on the nightstand, my boxers tangled in my jeans at the foot of his bed. And fragments of memory like the bones of a once breathing animal: his hands in my hair; my mouth, open, on his neck. The suspension of breath that signified the beginning, or the beginning of the end.

The hours stretch before me, pitiless. *He's at the library because he has papers due in a few days*, I remind myself every half a dozen seconds, *Not for any other reason*. In the bathroom I stand naked in front of the mirror, puzzling over my body, at my muscles strung with tension, the hair I sweep back from my face and hold pinned behind my ears. I don't want to shower. I don't want to wash him away, and I touch my finger to my throat, to the necklace he brought me from Greece. I haven't once taken it off.

I go into the back room and stand in front of the painting I started less than twenty-four hours ago. Blue, the darkest blue, scattered along the border of my canvas like I've chiseled the night sky and have nothing left to show for it but the slivers. I want to work, but I can't seem to pick up where I left off, and I end up sprawled on the couch, staring at the television. It's ten-thirty in the morning, and he'll be late.

But he's not. He's home before noon. I'm standing in front of the TV, my hands clasped behind my head, edging closer to hysteria. I've been pacing, replaying what I remember, inventing what I don't, and when I hear the front door open, I take one look at him and can't hold back any longer. I cover the distance that separates us and kiss him, the way I've longed to since the moment he walked in the door from Greece. Pressed against the wall, my hand cupping his neck, my thumb tracing the line of his jaw so I won't forget, so I won't ever forget. Wait, wait, wait, he whispers when we break for air, but I've waited long enough, and I ease him toward the sofa, my fingers finding the button on his jeans. I peel them back, then slide his boxers over his hips.

Prostrate between his legs, I give myself one long second to admire him. Then I lower my lips to his sun. He sucks in his breath as I trace his tattoo with my tongue; he's not protesting anymore. Instead, he rocks beneath me. Joel, he whispers, and the word serves as the most potent aphrodisiac. My name has never sounded so good. I don't even need him to touch me. I come the second he fills my mouth.

Then he sits up, pulling his jeans to his waist. James— I start, but he speaks, in the same voice I heard from him this morning. I have to get to campus, he says. I nod, struck by the magnitude of what we've done. He stands, yanking his tee shirt down over his abdomen, and before I can say a word, before I can pull him into my arms and beg him not to leave until we've put a name to what's between us, he's gone.

+ + +

I don't eat. I avoid the phone. I can't bring myself to touch the canvas from yesterday. Shadows lengthen on the hardwoods as darkness falls, and I close my eyes, picturing him in front of me, my mouth buried in his tattoo.

By the time his car pulls into the driveway I'm out of my mind. I need to see him, need him to confirm that what happened this morning, last night, wasn't a mistake. I need him to look in my eyes and tell me we're okay.

What're you doing? he asks, and I'm suddenly aware of how I must look to him, coiled in the chair beside the fireplace with no other diversion than a memory from hours ago. Nothing, I say, getting to my feet. I'm pained looking at the circles under his eyes and thinking that in any way I could have caused them. I'm hungry, he says, Let's get something to eat.

I've never been more aware of my body: my profile, my hands on the steering wheel, the flex of my thigh in my jeans as I press the Explorer's accelerator. There's not a sound other than the radio, not a word spoken between us. We order tacos; I silently accept his money.

An hour later, we're back in his bedroom. What are we doing? he whispers to me in the dark. It's not a question he wants answered, not that I could if I tried. When he tells me what he wants, I relent, without deliberation. I'd give him anything, I give him everything, and the night's black, black outside his windows. I don't care that I'm drowning.

+ + +

A cold front, a hard rain, and I'm not alone. I'm in his bed, dozing, curled in the center of his sheets, listening to the clack of his fingers on the keyboard. I wish he didn't have work, wish he didn't have papers to write, but I'll take the next best thing. I'll take him sitting with his back to me, tilting in his chair. I'll take him muttering over the research piled beside him, the words he's already written. I'll take anything he's willing to give, and I linger until he finally glowers at me over his shoulder. What the fuck, Joel, he says, Are you planning on staying in bed all goddamn day?

I scramble to my feet, and he looks away, like he doesn't want to be reminded that the reason I'm naked with half a hard-on is because he invited me in here himself. I pull on the jeans he stripped from me last night before he turned me over, before he fucked me so hard I'm aching now the way I did after I had sex for the first time. How's it going anyway? I ask, How's the writing? Shitty, he mutters.

I slip from his bedroom and pad down the hall to make a pot of coffee, even though my teeth already chatter from anxiety. Ten minutes later, he comes out of his bedroom and pours himself a cup. Can I get you anything? I say, Are you hungry?

Jesus. I'm worse than his love-struck sister, and I watch him take a sip, willing him to look in my direction and hating how weak I am in the midst of his power. No, he says, and he closes the bedroom door behind him. My finger automatically raises to my throat, to the necklace that over the past thirty-six hours has become my touchstone. If I close my eyes, I can still see our reflection in the mirror at the end of that summer, his arm clasped across my chest.

Peter calls that afternoon after the rain tapers, as I'm standing dazed in the back room. I don't think I have the steadiness to paint; my hands shake just looking at the canvas. When the phone rings, I dive for it, agree the second he asks if I want to play ball in spite of the weather. If I stay here, I'll fuck something up for sure; I've already spent ridiculous amounts of time loitering outside James's bedroom door, and I'm on the verge of returning if he doesn't come out soon. James interested? Peter wants to know, and I hesitate, then tell him I'll check. Yeah, James says, answering his door to my reluctant knock, I've got to get out of here.

I make every effort not to give myself away, but I play like shit and Peter finally nudges me, out of breath, his hands on his knees. What's wrong with you today? he asks. James cuts me a quick, nervous look. My silence assumed, my chest weak from the weight of our secret, and when I release the ball, James blocks me, his arm brushing mine. He's shaking too.

+ + +

The next day I'm riding high despite the fact that James stayed up almost all night working and left early for campus. I lie in bed after he leaves, marveling, the sheets faintly scented with his shampoo, our sex. I'm here, in his bed. I don't ever want to leave.

But the canvas I started a few days ago, a lifetime ago, beckons, and I stand for a minute at its threshold. Then I reach for my brush. I've never used colors so rich, so vehement; they suck me in and spit me out, and that's when my brush sweeps a thick scarlet line down the middle. He's probably the only one besides me who would recognize his face, and when he appears in the doorway and I finally lower my brush, I'm trembling again. He steps beside me; I try to decipher his expression, the code encrypted in his stance. Does it have a title? he asks, and the word comes unbidden to my mouth. *Crossing*, I say. He nods, slow and solemn, and when he turns his eyes to mine, I feel as if he's seeing me for the first time in days. You've never done anything better, he says.

That night, he pulls his shirt over his head as I sit on the edge of his bed. He wants the room dark. I unzip his jeans, bracket his hips with my palms. I don't need a lamp to find his tattoo, the sun that shone the first rays of light on this love, this desire. He moans as my tongue makes contact; I need the sound, need to feel his hips pulling away from me because that's not where he wants my mouth. He wants me here, and here, and I want to stay here, locked in this moment. I don't want to move forward or back.

He leaves the next morning for Fort Worth as he'd planned weeks ago. For the first time in years he doesn't try to convince me to come with him. I walk him to his car as if there's nothing fragile between us. Later, he says, ditching his eyes the way I've grown accustomed to the past few days, and I nod so briefly we might not know each other at all. I walk back into the house before he drives away.

+ + +

As I head downtown to meet my father for lunch on Christmas Eve, I call James from my cell phone. He never answers. I leave messages, each more desperate than the last; even I have to admit that. Sun reflects off the chrome of the car in front of me—it's warm here in Houston the day before Christmas—and when I get his voicemail, I hang up, then cut across all three lanes of traffic when I realize I'm about to miss my turn.

Fifteen minutes later, my father and I sit across from each other, a scotch apiece despite the hour. I've been polite since my arrival in Houston, though I can't bring myself to congratulate him on his marriage any more than I can look Catherine in the eye. She's been tender and deferential with me, which makes me feel defenseless and damaged. Anything we can do to make tomorrow easier for you…, she said to me in private this morning, leaving her sentence intentionally incomplete, but there's nothing that could make tomorrow any easier, nothing short of having James by my side. I close my eyes for one brief moment, thinking back to our trip home from Fort Worth last month and the way he rode me about allowing him to crash my father's celebration. If I hadn't been so vehement about excluding him, would he be here with me today?

He's not even answering the goddamn phone.

My father's intimate wedding last weekend precedes what will inevitably be a lavish affair tomorrow, and I'm going to have to make my way through that event on my own. I wish they could have celebrated simply, could have slipped away for their honeymoon without involving two hundred friends and colleagues. I'm not really up for the small talk, not up for dodging questions about what I do, who I'm dating.

I'm not asking you to lie, my father says, reading my mind. But you want me to deflect any question about what I do for a living, I finish. I don't think you can suggest you earn a living with your painting, Joel, he says. Then, as if he's managed to forget every year of my childhood, he adds: I think I've been more than kind.

I knew this would happen, knew I wouldn't be able to fight him. He's been patient long enough, and I steel myself against whatever diabolical plan he's been conjuring. If he tells me I have to move back to Houston, if he tells me I'm slated for Dallas, I don't know what I'm going to do. I can't imagine denying him and searching for some piece of shit job instead, can't imagine giving up the painting. And my father's all I have left. Though he hurts me again and again, I don't know that I'm ready to render myself an orphan. But that's where we're headed; the second I tell him I won't work for him, he'll cut me off, and not just financially. He might not refuse to take my calls; he might not ask me to surrender my key to his house. But he'll deny me emotional entry, and once he finds out I'm gay, the last vestige of his heart that holds a place for me he'll cauterize himself.

I know tomorrow will be difficult for you, he says in a voice that sounds almost gentle, and my eyes well with tears at this unexpected compassion. He gives me the privacy to compose myself, then sets his jaw as if he's come to a conclusion. I'm willing to overlook the deadline I imposed, he says, For the time being.

I wait for a wave of relief that fails to arrive. His change of heart, however beneficial to me financially, lends me an air of pathos I'm not sure I want, and I stutter an unintelligible response that he brushes aside, like a magnanimous king. I half-expect him to offer his hand for me to kiss, and I automatically curl into myself as if I'm trying to take up as little space as possible. I'm a six-year-old hiding from his father's ire, and when he bestows a sudden smile, I catch my breath. I want to drape myself over this impeccable white tablecloth and sob, because I'm mired in this fucked up relationship, because my mother's gone, because James hasn't called, not once, and I'm not in a position to lose him, too.

I swallow my emotion before my father can rescind his offer. Thank you, I say.

I'm almost back to the house after lunch when I wrench my cell from my pocket. James's phone rings again and again. Hey, I say when I finally get his voicemail, It's me. I've slowed to a stop two blocks from the house; I don't seem to have the capacity to move forward, but the words themselves tumble from my mouth. It's bad here, I say into the phone, shielding my eyes from the sun, I don't know why I thought I could handle this without... You can't imagine... I've left you a couple of messages, I know you're... Okay, this... This isn't...

A car behind me bleats its horn, and I jerk forward. Okay, I breathe, Okay, I'll talk to you later. I hang up, unable to believe as I pitch the phone onto the seat beside me that I've called him in such a rush of panic. If I knew his password, I swear I'd call to erase the message. Moaning, I cover my mouth with my hand, then grind to a halt in the middle of the street. I open the door and retch until I'm dizzy.

+ + +

I'm circulating. Armed with a glass of champagne, I smile, nod, make the smallest kind of small talk with my father's friends. I don't know half of them. The other half offends me; I know it's been almost five years, but they've accepted Catherine too easily, with too little rancor.

She's gorgeous, my father the envy of every man here tonight save for myself. A ruby-colored gown swivels around her ankles and dives toward the small of her back, where my father keeps a constant hand. He's given her jewels for the holiday, a diamond necklace as decadent as her smile, and it sparkles in the candlelight. Only once this evening have my father and I spoken, when I came downstairs dressed in a tuxedo. You're dashing, Catherine said, and my father grumbled something about my hair, which I'd managed to pull into a ponytail at the nape of my neck. The strands that didn't quite reach fell forward, and I tucked them behind my ear, embarrassed by the compliment. Oh Edward, she said, not realizing what she was doing, He looks just like you.

Now I sip my champagne, resigned to my conversation with Johnson McGarrity, who looks even more swinish than he did six years ago. We're standing beside the Christmas tree, the first one I've seen in this house since my mother's death. I don't recognize a single ornament. How are your studies? he asks, and I tell him they're fine. Who knows what my father has told him, what fabrications he's concocted? For all I know I've been saddled with a course load in UT's MBA program. I might even have a girlfriend, and I glance around the room until I find my father in the center of a group of well-wishers. What would he do if I told McGarrity the truth, if I told McGarrity that my hopes of hearing back from those galleries are

158

fast diminishing, that I've been checking my cell phone obsessively for a voicemail from my best friend, whom I've had the misfortune of fucking? I should mingle, I say, and he claps me on the back and sends me on my way.

How're you doing, Joel? Catherine asks, appearing beside me, and I'm struck by her sincerity, by the fact that she keeps her eyes on mine instead of roaming the room the way I might expect. I'm fine, I mumble, dropping my gaze to my champagne, and she squeezes my arm. She'd be proud of you, she says.

I'm not so sure she's right.

Slipping from her grasp, I flag down one of the waiters. I need a scotch, I tell him, Neat.

By the time my father summons me to give a toast I'm fairly fucked up. I stumble toward the fireplace, someone handing me a glass of champagne along the way. I've practiced what I want to say ahead of time, some bullshit my father might favor, but as I stand there in front of his guests, I lose every word. Through a fog of alcohol I swear I see my mother, just there behind the Christmas tree, one hand covering her pretty mouth. Her hair spills around her shoulders; I have a stark memory of holding a handful in my four-year-old fingers as I drifted off to sleep. I want to go to her, need her to make everything okay, but the second I step in her direction, she disappears. I squint up at the star on top of the Christmas tree. Hundreds of miniature white lights twinkle, then fragment as my eyes fill.

Show me what you've done, she says in my ear, but the memory that spins forward has me holding something other than my sketchbook. I lift my eyes to my father, who stares at me from across his desk. *What do you have to say for yourself?* he asks. I'm caught, trembling, and I shake my head to sever myself from the past. Then I catch a glimpse of Catherine. I'll ruin her celebration if I'm not careful, and I automatically raise my glass. Congratulations, I say, I wish you both many years of happiness. Here, here! someone calls, though I've slurred half the words, and as the room fills with applause, I skirt the crowd and let myself out the back door.

+ + +

Long after midnight, I'm still drunk. I light a fire in the library upstairs, settle with a cigarette into a wingback, and draw the smoke into my lungs. A glance at my cell phone has confirmed my worst suspicions, that despite the import of this day, my father's remarriage and Christmas to boot, James hasn't returned any of my calls.

I want to make excuses for him. I do. I want to believe that he's caught up in his family celebration, that he's enjoying time with his sister, even that he's consumed one glass too many from the bottle of wine I gave him to pass along to his parents, and that now he's in bed with his eyes shut tight, his breath like berries. But I have a feeling I know better. I have a feeling I've fucked up so royally I might never hear from him again.

I close my eyes and take in breath, edging it out from between pursed lips until I have nothing left to give, until nothing remains but guilt and shame. I shouldn't have tempted him. I should've held back, I should've been stronger. *We'd be fools,* I should've said, *To fuck with what we have.* Instead, I let him hold that joint to my lips, let him coax me into his gaze. And now he won't even take my calls.

I'm alone up here; my father and Catherine left for their honeymoon an hour ago, on their way to the St. Regis for the night before a late-afternoon flight to Paris tomorrow. Take care of yourself, Catherine whispered on her way to the car, giving me an impulsive hug, and I watched as they pulled from the driveway, then ducked upstairs when the taillights of their limousine disappeared around the corner. I can still hear some of my father's guests downstairs, occasional laughter, a trace of music so faint it's almost imagined. I'll be missed, I think. I should be down there, should take over my father's duties as host. But I can't think of anything but James, and I swirl the scotch left in the bottom of my glass, then look up as the door opens.

James stares back.

His presence erases every phone call that went unanswered, every minute of the past agonizing week, and vision or not, I move toward him. Wait, he says, but I already have my arms around him, my face buried in his neck. You have no idea how bad it's been, I whisper.

For just a moment I think he's going to deny me, and I brace myself for a rejection destined to bring me to my knees. Then he slides one hand through my hair.

Whatever he wants. Anything he wants.

An hour later, we stop at an I-Hop outside the loop. I smoke, drink coffee, jiggle my leg until James reaches under the table and touches my knee. Relax, he says, We're gone. I pick at my food, watch James eat his own breakfast and eventually half of mine. *Everything's okay,* I keep thinking, looking over at him. *He's here, everything's okay.*

I follow him home. Bloody light from the rising sun stains my dash, my hands on the steering wheel. There's a metallic taste in my mouth I can't seem to get rid of, and I run my tongue back and forth across my teeth, then light another cigarette and crack the window. That sun deceives; cold air filters through my Explorer and chills my arms. Shivering, I squint at the highway in front of me. I'm blind in more ways than one.

+ + +

He never tells me why he didn't answer my phone calls, why he didn't return any of my messages, and I don't ask. At night we sleep after sex that leaves me shaking with frustration and confusion and fear. We can't last, not the way he kisses me, skimming the surface of my mouth as if he's afraid of its depths. I want him to drown. I want his lungs to fill, I want to stop his breath. He doesn't look at me, shuts his eyes even in the dark, his hands in my hair the only indication I have that he sees me. And even that I question; at this length my hair feminizes me in a way I never considered until now. He won't go down on me, never jerks me off. Tokens he gives me when I'm so desperate I want to scream: a hand on my ass, a kiss planted hard on my jugular. I never imagined him such a callous lover, and I want to tell him to stop, to slow down, to take his time, because our potential's right there, shimmering like the cusp of an orgasm. But I don't say a word, and despite his approach, I come every time. This is James, after all. James holding my hips, James dripping sweat onto my skin. James's breath I'm breathing.

I try to show him what's missing, because I'm too afraid of the words. *This*, I say, with lips, hands, tongue. *This is how you cherish.* The middle of a bleak December afternoon and I lay him down in the center of my bed and lift his arms above his head gently, gently. I don't have to tell him to close his eyes; they're never open. My fingers find the button of his jeans, pull down so slowly he groans. His sun rises. Back arched, breath short, bottom lip caught between his teeth: I take in everything, the fingers of one hand wrapped around the shaft of his cock, the others deep, deep. My mouth slick with saliva and more, a taste usually denied me because of the precautions I take, a taste made all the more extraordinary because this is James. What are you doing? he moans, but he doesn't want me to stop. I close my eyes. *Cherish.*

On New Year's Eve we end up at a party. What did you expect me to say? James asks after Peter presses him into going, What was I supposed to tell him? By now I know better than to suggest the truth. So we show up together, uneasy in such a social environment, worrying over every shared smile, balking over every gesture no matter how platonic its intention. When I hand him a beer, he jerks away as if I've offered him my dick and not a Rolling Rock. I'm going to smoke, he mutters, and I watch him duck out the back door; a moment later, I see the flame from his lighter. Please tell me, Peter says, following my eyes, That you're not sleeping with him. I'm not sleeping with him, I say. Oh Joel, he says, At least tell me that he knows how you feel. I swear to god, I say, my voice shaking, I swear to god, if you fuck this up— You're taking such a risk, he tells me, and he sounds almost mournful, as if he has an idea of what's coming and knows it won't be good.

Late the next morning, James shakes me awake. Does Peter know? he asks, launching into an interrogation before I've barely opened my eyes, before I've even had a chance to gauge the tenor of my hangover. Know what? I mumble, and he whacks me on the shoulder. Does he *know*? he asks. What do you think? I snap. He buries his face in his hands like he's just been diagnosed with something terminal. I'm torn between wanting to place a soothing hand on his back and kick him in the skull. Why? he moans, Why did you tell him? I didn't have to tell him, James, I say, and he lifts his head. He *guessed*? he asks. How could he not, I mumble, After last night? Oh, he says, nodding, So this is my fault. That's not what I meant, I tell him, running my hand down my face. Sounded like it to me, he says.

I don't want him to look at me this way. I don't want to be someone he fucks surreptitiously, the way I fucked guys on the side for years. I want to be able to go to our friends, to Kyle, to Peter and Amy, and tell them we have something magnificent to say. I want to celebrate what we have here, what we've discovered, what we have a chance to become. James, I say, taking a deep breath, and he kicks me. Not hard, but hard enough, the heel of his bare foot catching the outside of my quad. We stare at each other, and then he kicks me again.

I'm on him. Palms to chest, I push; he goes right over the edge of the bed, and I fly after him. As his head hits the floor, he winces, and I use that second of disorientation to try to pin him down. But he heaves me off, grunting, wrestling me when I wriggle away from him. We're not using fists, I notice as we struggle for domination. Instead, we're grabbing each other's arms, holding each other back, our legs tangled together.

Then he has me. I buck beneath him, but he's straddling my waist, my wrists in his hands. Fuck you, I growl, and he forces my arms above my head and holds them there, his shoulders straining. His face is inches from my own, his breath hot and sour. Fuck *you*, he whispers, and I close my eyes.

He lets me go. Sliding onto his back, his arm to his forehead, he stares up at the ceiling. As I watch, one tear slips along the slope of his cheek. For just a second, I don't care what happens between us as long as he's okay. I lean forward and take his tear on the tip of my finger. He squeezes his eyes shut. Please, I say, and he shakes his head.

I do the only thing I can. I kiss him, my lips just above his heart. My hair spills across his chest, and after a minute I move lower until I'm circling my tongue around the edge of his nipple, then sucking it into my mouth. My hand sweeps down over his naked hip. I can feel him weakening, the surrender of his muscles under his skin. His dick is hard.

Everything, I think. *Everything I'll ever need is right here.*

+ + +

We need a vacation, I decide that night. Together, alone. If we can isolate ourselves miles from where anyone knows us, we'll be okay. We won't have to worry about what anyone else might think. He can get used to what's happening between us. I've had sixteen months to adjust to the idea of him, my entire life to understand what it's like to want another man. This is still so new to him.

I scout around and discover that we can be in Heavenly by the following weekend. This last minute the tickets cost a fortune, but I book the reservations anyway. Guess what? I ask the next morning, and he looks at me from under heavily lidded eyes, like I might be ready to suggest that we spend the next few hours indulging in some heavy drugs before we sacrifice a virgin to the gods. I plow ahead. I thought we could use a holiday, I tell him, handing over the itinerary. He glances through the information, the cabin I've reserved outside of Tahoe, six days and five nights. I know you have work, I say, afraid he's going to use his upcoming qualifying exams as an excuse, But I promise we'll be home in plenty of time for you to get organized for your semester.

He's quiet, fingering the itinerary. I don't know, he finally says. I lift my coffee to my mouth, afraid that if I don't have something to occupy my tongue, I'll plead with him instead of staying silent like I know I should. I have work, he reminds me, and I nod to let him know that I'm commiserating and not accusing him. He rakes his hand through his hair; we haven't showered since just before that party the night before last. We haven't done much of anything in the past thirty-six hours other than fuck and sleep and eat. If I weren't so terrified, I could live this way forever.

A holiday, he says. I nod again. We haven't had much of one, he admits, and I let go of part of a smile. He tilts back in his chair, considering. We could go skiing, he says. We could, I allow. Or we could snowboard instead, he tells me. Or go snowmobiling, I say, thrilled by what I can only interpret as a budding enthusiasm. Don't we need clothes? he asks, suddenly doubtful, Equipment? We'll figure it out, I say, shrugging, and he shakes his head. I don't want you buying a bunch of shit, he tells me. We can rent what we need, I say, It's not that big of a deal.

He falls silent again, contemplating. I watch him, wondering what he's thinking, if he's envisioning himself on the precipice of a mountain or buried under an avalanche of blankets at our cabin. Because that's what I want: not snowboarding lessons and cheeks so cold-chapped they're raw to the touch. I want a fireplace and a king-sized bed. I want ice crystals shimmering against the windows. I want to step outside in bare feet on a rustic porch and then, laughing, run back indoors.

We could figure this out, he says, startling me. Yeah, I admit, and he looks me in the eye for just a second before he turns away. I hold my breath, hold back from reaching for him. When he glances at me again, he's nodding. All right, he says, Okay.

+ + +

The day's thinning as we pull off the highway, the landscape desolate, more beautiful than I remembered. The only sound in the white evening light comes from the windshield wipers sweeping away a light dusting of powder; we've been quiet since we landed in Reno almost two hours ago. As we leave the road, the tires of our rental car crunch across gravel, a winding driveway nearly eclipsed by snow-covered trees. I slow to a crawl, unaccustomed to these driving conditions, though the path has been mostly cleared. James cranes his neck, peering into the dusk. Even I'm not expecting what appears at the break in the trees.

Lamplight glows from the windows of the cabin, a two-story affair with a picture-perfect porch. I pull to a stop at the end of the drive, and for a moment we sit in the stillness, taking in the scene in front of us. Then we're unloading bags from the trunk and making our way up the path to the entrance. Inside there's a warm rush of air, a fire already set to burn in the fireplace. Plush furniture faces the hearth, fresh flowers adorn the dining room table, and as I make my way through the swinging door into the kitchen, I find a fully stocked bar. Upstairs there's another fireplace, a bottle of champagne chilling in the corner, a bathroom the size of our living room, a Jacuzzi tub. I pause at my reflection. My bangs slip along the line of my jaw. I'm wearing flat-front, stone-colored khakis, a gray sweater. It's the same color as my eyes and the circles beneath them.

I turn to James. He's staring at the bed, the champagne, the bathrobes hanging in the open wardrobe; I know what he's thinking: that this cabin isn't just extravagant but romantic in a way he didn't expect and which I probably should've considered in more depth before making the reservation. Face flushed, he unwinds from his neck the scarf I picked out just yesterday at an after-Christmas sale. Want to go shopping? I'd asked, and he told me he had to work, the same excuse he'd given me every day since I booked our trip, an excuse I had started to find so suspect that I came close to asking him if he'd changed his mind. Afraid of the answer, I went shopping instead. Now I watch him ball his scarf in his hand. We could go to dinner, I say so he doesn't assume that I've been envisioning us lounging in front of the fire in matching robes. He nods, combing through the curls at the base of his neck. Yeah, he says, Okay.

We backtrack to a restaurant we spotted fifteen minutes before we reached the cabin. We're not walking into anything highbrow, but maybe that's okay. We've got big screen TVs instead, a cold pitcher of beer between us, and I feel for all the world like this moment might just be an extension of our time in college, when we sat across from each other in bars and fell into conversations we never wanted to end. Now we're five years older, six, and what we find to say to each other still holds us steady. He mentions Catherine in a low voice, and I open up just enough to tell him what I think of her, to admit that I can't imagine what she sees in my father. Maybe he's changed, he says, skimming his finger along the rim of his glass. He hasn't changed, I assure him. You should've told him about the portfolios you sent off last month, he says. Like he'd even care, I mumble. He shakes his head. Just wait until you have your own show, he tells me, and I let myself smile. My own show, I repeat, just to hear the words. Why not? he says, You're good enough.

I meet his gaze. This I'll take: his full attention, his admiration. For the first time since this whole thing started he stares right back. Then he ducks his head, the curl of an embarrassed smile tweaking his bottom lip. Delighted, I nudge his foot under the table; he looks up at me through lowered lids, blushing a perfect crimson he tries to hide behind his beer.

I am so in love.

We drive back to our cabin, that giddiness we felt at the restaurant riding shotgun. Inside I kindle the fire, and James wrests the cork from the bottle of champagne. Two glasses he pours, gold cascading over the sides. There's no need to ask what we're celebrating. I think we both know.

A little distance. That's all we really needed.

+ + +

I don't know why the hell they've entrusted us to take the snowmobiles out by ourselves. We have no idea what we're doing, and I hold my breath as James hits a patch of ice and skids sharply to the right. Then he recovers, glancing back at me and lifting one hand from the handlebars briefly enough to pump a gloved fist in the air, like he couldn't be any more exhilarated. He won't breathe underwater, even with a backup tank and a guide, but flying through avalanche country on a motorized sled doesn't even give him pause.

I'm skittish myself, liking the feel of the machine between my legs but leery of every potential hazard, every branch heavy with snow, every tree stump spotted a moment too late capable of sending me airborne. I lean hard into the snowmobile on the turns, accelerate too slowly up a slope and almost bury my skis in powder. But when I speed along a trail packed clean, the engine thrums. If the temperature weren't so cold, I'd take off my helmet just to feel the wind in my hair.

We're out most of the afternoon, the snow when we pull to a stop under a cluster of trees and tear our helmets from our heads so blinding we squint. We keep our voices hushed, as if we don't want to intrude on the silence of the mountain, as if the wrong tenor might cause the snow above us to collapse. I don't even want to light a cigarette; the flick of the lighter in the midst of all that magnificent quiet seems somehow obscene. We lean back in our respective seats and stare at the sky. The sun sheds the coolest light.

Back at the cabin early that evening James yanks a cork from a bottle of wine and pours us both a glass. We're sweaty and hot, and in the bedroom upstairs we strip layer after layer of clothing until there's nothing left. A bath, I think, my eyes skirting in the direction of the tub, but he shakes his head and pulls me toward the bed. His kiss isn't tender, exactly, and yet he's covering my mouth with his own. That's something, that has to be something, and when he rolls my hips away from him, when he raises them from the bed, I moan, low and reverential, a consecration of this moment, this day. He muffles the sound with the palm of his hand.

+ + +

The following night, we step from the car into wet, ripe snow. I turn my face to the sky, then to James. Flakes cling to his curls. But he ducks away from me when I move to touch him, looking over his shoulder at the empty parking lot as if he's afraid of who's behind us, who might be watching. So I settle instead for entering the restaurant beside him, where he gazes with a critical eye at the sofas encircling the fireplace, at the artwork placed strategically on timbered walls, as if he's planning on writing a review the second we make it out of here. Everything glows with a hint of candlelight; I was taking a risk when I made this reservation, the same risk I took when I booked our vacation. We're out, in public, where anyone can see us together and make assumptions.

As if he knows what I'm thinking, he mutters something about finding a restroom and disappears. I linger beside the fireplace until a waiter takes pity on me and asks if I want a drink. I order a martini, then drift toward a photograph displayed on the adjacent wall, something somber and quiet, branches laden with snow, ice crystals muted in the gray light of a long-ago day. The colors blend seamlessly with the gray leather sofas in front of the fire, the metal sconces above the mantle. I touch my finger to my throat.

Earlier this morning, behind our cabin, he tackled me to the ground. I blinked away snow until he raised himself above me, blocking the sky. With one gloved hand I touched the wave in his hair; I was wearing his hat, my hair loose and almost long. For just a second he closed his eyes. Then we were rolling again, laughing, sunk in a world of white.

But by noon he was antsy and pacing the hardwoods in front of the fireplace, muttering about how no one could live in such confining conditions for long. So we'll go out, I said, and he heaved a great sigh of relief, like he'd been thinking I might refuse him or tell him I was out of cash. Snowmobiles, he said, and I reached for my coat.

The mountain was colder, visibility in scarcer supply. The same sun that yesterday had dazzled the slopes now hunkered down beneath a bank of thick clouds, abandoning us to a world of white. On a whim I took off my helmet, breaking the rules and testing the wind. I was comfortable in a way I hadn't been just twenty-four hours ago. Ahead of me James concentrated on thick powder, patches of ice that hadn't existed the day before. He wouldn't remove his helmet, not until we stopped to drink from the water I'd stowed along, and even then, he avoided my eyes, as if I was going to give him shit for being so cautious.

Cautious: that's the way he was riding when I passed him up, wanting more, aching for the wind in my hair. He glanced over as I revved past, then accelerated until we were vying for position, closer than we should've been, skis tight enough to catch. I shouted something, smiling still, but of course, I couldn't gauge his expression, shielded as it was beneath his helmet. Turning back to the trail, I spotted the stump before he had the chance. One scream of warning and he was flying in one direction as his snowmobile plowed into a snow bank in the other.

The second I could, I made my way toward him; he was already stumbling to his feet. I helped him pull his helmet from his head. Are you okay? I asked, cradling his face in gloved palms, Are you okay? Give me some goddamn space! he yelled, shoving me aside, and I backed off, imploring him with my eyes to look at me so I could be sure he was all right. When he finally turned to me, he had only one thing to say. Wear your fucking helmet, he barked.

When my drink arrives, I take a subtle sip, keeping an eye on the photograph; I'm not inspired but subdued. Back at the cabin I'd invited him again into the bath, told him I'd take care of the ache in his shoulders, the tightness in his neck. I'm fine with Advil, he informed me, swallowing two with water from the tap. Stepping toward the toilet, he unzipped his jeans, then glared at me over his shoulder. I have to take a piss, Joel, he said when I didn't move, Or do you want to watch that, too?

I'm halfway through my martini, and he's still not back from the restroom. There's a part of me that wonders if I should go looking for him—maybe he whacked his head pretty good this afternoon, and he has a concussion we didn't suspect—and part that worries that he headed back to the cabin without telling me. I pluck an olive from my glass and chew half-heartedly, staring into a blur in the background of the photograph, what might be falling snow but could be a trick of the light. When someone steps next to me and leans in close, I gaze back as if he materialized from the world within that frame. You should see the one in the bar, he says, lips curved beneath a reddish-blond goatee. Cobalt eyes and tall, tall enough that reaching his mouth might take a bit of worthwhile effort. His eyes trip down the length of my body, then meet mine in a way that requires little interpretation; that quickly we've assessed each other, determined our potential, and I realize with a rush just how much I miss that ease. Then I think: *James*, and I glance again at the photograph.

The one in the bar, the man says, gesturing with his wine glass, Has far greater appeal. Oh yeah? I say, Why's that? He shrugs, shoulders twining beneath his shirt. *Five minutes*, I think, forgetting. *In five minutes they could be cupped in my hands.*

I never hear his reasoning. He follows my gaze and spots James watching from the doorway, narrow-eyed and pissed. Too bad, he murmurs, Unless…? He leaves his question hanging, a word so luscious that for a second I look back at him, stupid enough to consider the invitation. We're a thousand miles from home; who would ever know? But one look at James's expression as he stalks toward us and I'm shaking my head. Well, the guy says, and before James can reach us he slips away. Who was that? James asks, scowling, reaching for what's left of my drink. I can smell smoke on him; he's been outside sucking down cigarettes while I've been waiting. I don't know, I say, tempted to call him out but guessing he'll beat the shit out of me if I voice anything accusatory. Humph, he says, clearly not believing me. C'mon, I say, keen on distracting him, Let's sit down.

But twenty minutes later, he's still glowering. I've ordered a bottle of wine, and he nurses his glass with a gloomy resignation. When my goateed friend crosses the far side of the room with a jaunty wave in our direction, James clenches his glass in his fist. I want to soothe his jealousy, ease his mind. Would I sleep with that guy if I met him one night, unattached and uncommitted? Of course. Would I be interested in seeing what might happen if James gave any indication he wanted to join us? Maybe. The thought tempts me; I have a quick image of the three of us in a variety of tantalizing positions that makes my crotch swim with heat. But maybe if we actually found ourselves in that moment, I'd change my mind. Despite my myriad experiences, I've never been with two guys at once, and while that's more circumstantial than some dogmatic refusal to experiment, I don't know that I'd be willing when it came right down to it to share James with anyone else.

If I'm this uncertain, I can only imagine what he's thinking, and I realize that the only way I'm going to calm his mind, the only way he's going to understand that I'm not in any hurry to sleep with someone else, is to tell him how I feel about him. He needs to know the truth. And I'm better off telling him here than waiting until we get back to Austin and the preparations for his qualifying exams swallow him up. I'm better off telling him here, miles away from anyone we know. I'm better off telling him here than keeping this a secret any longer.

James, I say, and before I can say another word he hangs his head, because this time he knows what's coming. I plow forward anyway, knowing that there's no taking back these words, no way for him to misinterpret my meaning. A tremor that takes weeks to quell begins in the center of my chest, and still, still I speak. I'm in love with you, I confess, I'm so fucking in love with you, James, and I can't...

He's shaking his head, denying me, denying the truth, but I can see the way he's casting an eye back over the last few weeks, the last several months, picking up clues he's been avoiding. When? he says. What? I ask, and he says, *Since when?*

I don't want to tell him. I don't want to bring up that summer he went to Greece or the months I've spent in abject misery since. But I've started something I'm not sure I can stop, and when he slams his fist on the table, I say the only word that comes to my lips. Sun, I croak. What? he asks. I tighten my arms across my chest, my jaw shuddering from trying to hold everything in. What do you mean, *sun*? he asks, and I tell him everything.

By the time I'm finished James has drained our bottle of wine, and our waiter has figured out that we're not going to be moving beyond appetizers. I leave a handful of cash on the table without bothering to count the bills. There's the slightest chance as I slide my arms into my coat, as we walk into the cold hope of the night, that James will stop me, take me in his arms and end this agony. But he doesn't even look at me.

He won't even look at me.

At our cabin I stand in front of the fireplace, where the fire he built earlier has all but gone out. He shrugs out of his coat as I stare at the last of the embers, vermillion dying against the black. I want to go to him. I want to press my cold body against his own, feel his arms envelope me, hear the right words murmured in my ear. But he holds himself apart, rubbing his fingers back and forth across his mouth as if he's trying to erase the memory of my own. What am I supposed to say, Joel? he finally asks, I don't know what to say.

Any other time, I would've said *that's a first* and smiled as he brayed with laughter. Instead, I'm quiet, and he falls onto the sofa, covering his face with his hands. The picture he creates: his body long on an ivory throw, shadowed by the last of the firelight; if I thought for a second I could bring him back, I would.

Then he drags himself to his feet. I need a drink, he tells me, disappearing into the kitchen. A moment later, he's back, carrying a bottle and a corkscrew. Cheers, he says under his breath, drinking straight from the bottle, and though I'm nauseous, I take a long pull anyway.

He rekindles the fire. The wood snaps, hisses, and I watch as he slides the poker beneath the grate, stirring up the ashes. A few embers take flight, miniscule, brilliant, disappearing so quickly I wonder if I've imagined them. Do you remember when we went to Cancun? he asks. I nod, though he's not looking at me. He's staring into the fire as if he's remembering that trip, the sun on our skin, the taste of salt on our lips. That's where I should've taken him: Mexico. I don't know what I was thinking, shuttling him into the cold. In Mexico we'd be swimming. In Mexico we would've been so anxious to get to the pool that we wouldn't have been stymied by the roses on the bedside table or the candles encircling the Jacuzzi tub. We wouldn't have encountered the guy with the goatee.

You were fearless, he says. He's still stoking the fire, sliding the poker in and out of the grate as the logs shift in the light. I was terrified, he adds, And you were so sure of yourself. He looks at me over his shoulder. I didn't get that, he admits, You'd always been so...

He trails off, but I know what he means. You were drawn to me for a reason, Joel, he says, and that I can't deny. Replacing the poker, he slides his hands in the pockets of his jeans; he leaned against the desk in our dorm room so casually, as if he didn't give a shit what I thought of him. We went to Mexico, he says, And that dive changed everything.

He takes up the wine and starts pacing back and forth. I had this image of you, he says, I had this image of you, and then you had to put on that goddamn ventilator and drag me under the water. You didn't have to go, I tell him. Of course I had to go, he says, Aren't you listening to me? When he throws out his arms, wine splatters onto the floor. And then you flirted with the dive master, he mutters. You're jealous of the dive master? I say, startled, After all this time? I'm not jealous of the dive master, Joel, he tells me, I'm jealous of your fucking balls.

He takes another swig of wine, then wipes his mouth with the back of his hand. I can tell he's drunk; his gestures are turning sloppy, his eyes bloodshot.

I could've ended up with someone else freshman year, he whispers.

I feel like I've heard this before, like this isn't the first time he's tried to puzzle us out, and I don't know what to tell him. I just know what I want, and it's not the anguish in his expression when he looks at me. A rush of air leaves my mouth, a silent, concentrated scream as I realize just what I stand to lose here. Hey, he says, We're fine, we're good. I shake my head, and he takes an intoxicated step in my direction. Don't fuck with me, I say. Who do you think I am? he asks. He closes his eyes, and when he opens them again, I'm done in by his tears. I know who you are, Joel, he whispers, I know who you are.

+ + +

I'm throwing up. James has passed out downstairs under a colorless chenille throw, the fire nothing but ash. Cold ceramic tile chills my skin; I attribute my nausea to the martini, the wine, and not to what he's just promised. *We might as well try*, he said, *We might as well try to make something out of what we've started.*

He's waiting for me when I come out, and he squints, the chenille throw draped around his shoulders. Are you sick? he asks. I drank too much, I say, and he nods, scrubbing his hand back and forth across what's becoming a borderline beard. Me too, he admits, and my heart seizes. Will he even remember this conversation come morning? I wrap my arms around myself as he peels back the comforter on the bed. When I slide under the covers after him, he shifts until he's facing away from me. I want to press myself close to his body, lay my head against the solid plane of his chest. I want to throw my leg over his, press my lips against his throat and follow him into conjoined sleep.

I settle for listening to him breathe.

+ + +

Much of what we say, much of what we do over the next couple of days we veil behind a bottle or two of wine. The fire in the bedroom casts soft light on the walls, and every night, I watch the play of shadows long after he falls asleep. My own rest eludes me, the low-level anxiety I've felt since the morning after our first night together gathering in intensity, an emotional hurricane capable of pulling me under. I try to anchor myself where I can, clinging to whatever he'll give me: a half a smile I can just make out beneath his scarf and sunglasses one afternoon, fingers curled around my bicep an hour later, his breath hot in my ear.

Mornings are the worst. I'm already awake, and I watch him come to, witness the half a second before he remembers what we've done. He rubs his hand over his eyes, and I know he's steeling himself. You awake? he asks, his voice gravelly from too much alcohol and too little sleep, and before he can give me the time to answer he's leaving the bed, shoving his dick in his boxers with what I can only interpret as a grim resolve. But he'll find me later, after breakfast, after he showers. I'll be sitting in front of the fireplace, and he'll step in front of me, his hips level with the head I hold in my hands. He doesn't bother saying my name.

The night before we go home, he slips from my hold under the guise of a bedtime cigarette. He's spent the better part of the evening complaining about anything and everything: the wine we're drinking, the cold seeping under the door of the cabin, the logs in the fireplace, which he insists were too wet to light. Man, just shut up already, I say after he scours the honor bar and declares himself bored with his findings. I'm already regretting my tone, but I'm so tired of listening to him bitch that I can't stop myself. You're not paying for it anyway, I add, and his eyes narrow. I'm fucking hungry, he tells me, like that's the real issue here. I grab a packet of macadamia nuts from the bar and wing it in his direction. What's your *problem*? he asks with just enough trepidation that I realize he's afraid I'm going to call him on what I already know: that he doesn't have it in him to finish what we've started. Whatever, he finally mutters. Pussy, I say under my breath, and though I know, I *know* he hears me, he pretends he doesn't. I find myself relenting; I'm always relenting. James, I say, reaching for his arm, but he slides away from me. I'm going to smoke, he mumbles.

I see him through the window a few minutes later. He's forgotten his coat, and he hunches his shoulders, curved toward his cigarette as if it's a bonfire that might warm him. A slow inhale and the ember glows. As he lets out his breath, he glances over his shoulder and meets my eyes.

I've never seen him more miserable.

+ + +

I brace myself, waiting for the inevitable. James spends most of his time at the library, and I suppose I can't really fault him for that; his qualifying exams are just over two months away. I spend my time in the back room, knowing that if I don't go in there at all, I'm bound to drive myself insane overanalyzing everything that's transpired. When James comes home from campus, he stands silent behind me. I haven't even picked up a brush.

Five years have passed since my mother's death, and the night before James's classes start marks the anniversary of that awful trip to Houston. Every year, James remembers, and though he rarely mentions outright what happened, he finds a way to let me know that he hasn't forgotten. His quiet comfort has meant more to me over the years than little else could, and I count on his presence to soothe the pain that sometimes still crushes me.

This year, we sprawl in his bed post-coital. I've got the sheet pulled low around my hips, and he's sitting up, leaning against the headboard. We're both smoking; we've done nothing but, since we got back from Heavenly. I have a tight schedule today, he's saying, I might not be home until late. I nod, and he rubs his eye with the heel of his hand. I should shower, he adds.

I wait for him to give me something else, a word of acknowledgment of what this day means, a promise of the night. Don't let me stop you, I finally mutter when he's silent, and he stabs out his cigarette. A minute later, he goes into the bathroom to take a piss, and when he turns on the shower, I throw back the sheet and stand up. I've got a pair of jeans halfway to my hips before I realize they're not mine.

After he leaves I rub my biceps with my palms as I hunt around for a clean sweatshirt. Then, fully dressed, I crawl back in his bed and pull the covers up over my head. Pandora leaps to the pillow beside me. With one hand I stroke her fur until she settles, her tail flicking like a metronome.

When I open my eyes again and glance at the clock, I see that it's after noon. I feel it. My body's tight, my head aching; I've slept too long, and I claw my way out from under the blankets and give myself a cranky stretch, then cock my head. James still isn't home.

Just to be sure, I haul out of bed and look around, then open the door to the fridge after I've confirmed that I'm alone. I can't find a single appetizing crumb, and I shut the door again with a smack. Now I'll have to leave the house just to find something to eat.

Instead, I crack open a beer. Beer's always in plentiful supply; I can get downright drunk, I realize. I chug one bottle, then reach for another. A couple of beers aren't going to kill me, and they're doing a decent job of numbing the buzz at the back of my skull whenever I think about my mother.

Sometimes I wonder if I'm missing something, if there's something I've forgotten, something I should know but have managed over the years to repress. The thought makes me nauseous, reminds me of a dream I had once in high school. I was living my life, hanging out with my friends, and then I remembered that I'd killed someone, buried the body, lived years without discovery. The guilt was unreal, and I woke with a moan, then crushed my fist against my lips so I wouldn't be heard.

Shaking my head of the memory, I go into the back room, where I consider what I might be able to do before James returns. I haven't painted anything since before Christmas, since I finished *Crossing*. But when I look at my palette, at the containers of brushes and paints littering the table beside my easel, nothing comes. *Show me,* I hear my mother say instead, *Show me what you've done.*

I lift my beer to my lips, then plunk down in the chair beside the window, the one that holds James most nights when I'm working. He'll start out with a book, but I'll look up from my easel and find him watching me. We'll smile, our glances slight, subtle. Intoxicating.

He sat in one of our barstools as I stood between his open legs. When my hand dropped to unbutton his jeans, he sucked in his breath, then started laughing, still caught up in his high. But when I made him lift his hips so I could peel off his jeans, he moaned. Show me, he whispered, Show me what it's like.

Show me what you've done, my mother says, and I leap to my feet. Beer on an empty stomach isn't doing me any favors, and I go back into the kitchen, where I scoop up my keys and bang open the front door. I'll grab something out, and if he's hungry when he gets home, I'll take him wherever he wants and have a drink while he eats.

I just don't want to go through the rest of this day alone.

+ + +

Night fell an hour ago. I've spoken to him once, briefly; he told me he couldn't talk. In his absence I've gone through the beers on the refrigerator's top shelf, and I'm working my way through the ones on the bottom. And I've called my father, left him a drunken message I'm already regretting. I'm kind of having a hard day, I admitted, and the second I spoke the words, I hung up the phone. Breathy and effeminate: that's the last thing I want my father to be thinking when he hears from me.

I don't know what bothers me more: that James doesn't remember this date or that I'm not in a position to call and remind him.

Fine. I can make it through the evening without him. In less than five hours this day will be over for another year. So he doesn't remember, so what? I remember, and that counts for something. Closing my eyes, I try to summon her smile, the squeeze of her hand in mine. But she's lost to me, and I can't get past the words my father claims she spoke. *He was lying*, I say to myself, but sometimes I just don't know.

My eyes begin to bleed. The beer doesn't help, and I press my fingers against them for a while before I decide that this is bullshit. Bullshit that he's forgotten the date, bullshit that I can't call him and demand to know when he's coming home, bullshit that I'm supposed to stay here all night with nothing but the last of our beer and some shitty memories to keep me company.

Fuck this. If he won't come to me, then I'm going to him.

+ + +

I've left without a coat, and by the time I finally stagger into the building that houses the Classics department my teeth are chattering. I take the elevator upstairs to where I'll find the graduate student offices. Everything's quiet, and when I'm dumped off on the right floor, I find myself hesitating. The hallway's barely lit, doors shut and presumably locked. The only light spills from the end of the corridor, and after a minute I move in that direction.

He doesn't see me at first, and I stand in the doorway, watching him. He's engrossed in what's probably the syllabus for one of the classes he's teaching this semester, and in the glow of the computer screen he looks like the quintessential graduate student. Or professor: I can see him ten years from now, huddled over his work with the same intensity of expression. He'll be thirty-five, he'll have tenure. He'll spend his summers in Greece and come home rich with story. His students will adore him.

And where will I be? Will I still be cautiously approaching local galleries, then celebrating simply because someone agrees to look at my work? A couple of weeks, Cameron Mackey said, but it's been over a month, and I still haven't heard from him.

In ten years I'll be turning thirty-five. I will have lived almost half my life without my mother.

And what about us? I think, looking at James. How far will our relationship have deteriorated? Or will we have come out intact? Will I be the one he comes home to at night? Will I spend my summers in Greece because I'm invited, because he can't bear to leave me behind? Will we be everything to each other, everything we've always been and more?

Standing in his doorway, fearing the future, I catch my breath. He wheels at the sound. Hey, he says, startled, What're you doing here? I move toward him, then sink my knees in front of his chair and bury my head in his lap. Joel, he protests, trying to untangle me, but I tighten my arms around his hips. I'm not sure I can speak, and then something—my unexpected arrival, my collapse at his feet, the tears that glaze my eyes— makes him realize what he's forgotten. Ohhh, he says, Shit.

That's all I needed to hear. I shake my head at his apology, my hands automatically reaching for his jeans. We shouldn't, he murmurs, but he doesn't protest when I unzip them, then shimmy them over his hips. With one boot, I kick the door of his office closed, then lower my mouth to his tattoo and trace the rays of his sun. He leans back, and the chair creaks, the moan that escapes from his lips soft and inspiring. I lick him, suck him, slide one wet finger into his ass. His groan comes quiet and urgent to my ears.

Then he's finished. Come home, I say, not caring in this moment if he loves me or pities me. I'll take his smile, however resigned. Okay? I say, and he nods.

I see Pujan first. He's sitting in one of the chairs outside the office, backpack on the floor between splayed legs, and I can tell from his expression that he's been there a good, long while. Hello, Pujan says in a British accent that surprised me the first time I met him, How was your holiday? The blood falls from James's face, and Pujan's lip curls to the side, knowing and amused. You're the roommate, correct? he says, turning to me. I glance at James, who can't speak. Yeah, I mutter. Without thinking I offer my hand; Pujan regards it with some consideration, as if he's not sure he wants to touch it knowing where it's most likely just been. At the last minute he shakes, without getting to his feet. Nice to see you, he says. Then he turns again to James. Finishing some last-minute work? he asks.

I watch the chaos of emotion in James's expression, then reach for his arm. Let's go, I mumble, and he starts to stumble after me, then grinds to a halt when someone else appears in the hallway. This man has the look of an academic, the same absent-minded intensity James has been cultivating the past couple of years. James gulps, nods, sways beside me as his professor raises his eyebrows. Working late? he asks James. I believe he's a bit over-heated, Pujan says.

God, the audacity of that bastard. James's professor turns his eyes to me as if he's expecting an introduction, and when James fails to provide one, I extend a reluctant hand. Joel Grayson, I say, hoping my name will suffice. Ah, he says when I don't elaborate, his eyes traveling to James and back again, and I realize that by omitting mention of the nature of our relationship, we've essentially confirmed what he might suspect. He's my roommate, James blurts out, and something inside of me collapses.

Roommate: everything I wanted our freshman year, everything I craved when I suggested that we move into our own house the following summer. And now a cut so deep I almost miss the smirk on Pujan's face.

Well, James's professor says, but I'm already shuttling James in the direction of the elevator. Oh god, oh god, he's moaning even before the doors have finished closing, Oh god, oh god, oh god. I lean against the wall, biting my lip as he covers his eyes like he can't bear to face what's ahead of him. Pujan, he whimpers, He'll tell *everyone*. Maybe not, I mumble, though I don't believe that any more than James does. I touch his arm as the doors open, but he shakes me off, looking both ways into the empty corridor to be sure we're alone. I can feel my anger rising, mingling with the fear. He'll tell everyone, he insists as we push our way outside. So what? I say, So what if everyone knows? I step toward him, lowering my voice at the same time. Aren't we something good? I ask. My hand curves to caress his face, but he smacks my arm away, his eyes darting from side to side as if we're about to be ambushed. James, I whisper. My god, Joel, he wails, What do you want from me? I stare at him. Everything, I say, I want everything. He shakes his head. I can't, he whispers.

Two deaths on this date then. My mother's and mine.

Jennifer Hritz

4

For the next few days I barely make it out of my bedroom. I burrow into the covers, crawl periodically into the bathroom and hang my head over the toilet. Only when I'm sure the house is empty do I venture into the living room. Every so often, I tense at the knock on my bedroom door, the soft sound of my name. I never answer, couldn't if I tried. The cigarettes I've smoked have stolen my voice.

Friday afternoon as I'm scrounging for something to eat, a blanket thrown around my shoulders, Peter raps on the front door. Escape isn't possible, not with my Explorer parked at the curb and Peter rattling the handle like he's planning on coming in without an invitation. I help him out by yanking open the door. Go ahead, I say, Tell me you told me so. I never said anything to him, he says preemptively. I shake my head, though I can still feel that kick James gave me on New Year's Day. This isn't about you, I say. He steps through the doorway, his feet uneasy. You want to talk about it? he asks.

But he doesn't want to know anything, not really. He'll take generalities, but he doesn't want to hear that just four days ago, I was kneeling between James's legs. He doesn't want me to describe James's expression when he saw Pujan sitting outside of his office. He doesn't want to listen to me tell him that I managed to stave off tears until we got home that night, but that the moment James shut his bedroom door behind him I started bawling, and I've barely been able to stop since.

I shake my head; I swear he looks relieved. So what happens now? he asks. I don't know, I say, too overwrought to care about the tears that come to my eyes.

He doesn't stay long. An awkward pat on my back, a hesitant invitation to play basketball at some point, and he's headed for the door, throwing a take-care-of-yourself over his shoulder. I suppose I should be grateful that he took the time to drop by, awkward as he clearly feels, and I thank him as Kyle makes his way up the front steps. Though they merely nod in greeting, it's clear their visits were preconceived.

Oh dear, Kyle says, looking me up and down once we're alone, He really fucked you over, didn't he?

My eyes fill with fresh tears at the words. I do feel fucked over, and that I'm suffering at the hands of the person I love best in the world makes everything hurt that much more. Come with me, Kyle sighs, and I trail him into the kitchen, where he examines my paltry collection of wine; James and I drink those bottles faster than we can buy them. Selecting a Chianti, he uncorks the bottle with a few deft twists. Drink this, he says, pouring a glass of wine and sliding it toward me. I take a reluctant swallow, then follow him when he beckons me into my bedroom, where without a word he opens my windows and empties my ashtray into the trash can beside my bed. A January wind clears my room of a week's worth of smoke.

You drinking that wine? Kyle asks, stripping the sheets from my bed, and I automatically lift the glass to my lips. Don't you want to know what happened? I ask. I know what happened, he says, tucking the edges of a clean sheet neatly around my mattress.

Well, shit.

I take another self-pitying sip of wine. Don't you want to know why it ended? I mumble. I know why it ended, he says, But feel free to give me the gory details if you think that'll make you feel better. He's plumping up my pillows, smoothing the comforter in place; god, that looks inviting. Honey, he says, stopping me as I stumble toward the bed, You need a shower. I hesitate, running my fingers through my greasy hair. Do not let James see you like this, Joel, he adds. He's shaking his head, gathering my laundry into a pile. What do you mean? I ask, wondering if he thinks I still have a chance, that maybe if I get my shit together, James will change his mind. Joel, Kyle says, How much more power are you willing to give him?

A surge of anger suddenly quells my tears. He's right. James started this whole thing with his jealousy, his goddamn party favors. If he hadn't broken out that pot last month, I never would've caved. Hell, he never would've had the balls. And now when I'm good and hooked, he wants to cut me off. Kyle nods, seeing the change in my expression. You just ride that anger, he says, And protect your sweet self.

By the time I finish showering he's gone. My bedroom hasn't looked this clean since I unpacked more than five years ago: my bed's fixed, my trash can's empty, my floor's clear of laundry. Kyle left one window cracked, a small stick of incense burning, and I breathe in the scent, determined but without a plan. What am I going to do? Tell James off? Beg him to take me back? Promise that we'll keep what happened between us a secret? That if we can just be together, I'll never tell a soul? Would I even be willing to do that?

I would. God help me, I think I would.

The thought cripples me, and when I round the corner to the living room, the sight of James sitting in front of the fireplace finishes me off. I could stagger backward right here, up against the wall I painted a few years ago, and slide down until I'm flush with the floor. As I falter, he gets to his feet. Judging from his appearance, he hasn't been sleeping any better than I have; the thought makes me feel marginally better. If he'd let me put my arms around him, if he'd just let me soothe the circles under his eyes—

Can we talk? he asks, and I nod because hell, maybe he has a plan. Maybe he's spent the past few days trying to figure out how we can put this right. Because we could, so easily. We could be so much. I take a tentative step in his direction.

Joel, he says, I care about you.

Though grief brings tears to my eyes, rage rushes through me like a wildfire. I'd torch him if I could.

You *care* about me? I say. What do we do now? he whispers, all hunched and hangdog. Oh, I say, Did you not work that part out ahead of time? I didn't plan this, Joel, he tells me, and I shake my head. Bullshit, I say, You and your celebratory weed.

+ + +

The phone call from Cameron Mackey a few weeks later stops me from thinking that my mother might've had the right idea all along. I'm not catching you at a bad time, am I? he asks, You're not working? Uh, no, I say, because the fact of the matter is that I still haven't picked up a brush. But the second Cameron asks, I make my way to the back room as if I'd intended to go there all along. So, I've been looking through your slides, Joel, he says, And I'd like to see your work in person. Really? I say. When would it be convenient for me to drop by? he asks, I like seeing where my artists work.

My artists. What does that mean? I roll the words back and forth in my mouth, afraid to venture a guess. But I relish them anyway, halfway tempted to share them with James before I catch myself. Better to see what Cameron has in mind first. Better not to make more of a fool of myself than I already have.

When Cameron arrives a few days later—I've carefully orchestrated the appointment to ensure James's absence—I usher him to the back of the house. But he holds my arm, gazing at the painting on the living room wall. How old are you? he asks. Twenty-five at the end of the month, I say. And you have no formal training, he says. I shake my head, and he strokes one salt-and-pepper sideburn. All right, he nods, Let's see what you've got.

At first I can't tell what he thinks. He examines the paintings I've pulled while I rip at a hangnail, shredding the skin between my teeth. You really shouldn't bite your nails, he says absently, moving canvases aside to see what I might be hiding. That's new, I admit when he pauses at *Crossing*. He steps back, ruminating; my finger works its way again into my mouth. So? I finally ask when I can't take the silence anymore.

He offers me a show and laughs when I ask what that means. Two dozen paintings, he says, Give or take. Starting with *Crossing*, he points to half of what I've pulled, tells me I can choose the rest. These we'll group together— he starts. Wait a second, I say, I'm going to have my own show? October, I'm thinking, he tells me, That gives us plenty of time to plan.

179

Guess what? I say when James comes home from campus late that afternoon. I'm grinning in spite of myself, and without thinking he breaks into a smile the likes of which I haven't seen in months. I fall in love with him all over again. Tonight, he says, Tonight we have to celebrate.

I choose the wrong bar. If we'd gone somewhere quiet, if we'd had the time to share a drink and talk without interruption, we might've made some progress. But I suggest hitting a new bar not far from the house, and we find that we're not the only ones who had the same idea. Threading our way through the crowd, we try to snag a couple of stools but find the task impossible. We don't stand a chance of conversation either, and we order martinis so strong we recoil from the first sip. We plow through them anyway, leaning close to each other to make ourselves heard above the noise. Unable to sidestep someone trying to get the bartender's attention, James slides his arm around my shoulders, then blanches as if he's done something reprehensible. James, I say, the word lost in the throng. He sees my expression and tries to summon a smile. Nothing comes through but anger.

We leave as soon as we finish our drinks, James peeling out of the parking lot, tires squealing. He doesn't bother asking where I want to go next; he just heads home, where he plants himself on the back porch with a beer he doesn't drink and a fresh pack of cigarettes. Disconsolate, I sink beside him. So, congratulations, he says without even trying another smile. Thanks, I mumble. He sucks on his cigarette, then picks a stray piece of tobacco from his tongue. Joel, he finally says, his hands dangling between his knees, and when he trails off, I take a chance and touch his shoulder.

I want to make everything better, and I slide my hand up through his hair. At first he stiffens, but I hold steady, and he finally relaxes against me, leaning back into my hand, my chest. My world shifts into focus when he moans. Come with me, I whisper, and he follows me into my bedroom for the first time in more than a month. I missed this, he groans when I have his jeans down around his ankles. Not *I missed you*, but *I missed this*. For just a second I hesitate, but he's already winding his fingers through my hair, already saying my name. Pulling away would require a fortitude I simply don't have, and I put everything into this moment of connection, as if the future of our relationship rides entirely on the outcome of one blowjob.

If that's the case, I give shitty head. He comes with a shudder, then falls so silent I think he might be asleep. I hope he's asleep, because otherwise this quiet will kill me. Slowly I sit, elbows on my knees, head in my hands, and then he speaks, in a voice so clear there's no doubt that he's never been more awake. This was a mistake, he says.

I don't say a word. He pulls his jeans to his waist. I curl into the space he vacates, but sleep never comes.

+ + +

The next morning, he finds me in the living room, where I'm leaning against the bar, trying to summon the courage I'll require to broach the conversation I know we need to have, the one that kept me awake all night, the one that means the end of everything I know. We can't live together, not after what happened. Even if we could get beyond the past couple of months, last night changed everything. I close my eyes and think back to the pot we smoked the night I started *Crossing*. If I'd known ahead of time where we'd end up, would I have declined that first hit? Would I have turned away from his kiss?

I'm sorry, he mumbles, and I stare at him, at the hair slipping into his eyes, his shoulders crimped with tension. He shrugs without removing his hands from his pockets. I was kind of drunk, he says. You're lying, I say, And that makes me feel so much worse.

He hangs his head, contrite. I'm moving out, I tell him, and he jerks upright. What? he says. You can stay, I add, But I'm leaving this weekend. He's shaking his head, stepping toward me, then backing away. You can't leave, he says, You can't. James, I say, How can we possibly live together?

I'm surprised he hasn't suggested moving himself. If he was freaked out by the thought of Pujan telling people about us, then surely he realizes that by continuing to live with me, Pujan—and everyone else—can only conclude that we're sleeping together.

But maybe James doesn't care what people think as long as he can truthfully deny that nothing's happening. *By the time you finally got around to coming out*, he said the morning I was set to receive the results of that HIV test, *Most of my old fraternity brothers thought I was fucking you.*

Maybe he doesn't have a problem living with me. Hell, he probably likes feeling all progressive and inclusive. But maybe admitting that he's getting his own cock sucked is another story.

I think I'm going to throw up.

If you leave, he asks, How are we supposed to make this better? Maybe we're not supposed to make this better, I tell him, Maybe this has just run its course. But as I say the words, I'm grateful for the bar at my back. I honestly don't think I can stand. You can't believe that, he says. I don't know what to believe anymore, I tell him, and he buries his face in his hands. For one second I'm satisfied. But I love him too much to want to see him hurting, and I have to cross my arms over my chest to stop myself from moving toward him.

He'd just reject me anyway. Or we'd end up back in bed and have to start this conversation from scratch ten minutes from now.

What's in this for you? I ask, and he lifts his head. What do you mean? he says, his voice so hoarse I ache to soothe him. I manage to restrain myself as the tears in his eyes slip onto his cheeks. You're my best friend, he says.

I wouldn't know how to leave anyway. I don't know how to move forward without him. So I stay. I stay.

+ + +

We see little of each other. He's usually gone before I'm up in the morning, spends more time at the library than he has since I've known him. What's worse than anything is the way he makes excuses for how little time he's spending at home. I listen to him talk about how this meeting ran over and that student conference took longer than he anticipated; his lies leave me dizzy with grief.

His qualifying exams are the last week of March. Once he passes, he's considered a candidate for the PhD, and at that point he can start work on his dissertation. I'm not prepared, he admits one evening when we find ourselves in the living room at the same time. You'll be fine, I say, and he gives me a shitty look, like I'm not taking him seriously.

There are moments, many of them, when neither one of us wants to live here.

The first day of his exams, he comes home and stands in the doorway without taking his bag from his shoulder. Well? I say. I don't know, he admits, and when I press him for details, he says simply that the questions were more complicated than he expected. By now I know better than to reassure him.

On the last day he's so wiped out that he falls asleep on the sofa thirty minutes after he gets home. I finally shake him just before midnight when I think he might stay there all night. When do you think you'll hear something? I ask. Friday, he says, rubbing his eyes, Hopefully Friday.

He gets the call at the last possible minute, at a point when we're thinking seriously of bludgeoning each other if we have to wait for the news any longer. I watch him disappear into his bedroom with the phone in his hand, but as much as I strain to hear, I can't pick out a word. I resort to chewing on my thumbnail, then my skin, by the time he opens his door. He doesn't say anything, and I trail behind him into the living room. Well? I finally ask. They failed me, he says, dropping into one of the barstools. Shut up, I say, but he shakes his head like he's making his way through a dream. They failed me, he says. But..., I protest, I don't understand. He just stares in front of him like he's seeing the exam, combing through the answers to figure out exactly where he went wrong. I don't understand, I say again, What happened?

What happened, he repeats, What happened. He takes a deep breath, but even his exhalation doesn't slow the rush of blood to his face. What *happened*? he says. Jumping to his feet, he kicks the barstool. I wince as it crashes to the floor. *You* happened, Joel! he shouts, *You* fucking happened!

+ + +

I have to move out. I know I have to move out, but at the same time I know I'm incapable of initiating that change. Doing so would admit too much: that I've fucked up, that I'm on my own. If we stay here, isn't there at least a chance we can work this out?

He must feel the same way because not once has he suggested leaving.

Instead, he apologized the same night he accused me of sabotaging his exams. I didn't know what I was saying, he told me, leaning in the doorway of my bedroom with tears in his eyes. Don't worry about it, I mumbled, and he's been careful since not to suggest that his situation has anything to do with me. He's gotten feedback from his committee members, plans on retaking his exams next spring. I've never seen him so beleaguered. I watch him through the screen door as he smokes cigarette after cigarette, hate thinking that I'm the one who brought him to this point.

Kyle wants to set me up with someone. I tell him he can't possibly be that sadistic. Believe me, I say, I'm not fit company for anyone. He doesn't disagree but says he's not going to watch while I wallow around feeling sorry for myself. Let's at least go to lunch, he says, so I comply, knowing that the second he sees me, he'll change his mind. I'm right. Well, he sighs, You still look like shit. Tears fill my eyes, and Kyle shakes his head. C'mon now, he says in a soothing voice, beckoning for the waiter, Let's get you a nice glass of wine and sort this out.

By the end of our lunch Kyle's suggesting I take a vacation, if for no other reason than to escape what he's calling a "noxious home environment." Why haven't you kicked him out? he says. I've tried, I mumble. He's not a squatter, Joel, he says, but when he sees that I'm not going to change my mind, he tells me a trip might be in order. The thought of trying to coordinate something of that magnitude overwhelms me, and I pay lip service to his suggestion, tell him I'll look into the airfare. He pats my hand. You let me know if I can help, he murmurs.

I manage to fill my days. I sleep late, watch TV. Most afternoons I spend sacked out in a lawn chair in the backyard, a bottle of water within reach. I'm tan, and when I see my father at the end of July, he takes one look at me and gives his head a disapproving shake. I haven't seen him since the reception, and he started suggesting I make the trip to Houston back in April. I think he just wants to make sure I'm not whittling his money down to nothing with a drug habit or expensive whores. You must have a great deal of free time, my father grouses the second he sees my tan, and I sigh. Just because I don't have a nine to five job, I say, Doesn't mean I'm not working. No one has a nine to five job anymore, Joel, he informs me.

That night, after a few drinks, I tell him about my show. I've waited until I could catch him alone specifically because I don't want the invitation I offer to be in any way affected by Catherine's inevitable goodwill. I want to see how he's going to respond all on his own. I want to see if maybe James was right, if marriage has softened him. I want his face to crack open in a congratulatory grin, want him to admit that he was wrong, want to erase that awful conversation in his car on the way back from the airport after my trip to Europe. What does that mean? my father asks, Your own show? I tell him, watching his expression for even a flicker of pride. He rattles the ice in his glass with a grim belligerence. You're welcome to come,

I offer, willing—desperate—to let him in, but he just smooths his tie. Well, he finally says, and I wonder why the fuck I even bother.

+ + +

When Kyle appears on my doorstep the Friday before Labor Day and begs me to go out with him, my initial reaction's a firm no. A piece of ass will cure you, he promises. I'm not ready, I tell him, and he groans. Sweetheart, he says, That excuse is so last spring. I shake my head, and he gestures toward my ragged jeans and grimy tee shirt. Surely you're not going to let that ensemble go to waste, he says. I give him half a smile. Let's get you *out* there! he whines, and I hesitate just long enough for him to know he has me.

I realize, though, as we hit the usual bars, order the usual drinks, that I should've stuck with my gut reaction. I'm tired and out of practice, and I can't even smoke because Kyle's trying to quit. I slouch at the bar, refusing his invitation to dance, decide that he can't complain if I give him thirty more minutes. Impatient after fifteen, I tell him I'm leaving. One more drink, he says. I'm not up for this, Kyle, I say, closing out my tab. At least let me drive you home, he says. And steal you away from all this potential? I ask, squinting past him at the dance floor, Anyway, I drove *your* ass here. He sips from his cocktail, then sucks his teeth as if he's contemplating. But his eyes are already roaming the crowd. You'll make it home okay tonight? I ask, and he winks. Worst-case scenario, he tells me.

I'm sliding off my barstool when a friend of his approaches, and I move to leave before I end up stuck in introductions. But Kyle holds me back. I thought you didn't like the bar scene, he says to his friend, still clutching my arm. I shake him off as the guy murmurs an excuse, but before Kyle can introduce me himself, his friend sticks out his hand. Adam Atwater, he says. I mumble something that might pass for my name. Joel? he repeats, trying to confirm. I nod, eyeing the exit. What're you drinking, Joel? he asks. I'm on my way out, I tell him, but he's already gesturing for the bartender. Just one, he says to me with the kind of charm that tells me he's used to getting what he wants, Unless Kyle…? I scowl at Kyle, who grins in return. By all means, he says, Buy the girl a drink.

Pissed, I watch him fade into the crowd. I'm tempted to follow or head for the door without a word to his friend. But when I glance in Adam's direction, he has a twenty on the bar, and I heave a sigh of resignation. So, he says as the bartender slides two martinis our way. Plucking an olive from my glass, I listen as he tells me that he's only been in Austin for eight months, he's from Kentucky, he came here for work. As soon as he starts talking about his job as Director of Marketing for a computer manufacturer, I tune him out. If he wants to fuck me, there are easier ways to get to the point. I don't need to hear his whole goddamn story. What about you? he finally asks. Actually, I say, assuming my answer will be the final straw and readying myself for departure, I'm an artist. Really, he says, What's your medium?

He asks the question with such sincerity that I give him a second glance. His eyes, even in the dim light of the bar, knock me out. I could spend hours trying to coax that blue into being, and as they hold my own, I lose my train of thought. He's tall, taller than I am, and he leans against the bar with a calm insouciance that puts my half-gnawed cuticles to shame. Your medium, he reminds me. Right, I murmur, and when I fail to continue, his mouth curls to the left. A full five seconds pass before I realize I still haven't answered him. Acrylics, I say, Oils, watercolors. I find him nodding and surprise myself by admitting that I have a show coming up, my first. Well, that's got to feel incredible, he says.

His comment gives me pause. I *should* feel good right now. I should feel amazing. Just yesterday, I decided on the last of the paintings I want to include at my opening. I'm mere weeks away from the kind of success that last year I could only have dreamed of securing, and I've been so caught up with James that I haven't let myself feel a goddamn thing. You know what? I say, It does.

He grins. This time when he tells me a little more about his job, I listen, because he doesn't get too technical, because he has terrific anecdotes, because he's quick to turn the conversation over to me every few minutes. You want another drink? he asks when the bartender clears my glass. No, I say, I want to take you home.

But once I have him in my Explorer, I'm not sure what to do with him. I end up blathering that I've been trying to disentangle myself from this fucked up relationship before I finally just clamp my tongue between my teeth. Adam seems unperturbed by the way I've been rambling, looks through my CDs as I try to concentrate on the road. I kind of can't believe I have him in my car, and when I glance in his direction for the hundredth time, he takes my hand in his. Twenty minutes, he says, We can be at my place in twenty minutes.

But he lives way the hell out by Lake Travis, and it's longer than twenty minutes before we pull up to a brick two-story with impeccable landscaping. He's all grown up; inside he has more than a few pieces of mismatched furniture clustered around his fireplace, more than a dartboard and a half-assed painting of an arm on the wall, and I examine him more closely. He's wearing jeans and a shirt that complements his eyes, and though he wears the clothes casually, my guess is that he took care getting ready to go out tonight. His hair, thick and golden, betrays barely a hint of recession. He's thin, too, though he might have to work at that. I'd peg him at thirty, and when I ask, he says, Thirty-two. I sit on the edge of the sofa next to him, and his dog lumbers over to lean his head against my leg. Old and arthritic, he blinks at me with cloudy eyes. One paw in the grave, huh? I say, then redden at Adam's expression. Jesus. I don't even know how to make conversation anymore, and as if he knows what I'm thinking, he says, Have you been with anyone since…?

God, am I that ridiculous? Heat rises again to my cheeks; I don't even know what to say, and for just a second I think about getting to my feet and ending this right now before I can further humiliate myself. But he touches the tips of his fingers to my flushed skin.

I know it's been a while, but my god. No one has ever kissed me this way, not this slowly, not like I'm a jewel to be polished, an idol to be revered. He uncovers me, unearths me, peels back six months of celibacy and we're still fully clothed. Slipping the rubber band from my ponytail, he curls his fingers around my hair and moves in again to kiss me. That tug: I lose my mind, and I find the front of his jeans. What do you want? he whispers.

No one has asked me for so long that I don't know how to answer him. I'm afraid of saying the wrong thing, of making my desires known, of being rejected, refused. Does he honestly want to know, or was that question just part of his repertoire? Shh, he says, raising a finger to the furrow in my brow, Never mind.

He bends again to my neck. He's all soft moan and hot breath, and he's also making me wait, moving my hand away from his belt and linking his fingers through mine. We don't have to rush, he says, but I come up with a half a dozen reasons why I disagree. He pulls my tee shirt from my jeans, slow and painstaking, like he's unwrapping a present and doesn't want to tear the paper. I writhe with impatience, the wait excruciating. When his mouth meets my skin, I groan, but instead of relaxing into the sound, I feel myself freezing. With James I'd quickly learned to muffle my reaction, terrified he'd interpret my response for what it was: arousal coupled with sheer desperation. I'm suddenly naked, vulnerable, as self-conscious as I was my first time, and in a true self-defensive measure I shove him away from me. Hey, he says, but I'm already on my feet and reaching for my keys. There's no way I can stay.

Outside I gun the Explorer's engine, then bolt from Adam's driveway. Hands shaking, heart flying, I peel through the suburban streets. But by the time I make it to the outskirts of his neighborhood I'm fuming, pissed at myself for leaving, pissed at him for not holding me back. Cursing under my breath, I smack my hands against the steering wheel. If I'm going to blame anyone, it might as well be James. He's the one who put me in this position, he's the one who's left me so insecure that I can't succumb to what would likely have been the best sex I've ever had. I screech to a halt at the stop sign that will lead me to 620 and then back into my life.

My life. There's a joke without a punchline. For just a minute I think about what I have waiting for me at home. The back room? Given that I haven't painted a thing since last December, my work doesn't hold much allure. If anything, the thought of stepping in front of that easel makes me cringe. James? He wasn't even aware that I was going out tonight; his presence at home has become so scarce he might not realize I'm gone until tomorrow. I swipe my phone and check to be sure I'm not missing anything.

I'm not missing a goddamn thing except my pride.

Swinging the Explorer around, I feel my way back to Adam's street. Then I pitch my cell phone onto the passenger seat; I won't see it again for three days. When he answers the door, he doesn't say a word. He just steps aside to let me pass, and I kiss him, right there in his entryway. He kisses me back, winding his arms around me until I try to bring him down. Not here, he murmurs, Upstairs.

His bedroom's a clearing in the densest of forests. His walls crawl with shadows from the lamps on either side of his bed, a den of soft green that catches me first. He's not moving slowly any more; he's working my jeans over my hips as if he knows I could change my mind at any moment. Off, he says, indicating the tee shirt Kyle insisted I switch out for the one I was wearing earlier, and I pull it over my head. My abs crunch together, and he runs his hand across their flat plane. I sink back as his breath makes contact.

Sixty seconds later, I'm begging him to quit. He lifts his head, still so deep he can't focus. If you don't stop, I say, This is going to end really quickly. He kisses my hip, sucks hard on the bone, hard enough that the next morning in his shower, I'll trace my strawberry skin. Then he gets to his feet. I prop myself on my elbows, watching as he removes his shirt, unzips his jeans. Just this: my gaze held appreciatively, without judgment, and when he steps naked toward me, I sit up and straddle his legs. I know what I'm doing. I know what I'm doing, and I have no reason to apologize, and when his knees start to buckle, I pull him with me back onto the bed. He reaches into the nightstand for a condom, and I roll onto my stomach; he guides me back. I want your mouth, he says, and so I give it to him, releasing my breath. Into this space, we come. I don't ever want to leave.

+ + +

He's in the bathroom. I should be getting dressed, but I'm still in bed, surveying his room. He's no hippie. I think about my own bedroom, the metal blinds covering dusty windows, the candles burnt into puddles of wax, the full ashtray beside my bed. I can't remember the last time I washed my sheets. Adam's sheets smell like he pulled them from the dryer before he went out tonight. His furniture looks carefully chosen, too, like nothing he picked up on a whim or in one case snagged from a neighbor's curb. My money, I realize suddenly, I've used for beer and pizza, and seventy-dollar-a-tube paint. Adam spends his on home décor and martinis. I have half a mind to sneak across the room and check out his closet. I have a feeling he owns more than one suit.

Hey, he says, opening the bathroom door and leaning in the doorway. He has reason to lounge so casually, with hips that slender and long, tapered legs he keeps clean-shaven. I cycle, he said earlier when I asked. Now I reach for my tee shirt, knowing I probably wore out my welcome the second that condom came off. Take a bath with me, he says, and I blink. He inclines his head in the direction of the tub. C'mon, he says, It's big enough for both of us. Are you serious? I ask, and he says, Very.

He disappears again into the bathroom. I halfway think he's fucking with me. But then he peers around the corner, shaking out a bath sheet the color of bronze. You have somewhere else you need to be? he asks. No, I say. So, he says, C'mon.

Standing naked in his bathroom as the tub fills, I feel every bit as foolish as I did earlier when I made that gaffe about his dog. But he just pours bubble bath under the tap, then laughs at my expression. You don't do bubbles? he asks. Not since I was about four, I admit. Well, he says, That's all about to change. He churns the water with his hand, like a blond warlock, then shakes droplets from his fingers. Ready? he says, like we're about to go whitewater rafting, and we slide into the tub at opposite ends. We fit with legs scissored, the water sea-warm, frothy. I try to keep myself from smiling. You, he says, Have a beautiful mouth. Yeah, well, you have beautiful eyes, I mumble, sounding more like I'm criticizing him than bestowing a compliment. He holds a dripping hand in front of my face. What color are they? he asks. Brown? I guess, and he laughs, scratching the skin just below his earlobe and leaving a trail of bubbles along the line of his jaw, a gossamer beard. What about mine? I ask, closing my eyes. Yours, he says, Are the color of the first storm I saw when I moved here.

My chest tightens. You're very good, I say, pulling away from him, and he frowns. What? he says, You think that's a line? I don't say anything, and he grabs my foot with one soapy hand. Setting aside the fact that I've already gotten you into bed, he says, How many times do you think I've been able to use that in the last eight months? I shrug, though he has a point. He rubs the arch of my foot with his thumb, coaxing me into a smile, then slides his hand to my calf and pulls me closer.

Later, I'm leaning against his kitchen counter, eating the remnants of an order of kung pao chicken from a late-night delivery. My fingers are prunes. He's sitting in the living room, his head on his hand, watching as I pick at grains of rice with my chopsticks. He's chosen a CD, quiet and slow. The night's winding down, and I take a reluctant glance at the clock, then set down what's left of my belated dinner. I should go, I say. Yeah? he says, Why? Because it's almost three o'clock in the morning, I tell him.

He doesn't move. Instead, he smiles, like I'm a book he's reading and he's just now getting to the good part. That Explorer of yours turn into a pumpkin if you don't get home on time? he asks. Are you my fairy godmother? I snap. I half expect him to say: Do you want me to be? Or maybe he'll say something about his magic wand. I brace myself, waiting for him to fuck up. Tonight's been too smooth, too easy. He'll fuck up for sure.

Or I will.

But he doesn't say a word. He doesn't even raise his eyebrows, and after a minute I glance back at the clock. I should go, I mutter, toeing his kitchen floor with my bare foot. I'm dressed but like I have no intention of leaving: I'm minus a belt, my tee shirt hanging outside my jeans. I left my shoes upstairs. You have nice feet, he said in the bath, examining my arches. I get that a lot, I told him, and he laughed.

I don't want to leave. I want to know what it's like to spend the night here, in his room, in his bed. Eyes cast downward, I mentally list the reasons I should stay: I've been drinking (that was hours ago); I'm not sure I can find my way out of his neighborhood again (bullshit); I probably shouldn't drive without getting some sleep (bullshit times ten). I don't deserve him.

That one sticks, and I stare at the floor until he says my name in an authoritative tone I've yet to hear from him. Joel, he says, Come here.

+ + +

I stay for three days. I'm relaxed, and satiated, and I don't know if I could make it out to my Explorer even if I had the inclination to leave. Adam's indulgent, and we cook, watch movies, leave the house only on Sunday night when we realize there's nothing left in his refrigerator. We head to Central Market, buy on impulse, look over the wine selection. He holds my hand walking to the checkout line, and I don't give a shit who sees. When we get back, we make sandwiches, roast beef and cheddar on thick, grainy bread, feed each other plump black olives and lick our fingers. He touches the shell at the base of my throat, and I shake my head; he waves his hand like he's casting a spell, and I meet his mouth with mine. Then we play darts on the board in his game room late into the night.

You play? he'd asked the previous afternoon, pausing in front of the board, and I shrugged like maybe I'd thrown a dart or two in college. We playing for money? I asked as we threw the cork to see who would go first, and he raised his eyebrows. Sure, he said, If you've got some extra cash. I hid my smile and made a show of scouting around in his bedroom for my wallet and thumbing through the bills. I don't know how long I'll last, I said, But we can give it a shot.

I waited out a couple of turns before I let myself double-in. We were playing '01, starting at 501, and I acted like a novice, intentionally missing shots before I let myself get mildly lucky. You're not doing so bad, he said, and I ducked my head in feigned abashment. Maybe someday, I said, I'll play as well as you.

Nice! Adam told me as I started to catch up, and I murmured a thank you, then glanced down to make sure my toe was behind the throw line, like I might still be getting used to where to position myself. Luck, I said when I hit a ton. Adam turned to me in disbelief but kept his comments to himself until I doubled-out. Did you..., he said, Did you just *hustle* me? You should really be more careful about who you bring home, I told him. You should be more careful about who you *hustle*, he said. But he was laughing, and just before he kissed me, I said, Do you know how much you owe me? I don't have any cash, he admitted against my lips. Well, then, I said, We're going to have to find some way for you to work off this debt.

Monday morning, I wake with Adam sleeping quietly beside me. I've never spent the weekend with another man, not like this. In the past when I've gone home with someone, I've left as soon as the sex was over, stayed only a handful of times until breakfast the next morning. Not once did I spend the night at Darryl's apartment. And James—he made a point to leave his bed or ditch mine before I opened my eyes most mornings. Now this. I look around the room, at the casual drape of my clothes on the armchair in the corner, my wallet on top of Adam's dresser. I'm at home here, more at home than I've been anywhere in a long time.

The realization floods me with profound doubt, and I glance again at Adam. Last night, he wanted to give me a massage. C'mon, he said when I balked, I want to make you feel good. Fine, I finally muttered like I was doing him a favor, and he ushered me into his bedroom, where he lifted my shirt over my head and traced my spine. What, no oil? I mumbled, and he said he didn't have any. I've had one man spend the night here in the past eight months, he added, And I didn't give him a massage. Kissing the slope of my neck, he paused with his lips to my ear. Now would you please let me make you feel good? he asked.

I'm not jealous of what Adam's done here before me. I'm terrified that I'm the one who's different. I've committed way too many transgressions in my life to be wallowing here in Eden. I haven't painted a thing since last December. I've fucked up my only real friendship. My mother—

Instead of recognizing what's happened over the past few days as the miracle it is, I start to wonder if I should've left that bar the moment Adam met my gaze. I'm tempted to spend the rest of the day here, the rest of the week should he ask, and I don't think I can. I just don't think I can.

Stealthily, I separate the clothing I wore here from what I've been wearing the past several days. After a weekend of raiding Adam's wardrobe my clothes feel as if they belong to someone else. I pocket my wallet, slide my feet into my sandals. Indy, curled at the foot of the bed, watches me without raising his head. He can't possibly understand that I'm ducking out at daybreak because I don't want to have to explain myself, but I'm weighted down with guilt anyway. Avoiding his gaze, I poke around for my keys.

They're behind the dresser, Adam says, and I turn with a start. He's right; my keys are nestled against the baseboard. You don't want to stay for breakfast? he asks when I straighten. I should go, I say. When can I see you again? he asks. I'll call you, I tell him. You don't have my number yet, he reminds me, sliding into a smile that over the past few days has become as familiar as my own. I'll get it from Kyle, I mumble, backing away, and he frowns. Okay, he says, realizing I'm lying. I'll call you, I repeat, and I'm gone.

I'm almost home when I check my voicemail; I have no recollection of the miles I've traversed, the landscape I've passed. I'm still with Adam, in his bed, my eyes closed. We have the entire day ahead of us.

I might not have left. I might not have left at all.

And then James's voice fills my ear. Dude, where are you? he's asking, It's almost four o'clock on Saturday afternoon, and I want to make sure I don't need to call the cops. He laughs, a nervous titter I'd never associate with him. Call me back, he says.

Delete.

Okay, it's Saturday night, he says, Like, ten o'clock or something. There's a pause, like maybe he's going to say something else. Then he hangs up.

Delete.

Seriously, man, he says, It's the middle of the fucking night, and I have no idea where you are. He's pacing back and forth; I can tell by the creak of the hardwood floors. I can see him combing his hand through his curls. Would you just call me back, he says, So I'm not sitting around thinking you're the victim of some crime or something?

Delete.

Joel, he says. This time he sounds weary, like maybe he hasn't gotten much sleep. Sunday morning, he says, confirming my thoughts, And I just don't know what to do here because you won't call me back, and Peter doesn't know where you are, and Kyle won't return my calls. His voice muffles for a moment, like maybe he's covering his mouth or the phone itself. Can you just call me back? he asks.

Delete.

Fuck you, he growls as I turn onto our street, and my heart flies into my throat. I talked to Kyle, you prick, he's saying, I talked to Kyle, and he tells me that you've been too busy getting your cock sucked to call me back.

He's drunk. Drunk enough that his words run together, drunk enough that I hope to god he was calling from his bedroom or at least the front porch. I hope he wasn't driving. I can hear the sneer in his voice, the confusion, the jealousy; I'm tired of it all. Half of me wants to turn around and drive right back to Adam's, but here, here in my driveway, here in this house: this is where my life continues. Well, *fuck you,* James says in my ear, and then he hangs up.

My phone, when I check my recent calls, displays our number thirteen times.

And yet he's not waiting up for me. He's passed out on the couch, and he lifts his head with a snarl when I kick him with my boot. D'you miss me? I ask, and he scrambles to sit up, then drops back the second he feels what must be a ferocious hangover judging from what's left of the bottle of scotch he filched from my bedroom. Cradling his head, he moans; I stand above him like I've captured some long-elusive prey. I'm inclined to stamp my foot on my prize, but he breaks my heart, and I shake my head and walk away.

+ + +

The last weekend of the month, James goes to Fort Worth to visit his family. He doesn't invite me to go with him; he never does anymore. Frankly, I'm glad to see him go. Since Labor Day, we've been nothing but civil to each other, and we're both exhausted from the strain and sick of the hypocrisy. We smoke on separate porches, eat at different times; we're roommates and nothing more.

The morning after he leaves, I sit in front of the television with my eyes closed. I can't get Adam out of my mind. Those few days I spent with him have been the only reprieve in an otherwise miserable year, and I realize how ridiculous I sounded when I talked to Kyle and stumbled through an excuse as to why I don't think I'll be seeing Adam again. You have a self-sabotage streak I can't begin to understand, he told me, and I figured I didn't have much in the way of a defense. Look at the way I've been avoiding the back room, the way I shut myself off the second I finished *Crossing*. Then James. And now Adam.

Adam. I'm hard just thinking about him, and I slide my hand under my shorts, the same ones I wore yesterday. I could jerk off now, then think about the back room, my upcoming show. I'll be more relaxed, more focused—

A sharp rap on the door and my hand flies from my crotch. By the time I'm on my feet, the FedEx guy's already trotting back to his truck. *Jesus.* I kick the door open and reach for the package, my eyes scanning the address: Professor Fielding. Well, that's fucking premature. I shake the box; books, most likely, research for the dissertation he was supposed to start this fall. I'm tempted to shove it to the bottom of the garbage can, but instead, I plunk it on the bar, where Pandora eyes it with disinterest. I suppose I should call the bastard, tell him his package arrived. Of course, doing so sends a fairly clear message that I have nothing better to do than serve as his secretary. And he likely won't answer my call anyway. I'll get his voicemail, and then I'll have to leave a message, something brief and casual in a voice that reveals none of the misery I feel when I think about what's happened to us.

What am I doing here? There has to be a better way to spend a Saturday, and my mind once again drifts toward Adam. Then, before I can give myself time to reconsider I reach for my keys.

+ + +

Huh, Adam says, leaning in the doorway. He looks exactly as I remembered: tall and tan and like he totally has his shit together. I have half a mind to step forward and just see what happens. Instead, I offer him my most disarming smile, ducking my head in what I hope passes for proper contrition. I should've called, I admit. You don't have my number, he reminds me, but he doesn't sound entirely unfriendly, and I risk a laugh, taking care to look abashed. He smiles: score. Is this a bad time? I ask, and he contemplates an answer, his head cocked. What happens if I say yes? he asks, Do you disappear without a trace? If I disappear, I say, I'll leave my slipper behind.

We both look down at my sandals. They were nice once, ridiculously expensive; I remember charging them to one of my father's accounts. Now they're splotchy with old paint, frayed around the straps. My eyes travel higher to my threadbare shorts, my stretched-out tee, stained with what I hope might be paint but in reality is probably salsa from the tacos I picked up for breakfast. Did I really come over here without changing clothes, without showering? I resist the urge to lift my arms and sniff my pits. I was in such a hurry to put distance between myself and that house that I just bolted without looking in the mirror. Did I even brush my teeth?

Do you want to take a bath? I blurt out. His forehead crinkles. Or a shower, I say a little desperately, Maybe I could take a quick shower? He examines me from head to toe: my hair, which I barely took the time to scrape back into a ponytail; my rumpled tee shirt; my dirty feet. So far, he says, This is the weirdest second date I've ever had.

I laugh, kind of delighted that he's considering this a date given the way I just showed up on his doorstep like some foundling. He gives me half a smile. You know where to find everything, he says. I brush by him, probably giving off a robust scent of body odor. I'll be back, I tell him. I hope so, he says dryly, I can't wait to see what happens next.

Upstairs I take a quick shower, then scrounge around for a toothbrush and vigorously brush my teeth. Wiping the steam from the mirror, I can't believe I'm here, and again I have a fleeting thought that when I emerge from his bathroom, I'll find something to kill the mood. If he's already lying on his bed with his hand on his hard-on, I think I'm going to roll my eyes. But when I peer into the bedroom, I'm still alone. I get dressed in the same clothes I was wearing before my shower; I probably shouldn't root around in his drawers for something on the small side even if I had that luxury just a few weeks ago. Then, squeezing the last of the moisture from my hair, I open the bedroom door.

On my way downstairs I pass Adam's office. The last time I was here, I barely glanced inside, but something about the light causes me to stall in the doorway. Bookcases line two of the walls, his laptop open on his desk alongside a handful of photos. They're mostly of kids; I remember him mentioning a niece and nephew. I step a little closer to one of the bookcases for a quick glance at the titles, then lift the picture propped against one of the bookends. Adam, younger, his arms around another guy.

That's Bobby, Adam says behind me, and I whirl around, stammering an apology. He shrugs, coming into the room and standing beside me. That was taken in '87, he says, nodding at the picture I'm holding, He died in '93.

My eyes fall back to the photograph. Bobby's leaning against Adam, maybe a head shorter, but Adam has his own head lowered so they're practically cheek to cheek. I have the feeling, realizing that I don't need to ask Adam how his lover died, that I've stumbled on something more intimate than I've ever known. I'm sorry, I manage, and Adam gives me a quick smile, then holds out his hand for the frame. I've been tested, he tells me, In case you're wondering. I don't know whether to nod or pretend like it doesn't matter. More times than I care to count, he adds.

Downstairs he hands me a glass of wine, and we stand for a minute in front of the windows, staring out at the lake. When I saw this view a few weeks ago, I didn't even try to feign nonchalance. Now I rake my fingers through my still-damp hair, watching dust motes float in the lazy afternoon light. When I move to kiss him, he places his hand on my chest. No, he says, Not yet.

We eat dinner on his back deck, pasta he throws together with a handful of ingredients that have never seen the inside of my own refrigerator: sun-dried tomatoes, fresh garlic, a leafy bunch of basil. He hands me a small bag of pignoli and tells me to toast a handful. When I get distracted and torch them instead, he just laughs. But this is the last of them, he warns, handing over the bag, So keep your eyes on the pan instead of my ass.

My blush could heat the rest of our dinner.

Outside there's a breeze, just cool enough that Adam runs back in to get us both sweatshirts. I wind angel hair pasta around my fork; he sautéed everything together, the garlic, the tomatoes, then drizzled olive oil over the whole mess. The pignoli makes the dish, I tell him. You think? he says. Thank god I was here to help, I add. What would I have done, he agrees, If you hadn't shown up today.

I take some satisfaction in not having to wonder. Here we sit, with the stars spinning above us. For the moment we're here.

The sex is every bit as good as I remembered. He works his tongue from my collarbone to my ear, then licks all the way down my belly. He wants everything slow, brings me right to the point of orgasm before he backs off, laughing when I moan, half-annoyed, half-appreciative. Don't worry, he murmurs, as if I have any doubt, I'll get you there.

I bail as soon as it's over. I feel exactly the way I felt over Labor Day weekend: calm and comfortable and completely at home, and I know there's no way I can stay. I stand up, reaching for my shorts. Adam watches me through lowered lids without moving. Is this "I should go but let's get together for dinner next week?" he asks, Or "this has been fun but my life is complicated right now?" I can't really…, I mumble, trailing off. What? he says, Go to dinner, get involved? I reach for my tee shirt without answering. Joel, he says, yanking his own shirt over his head, I like you. I look over at him, and he holds up one hand. I like you, he repeats, But I'm not going to just sleep with you. I run my fingers through my hair, then pull it back into a ponytail. Will I see you again? he asks, and I shake my head. Then you can show yourself out, he tells me.

Whatever satisfaction I felt from the day disappears by the time I start the engine. I'm smarting with rejection, which makes no sense given the way I told him to fuck his parameters. Asshole, I mutter, but the word's barely a palliative, and I glance up at the second story windows as I back out of his driveway.

He didn't want me to leave.

+ + +

My mood blackens substantially over the next several weeks. I feel suspiciously as if I've cut myself off from something redemptive, and I don't understand why. For one thing, I could easily get in touch with Adam to apologize. I'm aware that I could've better handled my departure, don't like thinking about his expression when I told him he wouldn't be hearing from me again. But I can't bring myself to make the call, and the more time that passes, the more sure I am that I never will.

I'm not over James anyway. At least that's what I tell myself. Most of the time, though, I think what I miss is his friendship. The house just doesn't feel right; we don't know how to behave around each other anymore. If we find ourselves thrown together, we clear our throats until we can come up with an excuse to escape. I watch him sometimes when I think he's not paying attention, wonder if he's as lonely as I am, if he'd change anything, everything, if he could go back.

I keep dreaming about my mother. Not nightmares; nothing so intense that I wake in tears. But dreams disturbing enough that I'm pulled from sleep onto the back porch, where I'm forced to smoke alone. I hear her voice so clearly. *Show me*, she says, *Show me what you've done.* I hold a shaking cigarette to my lips, see her twining between the trees. She teases me, tortures me, until I finally traipse through the yard to convince myself of what I'm sure I haven't seen. My bare feet crunch through the fallen leaves. One pecan tree and then the next: nothing, not a single ghost behind either one.

Everyone's coming to my opening: Kyle, Peter and Amy. James. Are you sure you want to come? I asked James, and he gave me a wounded look I felt in my knees. Do you honestly think I'd miss your opening? he asked. That's the problem; I don't know what to think anymore. But I shook my head and told him of course not. I'm glad you're going to be there, I said.

I decide to give my work a shot because I know if I don't, I'll never be able to hold myself together at that gallery. People will want to know what I'm doing now. I have to have something to tell them.

I choose a time I know James will be on campus, which isn't so difficult since he's never home anymore. I invite Pandora into my space, thinking she might bring life to this moment, another heartbeat beside mine. Ready? I ask as she leaps to the windowsill, but I know I'm asking myself. Holding my breath, I reach for a palette, one I've used a hundred times. A gray, a green: blended together, they're the color of my eyes. A speck of midnight, a swell of scarlet. I've been here before, but I don't pull away; I always give in to what looks right.

Yet here I am, leaning so close to the canvas and staring with such intensity that I swear I can see every fiber. I move close, closer, the perfect daub of moss on the end of my brush. My heart trembles along with my hand.

Show me what you've done.

With a clatter my brush falls to the floor. Snot: that's the color I've chosen. Not the color of my eyes, a Texas sky moments before it breaks. Snot. I rock back, catching the easel with my foot, and the entire construction teeters. From her perch on the windowsill Pandora flees; I hit the edge of the table I bought just after I signed my lease. The easel rights itself, but I go down. Even when I hit the floor, I keep falling.

+ + +

How're you feeling? Cameron asks. Terrified, I say without thinking, and he laughs. His assistant hung the show a few days ago, and Cameron seems pleased with the final effect. Wine glass in hand, I move from one wall to the next, the last few years of my life spread out before me. Relax, Cameron says when I start to pace, Tonight's going to be beautiful.

Thirty minutes later, the gallery's packed, far more so than I expected. Congratulations, Joel, James says, touching my arm. Thanks, I murmur, too distracted for once to analyze the gesture. He's here with Peter and Amy; I see Kyle, too, and a handful of friends and acquaintances. The rest of this crowd I don't even recognize, and when Cameron approaches and hands me a glass of champagne, James steps quickly to the side; he's not my lover anymore. Ready? Cameron asks, and I nod.

As Cameron calls for everyone's attention, I take a quick breath. I can hardly believe I'm here, in this moment I've longed for since before I can remember. I can hardly believe my paintings are the ones that line these walls, that my work has summoned forth all these guests. My mother's missing, and my father. Adam certainly isn't here. I might never have another show again. But as I gaze around the gallery, I feel a profound sense of gratitude for even this one night, this one evening that mimics success.

Thank you all for coming out tonight, Cameron says after everyone quiets down, For the opening of an exceptional new artist.

There's a burst of applause, and then Cameron talks about looking over my slides back in February, seeing my work in person a few days later. There was little doubt, he says, That I'd stumbled across something extraordinary. I catch Kyle's grin, James's expression so soft it hurts. Then Cameron raises his glass, and a roomful of well-wishers follows suit. To Joel Grayson, he says, And his provocative collection.

I'm sure I don't deserve the wash of adoration that follows, the compliments I receive. I'm asked questions about my process, questions I don't even know how to answer, and I choke when one of the more outspoken patrons grills me about the portrait of my mother. Cameron saves me more than once, and after a while I start to get the impression that my reluctance to discuss my work has a certain intrigue. Overwhelmed, I watch as a couple to my right points out which paintings they like best and then discreetly, least. Everything cool? Cameron asks. Yeah, I say, Yeah, everything's cool.

Eventually, the evening slows. James leaves, and I watch the door shut behind him. The gallery's suddenly quiet, and I realize too late that I should've made plans for some kind of after-party. I'm too keyed up to go home, and I pat my pockets for my cell phone without success. I'm not sure who I would call anyway; I'm barely on speaking terms with the one person who truly understands how much this night means to me. Instead, I wander from painting to painting, until I find myself in front of *Crossing.*

Even though I regret the circumstances of this painting's inception, I've still been kind of proud it's mine. But now, standing in front of the canvas, I feel incredibly empty. I've painted nothing in almost a year, and every compliment I've heard over the past few hours means little when I think about that magnificent failure. So what if people like what I painted in the past? What's the point if there's been nothing since?

When the guy lingering beside me asks what I think, I shrug. You? I say, wanting to hear his thoughts. Yawn, he replies without hesitation, and for a moment I'm too taken aback to respond. I'm the artist, I finally stammer. I know, he says, amused.

I guess from his tone of voice that he's fucking with me and start to smile, then realize too late that he's perfectly serious. A year ago, I'd have come up with a wicked retort. Instead, I stare at him, speechless, as he backs up his critique with what begins to sound like irrefutable proof. Your color choice here, he's saying, gesturing to the scarlet streak bisecting the canvas, and I trace the line with my eyes. If I close them, I can remember the exact moment I swept my brush along his face. The sentiment's obviously sexual, the guy says, But so banal.

I gulp the rest of my wine, listening as he castrates me, confused as to why I'm not cutting him off. Shouldn't Cameron be running interference for me? But he's deep in conversation with someone near the door; I'm on my own, and the guy beside me finally turns in my direction. His eyes have the sheen of night water. Come to my place, he says, I'm having a party. I don't think so, I mumble, and he arches an eyebrow. Do you need an introduction? he asks. He offers his hand, leans in close. Jess Karr, he tells me, and I nod, shake, wince at his grip. His brow lifts like he's waiting for something. Then he grins. His eyeteeth are awfully fucking prominent. Come with me, he says.

By the time we get to his apartment, I'm no longer making my own decisions. Instead, I'm propelled by a force I can't control, and I gaze at the stained cement floor, the exposed ductwork, wondering what this space warehoused before Jess moved in with his ultra-modern furniture and impeccable artwork. When he coaxes me into his bedroom and offers me a line, I take the twenty and bend over.

Cocaine is nothing like Ecstasy. I'm rock solid, shot through with adrenalin and power. The fear I felt an hour ago standing in front of *Crossing* has disappeared. I'm an artist, a success, capable of painting anything I desire; I'm tempted to ask for a brush just to show everyone what I can do. But Jess pulls me back to the living room, introduces me to his friends. I catch someone's eye and then their hand. We grind in front of the open windows, untouched by the chill in the night air. I wipe the sweat from my forehead with the back of my sleeve. Everything's just so stark, so sharp. I don't ever want to come down.

When the door closes behind the last of his guests, Jess offers me a touch-up, a half a bump because I'm already plummeting. Then he shuts the windows and pins me to the glass, the city behind us a confusion of light. He has a sharp tongue and wields it like a dagger. My heart picks up speed. I don't climb as high, but I can feel my inhibitions melting, my senses crying out. Fuck, I say when his cigarette grazes my arm, and he smiles, his hand flat against my chest. *This is a bad decision*, I think as he unbuttons my jeans, but the words dissipate like smoke.

I fall further from grace.

5

Jess writes my first review. I find out when I pick up a copy of the *Chronicle* and flip to the Arts section, not believing for a second that my opening was important enough to warrant mention. When I see his name, my mouth falls open. Hunched in the driver's seat of the Explorer, my eyes snag on words no artist ever wants to see describing his work: predictable, uninspired, redundant. He's butchered every last piece, including *Crossing*. But it's the one of my mother that he finds most offensive. I'd pulled the painting—the first one I painted after she died—from the back of my closet, then thought after I'd spent some time examining it that I might seriously be better off with the watercolor of that full ashtray or my jeans coiled around my palette. But at the last minute I wanted her there. If she couldn't come to my show, at the very least I wanted her portrait.

In stark contrast to the languid brushstrokes that characterize the rest of this otherwise redundant collection, Mother *suffers from what appears to be a poor exploration of technique. Effective portraiture necessitates an honesty of vision, an authenticity of representation, yet Mr. Grayson betrays his subject with a blatant pedantry. A cryptic title fails to illuminate. Are we to assume irony? Obeisance? Only Mr. Grayson knows; or maybe not. If* Mother *is any indication, this is not an artist we can trust.*

I grab my phone and dial the *Chronicle*. What the *fuck*? I blurt out, my voice shaking when I'm finally connected. Excuse me? he says. Why didn't you tell me you were writing a review? I ask. Ah, he says, Joel. You totally fucked me over! I cry. Now that's a bit melodramatic, he says, sounding like my father. You publicly disparaged my work! I say, After you invited me back to your place and… and… Fucked you? he offers. What the hell is wrong with you? I ask, and he actually laughs. My review might be the best thing for you, Joel, he says, People will talk, they'll check out your show. But you've planted a fucking seed! I say. He doesn't seem concerned. People will make up their own minds, he says. You shouldn't…, I say, You shouldn't have… Fucked you? he says again, filling in the blank. I cover my face with my hands. I didn't hear you complaining on Saturday night, he reminds me. That's not the point, I inform him, and he loses patience. Listen, why don't we discuss this tonight at my place? he says, You can kick the shit out of me then.

Well, that's never going to happen. I hang up, smacking the phone against the steering wheel. I feel violated, and I pull my hands through my hair, thinking about everyone who might see that review, smile to my face, and pity me the second I turn away. What am I supposed to do now?

When I lift my eyes, I see a child. She's standing on the sidewalk in front of my Explorer, staring right at me as her mother fusses over a baby stroller. Wind whispers through her hair, lifts the edge of her dress. My breath softens to a hiccup, and I try to guess her age. Four maybe, five. She's wearing a sweater, cherry red. She doesn't take her eyes from mine.

Then her mother looks over at me and frowns. With the engine running I can't hear the girl's name, but I can tell that it's spoken with a sharp tone. When her daughter doesn't move, the woman jerks her around, glaring at me over her shoulder as if I have designs on her child, as if I've been contemplating shoving her in the backseat and then peeling from the parking lot. I should understand her expression, her instinct to protect, but for some reason my fury returns with a vengeance. I raise my hand, middle finger extended. The woman's eyes widen. Then she gathers her daughter to her side and hurries off down the sidewalk. I bury my face in my hands.

You want a little something? Jess asks that night. He's smiling, part vampire, part dealer. Whatever, I say, and he hands me a straw.

This, then: sheer exhilaration, a confidence that borders on euphoria. A body awareness I still can't believe. If you don't like my work, I say as he's peeling my shirt from my skin, Then why do you want me? If I don't like your work, he says, Then why do you want me?

The answer I have for him now will be different when I get back to the house just before dawn. In this moment I want hands, mouth, skin. Tomorrow's another story. As the sun rises, I'll flinch at the squeak of the screen door. I'll make my way into my room and huddle on the edge of my bed. My hands won't seem particularly steady.

But now, oh now. Right now, I'm perfectly in control. Right now, I know what I'm doing.

Right now, I'm a god.

+ + +

Jess was right about the review; a handful of others surface in the days following my opening. *Startling, risky, subversive*: these are the words I read, words so different from what I expect that I can't help but find every one of them suspect. The critics are playing off each other, writing for the sake of controversy or maybe to spite Jess, who probably took that gig at the *Chronicle* for the sole pleasure of vivisecting local artists; he obviously doesn't need the money, living in that converted loft. How am I supposed to believe what I read? *Startling, risky, subversive. Fraudulent*, I add, because how can I not? Even ignoring what Jess wrote about the portrait of my mother, I can't get past the fact that I haven't painted anything in almost a year.

Would it make you feel any better to know that you've sold nine paintings? Cameron asks when I slink into the empty gallery. Are you serious? I ask. He nods, gesturing me forward. This one, he says, indicating the canvas I finished last fall of the train tracks at Zilker, Went for seven hundred. Dollars? I say in disbelief, and he bursts forth with a raucous laugh I've never heard from him. Joel, he says, We discussed this ahead of time. Well, yeah, I say, But I didn't think...

He's already pointing to the next piece, the one James claims I painted in my sleep. I pulled it from my dreams, all right, stumbling from my bed one morning and into the back room without even stopping to get dressed. Everything's thick, gauzy, heavily-veiled. Beneath a diaphanous fog the barest hint of a figure, nude, bent beside a stone bench. This one, Cameron says, Eight hundred. Why? I say. What do you mean? he asks. Why are they selling? I ask, and he laughs again. I know what I'm doing, Joel, he says, And so do you.

By the time I leave I realize that I've made close to five thousand dollars, and Cameron believes I'll sell the rest. Even *Mother*? I ask, and Cameron gives me a slight smile. When considered in juxtaposition to the rest of your work, he says, *Mother* becomes quite curious, don't you think? I nod, but chill bumps crawl along my arms. Five thousand dollars, and in a few weeks my paintings will disappear into private homes and I'll never see them again, though it's not necessarily their absence I mourn. I just don't know how I'm going to replace them.

Congratulations, James says when I run into him at the house and tell him about my success. Thanks, I say. What happens next? he asks, and I give him a dirty look. He knows I haven't been painting, probably knows about that shitty review. But he stares back at me without malice, and I hesitate, then admit that I don't know. Maybe you shouldn't think so much, he says.

I want my friend. I want him back.

Maybe, I say, and he nods. For a minute we shuffle back and forth. Well, he finally says, cramming his hands in his pockets.

There's so much we could say if we dared to open our mouths. But we've already caused so much damage. I don't think either one of us feels prepared to let go of what we have left.

+ + +

A few nights later, I convince Jess to give me an extra bump for the road. He doesn't look happy; if I'm not at his sexual disposal, I'm sure he's thinking, then there's no reason for him to part with his supply. But I have an idea, and when I get home, I lock myself in the back room and snort that line right from the baggie. Then I clap my hands together and start rummaging through brushes I haven't touched in months. In my zeal I knock canisters from the table; they clatter to the floor. Ignoring them, I reach for my palette. Already I'm seeing colors.

One stroke, two, winding from the bottom to the top. Then crystals splintered by the sun. Blue like the sky, a peach so soft, so luscious I'm ready to take a bite. They cascade from the center, the simplest song. I can hear them now, and I cock my head, my paintbrush poised. But no. I'm only hearing James rattling the locked doorknob. Joel? he calls, but his voice comes to me like through a wind tunnel. In a minute, I pant. Turning back to the canvas, I wipe my mouth with the back of my hand. Paint stains my cheek; my skin bleeds the color of my palette. Then my brush strings the crystals together, links them with a single golden vein. James bangs on the door behind me as I step back to consider what I've done.

I'm better than I ever believed. The past year presents itself as a sabbatical, the purest *shavasana*. I was always working. Even when I believed myself blocked, I was always working. I release a cackle, high and heretical, and spread my arms wide. I am here, and I breathe in this moment as the door flies open and crashes against the wall. James stands in the doorway, fire furrowing his brow. My smile breaks wide and full. Come see, I say, Come see what I've done.

He steps toward me like he's walking on the thinnest sheet of ice. At any moment he'll plunge through the cold. Here, I say, reaching out to save him, Here. But he pulls away from me, frowning at my face. Paint? he asks, as if I'm going to lean close and admit that he's seeing blood. Paint, I say, drawing him in again, but he shakes his head. Are you *high*? he asks. Gloriously, I say, gesturing him toward the canvas, Now look.

He does, then turns back to me. What are you doing? he asks. Connecting, I say, Reconnecting. He swallows; I trace the motion with my eyes, touch his throat with the tip of my finger. The merest smudge of peach colors his skin. Don't, he says, his voice hoarse, Please.

But I'm already tired of him, and I turn back to my marvelous painting. You see? I say, You see what I've done? He doesn't answer me. I lift my eyes and catch the rising sun. You see? I murmur, You see?

+ + +

I wake to rain. The sound soothes me, like a cool hand on my forehead. Splayed sideways across my bed, I arch my back in a slow stretch, then let it fall. The sheet slips away; my skin, exposed to the chill, shivers. I pull the covers back to my chin, curling my fingers around the edge of the blanket, a habit I've had from as long ago as I can remember. Closing my eyes again, I doze to the steady rhythm of an autumn rain. I don't know the time, and I don't care. I don't have anywhere to go.

As I drift, I reconstruct last night. Time twists when I'm with Jess, turns back on itself. From one night to the next I can't remember what I've done, what I've let him do. I insist on condoms and not much else. Everything blurs together, the erotic with the downright foolish. I don't think last night was any different.

Today's… what? Friday? James teaches in the morning, spends most of the afternoon in the library. Nothing's going to interfere with his qualifying exams, not this time. He comes home with heavy eyes, a crease from his glasses on the bridge of his nose. Not that he'll let me get that close. His hand on my arm for one brief second the night of my opening was the first time we'd touched since last February, and there's been nothing since, except for the trace of my finger on his throat last night.

I bolt upright at the memory and stare at my hands. They're covered with paint. My hands, my arms, my feet when I throw back the covers: I've been working, and I leap from the bed. I remember! I remember how good I was!

But the canvas that waits for me isn't one of mine. I'd never disrespect color this way, never paint with such little regard for craft. I could never be this dishonest. And yet I've cheated, betrayed the brush in my hand, shown up at the temple with false rapture. Now I'm looking at the result.

Then I'm on my knees, surrounded by brushes, tubes of paint, everything I knocked to the floor in the middle of the night. Bending over, I vomit until hot tears run from my eyes. Until I have nothing left to give.

That night, I park myself in front of the television. I've showered, cleaned up the back room; at no time in my life have I ever felt more pathetic than when I was scrubbing that floor. The canvas itself I lugged into the bathroom, where I dumped it in the tub. Then I went to the shed out back and scrounged up some lighter fluid. I squeezed what was left onto the canvas, a lit cigarette between my lips. One inhale, one flick, and then I was ducking as a ball of fire shot toward the ceiling. I reached over, calmer than I expected, and turned on the shower. When the fire was out, I got myself a beer.

I'm still watching television when James comes home. Hey, he says. Hey, I mutter, sifting through my hair. He hesitates a moment, then goes into his bedroom; I wait, and a few minutes later, he returns with an incredulous expression. I slide my eyes in his direction without turning my head. He lingers for a moment, silent, then retreats.

I let him clean up the mess.

+ + +

James invites me to come with him to Fort Worth for Thanksgiving, posing the question as if he's afraid I'll take him up on his offer. I don't think that'd be comfortable for either of us, I say. He nods, looking miserable and relieved at the same time. What're you going to do instead? he asks, and I shrug. I'll probably get together with Kyle, I tell him, even though I've barely spoken to Kyle since the opening. Well, James mumbles, As long as you have something to do. I have plenty of options, I inform him, but the words I've spoken couldn't be further from the truth. Even my father and Catherine, knowing full well that I haven't made the trip to Houston even once since my mother's death, have made plans to visit Catherine's mother.

So on Thanksgiving morning I wake up alone, drenched in self-pity, and comb through the refrigerator for something to eat. I come up with an omelet, the date on the carton of eggs only slightly questionable. I eat standing over the sink without tasting a thing. Afterward, I sit in front of the television, lamenting my solitude, the loss of my friendship with James. The day passes slowly, beer by beer, and when the room starts to gray, I get up and switch on the lamp in the corner. The phone hasn't rung once all day.

Thanksgiving's bad, but it's nothing like Christmas. Determined not to go through another holiday alone and dreading the prospect of participating in the first real Christmas my father and Catherine will spend together, I start reaching out. First, I probe tentatively into Kyle's plans and hear that he's going skiing. Every year, he reminds me. I hesitate, on the verge of asking if I can crash his vacation. But before I have the chance he tells me he's invited some guy from college he's been hoping to nail for years and who's finally ready to party. Good for you, I say, my tone lackluster, and Kyle sighs. Can I assume you're not spending the holiday with your roommate? he asks. I don't need a lecture, I warn him, but he's already launching into a monologue about straight guys who cross over just long enough to experiment and the queers stupid enough to let them in. And he's still there! he says, You're still living with him! He can't afford a place of his own, I say.

Kyle groans. Don't tell me you're supporting him, he says. I'm not supporting him, I snap, and he says, Then kick that bitch to the curb, Joel! You don't understand! I say. Tears sting my eyes, and I force them away, though the shimmy in my voice betrays me. He wasn't just some straight guy looking to experiment, I tell him. Well, honey, he says, What has he done for you lately?

I hang up because I don't want to face his question and the answer it provokes. Instead, I call Peter, who sounds so surprised to hear from me that I realize I can't ask him outright about his plans. Amy and I are splitting time between our families, he says after our conversation eventually winds in that direction, What're you doing?

I hurry him into a goodbye without really answering him, then sit for a minute, the phone in my hand. My eyes shut when I think about Jess. I see him more often than I'd like to admit. Last night, I had to push him off me when he closed his hand around my throat, too hard to consider seductive. He was naked, white and thin, and when I shoved him away from me, he backed toward his bed, which was raised on a dais like a throne for a sultan. I wanted him to trip on the goddamn step. You could've crushed my windpipe, I said, and he laughed. Those teeth ruined his smile. You're a lot like your work, Joel, he said, A whole lot of drama on the surface and nothing noteworthy underneath.

I'm ashamed to say I didn't leave. I'm ashamed that I'm dialing his number. But I'm running out of options, and when he answers his phone, I come right out and ask if he has plans for the holiday. Doesn't everybody? he says.

That quickly there's no one left.

+ + +

The next day, I call my father at his office, worrying as soon as I dial his number that he's not going to want to talk to me in the middle of the day, that he's liable to remind me of the grueling hours he keeps and my failure to simulate a productive schedule of my own. But then he answers, sounding so smooth and professional I feel the faintest flicker of hope. I ease us into a light conversation, ask about his work and Catherine, tell him I've been keeping busy. Actually, I confide, I'm thinking about a trip. Oh? he says, and before he can ask how a vacation could possibly differ from my day-to-day I say, Any thoughts on where I can get in some good diving?

I never ask him for advice, never, and instead of lambasting me for spending his money, he starts ticking off places I might want to consider. Grand Cayman if you don't want to stray too far from home, he says, But I'd recommend spending some time in Australia. He tells me about a dive he took a few years back, a shipwreck rife with life. Spectacular coral, he adds. Think you can get the time off? I ask. Time off? he repeats. Yeah, I say, I thought we could go for Christmas.

He's silent. I start gnawing on my thumbnail. We haven't been diving together since Belize, I finally remind him. I remember, he says flatly; even now, seven years later, I cringe thinking about the way that trip ended. So, I say, trying to keep my voice calm despite the desperation I'm holding at bay, I thought we could rectify that over the holiday. The holiday, my father points out, Begins in nine days. We can be spontaneous, I say, then add in a smaller voice that makes me feel like I'm five years old: Can't we? Catherine's planning a traditional celebration, he informs me, citing the tree already decorated, the presents already purchased, the menu already planned. So we'll leave the twenty-sixth, I say, and he sighs not in resignation but with an impatience I know too well. I appreciate the flexibility of your *schedule*, Joel, he tells me, But I'm not at liberty to rearrange my work to suit your whims.

I don't want to hurt Catherine's feelings. I don't. She's been kind to me when she might have been cruel. But I can't spend Christmas there, not now. Not with James and me on such devastating terms, not after what happened in the back room a few weeks ago, not with what's starting to border on a dependency for a drug I wish I'd never tried in the first place.

I don't think I'm going to make it to Houston, I mumble. What? my father says. I can't go to Houston this year, I say, I can't. But you can spend thousands of dollars traveling across the world? he asks, his voice rising with every word, Do you have any idea how hard Catherine has been working to make this holiday memorable? I'm sorry, I whisper. You're goddamn right you're going to be sorry! he says.

I leave it to my father to break the news to Catherine. If I were a better person, I'd call her myself, apologize for bailing on the celebration she's putting together. Instead, I decide to get stoned out of my mind, then make the same mistake on Christmas Eve after avoiding a couple of her considerate calls. Sitting in front of the television, immersed in Christmas movies, I smoke myself into a stupor. When the urge to eat something hits me halfway through *A Christmas Story*, I rummage through the refrigerator and end up standing in the kitchen with my fingers in the olive jar. I eat one jalapeño-stuffed olive after another until I feel sick, then finally collapse on the sofa. I think about calling James, but I'm just lucid enough to hold myself back. Instead, I watch more TV, get into a six-pack, and then a twelve-pack. Around ten I make the decision that I should crawl off to bed and make it as far as James's room before a combination of nausea and nostalgia divert my course. I peel back his sheets, climb in, pull his covers over my head, pass out.

I awaken the dawn of Christmas Day in his bed. I've brought it all back, sleeping in here, and I bury my face in his pillow. I just want to go back in time, I just want him, I just want. I jerk off, and the instant I come I'm filled with regret and shame. Getting up, I strip the bed and stumble into the kitchen to throw the sheets in the washer. Then I shower, the water scalding, scrub every inch of my skin.

When James gets back from Fort Worth, he disappears into his room, then returns with an uneasy expression. Joel, he says, Did you… sleep in my bed? No! I say, Of course not!

He knows I'm lying.

+ + +

I make a mental list of New Year's resolutions, break them all within the first week. Jess's apartment holds too much allure, and I end up spending my time trying to recreate that initial high, smoke so many cigarettes my voice falls apart. We go to clubs I've never visited myself, wouldn't be able to find in the light of day because they're so nondescript, camouflaged in between sprawling industrial complexes south of town. They're always dank and dark, and they always reek of sweat, with an undercurrent of something unmistakably male. Jess and his friends drink overpriced cocktails, dance under shifting lights, lure me into the back. My weight drops, and when James finds me hitching up my jeans, my thumb threaded through my belt loop, I can't look him in the eye.

One night, I'm stupid enough—high enough—to let Jess convince me to show him the back room. Even under the influence of two thick lines I have the initial sense to refuse, but he waves away my hesitance with a distracted hand. What do you think I'm going to find? he says, Proof that you're everything I wrote in that review? Fuck you, I say, but I speak half-heartedly, my legs twined around one of his barstools, a beer in my jittery hand. Been there, he says, lighting a cigarette and winking at me, Done that. I show him my middle finger, then grimace at the memory that extrudes, that little girl in the cherry sweater. Why do you even care? I say. Who says I care? he asks, but he sounds hurt rather than bored.

I wonder if he could help me. Not that I need his help; under the shadow of intoxication I don't need a damn thing. But somewhere far beneath the sheen of this drug lies a paranoia so raw it bleeds. I needle it, lick it like an animal would a sore. What if there's something he could say that would help? What if with the knowledge he has as a critic he could point me in the right direction?

Sharp and alert, I manage the roads. Beside me Jess whistles tunelessly, gratingly. I grit my teeth, concentrating on the traffic, the lights, the feel of the leather steering wheel beneath my hands. Then we're crunching through the gravel and pulling to a stop behind James's car. With a single-minded purpose I lead Jess across the scabby lawn and up the steps. The screen door bangs open under my touch, but the front door sticks, and when I finally shove my way into the living room, James is waiting for me, his face frozen in disapproval. I don't even nod in his direction. This way, I say to Jess, but James blocks my path. I heave an elaborate sigh. James, I say, Jess Karr.

He recognizes the name. He must have read the review because his eyes widen. I have a feeling that even if Jess were to extend his hand, James might not return the greeting. But Jess hasn't offered a hand; instead, he's drifting toward the wall, the one with my painting. The second I catch his expression, I know I've made a mistake.

What the hell are you *doing*? James asks me, What's he *doing* here? Jess glances at us over his shoulder. Who's this asshole? he asks me, jutting his chin in James's direction. James gives him an incredulous look. I'm the asshole? he says, but Jess just shrugs. When'd you paint this piece of shit? he asks me, turning his attention away from James. Senior year, I mumble. Joel! James barks like I'm giving away state secrets, and Jess gives him a second glance. What's your problem, man? he asks. You're my fucking problem! James says, and now Jess looks him over, his lip curling in a gesture rife with sudden knowledge. Oh, I'm sorry, he says, Am I fucking your boyfriend?

I stop James just before he throws a punch, lock my hold on him as he thrashes against me. Son of a bitch, he's saying, trying to weasel out from under my arms. Jess taunts him, dancing around and throwing mock punches. Jess! I say, Stop! He does, reaching for the pack of cigarettes on the coffee table. Those are mine! James growls, and Jess lets a supercilious smile tweak the corners of his mouth, tapping the box against the palm of his hand. James, I warn, but he twists free of my arms. When I try to force myself between them, I'm the one who gets a blow to the head. I stagger backward, and then they're both reaching for me. Get the fuck out of here! James says, shoving Jess away. I'm not the one who just clocked him, Jess says. Please, I moan, sinking to the sofa, Will you please just stop?

James squats down in front of me, taking my chin in his hand. I haven't been so near to him, haven't looked him so closely in the eye, in more than a year. Shit, he mumbles, turning my head to the side, I really hit you. I grunt. Are you okay? he asks. Of course he's not okay, Jess says behind him, lighting a cigarette, He probably has a concussion. I don't have a concussion, I tell them, and he says, Then let's get out of here, Joel. You're not going *anywhere*, James tells me. I don't think it's up to you, Jess says, pulling me to my feet. He's not *leaving*, James says, grabbing hold of my arm. I can make my own goddamn decisions! I tell them, shaking them away, and they both look at me. Well? Jess says, and I hesitate just long enough for him to roll his eyes. He strides toward the door, his cell phone to his ear. Joel, he says over his shoulder, You let me know when you're ready to play.

I drop to the sofa as James peers through the window to make sure that Jess is heading toward 29th and not lingering on the sidewalk. I could've driven him home, I say. Yeah, he tells me, That would've been a great idea. I reach for the cigarettes, thankful for the diversion, for the simple act of breathing in smoke and letting it out again.

Can we talk about this? James says, Can we talk about what's happening to us? There is no *us*, I say, and he manages to look offended, as if I've spoken something other than the truth. Dropping to the coffee table in front of me, he pulls a cigarette from the pack. I hand him my lighter and watch as he lights up, sick and miserable. Don't you ever wish we could be the way we used to be? he asks.

I stare at the tip of my cigarette. If I pressed it into the palm of my hand, how long could I take the pain before I screamed? I bring it to my mouth, squinting at the ember as I inhale. I could do some damage if I was so inclined. I could pick up right where my father left off.

Or James could. I flick my eyes in his direction. He's courting his cigarette, an inhale here, an exhale there; he could put that energy to better use. And I'm not painting anyway.

What? he asks, frowning at my expression, and my coke-addled brain fails to consider the invitation I'm extending. His lips part when I open my palm, his cigarette suspended halfway to his mouth. What's wrong with you? he asks. What isn't? I say. But there's weight in my tone to offset my shrug, and when I lean forward, I don't bother to smile. C'mon, James, I say, Finish what you started.

He doesn't know me. He doesn't know me anymore; I can tell that's what he's thinking, and the realization penetrates me in a way his cigarette never could. James— I start, regretting this entire fucking evening, but he crushes his butt in the ashtray. I think we're done here, he says, getting to his feet. We were done a long time ago, I say.

He slams his way into his bedroom as Pandora slinks around the corner. Seeing me, she stops, save for one twitch of her tail. For a long moment we stare at each other, until her judgment feels so thick I hurl the remote in her direction. She doesn't even flinch.

+ + +

My show has wrapped. I've sold almost everything, earned close to fifteen thousand dollars. *Crossing?* I ask when Cameron calls, and he tells me no one has made an offer. I'll hang on to it for a while, he says, That'll give you a bit more exposure. I'm fine with that if only because I don't want the damn thing back where James and I have to see it every day. In the meantime, Cameron says, Keep working.

I hang up, then stare at myself in the mirror, disturbed by the clear pronouncement of my ribs when I lift my tee shirt, the sharp angles in my hips, my face. I turn my head to the side, examining my profile, startled by who I see staring back at me.

My mother.

Just before my birthday, I talk to my father. He wants me to come down to Houston, reminds me that because I missed the holidays he hasn't seen me since last summer. I refrain from pointing out that I'd invited him on a trip and he refused to meet me halfway. Maybe next month, I say. Meanwhile, he grumbles, I have no idea what's going on with you. Well, I admit, I sold some paintings. How much did that bring you? he asks, and I sigh. The money's not the point. I'd paint anyway, even if I knew I'd never earn a cent.

We've ceased talking about agreements, deadlines. He just deposits money in my account every month, and I spend it without a word. I should be happy; I've wanted for years for him to back off, to give me what I deserve without having to plead, but instead, I feel as if some kind of transaction has been enacted, and I can't quite figure out what's been bought, what's been sold.

What else? my father says, and before I can stop myself I tell him about Jess. I can't believe what I'm doing, the way I'm twisting Jess's name to a more feminine Jessica, admitting that I met her at my opening and that we've been seeing each other since. In my fabrication Jess crosses over, becomes someone my father can handle, someone of whom I don't have to be ashamed. I babble on, then finally stumble to a halt, afraid he's not going to believe me, or worse, accuse me of lying. But he just tells me he's happy to hear I'm making progress. Yeah, I mutter, Me too.

+ + +

James bails the week of his Spring Break, leaving me alone in the house for the first time since the holidays. I'm more lost without him than I expected, and the changing weather only serves to further confuse me. The warmth of the sun, the first unfurling of the leaves, find me blinking, stupefied by the changes the last year has wrought, and I park myself in one of the lawn chairs in the backyard, trying to recover. Over the years the straps have eroded, and half my ass hangs between the cracks. I pray for the sun to leach the white from my skin.

By the end of the week I've managed six days without the coke—Jess has left town, too, on the premise of an overdue vacation—and I'm feeling at least half as healthy as I look, the whites of my eyes, my teeth, shocking against my tan. I make a determined effort to straighten up the house, to wash my bedding. When the phone rings, I glance at the Caller ID and groan; I recognize my landlord's number and know what he's going to say. Our rent has gone up every year, and there's going to come a time when James simply won't tolerate the imbalance any longer. Don't tell me, I say, You're raising the rent. Actually, he says, I'm selling the house. You're selling my house? I ask, and he reminds me that technically, it's his. He wants it on the market as soon as possible, tells me James and I can stay through the end of the semester. Unless you want to buy it yourself, he adds.

He's joking, but my mind immediately analyzes the possibilities. Last year, when I turned twenty-five, I received some money from my mother's estate, and I haven't yet touched a dime. My father gives me plenty of cash, and I've been so preoccupied with all the shit that's happened the past twelve months that I haven't thought about what, if anything, I might want to do besides reinvest; really, the amount isn't anything that could change my life. Now I wonder if it might not be smart to use the money to buy the house. My father would have to cover most of the cost, of course, but for the first time in a long while, I feel excited. There's promise here, a sliver of hope. Hell, James can live here for free.

When he gets home that afternoon, I'm ready for him. I've showered, I've made myself presentable. I've got the windows open, hoping that will chase away the stench from all the cigarettes I've been smoking. And I've called my father to ask for help. I've never understood what you see in that dump, he told me, but when I let it slip that given its proximity to campus, the property value can only go up, he phoned the landlord himself. We'll close soon—this will be a cash deal—and I'll sign the money my mother left me over to my father. I couldn't have asked for a better solution, and I step forward as James drops his bag in the doorway. Want a beer? I ask.

He doesn't know whether to accept or decline, and the thought occurs to me that maybe he thinks, after all this time, that I'm trying to seduce him. You look like you could use a beer, I decide, opening the refrigerator and retrieving two bottles. What's up? he asks, accepting one, and I tell him I've heard from our landlord. He's selling the house, I say. So we won't be renewing our lease, he muses. We don't have to, I say, My father's buying the house. What? he says. I have some money, I tell him, Not much, but I'm signing it over to my father, and he's going to buy the house. I clap my hands together, almost gleeful. He'll buy the house, I say, And you won't ever have to pay rent again. He frowns, tugging on the bill of his baseball cap. Or you can keep paying, I add, If that makes you more comfortable.

He's quiet. With that baseball cap pulled so low over his eyes he might as well be twenty years old. Maybe I should move out, he finally says, like he's just tossing around an idea, like our relationship hasn't been leading up to this for more than a year. Look, I say, I don't mind picking up your share of the rent this summer while you're in Greece. It's not about the money,

Joel, he says. Okay, I say, So? It's not about the money, he repeats, and I snap, I know it's not about the money!

We stare at each other. We've lived together for almost eight years, he tells me. Oh, I say, Is there some kind of moratorium on the length of our friendship? He takes off his cap and runs his fingers through his crushed hair. I think we could use the time apart, he admits. You're going to Greece for three months! I say, How much more time do you fucking need? Why are you making this so difficult? he asks. *I'm* making this difficult? I say, This is *my* fault? You knew you were in love with me! he cries, And you let it happen anyway!

I want to hit him with something biting, something that will make him reel. But there's nothing I can say, nowhere we can go from here. We've come to the end, and I have to turn away so he doesn't see the tears burning in my eyes. Joel..., he says, but there's not enough conviction in his voice to sway either one of us.

+ + +

I'm dismayed by the thought of living by myself, and I can't stomach the idea of moving either. I don't think I have the stamina for that kind of change. So my father closes on the house, and I sign over what little of my mother's estate I owned.

James plans on finding an apartment as soon as he gets back from Greece. I can tell he's buoyed by the thought, by everything that's happening for him: his upcoming exams, which he's determined to pass; his trip; the prospect of being on his own. I haven't seen him in such a good mood for more than a year. He's even quit smoking, and I feel positively degraded going out on the back porch without him.

And then, a few weeks later, I discover another reason why he's always so goddamn happy. He has a girlfriend.

I've run into Peter. We haven't seen much of each other lately, but when I pull in behind him at the Party Barn, where I'm picking up a twelve-pack of beer, I honk my horn, and he pulls forward to wait for me. How's it going? he asks, and I shrug. He tells me about his job, his new apartment; I'm struck by the number of people I know who clearly have their shit together, in direct contrast to the mayhem that characterizes my own life. In the hopes of portraying myself as something other than the loser I am, I decide to offer up the news that I've bought a house. Sort of. James told me you decided to go through with it, he says, spoiling my surprise, Congratulations. He's moving out, I add. Because of Elizabeth? he asks.

I shouldn't be surprised; it's been over a year. But I still feel blindsided. What's she like? I ask. She's just some girl, he says, looking miserable for having brought her up at all, I'm sure it's nothing. If it's nothing, I say, Then why's he keeping her from me?

When James passes his qualifying exams a couple of weeks later, I offer to take him out to celebrate, just to hear what he'll say. He apologizes, fumbling and sheepish. I kind of have plans, he says. Oh yeah? I say, knowing he means with Elizabeth, and he stumbles all over himself trying to explain why he can't include me. I'd laugh if I wasn't so disgusted. I'd laugh if I wasn't so hurt I can barely look at him. Another time, he says. Yeah, I say, Right.

+ + +

You're gaunt, my father tells me when I finally concede to his persistent demands and drive to Houston for the weekend. Maybe it's the drugs, I say, and he informs me that if I'm trying to set some kind of precedent, I might as well leave right now. I was joking, I say, casting a semi-apologetic glance in Catherine's direction. She smiles, though she looks briefly concerned; I almost check my reflection in the mirror above the fireplace. Then my cell phone rings, and I divert my attention to the number on the screen.

Kyle. He's quit his job to start an Internet company, and on the few occasions we've spoken he's offered me work. Please, I've said every time, You know where you can go with that shit. Just before I silence my phone, I realize I could use a minute to regroup, and I mumble a quick excuse to my father and Catherine, then duck out the back door. I'm in Houston, I say, bypassing a greeting. Yeah? Kyle says, Well, guess who I just saw? Who? I say. Adam Atwater, he tells me, And he asked about you. He did? I say, not quite believing him. He did, Kyle assures me, lighting up a cigarette. The sound has me reaching in my pocket, but I've left all evidence of my habit in the Explorer. Instead, I lower myself to the edge of the pool, the water a welcome reprieve to the humidity.

What did you tell him? I ask, and Kyle snorts. Certainly not the truth, he says. What's that supposed to mean? I ask. Honey, he says, Do you honestly think I don't know that you're sleeping with the enemy? How the hell do you know that? I ask.

Kyle's silent. That prick, I say. He's worried about you, Joel, Kyle says. He's part of the fucking problem, I remind him, and he tells me that even so, James has a point. You don't know Jess, I tell him. We've met, he says, adding: I'm unimpressed.

Well, so am I, but I'm not going to tell him that. So you didn't say anything to Adam? I ask, changing the subject. No, he says, I didn't. Is he seeing anyone? I ask, trying to sound offhand, but Kyle isn't fooled. You know what this city's like, he says, Why didn't you go out with him when you had the chance?

I mull over his question at dinner that night as I try to figure out why after all these years I still want my father to like me, respect me, accept me. Not once does he ask about my work, not once does he mention my show, though I make a point to ask him about Permian. Instead, he's curious about Jessica. Yeah, I say, We're still seeing each other. He wants to know what she's like, what she does for a living; since I'm lying anyway, I tell him she's in information technology, then bask in his admiration for half a second before I remember that this is all bullshit. Do you have a picture? he asks. Sorry, I mumble, but he waves me off, full of good humor. I glance at

212

Catherine, who looks just as worried as when I first walked in the door. When are we going to meet her? my father asks. Soon, I say.

Needless to say, I don't sleep well that night despite a harder swim than I've had in months. I wake with the dawn and grab my trunks. Then I make my way downstairs where I put on a pot of coffee. Leaning against the counter, I wait for the coffee to brew, agonizing over the changes the years have brought to this kitchen, this house. Right here, I knelt on a chair turned backward, playing with a sink full of soapy water; right here, I sat with my watercolors spread around me and a brush too expensive for a six-year-old held in my hand. Almost seven years since she died and looking around this kitchen, I find it difficult to believe she even existed.

I'm tired of lying to my father. I hate wondering what that conversation between James and Kyle sounded like, I hate worrying about what Kyle might have told Adam. I hate Jess and his goddamn drugs, but I don't much like myself sober either. I rub a hand over my tired eyes, thinking about my mother. What advice would she give me if she could? But maybe I wouldn't be in this predicament, this perpetual purgatory, if she were here with me. Maybe if she hadn't died, my life would be completely different.

Joel? Catherine asks, and I jerk my eyes from the past. She's standing in the doorway, dressed in gym gear, her hair pulled back in a ponytail only slightly longer than my own. I straighten, then gesture to the coffee pot. Couldn't sleep, I admit, and she nods. She probably couldn't either; I'd realized last night that this weekend marks only the fourth I've spent with her since we met. We can't possibly be at ease with each other yet, though there's little doubt that she makes far more of an effort than I. Two years in a row I've received a birthday card written in her hand; several times I've come across voicemails letting me know that she's in Austin and—no pressure—but if I'm available, she'd love to meet for lunch. I've never returned her calls.

I wonder if she's happy, married to my father. I wonder if they fight. I wonder if she gives as good as she gets.

Mind if I join you? she asks, and I smother a sigh. She retrieves a mug from the cupboard and pours a scant tablespoon of half and half at the bottom. Cream? she asks, and I shake my head. She hesitates; I almost expect her to tell me I could use the weight. But she just leans back against the opposite counter. You headed out to the pool? she asks, and I tell her I'll be quiet, that I won't wake my father. That's not what I meant, she says. You taking a class or something? I ask, nodding at her clothing. I was thinking about it, she tells me, and I say, Looks like you were doing more than thinking about it. I don't usually find you alone, she confesses, as if stumbling across me in the kitchen at this hour might honestly induce her to change her plans. You're better off with the class, I assure her, reaching for the coffee pot. She holds out her mug, and I pour her some coffee, then fill my own cup. Joel, she says, How are you?

Unexpected tears spring to my eyes. I'm fine, I say, shaking them away, I'm good. Without thinking I take a swallow of coffee, scalding my tongue; she watches me with the same expression she wore two summers ago when she saw the scars on my arms. For just a second I think about blurting it all out, starting with my father's cigars. You're gay, she says, Aren't you?

My stomach bottoms out.

I'm right, she says, Aren't I?

There's no point in denial. Anything I say in my defense will just make me look that much guiltier.

Tell me he doesn't know, I say. He doesn't know, she says. Are you *sure*? I ask.

But she's telling the truth. If my father knew, I wouldn't be standing here right now. If my father knew, I'd have been kicked out long ago. Trust me, she says, He's far more concerned about the drugs. That was a *joke*! I cry, and now she actually looks afraid, as if she's blaming my appearance on an AIDS diagnosis. I slump against the counter. You don't know me, I whisper. I'd like to, she says, and for just a second I hesitate; I have to talk to someone. But then I shake my head. I need you to promise that you're not going to say anything to him, I tell her. I wouldn't, she says.

I think I believe her. No matter what Elisa promised back in college, I have a feeling she broached the subject with James. Of course she did. But one word from Catherine and my father would have nothing more to do with me. I think she knows that.

I've had a hard year, I admit, And I feel like shit, but I'm fine. I look her in the eye. Do you understand? I ask, and she nods. Joel— she starts, but I'm done. I let myself out the back door and head in the direction of the pool. She's smart enough not to follow.

+ + +

The next morning, I barrel my way north back to Austin. You'll have to bring Jessica soon, my father said as I swung my bag into the back of the Explorer. Sure, I said, avoiding Catherine's eye, and he gave me a good-natured cuff on the shoulder.

I put distance between myself and my debacle of a weekend, kill that conversation with Catherine as I follow the highway like I'd take a pencil to a familiar maze. With every mile my tension eases a little more, and I shake a cigarette from a fresh pack of Marlboros and crush the end against the lighter. Taking a long inhale, I let the windows slide down, let the wind fly through my hair. God, I miss my convertible. That sun would sear my skin on the trip back to Austin, even this early in the season, but sometimes I still wish I had my hands on that wheel. I would, if James hadn't taken my keys that day, if he hadn't been arguing with Darryl.

James. He's the only reason I'm heading to Austin. The back room certainly can't take credit for my trek north. Neither can Peter or Kyle. I have nothing much drawing me home except the off-chance that James and I might, despite everything, have something left to salvage. I don't like the idea of him talking to Kyle behind my back, but he's obviously concerned enough about me that he extended himself. And so what if he's dating some girl? That was inevitable, and anyway, I'm not jealous. I just want some of him, some of what we had. Especially after this weekend, I just want some of what we had.

I know he's leaving for Greece soon, I know he's moving out when he returns. But a handful of conversations before his plane takes off in a few weeks might make all the difference. I crank up the volume on the stereo, ruminating. I'll stop on the way home for some beer in case we're running low. A simple conversation in the swing on the front porch. Or on the back steps if that swing makes him feel as crazy as it makes me feel.

But when I get home, after I've stashed the beer in the fridge, I stop short in his doorway. The room's empty.

He comes home twenty minutes later, looking sick and apologetic. I thought you weren't coming back until this afternoon, he tells me, as if the only problem we have is my schedule. Oh, I say, Were you planning on moving back before then? He launches into his excuse, tells me that he got a call from one of his professors; she knew he'd be looking for a place to live by the end of the summer and has a garage apartment within his price range. I just figured I should take it while I have the chance, he explains. You're not even going to be here this summer! I say, incredibly hurt that he's in such a hurry to be rid of me that he'll pay the extra money for rent when he knows, he knows I'd have never made him pay a cent. I was afraid someone else would take it, he mumbles.

Does he not have any idea what I felt, coming home and realizing he'd moved out without warning me? How long has he been planning this?

Did your girlfriend help you move? I ask. What? he says. You heard me, I say, and he actually blushes. Sh-she's not my girlfriend, he stammers. You're fucking her, I say, Aren't you?

If I told him I was sleeping with his fourteen-year-old sister, his expression couldn't be more enraged, and I'm momentarily caught off-guard; he's more serious about her than I thought. I haven't mentioned Elizabeth, he says in a tight-ass voice, Because I didn't want to upset you. Well, thanks, I tell him, my tone saccharine, Finding out from Peter wasn't even remotely humiliating. God, I'm so sick of feeling sorry for you! he says, I'm so sick of the fucking responsibility! I never asked you to take responsibility for me! I say, I'm perfectly capable of taking care of myself! Well, congratulations, Joel, he says, You're doing a fantastic job.

I hit him. There's no thought involved; I'm just suddenly all arm, and when my fist makes contact, he stumbles backward, pulling the barstool down with him. He touches his lip, staring in disbelief at the blood and the way I'm standing above him, my hand still closed in a fist. Then he struggles to his feet.

I'm not quite sorry enough to stop him from leaving.

+ + +

The summer's hellish, impossibly worse than I could've imagined. Twice, twice, our air conditioner breaks. My air conditioner. I'm starting to regret my decision to buy the house. I could've moved into one of the apartment complexes not far from here or better yet, miles away. I could have a nice little patio and forego mowing my poor excuse for a lawn. Or at least writing out the check so someone else can do it.

But I'm kidding myself. How could I leave? This house is home, more home than I've ever known. I've unclasped his necklace and buried it in my dresser, but he's still everywhere I turn.

So I deal with it—the lapses of cold air, his absence—and I see too much of Jess, do way too much coke. I stay out all night, stumble in around five or six in the morning and find myself in the back room. In a coke-induced frenzy I take a box cutter to an acrylic in lavender and gray. I'm both repelled and attracted by the *thhhtt* the blade makes as I gouge the canvas. By the time I finish I'm shaking, and I wipe sweat and tears from my face with the back of my arm. Strips of canvas litter the floor at my feet. Noticing that I'm barefoot, I take that moment to traipse through the house looking for my shoes. I completely forget about what I've done, and when I pass the back room the next afternoon and see the mutilated canvas, I feel physically ill.

I should talk to Peter more but don't. He's consumed with work and Amy, and he calls one night to tell me he has some news. Can you meet me for a drink? he asks. Why? I say, afraid he's going to tell me that James and Elizabeth have eloped. But when I'm sitting across from him, he admits he's the one planning a wedding. Hey, that's great, I say, trying to muster up some enthusiasm, Congratulations. Thanks, he says, grinning with so much gusto I'm almost embarrassed for him. Have you set a date? I ask, and he tells me they're looking at next summer, mid-June. I'm hoping you'll stand up there with me, he says, Be a groomsman.

I flag the bartender and ask for a glass of water, realizing too late that I should've bought Peter a celebratory shot. But I think I'm going to be sick, and when the bartender sets my water in front of me, I take a long, shaky swallow. Are you okay? Peter asks with a curious expression. Did you ask James, too? I say. Is that a problem? Peter asks, and I shake my head. No, I say, Of course not.

I get the idea that I should pick up running again. I walk to the end of the block one humid morning, break into a slow jog, and can't believe how little air I can draw into my lungs. The cigarettes have taken their toll. I go a half a mile, probably less if I want to be honest, before I have to stop because I can barely breathe. I walk back to the house, my hand pressed against the stitch in my side, and when I'm back home, I scout around for Pandora, who senses my desire for at least a modicum of connection and flies under my bed. I'm all you've got, I remind her, because the fact of the matter is that James didn't just leave me when he moved out; he left his cat behind as well. I stretch my arm in her direction, and she hisses at me. Yeah? I say, Well, fuck you, too.

That night, I take one bump too many trying to maintain my high and end up pacing back and forth in front of the windows at Jess's apartment. You're going to have to calm down, man, Jess says from where he's crashed out on his bed. I glance over at him, at the casual sway of his cocked knee, the lit cigarette dangling from his fingers. You're part of the problem, I inform him. Why don't you come over here and tell me that, he says, setting his cigarette in an ashtray beside the bed. You think I'm lying? I ask, stepping toward him, and he pulls me down. Together we thrash, a complicated pile of limbs and misery. What's this? he says, yanking on my limp dick. Spit shines on his bottom lip, sparkling in the glow from all of his precious recessed lighting, and I turn my head away from him. He laughs, reaching for his cigarette. I wince when his elbow digs into my abdomen.

Propping his chin on the back of his hand, he takes a drag. As he inhales, a sliver of ash falls to my skin. I suck in my breath, and he closes one eye, examining my reaction. You like that? he asks. Fuck you, Jess, I say, rolling away from him, but he holds me back. You should be nicer to me, he suggests. Why? I ask, and he says, Because I'm not a bad guy. Who told you that? I say, Your mother? He chuckles; I can never tell what he finds truly funny and what he's stockpiling to use against me. His cigarette crackles when he raises his fingers to his mouth. Let me up, I say. What's the magic word? he asks, threading his legs through mine. Let me up, you prick, I say, but he just settles his weight more defiantly across my torso. *Prick* is not the magic word, he tells me. I try to push him off of me, but he catches my wrist, his cigarette between his lips. This time, the ash hits my chest. Get *off*, Jess, I say, and he laughs, the cigarette falling from his mouth. I scramble away as he moans over the burn in his sheet. What're you doing? he asks when he looks up and finds me rushing into my clothes. Don't touch me, I say, jerking away from him. Honey, he protests. Don't *fucking* call me honey! I yell.

By the time I get in the Explorer I'm shaking, great tremors that emanate from the core of my being. I screech to a halt on the side of the road and fumble in my jeans until my fingers close on the Xanax I filched on my last trip into Jess's bathroom. I have two pills in my palm, and I dry swallow them both, choking when they stick to my parched throat.

Hazards flashing, I sit in the Explorer until I think I can drive.

+ + +

James calls a couple of weeks later. I haven't spoken to him in three months, and I sink to my bed at the familiar sound of his voice. Twice he asks if I'm still there. Yeah, I say, rubbing my hand across my face, I'm here.

I meet him for lunch at noon, still a little high from the two quick lines I cut before my shower. They're a consolation prize from Jess. He's been tender with me, touches the back of my neck when I'm scrolling through my cell phone, reaches for my hand. Will you fucking stop already? I said last night when he tried to tuck a strand of hair behind my ear, I'm not your goddamn boyfriend.

James hasn't shaved in weeks. Nice beard, I tell him, instinctively reaching into my shirt pocket for a cigarette, and he strokes his jaw. I replace my cigarette with shaking fingers, remembering where I am. How are you, Joel? he asks. I'm great, I tell him without much fervor. I'm glad, he says.

I drink beer, order black bean enchiladas, feel like crying, will myself not to. He talks about Greece, his friends, his work, and when he asks about me, I excuse myself to take a piss, then stare at my reflection in the mirror. I look gray and unhealthy, and I'm incredibly conscious of how terrible I must look to him. How's your painting? he asks as I settle into the chair across from him again. Look, I say, Can we just… not…? We stare at each other across the chasm of our friendship. I missed talking to you this summer, he offers, I want—

I know what you want, I interrupt, You've already told me! He flicks his eyes apologetically at the couple next to us. Oh, am I embarrassing you? I ask, raising my voice, and he brings his eyes back to mine. Settle down, he says quietly. Then don't give me some bullshit story about missing me this summer! I say. I reach for my cigarettes again, then drop the box back on the table. I didn't hear a word from you all summer, I tell him, So don't expect me to just show up here and have lunch with you and tell you everything's okay so you can feel better about yourself! My nose burns, and I swipe it with the back of my hand. It's not okay, James, I say, It's just… not okay.

Joel, he says, You're bleeding. He gestures toward his nose, and when I look down at my hand, I see the blood. Maybe it's time for you to talk to someone, he says. The last thing I need is a fucking shrink, I say, tilting my head back, and he hesitates. I could go with you, he says.

Couples counseling. For this sham of a relationship. Right, I say, Because we do everything together, don't we?

6

I don't want to admit it, but I know James is right. I'm barely alive. I can't even remember the way the brush feels between my fingers, the sound of its stroke against the canvas. I need to get that back. I don't stand a chance if I can't get that back.

At the same time, I'm leery about opening myself up, about getting in a situation where I'm forced to talk about how I got to this point, this shitty place where I can't set foot in the back room without feeling like I'm going to burst into tears. I'd even take medication if I thought it would help, but I don't think this is something physiological, some mistake of chemistry I can correct. I'm here because I fucked up. And if I don't figure out some way to claw myself out, I have a feeling I'm going all the way down.

I make some tentative calls, and after I've left a half a dozen messages with various analysts without getting any callbacks I figure that the entire city's just as fucked up as I am but doing a better job of hiding it. Don't you sound eager, Kyle says when I answer the phone in a rush, and I blurt out that I'm thinking about getting into therapy and I'm waiting for a psychiatrist to call me back. The news momentarily silences him, and just when I'm starting to regret saying anything, just as I'm about to tell him I'm kidding, he says, I think that's a good idea, sweetheart.

Now I'm the one who's quiet. But he just says, If you're having a hard time finding someone, I might be able to help. You're in therapy? I ask, hoping that's the case so I won't feel like such a total fucking loser. Not at the moment, he admits, But I know someone. He lowers his voice conspiratorially. He's one of us, he confides.

Dr. Barrington returns my call within the hour. I tell him I'm interested in scheduling an appointment; he tells me his rates. They're exorbitant, and his next available appointment isn't until the end of September. Come fifteen minutes early to fill out some paperwork, he says, And bring a list of any medications you're taking.

I hang up, feeling better than I have in a long time. I start clearing the table, and once I get going, I can't stop. I clean the kitchen, scour through the refrigerator tossing out half its contents: moldy tomatoes; half-eaten pizza rigid with age; a jar of salad dressing Elisa bought so many years ago I grimace when I see the date. I clean the floor, actually get down and do it by hand with an old towel and Windex because there's nothing else in the house. In the bathroom I scrub out the tub until my arms ache, my hair swinging sweaty into the corners of my mouth. By the time I'm finished I'm starving, and I shower, then go out to get something to eat and come back with take-out Chinese. I set my plate of moo shui chicken in front of me, resolved, organized. I'm ready to move forward.

+ + +

In Dr. Barrington's office a few weeks later I balk at the paperwork I'm expected to complete. I'm not about to list the cause of my mother's death as suicide or divulge the excesses of my drug habit over the past year. Instead, I scrawl about having difficulty working, admit that yeah, maybe I'm a little anxious. I check the boxes that indicate I drink socially once or twice a week, then hand the papers back to the receptionist. I barely have a chance to sit down again before Dr. Barrington calls my name.

He's wearing jeans and a faded green golf shirt that's too tight around his biceps, and when I stand, he presses the palm of my hand with his own. Call me Bryan, he says, and I'm suddenly conscious of what I'm wearing: the tear in the leg of my khakis, the scuffed toe of my sandal. Remembering Kyle's comment, I yank my fingers away. But Bryan's nothing but professional. Please, he says, Come in.

He offers me a seat, and I choose a leather chair, casting an unobtrusive eye around his office, which reminds me an awful lot of Jess's apartment: hard edges, carefully placed art, a Persian carpet he must have bought at auction. Lighting fit for a confessional. I reach for a cigarette, then lower my hand.

I'm going to ask you a few questions, Bryan says, sitting down across from me, And then we'll see where we need to go from there, okay? I grunt in reluctant agreement, and he leans back, looking through my paperwork. I watch him from lowered lids. He's a good twenty years older than I am, his hair a muddy shade of brown but strewn with gray, lines crawling from the corners of his eyes. He has a nose like a hook.

So, what's up, Joel? he asks after a minute, You're having a hard time working? I nod, jiggling my foot. What kind of work are we talking about? he asks. I'm an artist, I mumble, and this time, unlike freshman year, there's no smile I have to suppress. He nods, taking quick notes with a black Mont Blanc. What else? he asks. What do you mean? I say, and he says, What's on your mind?

At first I don't know how to answer him, but then for some stupid reason I start telling him about Jess, that I met him the night of my opening, that he slaughtered my work but that I've continued seeing him. Why do you think you're sleeping with him? he asks when I lapse into a helpless silence. I don't know, I say. How's your sleep? he asks. Shitty, I admit. Do you take anything to help? he asks, and I mutter something noncommittal. What about alcohol? he asks, Recreational drugs? What about them? I say, thinking this session seems more like an interrogation than an attempt to get me back on track. Do you indulge? he asks. I shake my head. Not even an occasional beer? he says, and I give him a look. But I feel like I've given myself away, and I glance out the window. Sunlight drenches the skyline, and the sight, instead of inspiring me the way it might have once upon a time, depresses the shit out of me. Somewhere out there, Jess wanders around his loft; somewhere just north, in a garage apartment I've never seen, James holds Elizabeth in his arms. We're damaged, all of us, but no one more than I.

You've been depressed, Bryan says. He doesn't ask; he places the statement as fact, and I have a hard time swallowing. I can't paint, I tell him. Do you ever think about hurting yourself? he asks. No, I say. But my hands have started shaking; he's astute enough to notice. I'm going to write you two prescriptions, he decides, One for an antidepressant and one for anxiety. He tells me I'll get some immediate relief from the Xanax, but the Prozac needs a little time to reach efficacy. In the meantime, he says, Let's schedule an appointment for next week.

I leave with a wicked headache, but I call James anyway. I'm seeing a shrink, I tell him. Really? he says, like I might be fucking with him. I just left my first appointment, I say, and the sigh he releases could've filled the Hindenburg. I'm so glad, Joel, he says, I'm so glad you're finally getting some help. Yeah, I say, already irritated by his enthusiasm, Well, you're part of the problem, so... You can't keep blaming me for your shit, Joel, he says.

I hang up on him. I don't want to listen to his recriminations, and anyway, I'm pulling into the pharmacy. I'm salivating at the thought of release, and I wrench the cap from the Xanax the second the bottle's in my hand. This time, not coming down from anything but my own shit, I start to relax. Even before I'm home I can feel the slow *tick tick tick* of everything around me subsiding. This shit I could abuse if I'm not careful.

Curled on the sofa in the living room, the back of my hand resting on my forehead, I let myself melt, one minute to the next. Then I reach for the phone. I shouldn't have hung up on you, I say, and James tells me to forget about it, in a voice that suggests he was probably asleep. I glance at my watch. Somehow, it's midnight, but he's magnanimous despite the hour, despite the fact that he's likely not alone. Let's meet for dinner next week, he says, How about Wednesday? Wednesday works, I say. Soon, then, he promises, and I reach for Pandora. For once she lets me cradle her, and I slide right into a dreamless sleep.

+ + +

The next morning, I'm a little creaky from having crashed on the couch. My head's killing me, and my stomach doesn't feel much better; that's the Prozac, I'm sure of it. But I go into the back room anyway. In my absence dust has settled on the table where I keep my supplies, and I blow a wad of cat fur from my palette. I should probably spend some time straightening up, but instead, I reach for a tube of paint. I don't even care what color I've grabbed; I just want to see a coil on my palette. I just want to rub linseed oil between my fingers and then hold them to my nose, because that's the most powerful aphrodisiac I know.

But the longer I stand in front of that blank canvas, the harder my hands shake, and to compensate I swallow one Xanax too many and end up sprawled across the sofa with a cigarette that burns to the filter before I've managed more than a handful of drags. Shit, I mutter when I realize I've bled the day dry, and I make a mental note to pare back, to take just enough Xanax to steady my hands but not so much that I'm crawling into bed at night without having accomplished anything all goddamn day.

I find that the Xanax gets me through the morning but not if I have any intention of painting. Too much and I'm staring slack-eyed at the television, forgetting to flick the ash from my cigarette. Scaling back, I'm out of my mind, and by the middle of the afternoon on Sunday, surrounded by blank canvas, I think: fuck this shit. I'm out of here.

I go on a three day binge that I can't much remember after the fact. I have vague recollections of Jess hunched over his laptop, cranking out something for the *Chronicle* on a deadline as I stumble around his apartment; of hitting some club and then wandering off with a guy who might've had a nose ring; of arguing with Jess. I have the black eye to prove it, and I stare at my reflection in my rearview mirror on Wednesday morning after Jess finally kicks me out. No more, he said, and I frowned at his blood-encrusted lip, wondering if I threw the punch. I have no memory of hitting him.

Lost in the remnants of my high, I drive home, then sit on the front porch smoking cigarette after cigarette until the sun rises. Inside I struggle with the childproof cap on my Xanax, take two. Then I fall into my bed's embrace.

When the doorbell chimes long and hard—obviously not for the first time—I groan, then squint in the direction of the clock. Can it really be seven? At night? I throw the covers over my head, then tear them away when I hear the front door open and James call my name.

I'm staggering into my jeans as he appears in the doorway of my bedroom. Door was unlocked, he says, averting his eyes like he hasn't stripped me once or twice himself. Yeah, I say, scratching my hands through my hair. What happened? he asks, gesturing toward my eye, then tailing me into the bathroom, where I lean against the sink and peer into the mirror. I trace the swelling with my finger, then catch James's reflection. Viewed together, we're ridiculous. He's the picture of health, his cheeks flushed pink, his hair tousled into such perfection I half-believe he arranged it himself instead of just meeting the wind headlong. My own hair I haven't combed since Sunday, and I suddenly can't recall the last time I brushed my teeth.

I don't remember, I mutter, reaching for the toothpaste, and he gives me a closer look, like he's trying to ascertain exactly how many drugs I currently have in my system. You don't remember? he asks, and I shrug, shoving my toothbrush in my mouth so I don't have to answer him. He watches me, leaning against the doorjamb; how many nights did we spend in exactly this position, readying ourselves for whatever the evening had in store? I rinse my mouth, then edge past him.

We talked about getting some dinner, he says, following me. Yeah, I forgot, I tell him, and he nods. I shift my eyes away from him, in the direction of the window. Night's coming on thick, choking out the light. Well, he finally says, sighing.

Guilt-ridden, I offer him a beer. We can order a pizza, he suggests, as if I have any interest in trying to recreate the sort of atmosphere here we once indulged. Yeah, I say, dropping onto the sofa, Okay. Tell me about your therapy, he suggests, opening the refrigerator and extracting two bottles. What do you want to know? I ask.

Making his way through one beer and then another, James asks me questions—did I like the guy, do I think he might be able to help, did he prescribe any medication—until I finally moan. Look, I say, I really don't want to rehash the whole fucking session with you. I'm just trying to help, he protests. Well, I don't have the energy to go through this shit twice in one week, I tell him. Setting his mouth, he reaches for Pandora; I can't help but be pleased by the way she squirms out from under his hands. How's the dissertation going? I ask. Not well, he admits. Huh, I muse, taking a sip of my beer and knowing I couldn't sound any more insincere, That sucks.

+ + +

So how've you been? Bryan asks early the next evening. I'm sitting across from him in the same leather chair, wondering why I've bothered to come back. I almost didn't. I'm still reeling from the events of the past week, still find it hard to believe I snorted enough coke to stay high for something approaching sixty hours. Without the Xanax I'd be shaking hard enough for him to suggest rehab. Bryan watches as I work my thumb into my mouth. I've had a shitty week, I mumble. Mm, he says, Looks like you got in a fight. I don't elaborate, and he tries a different tactic. How's your anxiety? he asks, Has the Xanax helped? Maybe, I say, noncommittal. What about the Prozac? he asks, and I tell him I don't like it, that it makes my stomach hurt, that it numbs me out, though frankly, I'm not sure of anything given the amount of drugs I've consumed since I last saw him. He doesn't say anything, and I have a quick mental image of pulling the knot of his tie tight enough to choke him. I don't want to take it anymore, I add, I want to paint clean.

He's quiet, and I look down at my hands. He waits, one leg crossed over the other, without saying a thing. The technique's profoundly effective because after thirty seconds I can't handle the silence, and before I know what I'm doing I've started talking about James, how he dropped by last night, how we've known each other for eight years, how strange the house feels with him gone. I can hardly believe I'm spouting this shit to a stranger, but Bryan just takes notes with the same Mont Blanc, interjecting only once. This is a platonic relationship? he asks. No, I say flatly, I've been fucking him since freshman year.

If he's taken aback by my sarcasm, I can't tell. I cross my arms over my chest, my fists buried in my armpits. I won't tell him about my conversation with James on the front porch the summer I was seeing Darryl, or what transpired in the months following; those secrets are better left buried. But I find myself blathering about my decision to buy the house, about James moving while I was out of town. That must have hurt, he says. Can I smoke in here? I ask. Bryan shakes his head. I pull my hands through my hair. I miss him, I admit, I miss him, and I'm so fucking pissed that he left.

I go into the back room that night after my appointment. I'm clean for the moment; I've flushed the Prozac down the toilet against Bryan's advice. Your body needs time to adjust, he told me, And we can always try something else if the Prozac isn't effective. But I don't like the idea of trial and error, don't want to sample a half a dozen different meds hoping to hit on something that works. I just need to paint.

At the same time, I can't bring myself to dump the Xanax. The fix is just too easy, and I'm smart enough to recognize that I'm better off keeping that bottle in my medicine cabinet than finding too late that I'm in a bind. Anyway, I'm hoping I won't need the Xanax at all.

I take a tentative step through the doorway, into this room that houses my very spirit. In a gesture of supplication I touch my hand to my chest, then approach the canvas the way I might an altar. Breath audible, I take in the entirety of my easel, the wood pocked like an adolescent in serious need of Clearasil. The accumulation of more than seven years of drippings, blood spilled from my brush. And the canvas itself, white and bare, like the ghost of a lover.

Chestnut, gold, and a scarlet that almost two years later won't let me go: these are the colors I choose, a quiet mixing of pigment broken only by the scrape of the palette knife against the wood of my palette. Darkness reigns outside the windows, but here in the back room I have the right light to work, and I pick a brush from the container on the table behind me, then bow my head.

His face has angles I don't remember, fault lines that fill me with doubt. Twice I almost stop, let my brush clatter to the floor in defeat. Instead, I close my eyes, then loosen my hold on expectation. I'm here, in the back room, prostrating myself for the sake of connection. Whatever I'm offered I'm grateful to accept.

+ + +

I reach out to the one person in my life who's least likely not to silence his phone when he sees my number on the Caller ID. What'd you have in mind? Kyle asks, his tone indicating that he already has a party halfway planned. I was thinking lunch, I tell him. How about tea? he asks. Tea? I say, confused. High tea, he says, At the Four Seasons. He tells me he'll make a reservation, says he'll meet me on Sunday at three. You're serious, I say. Indubitably, he assures me.

I show up ten minutes late, irritated that I had to scour my closet for something befitting our destination. If I wanted to frequent the Four Seasons, I could've just called my father; he'd be more than happy to meet me here. I make my way over to Kyle, who looks me up and down before proclaiming me presentable. But you could be so much hotter if you tried, he adds as I yank out the chair across from him. I'm hot because I don't give a shit, I inform him, Now, do you want to tell me what we're doing here? He gazes back with a placid expression. Sighing, I pick up a menu, then perk up when I see that I can order champagne right alongside my Earl Grey. Do we get food? I ask. The food, he informs me, Is the very best part.

But scones do nothing for me, and after I mow through the tiny sandwiches on the bottom of that four-tiered tray I just signal for another champagne. You're feeling better, Kyle says, giving his index finger a delicate lick. A little, I admit. He's good, isn't he? he asks, The psychiatrist I recommended? You saw him too? I ask, surprised, and Kyle shrugs. I like to dabble, he says. But why? I ask, and he laughs. You mean because I seem so well-adjusted? he says. Well, yeah, I admit, embarrassed, Sort of. He's quiet for a minute, stirring his tea. I have my moments, he finally says, Just like anyone.

I contemplate that for a minute, watching him. Something compelled him to contact Bryan at some point, and I suppose I should be thankful. If not for his recommendation, I might be with Jess this afternoon, might be high out of my mind; I certainly wouldn't be looking at an evening in front of the canvas. But I feel uncomfortable all the same, like Kyle and I just discovered we're sleeping with the same guy. And the thin prick of jealousy beneath the discomfort: what's that about?

I take a good, long swallow of champagne as Kyle reaches for some kind of truffle. I don't know what he'd have done if I'd eaten my share; he's cleaned his way from one tier to the next without any help from me. So you're seeing him once a week? Kyle asks, popping the truffle in his mouth. I nod. He wanted me on meds, I add. And? Kyle asks, raising his eyebrows. I'd rather not, I say.

I can't tell whether or not he thinks I've made the wrong decision. But I'm certain I'm better off without them, especially when I get home, where I have the presence of mind to head straight into the back room. There I try to lose myself the way I have for years. Painting has never been so difficult, and I take repeated steps back, reminding myself to relish the simplicity of what I have in front of me—a dozen tubes of paint, a palette within reach—because if I get too caught up in criticizing the canvas, I'll never be able to continue. When over the next few days my brush feels too heavy, I trade it for a pencil and doodle in the margins of a menu from the pizza place down the street. Maybe I don't have to take everything so seriously.

I survive a week without the coke. I have a significant fucking headache, and my hands aren't as steady as I'd like, but I don't see Jess; I don't even speak to him. He leaves messages on my cell, which I ignore. I'm too busy making my way from one day to the next like I'm connecting the dots in a kindergarten assignment. I'm not sure of the final picture, but I know this much: I'm not going back to Bryan empty-handed.

+ + +

Bryan would've fit right in at the Four Seasons. That's what I'm thinking as I plant myself across from him on Thursday night; he would've been a better companion for Kyle. I'd been wearing a cashmere sweater I should've bought in a smaller size, the one pair of jeans without holes I currently own. Bryan's dressed in camel-colored trousers, an olive shirt with the collar unbuttoned. My session with him today probably wouldn't cover the cost of his shoes. Joel? he says, and I lift my eyes. He offers me a sliver of a smile, which I'm thankful to get. I have work to do here, and I'm slacking, picturing him at high tea with a glass of champagne in those thick fingers.

Sitting forward, I tell him what I've done: that despite repeated messages from Jess, I haven't called him back, that I've managed to make it through the week with minimal doses of Xanax, that—most importantly— I've been working. How does that feel? he asks, and I admit that right now, everything feels rote. But I'm working, I say, And that's something, right? What do you think? he asks, and I almost groan. Are you just going to turn every question around? I ask. What do you think? he says, but this time he's smiling, and for just a second I think about Kyle sitting in this office, eliciting the same response. I know one of your clients, I blurt out. Oh? Bryan says. Kyle Whittier, I say. Bryan nods, noncommittal, and I shrug. I hooked up with him a few days ago, I say, then regret my choice of words. I clear my throat. I mean, I say, We met for… lunch.

Bryan's silent, waiting to see where I'm going with this information. I guess…, I say, I guess I don't have a lot of friends. What about James? Bryan asks, and I blink. He didn't even have to look at his notes. What about him? I ask. Have you spoken to him? he asks. I shake my head, embarrassed both by my confession that I don't have a lot of friends—what kind of a loser can't scrounge up more than one person to meet for lunch?—as well as the deterioration of my relationship with James. A handful of years ago, I wouldn't have been able to imagine a time when calling James would precipitate an anxiety attack. Now I have no connection with his day-to-day, couldn't tell you if he'd given up coffee or needs a haircut. We didn't used to be this way, I mumble. How did you used to be? Bryan asks.

His question makes me ache, like I have a lover just out of reach. I don't know, I say, I used to be able to rely on him, I guess. I stare down at my hands, clenching and unclenching my fingers. I have paint under my nails; the sight gives me a subtle boost of confidence. There've been times,

I admit, When I've been blocked creatively. And James…? Bryan says. James kicks my ass into gear, I say. Are you blocked now? he asks. That's why I'm here, I remind him. Fair enough, he says, Does James know how you're feeling? I shrug. He must have some idea; he lived with me until recently, saw me crashed out on the sofa every afternoon, noticed the absence of paint on my hands. Whether or not he knows the extent of the paralysis is anybody's guess. Would he be willing to talk to you about what you're going through? Bryan asks. I don't know, I say, trying to picture myself making that call. I don't like the idea of feeling any more vulnerable with him than the past couple of years have rendered me. Still, I've always been able to count on him, always. When my mother killed herself— I say, then stop, realizing what I've done. I fold my arms across my chest. What did you want me to do? I mutter, Write on the fucking forms that she committed suicide? He doesn't say anything, and I close my eyes. Well, she did, I say sourly, She did.

I spend the rest of the hour talking about that Christmas just before her death. I remember the strangest details: the croissants we'd eaten for breakfast Christmas morning, the pattern on my father's tie, my mother's face shadowed with candlelight. But I can't recall anything of import from the holiday, even though I know there must have been tension or even arguments. Was your mother exhibiting symptoms of depression? Bryan asks, Were your parents having marital problems? I'm helpless to answer. Her death is the one certainty, and I can only imagine what horrors that means I've been repressing.

When my session ends, I limp to the door on the verge of tears. We're making progress, Bryan tells me, and I nod because I want to believe him, because if he's not telling the truth, I may just break down right here in the doorway of his office. He nods back as if he knows what I'm thinking. See you next week, he says.

+ + +

I call Jess. I'm ready to move on, and there's no way that can happen if I have access to what he's offering. Where've you been? he asks, and I tell him I'd rather not say. Well, that means you're fucking someone else, he says, sounding more bitter than I would've expected. I'm not, I say, Actually. Good, he says, Then you're free tonight. Jess, I say, I think I'm done.

He's silent, and I reach for my cigarettes and shake one into my palm. Are you still there? I ask after I've lit up and inhaled without hearing a response. Oh, I'm here, he says. I need some space, I tell him, and he says, Seems like you've had a good bit of that the past ten days. I need more, I admit. What does that mean? he asks. Honestly? I say, and he says, No, Joel, why don't you fuck with me some more? I'm not fucking with you, I protest, I just want a break. And that means you can't meet me for dinner? he asks. When have we ever gone to dinner? I say, and he tells me we can start now.

227

The thought of sharing a meal with him, of dating him—no. I won't go there.

No offense, Jess, I say, But I'm not interested. You realize, he says, That you're essentially telling me you've been using me for the past twelve months. I think we've been using each other, I say, and he hangs up.

The second the line dies, I start shaking. I've trashed my relationships over the past year and a half; I have little to say to Peter, I rarely see Kyle. James and I are one giant debacle. Minus Jess, I've got nothing to occupy my time, and even though I know that cutting myself off from an easy high has to be the best thing for me, I'm not entirely sure I can make my way without it. I have half a mind to call him back, to apologize, to tell him I was wrong. I am not addicted, I tell myself, and Jess's voice comes to me clearer than my own. *A hundred bucks says you're using by the weekend.*

I've been trying not to indulge in the Xanax Bryan prescribed, but now I reach for the bottle and hold it to my lips. Two pills slip onto my tongue, and I chase them with water from the bathroom tap, then sink slowly to the rim of the tub. Fifteen minutes for my hands to steady, and then I grab my cell. I broke up with Jess, I blurt out the second James answers, already bracing myself for his rush of enthusiasm. How do you feel about that? he asks, as if since we've last seen each other he's been reading up on how to relate to someone capable of violent emotional swings. How do you think I feel? I snap, and then instantly regret my tone. But I'm surprised to hear him answer my question. I think you're probably feeling a cautious optimism, he says, And I think you're probably a little freaked out that you've cut yourself off.

He knows me, he's always known me, and I cover my eyes with one hand. I need to see you, I say.

For the barest second he hesitates. Tomorrow, he tells me. Okay, I whisper, and he says he'll call me in the morning to work out the details. Relax, all right? he says, You did the right thing.

I take a bath; by the time I hang up I'm halfway in the tub anyway. I don't have bubble bath, and no one's here to tell me I have eyes like a storm, but I lean my head back and soak in the heat. The ceiling's still scorched from the funeral pyre I lit last fall, and I squint at the pattern, trying to make sense of what I see the way I used to examine the water stain on the ceiling of our dorm room freshman year. I'd lie awake at night, trying to pry apart that puzzle, trying to assign it meaning. At the time I didn't realize that I was really just waiting for him to come home.

+ + +

The following afternoon, I'm circling Town Lake with James. A *walk*? I'd said earlier this morning, and he told me he thought it might be good for us to have a conversation in a different venue. At first I was tempted to tell him to forget the whole thing. Can we seriously not handle a meal together? But then I caught a glimpse of the sky outside my window, and when I pulled open the screen door and stepped onto the front porch, I realized what had prompted his suggestion. We've finally been offered a break from the heat, and I laced up an old pair of running shoes. Your eye healed nicely, he said first thing. Yeah, I said, and that quickly we were on to something else. I'm not even sure what we're covering. We're just feeling the wind in our hair, the sun on our faces, and I concentrate on putting one foot in front of the other. Fresh air and sunlight: that's really what I needed today, though James at my side makes the weather that much sweeter. Surely that we're able to occupy the same space for more than a few moments without spouting vitriol means something. I've caught a scant glimpse of freedom, and I find myself thinking later that evening and again the following afternoon: maybe. Maybe.

The promise of possibility lures me into the back room, where for the second week in a row I paint every single day. I'm not thrilled with most of what I'm doing, have a dozen false starts in a pile. I just reach for a fresh sheet of paper. That I'm coming up with anything at all seems to me a vast improvement.

The next evening, I'm excited about seeing Bryan, about telling him that I've been feeling a little better, that I'm actually getting some work done. I pick at the paint caught between my thumb and forefinger, offer a guarded thank you for getting me to this point. You're the one doing the work, he reminds me. He's rubbing his temple with the butt of his pen, one leg crossed over the other. Today he's wearing a thick taupe sweater that broadens his shoulders, trousers carefully creased. Those three-hundred-dollar-a-session shoes. Why do I notice his wardrobe more than anyone else's? Because with few others these days am I this physically close for an hour at a time? Because I'm the slightest bit intrigued by the thin brush of hair on the backs of his hands, the casual shake of his wrist as he adjusts his watch?

Christ. I may be developing a bit of a crush.

I drop my eyes in case they're lighting up. When I glance back, he's watching me, waiting. I told Jess I was done, I say, reaching for a diversion. With your relationship? he asks. I hesitate, then nod. How did that feel? he asks. I knead the legs of my jeans; they're new, darker in color than I usually wear. I bought them today along with this shirt, a gray tee that makes my eyes smoke. And my hair: I've washed it, pulled it still wet into a ponytail at the nape of my neck. Now I loosen the rubber band and wind it around my fingers. I wasn't honest, I admit, In my first session with you. About your relationship with Jess? Bryan asks. About the drugs, I say.

I flinch in anticipation of his expression, but he's a blank fucking canvas. What kind of drugs are we talking about? he asks, his tone conversational. Mostly cocaine, I say, my voice matching the trembling in my fingers as they run through my hair, Sometimes a little E and Xanax to bring me down. He's taking notes with that Mont Blanc, probably thinking this would've been good information to possess before he started plying me with Prozac. I haven't touched anything for two weeks, Bryan, I say, More than two weeks. How often were you using before then? he asks. Every few days? I say, Maybe more. And how do you feel now? he asks. I take a deep breath. My work, I say, That's really all I need.

I assure him that I have no intention of contacting Jess, that even if I did, he'd probably tell me to go fuck myself. I have a vision for my life moving forward, I say, and that involves a brush in my hand.

I'm not making promises or anything, but I'm thinking about getting back into running, too. The weather's cooling off, and if I can just swear off the cigarettes, then I might be okay. I sit on the back porch in departing sunlight that night and smoke the last cigarette in my last box; I'm quitting for good. For the first time in so long my hands hold steady, and I stare at the paint blooming between my fingers. Yeah, I think. Every day's just a little better than the day before.

That night, James and I have the best conversation we've had in well over two years. He calls just when I'm starting to think about going to bed, whipped from three days of work. You sound good, he says. I feel good, I admit. Yeah? he says, What've you been doing? I'm just working, I tell him, and he lets go of a sigh so contented you'd think he was the one standing in front of my easel all day. I curl my hand around my bottle of beer, the one I've been allotting myself every evening provided that I've made it through the afternoon and come out the other end with something productive. What about you? I ask, and I can almost see him shrugging. The writing's slow, he tells me, But it could be worse.

We never talk about Elizabeth. A couple of times, James slips a "we" into the conversation; I don't know if he does so intentionally so I'll be sure to know that she's still in the picture or if he's unaware of what he's saying. I'm not sure that it matters. What we talk about instead is our history: our dorm room; the summer we dated Melissa and Cathleen; our trip to Mexico the summer after my mother died. One night, he reminds me of the time we drove outside of Austin city limits with a six-pack and came back screaming. I almost forgot, I say when we've finished laughing, and he says, How could you forget something like that, Joel?

I'm making so much progress. I get out of bed in the morning and head into the back room, excited by what's in front of me. Though I still haven't finished anything, I can't help remembering James's expression when he saw the painting of my mother the first time I picked up a brush after she died. *Process,* I say to myself. Right now I don't need to commit to the end result.

+ + +

When Kyle calls, I'm so thrilled to hear from him—to feel as if I, too, have friends and plans and a life—that I agree to meet him for dinner the second he asks. Well, don't you look fabulous, he says as I slide into a booth across from him, Did we go shopping? We did, I say, smiling. I'm wearing the same jeans and tee shirt I wore the last time I saw Bryan, and Kyle nods his approval, then glances under the table to check my footwear.

These boots look the same as the ones I wore nine years ago, and I feel a brief flicker of sadness looking at them. At one point James had them, too. I guess no one's perfect, Kyle sighs. He's still losing his hair, and his scalp gleams in the glare of the unsympathetic bulb hanging over our table. Without thinking I tuck my own hair behind my ears.

We keep casual company; only once does he ask a serious question. The good doctor, he says as our server drops off another round, He's still helping? I twist my hair into a ponytail, then let it fall toward my face. Yeah, he is, I say, omitting mention of that moment in Bryan's office during my last session when I realized I might have worked up a bit of a crush. I'm glad, he says, squeezing fresh lime into his drink, and I'm just about to thank him again for the recommendation when someone says, Hi!

I look up. The kid loitering at our booth has a head full of yellow hair that looks like it came right from a bottle. I give him a what-the-fuck look, but Kyle's smiling. Jack, Kyle says, sounding downright pleased, Good to see you. He waves a hand in my direction. Joel Grayson, he adds. Hi! the kid says again, so desperate I almost laugh. Yeah, I say, deadpan, You said that already. Kyle clucks his tongue. We've been doing some work with UT's business department, he tells me, and I nod. I should've guessed. Jack looks like every other college student trying to keep the same secret I was. What about you? Jack asks. What about me? I say, and he stammers over his words. W-what do you do? he asks. I roll my eyes in Kyle's direction. I don't know that I've ever been flirted with so badly. I'm an artist, I say. Really? Jack asks, Like, you paint?

Jesus, he's young. Self-conscious, too, and barely out of the closet. I glance at Kyle, who gives me a warning look. I shake my head, but Jack's already backing away. Okay, he mumbles, I guess I'll see you later.

Nice, Joel, Kyle says, like I've intentionally smashed Jack's heart into tiny pieces. What do you want from me? I ask, He's a kid. So were you, he says, Once upon a time. No, I wasn't, I say, taking a grim sip of my margarita. We both were, Kyle muses, looking in Jack's direction. I follow his gaze; Jack's with some girl, and the way he's squirming around in his chair I get the impression that she's nothing but a decoy. God, I remember that feeling. How old is he? I ask, and Kyle raises his eyebrows. You interested? he asks. Please, I say. He's eighteen, Joel, he says, And for some unfathomable reason he can't take his eyes off you. So what do you want me to do? I ask, and he says, Throw him a bone. Thanks for the advice, I say, getting to my feet and prying a couple of bills from my wallet. Unperturbed, he indicates Jack with the slightest tilt of his head. I shake my own, sighing.

But when I walk past Jack's table, at the last possible second I turn. He's watching me, and I hold his eyes, then let my gaze slide all over him.

+ + +

I'd like to hear more about your father, Bryan says at the beginning of my next session. I fold my arms across my chest. What do you want to know? I say. What would you like to tell me? he asks. You're the one who brought him up, Bryan, I say, and he clicks the cap of his Mont Blanc with the slightest smile, like maybe I've caught him out. You're right, he says. So what do you want to know? I ask. Was he abusive? he asks. Yes, I say.

For just a second I think I'm going to throw up. I press a hard fist to my mouth, then take a breath too shallow to do me much good. Across from me Bryan indicates the bottle of water on the table. I wrench open the cap. That was a direct fucking question, I tell him after I've gulped a mouthful. And you gave me a direct answer, he says, How did that feel? Like I might hurl on your Persian carpet, I say. So we're getting somewhere, he says.

I'm quiet, but Bryan's gaze holds such patience that I find myself relinquishing my secret, this secret from when I was six and I wasn't supposed to be in my father's study. I can still feel the doorknob turning in my hand, the oddest mixture of fear and excitement knowing I was doing something wrong. Even though my father wasn't there, his presence permeated the room.

And then, out the window I saw a bird chirping a song I couldn't hear through the panes of glass. I was struck by its tiny beak, the extension of its neck, the warble that though I strained, I couldn't quite make out. Climbing up on my father's desk, I tried to open the window. But the hinges stuck, and before I could stop myself I was flying backwards. As the decanter spilled, I caught a whiff of my father, the scent of money, of a well-aged scotch. When I realized that the papers covering the desk were soaked through, I burst into terrified tears.

That night, I cowered next to my mother. She'd cleaned up the mess, but there wasn't anything she could do about the papers I'd destroyed. He's very sorry, she said in a voice so contrite I might've assumed her the culprit. But my father wasn't interested in an apology and even less interested in one that came second hand. I was sure that even though I'd never gotten spanked, he was ready to hit me. When he raised his hand, I bolted. Upstairs I hid behind the bathroom door, waiting, trembling, crying, until I figured that maybe he'd decided not to come for me after all.

Downstairs I crept along the wall in the living room. When I got closer to the back of the house, I could hear them. And then, looking around the corner, I could see them. My father, all bulk beneath his dress shirt and tie, and my mother absorbing every blow. I couldn't move. I wanted to move. I wanted to stop him. But I couldn't. She finally collapsed, curled on the floor, and my father, turning, saw me. The front of his dress shirt was covered with a fine spray of blood. He didn't say a word, but I knew. I knew if I didn't step in the same thing would happen again.

I've repressed the memory long enough that the detail I remember shocks me. I can see her on the floor, her hands curved beside her lovely mouth. And the smell. I can smell her blood, his anger. But the image of my father is the most cohesive of all. I can visualize every line of his face, every wrinkle on his shirt.

How long did the abuse continue? Bryan asks. He never touched her again, I say, unable—unwilling—to keep the pride from my voice. I meant you, he says, and I look away from him. Years, I whisper. And your mother, he says, She wasn't aware? I scowl. Fuck no, I say. Bryan clicks his pen. What kind of a mother would she be, I ask, If she knew and let it continue?

I leave Bryan's office with a headache, scrounge around in the glove box with half an eye on the road, looking for aspirin, Advil, Xanax, something to obliterate the tension behind my eyes. There's nothing, and after almost sideswiping another SUV I give up. Each bead of memory triggers another, and I can't shake the idea that something's back there, waiting for me.

James calls on my cell when I'm almost home. Come over, he says, and I'm so tempted, especially since it's the first time he's invited me to his place. But I need time to rally for an expedition of that magnitude, and right now I'm having a hard enough time staying in my lane. Next week, I say, trying to be conciliatory, knowing he'll have plans with Elizabeth this weekend since his birthday's on Sunday. Monday's good, he says, and I agree, willing to say anything if I can just get him off the phone.

That night, I jerk off in the shower. I'm not thinking of James or anyone else I've been with the last few years; instead, I have the feel of his hand on my shoulder as I left his office this evening, the promise of absolution flooding my veins. I come, then sink to the bottom of the tub. Water slides down my face like tears.

+ + +

I don't know if I'm just releasing twenty years of toxins during my sessions with Bryan or what, but the painting's coming easier. I still haven't finished a single canvas, but I know that's coming, and when dusk falls the following Monday, the day I've agreed to meet James, I glance out the windows and grimace. For once I think I might be getting somewhere. I'm running out of yellow, and I've had to use a wringer to squeeze out what's left in the tube, but there's just enough for what I need, for what I'm envisioning. I look out the window again, at the way the sun's plummeting from the sky. I'm supposed to meet James in less than an hour, and I should be winding down so I have time to shower. Instead, I find myself rummaging for a brush with a thinner tip.

Twenty minutes later, I'm still in front of the canvas, and I swear if I have just another hour or two, I can get exactly what's in my mind into the paint. For the first time in so long I can finish what I've started. Wiping my hands on a cloth, I reach for the phone. I hate to get out of my head even this long; creativity can be flighty. But I can't let James leave his apartment thinking I'm going to be meeting him and then just not show up.

Hey, I say when he answers. Hey, he says, I was just about to leave. Well, don't, I tell him. Why? he asks, instantly concerned, What's going on? Nothing, I hasten to assure him, I'm just working.

If I was expecting him to celebrate the way he has in the past, I'm mistaken. So? he says. Can we meet tomorrow instead? I ask. I don't understand, he says, Do you have some kind of deadline or something?

The more time I have to spend explaining myself, the harder it's going to be getting back into the paint. Already I can feel the image I've been seeing loosening its hold, fading into the background. There's no deadline, I tell him, sounding more impatient than I intended, I just don't want to stop.

He's silent.

Look, I say, I'm working right now, and you know how difficult that's been for me. Yeah, he says, I know. So I'm sorry to cancel, I say, But if you can just meet me tomorrow night... I'm busy tomorrow, he informs me. Okay, I say, What about Wednesday? He sighs, like I'm totally fucking up some carefully constructed calendar. I remember too late that his birthday was yesterday and that I didn't call him. Wednesday doesn't work either, Joel, he says.

The paint's drying on my goddamn brush. At this rate I would've been better off meeting his ass. At least I would've ended a full day of work on a positive note. Thursday? I say, sounding a little desperate and forgetting that on Thursday nights I meet Bryan. All right, he concedes. I have therapy on Thursday, I say, Until eight. So eight-thirty, he says, sighing again in case I've missed that he's pissed.

I turn back to my easel the second I end the call. But I can't find the image. I try to coax it back, a lover gone astray, let my eyes fall to my palette. The colors shimmer in the light. I touch my brush to the paint, then try a half a dozen strokes. Nothing. I take a step away, go into the kitchen and pour myself a glass of water. Take a few deep breaths. I can lose myself again; I've been interrupted more times than I can count over the years, and slipping back inside has never been a problem for me. This time won't be any different. Cracking my knuckles, I go back to the canvas.

Gone. As fleeting as my short-lived career.

+ + +

The guy going down on me uses too much product. I don't know if it's gel or mousse or what, but every time I forget and try to slide my hands through his hair, I have to wipe them on his sofa. I don't think he notices. He's drunk; I wish I could say the same. I've had a few sips of a weak martini, a swallow of the beer he offered me when we got here. *Here* meaning his apartment, one of many complexes scattered along I-35 just north of downtown. I let him pick me up too fast, though at first glance he was just what I was looking for, the sole reason I went out tonight: bland good looks, indeterminate age. He could be anyone. Exactly what I wanted until I tried to run my hands through his hair.

I shift a little, glancing from the corner of my eye at my beer, which I've left out of reach. Just in case my perception's off, I stretch my hand. Nope. Muffling a sigh, I glance down at the guy between my legs. As if he senses my impatience, he drops lower, lapping at my balls like a dehydrated dog. Hey, I murmur, and he looks up, drunk enough that it takes him a second or two to focus. Hey, he says, hoisting himself off the floor like I'm offering him a kiss. You're good where you are, I tell him, my hand on his chest, and he drops obediently back to the floor. I try not to groan when he goes after my balls again. Here, I say, guiding him up and getting product all over my hands, I want you here.

I finally ease him back into a rhythm, then glance again at my beer. I should've taken that pause to slug the rest of the bottle. Suppressing a sigh, I take a look around the apartment, at the nondescript décor. This guy might have bought the whole set from Rooms To Go, lamps and motel art included. There's nothing inspiring here, not a single interesting photograph on the wall. Not even a dartboard or a map of ancient Greece.

I close my eyes, my thoughts drifting to the back room and what I left behind this evening. I've forced myself to work the past couple of days, even though I haven't managed to recapture what I lost when I made that call to James. The next morning, I slid a blank canvas onto the easel and with grim determination picked up a brush. I still couldn't find my way back, but I gritted my way through an hour's worth of work anyway.

The guy on his knees whimpers. I don't think he was expecting a marathon blowjob, and I squeeze my eyes shut in concentration. I can't even remember the last time I did this sober. With James, I guess, though I was always the one doing the work. Darryl, then.

No. Adam.

I'd stay with that for a while if I could erase Adam's expression the last time I saw him well over a year ago. *You can show yourself out*, he said, closing himself off the second I told him I wasn't dating material. I haven't seen him since. And now he's with someone else, according to Kyle. He might have asked about me, but he's with someone else.

This isn't helping. Opening my eyes, I look down and remind myself that there was a reason I let this guy pick me up tonight. I wanted someone banal, and now I've got him and the accompanying blowjob to boot. I should let him off the hook, yank on that sticky hair of his and tell him he can let up. I can jerk off when I get home like I did the other night.

But the other night I went somewhere I've regretted since. I'm sick of cliché: the gay guy who falls for his straight friend, the patient who fantasizes about his therapist. Still, Bryan's helping me more than anyone else has lately. He got me away from Jess, nudged me in the direction of the back room. I'm clean, so clean this blowjob feels like nothing at all.

Maybe I'll tell him when I see him tomorrow. Maybe I'll tell him what I did tonight, what I was thinking in the shower. His hand on my shoulder, on the back of my neck. My knees planted on that Persian rug between those leather loafers. His dick in my mouth, wet with saliva and pre-cum. And my name, murmured in appreciation at the way I've supplicated myself.

Yeah, that worked.

I didn't say I was proud of it.

+ + +

Sliding onto a barstool and ordering a margarita the following night, I wonder what the hell I was thinking, making plans right after therapy. I've spent most of the past hour talking to Bryan, and the mere articulation of whatever feelings I have for and about my father has left me more vulnerable than I would've thought. That I've given Bryan a starring role in my fantasies doesn't help. I'm not at all sure that what I need right now in the aftermath is an evening out, even with James. A hot shower and a Xanax sound far more appealing. I nurse my drink, my headache burrowed behind my right eye, and figure I should take solace in the few minutes I have to myself before James shows.

But nine o'clock approaches, and I'm still alone. I've moved on to a second drink, and I'm starting to get pissed that I'm sitting here when I could be stretched out on the sofa at home. I finally reach for my cell. Where are you? I ask when he answers, I've been sitting here for thirty minutes. I'm working, he says. What do you mean? I say. I'm writing, he tells me, his voice absent of apology, I'm not going to make it tonight.

He can't be serious. I know what it's like to get stuck in a moment of creation; I was just there myself a few nights ago. But I'd never leave him sitting at a bar.

Maybe we can get together over the weekend, he says. Over the weekend? I say. Or next week, he adds, reminding me that his life has no room for me on a Saturday night. You know what? I say, Never fucking mind. Hey, you have no right to give me shit about working, he says, *You're* the one who bailed on *me* the other day! I didn't stand you up! I tell him, and then, realizing this just might have been orchestrated, I say, What're you saying, that you wanted to get back at me? Don't flatter yourself, he snorts, but I'm not altogether sure I believe him, and the thought sobers me. Are we actually at a point where we're seeking revenge?

I've told you how much I've been wrestling with my writing, he's saying, I've told you that I'm having a hard time getting into any kind of rhythm. Do you think I don't know what that's like? I ask, and he says, That's why I think you could cut me some slack! I've been sitting here for thirty minutes, you prick, I say, At least I had the decency to call you before you left the fucking house. No one made you sit there for thirty minutes, Joel, he says, You could've left.

I'm not sure that's true. Five years ago, sure. Four years ago, three. But after what's happened to us the past couple of years, leaving this bar tonight would've meant something different, something I'm not sure I'm ready to admit. You know what? he says, I don't have time for this shit. What *shit?* I ask, and he says, I don't have the time to bicker about who fucked over whom. Well, we both know the answer to that, I tell him.

He's silent, and I fear for a moment that I've crossed a line and won't ever be able to navigate my way back. James— I start. I'm sick of the accusations, Joel, he says, I'm so sick of them. In truth he sounds weary, and I imagine him, his eyes closed, fatigue furrowing his brow. Yeah? I say, Well, I'm sick of having to beg for your company. *You're* the one who bailed on *me* the other night! he says. You're the one who moved out! I cry. Somebody had to move, Joel, he says, Somebody had to make a decision, and it sure as hell wasn't going to be you. What's that supposed to mean? I ask, because I distinctly recall telling him I was done the morning after I told him about my show. He was the one who wouldn't let me go. You'd sell your soul if it meant you didn't have to make a change, he says. He laughs, and the sound's unlike any I've heard leave his mouth in all the years I've known him. What am I saying? he mutters, We both know who owns your soul.

I rip into each word, rearrange them, dissect them for meaning. I'm not even breathing.

Joel, he says, I didn't mean that. Actually, I say, I think you did.

+ + +

Doors locked, blinds shut. This way, when he comes by—and I know he will—I won't have to see him. I've already left a message for Bryan, though I'll be lucky if he gets back in touch with me within twenty-four hours, luckier still if he can make the time to see me before next Thursday. And I've poured myself a scotch, a double. Just to steady my hands.

I turn the music up loud enough to drown out even the most persistent banging on the front door. Pandora flees the second she feels the bass. My phone I keep in my pocket on the off chance that Bryan rings, even though that means I'll have to field calls from James. They've already started, though at this point he's not leaving voicemails. He's just calling, testing to see if I'll pick up. I won't. I'm not ready for his apology.

I sit with my back against the wall, facing the front door. Because he'll show up when I don't respond. He knows he fucked up, and he'll come my way, repeating what he told me earlier, that he didn't mean what he said.

He'll be lying.

Pulling my knees to my chest, I stare at the door. If Bryan could see me now, he'd probably dole out some other diagnosis, add paranoia to what's likely a growing list of concerns. But I know what I'm doing; I know James.

I give him an hour at most.

He shows up in forty-five minutes. I get to my feet when I sense his footsteps on the front porch, fold my arms across my chest when the doorbell rings. Ten seconds and he's pulling open the screen door. I stay where I am as he knocks. After a minute he has the gall to test the doorknob, like he has the right to come into my house without a fucking invitation.

I can feel him pausing, and then I can faintly hear him traipse across the porch. I step into the hallway but stay in the shadows, away from the back door. Because that's where he's headed; he's walking around the side of the house and coming to the back porch. I think I hear the gate creaking somewhere underneath the music.

And there's the knock, like he's decided what the fuck, he might as well use his fist. C'mon, man! he finally shouts, oblivious to what the neighbors might think, Open the fucking door!

To think there was a time when I would've imagined this scenario impossible.

He bangs a while longer, then stops. But he doesn't leave; I swear I can hear him breathing, though that's impossible given the way I've cranked the stereo. If I got close enough to peer through the window, I might find him lighting up a cigarette on the top step.

But no. He quit smoking about a year after he quit fucking me.

I edge closer, and he waits, like maybe he's thinking that after all this time I might open up, like nothing more than a door separates us. Then he's gone.

I press my forehead against the door and release my breath.

How far will we have to fall before we hit bottom?

+ + +

Bryan's willing to see me on Saturday afternoon, and I fill him in on what happened, my voice hollow, my nerves shot. I've been bracing myself for another round of phone calls, the blow of James's fist on my front door. But he hasn't tried to contact me, and I wonder if that means he's finally given up. How would that make you feel? Bryan asks. I shake my head, my eyes full of tears I manage to suppress. I don't want to cry in front of him, think each time I leave his office that I'll give myself the space to break down as soon as I get home. I never do.

Bryan nods as if I've said something profound. I get the feeling he's impressed by the fact that I reached out Thursday night, that I'm ready to admit that the dissolution of my relationship with James isn't something I'm prepared to tackle on my own. I keep trying to remind myself that I've made the right decision coming here today despite being humiliated by this recent turn of events. Bryan knows how important James has been to me. He knows he's been the kick in the ass I've needed at times to get back to work, he knows how miserable I've been since he moved out. James is the single best friend I have, my only true family.

And he was still willing to wound me so mortally.

What do you think he might have said if you'd let him in on Thursday night? Bryan asks. He would've tried to convince me that I misunderstood him or that he didn't mean what he said, I tell him, At best I think he would've apologized. Do you want an apology? he asks. About as much as I wanted that Explorer my father bought me, I say, After he burned a hole in my arm. I look down at my hands; I've gone through the motions, planted myself in front of the canvas two mornings in a row. I have the paint under my nails to prove it. Not that I've come up with anything noteworthy. My heart has been somewhere else.

When I glance back up, Bryan's watching me with something like compassion. I shouldn't be surprised. Though he's careful to keep his distance, he's not entirely impassive. Who could be, hearing this shit? Still, if he can look at me like this, I must not be totally to blame.

Do you want to see them? I ask, the question so sudden that even I'm startled. Do you want to show them to me? he asks. But I'm already pulling my sweater over my head and turning my arm so he can see. Forgery, I say, deciding I might as well label them for him, Lying; showing up drunk one morning after being out all night. I press my index finger against the burn from that last cigar. This one, I say, I used against him when I wanted him to lease the house. What house? he asks. My house, I tell him, I knew he'd never agree if I didn't remind him of what he'd done. And the others? he asks. What do you mean? I say. What did you get in return for the others? he says.

I go through them again, citing my Explorer, floor seats at a Rockets game, a last-minute vacation to the Caymans, before I realize why he asked. Listen, I say, a little pissed that he intentionally tripped me up, I know what you're going to say. What am I going to say? he asks. That as long as I'm accepting these gifts or whatever you want to call them, he has some kind of power over me, I say. Does he? Bryan asks. Hell yes, I tell him.

For a long moment he just looks at me. I fold my arms across my chest. Don't you think I deserve something? I say, Given what he did to me? You tell me, he says. I think it's pretty clear how I feel, I say, and he says, Do you think there might be an alternative? Sure, I say, I could cut him out entirely and spend my life waiting tables. Waiting tables, he muses. Or whatever, I say, growing impatient with the turn this session has taken. Bryan nods, then casts a surreptitious glance over my shoulder, where I know he has a clock. Moments like these remind me that Bryan has no real interest in *me*, that if it wasn't for the money, he wouldn't be here at all. Time's up, I say without bothering to keep the bitterness from my voice.

You're angry, he says. Excellent observation, I tell him, Well worth the twelve hundred dollars a month I'm paying you. He doesn't say anything; he just watches me, like I'm a classic fucking nut case. You're not going to tell me to fuck off either, are you? I ask. Do you want me to? he says. Jesus, I say, You're incapable of a straightforward answer. You're not asking me straightforward questions, he points out. Fuck you, I say, Give me a straightforward answer. Ask me a straightforward question, he says, exhibiting such calm in the face of this minor meltdown of mine that I'd be embarrassed if I stopped long enough to think about it. Fine, I say, How old are you? Forty-seven, he says.

I'm taken aback, and I look him up and down. He's dressed up even though it's Saturday; I shouldn't assume I'm the impetus. For all I know he had a slew of patients before this appointment. Cashmere v-neck, winter wool trousers, those same goddamn shoes. How much did your shoes cost? I ask, and he looks surprised. I don't remember, he says, glancing down at them. Three hundred? I guess. Probably, he admits. I nod, jiggling my foot. Are you gay? I ask.

For a second I think he's going to tell me that whether or not he's gay has no bearing on my treatment. But he answers after the merest consideration. Yes, he says. Your father know you're gay? I ask, and he says, Does yours? I asked you a straightforward question, I remind him, but I know there's no way he's going to answer me. I've crossed the line, and I lean forward, elbows on my knees. Forty-seven, huh? I say, and he replaces the cap on his pen. He's shutting this down for today, and I'll have to make it until Thursday before I can see him again. I'm not sure I can go that long. I'm really not sure I can go that long, and I blurt out the first thing that comes to my mind. I wish you weren't my shrink, I say. Why is that? he asks, and I say, Why do you think?

I watch as he calculates an appropriate response, half-hoping he'll scrap what's right and take a step in my direction. God, I'm fucked up. Bryan— I start, but he's already adopting a mild tone that soothes my conscience. I've said nothing out of the ordinary; whatever feelings I might have for him are a result of the work we're doing together. Happens more often than you'd think, he says, shrugging.

So I'm a cliché, but he doesn't mind. That's something, I guess, and after we say our goodbyes I head home, forgetting until I turn onto my street that there's at least a chance I'll find James sitting on the front porch. I brace myself, already debating whether I'll stop and confront him or just drive on by.

But I'm worrying for nothing.

He's not here, and I'm alone.

+ + +

James doesn't call, but Catherine phones the following afternoon. She's smart, smart enough to get me to admit that she hasn't interrupted anything before she tells me she's in town. I don't think so, I say, and she laughs, a sound so fetching I almost join her. I haven't even invited you to dinner yet, she tells me. But I knew where you were headed, I say. Oh, c'mon, she says, I haven't seen you in months. Now you sound like my father, I tell her, and she laughs again. I promise not to take up too much of your time, she tells me, And you told me you don't have plans. He's not with you, is he? I ask, suddenly suspicious, but she assures me she's on her own. Dinner, she says, Nothing more. What else could I possibly have in mind? I say.

I meet her downtown at a restaurant so chic and trendy I realize too late that I should've dressed for the occasion. I suppose it doesn't matter; no one's looking at me anyway. Catherine could make a paper sack look *avant garde*, and as she unwinds her legs and stands to meet me, her wrap slides from her shoulder, revealing one slender arm. You're beautiful, I admit, letting her pull me close enough for a kiss on the cheek. Thank you, she says, managing to sound demure, And thank you for meeting me. You didn't give me much choice, I remind her. Ah, but now that you're here, she says, You can't imagine being anywhere else. Sure I can, I say, My couch with a beer and the remote.

But I've kept my tone light, and she smiles. For just a second I think about the way my father must have felt the first time she turned in his direction. Then I shake away the image and pull out her chair. Once she's seated, I settle myself across from her, my eyes dropping automatically to the wine list. I was thinking champagne, she says. Are we celebrating something? I ask. You mean other than your willingness to meet me for dinner? she says, and I grin.

I actually might have missed her.

When the champagne arrives, she omits ceremony and takes a sip. Relieved that she hasn't offered up a toast, I follow suit, and she leans forward as if she's on the verge of confiding a secret. You haven't asked about your father, she tells me. Is there something I need to know? I ask, frowning. No, she says, I just thought you'd want to know how he's doing. How's he doing? I ask. But I've spoken without inflection, and for just a second she looks hurt. Then she slides a pretty shoulder, unwilling to let my tone spoil our evening. He's quite well, she says, as effervescent as the champagne we're drinking, He'll be disappointed to have missed you. That's debatable, I say, But I'll take your word for it so we can move on.

She's quiet; I have a feeling she's considering challenging me, and I brace myself for a dissertation about my father's benevolence. But she changes her mind. Want to hear what's happening at my boutique next weekend? she asks, brightening. Absolutely, I say.

Banter carries us through our first course and most of the way through our entrées. She doesn't mention my father again, tells me instead about the fashion show she's organizing, the classes she's thinking of offering to underprivileged students interested in clothing design. I'm mildly impressed and baffled all over again why she's with my father. He's not known for his charity. But I keep my mouth shut and congratulate her efforts, emptying the last of the champagne bottle into her glass. What about you? she says, What's going on in your life these days?

Aside from the fact that whatever I say to her could find its way into my father's ear, I really have nothing but shit to report. I'm not going to tell her that I'm in therapy or that my psychiatrist has found his way into my fantasies on more than one occasion. I'm not going to admit that James and I just may have stumbled upon the point of no return. And I'm certainly not going to tell her about my work or confess that I haven't finished a single painting in so long that tears come to my eyes every time I step into the back room.

There's nothing much to tell, I say, draining the last of my champagne. Oh, I can't imagine that's true, she says, waving an airy hand. My eyes snag on her ring finger and the diamond my father planted there. They must be coming up on two years any day now. There's nothing to report, I assure her, and she gives me the coyest smile. Oh, c'mon, she says, What about Jessica?

She knows I sculpted Jessica for my father. She knows what she's really asking.

You're not my confidante, Catherine, I snap, and twin points of color appear high in her cheeks. I might as well have slapped her. I'm sorry, she says, I'm just… making conversation. Bullshit, I say, and she reaches for my hand. I yank it away. I wanted to apologize, she says, I wanted to tell you how sorry I was for what happened the last time you were home. Houston hasn't been *home* since my mother put a bullet in her mouth, I inform her.

She winces, and I throw my napkin on the table. Oh, please, she says when she realizes I'm leaving, We were having such a nice time. And then you had to ruin everything, I say.

I'm getting to my feet when Kyle swoops to my side, materializing out of nowhere like a fairy godmother with misguided timing. You're here without *me*? he pouts, leaning in for a kiss before I can stop him. I jerk away, but he's too busy fawning over my dinner companion to notice. *Enchanté*, he says, pressing Catherine's hand with his manicured own. Oh, Catherine says, looking dismayed, though whether that's because of the way our evening has deteriorated or Kyle himself, I don't know. Kyle, I say, grabbing hold of his arm so tightly he lets out a little shriek, This is Catherine Grayson. You're *hurting* me, sweetheart, he says, wriggling loose from my grasp. *Kyle*, I say, Catherine's my father's *wife*.

The change one sentence can bring. Kyle holds his fingers to lips so red they can't possibly be natural, then lets his hand drop and his voice deepen. Nice to meet you, he says to Catherine. Turning to me, he offers the first handshake I've ever had from him. Joel, he says, breaking my heart in all kinds of ways, Good seeing you.

I watch him walk away, feeling sick to my stomach. Then I turn to Catherine, who sits with her hands in her lap. I'm not seeing Jess, I say. Okay, she says. Kyle's a friend, I add, lowering myself to my seat. You don't have to explain, she whispers. Apparently I do, I say, Because I need you to understand that *you're* not my friend.

Tears come to her eyes; I can't afford sympathy. I don't know what kind of delusions you have about my father, I say, But at the very least you know what would happen if he found out.

She doesn't contradict me.

We're not going to have secrets, I say, I'm not going to fill you in on the latest gossip. I wasn't looking for gossip, she protests. That might be true, I admit, You've never been anything but kind to me.

The tears in her eyes spill onto her cheeks. Jesus. She's stunning even when she's crying.

My private life is just that, Catherine, I say, Don't ask me about it again.

I stay with her while she composes herself; I even walk outside with her, where we wait for the valet. Thank you for meeting me, she says just as her Audi swings into view. Highlight of my week, I say, and she gives me an appreciative smile.

I call Kyle before her taillights disappear. Bad timing, Kyle, I say. Oh my god, he breathes, I'm so sorry. Don't apologize, I say. But you kept trying to tell me who she was, he says, And I just couldn't keep my mouth shut. Nothing new there, I mutter. She's your *stepmother?* he asks. Are you on a date? I ask, changing the subject. I *am*, he says, He's delicious. He's right there, isn't he? I ask. He *is*, Kyle says, and I shake my head as my Explorer pulls to a stop in front of me. Well, I say, Have a good night. Breakfast tomorrow? he asks. Won't you have company? I say. Dinner? he asks, realizing his mistake, and despite the evening I've just endured, I find myself laughing. Sure, I say, Why not?

+ + +

On Thursday night I'm in my regular spot on a leather sofa in Bryan's office. Across from me Bryan clicks the cap of his Mont Blanc in a way that makes me grind my teeth. Despite hooking up with Kyle on Monday night and peppering the last few days with enough time in the back room to pretend I'm actually working, I'm amped up. I've brought Bryan up to date on what's been happening since I saw him last Saturday: that James hasn't called, that I met my father's wife for dinner. You've established some significant boundaries over the past week, he tells me, How do you feel about that? Exhausted, I say, and he nods as if he could possibly understand. I find myself annoyed with him today, and I slouch in my seat, wondering why. Maybe because he shot me down so unceremoniously last week, shrugging off my confession as par for the course. Couldn't he at least have told me he was flattered? I mean, he's forty-fucking-seven.

Let's talk about your mother, Bryan says, and I jerk upright. What? I say, Why? Why not? he asks. Uncapping his pen, he smooths the page in his notebook. I'm tempted to scribble it clean. I don't want to talk about her, I tell him. Already he's jotting something in his folder, and I groan; as if he knows what I'm thinking, he lays down his pen. What do you want to tell me? he asks, and I shrug. There's nothing much to tell, I say, She was a goddamn saint. He nods, encouraging me. She put up with my father, I remind him, She…

I was going to say, *She believed in me.* But maybe that's not entirely true. I slide the heels of my hands down my jeans, panic building at the back of my throat. Just when I think it's going to bubble over, spill into my mouth and force me to say something I shouldn't, I find a credible substitute. She put a paintbrush in my hand, I say.

As soon as I say the words, I have to repress a sudden, inexplicable urge to force my hand through the glass table in front of me. *What the fuck is going on?* So she might have questioned my abilities, so what? Maybe my father didn't hear her correctly. More likely, he was lying. You know, I say, I'm really not here to talk about my mother. Are you sure? he asks.

God, he's good. Turning my head, I stare out the window. I've watched autumn arrive from this office; I remember the sun on these buildings during my first appointment back in September. Now they fire their own light against a black sky. When I walk to my car, I'll have to brace myself against a November wind; before long I'll be looking at another holiday season.

The thought makes me want to scream.

He's still waiting for my answer. I can feel him watching me, and getting to my feet, I start to pace. I feel like a kid with ADD, my legs crawling with energy. I want to break into a run, throw open the door to this office and rocket down eleven flights of stairs to the cold street below me. But no. There's no one out there for me anymore, and I turn to Bryan. I have his attention, his eyes on mine. If I'd met you somewhere other than this office, I say, Would you have fucked me?

He doesn't even blink, and I start to laugh. Can't turn *that* question around, can you? I ask. He doesn't say anything; he probably spent the past five days reading up on transference so he'd be fresh for our appointment. Hey, I say, You wanted a straightforward question. Parking my ass on the sofa, I swing one leg over the other and look him in the eye. Would you or would you not have fucked me, I say, If we'd met at a bar instead of this office? A hypothetical isn't straightforward, Joel, he tells me, and I roll my eyes. You and your fucking nuance, I say.

Jumping up again, I hike the length of his office. He watches me without interjection until I stop right in front of him. Maybe you're just too much of a pussy to answer the question, I tell him. Do you think I'm a pussy? he asks, surprising me by repeating the word. I rock back on my heels, scrutinizing him. Dark hair, dark eyes, and that nose, like maybe he was smacked with a hockey stick as a kid. You're not even my type, I say, dismissive enough that I cause the slightest raise of his eyebrows. What's your type? he asks. Tall, I say, Blond. I shrug. Not you, I add, as if he doesn't see his own reflection in the mirror every day. Did your mother know you're gay? he asks. Of course she knew! I say.

Well, shit. I didn't mean to say that. Sinking back onto the sofa, I pull my hands through my hair. We never discussed it, I say, But she knew. And your father? he asks. He put a cigar out on my arm for cheating on a math test, I remind him, So what do you think? What would happen if he found out now? he asks, and I laugh, the sound thin and mirthless. I'd rather not guess, I tell him. Do you think he'd hurt you? Bryan asks. I'm not nineteen anymore, I remind him, and the second I speak the words, I frown, like maybe I've spoken them before to little effect. Then what's your motivation for keeping it a secret? he asks without giving me time to place the memory, and I tell him I have a vested interest in keeping the information quiet. Because he supports you financially? Bryan asks, and I narrow my eyes. I never told you that, I say.

But I'm guessing that was an easy assumption given what I've told him about my work, given the checks I'm writing him every week. Am I wrong? he asks, and I fold my arms across my chest. I think slipping me a little cash is the least he can do, I say, Don't you?

When I get home, I help myself to the first Xanax I've had in weeks, then crawl halfway under the bed trying to find Pandora. Inhaling a cloud of dust, I sneeze, whacking the top of my skull on the bedframe. Shit, I moan, touching my head and looking at my fingers to make sure I'm not bleeding. I lie still for a minute, feeling sorry for myself, then back out, wondering where the hell the cat's hiding now that I could use a little extra body heat. Climbing into bed, I close my eyes.

I'm tangled in the threads of the most intricate web. I can't pull myself free no matter how much I struggle. I'm aware of the spider before I see it, and there's an awful moment, excruciatingly long, when it's just out of my line of vision. Tears blister my eyes. And then it's before me, gray, enormous. I can't scream for the web in my throat.

+ + +

The next morning, feeling a little guilty about that Xanax, I lace up my shoes and hit the pavement. I might not be able to run as far as I could a couple of years ago, but that doesn't mean a mile or two won't do me some good. That rant in Bryan's office yesterday was the most exercise I've had in months. But as the air tears through my lungs, I realize that therapy has nothing to do with distance. I might not be smoking anymore, but I'm no better off than I was when I last attempted a run back in August, and I'm forced to slow to a geriatric walk just so I can make it home.

Frustrated, I kick off my shoes and climb back in bed, where I let the weekend pass me by. I sleep, I watch a few movies, I scrawl a few doodles in a sketchpad and call that work. How's the doctor treating you? Kyle asks when I rouse myself to meet him for brunch on Sunday. He indicates the cigarette he just lit, the one I've taken right from his hand. You told me you'd quit, he says by way of explanation. Yeah, I say, Well.

I stop at a convenience store for a pack of Marlboros on the way home, then spend the better part of the afternoon smoking on the back porch. I treat each cigarette like a long-lost friend, figure that between the coke and the smoke even Bryan would have to agree that I've made the right choice.

That night, I dig up James's address and head toward Hyde Park. When I spot his shitty car just north of 45th on Avenue G, I pull up to the curb and dim my lights. I can see his apartment lit up at the end of the driveway. He'll be working, scrunched over his computer or spread out across his couch with a stack of books beside him. I'll have the advantage of catching him off-guard. Fuck it, I think, placing one hand on the door handle, what's the worst that could happen?

And then headlights pierce my sideview mirror, causing me to duck in apprehension. I scrunch down in the front seat as a hatchback swings into the driveway and pulls to a stop.

She's wearing jeans and a coat, a color that's difficult to decipher in the dark. Balancing an armful of books on her knee, a few slide to the ground, and she bends over to pick them up, her hair spilling forward. As she straightens, she takes a quick look at my Explorer. I crouch lower, holding my breath, then peer through the window as she climbs the stairs to the apartment.

I don't wait for him to open the door. Instead, I drive home, where the house shivers with cold because I've left the windows wide open. I trek through the rooms slamming them shut. Then I yank a fraying sweatshirt from my dresser and reach for the Xanax. Nice and chill so I don't have to think about what I've been unearthing in Bryan's office or the way I'm doing my best to sabotage my treatment, the way I do everything else. So I don't have to think about James.

+ + +

James leaves a string of messages, none of which I return. I'm too afraid I've been discovered, too afraid that Elizabeth has figured out I was the one lurking across the street, and what am I supposed to say? That I didn't know if he was home? That I wasn't sure if he was alone? I could've just picked up the phone. Instead, I had to hide outside like a fucking stalker.

I've made some seriously shitty decisions the past few days. When I see Bryan, I'm going to have to admit that I've started smoking again, admit that I've dropped by James's apartment but was ultimately too chickenshit to ring his doorbell. I'll have to tell him I saw Elizabeth, that I've taken a few too many milligrams of Xanax.

And he'll want to talk about my mother again; I'm sure of that.

The lack of direction I've been exhibiting in the meantime scares the shit out of me, and I force myself into the back room because I'm not going to tell Bryan that on top of everything else I haven't been working.

I paint like an amateur, and I'm still thankful. I make mistakes that take me nowhere, dead end again and again and have to retrace my steps. I don't care. I'm tired and drugged and a coward in more ways than one, but right now, I have a brush in my hand, and that's all that fucking matters. In this moment that's all that matters.

+ + +

James catches me late Thursday afternoon as I'm trying to decide whether or not I have energy for another round with Bryan. I answer the phone without thinking, then snap to attention at the sound of his voice. What do you want? I ask, afraid he's going to call me out for skulking around outside his apartment. I've left you a few messages, he says.

A gross underestimate.

I thought we could meet for a drink tonight, he adds. Why? I ask. Because there's something I want to say to you, he admits. I think you've said plenty, I inform him, and that shuts him up. I don't feel good about silencing him. I don't feel good about this conversation in general, and I think about how easily I could let my finger slide over the button that will end this call, end this relationship for good. As I contemplate, I let the back door slam shut behind me. God, I miss that sound, he says.

No, he didn't. He didn't just say that. But he's telling me quietly that he has a Pavlovian response to the sound of the back door slamming shut that makes him want to light up. You don't smoke anymore, I remind him. That's true, he admits, But that sound makes me want a cigarette.

How many did we smoke on this porch? How many beers did we drink? How many conversations, how many words exchanged on the top step? I can see him sobbing here when he told me about Elisa, can hear the flick of his lighter the day he dissected my inertia before he was accepted into UT's graduate program. Fall, winter, spring, summer, season after season, year after year, and now I can barely handle hearing his voice on the other end of my phone.

Joel, James says, Hear me out. I don't know, I say, because I'm afraid that if I see him, I'll be right back where I started at the beginning of September. What happens if tonight goes badly? Do I end up at Jess's apartment? Do I set fire to the back room? I'm already alarmed by how much I've regressed in the past week. *How much power are you willing to give him?* I hear Kyle ask, and I shake my head. Please, James says.

Well, I never have been good at refusing him. And I did head over to his apartment on my own the other night, even if I couldn't have articulated my intention. So an hour later, he's sliding into a chair across from me at a bar down the street, unwinding his arms from his coat, slaking his fingers through his hair. I've used the time since we spoke to become increasingly suspicious of this meeting and my own motivation in agreeing to see him. I'm on my second beer, my third cigarette, and after I maneuver my way through this conversation I have to head over to Bryan's office for my next session. I'm not sure I have it in me.

How've you been? James asks. Fine, I say, tapping my cigarette against the edge of the ashtray, Great. How's therapy? he asks. Am I supposed to be checking in with you or something? I ask, and he sighs. I'm just curious, Joel, he tells me. Well, we both know where that's gotten us in the past, I mutter. Smoke streams from my nose, and he bites his lip. I cross my arms as our waiter pauses at our table, as James asks for a beer of his own.

I want to talk about what happened, he says once we're alone. He seems nervous, with those circles under his eyes and his hand combing obsessively through his curls. Okay, I say, relishing his anxiety, and he nods. That day, he says, That day I was supposed to meet you, I had a long day. A long day, I repeat. I shouldn't have taken it out on you, he says, I shouldn't have said anything about your father. You didn't, I remind him, You left that for me to infer. He's quiet, playing with the handle of his mug. I've realized, he says, That I wanted to hurt you. What? I say. I wanted to hurt you, he repeats.

Well, this is worse than I fucking thought. I have to focus on my cigarette, eyes squinting, so I can hide the tears that flood my eyes. Why? I finally ask. I don't know, he admits, cupping his hands around his mug, I've been trying to figure that out. Well, that's awesome, I say. Joel— he starts as if he's the wounded one. Stop, I say, pulling out my wallet. Please, he says, Don't leave. This conversation can't possibly get any better, James, I tell him. Please, he says, I want— For us to be the way we used to be, I finish, but he says: For you to meet Elizabeth.

Well, just go ahead and rub salt in that fucking wound, friend.

Why would I possibly want to meet Elizabeth? I ask. Because, Joel, he says, I think she's the one.

I stare at him for a moment before I suck the last drag from my cigarette and crush out the butt. If I hadn't palmed a Xanax with my beer thirty minutes ago, I might stand up and scream. Does she know about us? I ask. He looks away, and for a minute I swear he's going to say, *What about us?* But he just nods. So, what? I say, You're going to marry her? He shrugs; I almost feel sick. It's not that I want him for myself. I'm over him; I have been for more than a year. I'm just not over what he did to me. I can't believe how easily his life has fallen into place since he moved out, the way my own life has spiraled downward. He's moved on, and I realize with an acute sense of loss just how much that hurts. Well, congratulations, I say. You're leaving, he says flatly as I get to my feet. Forgive me, I say, If I'm not in the mood to celebrate.

I drive to Bryan's office because I have no one else to call for commiseration. The only two people who might understand the devastation I felt hearing James renounce me once and for all—the only ones who even know our history—are Peter and Kyle, and they're sick of the whole business and have been for months. But Bryan might be able to help, and when I get to his office, he invites me inside, then sits down across from me. I think this is the first time I've seen him wear a suit. Did you dress up for me? I ask. I had a meeting this afternoon, he says. That was a straightforward question, I say, smiling. No, he says, I did not dress up for you.

Chastened, I stare at my hands, which I've folded in my lap. James is getting married, I say after a minute. How does that make you feel? he asks.

Abandoned. Alone.

I get to my feet and walk to the window. The city spreads out before me against a backdrop of night sky. You ever think of jumping? I ask. Do you? he says casually enough that I know he's paying even closer attention than usual. Sometimes, I admit. I press my forehead to the glass and look down to street level, where Austin's just getting started for the night. From this height I feel so removed from everything. I don't know, I say, Don't you think it'd be easier to just… let go?

When I turn, I find his gaze sharp and alert, like he's thinking I might be hiding a firearm underneath my sweater. Lighten up, I say, I'm just thinking aloud. I lean back against the window, my palms on the sill. The glass feels cold; I can feel the chill through my clothes. How often do you think about suicide? he asks. I've spent the past seven years picturing my mother with the barrel of a gun in her mouth, I remind him. Do you own a gun? he asks. No, I say, But I'm sure I could find one if I put my mind to it. Have you thought about purchasing one? he asks. No, I say, sighing, And I'm not really going to jump from the window of your office either. Given your family history— Bryan starts. I'm a perfect candidate, I finish. You said yourself that you've spent the past seven years thinking about your mother's suicide, he tells me. That doesn't mean I've been planning my own, I say. How far have you gotten? he asks.

I don't answer him. Can I smoke in here? I ask. Are you smoking again? he asks. No, I say, rummaging in my pocket for a cigarette, I was just curious. There's no smoking in the building, he tells me when I extract one. Replacing the cigarette, I drop back down on the sofa in front of him. Why am I here? I say. Why do you think you're here? he asks. I don't really know anymore, I admit, I'm not seeing a lot of progress.

A deliberate shot to see if I can rile him. But he's implacable. What would constitute progress? he asks, In your mind? I shrug, and he watches me for a minute, then flips through his notepad. Can I share something with you? he asks. Whatever, I mumble, reaching for my cigarette again and then, irritated, shoving it back in my pocket. Since September, he says, You've stopped using drugs; you've ended a dysfunctional, year-long relationship; you've started setting clear boundaries; and you've started painting again for the first time in two years. He taps his pen against the notepad. You've also been examining what sounds like a very complicated relationship with your parents, he says, And you even quit smoking for a while, which seems to me a pretty good indicator that you can do it again when you're ready. He leans forward. Would you not consider that progress? he asks.

I don't want to see you anymore, I say.

For the first time since September I've caught him off-guard. What? he says. I don't want to see you anymore, I say. Joel, he says, We were just talking about suicide. We were talking about my mother, I remind him, And I don't want to talk about my mother. That in and of itself suggests that you should continue seeing me, he says. But I'm shaking my head. I'm thinking about the list he just gave me, evidence of the progress I've made. And all I wanted was to be able to pick up a brush. I came to you because I was having trouble painting, I tell him, And now I'm painting. Are you happy with the work you're doing? he asks.

A minor technicality. I'm no longer seeing Jess; I don't have cocaine binges to distract me. And if I'm not miring myself in this bullshit with my parents, then I'll have that much more creative space. James? Fuck him. I might be better off without him.

Thank you, I say, I don't think I could have made it to this point without you. Joel, it's my professional responsibility— Bryan starts. What the fuck ever, I say, Let's get a drink to celebrate.

He just looks at me the same way Peter did when he found out I was sleeping with James. Like he could predict the outcome and knew it wouldn't be good. For just a second I feel a modicum of doubt. Then I jump to my feet. I'm not going to second-guess this decision. I wish you'd reconsider, Bryan admits, rising to meet me. Not a chance, I say, offering him my hand. Call me if you change your mind, he says.

Driving home, I shiver with anticipation, smiling a smile so genuine I'm convinced I could captivate anyone I chose. I've made the right decision, and a glance into the back room confirms my thoughts. I'm working. And if for some reason I trip up, I have a refill on that Xanax.

So I'm okay. I'll really be okay.

I'm sure I'll be okay.

+ + +

I spend most of the weekend with Kyle, toasting my newfound freedom. I haven't seen you in such a good mood for *years*, he tells me, and I smile through a long-lasting drag. I'll kill the habit eventually, but for now I'm going to relish what I have going for me: a good friend with money to play and the promise of work next week.

Yet despite my grandiose expectations, I sleep late Monday morning, then stall long enough to convince myself that another day off won't matter. I'm gearing up for a burst of creativity, I figure, and deserve the time to let my thoughts coalesce.

But as I fritter away the hours, I start getting restless, and my thoughts turn inevitably to James. He hasn't called, and I'm not sure how I feel about that. I don't want to talk to him; I know that much. But I walked into that bar last week expecting an apology and instead got injury with intent and proof positive that he's moving on without me. He's not looking for us to be the way we used to be; he's getting married. Hell, for all I know, he might already be engaged. He's done with me, so done that he'll say shit just to hurt me. If that's the case, he doesn't want me in his life. And why would he? I'm a reminder of something he'd rather forget.

With that depressing thought in mind I trail into the back room, where I pick through what I've been working on since September. I'm hoping to find one painting I can come back to tomorrow, one I might be able to set right. Because even though I don't want to discount that I've been working, I haven't actually finished anything I've started. That has to change tomorrow.

I pull a few pieces that show promise, then suddenly remember something James said years ago. He'd wanted to know what I'd do if one day I picked up my brush and nothing happened. At the time I found the idea preposterous. But now I find his comment eerily prescient, and my response to him—I'd laughed—both dismissive and naïve.

To prove to myself that I know what I'm doing, I set my alarm for seven o'clock the next morning. I'm going to treat my work the way my father might his job. But the flaw in that reasoning becomes apparent as soon as I step in front of the canvas, Pandora winding around my ankles. Inspiration isn't something I can force; the past couple of months have already taught me that. Just because I'm showing up doesn't mean I have something to say.

For the first time in five days I feel some real trepidation. Maybe Bryan was right. Maybe I made a mistake. Maybe at the very least I should've kept my appointment for Thursday night.

I find myself reaching for my cell. But something—some vestige of pride, some alpha belief that I should gut this out—prevents me from dialing. I'm not willing to give up so soon.

I spend the rest of the week working, however loosely I might have to define that term, and when my father calls on Friday afternoon, I can't help but hope he's going to offer a last-minute invitation for Thanksgiving. As much as I don't like the idea of spending the holiday in Houston, especially after that impromptu dinner with Catherine a few weeks ago, I really can't stomach the thought of being at home alone either. I don't think I can deal with a repeat of last year.

I wanted to give you plenty of notice, he says, We're going to Anguila for Christmas. Really? I say, feeling a quick rush of excitement. So he liked last year's proposal after all! He just needed to control the plans, needed to book in advance. Well, that's fine. I haven't been diving in so long, and I close my eyes, thinking that a good, long breath underwater might be the perfect escape from everything that's gone wrong the last few weeks. I'll still have to maneuver Thanksgiving, but this gives me something to hold onto. A resort? I say, and he tells me that a friend of theirs has a house.

So this won't be just the three of us. I guess I can handle that. In fact, having some of my father's friends around as a buffer might honestly be helpful. I've never been to Anguila, I ruminate aloud, and my father says, Well, I'll let you know if you should put it on your list.

Wait, I say, I'm not invited? I thought that was understood, he says. I'm not *invited*? I repeat incredulously. How is that even possible? I just saw Catherine a few weeks ago.

Unless that dinner was the impetus. I close my eyes, picturing Kyle swooping toward me for a kiss. I can still see her expression, can still hear the chagrin in her voice. She might be leaving town for the holiday because she and my father have an invitation they can't refuse, or because at this point I make her really fucking uncomfortable.

Why would you be included, Joel? my father's asking, There won't even be anyone your own age. Well, Catherine's not far off, I point out, and I can sense him stiffening on the other end of the line. Last year, he reminds me, You couldn't be bothered to spend time with us at all. I invited you to go on vacation with me! I cry, and he says, With my goddamn money! This is un-fucking-believable, I say, I can't believe you're doing this to me! I will not continue this conversation if you're going to use that kind of language, my father says. I think I'm entitled to a little latitude, I say, Besides, you're the one who taught me the fucking word!

He hangs up. He hangs up, and I stare at the phone in my hand, then pitch it as hard as I can against the wall. Plastic shatters, and I whimper, then drop to my knees and crawl around, trying to find the parts I need to piece it back together. As soon as I clamp the battery in place, the phone starts to ring. How've you been? Cameron asks in response to my cautious hello, and I don't know whether to laugh or break into sobs. I'm all right, I say, and he tells me that he's collaborating with a few others to put together a showing of local artists at Laguna Gloria in February, and he'd like to include some of my work.

I jump to my feet and start pacing back and forth, suddenly full of energy, and as he outlines the parameters of the show, I think about what I have to offer, what I've been working on the past few days. Surely I have something worthy of consideration.

But my enthusiasm fades as soon as I look around me. Despite the work I've done the past couple of months, despite showing up in the back room every day this week, I have little to show, and I'm starting to think that the well of creativity has run dry. If I had the balls, I'd tell Cameron the truth. When do you need something? I ask instead. You have some time, he says, Have you been working on anything in particular? Maybe, I lie, and he tells me not to worry. You'll come up with something, he says.

But I'm not so sure, and after I hang up I give in and call Bryan's office. I'm willing to admit that I might have made a rash decision, willing to dig into the wreck of my past if that's what it takes for me to show up in February with even one finished piece. I'll see him tonight if he has time for me.

But he's out of town for the next ten days, and I dimly recall him mentioning a vacation a couple of weeks back. Some surrogate will be taking his calls while he's gone, and if I want to schedule an appointment for after he returns, I'll have to wait for his next available time slot, which isn't until the middle of December. But I'm one of his *existing* patients, I hiss, and the receptionist assures me I'm one of many. I'm happy to refer you to Dr. Campbell, she adds, as if I could possibly have any interest in starting from the beginning.

I hang up and sit cross-legged right there on the floor of the back room, then take a deep breath. I'm not meditating; I wouldn't even know how to begin. I've been up and down so much over the course of the past thirty minutes I don't know how to behave. But maybe if I stay here long enough, my pulse will slow. Maybe the tremor I can feel creeping into my hands will fade. I look around this place, this sacred place, and close my eyes.

I need something amazing.

+ + +

By the following Wednesday, the day before Thanksgiving, I've developed a case of full-blown insomnia. Maybe that's for the best. The dreams I've dreamed since I terminated my therapy have been epic, and invariably leave me more tired than if I'd never gone to sleep. But not sleeping at all isn't doing me any favors, and I drag my ass to my feet and gaze into the mirror. I've spent the night in the back room, trying to find a cure, cataloging what's going right for me: I haven't seen Jess in weeks; I'm clean except for the Xanax; I have a show in February and three months to come up with something.

The moment I hit on what I still have to accomplish, I boomerang the other way. I have a show in February and only three months to come up with something; I have no plans for the holidays, not Thanksgiving, not Christmas; I've cut myself off from the one person who has helped me the past couple of months; I'm on my last refill of Xanax; James is getting married.

No wonder I can't sleep.

I seriously need some caffeine, and so I head out, bypassing one coffee shop after another in favor of a parking lot that isn't already full. I'm starting to think I should just go home when I spot BookPeople from the corner of my eye. I can't really imagine finding the patience to open a book; on the other hand, I'm staring at a holiday with nothing but the television to keep me company. I don't think I can go there again. A stack of books might be just what I need, even if all it gives me is the illusion of industry.

I pick up a volume about Gerhard Richter, then linger at the shelves with a copy of *The Secret Life of Salvador Dali* before I wander into the fiction section, where I try to decide if I'm in the mood for John Irving or if I have the fortitude to grit through nine hundred pages of Wally Lamb. I'm ruminating, thinking about that Dali biography and realizing that I still need a jolt of caffeine, when someone says, Joel?

Adam Atwater's sitting behind me, tucked into an alcove of the fiction section. He looks like a wish come true, and I stare at him until he assumes from my silence that I don't recognize him. Adam Atwater, he says, his palm to his chest, Last year...

I know who you are, I say, charmed by his modesty, I'm just... I trail off, shaking my head. It's really good to see you, I confess, and he smiles, the easiest smile I've seen in months. It's good to see you too, he says. What're you doing here? I ask, Don't you have a job or something? I left the office early, he says. He tells me that his sister and her family were supposed to fly in this afternoon for the holiday, but they canceled because his niece has an ear infection. I have a refrigerator full of food, he says, And no idea how to cook a turkey. I pretty much subsist on Raisin Bran and take-out, I tell him. I'm a halfway decent cook, he concedes. I remember, I say, and for a moment we're quiet. So, what about you? Adam asks, What are your plans for Thanksgiving?

I don't know how to answer him. I find my situation too pitiful for words, and I'm not up for excuses or the beating to my self-esteem. I'm in town, I say, hoping I'm at least providing the appearance that I have arrangements for the holiday. He doesn't press, and I can feel myself relaxing.

I saw your show, he tells me. You're kidding, I say. You want to hear what I thought? he asks, and for just a second I think he's taunting me. He must have read Jess's review. But he's watching me with an earnest expression, and I finally nod. I went back a second time, he admits, I couldn't get some of the paintings out of my mind. No shit, I say, stunned. No, no shit, he says, giving me a half-smile. You went to my show *twice*? I ask, and he nods. Is that hopelessly transparent? he asks. I think it's nice, I say. That's what I was going for, he agrees, I wanted you to think I'm *nice* on the off chance that I ran into you.

I lower my eyes, but nothing in his tone suggests anger, and after a minute I look up at him. So, he says, and I balk at the change in his voice. I have to go, I say. Come to dinner with me tonight, he suggests. Uh, I say, drawing out the word as I formulate an excuse. C'mon, Joel, he says, You have to eat, don't you? Yeah, I admit. I can pick you up at eight, he tells me. Aren't you dating someone? I blurt out. Not for months, he says. I squint, feeling as if the sun has just barreled out from behind a sheaf of clouds. So, he says, I need your address.

Later that afternoon, after I get a good look at the circles under my eyes, I think about taking a nap. Instead, I find myself in the back room, submerged in paint. I haven't felt the impulse so strongly in months, and by the time the room's shadowed in dusk I'm almost light-headed. I keep going, captivated. Red, indigo, gold, dripping down my fingers, manacling my wrists. Taking a step back, I think about the last few hours, what I have ahead of me tonight, and believe myself saved.

+ + +

The doorbell rings exactly at eight. Hi, he says, and I want to laugh because he's making this all so easy. Hi, I say, and he grins. You look nice, he says, Clean. Funny, I say, gesturing him inside.

I've taken time getting ready tonight. I've showered. I've washed my hair. I'm wearing my favorite jeans, the ones with just a hint of rust-colored paint on the pocket from spending time in front of the easel. Very nice, he says, looking me over. You don't look so bad either, I say. He's wearing charcoal-gray pants, a blue shirt neatly pressed. I can't get over the color of his eyes.

Do you want a glass of wine? I ask. I do, he says, and I start to lead him into the kitchen but can tell from a glance over my shoulder that he's more interested in checking things out. I try to see my living room through his eyes: the leather furniture James and I picked out the fall before we graduated, the coffee table I never got around to replacing, the dartboard hanging beside the fireplace. Is this where you trained to hustle? he asks, and then he sees the wall, the one I threw up the winter after my senior year. You did this? he asks. Yeah, I mumble, and he lingers over the lines as I uncork a Chianti. You're kind of amazing, you know, he says. Well, I say, feeling like I have no right to accept that compliment given my current situation, but he shakes his head, taking the glass I offer him. I wouldn't lie, he tells me.

When he asks for a tour, I'm briefly grateful that I spent a few minutes straightening up before I showered. He pauses at the door of James's bedroom. There's not one piece of furniture in here, not one painting, and after a second he turns to me with raised eyebrows. I had a roommate, I say, It didn't work out.

In my bedroom he sees my bed in a tangle of sheets, a view from the windows of the chain link fence surrounding my backyard. The summer I moved in, I hung beads in the doorway of the closet, and they're still here, the ones that Pandora hasn't batted to the floor. I have a shitload of books, postcards tacked to my walls, a dresser spilling clothes, and I glance at him from the corner of my eye. Looks a lot the way I pictured it, he admits.

For just a second I think he's being critical, and I can feel my muscles take offense. But he turns a half-circle, and I realize that what he's actually telling me is that he thought about my room before tonight. Before tonight he wondered where I slept, and I give him a ridiculously happy smile that I try to kill the second I realize what I'm doing. What's next? he asks, coaxing it from me again.

I've left the light on in the back room, and Pandora slinks out of our way as we step through the doorway. You have a cat, he says, sounding surprised. She's not mine, I say, My roommate ditched her. *Right along with me*, I add to myself, then clear a path to my easel, a little blown away by the fact that I've led him in here at all. I sort of got preoccupied this afternoon, I confess, and he indicates the half-finished painting. You did this today? he asks. I nod, holding my breath; few people have ever seen anything so fresh. Gorgeous, he says. Now you're just saying shit, I tell him, nudging him with my shoulder. No, he says, I'm not.

We leave as soon as we're finished with our wine. He has a new car, a black VW Passat, and he drives me to dinner, a true date. We order a bottle of wine, and he tells me about his sister, his niece and nephew back in Kentucky, the horses his parents own. Do you ride? he asks, and I shake my head. He asks me questions that are just personal enough: where I grew up, where I've traveled, where I want to go next. I refrain from telling him that lately I haven't been thinking that far ahead. Maybe it's time, I think, watching him. Maybe I deserve more.

We relax over the last of our wine, split dessert. He takes the bill right from our waiter's hand. Let me split that with you, I say. You can get it next time, he tells me. All right, I hear myself agreeing, Thanks.

So are you coming over? he asks as we're walking out to his car. I cock my head. You never told me about your plans for tomorrow, he explains. I don't have any, I admit, and he laughs and tells me that neither does he now that his sister has canceled. So you have no excuse, he says. My place is closer, I tell him, but he shakes his head. I've got Indy, he reminds me. Oh, I say, Well, let's just run by my house so I can get my car.

I start yawning before we're out of the city. The sleepless nights have gotten to me, and by the time I pull into his driveway even the thought of falling into bed with him can't keep me awake. I don't think I'm going to be very good company, I confess. So we'll watch a movie, he says, We don't even have to talk.

A year has passed, but Indy remembers me. He stretches out on the floor beside the sofa, his tail thumping against my leg, and when I look up, Adam smiles. What do you want to watch? he asks. Whatever you want, I murmur, and then I'm gone.

I jerk awake an hour later and groan when I realize the time. So you're tired, he says, You can sleep as long as you want. I don't say anything, though I'm thinking about letting him convince me to stay. C'mon, he says, I promise I'll be a gentleman.

His kiss isn't what I expected, isn't what I remembered. His mouth feels so much warmer than I've conjured even in the depths of my dreams the past fourteen months, and for the first time in so long I don't have to try to make sense of what I'm doing. I missed you, he murmurs, and I close my eyes and kiss him with an abandon I didn't know I still possessed. Come with me, he says, grabbing my hand.

We climb the stairs to his bedroom, tripping into his bed just as Indy starts to whimper. Adam moans, vacillating. Give me a minute, he finally says, I need just one minute to let him outside. With a kiss he leaves me, and I sink into his pillows, then slide between flannel sheets. I don't remember a thing once I close my eyes.

+ + +

Indy's yawning in my direction, and I wrinkle my nose when I catch a whiff of his breath. Come have breakfast, Adam says from the doorway. He's already up, already dressed; when I squint at his clock, I'm stunned to find that I've slept all night and most of the morning. I can't believe that he invited me back to his house and I fell asleep before I could deliver. But before I have a chance to apologize he's indicating his dresser with a wave of his hand. Borrow whatever you need, he says before he disappears.

For a long minute I don't move. I'm in Adam's house on Thanksgiving Day, lounging in his bedroom while he makes me breakfast. And yesterday:

I remember the way I felt as I was working, the look Adam gave me when I showed him what I'd done. *Gorgeous*, he said, but *easy* is the word I keep circling. I could stay for breakfast, then let him pull me back upstairs when we're finished. I could say yes to every invitation he offers.

Or I can leave. My eyes automatically track to the jeans I dropped beside his bed last night. I could put them on and reach for my keys and tell him I have to go. I could head for my Explorer without a word. What do you think, Indy? I whisper, and he licks my hand.

When I step into the kitchen, Adam smiles. You like pancakes? he asks, bringing me coffee. I nod, wrapping my hand around the mug. I'm wearing his sweatpants; they're baggy and a little long. I'm thinking we should cook that turkey, he says. I thought you didn't know how to cook a turkey, I say, taking a seat. I don't, he admits, But I can call my sister. He slides the spatula under the pancakes to see if they're done. What do you think? he asks, Will you stay? I look down at my hands, at the faint streak of paint on my wrist. Yeah, I say, Okay.

We eat our pancakes with butter and syrup. In between bites we look at each other without speaking. Our bare feet touch beneath the table. I spent a weekend here more than a year ago, one golden afternoon a few weeks after that. Now I lick syrup from the tip of my little finger, quietly thrilled to be back. You're still tired, he says, tucking a strand of hair behind my ear. I shrug. You should go back to bed, he tells me, and I say, What about the turkey? But he shakes his head. Go, he says, Get some rest.

Upstairs I curl on my side, the feel of his sheets against my skin the only tranquilizer I need. He's cleaning up the dishes; I can hear the water running and the clink of silverware. Indy barks, and Adam's quiet voice filters up the stairs. I take a deep breath, hold the air in my lungs, and when I let it out, I have the sweetest dream.

I'm flying. Over a river, the water murky, muddy, shallow in places. I drop from the treetops, unafraid; I know I have the strength to pull out at the last minute. Skimming the water, I soar back to the trees before I hurtle downward again. I've never felt so alive. My body electric, every muscle in a state of suspended orgasm. I can do anything, I think, the realization surprising me. Anything.

+ + +

Everything tastes better than we expect. We've made mashed potatoes, gravy, green beans, and rolls to go along with the turkey and stuffing, and we compliment each other, drink a pretty good pinot. We laugh, a lot. I tell him about my dream, and he listens more intently than anyone's listened to anything I've ever said. You know what I think? he asks. I shake my head. I think, he says, You like sleeping in my bed.

He doesn't need to ask me to spend the night. There's no way I'm leaving. I've wanted you back since the moment you left, he says, and I know he's not feeding me bullshit. I let him unwrap the past fourteen months, the mistakes I've made, my wretched relationship with Jess, and when he gathers my hair in his hands, I give myself over to him. This I trust, in a way I haven't trusted anything for more than a year.

The next morning, we go downstairs for breakfast, then head upstairs to shower and end up in bed. This time, we don't leave. He keeps his hands on me, touching my hip, my shoulder, running his fingers down the length of my thigh. I'm unhinged by his attention. Tell me, he says, I want to know everything. I hesitate, terrified and excited. What's your favorite color? he asks, starting me out slowly. Scarlet, I say. So specific, he says, smiling, tracing the thin lines on either side of my mouth. I lean my head to the side, and he runs his fingers into my hair. You graduated from UT, he continues. I nod, closing my eyes. And the painting, he murmurs, Tell me about the painting.

I start with my first memory, of the taste of that paint, then work my way up to the show I have scheduled for February. What's it like to sell something? he asks. Affirming, I admit, And in a way it kind of sucks. I try to explain how painting enables me to resolve whatever I'm going through at the time, that I've always depended on the process itself. Once I've worked something out, I say, You'd think the end result wouldn't matter as much as whether I'm maintaining sanity, but... I tell him, a little embarrassed, that there's so much in the paint, so much emotion, that in some ways I feel as if I'm on display. You mean as opposed to the painting? he asks. Well, in a way they're the same thing, I say, But don't quote me on that. What about your parents? he asks, What do they think?

My father, I admit, has never considered my painting "work," has always been quick to point out that I'm not able to make a living without his financial contribution. That's incredible, Adam says, You're so obviously talented. I'm quiet. The mere mention of my father briefly dampens my convictions, and I feel a flicker of panic thinking about what I still have to accomplish before February. Hasn't he seen what you've done? Adam presses. No, I say, I haven't shown him a thing since high school. He didn't come to your show? he asks. I shake my head. What about your mother? he asks, Did she come? My mother's dead, I say, She killed herself when I was nineteen.

Then, inexplicably, I start to cry. Mortified, I sit up, mashing my hand against my mouth. Oh, honey, Adam says, Come here. He tries to put his arms around me, and suddenly a torrent of words gushes from my mouth: I'm telling him about the bathroom, the viewing, the funeral, my father's threat to keep me in Houston. He had me! I wail, He had me, there was nothing I could do! I babble about the burns, the stink of those cigars, that I had no choice in the matter given what I'd seen him do to my mother. The more I divulge, the more I remember. I feel like I've dropped my keys into a river and can almost see them just beneath the surface. I keep reaching, and reaching, until I finally squeeze my eyes shut. When I open them, Adam's watching me like he's wondering who the hell he invited into his bed. Oh shit, I groan. You're fine, he murmurs. I have no idea where that came from, I confess. You're fine, he says, Don't worry about it. Right, I mutter, Like you're not thinking you picked the wrong fucking day to run to BookPeople. He slips me a smile, and for a while we're quiet. Your turn, I finally add, only half-joking, and he hesitates. What do you want to know? he asks. What do you want to tell me? I ask, and this is what he says:

I met Bobby my junior year in college. We were taking the same contemporary literature class, though I don't think I could've told you who he was; he didn't make much of an impression. But one day, our professor asked Bobby to read his paper aloud to the class. I kind of checked him out then. He was wearing these cheap jeans and a god-awful shirt, and his face was just mottled with embarrassment. He was so shy, and he never could dress—I bought most of his clothes after we were together. But that day, I found him curious, in a sad sort of way. I couldn't imagine being so self-conscious myself.

A week later, I was at the library studying with a few friends, and when they eventually wandered off, I saw Bobby watching me. He was a couple of tables away, and as soon as I caught him looking, he ducked his head over his book. Huh, I thought, he's into me. I didn't even know he was gay. I kept my eye on him almost as a game. He didn't look up again—he just kept reading the same page over and over. And after a while I thought, you know, he's actually kind of sweet beneath that wardrobe. I got my books together, and I stood up, and the whole time he was pretending not to notice that I was getting ready to leave. And then I walked over and pulled out the chair across from him. You want to go out Saturday night? I asked.

He stammered over a half a dozen unintelligible words before he blurted out a yes. Do you even know who I am? I asked. Of course, he said, You're Adam Atwater. Then he introduced himself. He was so self-effacing. Yeah, I know, I said, You're in my lit class. I don't think he could believe I recognized him. I loved that, and I said, So are you going to give me your number or what? He wrote it down. I told him I'd call the next day.

But I didn't. I got busy, and when I finally got in touch with him on Saturday night, I didn't offer to take him out like I'd promised. I just asked if he wanted to come by my apartment. I figured I'd sleep with him, and that would be that.

I kissed him as soon as I shut the door behind us. He smiled; I can still feel his teeth against mine. And the kiss was good, too, better than I expected. But when I went for the button on those cheap jeans, he brushed my hand away. Like a girl, I thought at the time. I kissed him, thinking I'd hold out for a while and then try again. And that's the way we spent the next fifteen minutes, battling for position. I finally managed to get his jeans unbuttoned and halfway unzipped before he shoved me away. What the hell? I asked. You know what? he said, I really didn't want you to be an asshole. What's that supposed to mean? I asked. Do you have any idea how long I've liked you? he said, I mean, you haven't even offered me a glass of water.

He was right, of course, and I felt like an idiot. Whatever, I muttered instead of apologizing. I couldn't even look at him as he buttoned his jeans, and when he headed for the door, I didn't say a word. But at the last second I called him back. Listen, I said, I'm sorry. Whatever, he said, throwing the word right back at me and slamming the door behind him. I fumed for about ten seconds before I flew down the stairs after him. Give me another chance, I said, catching him halfway to his car. Why should I? he asked.

I didn't know what to say. I didn't know what answer he was looking for, and when he started to turn away from me, I swear to god I almost fell to my knees. I don't want to always regret this moment, I said. His smile blew me away, and I think I vowed right then to spend the rest of my days trying to make him smile again and again.

When we graduated, we stayed in Lexington, got jobs, and bought a house together. My parents loved him. I'd come out to them the summer before my sophomore year; my mother had suspected all along. My father hadn't, though, and he took some time coming around. But we're close anyway, the two of us. He was the one who taught me how to ride. Anyway, they both liked Bobby. And my sister thought he was great. I think maybe all three of them were just happy I was in a relationship; this was '86, '87, '88, and they were scared, I think. Everyone was.

We were good for a few years, happy. And then one day, I came home from work and Bobby was waiting for me. At first I thought something had happened to one of my parents or maybe my sister; Bobby never got home before I did. But he shook his head. I was already crying when he told me he was positive.

At first I didn't believe him when he told me he'd slept with someone else. You're lying, I said, Why are you lying? He just wasn't the type to cheat, and anyway, we'd been trying hard to stay monogamous because—well, because of everything. Adam, he said, Why else would I get tested?

When I realized he was telling the truth, I went into our bedroom, and I packed a bag. As soon as Bobby saw that I was leaving, he fell apart. Please! he cried, I'm sorry, I'm sorry! I shook him off and left him there, sobbing and begging me not to go.

Somehow, I drove to my sister's house forty-five minutes away. I cratered in her doorway, then let her pull me inside where I told her everything as her husband poured me a drink. I still appreciate that gesture; he'd just gotten used to having a gay brother-in-law, and now here I was, cradled on his couch with the news that my lover was HIV positive, and I probably was too. My sister cried along with me, holding my hands and telling me that we'd figure this out, that she'd help me however she could, they both would. She looked at her husband for confirmation, and he nodded. Their reaction was the first indication I had that I might not be alone and the sole reason I was able to fall asleep that night in their spare room. The next morning, I found them in the kitchen with their arms around each other. They didn't see me, and I watched as Ivan touched Julia's face with the tips of his fingers and kissed her. Then I went home.

Bobby was sitting on the floor in the living room, his back against the wall. He was still wearing the same clothes, a blue shirt and this terrible tie he'd bought on sale. He obviously hadn't slept, and he raised his eyes to mine. I laid down beside him and put my head in his lap. Neither one of us said a word. We didn't move for the rest of the day.

He didn't get sick for almost a year and a half. But when he did... I told my parents after he'd been admitted to the hospital for the tenth time. Bobby didn't want his own parents to know. We'd had a huge fight about them a few years earlier—he still hadn't come out to them by the time we graduated, and I'd gotten so upset with him that first Christmas when he told me he had to visit them alone. But he knew them better than I did. When they found out about us, they were furious. And when he got sick, I thought they'd want to make the most of whatever time they had left. But they didn't.

Bobby called them, and his father wouldn't even get on the phone. His mother asked him not to call back.

He died in March of '93. He'd been in and out of the hospital for months, but at the end I wanted him at home. Even with hospice there I wouldn't leave him. I couldn't. I slept in the chair beside his bed, holding his hand. His skin didn't feel human. It felt like an eggshell—dry and thin and brittle, and I wanted to cry, and I wanted to leave. I held on anyway.

I was there when he died. I wasn't even sure at that point if he was past consciousness. He hadn't talked in days. And then he said my name, so softly I wasn't sure if I'd heard anything at all. I looked at him, frowning, and he opened his eyes. They were the only part of his body that hadn't changed. Adam, he said in this beautiful, clear voice I hadn't heard in weeks. I'm here, I said, and he was gone.

His parents wouldn't come to the funeral. I didn't think his father would, but I thought maybe his mother... I called her myself, but she didn't come. I don't remember much about that day. I didn't cry; I didn't cry for almost six months. Not the day he died, not when his birthday passed, not when I slept with a friend of ours a few months after the funeral. I was too angry and too bitter. Not because he'd cheated on me and not because he'd put my own life at risk. I'd taken a test a couple of days after he told me, and we couldn't believe when I got the results back that they were negative. We were both so sure. I was relieved more because I don't know how he would've handled the news if the results were positive than out of any concern for my own health. But I was angry at him anyway. I had to watch him die. And even though I never said anything, he knew how much I hated him for that. He knew.

I didn't cry until I started feeling better. I was hanging out with my sister, and she was just pregnant enough with Lindsey to be able to feel the baby kicking. I put my hand on her stomach and felt that kick, that hard thump of Lindsey's foot against the palm of my hand, and I burst into tears. I miss you, I miss you, I said over and over. I miss you.

A couple of years passed. I started dating, a little. Once in a while, at the end of the day, I'd realize I hadn't thought much about him at all. Usually, that made me feel worse. And then, at the beginning of '97, I got the job here in Austin. But leaving Kentucky, selling the house—that was hard, and when I drove out here, I cried most of the way.

Sometimes I think I got the raw end of the deal. He died, I know, and he suffered, too, more than I'd ever thought it was possible to suffer. But I was the one who had to watch him die. I was the one who had to learn how to live without him.

Adam doesn't take his eyes from me as he talks. He's less emotional than I'd expect, though there are moments when he pauses long enough that I think he might cry. I don't know what to say when he finally falls silent. He's given me something, the magnitude of which I'm not prepared to handle. I know he's never told anyone this story. He's taken a chance with me, and I wanted to tell him five minutes in that I'm not worth the risk. I'm frightened by how quickly I've confided in him, by how generously he reciprocated. He draws his fingers through his hair, sadly, wearily, and I feel compelled to reassure him. I touch his face; he relaxes into the palm of my hand. Let's make love, he says, and I'm struck by how easily, how naturally talking about his former lover segues into this moment.

I'm not capable of this kind of honesty.

After we've showered we go out to pick up some dinner. We're both quiet, and on the way back to the house Adam pulls to a stoplight, then looks over at me without speaking. What? I say. He touches his hand to my chest, and then to his own. There's something here, he says, You feel it? Why do you like me? I blurt out, and he laughs. I don't know, Joel, he says, You just do it for me.

My sleep that night is wicked, but Adam's oblivious, and I'm enraged that he doesn't sense how much I'm struggling to claw myself from my dreams. Instead, he's quiet, peaceful, and the entire scene pisses me off more than I could've possibly imagined.

The sun's barely rising when the damage is done. He opens his eyes, propping his head on one hand. You're up early, he says, reaching for me in the gray light. I break away.

There's a moment of silence. Indy stretches from his place on the floor, wanders over to nose Adam's hand, and Adam scratches him behind the ears. You ready to get up? he asks, glancing back at me. Whatever, I say, swinging my legs over the side of the bed. Joel? he says, and when I look at him, he raises his eyebrows. What? he says, What's wrong? I don't answer him, and he finally slides across the bed and wraps his arm around my waist. His skin's so warm, and it takes me back a year, to the morning after our first night together. I'd sat up, calculating my escape, and he'd slid his arm around my waist and coaxed me into breakfast tacos and a blowjob. Now when he brushes my hair from my neck, I pull away from him and get to my feet. What're you doing? Adam asks as I grab my jeans. I don't need this, I tell him, I really don't fucking need this. Need *what*? he says. Your sweet fucking concern, I tell him, biting off every word. I throw my shirt over my head and spin around, trying to find my boots. What're you talking about? he says, What're you... are you *leaving*? Yeah, I say, I'm leaving. Joel, he says, bewildered, and I turn back, furious that he needs me to explain.

I don't need this! I say, I don't need to tell you... I don't need you to hear me, I don't need you, do you hear what I'm saying? I'm panting and sweating and out of control, and I say the one thing I know will render me unforgivable. I don't need you! I cry, Go tell your pathetic dead lover stories to someone who gives a shit!

I've never said anything so malicious, and I stare at him, horrified, as the color drains from his face. Adam, I lament, stretching out my hand, but he shrinks away from me. Please, he says, Don't touch me. I snatch my hand away from him. You should go, he adds. Gladly, I snap, flinging open the bedroom door. I bolt down the stairs, tripping and twisting my ankle. But I pick myself up, and I don't stop running until I'm outside.

By the time I get home I'm sobbing with rage and confusion, and my ankle's fucking killing me. I bypass Pandora, who glowers at me, then take the lid from the Xanax and dry swallow a couple of pills. Swiping a pack of Marlboros, I hobble into the living room and light a cigarette.

Thirty minutes and three cigarettes later, I'm able to breathe again, and I stare at the wall across from me. The colors haven't faded much over the years. I cock my head, holding the cigarette to my lips. Ash falls into my lap, and I flick it absently to the floor. What was it Adam had said Wednesday evening? That I'm amazing. Well. I pinch the edge of the cigarette between my lips and draw the last bit of smoke into my lungs.

Then I go to Home Depot, where I buy a gallon of black paint and a roller. Redecorating? the guy behind the counter asks. Something like that, I say.

When I get back to the house, I pry the lid from the can and dump half the contents in an old tray. Paint sloshes onto the floor. I ignore the mess I'm making, ignore the pain in my ankle, saturate the roller, then lift it to the living room wall. Press. Half the arm disappears. I laugh, suddenly manic, and dip the roller in the tray again. This time, I cover the thick blue paint streaking from the fingers. Taking a step back, I light a cigarette. Once the hand's gone, I know there's no turning back. I take the final drag on my cigarette and crush it out on the floor beneath me. Black paint dribbles down the wall, speckles the hardwoods, the clothes from last Wednesday. I squint my eyes at what I've done and smile.

There's no chance of salvation now.

+ + +

I've cleaned up the mess in the living room, though I can't bear to touch the wall. I got black paint on everything: the floors, the furniture. I've thrown the clothes away. There's a feel in the house I can't put my finger on, and I've ended up over the last week avoiding the living room entirely. I'm concerned, Kyle admits when I meet him at a bar, Are you still seeing your doctor? I don't know whether to roll my eyes or collapse into his arms. Because seriously, sweetheart, he says as someone steps between us, You do not seem well.

It takes the merest second to recognize the kid standing in front of me. I can still feel his eyes on me, can still remember fucking him with my gaze that day I met Kyle for dinner. H-hi, he stammers, his face already flushing. Joel, Kyle says, narrowing his eyes at me to convince me to behave, You remember Jack. Yeah, I mutter, Hey. Can I..., Jack says, Do you want me to buy you a drink?

There's something so innocent and unpracticed in his question, especially since I'm holding a full bottle of beer, that I can't help but say yes. Kyle lets me go, his eyebrows raised, and I follow Jack, watching as he leans over the bar. He's slight of build, and his jeans, a little loose, ride low on his hips. I suddenly realize he's about to buy me a drink with a fake ID. I don't think I'm what you're looking for, I tell him when he hands me a fresh bottle. Maybe you should let me make that decision, he says, but even in the dark I can see the rush of scarlet that spreads from his cheeks to his hairline.

I light a cigarette, and when he asks if he can bum one, I give him the box. He barely inhales, holding his cigarette with an awkward hand. I flag the bartender, and we knock back a couple of shots at the same time. By the time we finish a second beer and another shot I care a little less about what I'm doing. You want to get out of here? I ask, thinking that if we skirt the edge of the bar, we can bypass Kyle, who has occupied himself with a friend but keeps sending semi-concerned glances in our direction. I kind of live in the dorm, Jack tells me. Fine, I say, suppressing my groan, We'll go to my place.

But I've made a mistake, I realize as I open the front door of my house. Jack doesn't belong here in this maelstrom I've created the past couple of years, and his eyes skitter around the living room, snagging on the black wall. Beer? I ask, and he nods. I hand him a bottle, and he takes a nervous gulp. I know I'm expected to make the first move, and I pull him toward me without preamble. There's not a line on his face. He returns my kiss, his mouth slow, new; I hate the way my body automatically responds: the catch of my breath, the rush of blood between my legs. I want him on his knees, but I'm already feeling guilty about bringing him here, especially since he let it slip on the ride over that he turned eighteen the day after Halloween. What'd you do, skip a grade? I asked, and he told me he started kindergarten early. He's barely legal.

I also have the distinct, unsettling impression that I'm his first. He hasn't said as much, but there's something in the way he looks at me when I reach for my beer that makes me feel like I've been chosen. If not, then I'm pretty close to the top of the fucking list.

Leading him to the sofa, I kneel down in front of him. You want to tell me what you want? I ask, but he just gapes at me like he can't believe this is even happening. I tug at his zipper, slide his jeans over his hips. That smooth skin below his navel, that line of baby fine hair: he's young. I could devour him if I didn't have a conscience. Maybe I don't. If I did, I wouldn't have brought him here at all, because he's not in this for one night, trust me. I can tell from his expression, a look that's half disbelief, half adoration. I can tell, because not all that long ago I wore the same look myself.

I have a choice here. I can make this a night he'll go to again and again when he's on his own. He'll find me in his memory because I have the option of doing right by him, of telling him we should scrap this sofa shit and go into my bedroom, where I could lay him out long on my bed. I could throw an old tee shirt over that lamp on my bedside table to color the room. I could take twenty seconds to light a candle; I could offer him a massage. Others have done the same for me, and I have an opportunity to return the favor. Because he's young, so young. Whatever this night looks like will spill over into the rest of his life. I could make this moment perfect. I have that power.

Or I can take him here, in the living room, without a condom. Because he'd let me get away without one, I know that for sure. I know exactly the inflection I'd need to convince him to let me fuck him without obstruction. I could fuck him right here and drive him back to his dorm and tell him I never want to see him again. Or I could string him along, pretend I care about him when I'm interested in nothing more than his virgin ass. I don't have to be good to him. I don't have to be kind, and that's an entirely different sort of power.

But I'm not that cruel, and I bring my mouth back to Jack's and part his lips with my tongue. He shudders as my hand wraps around his cock, and then he comes without warning.

Well, that was a lot of mental work for thirty seconds of nothing. Jesus, he's young, and when he starts to apologize, I moan. Are you...? he asks, catching his breath, Can I...? I remove his hand from my crotch. Please, I say, I'm fine.

I take him home as soon as he's dressed, mumble an excuse about having an early meeting with a gallery tomorrow, a bullshit lie I wish to god were true. In front of his dorm I accept a chaste kiss, write his number on the palm of my hand when he offers me a pen. The second I get back to my house, I scrub it clean.

+ + +

I find myself looking for Adam's Passat everywhere, haunt the fiction section at BookPeople hoping to conjure a reconciliation. I have no plan in the event that I run across him, but I can't seem to help myself, and I end up with enough books to carry me through what's likely going to be another shitty holiday.

Jack calls. I have no idea how he got my number—unless Kyle gave it to him, and I find that hard to believe. He's already reamed me for leaving that bar with what he says is a borderline minor. Weren't you the one who told me to throw him a bone? I asked. A bone, he said, Isn't a blowjob. Trust me, I muttered, We never got that far.

Jack has finals next week, and then he's going home for Christmas. Where's home? I ask, and he names some small town south of Houston. I don't have to ask if his parents know he's queer or what his Christmas will be like. I already know the answers. He talks about school, his classes, tells me that what he'd really like to do is write screenplays. But I figure I need to be more realistic, you know? he says, I mean, how many people out there want to write screenplays? The conversation trails off. He wants me to ask him out, and I can't. I just can't. Maybe..., he says, and I tell him I have to go.

James calls, leaving a carefully composed message I don't know whether or not to return. He wants to talk; I can't imagine why. We have nothing left to say to each other, and I can't imagine what good could possibly come from another attempt. We're our very own train wreck, a codependent disaster. Neither one of us can tear our eyes away.

At the same time, I miss what we had, what we were to each other, and one afternoon in a fit of nostalgia, I decide to fuck it and drop by his apartment, checking to be sure Elizabeth's car is missing from the curb. Well, shit, he says, looking just as stunned to see me on his doorstep as I am to find myself here, Come on in. You have any beer? I ask. Sure, he says. I look around the tiny living room, trying to picture him here, studying, watching television. With Elizabeth. My eyes automatically glance in the direction of the bedroom. I'm glad you came, James says, handing me a bottle, I was starting to think... We both stare at the floor. Do you think it's possible, I say, For us to have a normal conversation?

We don't discuss Elizabeth or my therapy or what happened between us. Instead, we talk about what Major Applewhite and Mack Brown are going to do for the Longhorns and joke about Peter getting married next summer. Jumping up to get us both another beer, he tells me I wouldn't believe his sister. She's what now, I ask, Thirteen? Fourteen, he says, And she has all these guys calling her, sixteen-year-old guys who can drive. We shake our heads, and he pauses, his bottle poised before his lips. She asks about you, he says, They all do.

I stay for three hours. We haven't spent so much time together since he moved out, and I think we're both surprised that we've managed not to tread on anything unpleasant. I'm glad you came, he tells me, walking me to the door, and then he hesitates, and I know he's going to fuck up whatever progress we've made. Come to dinner with us, he suggests. I stop, stuck on the word he's used. *Us.* I'll be through with everything by the middle of next week, he's saying, I'll call you. He pats the door. I'll call you, he repeats, as if he's trying to convince himself. Yeah, I say, Why don't you.

+ + +

The thought occurs to me that if I'd gone ahead and booked an appointment with Bryan before Thanksgiving, I'd be getting ready to see him. Maybe not today but soon. I've fallen off the fucking rails; there's no doubt about that. At the same time, I'm relieved I held off from calling him. I have a feeling I would've canceled anyway. Admitting that I'd overestimated my progress would be one thing; telling him about my behavior over Thanksgiving would be another. And I brought Jack back to my place, stopped off at James's... how much more masochistic can I get?

Considerably, apparently, because when James makes good on that promise to invite me to dinner, I agree. I'm in the back room when he calls, though I'm not working. I haven't painted anything other than the living room wall since the day before Thanksgiving. I told you I'd call, he reminds me. You did, I say, Congratulations. C'mon, Joel, he says, I'm trying here. What do you want from me, James? I say. Come to dinner with us, he tells me. I'm busy, I inform him. I haven't even suggested a time, he says. Yeah, well, I mutter, I'm busy in general.

But he's not going to be put off so easily, and he reminds me that he's planning on going to Fort Worth for the holiday. Why do I get the feeling that if I turn you down now, I won't hear from you again? I say, and he tells me I'm being melodramatic. Anyway, he continues, Elizabeth wants to get to know you.

That can't be true. She can't possibly be that open-minded.

Look, James finally says, I'm not going to beg you. So it's now or never, I say, and he sighs. It's an invitation, Joel, he says, Not a fucking ultimatum.

I don't know how I get through the meal. Elizabeth's beautiful: springy auburn hair, heart-shaped face, perfect smile, and she tells me about her job in public relations for the city, talks about the trip she and James are making over New Year's so James can meet her parents, prattles on about their first date. Her agenda couldn't be any clearer. She's marking her territory, letting me know that whatever my history with James, the only place left for me moving forward will be on the sidelines. James stares down at his plate, refusing to meet my eyes. Well, he wanted to hurt me last month, and that still seems to be the case. Otherwise, he'd never put me in this position.

Elizabeth brushes her hair behind her ear with a delicate gesture; though she wears no ring, I can already see the diamond on her finger. I don't think I can do this anymore, and I drain the last of my beer. Oh, she says mournfully, seeing me stand, You're not leaving, are you? Honestly, I say, I think we've all had enough. But I've barely gotten to know you, she protests. Let him go, Elizabeth, James mutters, and I narrow my eyes in his direction. He glowers back at me like this wasn't his goddamn idea. You know what? I say, deciding that maybe it's time for my side of the story, I think I'll stay. Fine, James says, smacking his hands on the table and getting to his feet, Then we're going to need more beer.

Elizabeth and I stare at each other after he leaves. You don't like me much, do you? she finally asks. How could I? I say, You've spent the past hour putting me in my place. Tears spring to her eyes. Her blouse has tiny, pearl buttons; I can see them slipping through James's fingers. I don't understand, she whispers, and I open my mouth, the barb ready on my tongue.

And then suddenly, I realize. She doesn't know.

I suck in an audible breath, and Elizabeth frowns, a pretty pucker of her forehead that I realize couldn't be any closer to sincere. *She doesn't know?* I'm thinking, *she doesn't know? How can this girl be the one if she doesn't know?* Joel? she says, but I'm sitting across from James at that bar when he told me she was the one. *Does she know about us?* I'd asked, and for a second I thought he was going to say, *What about us?* Then he nodded, and now I freeze his expression: hand cupped around a mug of beer, shoulders hunched, eyes averted.

I've been erased. He's going to marry this girl, and he has no intention of ever telling her what happened between us.

And he lied to me, he lied.

What'd I miss? James asks, yanking out his chair, and when neither Elizabeth or I answer, he looks from one of us to the other. *Eight years,* I think, staring at him, *I've known you for eight years.* Joel? he says, and I say: Fuck you.

Under a weeping sky I stumble through the parking lot. When Jack appears beside me as I'm opening the Explorer's door, I jump, then start to laugh. Of course he's here. Of course. You coming or going? he asks. Neither, I say, Both. You want to get something to eat? he asks. No, I say, and he shivers in the drizzle. I glance back at the restaurant; I half-expect to see James barreling through the night after me. But Jack and I stand alone. We stand alone.

My roommate left for the holidays, Jack volunteers. Perfect, I say.

Halfway there, I almost turn back. But I don't. Instead, I park behind him, and we walk together up to the entrance. The smell, when he opens the door, almost knocks me backward. He's in a different dorm, but the smell's the same. The smell's exactly the same.

By the time we make it to his room I can't contain my fury. You want a beer? he asks as I clench and unclench my fists. Okay, I say. He has a mini refrigerator just like the one James and I had, and he bends down, then hands me a can of Keystone Light. You want to listen to some music or something? he asks, indicating the CDs on his bookshelf. No, I say, Not really. I shake a cigarette from the box I'm holding and dig in my pocket for my lighter. You can sit down, he offers, indicating one of the beds as he disappears into the bathroom, I'll be right back.

I lie on his bed, my hand propped behind my head. There's no water stain on the ceiling in the corner by the closet. James's clothes aren't folded in the dresser. My sketchpad isn't beside the bed along with a half a dozen pencils sharpened to a point.

I'm not nineteen anymore.

When Jack opens the bathroom door, my cigarette's one long ash. I lean over the side of the bed and grab his trash can, grind the butt against the metal. My hands seem surprisingly steady. Get undressed, I say, and he looks surprised. O-okay, he stammers, and I lean back on the palms of my hands and watch as he strips. His shirt first, pulled over his head and revealing a smooth plane of white, then his jeans; I can tell he's nervous by the way he tosses them on the chair beside the desk, by the way he wads his boxers into a ball, then drops them on the floor.

I'd bet the back room that he just brushed his teeth.

I fuck him standing up, bent over his desk. He laughs at first, then tries to slow me down, begs me to take it easy. C'mon, Joel, he says, and I finally have to cover his mouth with the palm of my hand. He'll have bruises on his hips in the morning, but I can't seem to loosen my hold. I haven't used a condom, and my saliva isn't enough; I can tell it's not enough. He whimpers beneath me, and I press my mouth to his ear. Shut up, I whisper, Please, just shut the fuck up.

Outside the rain hasn't let up, and the Explorer's cold, so cold. I blast the heater, blow on my hands. I'm not even halfway home when I have to pull over. I lay my head on the steering wheel, the rain diamonds on the windshield, and cry harder than I have in years.

+ + +

I spend the holiday trying to convince myself that I can recover from the past couple of years, that I can live with myself after what I've said to Adam, after what I've done to Jack. I'm not a bad person. I've made mistakes, but I can do good.

I haven't heard from James. That surprises me, a little. I expected more from him: to hear him banging on my door at three o'clock in the morning, maybe, or to be assaulted by a dozen phone calls. There's been nothing, though, and I've stopped listening for his footsteps on the front porch. He's probably out of town by now anyway, in Fort Worth for Christmas and heading south after the holiday to meet Elizabeth's parents. Still. An apology, I thought, at the very least. After eight years, I thought at least an apology.

In the absence of human contact I realize that I have to figure out a way to cope on my own. I take a sheet of paper just as it's getting dark on Christmas Day and make a list, a sort of jump-start on New Year's resolutions, never mind that reading over them leaves a gritty taste in my mouth. I stare at the paper in my hands, determined, penitent: I will paint. I will manage to get enough work finished that I can swing the February show. I will not dwell on my relationship with James. I will not say anything cruel to anyone. I will not fuck over eighteen-year-old kids.

I will move on.

I awaken the next day, the twenty-sixth, and head into the back room. I'm wary but committed, and I pull acrylics because I know they'll get me through the day with the least amount of effort. Everything's gray except for one blinding stroke of fuchsia that appears from out of nowhere and sucks me in. When I look up, the day's already dying. Tears come to my eyes. If I've gotten this far, surely I'll be okay.

I shower, check my cell for messages I'll never receive. At this very moment my father and Catherine have likely wandered in from the beach; they'll be tired and gritty with sand but full of anticipation for their evening. James and Elizabeth must be in Fort Worth or maybe Houston. I wonder if over the last few days James confessed to anything. I'm thinking he didn't. I'm thinking Elizabeth wouldn't understand, and that's why he never told her in the first place. I'm thinking he made some bullshit excuse as to why I left.

Who else? Cameron Mackey's hardly a friend, not the sort of friend who might check in over the holidays. Since his engagement, Peter has been virtually unavailable. And Kyle told me the night I went home with Jack that he was meeting a friend of his in Aspen for the holiday. I'm an old lady with a cat, I think, glancing at Pandora. But I have my work, and that's enough. That's more than enough.

I run out for something to eat and get to the end of the block before I realize I've forgotten my wallet. Swinging into the nearest driveway to turn around, I glance in the rearview mirror. White Christmas lights fill my field of vision. I back up, then check the rearview mirror again, frowning. I can feel something long repressed wriggling to the surface. At the edge of my driveway I throw the Explorer in park, and by the time I get to the porch I'm on my hands and knees. I crawl to the top and can't make it any farther.

The day after Christmas, sophomore year, and I can't keep my grades a secret any longer. My mother handed them to me this morning; she'd hidden them after all, kept them from us until after the holiday. Now my father's waiting in his study, and as I close the door behind me, I'm suddenly sick to death of the entire scenario. The expression on his face, his posture behind his desk, the thick smell of cigars: I'm tired of it, tired of the ten plus years of dealing with this bullshit, and the conversation gets off to a bad start. You're not going to be happy, I tell him, handing him my grades. As he looks them over, I sink to the chair across from his desk, pulling the collar of my sweatshirt up over my chin. What do you have to say for yourself? he finally asks. Ethics was tough, I mumble. That might explain the F, though I doubt it, he says, But how can you justify the C's in the other three classes? I don't have an answer for him, and he watches me for a minute, then sits back in his chair. You're taking this better than I thought you would, I admit. I've learned by now not to expect much from you, he says.

He knows just what to say to hurt me, and before I can think about what I'm doing I'm backtracking, telling him that the Ethics professor talked in circles, it was an eight o'clock class, the Spanish final was harder than I expected… He shakes his head throughout my explanation, and I eventually trail off. Reaching for the decanter of scotch on the table behind him, he refills his glass. What we have to decide, he says, speaking as matter-of-factly as he might if I were a business problem to solve, Is how best to deal with this situation.

I'll do better next semester, I say, I'll study harder, I'll make sure the grades come up. He doesn't remind me that he's heard these promises before. Instead, he wants to know what I've decided about next semester. He'd given me a choice after loading me up with the requisite introductory business classes of going with Statistics or shifting gears and registering for an upper-level science class. Horrified by the prospect of either, I'd scrapped his advice and gone with Drawing Foundation. I'd trembled as I registered, partly from fear but mostly from anticipation. My life, I kept reminding myself, this is my life. I thought I could get far enough into the semester before he found out what I'd done that by then dropping the class wouldn't make financial sense. But my success was predicated on him forgetting that he'd given me a choice in the first place. What did you decide? he asks now.

I tell him in a voice so low he has to duck his head to hear me. His lips thin at the news. Well, you'll have to drop the class, he says.

In his mind he doesn't need to say another word. I'm not so stupid that I'd ignore his order, and even if I was, he knows what he can do to change my mind. But as I stand there in front of this man who looks so much like me, I make the decision not to be bullied any longer. No, I say, and he raises his eyebrows. Excuse me? he says. No, I say,

I won't drop the class. Yes, he says, setting his glass on the desk with a smack, You will. I won't, I insist, and he takes a step toward me.

Springing from my chair, I duck under his arm and make it to the door, but he catches me with my hand on the knob. I'm shoved against the wall, so hard that for a second I can't move. Then for the first time I fight back. But he blocks my swing as easily as if I was simulating a punch, his own fist catching me on the chin. I falter, and he grabs my wrist and twists, pushing me backward at the same time until I'm flush against the door. Please, I whimper, because he's hurting me, he's hurting my wrist, and this isn't the hand I can harm. Don't you disrespect me, Joel, he says. Okay, I say, I'm sorry.

He gives me one last shove for good measure. Holding my hand to my chest, I test my wrist to assess the damage. My father looks at me from under lowered lids; I'm a pussy. He doesn't even have to say the word for me to know what he thinks. But I could've just as easily been looking at weeks without being able to work, and as he turns away from me and reaches for his drink, I realize that if I let this go, I'm never going to escape. I can't live this way from holiday to holiday. I can't worry that when I'm gone, he'll turn to my mother. I'm no longer a child, and I'm on him with a roar.

Scotch spills onto our clothes as the glass falls from his hands; I'll smell it all the way back to Austin. From the corner of my eye I can see the smoke from the cigar on his desk, and when he closes in, I start to struggle. But he's not interested in making me burn. Instead, his hand closes around my throat. I can feel my eyes widen as he cuts off my airway, as my mouth opens without reward. I'm writhing against him, frantic for release. If he ever lets me go, I'll have bruises on my neck I'll have to hide.

As the edges of my world begin to gray, I meet his eyes. I'm looking into a mirror, and then breath tears through my lungs, ragged and pure. I drop to the floor. He's pacing back and forth, snorting like a stallion, an animal caged. I've never seen him like this, and I never want to again. You can't do this anymore! I cry, I won't let you do this anymore! I take a deep breath and a leap of faith. I'll tell her, I say, I'll tell her everything.

The room waits, and so do I, in a silence so thick he might as well still have his hand around my throat. I can't decipher his expression. He's wrestling with something, and when he finally speaks, the words fall from his mouth without triumph. Do you honestly think she doesn't know? he says.

For the first time in my life I'm more afraid of his words than I've ever been of his hands.

I'm halfway through the living room when I see her. I can read every lie in her face. She knows, she's always known, and when she steps toward me, I push her out of my way. Joel! she cries, stumbling. I catch our reflections in the mirror in the foyer. I am no son of hers. Please! she says as I throw open the front door, but I already have my keys. In the chill of the night I race to the Explorer and lock myself against her. She pleads with me, hammering on the window, and for just a second I wonder what would happen if I opened the door and slid into her arms. Through the glass we gaze at each other, my mother's hand reaching for mine. She wears her hair long, in thick, dark ropes that fall past the shoulders of a gauzy white blouse. Tears roll down her cheeks. Joel, she says, my name muffled by the glass, and I cover my eyes and cry.

Then I turn on the ignition. As I pull away from the house, I throw my eyes to the rearview mirror. White Christmas lights frame the last image I have of my mother alive: on her knees, in our driveway, her head buried in her hands.

Pandora curls up warm on my lap three weeks later. I haven't talked to either of my parents. James, when he answers the phone, makes excuses, takes messages from my mother, who's called at least once a day since I left. The messages that make their way to the machine I erase without listening. There's nothing she could possibly say that I want to hear. I'll be happy if I never hear her voice again.

Classes start tomorrow, and James sits beside me with his calendar in front of him. I stare at the television, my legs crossed on the coffee table. Latest beer beside my boot. When the phone rings, neither one of us moves. James finally sighs and reaches for the receiver. I watch his face turn ashen. Joel, he says.

+ + +

That final image of my mother is so real, so substantial, so catastrophic, that I can barely get out of bed. I was on the front porch for hours Saturday night before I finally groped my way into my bedroom, but I couldn't sleep. I still can't. I can't cry either. Instead, I will the phone to ring. I need to talk to someone, anyone, and realize as the twenty-seventh passes in silence that there's no one left.

I run out of cigarettes on the thirtieth as the sun's setting, and I go to the nearest convenience store to buy a box. I smoke a cigarette on the way home, another sitting in the swing on the front porch. Tapping the ash onto the floor beside me, I feel a mild buzz; I've had nothing to eat in days. Then I go back into the house and take a shower, pull on jeans and a sweater, my boots.

Finding my way isn't a problem. I could make this drive even in my sleep, and I pull up to his house just after seven-thirty. He has Christmas lights, the icicle kind, and a couple of reindeer in the front yard, and I find myself laughing under my breath as I trudge up the sidewalk. I should've known. There's a wreath on the front door, too, fresh pine, and I inhale with closed eyes, then reach out and press the bell. After a minute I hear footsteps, then voices. I hadn't considered the possibility that he might not be alone.

When the door swings open, I stare down at the little girl standing in front of me. Uh…, I say, taking a cautious step back. Who're you? the girl asks, but before I have the chance to answer I hear Adam. He's heading in my direction, and though I can't make out what he's saying, I'm instantly reassured by the sound of his voice. Who're you? the little girl says again, and then Adam appears like the answer to a prayer. His face falls at the sight of me.

Who's that man? the little girl asks, tugging on his sleeve, and he nudges her through the doorway. Go find your mom, Lindsey, he says, and she protests but allows Adam to close the door behind her. I try not to be too shaken that he hasn't invited me inside. Your niece? I ask, but he ignores the question. What're you doing here, Joel? he says. I kick at the ground with the toe of my boot. I came to apologize, I say. He stares at me, and I fold my hands together. If I thought falling to my knees would do any good, I swear I would. I'm sorry for what I said to you, I say, I'm sorry for… leaving the way I did. You're more than a month late, he tells me. I know, I say, I know, and I'm sorry.

Pursing his lips, he looks at the sky like maybe he's going to find his next line in the stars. From over his shoulder the blinds part, and Lindsey peers out at us; she must be here with her parents and little brother, and I'm suddenly embarrassed that I've just dropped on his doorstep with a bullshit excuse for treating him so badly. No wonder he hasn't asked me to come inside. I'm lucky he's taking the time to talk to me.

For just a second I wonder what might have happened if I hadn't let Thanksgiving end on such a shitty note. Would we have continued to see each other? Would I have been included in the Christmas celebration he likely spent with his family? Would I even now be curled up beside his fireplace, drinking a glass of wine and talking with his sister and brother-in-law or laughing with their kids? Heartbreaking, to think I came so close.

Adam sighs, and I'm pulled from a future that never materialized and back to this moment, where I stand in the cold and he talks to me with a closed door behind him. Apology accepted, he finally mumbles, and I'm so stunned, so grateful, that my legs waver. He folds his arms across his chest as I steady myself. So, your sister's in town? I ask. Yeah, he says. Do you think, I say, I mean, I know you have company, but do you want to maybe get a drink or something? He's quiet, and my face flushes. No, I agree, I know you probably can't leave. I bury my fists in my armpits, my shoulders hunched. Maybe tomorrow though? I offer, Or whenever they leave? Adam tilts his head in a gesture so sweet I can't help myself. Or maybe, I say, slipping him half a smile, We could take a bath.

He looks at me with such fury I take a step back. You are not welcome here, Joel, he says, and I force myself to nod. Oh, I say, my voice so small I might as well not be speaking at all, Okay.

He turns away from me and shuts the door behind him. I stumble to the curb. Behind the wheel my blood pressure rises. I'll never drive this way again.

+ + +

I wonder if I've known all along that this is where I'd end up, in the back room surrounded by canvas, a box cutter in my hand. Dragging the blade across the tip of my finger, I watch as blood slides beneath my nail. With my finger in my mouth I shove Pandora out the front door, for good. Then I pull my sweater over my head. Barefoot, clad in nothing but jeans, I go into the bathroom and take a deep breath.

My skin parts without complaint. Pressing the box cutter into the flesh at the base of my palm, I cut upward toward the crook of my arm. Then I shift the blade to my other hand. This cut's deeper, partly because I'm not as adept with my right hand and partly because by now I'm slick with blood. Behind me the bathtub fills. Everything's covered in blood: my arms, my feet, my jeans, which I strip with crimson hands. Then I slide into the tub and stare at the blackened ceiling. I almost hear my name.

+ + +

I sense movement before I open my eyes. Disoriented, I take in a white room, a woman with long, dark hair. Mom? I whisper, and there's a cool hand on my forehead. I stare at the woman in front of me, then slowly realize what happened: I'm here, I'm alive. This woman is not my mother. Tears slip from the corners of my eyes, into my hair. There's a strange sensation in my arm, and then whatever it is I've been given knocks me out.

The next time I awaken, I swear I see Adam. Frowning, I try to speak, and James's features fall into place. He's sitting in a chair beside me, and he looks like shit but manages a smile. I run my tongue along the edge of my lips. Reaching for my arm, he changes his mind and ends up settling his hand on top of the blanket instead. I watch his fingers move back and forth. Joel, he starts, and then he breaks into sobs. I conjure every scrap of strength I can gather. Get out, I say. He draws the back of his hand across his eyes. What? he gulps, and I say, Get *out*, James.

He backs away from me, then flings open the door. I take a deep breath, bracing myself for an onslaught of tears. Nothing happens. That guy that was here? I say when the nurse appears, and she nods. I don't want to see him again, I tell her. All right, she agrees, and I close my eyes. I don't want to see anyone, I whisper.

+ + +

Dr. Herrera, the woman I'd mistaken for my mother in those initial seconds after awakening, drops by with stultifying regularity to check on me. How're you feeling? she asks each time, as if she expects the answer to change. I want a cigarette, I tell her, and she says that as soon as I'm stable, I can smoke all I want. We'll get you feeling better, she promises, and I don't make the mistake of believing her.

The afternoon of my transfer to the third floor, where I'm going to be facing weeks and maybe months of therapy, I'm lying on the bed, curled on my side, my hands between my knees. I'm wearing jeans and a sweatshirt, tennis shoes. I have no idea how the clothes have found their way into my hospital room; I'd rather not imagine James or my father combing through my closet. Somewhere just beneath the surface I know I want a cigarette, the same way I know I can't have one. When I blink, the room disappears beneath my eyelids, then reappears. Everything's muddled. Not just my thoughts, but my breath, the beat of my heart.

I start to drift off, but the sound of the door opening brings me back. At the sight of my father I crawl into a sitting position. He's wearing a suit, and I swallow, acutely aware of my torn jeans, my ragged ponytail. Miles of gauze around my wrists. Joel, he says, though he can't meet my eyes. How did you get in here? I ask, bringing my knees to my chest, and he smooths the front of his shirt, his tie. He looks polished and poised, and I'm suddenly conscious that I haven't showered in days and days. Loosening my ponytail, I comb my fingers through the knots in my hair. I shouldn't be kept from my own son's room, he's saying, and I can almost hear the arguments he must be having with my doctor, with the nurses on duty. He steps toward me; I try to hold back the shudder I can feel starting in my abdomen. This, he says, gesturing around the room, a gesture that I imagine includes my own pathetic self and whatever edicts I might have set forth about visitors, This…

He's not going to hurt me. I don't think he's going to hurt me, but I don't want him to touch me, and when he places his fingers on my shoulder, I scream. Hands covering my ears, I scream and scream. My lungs propel me beyond my father's expression, the slam of the door, the pinprick of the needle in my arm. I scream through it all, one continuous, glorious howl, and the sound takes me beyond even myself.

PART THREE

Jennifer Hritz

1

May 1999

I run every day.

I started early that morning, my first in Mexico. Sleeping late isn't possible; none of the windows have blinds, and the heat's unbearable, especially once the sun rises. After six weeks I'm still trying to get used to living without air conditioning. When I wake up a little after dawn, my hair's damp, my skin flushed. I look as if I've been indulging in some stellar sex, but of course, that's not the truth. I haven't been with anyone in months.

I run along the beach, just beside the water. I never meet a single person, even though I'm able now to make it almost four miles without feeling as if I'm going to pass out. The first time, I puked at the half-mile mark. Now I'm stronger, especially since I've given up the cigarettes. And the sand's good for my ankle. I don't think it ever quite recovered from that fall down Adam's stairs.

That first day, after I'd driven into Tulum to stock up on bottled water, beer, an odd assortment of food, I realized I was ready. I knew I'd work that afternoon, and my scalp prickled at the thought. A precarious claim, artist. The work on my wrists was all I'd come up with in a while.

But when I got back to the house, I stretched, then applied gesso to the canvas, opened fresh tubes of acrylic. Dipping my brush into paint the color of the sea, I touched the canvas and waited for something to restrain me. But the color anesthetized the white, and I dug more deeply, allowing myself the luxury of immersion.

That night, I sat on my front porch with a lukewarm beer. As the sun bled, I stripped, then waded into the sea until the water encircled my waist. With the crest of the next wave I held my breath and dove.

I've gotten into the habit of painting after I run, after I've showered. I stand in front of the canvas, the brush between my fingers, and work for a few hours before the heat drives me from the house and into the water. I'm dark, my skin dry, the lines in my face more pronounced than they've ever been. I keep my hair tied back.

I'm not lonely, though I talk to no one. Really, there's just not much need for conversation around here. I'm isolated, a good ten-minute drive from the nearest town, and even though I'm on a first-name basis with the guy who owns the makeshift grocery store at the edge of the highway, I'm still at a point where I can't seem to find the Spanish words I need. He's an older guy, speaks a little English, gives me the coldest beer from the back of the cooler. He pronounces my name with an h: ho-el, and the sound always makes me think of peppermint.

I haven't talked to James. I haven't talked to anyone besides my father, and it was past the middle of March before I felt in enough command of my emotions to handle even that. I called him from the hospital from Dr. Herrera's—Lydia's—office. She sat beside me in the chair across from her desk while I dialed his number, and when he answered the phone, I wanted to grip her hand in my own. I didn't, though, and once my father got over the initial shock of hearing my voice, I told him what I wanted. I'd been thinking about Mexico since the beginning of the month, knew I wouldn't be able to deal with going home so soon. He was quick to give me whatever I wanted, and I got off the phone after five minutes not knowing whether to laugh or cry. I've only spoken to him once since then, when I found the house and needed him to arrange the lease. He responded without hesitation, and though part of me wanted to believe his eagerness to accommodate telling—I'd probably so embarrassed him that he was prepared to help me flee the country—I also felt a profound appreciation for his willingness to help. Telling Lydia how I felt, I couldn't quite believe the sentiment, but there was no getting around the fact that without his assistance my fledgling idea to spend time in Mexico would never have gotten off the ground.

Though I told Lydia a great deal, I didn't tell her everything. I couldn't; there was just too much, and anyway, the second I started feeling even remotely like myself, the only thing I wanted was to get out of there. All that talking, all that emphasis on working through my issues. She wanted me to keep a journal, for god's sake. If I'm repressing, I told her, Then maybe there's a reason. She didn't buy that, coaxed me over an eight-week period into telling her more than I wanted. About my relationship with Jess. About my therapy sessions with Bryan. About my father.

I never mentioned my mother.

Instead, I talked about James. She didn't bat an eye, just nudged the box of Kleenex across the coffee table. I took one tissue, and then another. She didn't say a word, and when I finally shook my head and crumpled the tissues in my fist, she asked me to start from the beginning. What do you want to know? I said.

When Lydia finally told me that James had been trying to contact me, I laughed. Well, that makes sense, doesn't it? I said, He feels guilty. The thought gave me satisfaction. Cruel, I know, but I couldn't help thinking that maybe in some small way he got what he deserved.

Most of the time, though, I'm able not to think too much about what's happened over the past few years. I concentrate on the day-to-day, on the painting, the running, and one day bleeds into the next easily, seamlessly. Most nights, I swim before I go to bed, wade until I'm deep enough for the waves to knock me off my feet. When I come up for air, the whole sky wide above, I feel calmer than I have in years.

I steer clear of tourist traps. I'm pretty safe if I stay out of Tulum, and I try to buy food and water in bulk to avoid having to go into town too often. The couple of restaurants I frequent are small, cheap, innocuous, and I never see anyone with skin lighter than mine in either of them. Juan, the guy from the grocery store, tells me of a bar where I could meet some other Americans, but I shake my head. Not tourists, he clarifies, Not tourists. But I tell him I'm not interested. I'm more than content keeping company with myself.

Lydia was concerned when I told her of my idea to come here. I'm not sure isolation's best for you right now, she said, frowning, and I told her that with all due respect maybe it was time for me to figure that out on my own. She wanted me to continue my therapy, said I'd be better off either staying in Austin and seeing her once a week, or at the very least reestablishing myself somewhere else and seeing someone new. She'd told me once early in my treatment that if I felt more comfortable working with Bryan, he'd be happy to accommodate. So he knows what happened? I said, and she reminded me that his name was on the prescription bottle I'd left on the bathroom counter. I thought back to that moment of elation I'd experienced the last time I was in his office, when I was so certain I didn't need him anymore, and I was humiliated enough to groan. No, I said, I'd rather work with you.

You've come a long way, Lydia told me the day before I was released, But you still have a long way to go. I put my arms around her, wistfully. She hugged me back, patted my shoulder. That was the closest I'd been to anything maternal in so long that my chest hurt from trying to keep everything in. I almost broke down at that moment, might have if she hadn't pulled away at just the instant the words came to my lips. Call if you need me, she said, and I nodded instead.

I live carefully. I run, I paint, I dive, I paint, I sleep. When I dream, I paint. I break occasionally for meals, which I eat in solitude. I want nothing to disturb the rhythm I've created, nothing to get in the way of what I'm trying to do here: Get well. Paint. Get well. Paint. Paint.

I talk to none of my friends from Austin, think even less about them. I'm not ready, don't know that I ever will be. I figure I've alienated just about everyone, remember with a start one night that Peter's getting married and I'm supposed to be in the wedding. I systematically dismiss the thought. I'm sure he's asked somebody else by now. And anyway, I could never face James.

James. Peter, Kyle, Jack. Adam. If I dedicate my energy worrying about what they think of me, lamenting what happened, what could've been, I won't be able to function. Some mornings it's hard enough to get out of bed, to run, to work, without having to also assume responsibility for all the damage I've caused. They're better off without me, I'm sure.

And I have to work. I have to. I'm dead without it.

+ + +

I stick to the beach in front of the house during my morning run. I traverse the same stretch of sand day after day without variation; I'm not interested in exploration or a chance encounter. I just want to run, and then make my way back to the house. But there's a strange rise in the coastline about two miles into my route—about the point where I usually turn around—that beckons, and one day, I simply keep running. I have a good pace, and I go with it, clear another mile as the sand gives way to clumps of vegetation, then rock. I climb, breathing harder than I would've expected. The hill's kicking my ass. Five excruciating minutes later, I reach the top.

The drop's easily seventy feet, the water beneath me a smooth sheet of turquoise. I catch my breath twelve inches from the edge. Sweat drips from my chin. I'm tempted to jump. To just strip off my clothes and jump. Take the fucking risk. Instead, I peer over the cliff, hesitating. The water looks deep; I swear I see fish.

As the sun darts out from behind a sheaf of clouds, dazzling the water, I look up at the sky, a thin robin's egg blue, the color of the sea improbable in contrast. Taking a rock in my fingers, I bring my arm back and hurl it over the side. I can't hear the splash as it enters the water, and I stand for a minute, then inch from the edge and head back the way I came.

That night, when I drive into town to get something for dinner, I stop to talk to Juan and buy a six-pack of beer. He smiles when I tell him what I found this afternoon. *Mucha gente salta*, he tells me, and I say, Really? He nods, ringing up my beer, and I hand over my money. *No todos viven*, he confides in a lower voice. He slides the cash in the register, tells me that more than a few suicides have jumped from that cliff, more than a few kids on a dare. I wonder if he chose the words because he noticed my scars; I have the urge, suddenly, to cross my arms. How deep? I ask, and he laughs, says that depends on the tide. Looks safe enough, I mutter, not wanting to sound like an amateur. He grins. Tells me things aren't always what they seem.

+ + +

By the end of May I'm starting to run low on cash. I'm not guilty of reckless spending; in fact, I've spent considerably less than I anticipated. I have little to blow money on here other than food and beer. But my father stipulated that we'd give this thing a go for a couple of months and then reassess the situation. I'm not really concerned about a deadline; he's not going to make me come home, not under the circumstances. I think he's still too taken aback by what happened to press. But the mere fact that I have to initiate contact unsettles me, and I put off making the call until I'm looking at a weekend without beer.

Joel! he says in a hearty tone that stuns me, How are you? I stutter a response; I'd been convinced he wouldn't want to hear from me, and instead, he sounds relieved. I've been wondering about you, he continues, How you're doing, how you're making out down there. Actually, I admit, I need money.

He's silent. I wince. Of course, he finally says, Why else would you be calling?

I take a mental step back. Count to five, a strategy Lydia suggested I employ for moments such as this. Breathe, she said, Try not to react so impulsively. I'm sorry, I say, That was crass. You could at least tell me how you're doing, he grumbles. I'm fine, I say, I'm doing well. He's quiet, and I add softly: I'm feeling so much better, Dad.

The admittance is a huge concession. I'm used to telling him nothing of value about my life, and though I'm talking to him in part because I rely on him financially, I realize as I'm waiting for him to respond that I need him to know something of what I've been through and validate that somehow. Not that he could ever understand. But I'm hoping for a kind word: he's relieved to know I'm improving, he'll do anything he can to help, financially or otherwise.

Instead, he tells me I might want to pass along the information to some of my friends. I'd told him back in March that I didn't want him speaking to anyone, didn't want him telling James or anyone else where I was, what I was doing. I can't stand the idea of them talking about me behind my back, picking me over, though whether I like it or not, I've probably been the subject of more than one conversation. I'm not interested in talking to anyone, I remind him. I understand, my father says, But you should at least contact Adam.

A quick shock of excitement courses through me at the mention of Adam's name. I've avoided any thought of him the past four months, and now without warning everything comes back: every word, every glance, every kiss more vivid than the moment we first exchanged them. You of all people, Joel, my father's saying, and I pull myself back to the present. The thought occurs to me that my father shouldn't know the first thing about my relationship with Adam or even that he exists. I suddenly have a very bad feeling I've misinterpreted something tremendous.

How do you know Adam? I ask, and my father pauses as if he thinks I might be fucking with him. What do you mean? he says, I met him the night he found you.

Everything stops. The lavender spread of the night sky, the murmur of the ocean, my heart. In the sudden absence of sound and motion I see him—Adam—sitting across from me that first moment I awoke in the hospital, and I watch in horror as his face blurs into James's. I thought

James found me, I say, lowering myself to the top step of the porch. What made you think that? my father asks.

I don't know what to say. That I assumed when I saw James sitting beside me in the hospital that he must've been the one? That I felt a faint glimmer of gratification when I imagined what he must have felt walking into that bathroom? Not that the reason for carving up my wrists had been to punish James. But he'd hurt me so deeply that I couldn't have come up with a better way to retaliate if I'd tried.

Adam. My god, he must hate me. As far as he's concerned, I've known all along that he was the one and I've never tried to contact him. I listen with dismay as my father tells me that he'd received the phone call from Adam himself in the early morning hours of New Year's Eve, that James hadn't even arrived at the hospital until later that day. He was with his fiancée, my father says, They were out of town. And I realize that James's plans had never changed at all, that he was with Elizabeth, exactly as he'd told me he'd be. My father himself had contacted him.

I don't stay on the phone long after that. My father knows little else, can only tell me that at first Adam was belligerent about getting information, but that the frequency of his calls has tapered because my father has refused to tell him anything. At your request, he reminds me. He has no idea where I am? I ask. No, he says, None.

I sit on the porch for more than an hour after I hang up, the initial reason for the call to my father long forgotten. By the time I drag myself back into the house it's almost ten, later than I'm usually awake these days. I crawl into bed still holding the phone, then curl on my side facing the open window. I'm sure I won't be able to sleep. And when I finally do drift off sometime after midnight, I dream I'm underwater without gear. I'm okay for the moment, but I know I won't make it much longer without surfacing. I'm just starting to lose my shit when I see someone in front of me. The figure turns, arms outspread, at once becomes everyone I know. I watch as my father, my mother, James, Adam, morph one into the other, and I extend my hand. I wake before I find out if I've been saved.

+ + +

When I hear Adam's voice, I lose my own.

I've prepared ahead of time what I want to say, how I can approach him after all these months, but when he answers the phone, the words I've practiced over and over the past few days suddenly fail me. Hello? he says again. Taking a deep breath, I come up with a few garbled syllables that sound remarkably like nothing, and after the briefest
pause, amazingly, he says, Joel? Yeah, I whisper. Oh, Joel, he says, Joel, Joel. He speaks my name with such ardor, such gratitude, that my lashes instantly thicken with tears. How are you? he asks, and I start to laugh even as the tears creep from the corners of my eyes. I brush them aside with the back of my hand, sitting there on the bottom step of my rickety front porch. Okay, I tell him when I think I can speak, I'm okay.

He makes no attempt to disguise his own emotion. I'm so glad you called, he keeps saying, I'm just so glad you called. He finally releases his breath, apologizing; I tell him I'm the one who should be saying I'm sorry. I owe you an explanation, I say, and when he tries to assure me he doesn't need one, that he's just thankful I'm all right, I cut him off. Please, I say, I need to tell you why I haven't tried to get in touch with you.

He listens without interjection, and at first I'm afraid he doesn't believe me. I wouldn't necessarily blame him; the story sounds implausible in the telling. At some point, I imagine he's thinking, I must have talked about this with my doctor. But he doesn't say a word, and I finally end up telling him about James. Not that we'd been involved, but that we'd been having problems, that we had a falling out a couple of weeks before Christmas, that when I was told repeatedly that my friend had found me, I just assumed Lydia was talking about James. No one even mentioned your name, I say, And after our last conversation I thought I'd never see you again.

He doesn't say anything, and I lapse into silence, burrowing my toes in the sand. I'm convinced he thinks I'm lying, and I'm trying to figure out what else I can say to persuade him I'm telling the truth when he asks in a strained voice if I'll ever be able to forgive him. For what? I ask, astonished, and he says, For what I said to you that day. I almost laugh; only Adam would overlook everything I've done to him, everything I've said, and fixate on the one wound he inflicted himself. Adam, I say, There's nothing to forgive. He doesn't seem so sure, tells me that the reason he came to my house at all was because he felt uncomfortable with what he'd said to me. You just appeared at my front door out of nowhere, he says, And I wanted you to feel as devastated as I felt the morning you left. He tells me he regretted what he said as soon as he shut the door behind him, that he thought about calling me. I even picked up the phone, he says, But my sister was there, and her husband and the kids…

He trails off. Why did you come inside? I ask, When I didn't answer the door? He laughs, the sound short and bitter. I saw your cat, he tells me. Pandora? I say, surprised. Whatever, he says, I saw your stupid cat, and I opened the door to let him in. Her, I correct him. I opened the door, he says, ignoring me, And I saw the wall.

I close my eyes. I can't bear to think of what I've done either; I'd made arrangements a week before I even left the hospital to have the wall painted a nice, antiseptic white, knowing I wouldn't be able to walk through the front door otherwise. I'd still been apprehensive turning the key in the lock when I went back to the house, briefly, to pack up a few things before I left for Mexico, but when I opened the door, I found the wall as barren as the first time I saw it at the end of my freshman year. Even so. I hadn't been able to stand there for long.

I knew, he says, Before I got to the bathroom I knew.

He sounds matter-of-fact, detached, and I think for a moment, sitting there on the front porch in the hot wind, that I'm going to be sick. There was so much blood, he tells me, and I lean over my knees, spitting thick ropes of saliva into the sand. Joel? he says. But I'm too busy trying to erase the image he's just conjured, reconcile that with another. My knees hitting the cold tile, James's arms around me. Okay, he whispered, Okay. I wipe my mouth with a closed fist. Joel, Adam says again, and I clear my throat. I'm here, I say.

So, he says, making an effort to change the subject, Where are you anyway? Mexico, I tell him, A hundred miles south of Cancun. Are you in some kind of treatment center? he asks. No, I say, finding the idea both amusing and insulting. I tell him I flew to Mexico the day after I got out of the hospital, that I needed to be someplace where I could concentrate on work without having to think about anything else. There's not much to do here other than paint, I tell him. And are you painting? he asks. Yeah, I admit, I am.

We talk for another ten minutes. I tell him about the house, about not having air conditioning, and I ask about him. Work, you mean? he says, and I realize I don't want to know the impact my suicide attempt has had on his social life. Sure, I say. I'm inundated, he tells me, Everyone's freaking out about Y2K. I guess I'm a little out of the loop, I confess, I have pretty limited access to the outside world. I wish I could say the same, he assures me, but I have my doubts. Personally, I think he thrives on this shit.

Well, he finally says. Yeah, I say, I'll let you go. Can I call you? he asks, and I smile, the movement strange after all this time. I know I don't deserve his forgiveness. Yet he's offering it anyway, wants to talk to me again. Yeah, I say, You can.

+ + +

But he doesn't call. Not that day, or the next, or the next. Shaking off the doubt, I concentrate on my work, but by the end of the week I have to acknowledge the possibility that I might not hear from him again. I run toward the cliff, wiping perspiration and grit from my face as I make the climb. When I reach the top, I squat, the backs of my calves sticky with sweat. Clouds skirt the morning sun, cast shadows across the water. Rocking forward, I hang on to the edge with one hand as I try to better estimate the drop. How many seconds before I'd hit the water? And no promise whatsoever that I'd surface.

When my calves start to cramp, I straighten. There's a strange feel here that I didn't notice last time; I can almost hear their voices. I look around me at the expanse of ocean, at the sky above. This is an awfully lonely place to die.

He calls that night when I'm already in bed, when I've pretty much reconciled myself to the fact that he asked for my number out of some warped sense of responsibility, or maybe pity. Am I calling too soon? he asks right away. Actually, I confess, closing my eyes and shaking my head at my candor, I've been wondering why you haven't called. And here I've been trying to give you space, he tells me. I groan. *You* could've called *me*, he points out. I wasn't sure you wanted to talk to me, I admit.

He's quiet for a moment, as if he's been wrestling with that very thought. No, he says, I want to talk to you.

We're on the phone for over three hours. We don't discuss anything serious; maybe that will come later. Instead, I tell him about the diving I've been doing the past few months. He talks about cycling, and I mention that I've gotten back into running, that I go every day, that I haven't taken a day off in months. That's the way my job's been lately, he says. We laugh and find ourselves approaching midnight before we've managed to say half of what we want. I should probably get to bed, he tells me, his voice a good octave lower than when our conversation first started. Okay, I say, but neither one of us makes a move to get off the phone.

When we finally hang up, I can't get to sleep. I end up going for a run in the moonlight, slow to a walk and surrender to the rush of blood in my legs. I'm full of the sound of his voice, and I close my eyes, the wind tugging at my hair.

I feel closer to something good than I've felt in years.

+ + +

For the next few weeks I barely touch the ground. We talk almost every day. He's the only person I'd ever allow to interrupt my work, and I end up sitting against the wall in the front room, my fingers leaving smudges of paint on the phone. Mostly, though, we talk late at night after I'm already in bed. Calling him becomes my nighttime ritual: I shower, I crawl under the sheet, I dial his number. We talk for an hour, maybe more, and when he tells me he has to go, I try to coax him into another ten minutes.

Our conversations aren't superficial, but they're also not as substantive as you might expect. We talk about nothing unpleasant, and I'm quick to change the subject when I think we're headed in that direction. I've heard enough of his shit for a while, I figure, and god knows he's heard enough of mine. So instead, we talk about the Austin music scene, and books we've read, and debate the best place to get a classic margarita on the rocks. Sometimes, I sense a bit of impatience on his part, as if he's looking for me to say more. But I hold my ground. I'm not interested in rehashing the past.

I'm still working, though even I have to admit that my attention span's not what it was when I first arrived here. I know he might call at any moment, and more often than not, I find myself standing at the easel, the end of the paintbrush against my lips, daydreaming. I work best in the early morning, fresh from a hard run and at least a little bit of sleep. It's the middle of the day that leaves me restless. What've you been doing all afternoon? Adam asks, calling me on his way home from work. Failing to concentrate, I say.

+ + +

Mid–June, Adam tells me he's heading to Kentucky to visit his family, and though he's vague about the motivation for his trip, I know why he's going. Father's Day is the twentieth. I don't think I've acknowledged the day in years, probably since my mother died. So this is what you get for impregnating women, I thought one year when I was maybe seventeen, watching as my father grudgingly opened a dress shirt and tie.

Thinking back, I try to remember what we did that last Father's Day we were all together before I started college. My father had suggested going out for dinner, but my mother convinced him we'd have far more fun staying at home, hanging out by the pool. We'll have a barbeque, she said delightedly. My father was skeptical, and in fact, the idea turned out to be disastrous. I distinctly recall him standing over the grill, red-faced, sweating, pissed. I gave him a tie that year, I think. I gave him a tie every year.

I wonder how he feels about the fact that I never see him on Father's Day, never send a gift, never call. The more I speculate, the guiltier I feel. Honestly, our last conversation was better than I expected. Once he realized that I'd misunderstood who found me, he was patient, even kind. And I can't overlook that he's held to his end of the bargain, has not only provided me with the financial resources I need to stay down here, but has also kept my friends at bay. I can just imagine Adam's persistence those first couple of months; the phone calls must not have been easy for my father to handle. He deserves the benefit of the doubt.

Still I procrastinate and end up making the call late in the day when for all practical purposes Father's Day has ended. I'm mildly worried Catherine will pick up; I haven't spoken to her since she was in Austin last year, though she sent me a letter when I was in the hospital, a letter I wasn't sure I wanted to receive and regretted reading after the fact. Her words couldn't have been any more sympathetic, and I couldn't have been at any more of a loss. What was I supposed to do? Write her back? Tell her that I appreciated her concern, but I was more than fine? She had plenty of evidence to the contrary. So I did nothing, and now I take a deep breath. Happy Father's Day, I say when I hear my father's voice.

I've startled him, and I start picking at the paint along the doorjamb. I bet he thinks I'm calling to hit him up for cash, and when he asks how my money's holding out, I almost groan. I have plenty of money, I inform him, That's not why I'm calling. He makes a sound I can't quite interpret, and I feel myself flushing. I've called him with the best of intentions, and it doesn't seem that he can get past his own assumptions. Closing my eyes, I try to count, the way Lydia suggested. But before I can get anywhere my father speaks. If you need some extra cash— he says. I don't need extra cash! I say, I was calling to wish you a happy fucking Father's Day! Don't forget that I'm paying for you to stay down there, he says in the tight-ass tone I've grown accustomed to over the years. Jesus, how could I forget? I scream, How could I ever fucking forget?

Two minutes in and I'm shouting obscenities. I hang up and lower myself to the top step, where I try to calm my breathing. He could've at least entertained the possibility that I might be sincere. Even if I had been calling for money, he has no right to make me feel guilty. He set the stage for our relationship years ago.

By the time Adam calls that night the last thing I want to hear about is his storybook fucking family. Did I call at a bad time? he asks when I answer the phone. Oh, no, I say, my snarl evident, You're just fine. Are you sure? he says. How was your trip? I ask, ignoring his question. Good, he says, Pretty great, actually. He tells me he was able to spend time with his sister, her kids, his nephew has just started riding, it was all so fucking great. I don't say a word. Are you still there? he finally asks. What'd you get him? I say. What? he asks. I wrap my finger around a thread unfurling from the hem of my tee shirt and yank it out. Your father, I say, What'd you get him for Father's Day?

Adam's quiet. Don't give me some bullshit story about not having seen your family in a while, I say, Tell me what you got him. A saddle, he says, He's training a new horse, and he wanted a saddle. Hmm, I muse, Did he like it? What's going on here? Adam asks, Are you upset with me or something? Hey, I just want to hear about your weekend, I tell him, You're the one who said you had such a fantastic time.

He doesn't say anything. I start to pace. So, did you have some kind of celebration? I ask. I'm not going to do this, Joel, he tells me. I bet you had a party, I say, my voice tight and accusatory, I bet you had a fucking cake. You know what, Joel? he says, I'm sorry I called.

I go for a run, lace up my shoes and hit the sand, make a four mile loop in the dark. Coming back to the house, I strip off my tee shirt and wipe the sweat from my face as I'm reaching for the phone. I think that was textbook displacement, I tell him when he answers, and he actually laughs. I pull a bottle of water from the fridge. I had a shitty conversation with my father tonight, I confess. That's too bad, he tells me. Yeah, well, I say, I shouldn't have taken it out on you, and I'm sorry for that. That's okay, he says, sounding surprised by my apology, Forget about it.

There's a part of me, over the next few days, that feels compelled to call my father to apologize. But I can't quite forget how quick he was to assume the worst, to put me in my place. I don't want to hear further insinuations about my intentions. I'll have to talk to him soon enough anyway. The money he deposited in my account at the end of May won't last forever. I should breathe while I have the chance.

+ + +

Though Adam and I talk every day, I've never told him about James. Why would I? The most he knows, the most I've ever told him, is that I had a roommate, and he moved out. I'm trying to keep my phone calls to Adam light, trying to avoid the weightiness that characterized the last weekend we were together, and if that means we spend more time discussing the weather than what keeps us awake at night, that's fine with me. That we're talking at all seems to me more relevant.

I've been trying my best not to think about James anyway. I'm still struggling with the notion that I was slashing my wrists at the same moment he was road tripping with Elizabeth, ringing in the new year. Though I'm loath to admit my dependence on someone who obviously hasn't been there for me for more than two years, I can't help feeling as if I've been cast aside.

One night, I'm in bed, propped on my elbow, my head cradled in my palm. Adam and I have been on the phone for more than an hour, and he's told me several times that he has to go, he has to get some sleep, he has way too many meetings tomorrow to stay up so late. C'mon, I say, Haven't you ever pulled an all-nighter? Not since college, he says, and I'm about to say the same until I remember that less than a year ago, I was consuming so much coke that I was capable of pulling all-nighters back-to-back. Adam doesn't notice the way I've paused. What were you like in college? he asks. Closeted, I say, and he laughs. All four years? he asks. The first three and a half, I admit. Who'd you tell first? he asks, and I swear I feel such a sharp sense of alarm I hear ringing in my ears. My roommate, I mumble, and then for some unfathomable reason, I say, I slept with him. He told me, Adam says.

I count to five. What? I say. He told me, Adam says, A while back. I try counting again and can't make it past two. *What?* I say. I don't mean to upset you— Adam starts. Wait a minute, I interrupt, You know *James*? Joel, he says, Of course. They met when I was in the hospital, Adam tells me, and they've gotten to know each other better over the past six months. You're *friends*? I ask incredulously. Well, yeah, Adam says, I guess we are. I don't believe this, I tell him, and he says, You honestly thought we didn't know each other? Does he know you've been talking to me? I ask. Joel, Adam says, Of course he knows. What have you told him? I ask. Just that you're in Mexico, he says, Just that you're okay. You had no right, I tell him. He's been worried about you, Adam protests. You had no right! I cry, You have no idea what happened between us!

There's a silence heavy with contradiction.

Oh shit, I moan, What did he tell you? Not much, Adam says, Just that you were involved, that you couldn't make it work. I groan. Why would he tell you that? I say, How did that even come up in conversation? You have to understand the context of the situation, he says. There's no fucking context that makes that conversation okay, I tell him, and he says, You're wrong.

The morning after I kicked James out of my hospital room—the morning after Adam and James met for the first time—the two of them agreed to meet at my house to get some of my things to take to the hospital. When Adam arrived, James was sitting cross-legged on the coffee table in the living room, drunk, staring at the wall I'd covered with black paint. He had a bottle of scotch beside him, and despite the early hour, Adam joined him for a drink. Over the course of that drink James confessed that we'd slept together and hadn't been able to cope. He was beside himself, Adam says, And consumed with guilt because he'd convinced himself that what you'd done was directly related to what had happened between the two of you. They talked for a long time, until James finally admitted that he couldn't handle going through my shit. So Adam took care of that himself, the same way he'd taken care of arranging for a cleaning service.

I'm amazed by how much James has managed to leave out, how selective he was about the details. Adam has no idea how my relationship with James came about, that the final blow was James's repudiation of our relationship when it came to Elizabeth. All he revealed is that we slept together and couldn't make it work. Really, it's almost laughable.

What bothers me even more than the fact that Adam knows is his wholesale acceptance of what James has told him, his failure to ask for my side of the story. I can't believe he's so willing to take James's word without any regard for our own history. But before I have the chance to demand the opportunity for rebuttal he says, Look, I have to be honest about something. He pauses, and I get the impression that whatever's about to come out of his mouth he's wanted to say for weeks. For months you thought James was the one to find you, he says, And you never called him. He hesitates. Don't you find that... indefensible? he asks. Indefensible? I repeat in disbelief. All right, Adam concedes, Maybe that's a little strong. You think? I say. You should call him, he suggests, Just to let him know you're okay. You've already told him, I remind him. I still think he'd like to hear it from you, he says, and then, realizing just how pissed I am, he says, Look, I'm not trying to tell you what to do. Are you sure? I ask, You're doing such an excellent fucking job.

We don't speak for almost a week. I go through the motions, I run, I paint, but at night I have plenty of time to wrestle with what he's said because he doesn't call. Lying in bed, my eyes wide to the night, I catalog James's every indiscretion. By the time I'm finished I'm rigid with anger and utterly incapable of rest. And so the week passes, until my body can bear up no longer.

I watch the storm come Monday morning at first light. I've not slept, and I stand for a while on the porch, then shut the door as the rain intensifies. I end up back in bed not because I have any grandiose expectations of sleep but from an almost primitive desire to protect myself. Nestling in the corner where the bed meets the wall, I sink lower and lower until I'm curled beneath the sheet. Black clouds kill the last of the dawn.

I awaken drenched in sweat nine hours later and step outside into afternoon sun. With the sand packed beneath my feet I make good time. Standing at the edge of the cliff, the sea unfolding before me, I take stock. The problem is that for every betrayal I've recorded I remember a dozen selfless acts.

I call Adam that night, armed with nothing but an explanation. Please, I say when he answers, Give me the benefit of the doubt.

I tell him everything that happened between James and me, from the beginning. Yes, James and I slept together; true, that we hadn't been able to cope. But James was the one who sat next to me on the front porch and practically offered himself up. Then, when I finally told him how I felt, he let it continue. And the clincher, I tell Adam, was hearing James assure me that Elizabeth knew about us, only to find out he'd lied. The situation was considerably more complicated than James led you to believe, I say. Why didn't you tell me any of this the other day? Adam asks. Because you didn't seem all that interested in my side of the story, I say. Leaning back against the kitchen counter, I stare out the open window over rough dunes, rocks bleached white by the moon. Because it's incredibly fucking painful to talk about, I add.

The headache that's been plaguing me all week, the one that disappeared long enough for me to sleep this morning, has returned with a vengeance, and I make my way down the hallway in the dark. I'm suddenly so tired. Look, I say, ready to end this conversation, My relationship with James… that's my business. I understand, Adam says. I'm serious, I tell him, I'll talk to him if and when I'm ready.

Crawling into bed, I pull my tee shirt over my head, lifting the phone away from my ear. Anyway— I start. Don't hang up, he says, anticipating my next move. I unbutton my shorts, then kick them onto the floor. Even at this time of night the air feels thick and warm, and I lift my hair off the back of my neck, then reach for the rubber band I've left on the bedside table. I don't see how you manage down there without air conditioning, he says when I tell him what I'm doing. I don't wear much, I admit. Really, he says, sounding interested, What are you wearing now? Nothing, I say, and he groans. Nothing? he says. Not a thing, I tell him, What're you wearing? Pajama bottoms, he says, Pajama bottoms and a ratty tee shirt. Sounds hot, I tell him. Are you in bed? he asks. Yeah, I say. You want to come? he asks in a near-whisper. I answer in a hush, ask what he has in mind. Why don't you let me tell you, he says.

Afterward, I can't bear to hang up. I miss you, I murmur, so close to sleep that I have little trouble saying the words. God, Joel, he says, I miss you, too.

+ + +

The following night, Adam tells me he has some time off next weekend. The words come that plainly, that simply. I have a few days off next weekend, he says, Because of the Fourth. I miss the point. You doing anything interesting? I ask. I don't have plans yet, he says. I ramble on for a minute or so about the Fourth of July and fireworks and that there's not much celebrating going on where I'm living right now before I change the subject. So what're you wearing? I ask. Later, I realize I should've paid attention to the moment of silence I heard before he answered me.

A couple of weeks after that conversation, I catch him as he's walking in the door from work. You're not going to believe what I did this morning, he tells me. You won a game of darts, I say. He laughs and says I'm not even close. I signed a contract to put in a pool, he tells me. No shit, I say, and he says they're breaking ground next week. I'm getting a diving board, he confides, And maybe a slide. Well, if your neighbors don't already know you're queer, I say, They will now. He chortles and tells me that's exactly what Gary said. Who's Gary? I ask.

He pauses, like he's realizing that he just fucked up. This guy I'm seeing, he finally admits. You're seeing someone? I moan. Yeah, he says. For how long? I ask. Three months? he replies, as if he's not really sure himself, We're... you know.

I don't know. I don't have any idea. I can't believe he's seeing someone. All this time we've been talking, and he's been with someone else.

I manufacture a reason for getting off the phone. Aw, c'mon, Joel, he says, You don't have to go. I really can't talk right now, I tell him. And I can't. I'm not even sure how to breathe. I just don't understand. How could I have misread the past couple of months, the last fifty phone calls?

And the sex. The words he's whispered, the nights we've shared... I'm pissed. I thought we had something here, and all along he's been fucking someone else.

I have one question, I tell him when I call him back. Okay, he says slowly. Why have you been talking to me for the past three months if you're seeing someone? I ask. Can you hang on a second? he says. He covers the receiver with his hand, and I hear him talking to someone in the background, the sound muffled. *Shit*, I think, *Gary's with him now!* Are you there? Adam asks a moment later, and when I grunt a yes, he says, I've been talking to you, Joel, because I like you. You like me, I repeat, and he says, What's wrong with that?

I don't say anything. Seriously, he says, I'd like to know. You never even mentioned him! I cry, and he tells me he didn't realize he needed to. I'm sorry if you think I misled you, he says, But what did you think was going on here? We've been talking every day! I tell him, We've been... I hear him take a deep breath. Look, I don't want to negate what's happened between us, he tells me, But I'm far more interested in the real thing. You've never suggested getting together, I protest. Will you listen to yourself? he says, You left the country, for god's sake. So? I say, and he says, So I figured you'd let me know if and when you were ready for me to visit. All I had to do was tell you I wanted to see you? I ask. That would've been a good start, he informs me.

I don't bother counting to five. I want to see you! I blurt out, Come down! When? he asks, and I say, Whenever! Okay, he says. Okay? I say, and he tells me he can be there Thursday afternoon. What about Gary? I ask. What about him? he says. Won't he be upset? I ask. Probably, Adam admits, But he's a big boy. I slip the tip of my thumb in my mouth and start gnawing on the nail. I have company now, he tells me firmly, But I'll call you tomorrow. Tell Gary I said hi, I say, and he laughs.

+ + +

I take one look around the front room of the house I'm renting and panic. For the past few months I've been working solely for myself. I might, after the fact, examine a certain canvas and try to imagine contacting Cameron, but for the most part I've been concentrating on the process. I'm interested in the healing properties of my work, and I can sense the ways in which the spirit of what I've been doing has infused this house. I feel suddenly protective of my space. I want to see Adam, god knows I want to see Adam. But I'm not at all certain I'm ready for him to come *here*.

Are you alone? I ask the following night. I wouldn't have answered the phone otherwise, he tells me, and I feel a furious rush of jealousy. How'd Gary react when you told him you were coming here? I ask. Well, he wasn't thrilled, he says. I get the impression I shouldn't have asked, and I move quickly so he doesn't have time to get pissed. Look, I've been thinking that maybe it's not such a good idea, you coming here, I say, The house... the house is small, my shit's everywhere, I don't have air conditioning... You don't have air conditioning, he repeats. Right, I say, But I've checked out a couple of places up the coast, and I don't know, I thought you could tell me which one sounded good to you. What are you saying? Adam asks. I thought we could meet someplace less... someplace more... neutral, I tell him. Are we at war? he asks. No! I say, I just... I don't think... Relax, he says, I thought you were trying to tell me not to come at all. I wouldn't do that! I say, though I'm struck by the fact that yeah, that's exactly the sort of thing I'd do. He's nice enough not to belabor the point.

So tell me about Gary, I can't help asking before we hang up. Why? he says. Where'd you meet him? I ask. He's my accountant, Adam tells me. Your *accountant*? I say, laughing. What's so funny about that? he asks, though he sounds as if he's smiling. You've been seeing him for three months? I ask, and Adam says, Closer to four at this point. *Four months*, I think, *shit*. So, do you like him? I ask, posing a ludicrous question given the amount of time they've been together. This is getting tedious, Adam tells me. Hey, I say, I'm just trying to get a feel for the other guy you're sleeping with. What else do you want to know? he asks. I don't know, I say, What does he look like? He's about my height, Adam says, He has brown hair and brown eyes. I mull that over, unhappy with what I'm conjuring. Is that enough information? Adam asks, Or do you need his dick size, too?

That shuts me up, and he sighs. Look, I like him, Joel, he says, He's a nice guy, the sex is good. He lowers his voice. The thing is, he says, I'm coming to see you.

+ + +

The morning Adam arrives, I run as the sun spills over the horizon. This time, I barely make it to the top of the hill without collapsing; I've been unable to sleep the past few nights, nervous as I am about this visit.

When I finally stop and bend down to stretch my hamstrings, sweat drips from the tip of my nose. I straighten, swaying slightly from exhaustion, then sink into a sitting position, my legs hanging over the side of the cliff. There's a kick to the wind today, and small whitecaps peak across the green. Sunlight rains across the water, across my face.

I should jump. I close my eyes, picturing the moment my feet leave the earth, the sky blue blue blue overhead. The feel in the pit of my stomach terrifying, and wonderful, and I know that even with my mouth open I won't be able to scream.

I wonder how deep, how cold. I wonder whether sunlight penetrates the ocean floor. I wonder if I'd make it back up.

Planting my palms beside me, I get to my feet. But as I straighten, I slip, my right foot shooting out from under me. My arms spin, suddenly frantic for control: loose sand, pebbles, flying. I almost pitch right over the side, then catch myself at the last second and take a giant step back. Jesus, I think. I'm not ready for this.

+ + +

I'm back in the land of the living, no longer marooned on an island of my own making, and I check in to our resort already feeling a little overstimulated. I'm just thankful for Adam's forethought, for his suggestion that we book a resort that doesn't allow children, that doesn't cater to a crowd intent on partying. Our resort's small, private, and quiet, though I'm so used to solitude that I find myself reeling as I'm shown the grounds, the multiple pools, the stretch of beach blooming with umbrellas. In our room I splash my face with cold water, shake my hair loose from its rubber band. My skin below the waistband of my shorts looks fish belly white.

A knock at the door and I'm staring at Adam. Freshly cut hair, a tan I didn't expect. A smile I'd marry if I could. Hi, he says, and I pull him inside and kick the door closed.

We fall into the moment as if it's our last. Our mouths, our legs entangled, and we stumble backward into the room, my head banging against the door. He murmurs an apology against my lips; I don't take the time to respond. It's just been so long, and he's right, even the best of the phone calls over the last month can't compare with the feel of his hands, his tongue. He kisses my throat, licks my neck; I peel back his shorts. When I slide my hands down his hips, he moans, the sound the most perfect I've ever heard. Our foreheads press together, his fingers covering mine.

Then he blanches.

My scars, almost seven months after the fact, don't look much better than they did at the outset. I imagine that whoever was working the emergency room must have been more concerned with saving my life than with anything cosmetic, and as a result, I have crooked fucking lines traveling from my wrists to the hollows of my arms. Sometimes, catching a glimpse of them, I'm surprised and a little disappointed by my lack of precision, an analysis which in turn makes me feel that much more fucked up for caring. I don't hide them; living alone as I have the past few months, there's been no reason, and aside from that one uncomfortable moment in Juan's store, there's been little reason to feel ashamed. Gazing down at the damage, though, I'm suddenly aware of how they must appear to someone who has never seen them.

Hey, I whisper, and Adam's grip on my wrists tightens. Do you have any idea what you put me through? he asks. Probably more than you can imagine, I tell him, and he sinks suddenly to the bed. I'm not sure which emotion I'm less equipped to manage: his anger or his grief. Maybe I should go, I mumble, and he looks up at me, incredulous. Is this just what you do? he asks, Bail the second things get complicated? Well, you're obviously pissed— I start, and he says, Excuse me for having a human fucking reaction, Joel!

I've never heard him curse before, and the word sounds terrible coming from his mouth. The last time I saw you…, he says, shaking his head, You have no idea what it was like for me, Joel, and you've never bothered to ask. He looks down at his hands. You don't have it in you to ask me now, he says.

He's right. I don't have the courage to ask such a question, or the strength to hear the answer. But I have a feeling that if I stand before him in silence, the next few minutes will find him packing his bags. The words break from my throat, hoarse and painful. Tell me, I say.

Though I'm standing when he starts talking, I'm sitting on the floor by the time he's finished. He's on the edge of the bed, hunched over, his hands between his knees. Only part of what he says can I process; his own memory seems fragmented as well. I'm left with singular images that simultaneously conjure an aching sympathy and, unexpectedly, fury. She's done this to me, and listening to Adam, I can't believe I've risked imposing the same sentence on anyone else.

I see him, stripping towels from the bar in my bathroom and wrapping them around my arms. Dialing 911 from his cell and panicking when he can't remember my address. Holding himself together at the hospital, then breaking down the second he sees his sister. Passing on the information to my father, knowing our history and my mother's. Believing that I'd change my mind about having visitors, then going months without hearing a thing. All I could think…, he says. He presses his fingertips together like he's trying to catch hold of the right words. I felt very out of control, he tells me, adding that over the next couple of months he quit cycling, slept around more than he should have. Then everything started to normalize, he says. Why? I ask, and he gives me the wryest of smiles. I met Gary, he says.

This time, we move more slowly, with greater deliberation. We're both a little drunk; we've gotten into the mini bar, and I've whipped up cocktails strong enough to bite the tongue. We sip from heavy glasses as sunlight shadows the floor, the sheets, our bare skin. I'm cold, unaccustomed to the air conditioning, and I shiver when Adam's mouth presses against my shoulder, the hollow of my left arm. I'm just intoxicated enough to let him kiss the ragged lines of my scars. My hair falls dark across the pillow, across my face, and I watch as he takes another drink, trailing the tip of his finger from my navel, down, down. I close my eyes. Open myself up to the warmth of his body.

+ + +

We live a blissful few days, save for one mistake I make on our first morning. My eyes had opened at dawn, aware of the sunrise despite the darkened room and the way I'd buried myself under a pile of covers to escape the air conditioner, which Adam balked at setting above seventy-eight degrees. I'd stolen from the bed and snaked my running shoes from my zippered bag, which I hadn't gotten around yet to unpacking. Dressing in silence, I slipped from the room before I could wake him. On freshly raked sand I ran, then discovered when I made it back to our room that he hadn't been happy to find me gone. If I'd left for good, I would've taken my suitcase, I pointed out, and he folded his arms across his chest. I hastened to reassure him. No problem, I said, I'll wake you from now on.

We're on the beach early, where the sun warms my chilled skin. Adam's tan, too, with patches of white skin I find fascinating. The cycling, he reminds me, stroking sunscreen on his calves, and I gaze at him until he finally asks if I just want to go on back to the room. Yes, I say, Please.

By Saturday afternoon I've lost count of the number of times we've made love. We lie in bed, fingers entwined, and I study him, the thick comb of his lashes, the curve of his mouth. I want to give him more. Do you want to see where I'm staying? I ask. Oh yes, he says.

We drive south without speaking, then turn off the highway and head in the direction of the water. The house rises out of the sand in all its pink glory. When I saw it for the first time, I was stunned by the color, a fuchsia so bright my eyes ached even beneath my sunglasses. I'd stood there, mouth agape, knowing that the wide open windows meant I'd been naïve enough to lease a house without air conditioning. Now Adam follows me through the sand and up the front steps. I move aside once I've pulled open the screen door. He steps gingerly, as if he's entering someplace sacred.

Do you want anything? I ask, Water or a beer? But he shakes his head, drawn toward the canvas I left just two days ago. I've been a little obsessed with Starburst colors, those bright candy squares of yellow and orange and green. For this canvas I've chosen strawberry, rich and intoxicating on the left side of the canvas, but bleeding to pale as the color scrolls to the right. I'm still working, I admit, and he gives me a quick smile. The bedroom's back here, I say, leading the way.

There's little in here that's mine, but somehow, the room—the house itself—feels more intimate than I could have imagined. No television, Adam says as I open the windows, No stereo, no computer. I sit on the bed, tilting my head in the direction of that coastal breeze. No air conditioning, he adds. Well, I say, reaching for his hand and pulling him down beside me, It's all about the painting.

The sex is different from any I've known. There's no music, no television, no white noise from the air conditioner. Everything's so sharp, so clear. If I didn't know any better, I'd liken the experience to sex on drugs, but really, there's little similarity. We move without illusion. My name, muffled against the ridge of my shoulder; the taste of his skin at the base of his spine; the commingling odor of sun and pool and sweat and the one condom he brought. My senses are far more present than they've ever been, and the orgasm they produce shakes me in a place I believed unreachable. I offer no words, but whatever he sees in my expression must be enough. You, he whispers, You.

+ + +

I'm with Bobby, Adam's lover. Adam's former lover, I correct myself in the dream. We're diving without oxygen, and we're someplace familiar; I'd swear we were mere yards from my house. We're moving in tandem, though as the temperature drops, Bobby swims ahead. No problem, I think, I've done this before. A vivid image of Carla appears before me, then fades. Bobby gestures for me to rise to the surface. Don't be such a pussy, he says when we break for air, We're talking maybe thirty seconds. I shake my head, confused. Whatever, he says, I'm going down. He smiles, leaning toward me. Get it? he says, Going down?

My dick's instantly hard, and I feel a wave of conflicting emotions. Surely Adam's around here somewhere? Bobby's smile broadens. He moves closer, close enough for me to feel a shock of cold breath on my neck. His hand cups my balls, squeezes gently. Get it? he whispers again. Aren't you dead? I say, but he drops beneath the surface. I watch as the water closes above him as if he never existed at all. Then I follow.

Thirty seconds, he'd said, but we're down longer. He reaches the end of the cave ahead of me, spills into gorgeous light. C'mon, he calls back, You're not going to believe what's on the other side! I push myself forward, my arms, my legs furiously pumping, but I'm getting nowhere. Wait! I yell, wasting the very breath I've been rationing. He pauses, but the light begins to fade. I claw the rock as the water blackens. Then I feel him right beside me. You're dead, he says.

I jerk awake, then let the pieces of my reality fall into place. The dream seeps into my unconscious, unpleasant, unwelcome. What's wrong? Adam murmurs, curving closer to me. Shh, I whisper, Go back to sleep. But he turns on the bedside light. Tell me, he says, and I rub the back of my neck with one hand, eyeing the clock. We've been in bed less than an hour. One hour in and I'm already having nightmares.

I let him stroke my back, though the air conditioning against my bare skin makes me shiver. Did you have a bad dream? he asks. I don't say anything at first; the truth's just too creepy. But then I tell him about the dive I took in the fall of '95 when I fled the country because of James. I describe how Carla and I fell out of the mouth of that cave into a warm pool, tell him I'd never be able to capture the brilliance of those colors even if I tried. I left that space perfectly relaxed, cocooned in the certainty of my breath. Would you have done it? I ask, Taken the chance not knowing what was on the other side? I pose the question thinking of the cave, but it's that cliff that takes up position in my mind, and I shudder as I feel my foot slipping on the rock, my arms furiously pinwheeling. Adam barely thinks before he answers. Of course, he says, the lamp illuminating his skin as if he's some kind of god, You only live once, right?

+ + +

Less than an hour before he has to leave for the airport on Sunday morning, we're still in bed. So what now? he asks, kissing me, his mouth rough against my own. He hasn't shaved once since we arrived, and his jaw's lined with gold. I'm enthralled. You could come back next weekend, I offer, and he indulges my answer with a smile. Why don't you come to Austin instead? he asks. But I shake my head. I'm not there yet, I say, and he nods without taking his eyes from mine. I lean in for a quick, reaffirming kiss. Come back next weekend, I say, I'll pay for your ticket. He tucks the blanket around my shoulders, reminds me that I'm leasing a house without air conditioning. I'm living without air conditioning because I'm too lazy to look for something else, I tell him. Still, he says, You work too hard to be buying me plane tickets.

I laugh, though there's residue beneath the humor: of bitterness, and regret. I appreciate the compliment, I say, But I can't support myself with my work. So how do you manage? he asks, and I work my fingers toward the soft skin on the inside of his thigh. My father pays for everything, I tell him. He pulls back, though he winds his hand through mine. What do you mean, everything? he says, You mean rent and gas and… food? He sounds incredulous, and I feel a faint sense of foreboding. I told you this months ago, I tell him, but he looks at me as if I've just announced that I'm straight, and married with a couple of kids. You told me your father helped you out, he says. He does, I tell him. I thought you meant he gave you a few bucks now and then, Adam says, I thought maybe he helped you out with your medical insurance or that he'd bought you the Explorer. Well, you thought wrong, I tell him. Obviously, he says, extracting his hand from mine. Well, what did you think? I say, getting defensive, That my paintings were bringing in so much cash that I could decide on a whim to live in Mexico?

Adam presses his lips together. I don't know, Joel, he says, I guess I thought you were earning some money from painting but that you had some kind of supplemental income. Doing what? I ask, Moonlighting as an accountant? He gives me a dirty look, and I immediately regret the insult I've lobbed at Gary. I thought maybe you commissioned yourself out, he says, Or that you took an occasional part-time job to save money. He grits his teeth. I thought maybe you had some money from your mother, he says. It wasn't much, I tell him, sitting up, Believe me. For a minute I think he's

299

going to apologize for bringing her up at all. But then he says, Have you *ever* worked?

His question obliterates every positive comment he's ever made in regard to my painting, every indication that he respects who I am, what I do. I stare at him, unable to believe that after everything we've shared this weekend he could say something so cruel. Fuck you, I say, and he sways as if I've actually struck him. Fine, he says, I have a plane to catch.

Stunned, I watch him get dressed. He's tossing clothes in his suitcase haphazardly, a sure sign that he's upset. This isn't ending the way I expected, he tells me. You're the one crucifying me because I'm taking what I'm owed, I say, getting to my feet, and the look he turns in my direction contains both pity and repugnance. I scramble for justification. You know what he did to me, I cry, holding out my arms, I told you what he did to me, I told you what he did! You did that to yourself, Joel, Adam says.

I take a step back. I'm sorry, he says, That was blunt. No shit, I say, and he looks at his watch. Please, Joel, he says, I really don't want to leave like this. He steps toward me, and I hesitate, then let him slip his arms around me. I know what you've been through, he says, lowering his voice, And I know how seriously you take your work. He pulls me closer. I didn't mean to trivialize either one, he whispers.

He presses his lips to my hair, then curls a strand behind my ear. I just don't see how anything good can come from your father supporting you, Joel, he says, and I groan. What do you want me to do? I say, breaking away from him, Get a job waiting tables, paint when I get off at midnight? That might be healthier, he points out. I shake my head. There's no way you could understand, I say. I know he hurt you, Adam tells me, and I say, Then you know that he owes me! Don't you see that it'll never be enough? he asks. Maybe you're right, I tell him, But in the meantime I'm going to take what I can get.

He looks like he doesn't trust himself to speak, and I alter my voice so I sound like I'm negotiating with a hostage taker. This is just what we do, okay? I say, He gives me money, and I pretend to be the son he's always wanted: straight and employed and— Whoa, whoa, whoa, Adam interrupts, He doesn't know you're gay? Why would I tell him? I ask. I thought you were out! he says. I am out! I insist. Right, he says, Except to your father, who happens to be supporting you.

We stare at each other, until he buries his face in his hands. I'm suddenly shot through with anxiety. Adam, I say, My relationship with my father... this is all just peripheral! Oh, Joel, he says, and I stiffen at the condescension in his voice. I am not some closet case! I shout. I never said you were, he says, and there's truth in his tone; whatever he thinks of me, I'm far worse.

You have a plane to catch, I say, the words leaving my mouth with a finality I hadn't intended. So this is it, he says.

He doesn't want me to walk him out. Let's just say goodbye here, he tells me. I still have my arms folded across my chest, but when he steps toward me, I let them fall. One kiss, so tender that tears come to my eyes. See you around, Joel, he says. When? I want to cry. God, tell me when. But I say nothing at all, and he picks up his bag and opens the door. Tosses a half-hearted smile over his shoulder, and he's gone.

+ + +

For the next few weeks I'm stuck in a purgatorial quagmire. Adam doesn't call. I'm hurt, though I'm not surprised. I'm the one who stalled the forward motion of our relationship, refusing to be flexible about where we could see each other, admitting my dependence on my father for money and my lack of forthrightness when it comes to my sexuality. But god. I miss him, and I'd hoped that maybe, once he got back to Austin, he'd feel the same.

I think he's trying to work things out with Gary. That's my bet. I think he came to see me, figured out at the last minute that I wasn't in a position to do much of anything, and called Gary the second he got home to see what they could salvage. I'm sick at the thought, but I have a feeling I'm right, and when I stumble from my bedroom each morning and stand in front of that Starburst canvas, inspiration eludes me. *You mean rent and gas and... food?* he'd asked, and I still argue with him, though he's no longer around to hear me.

I'm not painting, but I'm not doing much of anything else either. I don't run. I don't swim. I don't dive. At night, in a torpor brought on by a little too much beer and way too much time, I sit on my porch and stare at the ocean in front of me. There's a faint line on the horizon where the water ends and the sky begins, and I concentrate on that thin stroke of gray as I nurse my last drink of the day. I usually go to bed just drunk enough to recognize the folly in trying to contact him.

One night at the end of August, blinded by malaise and a summer storm, I hike to the cliff. The ocean roils beneath me, swirls into eddies I can barely see because of the rain that slakes from the sky. Lightning crackles through the clouds, and I sway at the edge of the cliff, thinking of that moment in Bryan's office when I pressed my hands to his window and asked if he ever thought about jumping. If I wanted to let go, now's the time. I peel a beer from the carton I've hauled up here with me and raise the bottle to the sky, like I'm offering some kind of cosmic toast. Fuck you! I shout. My voice drowns in the elements, and furious, I scream the words again. I want them to carry across countries: to my father and his well-meaning wife; to James and his perfect fucking girlfriend; to Adam, who teased me into believing I stood a chance. I rail at the night, rain soaking my hair, my clothes. I want to reach my mother, whose blood flows within me, makes me everything I am and everything I'm not. Then I suck down my beer and hurl the bottle over the side. Another and another, until my fist fits around the neck of the last one. I'm at the edge; a gust of wind and the sea will rise to meet me.

But the sky suddenly calms, like it's been given a nice dose of lithium. I wipe tears and rainwater from my face as the clouds open. I'm left with a moon, white and full, to light my way home.

The next morning, I take a hard look at my options. I don't know how I'm going to manage living in that house again; I don't know what I'll do if I run into James or Kyle or Peter. And I'll have to see my father. I'm sure of that. He's not going to accept me returning to the States without seeing him. But Adam's there, and that's enough. That should really be enough.

+ + +

I put off calling Adam until a couple of days before my flight. I'm packed; I've had my work crated and shipped. I want to be sure I'm finished here, that I have no choice but to leave regardless of Adam's reaction. Because he might not be excited. He might actually be pissed. I might have to rally to win him back.

I'm coming home, I blurt out when he answers, and there's a long pause. You mean, for a visit? he asks cautiously. No, I say, For good. I start cracking my knuckles. I'll be back Friday afternoon, I add, And I was thinking…

I don't finish my sentence, half-hoping he'll finish it for me. He doesn't. I was thinking— I start again, and he interrupts. The day after tomorrow, he says. Yeah, I admit. He makes an odd sound I'd take for a laugh if I didn't know better. Six weeks ago you didn't think you could handle coming here for the *weekend*, he reminds me, And now you're coming home for good, and you what, want to pick up where we left off?

He's pissed, all right, and I bite my lip. You're unbelievable, he says. I know, I say, I know, and I know you're probably with Gary.

He doesn't contradict me.

The feel of his hand on my chest as we sat at that stoplight last November, conviction I could barely imagine in his eyes, and the next morning, I cast him aside as if everything he'd offered meant nothing. I can't let that happen again.

Last Thanksgiving, I say, You said you thought we had something.

He's quiet, but I know he remembers just as well as I.

I think you're right, I tell him, I think you're right, and I'd like to try. Your timing sucks, he says flatly. Why? I moan, Are you and Gary…? This isn't about Gary! he insists, This is about you acting as if you have the prerogative to walk in and out of my life as it suits you!

I instantly regret postponing this phone call. I should've talked to him the second I started making plans. If he's not an option, I'm so fucked. There's no way I can go back to Austin by myself. There's no way I can do this alone. Adam— I start, and he cuts me off. Why should I open myself up to you again? he says, Why should I let you back in?

I have a feeling he doesn't want to hear that I'm afraid to get off the plane unless he's waiting for me. I think he wants a declaration, a commitment of some kind, and the best I can offer him is some bullshit about knowing I have issues. And an apology: he deserves one after the way I behaved. I sent him away without consideration, because I felt stupid and foolish, because I couldn't admit he was right. Adam, I say, not sure where to begin, then reach back a dozen years and borrow his own words to Bobby. If you hang up now, I say, You'll always regret this moment.

He's quiet, and I close my eyes, throw a silent benediction toward the sea. If I'm the first to speak, everything's lost. He sighs; still I wait. I'm not my father's son for nothing. All right, he finally says, Give me a call when you get back.

I hang up before he can change his mind.

The next morning, I get my hair cut, drive all the way into Playa del Carmen and ask at one of the resorts for a recommendation. The stylist, when she has me in her chair, doesn't want to touch me. *Demasiado*, she keeps saying, Too much change. But my hair hangs below my shoulders, tangled from four months of wind and salt. Take it, I say, Take it all.

When she's finished and I look in the mirror, I feel like I'm staring back in time. I touch my smooth neck, run the heel of my hand above my ear. I half-expect to see James hovering behind me.

Well. There's no turning back now.

Jennifer Hritz

2

From the safety of the cab I eyeball the house, the status quo in Mexico suddenly looking a lot more appealing. I've only been back here one time since I was released from the hospital, and I didn't spend the night. I couldn't; I'd been terrified that once I walked through the door, I wouldn't be able to get out again. Instead, I went into the back room, packed up the few things I needed, and bolted. I'd been careful not to look in the direction of the bathroom. I hadn't even taken a piss; I'd held it until I got to the airport.

Now the driver gives me an impatient look. You getting out or what, man? he asks. I reach for my wallet, and as the cab pulls away from the curb, I cross the lawn, a path I must've taken thousands of times in the past eight years. But nearing the porch, my legs calcify, and I have to coax myself into putting one foot in front of the other. With a trembling hand I unlock the door.

Nothing's changed. Nothing's changed at all, and I have a frightening suspicion that if I take a look in the kitchen, I'll see the bowl of cereal I tried to eat a few days after Christmas, Pandora's cat food in the dish beside the refrigerator. I flick my eyes around the living room, settling for just a moment on the near-empty bottle of scotch on the coffee table, then walk down the hall and pause in the doorway of my bedroom. The blinds have been closed against the sun, but I'm able to make out the mess of bedcovers, clothes on the floor.

Inching forward, I stop when I can touch the doorframe of the bathroom with the palm of one hand. With the other I flip on the light. I know everything's been cleaned, but once the light illuminates the floor, the tub, my knees start to fold in on themselves. The room's neat, clean—cleaner, really, than it's been in years. One folded towel hangs over the edge of the sink. Otherwise, the room's empty; even the shower curtain's gone.

I back out of the bathroom, grabbing the handle of my bag without breaking stride. The Explorer's steering wheel feels strange under my hands, and twice I misinterpret corners, accustomed as I've been the past six months to the Jeep, but the highway stretches before me, and I make it to Adam's house in less than twenty minutes. When he opens the door, I stumble forward, into his arms.

Joel, Joel, he protests, untangling himself, What're you doing here? Casting a quick glance behind him, he pushes me away, his fingertips on my breastbone. I thought you were going to call, he says, closing the door halfway behind him. B-but I thought, I stammer, But you said… He's shaking his head. You can't just show up, Joel, he says, I have a life, I have—

He stops, but I know what he was about to say. I've taken note of the unfamiliar car in his driveway. I just haven't wanted to admit to myself who parked it there.

Babe? someone calls from inside the house.

Well, that's Gary. I can tell by the way Adam closes his eyes. Babe? Gary calls again, and Adam gives me a grim look. Come on, he says, We might as well get this over with.

Gary meets us in the living room, smiling without suspicion. I'm dismayed to find him attractive. Thick hair, midnight eyes: I can see why Adam likes him. I might have considered him myself if I'd ever had the need to hire an accountant. But the thought of him *here*, in a place that should've been mine: I was foolish for ever leaving. Gary, Adam cautions, stopping him before he can offer his hand, This is Joel.

Gary's smile disappears. What're *you* doing here? he asks me. Gary, Adam says, Please. Clapping his hands together, Gary conjures another smile. Right, he says, Where are my manners? He gestures toward the kitchen. We were just about to order some dinner, he says to me, Would you like a beer? I hesitate, glancing at Adam. Better check with Daddy, Gary agrees, and I recoil. Let's keep this civil, Adam says tightly. What's he *doing* here, Adam? Gary asks, losing his patience, and Adam looks over at me. I get the impression that he expects me to answer, and I take a deep breath so I can speak without the element of hysteria I felt flying down my front steps thirty minutes ago. I was going to call, I say, I was going to call, but I got home, and I just… I couldn't…

Adam softens, and catching the change in his expression, Gary says, You've got to be kidding. I give him a dirty look, and miraculously, Adam joins me. I can't believe you're willing to put up with this shit, Gary says to him, You told me you were through with him. I am! Adam snaps.

Every hope I've harbored vanishes. They both step forward when my legs fail, and the thought occurs to me, fleetingly, that under different circumstances Gary and I might have been friends. Together they ease me into a chair, and then Gary steps back, crossing his arms over his chest. But Adam can't let go of my hand, can't stop himself from cupping my cheek in his palm before he catches himself and casts an anguished glance over his shoulder. Gary— he starts, but Gary has already turned on his heel. Adam's half a step behind him. Give me one hour, Gary, I hear him say a minute later as the front door opens, Just one hour.

He's cutting me loose. That's why he needs an hour: to let me down as gently as only Adam could. He's too nice and too sympathetic to what I've told him about being incapable of staying in my house to just kick me out. But I have little expectation that I'll be here tomorrow morning, that I'll be here for more than the time it takes for him to remind me of everything I've done wrong.

By the time Adam appears in front of me again, looking as if he has the barest command of his emotions, I've wrapped my arms around myself, and I'm holding my jaw tight to keep my teeth from chattering. You're cold, he says, but I stop him when he moves toward the thermostat. Trust me, I say, It's not the air conditioning.

He looks stricken, and he stares down at his hands, which he clasps, then opens. I have a boyfriend, he says as if he's reminding himself. He glances up at me. And I like him, Joel, he confesses, He's good to me. Then why did you tell me to call? I whisper, and he shakes his head. Because from the moment we met, he says, I haven't been able to get enough of you.

His words thrill me, trip the beat of my heart. Adam, I say, reaching for him, but he pulls away from me. I need to know what to expect from you, he says, I need to know that if I invite you to spend the night, you're not going to bail in the morning.

I flinch. He has every reason to doubt me; I've certainly never given him an opportunity to trust me in the past. But I've come all the way back to Austin to be with him, and I remind him of that in a low voice. He shakes his head. Your presence here isn't enough, Joel, he says, I want all of you, or I don't want you at all.

I'm stunned by the ultimatum, though I shouldn't be. He's been working up to this since the first night we spent together. I'm amazed I've been able to string him along the way I have the last few months, the past couple of years. I'm at a crossroads, not the first one I've encountered, and despite the fact that I'm scared shitless by what I'm about to commit, I'm not going to make the same mistake again. I'm willing to try, I say, Isn't that something?

He doesn't move, and I hold my breath. Why'd you cut your hair? he finally asks. I look younger, I admit without answering him, and he grunts. Am I that much of a liability? I ask. You're definitely a risk, he says.

He goes upstairs to call Gary, telling me he can't make any promises about how long this conversation might take. I'm not exactly in a position to argue, and to give him some privacy I make my way out the back door. I've forgotten about the pool, and I stand for a minute in the bright sun, blinking as if I'm seeing a mirage. The water ripples softly in the breeze coming off the lake, and I trip down the steps and pry off a sandal, then dip my toe in the shallow end. The pool's probably too warm this late in the summer for Adam, but given my low threshold for temperature variation these days, I find the water pretty much perfect. Kicking off my other sandal, I lower myself to the edge of the pool and slip my legs beneath the surface.

When the back door slams shut, I open my eyes. He's hurt, Adam says before I can ask, And he's angry, and he has every reason to be pissed.

Less than twelve hours ago, I was standing with my feet in the ocean's froth, my ears tuned to the pounding of the waves. Now I'm here, and I watch as Adam comes toward me, pulling his shirt over his head. I can't move, can't breathe, can't even look at him, he's so beautiful. We're swimming, he says when I get to my feet and take a step in his direction. He unbuttons his shorts, and I scan the perimeter of his property. But he doesn't care about being seen. Dropping his clothes, he steps to the diving board. After a moment I follow.

We don't race; this is no competition. We just swim, our strokes quiet and clean, and when he finally hooks his elbows over the side of the pool and tilts his head toward the sun, I take a chance and move toward him. Sun hot on my head, his hands pool-cool. And that kiss, like he's been saving up for this moment for the past six weeks. Relax, he murmurs, This part has never been a problem for us.

Later, I'm half-asleep as he runs his hand across my scalp. The haircut, he mutters, I'll need time to get used to.

+ + +

I've arrived at Adam's house at the beginning of Labor Day weekend, and I find it poignant that we've come full circle. We've known each other for two years, I tell him Monday morning as we're lying in bed. And we've spent about two weeks of that time in each other's company, he tells me. At first I think he's being snide, but then he smiles, and I relax into his arms. Friday morning, I'd awakened to him watching me; I jumped, and he instantly stiffened, preparing himself for what he obviously regarded as my impending departure. I automatically shifted into defense mode, until I remembered to breathe. He's given up so much for me and has so little reason to trust me, and I opened my hand to his. Hey, I whispered, and the relief on his face just about crushed me. I'm working with such a tremendous deficit.

But we can't stop smiling at each other, touching each other, saying each other's name. Catching his reflection in the mirror after we've showered, his face holds the same flush of intoxication as mine. We've been nowhere outside of the house, seen no one, spoken to no one. Do you miss him? I ask, meaning Gary. Honestly, Joel, Adam says, You haven't given me the chance.

Monday night, we lounge on the sofa, paying little attention to the television murmuring in the background. Are you nervous? he asks. He's talking about my plan to revisit my house tomorrow, and I wind my fingers through his, halfway wishing that he'd offer to blow off work so he can join me. Mm, I say. Mm? he asks, raising his eyebrows. Mm, I repeat, moving our hands below my waist, and he lets me off the hook.

The next morning, he leaves for the office, and though he told me I could crash at his place until I feel suitably prepared, I head home instead, resolved to cleanse the rooms of their awful fucking aura. My first order of business: stash what's left of the bottle of scotch in one of the top cupboards in the kitchen. Then, my bag still in the doorway, I start cleaning. I scour the refrigerator, the sink, the kitchen counters. I whip out a piece of paper: cereal, milk, beer. I take the list with me into the living room, buoyed by momentum, and shake out the blanket crumpled on the couch. I shove a handful of CDs in the stereo. I work the entire morning, and by lunch I've finished the front of the house, and I'm ready to start on the bedroom. How are you? Adam asks when he calls. Managing, I say, You? I'm buried, he tells me.

I tackle the bedroom, then head into the bathroom as the afternoon's waning. There's no reason to clean in here; wiping my hand along the edge of the sink, I can't even come up with a fine film of dust. But I've got to bathe at some point, and I strip, then stand with my arms folded across my chest as the water heats. When I step into the shower, water splatters onto the bathroom floor now that the shower curtain's gone. I hurry to finish, then slip as I step from the tub and whack my knee on the porcelain. The skin takes on a spoiled color.

I have good news, Adam tells me when I get to his house that night, And bad. What's the bad news? I ask, and he admits that he has to leave town tomorrow, a spur-of-the-moment business trip that can't be helped. What's the good news? I sulk. I'll be back by the weekend, he says. *That's* the good news? I say. I've told him nothing about my day, haven't mentioned the shift in the house as I moved into the bathroom, but he seems to know what I'm thinking. Why don't you stay here while I'm gone? he asks, and I tell him I'm going to have to get used to staying at my place at some point. Why don't I leave you a key anyway, he says, Just in case.

The next morning, he leaves for the airport, and I go home, where I try to figure out why the boxes I've had shipped from Mexico haven't arrived. I need to see those paintings again, need them to affirm that I'm okay here, because right now all I can see is that white fucking wall in the living room. Where are they, where are they? I mutter, realizing as I glance around without finding her that I'm talking to Pandora. She's long gone, with James from what Adam told me. He took her the day after I was admitted to the hospital.

The reminder makes me grim. I stalk around the house, in and out of James's old bedroom, into the back room. I'll have to reorganize in here, though I hesitate to begin until I'm sure my work has arrived intact. I end up on the top step of the back porch, where I suddenly develop an intense craving for a cigarette.

Adam calls from the hotel that night. I'm curled in the center of my bed, listening to the click of the ceiling fan, inventing nightmares in the shadows thrown by the sliver of moonlight skipping through my blinds. I find it difficult to believe that I've ever been comfortable here, ever slept a full night in this bed. You doing all right down there? he asks. Yeah, I say, slipping into his voice. If I keep my eyes shut, I can imagine I'm in Mexico; I can pretend that this conversation is one of many we had over the summer. You're sure you're okay? he says just before he hangs up, and not wanting to break the spell, I murmur, I'm good, I'm good.

But once I hang up, the moment's gone. I'll never make it until morning, and I finally throw off the covers and head for my Explorer. I drive to Adam's, where I let myself in with his key and climb the stairs to his bedroom. I'm at your place, I say, waking him at his hotel. I like the idea of you in my bed, he admits. He's probably afraid that the timing of his trip will send me packing, and I close my eyes and promise him I'll be here waiting for him when he gets home. Trust me, he says, I'm counting the days.

+ + +

I call Kyle. I'm going to have to talk to him eventually, and I'd rather the encounter take place on my own terms. When he answers his cell, though, I realize just how far I've pushed him. Eight months, he says, sounding more bitter than I expected, Eight months you've been gone, and I've had to hear every little scrap through Adam. But now I'm back, I tell him, and he says, So where are you taking me tonight? I'm startled into silence, and I can almost see him shaking his head. You're lucky I'm free, sweetheart, he says.

That evening at his place, he holds me at arm's length, exclaiming over my haircut, *tsk tsk*-ing about the scars on my arms. Hooking one hand around my neck, he kisses my cheek. You look good, he assures me, gesturing me inside and offering me a glass of wine. He makes quick work with an enviable bottle, as if he might have been born with a corkscrew in his hand. So you're with Adam now, he says, pouring me a glass. I blush, to my surprise as well as Kyle's. Mm-hmm, he says, Sent Gary packing the moment you got back in town, huh? You heard about that? I ask, and he leans over his bar. Honey, he says, I hear about everything.

I'm not sure I want to delve any deeper into that remark, and I carry my wine into the next room and drop into the nearest chair. Kyle stretches out on a plush chaise lounge that would look far better next to his opulent bed. What about you? I ask as he adjusts the hem of his shirt, Are you still seeing that guy you met in Aspen? He almost chokes on his wine. Darling, he sputters, you *have* been gone a long time. With a faint smile he tells me that the Aspen boy hadn't lasted long, that no one ever does. I'm destined to be alone, he says with a pout. How can you be alone? I say, grinning, When you're here with me?

I find that I'm enjoying myself far more than I expected. He plugs me with the latest gossip, insists I traipse into his closet to check out his fall wardrobe, asks my advice about the new bedding he wants to buy. I want something understated, he confides, You know, to offset my performance. There's so much lightness here, and I accept his offer of a second glass of wine, suddenly thankful that I came.

Only when the evening's winding down does Kyle turn serious. You know, Joel, he says, staring off into the distance, You should've called me. I finger my drink, discomfited by the admonition and well aware that if I let him, he'll work himself into a rant. I know, I say, And I'm sorry.

He walks me to the Explorer under a soft September sky. There's barely a hint of autumn in the air, but it's coming. In the wind I can feel the season coming. You talk to your ex? Kyle asks as I'm opening the door, and I give him a sharp look. Though I've thought of James often over the past few days, I haven't spoken to him once, haven't considered contacting him. It's all just a little too much: Adam, the house, Kyle. I don't know that I'm prepared for another confrontation.

I saw him, you know, Kyle says. You did? I ask, and he nods. Then he hesitates, as if he's trying to decide what to tell me next. I don't want to know, I say quickly before he can confide anything else, and instead, he thanks me for an evening well spent. I'll hear from you? he asks. Count on it, I say.

I call Adam on my way back to his house and tell him where I've been. I'm so glad, he says. You're coming home soon, right? I say, Because this… This what? he asks when I don't finish. I swallow, the stress of reentry finally catching up to me. This is harder than I expected, I admit. Tomorrow, Joel, he says, I swear.

+ + +

The work I've shipped from Mexico is waiting for me when I get home the next morning. Jubilant, I haul the boxes inside and start clearing out the back room. Half-dried tubes of acrylic, old brushes, strips of canvas, I pitch into a garbage bag. Before I become too maudlin I lug the paintings I was working on last fall, including the one I started the night of my first date with Adam, to the curb. I straighten stacks of drawing paper, I clear the table, I categorize the supplies I'll need going forward. I even sweep the hardwoods. When I'm finished, I reach for the first box, practically shaking with anticipation. I just want to set them up, each and every canvas, surround myself with what I've done.

But the colors don't seem right. Frowning, I take a step back, then open each of the boxes in succession, line every canvas against the wall. My eyes slide from one painting to the next, each more garish than its predecessor, until they finally stop at what I'd considered my best. I'd used a tangerine so bright I'd been able to see the color in my dreams, could probably still find drops of it on my shorts if I looked for them now. I'd been beside myself, trying to capture the last of the sun before it set, the night after I first talked to Adam. Standing here, the canvas ablaze in front of me, I suddenly understand what's happened. That same mania, that same hysteria I felt when I came home from Adam's last Thanksgiving, followed me all the way to Mexico. I'd assumed that because I'd been able to paint at all that I was okay. I hadn't finished anything in so long, and I'd somehow deluded myself into believing that completion itself was enough. The thought never occurred to me that from the moment I set down that roller of black paint I'd been finishing what I started.

When Adam comes home that night, I don't tell him what I've discovered. I need some time to digest what I've encountered, time to figure out what to do now. So what happened with your work? he asks. I think I need some space, I admit. What do you mean, space? he asks, and I tell him I worked my ass off all summer and when I expend that much energy, I like to take some time before I come back to the paint. A fresh perspective, I say, and he nods so easily that I convince myself I'm telling the truth.

Space. Perspective. A little time off and I'll be fine.

+ + +

Adam leaves for the office by seven-thirty most mornings and doesn't come home for a good twelve hours. I flounder in his absence. I sleep late, I watch movies, I even go to my house under the pretense of painting. But the truth of the matter is that I'm not accomplishing much of anything. I end up with entirely too much time on my hands, a circumstance that reminds me vaguely of my freshman year in college, and more vividly of the fall after my trip to Europe.

I search for distractions and finally work up the nerve to call Peter. He sounds stunned to hear from me, so stunned that I'm embarrassed I've called. He and Amy are doing well, he says; they're moving to Denver at the end of the month. We should get together before you leave, I suggest, guessing that'll never happen. Yeah, yeah, he says, playing along, That'd be great. Saddened to realize that for all practical purposes our friendship has ended, I figure the least I can do is apologize for missing his wedding. No big deal, he says, I was just glad when James told me you were okay.

James. I still miss him terribly, and I toy with the idea of getting in touch with him, go so far as to pick up the phone one afternoon before I realize that Elizabeth might be the one who answers. But the longer I go without initiating contact myself, the more likely it is that he's going to take me by surprise.

And he does, sooner than I would've thought.

I'm in my backyard assessing the damage from a storm that must have blown through months ago. I'm gazing skyward, trying to figure out whether or not a strong enough wind has the potential to send what's left of one of the pecan trees crashing through my bedroom window, when the gate on the side of the house creaks. I glance over. James stares back.

I find myself fighting for sudden control: of my breath, my tears. My god, it's hard to see him. He's lost the beard, but his hair's just as unkempt as it was when he got back from Greece last year, and he raises a self-conscious hand to his neck as if he knows what I'm thinking. Hey, he finally says. I attempt a smile, which fails. Can I come in? he asks, indicating the yard. He raises the latch without waiting for an answer—a good thing, as I seem incapable of speech. Adam said you were back, he tells me, letting the gate clang shut behind him and shoving his hands in the pockets of his shorts. I nod. I thought…, he says, I thought we could get dinner… He trails off, the invitation probably sounding as ludicrous to him as it does to me. Or a drink, he adds. He laughs skittishly. I could use a drink, he mutters under his breath. There's beer in the fridge, I blurt out, though inviting him inside could well destroy what I've been trying to rebuild the past nine months. Yeah? he says, raising his eyebrows, and I nod.

Following me into the house, he waits as I take two Shiners from the refrigerator. I hand him a bottle with a shaking hand; he seems less than stable himself. How are you? he asks. Okay, I say, Good. He nods, and I return the question. Fine, he says, I'm fine.

There's a silence I can barely take. The past couple of years cripples us, and now that we're beyond the pleasantries, I'm not sure either one of us knows how to proceed. We stare hopelessly at the floor, and then at last James clears his throat. So you were in Mexico, he says. Yeah, I say, settling myself on the sofa and gesturing for him to sit as well, South of Cancun.

We talk a bit about what life was like down there. I tell him about the diving, the running; I think he's just grateful to hear me speak. After a while I offer him another beer, and he waves me back to my seat when I stand up to get him one. There's something disconcerting about seeing him pull the bottle from the fridge, tossing the cap onto the counter, and when he automatically drops sideways in the chair the way he always did, his legs draped over the arm, I shake my head. What? he asks, catching my eye. This is just strange, I admit.

An embarrassed silence passes, and he rights himself and plants his feet on the floor. What about you? I ask, Did you graduate? He frowns, as if he wishes I hadn't asked. No, he says, Things have been kind of… fucked up. My spine stiffens at what must be an accusation; he takes a swallow of beer and plunks the bottle on the coffee table. You painted, he says, jerking his chin at the wall across from us, and though his tone's casual, I'm struck by the way we're jockeying for power. Yeah, I say, and he nods. You paint some when you were in Mexico? he asks, Or is this all you've done lately? What, I say, Adam hasn't told you that, too?

We both start at the acidity in my tone. I suddenly have a headache, and I press my fingertips to my forehead. I didn't come here to stress you out, Joel, he tells me, sounding annoyed. Why did you come? I ask, and he looks so unhappy I just might burst into tears. I thought we could talk, he finally says, I thought we could at least talk.

Swigging some of his beer, he looks me over. You look good, he offers, but he's speaking grudgingly, like maybe he's afraid I'll hear the compliment and get the wrong idea. I glance down at myself. You look…, he says. What? I ask when he doesn't finish. I don't know, he mumbles, Together. What'd you expect? I ask. He rolls his shoulders, but I can see him glance at my arms from the corner of his eye. I turn them over so he can get a better look. Jesus, he says, his voice cracking, Jesus, Joel.

I'm not prepared for his reaction; if anything, I expected to incur his wrath. How could you? he asks, How could you do it? It was easier than you'd expect, I tell him. God, how can you be so cavalier? he asks, wiping the corners of his eyes with his thumb and forefinger, Didn't you think… didn't you realize that people care about you? That was a little hard to believe under the circumstances, I tell him, and he stares at me. You blame me, don't you? he says. I don't answer him. What happened wasn't my fault! he says, though he sounds as if he's repeating something someone else has told him many times. I don't contradict him, but in his mind my silence seems as good as an indictment. How can you not take responsibility for what you've done? he says, How can *you* accuse *me* when *you're* the one who cut yourself?

I think you should leave, I say, and he smacks his hands against the chair. Why not? he says, God forbid we ever talk about anything. He gets to his feet but stops halfway to the door. Did it ever occur to you to think about how devastated Adam would be when he found you? he asks. Adam wasn't supposed to find me! I snap, and now he smiles thinly. That's right, he says, That was supposed to be *my* punishment. You fucked me over, James! I cry, You were my family, you were all I had! God, do you know how much pressure that is? he asks, To be someone's everything? Fuck you, I say, my voice breaking. I didn't mean to hurt you, he says, I never wanted to hurt you. You didn't even tell her! I say. What did you want me to say, Joel? he asks, I didn't want to lose her! Then why did you insist that I meet her? I ask, You had to have known she'd find out! I left the table to buy a pitcher of beer, he says, I didn't think you'd even have time to tell her you're gay!

I take a step back. He crams his hands in the pockets of his shorts. You didn't tell her I'm gay? I asked. I didn't know how, he mumbles, I didn't know what to say. How about the *truth*? I say, How about that you used to fuck me? He flushes, and I'm enraged by this chronic Puritan streak, the same one that destroyed us. Come here, Joel, I say, mimicking him, I want to fuck you from behind, I want to fuck you standing up, I want to fuck you in the back room. Joel, he pleads, Stop. God, you can't even think about it, can you? I say, You started this whole fucking thing, and you can't even bring yourself to hear me say the words! You should've told me how you felt about me! he shouts. That wouldn't have made a goddamn bit of difference, I say, You knew what you wanted, and you didn't give a shit what that did to us!

The tears in his eyes will never be restitution enough. Get out, I say, Get the fuck out of my house. But when he reaches the door, he stops, one hand on the knob. We're not going to be able to salvage this, he says, Are we? I fold my arms across my chest, though the gesture's meant to stop my heart from spilling onto the floor. D'you think it's worth trying? he whispers. I don't answer him, and he opens the door.

I cry for a long time after he leaves. The phone rings, but I keep to myself, and gradually, the room blackens. By the time Adam bangs on the front door the skies have opened. Did James call you? I ask as he scans my expression, and he nods, pausing when his eye catches the living room wall. He hasn't been here since the day after he found me. I had it painted, I tell him wearily. Okay, he says, but he glances at the wall again, as if it's alive, as if at any moment it might lunge toward him, jaws wide.

Do you want a drink? I ask, I could use a drink. I go into the kitchen, where I take the scotch down from the cupboard and pour us both a glass. A warm flush spreads through my chest when I swallow. Did you know he was coming here today? I ask. Adam hesitates, and I shake my head. You should've warned me, I say. He asked me not to say anything, he tells me, setting his glass on the bar without taking a sip. But I'm the one you're fucking, I remind him, and he presses his lips together so tightly they turn white. He has a longer history with you, he says, And certainly a more complicated one, and he asked me a favor I wasn't about to deny. I pour myself another drink, pissed. And for the record, Joel, he adds, I'm not *fucking* you.

We don't stay in that house long. I offer Adam a dry shirt, but he waits for me in the living room and pulls it quickly over his head when I return. He doesn't want to be here any more than I do, and we linger just long enough for the rain to taper. Once we're back at his house, he's all compassion, and he leads me into the shower and then the bedroom, where he brings me hot tea as if I'm sick. I accept the mug, the ceramic warm in my hands. Shitty day, I confess after the first few sips, and he nods.

+ + +

Masochist that I am, I call my father a couple of days later, knowing he'll probably be angry when he finds out I've been back in Austin for more than three weeks and haven't bothered to contact him. I'm right; initially, he's pleased to hear from me, but he changes his tune when he realizes he's the last to know I'm home. Should I assume you'll be making a trip to Houston? he asks, and I wonder if he's made the suggestion to punish me or if he truly wants to see me. I don't know, I sigh, but he manages to bully me into accepting an invitation for the very next weekend. He stops short of reminding me how much financial assistance he's given me, but there's no question the thought's there, ready to be articulated should I put up a fight. I don't have the strength.

I could go with you, Adam offers when I tell him the news. I give him a look. I thought you were ready to try, he reminds me, and I explain, painfully aware of what happened the last time we touched upon this subject, why even if my father suspects, I need to keep up the charade. I end up sounding ridiculous. You know better than anyone what can happen, I finally tell him, hoping to latch on to some kind of comparison, Bobby's parents refused to speak to him once they found out. Bobby's situation was completely different, he says tightly.

I shut up, regretting having said anything. Look— I start again after a minute, but Adam holds up his hand. You already know what I think about this, he says, I'm willing to make the trip, but if you don't want me to go, then I'll just see you when you get back. I eye him, trying to gauge how much damage I'm causing. I'm not saying another word, he says.

So the next Friday, I'm in Houston, alone, ringing my father's doorbell, trying to forget that the last time I saw him I was screaming in a hospital bed. Glad you could make it, he says when he opens the door, offering his hand as if I'm one of his business associates. I take his lead and nod when he offers me a drink. You look well, he says, and I suppress the urge to glance down at my arms, which I've covered with a long-sleeved shirt despite the weather. You're certainly tan enough, he adds.

The remark sounds disparaging, though I don't necessarily think that was his intent. Glad to see you've gotten rid of that hair, he adds, shifting his gaze as Catherine appears. Hey there, she says, abandoning pretense and drawing me into a hug. I let her cling to me for a moment, then gently extract myself from her arms. She means well; I know that. You look divine, she says, touching her hand to my hair. Thank you, I mumble.

Catherine has prepared dinner for us, a kindness which makes me cringe. She's trying to turn this weekend into some kind of reunion, and we gather around the dining room table under so much candlelight that the walls themselves seem to flicker. Joel, my father says, pouring me a glass of wine, Tell us your plan. My plan? I say, and he winks, a gesture I find unsettling given that I can't be sure whether there's mirth in its intention. What are you planning on doing with your time? he asks, Now that you're back in Austin.

His question hurts because I have no answer. Every disaster I created in Mexico scrolls through my mind's eye. I don't need to lobby for time and space to paint. I have all the time in the world and absolutely no way to fill it. I don't know, I admit, and my father frowns. I think he expected me to argue with him, but when he glances at Catherine, I realize they've discussed my situation ahead of time, and at the very least he agreed not to talk about money this weekend.

I wonder what else he might know. By now Catherine must have guessed the particulars of my relationship with Adam. Does my father have any idea? I can't tell from the way he's ruminating over his wine, from the precise movement of his knife across the filet on his plate. But no. I wouldn't be sitting here if he knew, wouldn't have been invited this weekend at all. I take a long breath, and Catherine saves me from having to answer any more questions about my direction—or lack thereof—and asks me instead some light-hearted questions about Mexico, which I struggle to answer. I keep thinking my father's going to tell me that after all these months I have a responsibility to contribute more to the conversation, at least for the duration of one meal. But he's quiet, gazing out the window in the direction of the pool. I have a fleeting memory of standing beside him at some point when I was in college, talking about nightswimming. My sophomore year?

That might have been mere weeks before she died.

After we've finished eating my father and Catherine let me escape to my old bedroom. They're probably happy to see me go; that dinner couldn't have been any more uncomfortable. Trailing my fingers along the bookcase still filled with paperbacks and high school paraphernalia, I wonder how many nights I've slept here. Although we occasionally took vacations, I rarely spent the night elsewhere, never once stayed with a friend. I try to picture Adam here. He'd be more out of place than I am.

Crossing to the window, I part the drapes. Moonlight glances off the water in the pool. I've climbed out of this window; I've been sneaking out of the house since I was fourteen. The room overlooks the backyard, the window opening onto a sloped roof. If I'd had the courage at some point, I probably could've jumped right from the rooftop into the deep end of the pool. I spent more than a few nights when I was in high school sitting on this roof, staring up at the night sky, fantasizing about a life where I'd live free of my father, my bewildering sexuality. And if I crept along the edge of the roof closest to the house, I could hook my foot along the gutter and shimmy down the latticework altogether. I don't think my father ever suspected, at least not until he caught me the summer before my senior year in high school. I'd been too drunk to come in the way I'd left, and I used my key to open the back door. My father had already been awake, and he'd forced me to tell him what happened, torn down the latticework later the same day.

My mother wasn't happy. The roses were in full bloom.

Now something makes me open the window. The night's sticky, humid, but I haul over the side anyway. At this age I barely fit, and for a second I'm afraid I'm stuck. Shit, I mumble, concerned more with the possibility of my father discovering me in this position and less with actually being trapped. I rock to the side, then tumble out the window and fly down the slope toward the pool. I stop myself just before I roll over the edge. Scrambling to my feet, I back up until I'm flush against the side of the house.

God. The view's just as I remembered.

+ + +

My father doesn't work on Saturday. I can recall very few times when he's taken the entire weekend off, and when I wander downstairs mid-morning, respectably hungover, I anticipate finding him dressed for the office. But he's sitting at the breakfast table by himself in a pair of swimming trunks and a golf shirt. I'm going for a swim, he says, omitting a greeting, Why don't you join me.

I get the impression he hasn't made a request. Suppressing a sigh, I go upstairs to change, and by the time I get my ass outside he's already in the pool. I stand for a minute, watching him. He looks good, despite his age, though I notice that his hair's a little thinner in the water than he's probably aware. I can't help feeling the tiniest bit smug. Are you going to join me or not? he asks, coming up for air.

I'm not sure how many laps we swim. I can't waste energy trying to count; I'm working too hard to keep pace with him. I had no idea he was in such good shape. I've only missed a couple months of running, but my lungs burn, and as we turn for another lap, constantly changing places, always within a mere twelve inches of each other, I start to think maybe he's intentionally trying to humiliate me. I mean, my god, the man's what? Fifty-four? Fifty-five? The thought gives my stroke an additional edge, and I pull ahead of him, making it halfway across the pool again before I realize he's not following me.

You're in terrific shape, he gasps when I surface. Thanks, I say, careful not to reveal how much I'm struggling for breath as well. Have you been working out? he asks. I've been running every day, I admit, though in truth I haven't been even once since I got back from Mexico. Well, you're doing something right, he says. I follow him as he gets out of the pool, so pleased with the compliment that I start chattering about how many miles I've been logging each week, how difficult I found running in the sand. He reaches for a towel and runs it across his hair; I grab one myself. So you've been swimming a lot, too, huh? I ask.

My father doesn't answer. I'm shaking water from my hair, droplets spattering the brick at my feet, and I finally look up at him. Yes, he says, dragging his eyes from my arms, Nearly every day. He squints into the morning sun. Dad, I say, and he drops his towel on one of the chairs and pulls his golf shirt over his head. We have dinner reservations at eight, he tells me, apropos of nothing. Dad, I say again, and he lowers his voice. For god's sake, Joel, he says, Cover your arms.

+ + +

Dinner that night reeks of discontent. I've dressed in a lightweight sweater, and I pull my sleeves to my wrists. My father ignores the movement, but Catherine gives me a pitying glance which completely discomposes me. He must have told her what happened. I pick my way through my salad, drink more than a fair share of wine, listen to my father talk about business, the country club, his latest round of golf. I don't have a word to contribute. I'm still trying to accept that nine months ago I tried to kill myself and he doesn't seem to find that worthy of discussion.

I haven't planned on calling Adam this weekend, given that I know too well how he feels about my trip, but when I check my voicemail, I find that he's left a message telling me he's thinking about me, assuring me that I can call him if I want. He's gone out of his way to be kind, a concession I know I don't deserve. I look at the clock, figure I'm just drunk enough to ignore the time. How's it going, baby? he asks, and I shut my eyes, close to weeping at the term of endearment. I'm okay, I tell him. Have you been drinking? he says, You sound a little trashed. Maybe, I admit. Oh, he says.

What about you? I ask, What've you been doing all day? Not much, he says, Missing you, mostly.

Already feeling better, I nestle under the covers. What's it like down there? he asks. Dismal, I say. Oh, Joel, he says, Why? I don't feel like getting into it, I say, I'd rather talk about you. Okay, he says, and I can tell he's smiling. Tell me about your cycling trip, I say. I cut it short, he tells me. Oh yeah? I say, falling into his voice, Why is that? Actually, he says, hesitating, I had lunch with James.

I close my eyes.

Please don't read anything into this, okay? he says, We had lunch: no big deal. He tells me that James called on the spur of the moment, that they figured the timing was probably good since I wasn't even in town. I try not to think of the two of them cozying up to a table somewhere, talking about me. I'm hanging up, I say. Joel, he protests, and I say, This is so not what I need to hear from you, Adam. You're right, he says, I shouldn't have said anything. You shouldn't have met him for *lunch*, I say, and he's quiet. Can we talk about this tomorrow? he finally asks. Why? I say, Are you with him right now or something? Of course not, he says, taking obvious pains to remain calm, I'd just rather fight with you in person. Great, I mutter, That gives me something to look forward to after my shitty weekend.

I hang up, dropping my cell phone beside me. I'm trapped. If I go downstairs, I'll have to contend with my father. Catherine will likely try to corner me if I slip outside by the pool; she's been wanting to get me alone all day. If I stay up here, I won't be able to get the image of Adam and James out of my mind. And if I go back to Austin, I'll be walking into a fight.

Goddamn him. How could he hear me out that night in Mexico, agree that James fucked me over, and then accept an invitation to lunch? Getting to my feet, I pry open the window. I slither through the opening, then hunker down against the side of the house. I'd kill for a cigarette, a joint, a beer. Instead, I stare up at the sky. This same moon illuminates Adam's bedroom, shines across a Mexican sea.

I'd sketch its beam, if only I could.

+ + +

Good of you to come, my father tells me the following afternoon like I had any choice in the matter. No problem, I say, swinging my bag into the back of the Explorer. He's already written me a check, told me he figured I'd probably need some extra cash now that I'm back in the States. To get reorganized, he said, and I just pocketed the check without a word. I wish we could've talked more, Catherine says, and I give her a rueful smile as if I totally agree. Next time, I promise.

I can't back out of their driveway fast enough.

I've debated going straight to my own house in a gesture Lydia would assure me is patently passive-aggressive, but by the time I get back to Austin I'm so pissed off that I drive straight to Adam's, where he makes the mistake of trying to gather me into his arms. I'm not happy with you, I say, pushing him away. I'm sorry, he apologizes, I should've talked to you first. The timing's not the issue, Adam, I tell him. Jesus, how can he not understand? He *hurt* me, I say, More than my father ever did.

Oh honey, Adam says. He reaches for me, but I back away and sink into the sofa. Sometimes I want a cigarette so badly I could scream, I say, running my hand through my hair. I cut my eyes at him; he doesn't look surprised. I suspected, he admits, I figured you couldn't live with James and not pick up the habit. James smokes? I ask, and now he looks confused. Yeah, he says, Obsessively.

Well, I must not totally despise him, because I feel a tiny spark of sympathy at the news. Something must have pushed him over the edge, and I automatically glance down at my arms. He's had a hard time, Adam adds quietly. Tears come to my eyes, and he reaches for my hand; this time, I don't pull away from him. I hate going to Houston, I whisper. I know, he says. I hate my father, I say, But god, I want him to like me. I laugh, the sound uninviting. How's that for fucked up? I ask, but Adam shakes his head. He's your father, Joel, he says, squeezing my hand. What did you think of him? I ask, and he sighs. He was terribly concerned when I called him last year, he says, and I feel a sad little prick of affirmation at the news. He cares, at least a little. And he was angry, Adam adds. Angry? I say, Or embarrassed? Adam hesitates, and I withdraw my hand. Please— he says, but I cut him off. Trust me, I say, You're not telling me anything I don't already know.

We're quiet for a moment. He wanted to know how you knew me, he says, He told me you'd never mentioned me. What'd you tell him? I ask. That I knew plenty about him, he says. You said that? I ask, gazing at him in frank admiration. If I hadn't been trying so hard to be diplomatic under the circumstances, he says, I could've said much worse. Sometimes it scares me how much like him I really am, I admit. There's no comparison, he says, and I close my eyes. I look like him, I say. Yeah, Adam says softly, You do.

That night, under cover of darkness, I tell him the rest. Not about my mother; god, not about her. But about Jess, and Bryan, and what I did the night I realized James's loyalty to me ran more shallowly than I'd ever imagined. He listens without judgment, and when there's nothing left to say, I turn to look at him. I can barely make out his expression. Joel, he whispers, and I need no other word to know his mind. He reaches for me, his hands sweeping the length of my body, and I relinquish what I believe to be the last of my fears. Accept his touch as the last step toward deliverance.

+ + +

The weather's turned too cold for the pool, but that doesn't stop us from spending most of our free time outside. We grill just about every night and eat at a table beside the water, where we eventually determine that the atmosphere's just too pretty not to share. I suggest Kyle, and Adam suggests some of his cycling friends, and I decide not to worry about what anyone thinks of me.

We spend most of Saturday afternoon in preparation, open the door that evening to a handful of friends. We offer them drinks and an elaborate array of *hor d'oeuvres*, then sit outside in the cool autumn wind and smile when they praise what we've done. Halfway through the evening, Kyle pulls me aside. You, honey, he says, Look better than you have in a long time. I think he might be right, and I know the reason happens to be sitting a few feet away. I watch Adam talking to some guy he cycles with on the weekends; he glances up, smiling a delicious smile I can feel working its way down to my toes.

I still can't believe my luck. He could've tired of me already or decided he missed Gary. Instead, we're throwing parties, and I raise my glass to my lips, gazing at this small crowd of Adam's friends, at that beautiful pool glowing in the night. The thought that I was teetering on the brink of that cliff just a little over a month ago catches my breath.

I think that was a success, Adam tells me as we close the door after the last of our guests. Especially for Kyle, I add. He'd disappeared around the corner of the house with Adam's cycling buddy, Scott, come back looking pleased with himself. Scott has a boyfriend, right? I ask, following Adam into the kitchen, and he shrugs. Of sorts, he says, He's pretty promiscuous. He starts clearing the counter of martini glasses; I'm suddenly bothered by the nonchalance in his tone. What does he do when I'm not around, I wonder, when he's traveling? Are you? I ask, and he gives me a strange look. Am I what? he asks. Promiscuous, I say. What do you think? he asks. I shrug, avoiding his eye, but I see him lean back against the counter, his arms across his chest. Have you ever been in a monogamous relationship? he asks. Not really, I say, thinking briefly about Darryl. Does it count if every time you fuck your boyfriend you're thinking of someone else?

Monogamy isn't easy, Adam informs me. Well, shit, then, I mumble, Forget it. I brush a few crumbs off the island, aware of his eyes on me. You were monogamous with Bobby, I remind him, and he gets quiet. Believe me, he finally says, It wasn't easy. And Gary, I say, He was pissed you came to Mexico. Gary and I didn't have an agreement, Adam tells me. Then why was he so upset that you came to see me? I ask. Because, he says, He knew I was in love with you.

We both start at the way I've sucked in my breath. Shh, he says, placing a hasty finger over my lips, Don't say a word.

+ + +

I'm not working, but I don't much care. All I want, all I need, is him. When he's at the office, I busy myself with the mundane: I nap, I shop, I hold mini-dart tournaments with myself. Basically, I wait until he's free and then saturate him with my presence. He's a deliberate lover, a careful lover, though saying so makes him sound inhibited. He's not. He's actually the opposite, and sometimes I feel the slightest bit self-conscious knowing what he's done. I've pressed him for details about what his life was like when he was younger, what his life was like before Bobby, after Bobby, and he's complied, though he always shakes his head. Why do you want to know? he asks. Because, I say, I want to know everything about you.

He lavishes me with attention, and I lap it up as if I'm deserving. You're good, Joel, you're so good, he says each night without provocation. These words he murmurs in the dark, in my ear, in the swell of our lovemaking, and each time, I want to swallow them whole. I've been waiting for them, for him, my entire life.

Sometimes, despite the satiety I've found with him, I have an odd feeling I've forgotten something. My work, I think, I miss my work. Then I dismiss the thought, too preoccupied with Adam to give a shit.

Really, I'm okay. I really think I'm okay without it.

+ + +

We're going to Kentucky for Thanksgiving so I can meet Adam's parents. I can't believe how easily I've accepted his invitation, and neither can he. I kind of expected a litany of excuses, he says. So did I, I tell him, and he laughs. He wants to leave the day before the holiday, spend the entire long weekend with his family. You realize this is the first time I've met anyone's parents, I tell him. Well, he admits, You're only the second guy I've brought home. They might hate me, I warn, You should at least prepare yourself for the possibility. They're not going to hate you, he says, They're going to love you. He kisses me, his hands cupping my face. I love you, he reminds me, And they will too.

Kyle's having a Halloween party. And don't you dare arrive without a costume, he tells me. I groan, but Adam loves the idea. That's because you haven't spent most of your life pretending to be someone else, I inform him. C'mon, he says, We'll think of something outrageous.

We start ransacking costume shops, trying on cowboy hats and combat gear, and then, while Adam's examining a mask of Bob Dole, I find a long, white wig and beard, white robes. I squirrel them away to the dressing room, then come out a few minutes later and tap Adam on the shoulder. Let there be light, I intone, folding my hands together and donning my holiest expression. Oh honey, he says, amused, I don't think you can pull that off. I turn toward the mirror. Actually, I look pretty convincing, except for the eyes. What do you think? I ask, You feeling devilish?

We keep our costumes a secret, get dressed the night of Kyle's party as excited as if we're kids about to go trick-or-treating. You look amazing, I tell him, checking out his costume. He's wearing shiny red spandex, a red fitted cap with horns, and he's drawn an evil mustache above his lips, a triangular goatee on his chin. Too bad we have to cover your ass with that forked tail, I tell him. You look positively irreverent, he says, and I grin.

We open the door of Kyle's condo to a plume of cigarette smoke and an array of characters from different centuries. Kyle, dressed in a cat costume I know he wore a few years ago, intercepts us before we can get past the entryway. A bit of a stretch, don't you think? he asks me. Adam laughs, and Kyle raises one claw and hisses half-heartedly. What happened? I ask, indicating his costume, You promised me tulle and sparkles. Oh, don't get me started, he says, Or I'll be blubbering all night. Stroking his whiskers, he leans a little closer, tells us the costume shop misplaced his order. I feel just like Mrs. de Winter, he confides, blinking back manufactured tears, You know, having my big day spoiled. Sighing, he tells us we should get a drink. And have a good time, he calls as we make our way to the bar.

We do have a good time, for the first couple of hours. We drink margaritas and dance to old disco music and field comments from people who find our costumes either offensive or hilarious. There's an angel around here, too, the giant cockroach tending bar tells us. Thanks for the tip, Gregor, I say.

Around midnight we run into Nathan, Adam's intern. Hey! the kid shouts, breaking into an exuberant smile. He's dressed as a pirate, with a patch covering one eye. I can't see a fucking thing, he tells me, and then to Adam, he says, I can't believe you're here! Adam introduces me, looking mildly embarrassed to be caught at the same party as one of his interns. You guys look awesome, Nathan says, examining us, I was supposed to come as a devil, too, but I looked like shit in the costume. His eyes slide down Adam's torso. You manage just fine though, he says as if I'm not even here, and then he flicks his attention back to me. Hey! he says, My boyfriend's dressed as an angel! Scouting around, he stands practically on tiptoe. Where is he, where is he, he's muttering. Well, I say, noticing my empty glass, but Nathan lets out a triumphant cry. Jack! Nathan shouts, and Jack turns.

He's dressed as an angel, in a white gown with iridescent wings. Ohhh shit, I breathe, but Nathan's already reaching for Jack's hand. Jack, this is Adam Atwater, Nathan tells him, and though twin spots of color appear high in Jack's cheeks as he recognizes me, he extends his hand to Adam. I've heard a lot about you, Adam tells him, and Jack looks startled, until he realizes that Adam means because of Nathan. I stare at the floor until Adam introduces me. Hey Jack, I mumble, smart enough not to offer my hand. Do you two know each other? Nathan asks, surprised. Yeah, I say at the same moment Jack says: Barely.

There's a part of me that hopes Adam won't understand what's going on, might not remember what I confessed a few weeks ago. For now he just looks confused, but I'm unlucky enough to witness the moment he realizes who's standing in front of him. Looking at Jack, I can understand the horror in his expression. Jack might be on the verge of nineteen, but he looks younger, especially dressed like he's just arrived from heaven. I'm going to get another drink, Jack mumbles, turning away, his wings shimmering in the candlelight. Um, Nathan says apologetically, staring after his boyfriend, and I mutter an excuse and slink after Jack.

Hey, can I talk to you? I ask, catching his sleeve. What do you want? he asks, and I gesture him aside. I want to apologize, I admit. You've got to be kidding, he says, After all this time? I've been out of the country, I say, feeling the faint flush of humiliation on my cheeks, and he nods. Yeah, he says, I heard.

He pulls a pack of Marlboros from somewhere up his sleeve, then gestures for me to follow him outside onto Kyle's deck. We're alone for the moment, and he turns away from the wind to light his cigarette. As an afterthought, he offers one to me. No thanks, I say faintly. He taps his cigarette over the balcony. You heard I was in Mexico? I ask, and he smirks. That's one way of putting it, he says, and I blink, suddenly grateful for the robes covering my arms. He brings his cigarette to his lips. You all better now? he asks, and I nod uncertainly. Last year, I say, I wasn't really...

I falter, and he raises his eyebrows. Whatever, he says, dragging on his cigarette. His fingers are long and thin, remarkably similar to my own; I never noticed. So how long have you been seeing Adam? he asks. Not long, I say, A couple of months. Nathan says he's a good guy, he tells me. He is, I murmur, and Jack nods. You don't deserve him, he says, so casually that I think I haven't heard him correctly. What? I ask, but Jack doesn't repeat himself. Instead, he adjusts his wings, checking his reflection in the window. Jack, I say, holding him back, I really am sorry. You're the one who has to live with yourself, Joel, he says.

I don't try to find Adam. Instead, I head right for Kyle's bedroom, where I think he has some excellent weed tucked away in his closet. But all I see is a bottle of tequila and a solitary shot glass. Everything okay? Kyle asks, spotting me as I close the door, but he looks like he's having way too much fun at his own party to take the question seriously. Fabulous, I say.

Thirty minutes later, we're sitting around the table in his kitchen: me; Kyle; Kyle's super straight neighbor; and Adam's friend, Scott, who Kyle's been sleeping with surreptitiously since the night of our cocktail party. We're slamming shots; I've had enough that I don't feel the liquor's heat anymore. And I'm smoking. I grabbed the cigarette right from Kyle's fingers myself. When Adam appears in the kitchen, I barely glance his way.

I've been wondering what happened to you, he murmurs, bending down beside me. I shrug, my cigarette between my lips, my beard pulled below my chin. Take a seat, girlfriend, Kyle offers, kicking an extra chair in his direction, and Adam sits. Shot? Kyle asks. Adam nods, and Kyle pours, then slides the glass across the table. I've lost count of how many I've had, think the one in my hand might be number three. Adam watches me drain my glass. We're leaving, he says the second I set it down. I'm okay right here, I tell him. This isn't up for debate, he says.

Outside we head toward his car without speaking. When I stumble over my robes, he holds me up with grim resignation. I shake him off, falling into the front seat of his car with such force I think for a second that I'm going to hurl. I almost wish I would. Aren't you going to say anything? I ask as he gets in beside me and fastens his seatbelt, and he cuts his eyes at me. What do you want me to say? he asks. I rest my head against the window, my cheek hot against the pane. He's young, he admits, and I grunt. Adam shakes his head, pulling away from the curb. I mean, my god, Joel, he says, He's just a kid.

I fall asleep or pass out, and when we get to his house, I pry open my eyes and fumble for the door handle. I'm going home, I tell him, climbing from his car and steadying myself against the bumper. Yeah, that's exactly what you should do, Adam says, Drive. You don't want me here anyway, I tell him, feeling the full weight of his condemnation. You're drunk, he says flatly, And I'm not letting you leave in this condition.

Dragging my feet, I follow him inside, where I fall into one of the kitchen chairs as he opens the back door for Indy. I told you how old he was, I mutter. He shakes his head, and I start picking at a hangnail. I told you how old he was, I repeat, pulling the skin with my teeth. Seeing him caught me off-guard, he says, I think that's understandable. I wince as my skin rips, then suck on the blood welling beside the nail. He said I don't deserve you, I say. He doesn't even know me, Adam tells me. But he's right, I whisper.

Upstairs I take a handful of Advil. I'm going to take a shower, Adam tells me. Okay, I mumble, knowing I probably shouldn't crawl between his sheets reeking as I do of alcohol and cigarettes. When I close my eyes, the room spins crookedly, like a malfunctioning carousel. After a minute I give up. I drop my robes on the floor beside the bed, then turn back the sheets and climb inside. The nightmare hurtles toward me.

I'm sitting at a table with my mother. She's talking, though I can't really hear her voice, can't make out what she's saying. I'm just so in awe of her presence, of her physical being: she's here, in front of me, she's here. She looks exactly the same, and I'm staring at her, so thankful, when she turns her beautiful smile in my direction. Then with a meat cleaver she cuts off my hand. The action's clean, swift, precise. The smile never leaves her face.

I wake with a moan, my hand crushed to my mouth. Stealing from Adam's bed, I make my way downstairs in the dark, where I sit on the sofa with my knees to my chest. My dream breathes just behind my eyes: her smile incredible, macabre. I bury my head deep in the crook of my arm; I can still smell smoke and liquor from Kyle's party on my skin, my breath. It takes a few minutes for me to realize that I'm rocking back and forth. Then I hear Adam coming down the stairs, padding across the floor. Joel? he says, and I lift my head.

I had a dream, I say. About what? he asks, lowering himself to the sofa beside me. She cut off my hand, I tell him. I look down for confirmation, surprised to find my limb intact. Who? he asks. My mother, I say. Oh, honey, he sighs. He strokes my arm with the tips of his fingers until I'm shivering. She knew, I say, and the words, finally spoken aloud, terrify me. She knew, I say, She knew what he was doing. It was just a dream, Adam tells me, You just had a bad dream. I yank my arm away from him. It wasn't a dream! I say, She knew what he was doing!

Bawling, I tell him everything I remembered last Christmas, everything I haven't let myself acknowledge since then. Your father was lying, Adam says. He wasn't! I insist, He wasn't lying! I tell him about leaving his office and seeing my mother, how she tried to stop me, how I ignored every message she left for me once I got back to Austin. It wasn't your fault, Adam says, knowing where I'm going, What she did wasn't your fault. But even if he's right, that's not the point. I hate her! I cry, I hate her, and I don't know what that means! Joel, he says, Honey. Don't you see? I wail, She's the one who gave me the painting! I cover my face with my hands. What does that mean? I say, Tell me what that means!

At first I fight back when he puts his arms around me. Don't touch me! I cry. Okay, he says, All right. But he manages to pin my arms to my sides, holding me so fiercely that even as I struggle against him, I can feel myself surrendering. He staggers under the sudden addition of my weight. Shh, he says, over and over, Shh.

I kiss him while I'm still crying. His mouth tastes faintly of sleep. Wait, he murmurs, but I shake my head. He's the one thing that makes me feel like I know what I'm doing, and I say at the edge of his mouth, Please. No, he whispers, trying to stop my hands, and I moan. Please, I say, Please don't tell me no. Joel, he says, hesitating. Please, I say, but the word doesn't make it past my lips as anything audible.

+ + +

Upstairs I lie in Adam's bed. Sit up, he says, dropping two pills in the palm of my hand and passing me a glass of water. I swallow whatever he's given me without protest. I feel as if my insides have been scooped out, all that pulp and mush and string scraped away. When Adam gets into bed beside me and touches my shoulder, I think I might just cave in on myself.

The next morning, I wake belly down, my hand curled tightly beside my mouth. I'm alone, and a quick glance at the clock confirms that Adam's probably been at work for hours. I didn't even hear him leave. I sit up, my abdomen creased with prints from the sheet, then hold my aching head in my hands. I have a feeling that if I don't get up now, if I don't get something in my stomach, I'm either going to hurl all over these flannel sheets or I'm going to fall dead asleep again and not wake at all until he comes home. That's the last image I want him to have of me after last night: crashed out in his bed on my sixteenth hour of sleep.

Getting to my feet, I pull a pair of pajama bottoms from the drawer Adam cleared over Labor Day weekend. Then I reach for one of his tee shirts and go into the bathroom to brush the night from my mouth. I don't see how I missed Adam showering this morning, and with renewed humiliation I reach for my cell. I owe him a call.

But I find him downstairs, sitting at the breakfast table, his laptop open in front of him. Why aren't you at work? I ask. I thought I'd work from home today, he says. I fold my arms across my chest. How are you? he asks. Fine, I say, shrugging, and his brow furrows. I try a laugh. I don't know what happened, I mumble, I had way too much to drink. Please tell me you're joking, he says, Please tell me you're not going to blame what happened on one too many tequila shots.

I turn away from him and reach for the coffee pot. I'm fine, I tell him, Really. But I have to lower the pot because my hand's shaking. We need to talk about this, Joel, he says, I want to talk about this. But I don't! I say. I clear my throat. I don't, I tell him more calmly. I set the pot on the counter. You should've gone to work, I say.

I head home thirty minutes later. You can sleep here, he points out when I tell him I need some rest. Please, I say, Just give me some space today. He doesn't look happy. I'll call you later, he says, Or maybe I'll just come by. Why? I say, Are you afraid you're going to find me hanging from the rafters? Tears spring to his eyes, and I blink. Sorry, I mutter. Get some rest, he says, Get some rest, and I'll talk to you later.

Standing at the threshold of my bedroom, though, I know there's no way in hell that I'm going to be able to fall asleep here, and I'm more than a little annoyed that Adam had that figured out before I even left. I should've stayed at his house, should've stayed in his bed. I end up calling him from my cell at the foot of his driveway in the middle of the afternoon. Ten seconds later, he's opening the front door. I couldn't sleep, I say. Okay, baby, he says, pulling me close, Okay.

+ + +

The next week passes with little reference to what happened on Halloween. Not that Adam hasn't tried to get me to talk; I've just cut him off before he can get going, and after the first few attempts he drops the subject entirely. By the weekend he's grown quiet himself, though he rouses himself into extending an invitation for dinner Friday night. Just the two of us, he adds, as though I'd assumed that, despite our circumstances, I might be thinking he was planning a party.

I'm waiting for him when he gets home from work, and I watch television from his bed while he's showering. You wearing jeans? he asks, opening the bathroom door and taking in my prone position. I'm not planning on changing, I tell him. He nods, drying off. There's nothing left of his tan—or mine, for that matter—and his skin's a silky white, luminescent in the light from the bathroom. His legs are freshly shaven, too; I can tell from the prick of blood on his ankle where he must have cut himself. He hasn't had the time for a wax. Eyes on the television, he rubs his hair with his towel, then looks over when he feels my stare. Come here, I say. He hangs the towel around his neck, but he doesn't move. C'mon, I say, We don't have a reservation, do we? He shakes his head. Come here, then, I cajole, and he steps to the edge of the bed. I sit up, straddling his legs. Palms spread, I place both hands on his quadriceps, the skin smooth, warm. When the muscle in his left leg jumps, I glance up at him. You riding tomorrow? I ask conversationally, sliding my hands around the back of his legs and cupping his ass. Yeah, he says. Who're you riding with? I ask. He runs one hand through my hair without answering.

I've been using him—using this—the past five days. I can't get to sleep at night without him, can't get my mind off of what's happened long enough to relax. I take him desperately, like a drug, craving whatever soporific release he can offer me, however momentary. He's aware of what I'm doing. But he never refuses me, never, and I capitalize on his generosity. Go to him again and again.

We don't make it to dinner. I should shower again, Adam murmurs, and I look over at him, at the fine sheen of sweat on his chest. Go ahead, I say, but he just rolls over and closes his eyes. I place one hand on the small of his back. Joel, he says. Hmm, I murmur, sliding my index finger up his spine. I think you should get back into therapy, he says. I let my hand fall. I'm so glad you told me, Joel, he whispers, I'm so glad you told me, but I think you need to talk to Lydia.

He's right. Of course he's right. I haven't worked in months, haven't painted a thing since I got back from Mexico. My self-imposed break has taken on a life of its own. And my mother…

I can't imagine what you're going through right now, he's saying, I can't imagine what you're feeling, and I want to help, I want to help, but I don't know what to do. He pauses, and I realize he's on the verge of tears. Please, he says, catching my hand, Think about what I'm saying. I nod, and he kisses my fingers. I love you, he whispers, I just want you to be okay.

But I'm not okay. I'm not, and at the beginning of the next week I break down and make an appointment. To be honest, I'm lucky Lydia's available; with the holidays approaching people are freaking the fuck out. But we have a history, and she has a cancellation, and she manages to squeeze me in.

I don't say anything to Adam until the night before my appointment, partly because I want the flexibility of backing out if I think I'm not going to be able to handle going after all, but mainly because I know he'll react with such relief, such gratitude, that the pressure will suffocate me. He reacts true to form. God, thank you, he says when I tell him, Thank you for agreeing to go. He offers to come along, and though I know he's just trying to be nice, I can't help remembering that James suggested the exact same thing before I started seeing Bryan. Thank you, I say, But I need to do this myself.

I meet Lydia at her office the following morning, already feeling nauseous. Entering the building, I eye the nearest trash can, wondering how pathetic holding onto the rim and puking up last night's dinner would render me. But the moment passes, and I make my way up the stairs and into Lydia's office, where I collapse into a chair in a waiting room I haven't seen since March. Her décor is nothing like Bryan's, and if I'm honest, I have to admit I'm glad. Bryan's office reminded me of Jess's apartment, which always left me with an uncomfortable whiff of my father. Money, I suppose, and it's pretty clear that Lydia's not in this for the cash. She's half the price of Bryan, and while that would probably buy her a decent pair of shoes, she apparently doesn't funnel her proceeds into either her wardrobe or her office. Walls the color of a pale sunset, furniture that looks more like she's scavenging area thrift stores than showing off her latest find. I think she gets her clothes there, too.

Bryan helped me; he did. But there's something about Lydia that calms me in a way Bryan never could.

When she opens her door, she looks so pleased to find me in her waiting room I can't help smiling. Joel, she says as I get to my feet, I'm happy to see you.

I end up telling her everything: that I've been to Mexico, that I've gotten in touch with Adam, that we're trying to make something work but I can't seem to come to grips with some of my history. I describe in as neutral a voice as possible what happened after Kyle's Halloween party, about my dream, about my mother. I don't cry, but I'm shaking, hard enough that I don't dare take a sip from the cup of water in front of me. Tell me, she says when I'm finished, What would you like to happen?

I don't even have to think.

I want to work, I say, God, Lydia, I just want to work again.

She tells me that over the next few days she wants me to think about painting. Don't dwell on the work you did in Mexico, she says, Don't think about starting something new, just think about the act itself, that moment when you're inside what you're doing. I nod, and she nods back. Okay, Joel, she says, I'll see you next week.

+ + +

I feel marginally better over the next few days, though I'm more tired than I've been in a long time. Adam and I spend a quiet weekend at home; he gives me space, doesn't suggest I give him a recap of my session or ask what I've been thinking since. Anything I can do, he says on Sunday evening, and I'm not sure whether he's posing a question or simply offering his support. Either way, I feel indebted.

I try to take Lydia's advice. I close my eyes more than once: in Adam's bedroom when he's at work, in the shower, in the afternoon glow of the back room, and I try to summon that moment when everything's yet before me. I can conjure nothing. Oddly, the thought doesn't reduce me to tears. Instead, I'm numb.

I don't understand, I say to Lydia during my next session, What am I doing wrong? She tells me I have to be patient, that I can't expect to spend an hour with her and find myself changed. But I want..., I say. I know, she says when she sees that I can't finish my thought, And trust me, that's half the battle.

We don't schedule an appointment for the next week, during the Thanksgiving holiday. Instead, we arrange to meet on the third of

December, a date that sounds hopelessly distant when I think of all I'm going to have to maneuver before then.

I'm not looking forward to the holiday. Don't get me wrong; I don't want to be alone. But in light of the past few weeks I'm not up for meeting Adam's family, and he knows it. They're going to love you, he repeats once too often, and I realize that someone in his family—most likely his sister, Julia—knows more about me than makes me comfortable. But I don't bail on him. This much, I think. I owe him this much.

His family receives me with little acrimony, considering. This, Adam says in a tone of reverence when we arrive, Is Joel. His mother gives me a guarded hug; his father shakes my hand. Thanks for having me, I mumble, and Adam slides his arm around my shoulder, right in front of everyone. I think I'm the only one who sees the look his sister gives her husband.

That first night, we eat an early dinner for the benefit of Adam's niece and nephew, who spiral around the dining room table with excitement. They're never going to eat, Adam, Julia protests when he jumps up and starts passing out gifts halfway through dinner, but she's smiling, and walking behind his chair a moment later, she kisses the top of his head. He reaches up and takes her hand.

As soon as I'm able, I escape to the bathroom, where I rummage quietly for the Tylenol. I take a small fistful, and by the time I get to the living room Julia and her husband are herding the kids into the bathroom, and Adam's mother is talking about getting the dishes cleared. Let us help, I offer, and though she waves us back to our seats, we insist. Lindsey and Rye tumble into the kitchen to say good night as we're finishing; Adam swoops them off the floor, and they shriek. Don't let the bed bugs bite, Adam tells them. Lindsey giggles, but Rye's forehead creases. Bugs? he asks, turning to Julia. Of course not, she says, frowning, There are no bugs.

We settle on the sofa in the living room after Lindsey and Rye go to bed. Adam slings his arm around me, his thigh pressed against my own; Julia seems just as discomfited by our proximity as I am. I've never been so demonstrative, and I can't help but hold myself stiffly, as if I'm waiting for a reprimand. So how are you, Julia? Adam asks. I'm great, she says, How are *you*? Good, he says, glancing at me, We're good.

We're up later than I'd like. My headache hovers just along the periphery, and I drink one too many bourbons trying to kill it for good. We finally make our excuses just after midnight, then head into Adam's old room. We get to stay together? I'd asked before we arrived, and he laughed. You all right? he asks now, noting the look on my face, and I nod. Good, he says, kissing me. He starts to unbutton my jeans; I shrug away. I need a shower, I tell him, and he ushers me into the bathroom. Towels, he says, indicating the linen closet, Soap, shampoo. Thanks, I say, and he touches my arm. Relax, Joel, he says.

I stand under the shower, head hung, eyes closed, and think about where I was last year at this time. With him, on the cusp of possibility.

Considering everything that's happened since, I can't believe I'm here. I tilt my head to the side, willing the water to loosen the knots from my neck. What causes me the most trepidation is trying to picture myself a year from now. I can barely feel this moment; I'm dead mentally, emotionally. Creatively. I touch my hand to my naked chest. Sometimes I'm surprised that my heart still beats.

+ + +

Thanksgiving Day wears me out. I had trouble falling asleep, and I awaken ridiculously late as a result, a faux pas not lost on Julia, who asks when I appear in the kitchen well after ten if I've had a good rest. Something about the way she's posed the question embarrasses me; Adam and I aren't used to being quiet. You want some breakfast? Adam asks, wrapping his arms around me. Maybe just some coffee, I say, extricating myself.

By dinner I've heard Bobby's name at least a half a dozen times. Julia's the one doing the talking, mentioning his name casually, in a way anyone would: as she relates an anecdote, reminisces about a previous holiday. But her comments become increasingly pointed, and by the time we've finished dinner Adam looks hurt and confused. I'm sorry, he says when we catch a moment alone, I don't know why she's talking about him so much. Maybe because they've never seen you with anyone else, I tell him, Maybe because they liked him. I fold my arms across my chest. Maybe because his picture's everywhere, I mutter, and he glances around the living room, startled. I didn't realize, he says. He starts taking photos from the bookcase, the desk. You don't have to put them away, I tell him, but he shakes his head, stacking the frames on a shelf in the closet. I want them to love you as much as I do, Joel, he says. That's not going to happen, I tell him. They like you, he protests, and I say, They're tolerating me, Adam.

He lowers himself to the edge of the sofa, his hands between his knees. Would I have liked him? I ask, knowing I don't have to explain who I mean. I don't think so, he says, shaking his head, You really wouldn't have had much in common. He crosses one leg over the other; he's wearing jeans, and the material wrinkles softly around his knees. I don't compare the two of you, you know, he says. I snort. I don't, he insists. Don't you ever think about the fact that if he hadn't died, we wouldn't have met? I ask. Not really, he tells me, and I say, You're lying. He looks away, then shakes his head. Who knows what would've happened? he says, I mean, maybe if he hadn't gotten sick, we would've stayed together, maybe we would've split up, maybe you'd be— Dead? I interject. I was going to say with someone else, he tells me. He reaches for my hand. I love you, Joel, he says, It's just that simple.

I'm not so sure. He's said the words on four separate occasions; I can't bring myself to say them back. Each time I hear them I lock them away for safekeeping, but I don't return them, not once. I don't know why, I mutter now. I know you don't, he says, removing his hand from mine, And I think that's part of the problem.

+ + +

Friday starts off a little easier. We make brunch, hang out with the kids for a while, then traipse up to the stables to look over the horses. You up for a ride? Adam asks me, and ten minutes later, I find myself astride one of the older mares. Adam rides casually, holding the reins lightly in one hand; I'm gripping my own, my knees digging into the saddle. You look sexy up there, he tells me, lowering his voice so no one else hears. Then this is all worthwhile, I allow.

That evening, while Julia and her mother are doing some early Christmas shopping, Adam offers to give Rye a bath. Would you? Ivan says. Joel and I can manage, he says, and I look at him, eyebrows raised. Adam just smiles, snagging Rye on his next pass through the living room. Rye shrieks with laughter, lets Adam tuck him upside down under his arm. Have you seen Rye? Adam asks me. I think he's in the kitchen, I say, and Adam traipses into the kitchen as Rye giggles. Found him! Adam shouts, and a moment later, he returns with Rye riding his shoulders. Rye looks impressed; Adam's taller than Ivan, and Rye reaches one little arm to the ceiling to see if he can touch it. Almost, Adam says, heading down the hallway toward the bathroom. I follow, watching them pause in the doorway so Rye can duck his head. You're going to pee before you take a bath, right? Adam says, lowering his nephew to the floor, and Rye giggles.

When Rye's finally in the bath, he looks up at me. I'm leaning against the sink, my arms crossed over my chest. Play, he says, and I glance at Adam, who's sitting on the edge of the tub. I think your uncle wants to play with you, I tell him, but Rye's extending a pudgy hand in my direction. I take the plastic submarine from his fingers. You want me to play? I ask, and when he nods, I roll up my sleeves. I feel kind of touched, and I duck my submarine under the water, turning the periscope in Rye's direction. Enemy has been spotted at three o'clock, I say, muffling the words with my hand so I sound as if I'm speaking into a radio. Rye laughs. Incoming, I say, sending a wave of water Rye's way. You're good with him, Adam says, smiling as Rye cracks up. Yeah, well, don't get any ideas, I tell him.

We play for a while, and then Adam soaps Rye down. Slippery, Rye says, patting his belly. Shit, he's cute, and when Adam hauls him out of the tub, I dry him off with a towel. Lindsey's back and she's looking for you, Ivan says to Adam, appearing in the doorway. Okay, Adam says easily, scooping toys onto the bathmat. I'm patting them dry when I see Lindsey. Her lips look especially pink, as if she's been sucking on a peppermint. Hey, sweetheart, Adam says, but Lindsey looks right past him. Did you cut your arms? she asks me.

Adam sucks in his breath, and I hastily slide my sleeves to my wrists. Mama says you cut them, she tells me. Your mother should keep her mouth shut, Adam snaps. Adam, I say, but Lindsey seems unfazed by such blasphemy. Did you have an accident? she asks. Something like that, I say, and she looks skeptical, like she's caught me in a lie. Mama says you did it on purpose, she says. That's enough, Lindsey! Adam says. Lindsey looks solemnly at her uncle, then again at my arms, though there's nothing now to see. Did it hurt? she asks.

This time, Adam doesn't say anything. They're both silent, waiting for my answer. I tear my gaze from Adam's and focus on Lindsey. She has a fantastic elfin face, smoky blue eyes. A little, I admit. Can I see? she asks, and I hesitate, then slowly push back my sleeves. She examines my arms with all the detachment of a coroner. Did you use a great big knife? she asks, and then Julia's sweeping Lindsey out of the bathroom without giving either one of us time to respond.

Not that we'd have the wherewithal. Adam doesn't move from his position on the floor, and after a minute I start dropping the toys in a bucket beside the tub. A great big knife, he says, and I sit back on my heels. I used a box cutter, I say, and he flinches, as if it's his own skin I'd cut. I'm sorry, I say, I thought you knew. He shoots me a look of fury. Oh, I know, he says, I was the one who stopped you from bleeding to death, remember?

Julia barely speaks to me the rest of the evening. I keep waiting for Adam to intercede, but he doesn't. I decide to turn in early, make apologies halfway through the movie we've rented. No one persuades me to stay.

I lie in Adam's old room, thinking about Bobby. He slept here, made love in this bed. He was alive, as alive as I am right now, and now he's what? Six feet under? Fragments in Adam's memory? If Adam hadn't found me that night, if he'd gotten caught up in his family, if he'd decided I wasn't worth the time after all, would he even know I was gone? I picture my house sold, my Explorer parked in my father's garage. My paintings in a landfill somewhere, my clothes on someone else's back. I'd be a wisp in the ether, something barely remembered, nothing.

The next morning, Adam's quiet and hungover, and Julia chooses the wrong moment to confront him about last night. They argue in hushed voices while Adam's parents take the kids riding. Lindsey's a precocious child, Ivan finally says. He nods to himself, then inclines his head in the direction of the kitchen, where Adam and Julia are under the apparent impression that we can't hear what they're saying. Julia's very protective of him, he adds. No shit, I say, but he shakes his head. You'd understand, he tells me, If you knew what he went through with Bobby.

I ask Ivan if I can borrow his car. He silently hands me his keys, and I make my way to the nearest convenience store, where I buy a pack of cigarettes. Leaning against the hood, I light up, smoke one cigarette straight through to the end, then light another.

When I get back, Adam and Julia are no longer speaking to each other. I don't want to be responsible for coming between the two of you, I tell him, and he says, You don't want to be responsible for anything! I take a step back, and he blinks. We've got to get out of here, he says, We have to get back home. He goes in search of a phone and actually calls to see if we can get an earlier flight; everything's booked. He's practically in tears. Adam, I say, We're fine here, we're fine. He shakes his head: no, no. We're fine, I say, We're leaving tomorrow.

I convince him that we need to do our best to put up a front for his parents. I'm determined not to be the source of any more trouble, especially since they've gone out of their way to make me comfortable. Twenty hours, I say, looking at my watch, We can handle that.

That afternoon, I try to make myself scarce so Adam can spend the little time he has left with his family. He's barely had the opportunity to talk to his father alone, and he disappears with him at one point; I see them later from the back porch, where I'd been hoping to sneak a cigarette. They're talking, Adam with his head down and Mr. Atwater with his hand on Adam's shoulder. His father's nothing like my own.

Mrs. Atwater's kind, though I know she must be worried. She sends Julia to the store while Rye's napping, while Ivan's watching a video with Lindsey, and invites me into the kitchen for a cup of tea. I follow apprehensively, but she just sets a pot between us. You know, she says after a moment, sitting back in her chair and tapping the rim of her cup, You're very much like I expected. I look away; I'm aware I haven't made the best impression. But she smiles and tells me that's not a criticism. A mother knows her son, she adds. I shift, but she's gazing into her cup, and she doesn't notice. He loves you very much, she tells me, and I suddenly have the strangest feeling that she can almost see why.

At dinner that night we're all quieter than we've been since Adam and I first arrived. Salad passes from one of us to another, wine pours into glasses, and finally, after Lindsey and Rye have wandered off and we're sipping our coffee, Adam's mother says, You know, Joel, I don't think that I've asked about your work.

Such a generous question, and such a terrible one, as well. What do you want to know? I say. Are you any good? she asks, and before I can cry or run or admit the truth, Adam says, He's wonderful. He looks at me, naked in his longing. Some of his paintings, he says, Haunt you for weeks, months after you've seen them. He leans forward, speaking with such fervor that his voice trembles. Some of them, he says, I can't get out of my mind.

His parents exchange glances. Well, his mother says soothingly, as if she's trying to smooth the edges for him, and he turns to me. I don't think you realize how incredible you are, he says. I murmur a thank you, wondering which paintings he could possibly have in mind. I'm serious, he insists. I take a closer look at him and then at his wine glass, trying to tally how much he's had to drink. I'm not drunk! he tells me. At any rate, Mrs. Atwater continues, I find it refreshing that in this day and age you're able to make a living doing something you love.

I murmur something unintelligible, well aware that we're treading on unsteady ground. But Julia steps in. You don't really earn a living with your painting, she says, Do you, Joel?

So he told her. He's told her everything, and I don't have the energy for pretense any longer.

No, I say, I don't.

Excusing myself, I slip out the back door before anyone can stop me. Night chill coaxes me behind the stable, where I light a cigarette, cupping my hand around the flame to block the wind. Hey, Adam says in a low voice a minute later, sliding his hands in his pockets. I nod, making no attempt to hide my cigarette. Can I sit? he asks, gesturing toward the bench I've chosen, and I shrug. He lowers himself beside me without removing his hands from his pockets. I'm sorry, he says, inclining his head in the direction of the house, I probably shouldn't have confided in her. Hindsight, I agree, but he doesn't smile.

When we get back…, he starts, but he doesn't finish his thought. When we get back, what? I ask. We just need to go home, he mumbles, and I take another drag from my Marlboro. Why? I say, Are things so different there? He gives me a hurt look, and I turn my attention to the sky.

You're not painting, he says after a minute. No, I say, finishing off my cigarette and crushing it against the heel of my shoe. Why not? he asks. I start to shrug but find that I can't be so cavalier about something that has always defined me. There's nothing there, I tell him. So that's it? he says, You're just going to throw away a lifetime of work? There's nothing there, Adam, I say. What's that supposed to mean? he asks. You know what it means, I say, You saw what I did in Mexico.

He has the decency to look away. If that's the best I can do— I say, and he says, That's not the best you can do, I've seen what you can do! He stands up and starts to pace. Have you talked to Lydia about this? he asks. Of course I've talked to Lydia, I say irritably. What does she say? he asks, and I give him the same line Lydia gave me: I can't expect everything to change overnight. She's right, he says, You just have to keep seeing her. I'm not sure I have the energy, I tell him. Maybe it's time to try medication— he starts. I groan. Do you honestly think I have any interest in feeling more dead than I do right now? I ask, and he starts to cry. You're slipping away from me, Joel, he says, I can feel you slipping away. Stop crying, I snap, I can't handle your pain, too! He covers his mouth with his hand; sometimes I can't believe my capacity for cruelty. I just want to help you, he whispers. I am not your reclamation project, I tell him.

You're right, he finally says, You're not.

THE CROSSING

3

I derive little pleasure from the weeks following Thanksgiving. The Christmas lights, the decorations, the approaching parties provide greater consternation this year than they have since my mother's death, and I quickly decline each of Adam's invitations. He suggests visiting the Trail of Lights; I tell him I'm not up for the crowds. I give him the same excuse when he mentions a shopping excursion, add that the commercialism of the whole season really gets to me. Let's do a tree then, he says, No crowds and we already have everything we need. I acquiesce, but when the time comes to string the lights, I sit in the armchair with a beer and watch him instead. He's meticulous and ends up with a beautiful tree; I do no more than congratulate him on the accomplishment.

I don't know what he wants from me, I say to Lydia, What does he expect? I've already told her about our visit to Kentucky, about our conversation the night before we came home. What do *you* think he wants? she asks. I don't know, I say, shrugging, For me to be okay, I guess. She presses her lips together without taking her eyes from mine. I get the impression she knows something I don't.

My father calls. He and Catherine are heading out of town for the holiday. Aruba? I say, and he tells me they're planning a short weekend in New England. Catherine wants a white Christmas, he says. I grunt. My father pauses at the sound, then tells me he didn't call to start an argument. Why *are* you calling? I ask. Catherine thought you might like to come down for a visit, he tells me, We were thinking next weekend.

Adam and I are supposed to go to a party next weekend. Scott issued the invitation weeks ago. We've committed, though to be honest, I can't imagine I'll be in the mood. I don't know, I say, Next weekend I'm busy. Well, I'm going to need a decision soon, my father informs me, Because that's the only free weekend we have. Fine, I sigh, I'll be there.

Scott's party is next weekend, Adam reminds me when I break the news. Well, this is the only time my father can see me, I say, So what do you want me to do? Stay here! he says. Adam, I say, I can't refuse to see him. Why not? he asks, and for the first time since our last morning in Mexico there's real challenge in his voice. Do you want me to leave? I ask, afraid of his answer. No, I don't want you to leave, he says, gritting his teeth, I want you to call your father back and tell him you're not coming.

Well, that's not going to happen, and when I see that we're at an impasse, I let myself out the back door, where I lean against the railing of the deck and fumble in my pocket for a cigarette I don't find. How long, I wonder, before *that* habit dies? Instead, I stare into the night, at the glimmers of light surrounding the lake, houses outfitted for the holiday.

I'm not sure I have the energy to make it through the twenty-fifth. I'm not sure I have the energy to make it through the weekend.

The door opens, and Adam steps beside me, his eyes on the view. Pretty, he murmurs, and I nod. He's already found fault with me; why make the situation worse by admitting that the same lights he admires trigger in me a decade-old anxiety? But on a subconscious level he seems to know what I'm thinking because he moves a little closer, until his arm brushes mine. I don't like fighting with you, he says. I don't like fighting with you either, I mumble, and he says, Let's not then.

He threads his fingers through mine. You're cold, he says. Pretty much all the time, I admit, and he pulls me into his arms. We'll figure this out, he says, Okay?

I'm not sure what he means, if he's talking about the holidays or the trip I'm making to Houston next weekend or my relationship with my father in general. I tell him what he wants to hear anyway. Yeah, I say, Okay. We'll figure this out, he says, We have plenty of time.

+ + +

My father's selling his house. I don't know why I'm surprised; I would've expected him to sell long before now. But he could've found a better way of telling me than sticking a sign in the yard, and when he opens the front door, I say, immediately forgetting all the prep work I've done with Lydia, You're selling the house? Catherine's standing behind him with a hesitant smile. We just signed the paperwork today, she says. I look at my father, who nods. Why didn't you tell me? I ask, knowing the question makes no sense whatsoever, and even my father seems taken aback. I hardly consider my father's house my home. Still. My mother lived here.

And then I think: sell the fucker.

I get ready for dinner that night with a scotch beside me on the vanity in the bathroom. We're going out to celebrate. I feel as if my father's washing his hands of the years he lived here with my mother, with me, and even though I might have my own reasons for wanting to forget those years, I'm not necessarily ready to participate in his repudiation of the past.

Dinner, though, isn't half-bad. My father has invited another couple, and they're actually pretty cool. Carlton tells me while his wife and Catherine are talking and my father's arguing with the sommelier that he hasn't lived in Texas for long, and he's never been to Austin. I hear it's pretty laid-back, he says, and I tell him that's true, that the population has exploded in the past five years, and the cost of living's getting kind of ridiculous, but it's worth every penny. You have a girlfriend? he asks as my father's turning back to our conversation. I give Catherine an inadvertent glance. No, I say, shaking my head and realizing too late that I never told my father I cut ties with Jess. But he obviously knows, either because Catherine confided the news at some point or because no one by that name—of either gender—came to see me when I was in the hospital. In any case, he doesn't look surprised, and before Carlton can pursue his line of questioning, Catherine suggests that my father tell everyone about the plans for their new house.

There's more laughter at dinner than I can remember there being at any meal with my father in years. Carlton's wife has a sense of humor that matches her husband's, and the two of them tell us a few anecdotes about their children that have us practically in tears. As we're finishing our meal, my father catches my eye and grins. Let's have an after-dinner drink, he says, and though he offers the suggestion to the entire group, he's looking right at me. Yeah, I say, Okay.

We go into the bar, where we secure the sofa and chairs in front of the fireplace. Why don't you let me get this? Carlton asks after my father has beckoned the waiter. But my father, ever the patriarch, shakes his head. He orders for us all, his voice quiet, assertive; people listen when my father speaks.

The drinks arrive, and I take a sip of my scotch. Beside me on the sofa Catherine and Carlton's wife are drinking cosmopolitans, talking about planning a trip to Costa Rica, and I turn again to my father. He and Carlton are sitting in wingbacks which straddle a small table perpendicular to the rest of us. My father's drinking scotch, of course, and I notice that Carlton's drinking the same. He sees me looking and raises his glass in acknowledgment. My father actually smiles. I can't recall the last time I've seen him so remarkably at ease, and I'm trying to pinpoint the moment when he reaches into the pocket of his suit and extracts a cigar case.

I stiffen. Sliding a Cohiba halfway from the leather, he allows Carlton to take the cigar himself. There's an offhand remark about the aroma as Carlton draws the cigar across his upper lip just below his nostrils, and then my father turns to me, the case extended. He's still nodding his head in agreement to Carlton's comment, but as he meets my eyes and realizes what he's done, he balks. For a long, unpleasant moment we stare at each other. Don't you smoke, Joel? Carlton asks curiously, and my father snatches the cigar case from within my grasp. No, I say, I don't.

My father doesn't look at me. He seems greatly embarrassed, his cheeks flushed the same pink as Catherine's drink, and Carlton has to repeat his request for a cigar cutter. My father fishes in his pocket and hands one over. Carlton trims his cigar with relish as my father silently passes him a lighter. Joel, Carlton says, You don't know what you're missing.

I excuse myself. Crouched down on the asphalt at the back of the restaurant, I call Adam's cell from my own. When he finally answers, I burst into tears. Joel? he says, and I start wailing. Okay, baby, he says, Hang on, hang on. The sound of Scott's party dims, and I hear a door closing. Okay, Adam says, What's wrong? I blurt out a mostly incoherent reply, still crying. Look, I need you to calm down, Joel, he tells me, I can't understand you. Taking a deep breath, I wipe my face with the back of my hand. Tell me what happened, he says.

By the time I'm finished I'm speaking entirely without emotion. Adam's the one who's furious, and I straighten, taking a furtive look back toward the restaurant to make sure I'm not being sought. I want you to come home, Adam's saying, I want you to get in your car, and I want you to come home. I can't, I say, and Adam says, Yes, you can. I can't, I insist, I've been drinking for the past three hours. Then I want you to go to a hotel, he tells me, and I realize with a twinge of guilt that I've destroyed his evening by calling him. I'll be fine, I say. How can you even go back there with him? he asks, and I start walking toward the restaurant, grit from the parking lot crunching beneath my shoes. I guess I think I don't have a choice, I say.

My father and I don't talk about what happened. He doesn't even look at me, doesn't say a word until the next morning when he finds me loading the Explorer. You're heading back early, he observes, and I shoot him a look that makes him turn and go inside. I leave without saying goodbye.

When I get back to Austin, Adam's waiting for me. He looks tired and hungover and way older than thirty-four, and I'm well aware that I'm the one responsible. Still he takes me in his arms and tells me he loves me, the words whispered against my hair. I push him gently away.

+ + +

We have a bad week. I think we both know we're approaching some kind of confrontation, and we pick at each other without actually fighting, saving our strength for whatever's coming.

I've agreed to go to Adam's office Christmas party, and frankly, I think that's part of the reason I'm in such a funk. We haven't been anywhere together, not since Kyle's party on Halloween, and as the occasion approaches, I find myself wondering how I've managed to get myself roped into not only going out but going to a holiday celebration for a computer manufacturer. Why do you want me to go anyway? I ask him midweek. What do you mean? he says. Won't I make some of your colleagues uncomfortable? I ask, and he narrows his eyes. I work my ass off for that company, he tells me, I'm not going to leave you at home just because someone might not be able to handle seeing us together. I find his insistence on including me a bit incendiary and would probably assume he was using me to make a point if I didn't know him any better. But I think he just truly wants to be with me, and that makes me feel even more like shit for wanting to bail out.

Saturday morning there's a snap to the air when we let Indy outside, and we light a fire in the fireplace and curl up on the sofa, cradling our coffee mugs. I could stay here all day, Adam murmurs, and so we do. We don't turn on the television, we don't pick up a book. We don't talk. We just stare into the fire and drink coffee, and when I move my cold feet into his lap, he simply shifts to accommodate them. There are moments when I think everything might be all right.

We have such a good day together that we're pressed for time getting ready. I've never seen you in a suit, he tells me, knotting his tie. It's been a while, I admit, and he steps closer. You look good, he says.

We haven't tired of each other. I want him just as desperately as I ever have, and there's no doubt in my mind that he feels the same. But there's a yearning in his gaze that I can't quite reconcile, and every time he touches me, I'm that much more aware of what I'm holding back. We're going to be late, I murmur, and he nods.

+ + +

Pulling up to the Driskill, I see a swirl of holiday revelers spill onto the sidewalk. Ready? Adam asks beside me, and I eye the twinkling white lights with trepidation. I should've protested, should've bagged, should've claimed a migraine. C'mon, he says, knowing what I'm thinking and catching my hand, I promise it won't be that bad.

But upstairs he's accosted before we can even make our way to the bar. He's well-liked, I discover, and well-known, and he introduces me to more people in ten minutes than I could possibly want to meet in a lifetime. A pianist draws Christmas melodies from a grand piano in the middle of the room, and I agree with one of Adam's colleagues when she confides that Christmas is her favorite time of year. Adam touches my shoulder; he's concerned about me even here, even now. When we finally reach the bar, I ask for a scotch, then down it in one gulp. Adam orders a glass of wine, takes one sip. I realize with dismay that I'm expected to pace myself.

A couple of hours later, we've listened dutifully to a series of congratulatory speeches interspersed with anxious jokes about Y2K, and made our way through the buffet line. I've nothing left to say to the woman seated on my right; she wanders off, and I stare into the solitary candle in the center of the table, debating whether or not I should head to the bar for a third glass of wine. Are you all right? Adam asks, leaning toward me. He seems concerned that my companion has left the table—she was obviously keeping me quietly occupied—and I see him glance at my wine. Instead of bristling, I say, My second. I wasn't counting, he says. Bullshit, I say, though not unpleasantly. He rewards me with half a grin, then catches someone's eye and raises his hand in greeting. Come with me, he says, pushing back his chair.

I follow him, automatically extending my hand when Adam introduces me. I'm offered a puzzled expression in return. My partner, Adam clarifies, and I'm far more taken aback than Adam's colleague. Ah, the guy says without animosity, but the second etiquette allows, I excuse myself. At the bar I ask for a glass of water, and holding my drink, I head for the vacant sofa near the staircase. Music bellows from one of the adjacent rooms, heavy on the bass; after a moment I recognize the unmistakable sound of the Village People. Someone wanders past, tie loosened. The party's obviously morphing into a less formal affair.

Partner. I broach the word tentatively, as if it's blown glass capable of shattering in my hands. I've not thought beyond the terms *boyfriend*, *lover*. I've not thought beyond the immediate. I see Adam only as a means of getting me through, of holding me together. He's what brought me back to Austin, he's what gets me out of bed every morning. I can't get along without him. Sitting there at the top of the stairs, I think about what he's given me, what I've refused to reciprocate. He's asked for so little. And yet from the moment we first met, everything has been about what I want, what I need. I think back to a recent session I had with Lydia; I remember complaining about Adam's frustration when I refused to get excited about the holiday. What does he want from me? I'd whined. How egotistical. He wants the same thing from me that I ask of him, the same thing I wanted from James all those years ago: everything.

From here I can see him, an untouched drink in his hand. He's one of the better-looking men here. But I've seen the aftermath of the past year in the lines around his mouth, the shadows under his eyes. I might be compensation enough if I offered myself to him unreservedly, wholly. Instead, I make him beg for every morsel, and then, once I've finally opened up, I punish him for loving me. I shouldn't have to apologize for wanting to be with you, he told me yesterday, and he's right. How can I think in terms of partner? I haven't even been his friend.

He must sense me watching because he looks up and smiles a smile only I know. Tears come to my eyes, and I blink them away as he approaches. I'm sorry, he says, gesturing with the same hand that holds his wine, Are you okay? I rise slowly to my feet. I think you should go to Kentucky, I say. What are you talking about? he asks. I'm not giving you what you need, Adam, I say, I'm not giving you what you deserve. Joel, he says, Please. He touches my arm, to lead me back into the center of the room, and I pull away. Adam, I say, I don't know that I ever will.

The words take great courage. If I leave him, then I'm alone, and I'm not sure I can do alone again. Not here in Austin, not now. But I say the words anyway, certain at the very least of their honesty. Is this about what I said? he asks, Is this because of the way I introduced you? What we're doing here isn't fair, I tell him. To whom? he asks, Shouldn't I get to be the judge of that? Adam, I say, You know I'm right. You're tired, he says, dismissing me, We can talk about this in the morning. No, I say, and he makes a strangled sound deep in his throat. I know I don't possess the kind of resolve I'll need if he breaks down. Please, I say, Please don't cry. You're breaking up with me at my Christmas party! he protests, but he gets himself under control. Go to Kentucky for Christmas, I tell him. And when I come back? he asks. I shake my head.

I leave him at the top of the stairs, my own tears so blinding that I misjudge the last step and slip, my shoe sliding out from under me. Brushing off the attention of the employees who witness the incident, I stagger through the doors and into the night. Taxi? the doorman asks, already stepping to the curb, and within seconds the car door closes behind me. Hunched in the backseat, I meet the driver's eyes in the rearview mirror. Just drive, I say.

+ + +

One o'clock in the morning. I've changed into sweatpants and a long-sleeved tee shirt, and my bare feet wear the same path in front of the television over and over. I've submerged the phones in six inches of water in the kitchen sink; this way, I figure, I'll have a good thirty minutes to talk myself out of what I'm doing if I get in the Explorer.

I know I've made the right decision, the first really good decision I've made in a long while. I keep trying to remind myself of that when I picture Adam's expression the moment I turned away from him. He's hurting now, I know he's hurting, but he'll be so much better off without me.

I'm still pacing when I hear the knock, and I pause mid-stride. God, not him, I think. Anybody but him. But James stands on the other side of the door, his hands in the pockets of his coat, his collar turned up against the wind, his hair wilder, longer than I remembered, though the color's as familiar as the floor beneath my feet. I simply can't ignore the years of grief on his face.

How is he? I ask, letting him inside. Devastated, he says, adding: You don't look much better. He examines my posture, the fold of my arms across my chest, my eyes rimmed in red. I don't trust myself to say anything, and after a minute he shrugs out of his coat and lays it over the back of one of the barstools. He looks thrown together, as if he was asleep when Adam called and he just got out of bed and dressed in whatever he found on the floor. Now he stares at the living room wall, stretched nakedly across from us. Did he tell you about my mother? I ask. He nods. What did he say? I ask, and he hesitates. That she knew, he admits.

He says those words and I bawl like a child, soaking the collar of his shirt when he locks his arms around me. Okay, I keep expecting him to say, Okay. But he promises nothing of the sort, and I realize how much time has passed, how much older we are, how much less gullible. The thought makes me cry all the harder.

When I finally push him away, his eyes are as watery as my own. How's Elizabeth? I ask, ready to change the subject, Did you propose to her yet? Yeah, he says.

I need just a fraction of a second to cope with his answer. We've fucked, right here in this room, right here on this couch, and our ghosts haunt me just enough that I catch my breath. So, what? I say, She turn your ass down? No, he says, stroking his jaw as if he's still trying to figure that out, She didn't. He glances at me, and our eyes lock. Congratulations, I say.

He leaves as the sun's rising. I practically have to kick him out. I'm fine, I tell him for the hundredth time, I'll be fine. But as he starts down the steps, I call him back. Thanks, I say, For coming tonight.

He grins, and for the briefest moment it's as if he never left.

+ + +

I spend Christmas alone, for the third year in a row. James invited me to come with him to Fort Worth; I'd been stunned by the proposal and told him I appreciated the offer but couldn't imagine spending the holiday with his fiancée. Oh, Elizabeth's not coming, he said, You know—our last holiday alone with our families and everything. Well, that's even more reason for me not to go, I told him. He doesn't seem at ease with my decision, says he'll give me a call from his parents' house. I think he's worried about what I'll do, left to my own devices.

Adam's gone to Kentucky. James told me in the same conversation he extended the invitation to Fort Worth. I'm glad. I wouldn't have been able to bear the thought of Adam staying home alone, and god knows what kind of mistake I might've made halfway through Christmas Day if I'd known he was by himself.

I have a lot to tell Lydia that week between Christmas and New Year's. I've spent most of the past ten days crying, and I wipe my eyes with the back of my hand. They've been pothead red for days, and I have a perpetual headache no amount of Advil seems to kill. Have you spoken with him? she asks, and I shake my head. I don't want to talk about him anymore, I say, I just want to know where I'm supposed to go from here.

+ + +

Kyle finds out about my breakup belatedly, prone as he is to skiing over the holiday. He calls the second he hears the news. Let me take you out to dinner, he says. I don't think so, I tell him, but he says I have two choices: I can go to dinner with him or I have to go out with him tomorrow night to a New Year's Eve party. What about Y2K? I say, Aren't you worried about your business? If there's a problem, he tells me, We're all going to be screwed.

I go to dinner with him because there's no way in hell I'm going out on New Year's Eve. But I shake my head at his suggestion of drinks and tell him I'm entitled to at least a brief period of mourning. Then I go home. I've spent more time in my house in the past week and a half than I have since last year, and I suppose I'm starting to get used to the place again.

The next morning, I go for a run, my first since my return from Mexico. I'm starting from scratch—again—but I resolve to keep up the habit. No more cigarettes either—I've had way too many since Thanksgiving. I make it two miles before I have to stop, figure that's probably not quite as bad as it could be. I'll run again tomorrow, I think, even if there's chaos all around me.

But the world doesn't collapse. Nothing happens at all, in fact, and I'm strangely disappointed. All that buildup and then… nothing. Life goes back to normal for most people; I kick around my house, trying to figure out what I want to do now. Occasionally, I peer into the back room, but I never go inside. I've lost what I had, or thought I had, and there's no point in pretending I haven't.

Weeks pass. I still see Lydia, and most of the time I feel better talking to her, though I'm not sure I'm making any progress. We rehash the same old stories, muddle through the same old shit, until one day I just blurt out that I'm not ready to forgive either one of my parents. Regardless, she says, You have to find a way to live with what they've done. What do you think I'm doing now? I ask. What're you doing now? she echoes, and I groan. You're trying to tell me that I'm not really living, I say. Are you? she asks. I stare at the poster on the wall behind her, a stupid picture of a kitten clinging to a tree branch. *Hang in there!* the caption encourages. I don't know, I finally tell her, and she says, infuriatingly, Yes, you do.

I don't hear from Adam. I'd been vehement standing at the top of the staircase at his Christmas party that he not get in touch with me, and he complied with my wishes. I hear about him, though, mostly because of James. He's been good to me, comes by for an occasional beer, drags me out for lunch or dinner. He's putting the finishing touches on his dissertation, hoping he can get all of his rewrites done before his defense at the end of March. What does Elizabeth think? I ask one afternoon when I agree to meet him for a drink. She hasn't read it yet, he tells me. No, I say, What does she think about you spending time with me?

For a long moment he stares into his beer. Well, he finally admits, She's not happy.

I've been wondering how long this could last, but now I can imagine. I'm not going to be invited to their apartment; I'm never going to see him on a Saturday night. Hell, I'll be lucky to get a wedding invitation. But he surprises me. You're part of my life, Joel, he says, She's just going to have to accept that. You sound awfully fucking certain, I tell him, and he shrugs. Look, I'm not going to lie, he says, You're not a favorite topic of conversation. I signal the bartender for another beer. I don't know, he says, sighing, I don't think I did myself any favors by not telling her from the beginning. You didn't do any of us any favors, I inform him, and for a second I think he's going to get pissed. Instead, he seems to be sitting with what I've said. You're right, he finally says, I didn't.

The bartender replaces my glass with a fresh beer, and I take a thoughtful sip from the head. I think..., James says. What? I ask when he doesn't finish, and he hesitates. I think she's worried something could happen, he admits. Between us? I ask, incredulous. He nods. Did you tell her there's not a chance in hell? I say.

I swear to god he looks wounded, and I take a closer look at him rubbing his thumb back and forth on the handle of his mug, his hair curling over the collar of his shirt. He could use a shave; he could always use a shave. And that mouth, that mouth I dreamed of kissing, until fantasy became reality and shattered any illusions I had about how close he held my heart.

I keep telling her I'm not going to cheat on her, he says, color rising in his cheeks.

Then he turns to me, and his gaze holds more than I'm capable of handling when I'm still nursing my own self-inflicted wounds. The space between us comes alive, with story both real and imagined. I'm caught, like Chloris in Botticelli's painting. Breath falls shimmering from my mouth, ushers in what I hope to god will be a different era.

Anyway, he mutters, turning back to his beer and breaking the spell. Have you talked to Adam? I ask, and he tells me that Adam's keeping to himself, that he's busy with work, that he's still cycling. Does he ask about me? I say, not sure I want to know the answer. James nods. What do you tell him? I ask. The truth, he says, That you're miserable without him.

+ + +

I turn twenty-eight. Kyle offers to take me out to celebrate; I refrain from telling him I'm not sure there's reason. When I check my reflection that night, a few minutes before he's supposed to arrive, I'm struck by the oddest sense of déjà vu. I lean closer to the mirror, frowning, then place the memory. I'd done the same thing when I turned nineteen. I'd stood in front of the mirror in my dorm room, looking at my reflection, trying to analyze what I saw staring back at me. Now I'm nine years older. Nine years, and I trace the outline of my face, struck by the magnitude of all those months, weeks, days, hours. Nine years since my nineteenth birthday. Almost ten since I met James. Eight since my mother died. Six since I graduated from college. Two and a half since I met Adam, since my show. Fourteen months since I cut up my arms.

By the time Kyle arrives I'm weepy, and he pats me on the back and sniffles when I tell him what I've been thinking. I'm tired of being so emotional, I say, pressing my thumb and finger into the edges of my eyes. Nothing wrong with a good cry, he says, so earnest I have to laugh.

My father calls the next day. I answer the phone, bracing myself for a belated birthday greeting, but he's calling to talk about the progress of his new house and how the closing date has been pushed back another month. So you're looking at the end of June? I ask, and he says he's not optimistic that they'll meet even that deadline. At some point you'll need to clear out your old room, he tells me. I grimace. That'll mean another trip south. But I say okay, figure July is still a long way off.

+ + +

Adam's seeing someone.

I find out a couple of weeks after my birthday just as the weather's starting to warm. I'm sitting in the swing on the front porch, talking to James, and I ask the question about Adam casually, not expecting any change in the answer I've been hearing since December. But James hesitates. What? I say, Tell me. Yeah, he says, He's kind of seeing someone.

I can hardly blame Adam for moving on. I made it perfectly clear that he didn't have a future with me. But god, this hurts. I don't really know that much about him, James confesses, adding: I don't think it's serious. It's serious enough that he'd tell you, I point out, Knowing you'd tell me. James doesn't say anything for a minute, then ventures a guess that maybe Adam made the whole thing up to get me back. No, I say, Adam doesn't work that way.

Gradually, over the course of the next couple of weeks, I dig up some information, partly from James and partly from Kyle. After the fact I wish I hadn't. The news leaves me cheerless, as everything does these days, and I finally tell them both that I've heard enough. I just can't handle any more.

I sleep with a couple of different guys in the weeks following the news. Both encounters leave me disheartened and feeling suspiciously the way I used to feel years ago, sneaking around behind James's back to get what I needed. The first guy I pick up and take back to the house, then decide halfway through a blowjob that this isn't what I want after all. As soon as we're finished, I kick him out, then sit on the sofa thinking about all the shitty sex I've had in this house. Certainly the few girls who spent the night in that first year or so. James himself, after the first time, because sleeping with him scared the shit out of me. Even when the sex was decent—with Darryl, for example—my feelings for James killed the experience.

And Adam. He never touched me in this house, not once.

The second guy I hook up with runs into me one night at Central Market about a week after I kick the first guy out. He literally plows into the back of my Explorer as I'm waiting to pull onto Lamar. I get out of the car to inspect the damage, then end up following him to a nearby park. We fuck in the back seat, and afterward, by the shaky way he zips his jeans, I get the feeling that he's married and probably has a few kids. I check his finger for a ring, but that doesn't mean a thing; he could've easily pried the ring loose. So I just come right out and ask. He's angry enough that I know I'm right. Hey, man, I say, Your business. You're goddamn right, he answers, slamming the door behind him. I watch him drive away, then dig around in the glove box until I find a lone cigarette. Sitting there in the front seat, the window cracked, I smoke, the groceries melting on the seat beside me.

I think about that summer James went to Greece for the first time, before I realized I had feelings for him. I'd slept with a dozen different guys that summer, run through them as if I'd never have the chance to be so cavalier about sex again. Maybe that's why when he walked back through the door, I fell so hard. I missed the intimacy we shared, an intimacy I'd never had with anyone before him, that I've had only with Adam since.

Now I realize that if I can't have Adam, I'd rather have no one at all.

+ + +

Cameron calls at the beginning of April. I haven't spoken to him since I got back from Mexico, though he left me a couple of messages last fall.

He'd gone ahead with the show at Laguna Gloria without me, but now he wants to check in. You're a difficult man to reach, he says, and I apologize, embarrassed for never getting in touch with him. Not a problem, he assures me, I'm sure you've been keeping busy. I grunt. The reason I'm calling, he says when I don't elaborate, Is because I wanted to know what you've been doing lately, what you've been working on, what you might have to show me. Nothing, I say, and he seems momentarily taken aback, then offers something about understanding why I might want to take some time off. Do you have anything… marinating? he asks. Not really, I say. Okay, he says slowly, Well, if you want to give me a call, you know you can.

I'm about to hang up when he stops me. *Crossing* sold, he says.

Well, I'll be damned. After all this time. How much? I ask. Three thousand, he says. Are you serious? I ask, and for the first time since I met him he sounds sheepish. Your… sabbatical, he says, Pushed the price a little higher. Imagine how much you would've gotten if I'd succeeded, I tell him, but he doesn't laugh. I can send you the check, he says, Unless you want to drop by the gallery… Can you just send it to me? I ask, knowing I don't have the heart to step through those doors. Of course, Cameron says, Good talking to you, Joel.

I go into the back room and shuffle through the papers on my desk until I find the cards we printed up a couple of years ago to announce the opening. I stare at the card, at *Crossing* in miniature, and my heart quickens. Not because of what was going on in my personal life at the moment of the painting's creation but because of what the piece represents: the pinnacle of my short-lived career. The painting's not bad. Even now, more than three years removed from its conception, I can appreciate the texture, the color, the outline of James's face. I can see the anguish I'd felt, that night I finished, and somewhere beneath the surface I can make out the faintest hint of possibility.

I choose a tube of acrylic, a warm taupe, something quiet, subdued. I take the cap from the end and squeeze. Paint coils onto the palette. I pick another tube, and another, thinking, always thinking about what I want to avoid: anything gaudy, anything that might remind me of what I did in Mexico. Taking the palette knife, I mix the paints until they yield a silvery fawn color that clings to the end of my brush. I close my eyes the way I used to, trying to give whatever's there the space to breathe. Then I reach out and touch the white.

After two hours I give up. I've sullied sheet after sheet of paper, opened tube after tube of paint, and nothing's made a difference. Whatever I had no longer exists, and I wash the brushes and my hands. The colors blur together, turning the water at the base of the sink a disagreeable brown. When I'm clean, I shut off the faucet and go into the back room, where I stand for a minute in the failing light. Then I shut the door.

+ + +

I've agreed to meet Kyle for dinner, and when I get to the restaurant and see that he hasn't arrived, I ease myself onto a barstool and order a beer, ruminating. I've just told Lydia I don't want to see her anymore. I'm feeling better, I said, I'm happy with the progress I've made since November. I'm concerned, she admitted, and I sighed. Lydia, I said, You're always concerned. I'm not convinced you've thought this through, she told me. You know what? I said, I'm tired of thinking.

And I am. Tired of thinking about my mother and what she allowed to happen. Tired of thinking about my father and his zeal for the life he's constructing with Catherine. Tired of thinking about Adam and the ways I've hurt him. Tired of thinking about how different my life might have been if James and I had never crossed that line. I'm just tired, and that's probably part of the reason why Lydia was able to coax me into scheduling my next appointment.

I should know by now not to make plans right after therapy. I should be enjoying this beer from the comfort of my front porch, even though that would mean sitting by myself. I suppose I should be thankful that I still have a couple of friends interested enough in my recovery that they'll do anything they can to get me out of the house, but I'm not sure I wouldn't be better off at home.

A moment later, I see that I'm right. I'm absently licking a bit of foam from my lip when I see Adam. He's at the hostess stand with another man. His lover, I realize as they join hands. He's with his lover, and I'm suddenly so grateful for the barstool beneath me. All this time, I've been able to pretend Adam wasn't serious about this guy, but here's the proof. I stare at them, unable to look away, until Adam meets my gaze. I lift my hand; he says something to his date without taking his eyes from mine. Then he walks across the bar in my direction. Hi, he says when he reaches me, and the emotion I hear in that one-syllable greeting squeezes my heart. Hi, I say. How are you? he asks, and I shrug. There's no point in lying. You look good, he offers. You do too, I say.

He does. I find it painful to look at him for longer than a few seconds at a time. I keep flicking my eyes around the restaurant, down to the floor, anywhere so I won't have to light on his face. How's work? I ask. Work's, he says, You know. I nod. Are you painting? he asks, and just then, his date steps beside him. Our table's ready, he says, putting a hand on Adam's arm. Give me a minute, okay? Adam says without introducing us. His date backs off; it's the closest I've ever seen to Adam being rude.

Are you here by yourself? he asks once we're alone again, and I shake my head. I'm meeting Kyle, I tell him. This is nothing, you know, he says, gesturing in the direction of his boyfriend, It's really… nothing. I examine the hardwoods beneath my feet. You don't have to…, I mumble, I don't expect you to…

I miss you, Joel, he says, and I have to swallow because god, I miss him, too. Can I call you? he asks. I shake my head, and he squints, his eyes at a point above my shoulder. Okay, he says. He looks back at me and makes an attempt to smile. It's really good seeing you, he tells me. He holds out his hand, and I slip my fingers into his, almost losing my resolve at his touch. But then he removes his hand from mine. Goodbye, Joel, he says.

That night, I dream I have a child. Awake, I find the idea laughable. I'll never have a child. But this dream feels so real, so palpable. I'm wearing my baby in a sling, and every time I glance down, he stares up at me with eyes the color of slate. The dream shifts, and I'm suddenly with my mother. The baby's nowhere to be found. Where's Joel? she asks, frowning. Mom, I say, I'm right here. She looks through me. Where is he? she says impatiently, Where's Joel?

+ + +

I talk to my father. He wants to know when I might be making the trip down to Houston to sort through my things. Soon, I promise, and he tells me they're looking at a closing date at the end of July, so I'll have to be sure to come before then. Fine, I say, performing a quick, mental calculation of how many weeks that leaves me, I'll be there.

James will be graduating soon. He's getting married at the end of July. Then he and Elizabeth are moving to Chicago, where James has landed a coveted, tenure-track position. I can't really picture him someplace so cold, and truthfully, I think he's apprehensive. I wonder how I might have regarded the news of his departure six months ago, a year ago, three years ago. And now he's getting married, too. There've been moments in the last few weeks when I could've sworn he was about to ask me to be in the wedding party; I'm glad he had the sense to abstain or that Elizabeth has convinced him to choose someone else. I have no business standing next to him on his wedding day, not under the circumstances. Thinking about the ceremony itself, though, I realize that Adam has probably been invited. James and Adam are friends, after all, irrespective of their relationship with me. I'm not trying to put you on the spot, I tell James when I ask. Actually, he says, Adam's not coming. Because of me? I ask. Well, he has a point, James says, Do you really want to see him?

I do. I do, at the same time I know seeing him would set me back weeks, months. But god, what I wouldn't do for just a glimpse of him, for one smile aimed in my direction, to hear my name coming from his mouth one more time. No, I say unhappily, I guess I don't. By the way, James says, so casually I want to bludgeon him, He's not seeing that guy anymore. He's *not*? I say, When did that happen? Couple of weeks ago, he says.

Right after I ran into him.

When were you going to tell me? I ask, but he shakes his head. You're not going to call him anyway, Joel, he says, So what difference does it make?

+ + +

The knowledge that Adam's no longer seeing someone leaves me even more angry and depressed than I already was. I hunt around for someone to blame and end up, as usual, with my father. He's the root cause of all my problems, and she's not exactly irreproachable either. Between the two of them, I never stood a chance.

What would you say to her if you could? Lydia asks during my next appointment. I'm not role playing with you, I tell her, unscrewing the top from the bottle of water I bought on the way here. We're weeks away from summer, but the sun's already merciless. Why not? she asks. Because it's pointless, I say between sips, Because I'm not going to say anything earth-shattering. Why don't we try? she says. She uncrosses her legs, sitting up straighter. Let's pretend I'm your mother, she says, What would you like to tell me?

I set down my water. My mother didn't wear glasses, I tell her, and she actually removes hers. Folding my arms across my chest, I look up at her through lowered lids. She had hair like yours, you know, I say. Did she? Lydia asks. Well, no, I admit. My mother's hair was straight and smooth, and she usually wore it up, pinned off her neck in some complicated arrangement. But when I saw you for the first time, I say, In the hospital... I reminded you of her? she asks. For a second I thought maybe my entire life was just a really bad dream, I say, my voice unraveling. Lydia's quiet. I cover my face with my hands. What are you thinking right now? she asks after a moment.

That I never returned her calls.

That I erased her voice.

That I pushed her over the edge.

That I've never hated anyone more.

I want her gone from my memory, I whisper, I want them both gone. That's not possible, Lydia says, You have to embrace what happened to you. Embrace what? I say, That my father burned the shit out of me, that my mother let it happen? The good along with the bad, she tells me. Fuck that, I say. If you want to start feeling better, Joel, she says, You really don't have a choice.

+ + +

My father wants me in Houston for the Fourth of July. He says I should come the weekend prior, says that way I'll have a couple of days to root through the boxes in my closet and figure out what I want to take, what I don't care if he pitches when the movers arrive in a couple of weeks. I'll be finished by the end of the weekend, and I'll have a day or two to relax by the pool. I was thinking of inviting a few people over for the holiday, he confides, Just a few people, something tasteful. I'm unimpressed. You know what? I tell him, I'm busy that weekend. But he wheedles his way into making me change my plans. I thought we could use the time to look around for a new car, he tells me, slipping into a more persuasive tone, Isn't it about time to trade in that Explorer?

I want to tell him I can't be bought. I want to tell him I don't want to come. I want to tell him he can keep whatever shit I still have in that house, all my crap from high school and junior high; I want none of it. But I can't bring myself to refuse him, and I try to focus instead on what I'll get out of this arrangement. I'd like a new car. The Explorer has almost fifty thousand miles on its odometer. And I could use a change anyway. So I go down there, I think. I go down there, I put up with my father for a few days, and I drive back in a brand new Lexus coupe because this time, I'm going to take him for all he's worth. Sounds like a plan to me.

What's with you? James asks a few days after I've agreed to spend the Fourth in Houston, and Kyle poses the same question in a slightly less antagonistic way during a different conversation. You know Adam broke it off with that guy, he adds. I grind my teeth and tell him I've heard, I've heard. But you're not going to call him, he says. No, I say, So back the fuck off. Kyle clucks his tongue. I don't want to think about him anymore, I say, There's just no point.

+ + +

I count the days until June thirtieth, mentally drawing a big, black line through each number every night as I lie in bed. I have the uncomfortable feeling that instead of crossing off the days leading up to some event, like Christmas when you're a kid or the end of the semester when you're in college, I'm simply crossing off days of my life. I picture myself going down to Houston, getting through the weekend, coming back and finding weeks later that I'm still crossing off each day. There, I think, imagining the calendar inside my head. One day closer to death.

Maybe you should look at this visit as an opportunity, Lydia suggests when I see her the day before I leave. What do you mean? I ask, and she reminds me that I don't spend much time with my father, that I'm going to Houston specifically to rummage through my old room. Maybe the two of you can do some of the work together, she tells me. Have you not been paying attention for the past year and a half? I ask. She doesn't say anything. Look, I appreciate the positive attitude, I say, But my father's not interested in bonding over old photographs. What do *you* hope to get out of the weekend? she asks, trying a different tactic. A new car, I say.

I'm not in the best mood heading south, and I wriggle around in my Explorer, thinking the seat somehow too small for my frame. When I finally get to Houston, I find there's been a change of plans. Catherine's mother has had a stroke, and Catherine's already left for Dallas. My father has a flight that evening, has just made arrangements for a cab when I open the front door. Why didn't someone call me? I ask, so rattled by the news that I forget to offer up any sympathy, I could've turned around. You have plenty to keep you busy here, my father informs me. But when are you coming back? I ask. I'm not sure, he says, Probably in a few days.

I don't like the idea of being in this house by myself. I haven't stayed here even one night alone since my mother died.

Should I just go back when I finish? I ask, thinking maybe I can tackle the room tomorrow and that way I'll only have tonight to contend with.

Don't worry, Joel, my father says, completely misinterpreting my reasoning, You'll get your car. I wasn't thinking of the car! I tell him. Just take care of that room, he says, And I'll try to get back by the end of the weekend.

He leaves, and I watch from the doorway as the cab circles through the drive. Long after he's disappeared from view, I stand there, reluctant to turn around. But I finally shut the door, and folding my arms across my chest, I look around the living room. Really, it bears little resemblance to the home I knew growing up. Even the accents—the paintings on the walls, the candleholders on the end tables—are different. And yet, if I relax my eyes as if I'm trying to find the picture within the picture, I can see her. Standing at the window or crossing the dining room, her hair pulled gently away from her face. I inhale, imagining I smell her, too. She smiles at me. *Show me*, she says, *Show me what you've done.*

Enough of this shit.

With a gritty determination, I turn on the stereo and fuck with the dial until I hit on a radio station playing house music with few commercials. I order a pizza. I crack open a Rolling Rock, then wander into the living room to wait. Maybe this weekend will be liberating, I think. I mean, how often do I get the chance to breathe in my father's house?

But there's no breath to be had at all. The house holds too many opportunities for me to get into trouble, and by the time I've finished my pizza and exhausted the possibilities on television I've started investigating rooms I have no business entering. I'm not looking for anything in particular, but I seem unable to stop myself from venturing into my father's bedroom, and then his bathroom. Catherine's had the wallpaper replaced with a rough, textured paint, the color a tempestuous blue-gray, but I remember what went on here just the same. With a detachment that surprises me I stare hard into the moment I saw my mother's blood. If anything, I'm more moved by James's arms around me than anything else I experienced that night.

Wandering through the downstairs, I poke around the bar, then get myself another beer and head to the second floor. But no one has ever spent much time up here, and aside from my old bedroom and a series of guest rooms there's not much to see other than the library. I plunk myself down in the wingback, my feet on top of an ottoman. I slept with James, right here, right in this spot. The night of my father's wedding reception I slept with him, even though I didn't want to. I wanted, the moment I saw him standing in the doorway, to get in my car and drive back to Austin. But I'd been too afraid not to touch him; after all, I hadn't spoken to him in days. So I let him fuck me, and when he was finished, I simply pulled my pants back to my waist.

I get a little drunk, reminiscing up there in the library, making quick forays back to the kitchen for more beer. When I run out of Rolling Rocks, I start in on Heinekens, whittle those down until just a couple remain the next time I look in the fridge. Sometime after midnight, I go outside, where the pool laps at my feet. Taking off my clothes, I lower myself into the shallow end and wade around for a minute before I dunk my head. I stay outside long enough for the beer to wear off, long enough to have a substantial headache when I go back inside.

Then I figure that as long as I'm making the rounds, I might as well take a look in my father's study.

I haven't been in this room since the day after Christmas my sophomore year in college, and I stand just inside the doorway in my shorts, a towel wrapped around my shoulders. The air conditioner bites. Unlike the rest of the house, this room hasn't changed, and my eyes fall on my father's chair, his desk, his expensive fucking humidor. There's a decanter of scotch on a long table and a couple of glasses. Rubbing my hands, I pour myself a drink, then sit down on his side of the desk.

I've never sat in this chair, never. Joel, I say, mimicking my father's voice, which isn't all that hard since we sound practically the same, If you fuck up one more time, I'm going to pull you out of school. I point my finger at the empty chair across from me. I'm sick of having to make excuses for you, I say, Who the hell do you think you are?

There's a mirror on the far side of the room, and when I lean over the desk, still ranting at my imaginary self, I catch my reflection. Christ. I would've barely been able to differentiate between the two of us.

I make myself another drink, and then another. Sitting there behind my father's desk, I get downright shitty, and after a while I have to lay my head near my father's computer.

And then in a moment of weakness I call Adam.

Four o'clock in the morning, easily, and he answers the phone, his voice still filled with dreams. My eyes pool. Hello? he says again, and I hang up. When the phone rings ten seconds later, I answer without saying a word. Hello? Adam says in the silence. My voice stalls. Hello? he says, Is anyone there? After a pause he asks tentatively, Joel?

I hang up. He doesn't call back. I finish my scotch and set the glass on the table behind me. Then I stumble upstairs and pass out.

+ + +

I wake up in my old bed mid-morning, my mouth coated with a thin film that no amount of brushing seems to eradicate. I'm hungover, not so much that I need to get back in bed but just enough that I can't consider baking outside by the pool in the July heat. I sit in the kitchen, my hand around a mug of thick, black coffee, trying to forget that I've called him, drunk, in the middle of the night, no less. And he knew it was me.

My father phones late that afternoon, interrupting my nap. Catherine's mother isn't faring well, and he won't be back until the Fourth at the earliest. I assume you'll still be there, he tells me. Maybe, I say, I'm not sure. So you're finished with the room then? he asks.

I'm back in the pool that evening. I've temporarily lost my taste for beer, for scotch; at any rate there's not much left of either. I float, procrastinate. I've opened the door to my closet; I'll need a good week to get through the boxes I've found, some of which I know weren't in there my last trip down. I haven't opened even one.

But I start late that night at an hour which should be seeing me off to bed. Old clothes, bits of paper, pictures I haven't seen in years cover the floor. I weed through it all, separating the few items I want to keep from the shit I have to throw away. When I've emptied a few boxes, I go downstairs for a trash bag, then crawl around on my hands and knees, scooping up my past, the random Kodak sticking to my palms. Sliding another box across the carpet, I dump the contents in front of me: a satire I had to write for my senior English class; a ticket stub from a basketball game; a picture from Homecoming my junior year, the one year I went. I dig deeper, come across report cards from junior high.

I don't know why I'd keep any of this shit.

Momentum carries me for a while, but by three in the morning the task of sorting through my childhood gets the better of me. I crash right there in the closet, my head on my arm, and dream an unsettling dream.

There's a Christmas tree, and behind the tree a window that looks out onto a loose coating of snow. I have a vague feeling I've been here before. I'm standing beside the tree, talking to someone, when I hear my name. A glass of mint-colored holiday punch in hand, I turn. My mother, dressed in gray silk, nods in the direction of my friend. Her hair falls in waves. Well, she says in a voice like the tinkling of jingle bells, Who's this? She holds out her hand; James takes her fingers lightly in his own. He's smoking a cigar. Winking, my mother leans toward me. What have you done? she asks.

I open my eyes. I can still hear her voice, her merry laughter as she tried to catch me in a lie.

My mother knew; she would have had to know, from the time I was very young. After all, I knew, and I was closer to no one but her in those early years. Even though I never said a word, mystified as I was by my own longing, she would've known. I'm just as certain that she would've never repeated her suspicions to my father. If he knows, he's figured out all on his own.

There was one night, my junior year in high school, that would've been impossible for her to ignore. I was seventeen. I'd had little experience up to that point: the guy I'd let take me to the beach; another who worked at one of the record stores at the mall. He'd told me to come by after work, and I got halfway through my first blowjob before his manager stumbled upon us. I ran out of there in a panic, then stopped on the way home to jerk off in the front seat, ashamed before I even came. And then, when I was seventeen, I got picked up in the middle of the day during Spring Break.

I'd been at the Contemporary Arts Museum for most of the morning, but I left after noon and wandered through Montrose. I knew exactly where I was but not what I was doing, and when I stopped at a café to get something to drink, the guy who'd been sitting at a table with his friends, the one who'd already stared at me with such blatant provocation that I stammered ordering a Coke, appeared beside me. How old are you? he asked. I was too taken aback by his approach to reply, and he nodded in the direction of his friends. They think you're in high school, he said, At best a young eighteen. He gave me half a smile and said his bet was nineteen and home from college for Spring Break. Who's right? he asked, and I said quickly: You are.

I left with him five minutes later. He told me he didn't live far, and when we were in his car, I asked his name. Michael, he said, amused, What's yours? At his house he offered me a beer, and I accepted but barely had a chance to take a swallow before he had my shorts around my ankles. You've done this before, right? he murmured, noting my expression. Yeah, I said, feigning offense, but he discovered my lie soon enough, after he coaxed me into his bedroom. I automatically rolled over onto my stomach, and he said, rolling me back, I want you this way. I'd been confused—and hopelessly naïve—and he frowned. But he opened my legs, positioning himself between them; I remember thinking that his biceps were huge. Then I bit into the flesh of my tongue, my eyes squeezed shut against pain I hadn't expected.

I thought you said you'd done this before, Michael murmured, and when I hesitated, he pulled away from me. Wait a minute, he said, Have you ever done *anything*? I drew my knees to my chest and told him in a low voice about the beach, the blowjob in the back of that record store, wanting to prove to him that I wasn't a total novice. He watched me over one ropy shoulder. Are you really nineteen? he asked, and when I shook my head, he buried his face in his hands, moaning that he should've listened to his friends, he should've listened, they were always right.

I reached for my clothes. But he touched my hand.

Relax, he said, It's supposed to hurt at first. I concentrated on my breathing, tensed the second I felt him inside of me. Relax, Joel, he said, his lips to my ear, Your world's about to make sense in a way it never has.

I didn't see him again, though I asked as he was driving me back to my car if I could. You've got to be kidding, he said. I was thoroughly humiliated, though now I can see his point. But when I got out of his car, he softened the insult and called me back. Hey, Joel, he said. When I bent down, he gave me the same smile he'd given me at the restaurant. You're going to be just fine, he told me.

That evening, helping my mother set the table for dinner, I could still feel him. I'd bled—not much, but enough to remind me of the incredible experience I'd had that afternoon—and I went about the business of carrying plates and forks and knives to the kitchen table without paying attention to what I was doing. My mother was making iced tea, but I felt her looking at me. She hadn't questioned where I'd been all day; she never insisted upon knowing my whereabouts the way my father did. I was filling the glasses with ice, hot and distracted, when one of the newscasters on the television mentioned AIDS. My mother and I both looked at the TV at the same instant, and I flushed, both with self-consciousness as well as fear. Michael hadn't used a condom. So, my mother said half a minute later, You had a good afternoon? Yeah, I said, It was good. I stared at the tile beneath my feet, then raised my eyes when I felt it was safe. She was looking right at me, and I knew. I knew she knew.

The subject never came up again. Whatever thoughts she had about the matter she kept to herself. And now I wonder: what would she have thought of James, of Adam? What would she make of my friends, what would she think of my singular, unsatisfying encounters? Would she accept me? Or would she be as horrified as I imagine my father would?

I'm not sure why I care. I've had enough bullshit to contend with as a result of her suicide, not the least of which has been an oppressive, dirty guilt. Since last year, I've had to constantly remind myself that even if my refusal to return her phone calls that January pushed her over the edge, I had plenty of reason not to want to speak to her in the first place. My hatred for her is so intense that most days I can't recall a single nice word she ever said to me, a single nice thing she did.

+ + +

My father phones to tell me that Catherine's mother has improved. I pull out of the madness in my closet enough to ask him to pass along my wishes for a quick recovery. But he's already moved on, tells me he'll be back mid-morning on the Fourth, says if I'm planning on staying for a couple of days he might be able to take some time to look around for that car. If you've finished your work, he adds, as if I don't understand I'm supposed to uphold my end of the bargain. I'll be done, I tell him. Have you found anything interesting? he asks. What do you mean? I say.

An hour later, I find some of my mother's belongings. He's left them to me to go through. I thought he'd gotten rid of everything, and I stare with increasing apprehension at the pile I've just dumped in front of me before I gingerly take a loose photograph in my hands. I don't know that I would've recognized her with her short hair and graduation cap. Her high school yearbook, a diary filled with short, exclamation-filled entries; I snap that shut before I see my father's name. Then, digging deeper, I start coming across her work. Watercolor after watercolor, paintings I'm seeing for the very first time, paintings I used to beg her to show me when she was still alive. I follow the curve of her brush, trace the letters of her maiden name with my eyes. Charlotte Brennan, dead by her own hand at forty-two.

I could've so easily followed in her wake.

I bundle up the paintings and photos and cram them in the trash bag. The yearbook follows along with her diary. I'm tempted to take everything outside and start a bonfire. Burn the shit. Instead, I move on to the next box with shaking hands.

I'm not leaving this house without a fucking automobile.

+ + +

The early morning hours of July third and I'm deep in the closet. I have a stack of clothes on the floor beside the dresser. The old paperbacks I've packed in boxes. A handful of pictures I want to keep, and twelve trash bags line the hallway filled with what I don't. I have only one carton left.

The album appears from beneath thin sheets of tissue. It's worn, tattered at the corners. Holding my breath, I sit back on my heels and open the cover.

She kept everything.

Mesmerized, I turn the pages, reacquainting myself with my very first work. Finger paints, watercolors, chalk: it's all here. I find what might have been my first painting ever, a swirl of cerulean with a hot scarlet center. There's a watercolor I remember painting in the third grade, beach umbrellas in the rain. A sketch I finished on our skiing trip, a chalk drawing of my mother by the pool, a funny portrait of my fourteen-year-old self with braces. Kneeling on the floor of my closet, holding my childhood portfolio in the palms of my hands, I start to cry.

After my mother's death I practically martyred her. I buried her transgressions along with her body, until I was forced to admit her complicity in my abuse, an offense I haven't had the wherewithal to combat. Since then, I've been carrying her sins around with my own, bitter and resentful; it's impossible to hate your parents and love yourself.

When I was eight, and ten, and twelve, I wanted her to save me. I knew she couldn't, but that didn't stop me from dreaming, just the same. I adjusted to our role reversal, secure in the knowledge that at least I was protecting her, graduated from high school and left for college with fragile self-esteem. I'm sure that's why I was drawn to James. He seemed so confident, so self-assured; I wanted the same qualities for myself.

My father told me six years ago when I got back from Europe and he wanted me to take that shitty job in Dallas that my mother didn't think I have what it takes to make it as an artist. Part of me didn't believe him; at that point he probably would've said anything to get me into the business world. But maybe he was telling the truth. I think it's possible that she confided her fears to him in a moment of doubt. All this time, I've made the mistake—and so has he—of assuming she meant I didn't have the talent.

My mother wasn't concerned about my talent. She'd never been concerned about my talent. But she knew me, and she knew what my father was doing to me. She knew I'd start to question my abilities. I'd vacillate between periods of intense creativity and drought. I'd come up against a particularly savage block I wouldn't be able to get past. And then, I'd just give up, stop painting altogether.

I'm amazed by how accurately she's managed to forecast my life.

I've been trying for months now to figure out how I've gotten to this place, this unhappy place where I can't seem to commit myself to a relationship, where I'm afraid to face the canvas. I'm so lonely, and so incapacitated creatively, and my god, it's such a fucking effort to get out of bed in the morning. I think about the future, about what I have waiting for me, and I swear that what I see seems so devoid of purpose that half the time I wish Adam had never found me.

Show me, my mother said, *Show me what you've done.*

I stare at the paintings my mother has saved, gaze at the one that might be my first, blue the same color as a Yucatan sky. Did I finish this painting the same day I stuck my brush into that well of scarlet, and then into my mouth? Even then, I knew I'd never forget the taste.

My earliest work is completely unselfconscious, my latest naked with self-doubt.

Am I capable of saving myself? I've never believed I had the strength. The times I've tried—just before I carved up my arms or when I sat down with my makeshift list of New Year's resolutions—I've failed. I'm not sure why this time would be any different.

Setting the album beside me, I go back into the hallway, where I rummage through the trash bags until I find my mother's watercolors. Then I go back to the closet, where I sit down and slowly sift through them again. Comparing my first painting to what could be one of her last, I find no similarities, no sign that I was somehow picking up where she left off, somehow continuing her legacy. Her painting stands on its own, would have garnered a more impressive critique from Jess than my own work did. He would have liked the simplicity of these lines. He would have appreciated her subtlety, colors so ethereal I feel lighter just holding the painting in my hands.

My mother had something. The knowledge hits me with a pang—not because I'm jealous, but because she could have developed her talent into something exquisite. She should have had her own shows, her own reviews. She shouldn't have had to funnel her passion into me, though I'm so grateful she did.

I didn't push my mother over the edge. Neither did my father. She took the leap herself the moment she stopped painting.

I reach again for my album. All that blue, punctuated by a scarlet I might as well have squeezed from my own heart. I run my fingers lightly over the canvas in front of me, reading the soft welts of paint for meaning as if I'm blind. Suck in my breath when I realize what I've been missing, all this time.

Faith.

+ + +

I'm waiting for my father when he gets home mid-morning on the Fourth, just as he promised. Are you finished? he asks, speaking with the same tenacity he used to speak about my grades. Yeah, it's done, I say, following him into the dining room. He nods, rifling through the mail on the table. He's dressed in a suit; I'm wearing shorts and a tee shirt I stole from James years ago, the word LIFEGUARD emblazoned on the back. I need to talk to you, I say. He raises his eyebrows, and I forge ahead, past the irritation already clouding his face. First of all, I say, I'm gay.

His expression suggests he's more surprised by how calm I sound than with the revelation itself. The realization strengthens my resolve, fills me with a surge of unexpected empowerment, and I have a hard time not breaking into a smile. My guess is that you've known for a long time, I continue, and when he doesn't contradict me, I say, Frankly, I'm tired of skirting the issue. How am I supposed to respond to this? he asks. How would I like you to respond? I say, Or how do I expect you to respond?

I don't have time for this, he snaps, and I reach for the folder on the buffet behind me. I've spent the past twenty-eight years preparing for this moment, and despite the way he's treated me, I almost feel sorry for him. There's no way he could have prepared himself for what's coming.

I think it's time we got everything out in the open, I say.

A modicum of trepidation slips beneath his expression. I've been thinking, I say when I see that I have his attention, That somehow you'd get around to liking me. I stare down at the glossy surface of the dining room table. My reflection stares back, and after a moment I look up, into my father's eyes. I don't think that's going to happen, I say. He opens his mouth to speak; I hold up my hand. I don't mean that you don't care about me in the sense that I'm your son, I say, But let's be honest: you don't like me. I laugh, abruptly. How could you like me? I say, You don't even know me.

My father presses his lips together, and despite the relief I feel finally speaking the truth, the realization that he agrees temporarily discomposes me. We stand together in an awful moment of honesty, until I gather myself together. I've been worrying for years now that the wrong word or the wrong look or the wrong information would get me cut off, I tell him, But I don't think that could ever happen. I shake my head, realizing for the first time that he's needed me just as much as I've thought I needed him. I thought you owed me, I say, trying to explain to him, to myself, why I've allowed this situation to continue, I thought you owed me for what you did to me, what you did to her. How dare you? he asks, How *dare* you accuse me? I think I'm finally starting to understand, I say, ignoring him, That if I allow you to support me, I'm just as bad as you are. I run my hand through my hair, momentarily stunned by the money I've taken from him over the years, the cars, the gifts. Maybe I'm even worse, I admit.

I lay the folder on the table. I don't want any more, I tell him, I'm out.

Before he can protest I explain what the folder contains: a timeline for buying back with interest the house in Austin. The money I earned from my show he can consider a good faith down payment. I'm keeping the Explorer for now, I add, But I'll sell it when I get back to Austin and send you the cash. I hand him my checkbook for good, then take my wallet from my back pocket. I've sold all those paperbacks, every album I could find. I have three hundred dollars to my name, I tell him almost gleefully, and the mention of an exact amount pulls him from his daze. But Joel, he says, How will you live? Free, I say, understanding the word for the first time in my life, I'll live free.

Thirty minutes later, I'm ready to leave. I load everything—of mine, of my mother's—into the back of the Explorer, then go up to my old room to be sure I haven't forgotten anything. Aside from the furniture there's nothing left, not in any of the dresser drawers, not in the desk, not in the closet. I stand in the middle of the room for the last time, then take a deep breath. When I leave, I close the door behind me.

+ + +

I start painting that night, the moment I get back to Austin. I drop my bag right in the doorway, search through my paints until I find exactly what I need. The wall opens up in front of me. I work all night, and when the next day dawns, I keep going, suspended in a state of grace. When I'm finished, I sink to my knees, swept with gratitude.

Right there on the living room floor I fall into a beautiful sleep, and the first thing I do when I open my eyes is reach for my phone. Adam, I think. He's the only one I want.

I should've known you'd call today, he says without bothering to say hello, and I have to steel myself against the bitterness in his tone. How've you been? I ask. I had Indy put to sleep, he says, and my enthusiasm dies in my throat. Oh, Adam, I say, picturing his dog's sweet face, I'm sorry. Yeah, he says, clearing his throat, Well, he was twelve, so.

He's trying to sound matter-of-fact, but I know what losing Indy means for him. I wish so much I could have been there. Adam— I start. You called me last weekend, he interrupts, At four in the morning. Yeah, I admit, and he wants to know why, why I called, why I wouldn't speak to him, why I'm calling now. I mean, it's been six months, Joel, he says, bewildered. I know, I say, And I want to explain, but I need you to come over here. You've got to be joking, he says. I realize I have no right to ask, I add. You're right, he says, You don't.

I accept his derision; god knows it's well-deserved. But I've caught the tremor in his voice, and I say the one thing I think might sway him. I told my father, I say. Yeah? he says, Congratulations.

My eyes fill, not because of his sarcasm, and not because I can't bend him to my will, but because of how terribly I must have hurt him to make him react this way. I'm sorry, Adam, I say, I'm sorry I haven't been the man you deserve.

In the silence that follows I tell him what else I've done. I don't understand, he says, How are you going to live? Wait tables? I suggest, the idea sounding only half-bad, and I repeat the word with more conviction. I don't understand, he says again. That's why I need you to come here, I tell him.

I meet him on the front porch thirty minutes later. He looks beaten down, and broken-hearted, and god, I just want to take him in my arms. He hasn't shaved in days, and I realize that whatever he's been going through with Indy has taken up more than just the past few hours. Joel, he says, Why am I here?

The paint's still wet in places. I stare at the wall, scrutinizing what I've done; I feel as triumphant now as the moment I set down my brush. Both arms begin at the shoulders; I'm not ashamed of the scars that run from the wrists to the elbows, or the welts that mar the flesh on the inside of the biceps. I'm more interested in what the hand holds, in the scarlet background that frames the flesh. I resist the impulse to touch a patch of paint just in front of me, then glance at Adam.

He's standing with his arms across his chest, and he's crying, so quietly I can't hear a thing. Oh, baby, I say, and before he can tell me he's okay, before he has a chance to start apologizing and get himself under control, I fold him into my arms. Cradling his head on my shoulder, I hold him, and this time, I let him cry.

Later, we sprawl on the sofa, our hips touching, our hands entwined. I gaze at the wall, at the paintbrush caught between the fingers of that hand, at the promise of my future. I love you, I say, I love you, Adam.

He doesn't open his eyes. He doesn't say a word. He just squeezes my hand.

DISCUSSION QUESTIONS

1. From the very beginning of *The Crossing*, Joel and James seem to have a unique bond. Describe the ways their friendship changes over the course of the novel. How does sex complicate their relationship?

2. Describe Joel's mother. What do you think of her relationship with her husband? Her son? Do you agree with Joel's initial contention that he pushed her over the edge? Or were there larger forces at play that prompted her suicide?

3. Finances inform at least part of Joel's decision not to break ties with his father. At one point, after his father has agreed once again to continue supporting him, Joel says he "can't quite figure out what's been bought, what's been sold." How would you answer this question?

4. Joel groans when James intimates that Joel has easier access to sex, hoping that his best friend isn't "going to make some generalization about gay men and promiscuity." Think about your own biases and judgments about this topic. Does Joel seem to fit a stereotype in this regard? Or is his character more complicated than that?

5. When Joel meets Adam Atwater, they fall into a weekend of some intensity. Why do you think Joel is so drawn to Adam? What characteristics in Joel does Adam find compelling?

6. Describe Joel's relationship with his psychiatrists. How do Bryan and Lydia help him? In what ways do they hinder Joel's treatment, consciously or unconsciously?

7. From the time Joel comes out to James—arguably even before—James is supportive. At what point does that support cross over into curiosity? At what point does curiosity become something more?

8. When Joel spends Thanksgiving weekend with Adam, he ends up telling him about his mother's suicide as well as the abuse he suffered as a child. Why do you think he confides in Adam? How does Adam respond? At the end of the weekend why does Joel "say the one thing I know will render me unforgivable?"

9. Joel's living room wall sees a frenzy of activity: A last-minute painting; a coat of black paint; a coat of white; and finally, a painting of an arm, fingers holding a paintbrush. Describe the course of events that led to each iteration, and discuss what that final painting signifies for Joel.

10. Catherine couldn't be any more different from Joel's mother. Why do you think his father fell for her? What do you speculate about their relationship? Do you like her? Do your feelings change once she meets Kyle and you're left to wonder why she reacts the way she does?

11. Joel is a master of self-sabotage, and that can sometimes be frustrating for a reader. Did you find yourself getting impatient with Joel? Or as you learned more of his story, did you lean in the direction of compassion?

12. The scene in Jack's dorm room might possibly be the most difficult for many readers. How did you feel reading that scene? Is there any way to contextualize that scene within Joel's larger experience without negating the gravity of what he does to Jack? How do you think Joel felt before, during, and after?

13. At the beginning of *The Crossing*, Joel is still getting used to having his own space to work, and very few people have ever experienced his art. How does Joel's relationship with his work change over the course of the novel? Where do you think he'll go from here?

14. If you've read *I, too, Have Suffered in the Garden*, you're very familiar with Adam's story. How does knowing what happened prior to 2005 impact your perspective of Adam's relationship with Joel?

ACKNOWLEDGMENTS

Joel's story has been decades coming, and I'm certain to overlook some of the many talented people who helped this project come to fruition. But among those I can count as my friend:

Virginia Hassell with Big Star Creative has been a huge supporter from the beginning, and I'm indebted to her for carrying on a design aesthetic set forth by Jennifer Elsner with Viewers Like You. Josh Baker with AzulOx blew me away with a photography session that brought to life a scene that was years in the making and helped anchor the cover for this novel. Evan Shaw and Addison Roush, the actors who participated in the shoot, were nothing but professional, and left me giddy at the end of the evening. David Shields determined what typesetting best fit my previous novel, and his vision impacts this project as well.

Kristin Dorsey has read this novel more times than I can count, in multiple iterations. Her editorial advice permeates this book. Jennifer Seth also started again from the beginning more times than I can count; for her feedback I'm hugely indebted, as well as for her constant support and encouragement. Amie Stone King deliberated over multiple drafts and has served not only as a careful editor but as a brilliant marketing machine. I'm lucky to have her on board.

Without early readers this project might have stalled at the gestational stage. Olga Valenzuela, Maureen McGinn, Beth Rindfuss, Kathryn Schuetts, and Kim Whiteman were willing to take on the challenge of reading a fledgling manuscript (without page numbers!), and I'm grateful to them for their enthusiastic notes. Robert Stearn read brief passages and gave me much-needed feedback. His willingness to answer every question I asked him I will always appreciate.

Officer Lisa Lamkin of the Friendswood Police Department methodically answered a series of questions about DWIs. Any discrepancies in this novel are entirely my own; her feedback was thorough and exhaustive. Dr. Dan Skoglund and Kristen Skoglund answered multiple questions about anti-depressants, anti-anxiety medication, and suicide. Cathy Savage gave me a better understanding of the Austin art scene in the mid-nineties and taught me about light tables and loops. Brian Falbo filled me in on the finer points of playing darts, and Wendy Betron made me laugh as she told me about partying at the University of Texas. Without the advice of each of these individuals this novel would be sorely lacking in color.

I'm thrilled to have parents who support my work, and I want to take this opportunity to thank my mother, my father, and my brother for reading early portions of this manuscript and for understanding that these stories need to be told.

Katherine Torrini spurred me on when I was lacking faith; her coaching and artistic example continue to inspire me.

A special thank you to the Writers' League of Texas, as well as the Houston Writers Guild, for their encouragement and support—and for awarding me contest wins.

Ken Jones, a thank you hardly does the support you've given me justice. And yet: Thank you.

And for my son, who rolls his eyes when I get lost in my head but who shows a similar inclination himself: I appreciate your love and support.

THE AUTHOR

Jennifer Hritz is the author of *Smoke and Glass, The Crossing,* and *I, too, Have Suffered in the Garden.* Winner of the Chris O'Malley Fiction Prize, she holds an M.A. in Literature and Language, as well as a Ph.D. in American Literature. Her short stories have been published in *The Los Angeles Review* and *The Madison Review.* She lives in Austin, Texas. Readers may visit her website at www.jenniferhritz.com.

Interested in Adam's story?
Keep reading for a sample of
I, too, Have Suffered in the Garden.

1

March 1990

Bobby kneels in the dirt behind the house, his hands deep in the earth. Beside him Indy wags his tail, a brush of soil across his wet, black nose. I stand with my arms crossed over my tee shirt, trying to keep warm. It's too early, I say, but I'm ignored by Bobby as well as the dog. The branches of the maples rattle like old bones; green buds that seemed on the brink of unfurling just last week curl inward, away from the chill. Shivering, I watch as Bobby takes one of the plants from its plastic container and plucks at its roots, his fingers deft but gentle. I'm cold, I say. So go inside, Adam, he says, depositing the plant in the hole he's dug and packing it with dirt.

I don't want to go inside by myself. I want him to come with me. I want him back in bed. I've been missing him all week; I left last Monday for a business trip that lasted a day longer than I expected. When I finally got home last night, he was already asleep, and he turned away from me when I slid my hand over the slope of his hip. Tomorrow, he murmured, but he took off for the nursery before I was even awake, and now he's emptying the next plant into the palm of his hand.

We'll have another freeze, I inform him, examining the sky like I know what I'm talking about. There's not a trace of the sunlight that spilled golden through our bedroom windows last Sunday morning, warming our skin as we made lazy, sleepy love. Afterward, I'd pulled my grandmother's quilt over our heads, and we'd lain together under a patchwork of color as rich and vibrant as stained glass. Today the clouds hang ominous and low. Looks like rain, I conclude, and Bobby sighs. Adam, he says, sitting back on his heels, Are you going to help me, or are you just going to stand there and complain?

I go inside. Heat rises from the floorboards and thaws my bare toes. For three hours he works, disappearing around the corner of the house at one point and coming back with the hoe. I'm reheating the soup he made last night when he opens the back door, stopping in the laundry room to peel off his muddy jeans and toss them in the washer. After he goes into the bathroom to shower I sweep Indy's paw prints from the floor.

We'll have tomatoes, he says a few minutes later, joining me at the table. Maybe, I admit as he tears off a piece of toast and gives it to the dog. Catching one of his hands, I examine his thumb, then run my tongue across the whorls on the pad, tasting soap and the singular tang of his skin. Mm, I say, but he pulls his hand from mine. I'm hungry, he says, Let's eat.

The rain starts that night as we're getting ready for bed. I told you so, I say, staring out the window. Plants like water, he tells me, his tone mild. He's lying on the bed, the dog stretched beside him, shedding long, blond fur on my grandmother's quilt. Does he have to be up there? I ask, and Bobby rolls his eyes. But he nudges the dog to the floor, his sweatpants pulling away from his tee shirt and giving me a glimpse of fine, white skin.

I'm allowed one kiss before he moves away. The gardening wore me out, he claims. You've already used that excuse today, I tell him. But he stops me when I try to kiss him again.

That night, I dream of snow, falling from the sky like confectioner's sugar. Giddy and excited, I watch from the window, hoping it will stick. C'mon, Bobby says, taking my hand, and I follow him outside without my coat. I'm thinking of the sled Julia and I got for Christmas one year and the hot chocolate that waited for us after our first dizzying trip down the hill behind the stable, my mother's smile as wide as her arms. But this is no snow from my childhood. The moment we step from the porch we feel the sting, and I turn to Bobby in dismay. Ice, he says, wincing. Barely audible at first, the sound crescendos until the clatter of sleet drowns out even our voices. Bobby hunches deeper into his sweatshirt, and when I reach out to him, I realize I've misjudged our proximity. I try to ignore the sharp prick of fear along my spine. Holding my hands over my head for protection, I squint into the storm. Bobby? I call. I can't see him, and I spin around, losing my sense of direction in the process. Panic robs my breath, but I scream his name with what little I have.

I wake with a sob to an empty bed. Sleet rattles against the windowpane, and when I realize he's gone, I bolt. Without the benefit of light I stumble toward the back door, where the dog waits, whining. Hush, I say, Hush.

Ice nettles every exposed surface of my skin as I run across the yard. Help me, he begs, throwing me a towel, but the sleet comes too thick, and the weight of the towel crushes everything I'm trying to protect. Bobby, I say, giving up, but by then he's kneeling on the ground, his head in his hands. Despite the torrent of ice, I can hear him crying. Jesus, Bobby, I say, dropping beside him, We'll replant. He rocks forward, moaning, scaring me. Bobby, I plead, but he presses his forehead to the ground.

Inside, once I've gotten him out of his wet clothes and wrapped him in the quilt from our bed, once I've wiped the dirt from his face, I sit in front of him. Tears still slip from the corners of his eyes. I don't understand, I say, catching one with the tip of my finger, Help me understand. I've never seen him look so wretched, and I finally take his face in the palms of my hands and kiss him, until his mouth softens under the weight of mine.

The next morning, we stand in the garden without speaking. Sun warms the ice caught in the shriveled leaves of the plants we hadn't been able to cover. I bend to pull a towel from a row of tomato plants, the material stiff and hard in my hands. We'll replant, I say. I shield my eyes from the sun, listening to the steady drip of the gutters. In a few weeks, I promise, We'll replant in a few weeks.

The tomatoes come late that summer. They hang huge and round and red from the vines, and still we can't bring ourselves to pick them. A bounty, I proclaim, even as I watch their skins split and spoil. A waste, Bobby says, and I lower my eyes.

2

June 2005

We're supposed to have dinner together tonight at home. Eight o'clock, Joel told me before I left for work this morning, but I know better. He's running tonight, and he has a tendency to lose track of time when he runs. I bought him a sport watch a few years back, but he refuses to wear it, claiming he doesn't like the feel of it on his wrist. So you'd rather I sit around waiting for you, I say, but he just laughs. I cycle for hours at a time on the weekends, he rationalizes, and I can hardly get upset because his run takes longer than he expects. But I can, and do, and realize if I take a step back that what's really at work here is a little jealousy. I've seen him emerge from his studio, dazed and stumbling over his words, lost in whatever he has in his head; running has the same effect on him. He'll go out tonight, promising me he'll be back within the hour so we can cook something, then show up long after I've given in to the frozen pizza I've insisted we buy or the Ding Dongs I've stashed at the top of the cupboard. Where the hell have you been? I'll ask, and in a voice drunk on his own exertion he'll tell me that he didn't realize the time. I'll watch as he pulls his sweaty tee shirt over his head, as he peels off his shorts, his legs trembling, and I'll have to bite my tongue to stop from asking how he couldn't notice that the neighborhood was shutting down around him. He'd just remind me that we're living in the middle of suburban hell anyway, and that would only start a different argument.

But he's in the kitchen peeling carrots when I get home, later than I promised since I assumed he'd be gone. Where've you been? he asks, and I set my laptop beside the table with a sigh. Drinks, I say, lowering myself onto a barstool. He looks up at me, grazing the tip of his finger with the vegetable peeler. I wince at the blood, but he doesn't miss a beat, automatically turning away from me and holding his finger under the faucet. Watching him, I think of the nachos and margaritas Trainor and I ordered, the beer I had at Trainor's apartment. I'd set my bottle on the flat plane of his abdomen, traced the circle of condensate that appeared when I raised the bottle again to my mouth.

Salmon, Joel says, turning back to me, though I haven't asked what he's preparing, and my stomach groans at the thought. What about your run? I ask. He shrugs, whisking the peeler across the last carrot in three swift strokes. I haven't seen much of you, he says, and I can't tell whether or not his tone carries accusation. I can't help that I had drinks, I mumble just in case. He gives me an odd look, reaching for a glass of wine I hadn't noticed and indicating the bottle. I'm not really in the mood, I mutter.

An hour later, I'm rummaging through the medicine cabinet, looking for some Pepto-Bismol or anything else that might settle the roiling of my stomach. I'd managed to eat half my fish before confessing that drinks had turned into dinner; Joel gave me a look of barely disguised disgust. Now he appears behind me as I'm drinking straight from the bottle. You all right? he asks, and I nod, holding my fist to my mouth and doing my best to suppress a belch. He shakes his head, reaching for his toothbrush. He's a fanatic about his teeth; he's a fanatic about a lot of things now. I watch him squeezing the toothpaste, pressing the tube exactly in the center, right where it makes me crazy. So are you down for the count? he asks, starting to brush, and I say, What do you mean? He holds up a finger, and I mash my lips together and wait until he's finished. I thought we were going to hang out, he tells me, wiping his mouth with the back of his hand. What did you want to do? I ask.

It's been a few weeks, easily, more if I want to be honest with myself. I know I need to make some kind of overture if for no other reason than to throw him off track. I've made way too many excuses lately. But guilt precludes me.

It's been a while, he tells me, and I hurry to say: Not that long. He bites his lip, a habit I used to find endearing but which I swear now raises my blood pressure. I don't feel good, I tell him, What do you want me to do? He tilts his head to the side as if he's actually considering the possibilities. You could eat one less dinner, he suggests, and I put the Pepto back in the medicine cabinet and shut the door with a snap. So now I'm fat, I say, and he groans. No, he says, Now you're exhausting, Adam. He turns away from me. I'm going for a run, he mutters, I won't be late.

A lie if I've ever heard one. I listen for the slam of the front door, then stretch out across the bed once I know I'm alone. I could sleep if I let myself; betrayal wears me out, and I wonder, not for the first time, if Trainor's worth all this grief.

I first met Trainor in the fall of '02 at a technology expo in Vegas a couple of years after Joel and I got back together. I didn't sleep with him then, though I could have, and we kept sporadic contact from a purely professional standpoint. I suppose I'd seen him a half a dozen times when the position at Fusion Technologies, the computer manufacturer I work for, became available last year. I called him personally, flew him down for an interview. He seemed a good fit—for the position, for the company— and I offered him the job on the spot.

Joel didn't like him from the beginning. They met a few weeks after Trainor started, when there was nothing more serious between us than a fierce flirtation. He's a player, Joel informed me after spending all of five minutes with him. Well, he can't have me, I said, which at the time I thought was less of a lie than pretending I didn't want him. When I finally slept with him this past January, all I felt was relief, though I suspect that wasn't because I'd been able to let go of all that pent-up frustration I'd carried around for two and a half years. I actually think I'd been waiting to slip. Sometimes I think I even orchestrated the entire thing.

Hauling myself to my feet, I go into the bathroom. A shower might revive me, and I get undressed, taking a good, hard look at my reflection. Fat may be a stretch, but I'm definitely thicker, especially around the middle. I grab a chunk of skin between my thumb and forefinger. I need to get back on my bike, but telling Joel I'm going for a ride is the easiest way for me to see Trainor on the weekends. I can't very well come back from what he thinks is a three hour ride and tell him I need to work out. So I'm not exercising, and it probably doesn't help that I'm eating nothing but crap. That's Joel's fault; if he wasn't so obsessive about everything he put in his mouth, I wouldn't feel the need to sneak junk at work. I'm lucky to find him drinking a margarita anymore: too much sugar, he says. He wants everything organic, everything whole. At first I laughed when he stopped eating meat, and gave him a hard time about the fact that he'll still eat fish. Nothing with a face, Joel, I said, Nothing with a face. I should've kept my mouth shut. Now he carries a list of sustainable fish in his wallet, and I can't eat a steak without hearing that what I'm eating will rot in my stomach. You should treat your body with more respect, he chides, and I want to kill him. Opening his veins in his bathtub a few years back falls a little short of reverence in my opinion. Don't try to tell me that the coffee I need to get me going in the morning compares even a little with the massive amounts of cocaine he used to shove up his nose.

I step into the shower and close my eyes. Honestly, Joel hasn't said a word about the weight I've gained, though it must be fifteen pounds by now. I know his comments stem more from his concern about my stress level, from the way I'm handling my father's illness, which pretty much consists of outright denial. I know he just wants me to be healthy so I can deal with the tension at work, so I can make another trip home. But sometimes I get so sick of listening to him. Sometimes I just want a cheeseburger.

I'm getting out of the shower when I hear him coming up the stairs. Wrapping a towel around my waist, I nod as he appears in the doorway. Hey, he says, and I can tell from the tone of that one word that he's forgotten whatever friction existed between us before he left the house. How was your run? I ask as he pulls his shirt over his head. Good, he admits. He kicks off his shoes, then hooks his thumb under the waistband of his shorts and yanks them down. I lean against the sink, watching him.

His belly's flat, flatter than Trainor's and certainly flatter than my own, and his legs quiver with muscle. He runs and takes the occasional yoga class, and he looks better, in fact, than I've ever seen him look. Want to join me? he asks, taking note of my expression, but I shake my head. He's high enough from his run to shrug.

Once he's in the shower, I go into the bedroom and rummage for a pair of shorts. I should be heading to bed soon—I have a string of meetings starting at eight o'clock tomorrow morning—but I have a feeling Joel won't let me off the hook so easily. I can't help feeling the slightest bit coerced. Though that's nothing new; sometimes I think I've felt that way from the moment we got back together.

We met over Labor Day in '97 and spent what I interpreted as a pretty fantastic weekend together before he bailed on me. I saw him again a few weeks later, and then not again for over a year. By the end of another long weekend I believed we'd crossed into a serious intimacy. But he bailed again, and when he came looking for me a few weeks after that, I told him he wasn't wanted. Hours later, I found him in his bathtub, his arms wide open.

We didn't speak for more than five months, and when he finally called, he told me he was living in Mexico. I went down to see him, and though that trip didn't end the way I envisioned, within a couple of months he'd moved back to Austin, and I broke up with the guy I was seeing so I could be with him. We lasted all of four months before he left me again.

I've never felt so alone. Not when Bobby was first diagnosed, not when he died, not when I moved here to Austin, not any of the other times Joel walked out on me. I tried to convince myself that I should feel lucky. After all, I'd loved two men in my life, and what I shared with each of them was probably more than most people ever experienced. Instead, that made losing them all the more brutal.

Six months later, Joel called, the same day I had Indy put to sleep. Bobby was the one who'd brought him home as a puppy, all soft paws and tail, one Saturday morning after we bought our house. Okay, I know I should've talked to you first, he said, already anticipating my argument, But Adam, look at him. He turned him toward me, cupped in the palms of his hands as if he was sheltering something sacred. Maybe he was. Considering what he'd been through, he deserved to be loved without condition. I took one look at him, at the gentle curve of his fingers around that dog, and knew I couldn't object.

Indy lived for almost thirteen years, through Bobby's illness and death and my move to Austin at the beginning of '97. When his incontinence started a few months after Joel and I broke up the last time, I took him to see the vet, who'd looked grim. Indy would not go fast, I was told, and I should give serious thought to putting him to sleep. But I couldn't do it. I just couldn't let him go, and I kept him alive much longer than I should have, much longer than was humane. He lost his hearing and his sight, and by the last week I was carrying him up and down the stairs because he wasn't capable of getting around by himself. One day, I stumbled, dropping him to the floor, and when I tried to scoop him up, he snapped at me. I crouched down and hauled him into my arms, where he whimpered so low and pitifully I couldn't bear it any longer. I took him to the vet that day.

Joel called the moment I got home. I'd been waiting for months for him to contact me, and now, my hands still warm from cradling Indy's head in my lap, I had Joel on the phone, telling me he needed to see me, telling me he had something to show me. I almost told him no. But he was persuasive, and I was vulnerable, and I eventually agreed to meet him at his house. The moment I stepped through his front door, I burst into tears. The living room wall, the one I'd found covered with black paint the day I found him in a bathtub of blood, held what I think might just be the best work he's ever done. I'm not the only one to think so; before he sold the house he knocked down the wall and delivered it over to a local gallery, which in turn sold it for $8000. That day, I stood in front of his painting, weeping, and he took me in his arms and whispered apologies until I sank to the floor beside him. I love you, he said for the first time, I love you. I just held his hand, my eyes shut tight.

Almost five years later, he's done everything he promised. Sometimes I'm still astonished when I think about how he's changed. I couldn't have asked for more, and yet, there are moments when I find myself feeling just a little bit bitter about the way he made me suffer.

I get in bed and reach for the remote, clicking through the channels as I ready myself. I know what he'll want as soon as he steps from the shower. But he surprises me. What're you doing? I ask when he comes into the bedroom and starts getting dressed. I have..., he confesses, swirling his hand beside his head to let me know that he's thinking about his work, and even though I should be thankful that he's letting me off the hook, I can't help feeling hurt that I'm losing out to his studio. I thought you wanted to hang out, I say, as if he's been the one putting me off all evening, and he actually hesitates. I cringe. Go ahead, I assure him, We'll have time later. When? he asks with a wry grin, but he's already moving toward the door. We'll be fine, I mutter, and he disappears.